THE HUNCHBACK
OF NOTRE-DAME

Victor Hugo

The Hunchback of Notre-Dame

Revised Translation and Notes by Catherine Liu

Introduction by Elizabeth McCracken

THE MODERN LIBRARY

NEW YORK

2002 Modern Library Paperback Edition
Biographical note copyright © 1992 by Random House, Inc.
Introduction copyright © 2002 by Elizabeth McCracken
Revised translation and notes copyright © 2002 by Random House, Inc.

LIBRARY OF CONGRESS CATALOGING-IN-PUBLICATION DATA
Hugo, Victor, 1802–1885.
[Notre-Dame de Paris. English]
The hunchback of Notre-Dame = Notre-Dame de Paris / Victor Hugo ; revised
translation and notes by Catherine Liu ; introduction by Elizabeth McCracken.
p.   cm.
ISBN 0-679-64257-9
1. France—History—Louis XI, 1461–1483—Fiction. 2. Paris (France)—
History—To 1515—Fiction. I. Title: Notre-Dame de Paris.
II. Liu, Catherine. III. Title.
PQ2288 .A345 2002
843'.7—dc21   2002018917

Modern Library website address: www.modernlibrary.com

Printed in the United States of America

Victor Hugo

Victor-Marie Hugo was born in 1802 in Besançon, where his father, an officer (eventually a general) under Napoleon, was stationed. In his first decade the family moved from post to post: Corsica, Elba, Paris, Naples, Madrid. After his parents separated in 1812, Hugo lived in Paris with his mother and brothers. His literary ambition—"to be Chateaubriand or nothing"—was evident from an early age, and by seventeen he had founded a literary magazine with his brother. At twenty he married Adèle Foucher and published his first poetry collection, which earned him a small stipend from Louis XVIII. A first novel, *Han of Iceland* (1823), won another stipend.

Hugo became friends with Charles Nodier, a leader of the Romantics, and with the critic Ste.-Beuve, and rapidly put himself at the forefront of literary trends. His innovative early poetry helped open up the relatively constricted traditions of French versification, and his plays—especially *Cromwell*, whose preface served as a manifesto of Romanticism, and *Hernani*, whose premiere was as stormy as that of Stravinsky's *Rite of Spring*—stirred up much protest for their break with dramatic convention. His literary outpouring between 1826 and 1843 encompassed eight volumes of poetry; four novels, including *The Last Day of a Condemned Man* (1829) and *Notre-Dame de Paris* (1831); ten plays (among them *Le Roi s'amuse*, the source for Verdi's *Rigoletto*); and a variety of critical writings.

Hugo was elected to the Académie Française in 1841. The accidental death two years later of his eldest daughter and her husband devastated him and marked the end of his first literary period. By then politics had become central to his life. Though he was a Royalist in his youth, his views became increasingly liberal after the July revolution of 1830: "Freedom in art, freedom in society, there is the double goal." Following the revolution of 1848, he was elected as a Republican to the National Assembly, where he campaigned for universal suffrage and free education and against the death penalty. He initially supported the political ascent of Louis Napoleon but turned against him when Louis-Napoleon established a right-wing dictatorship.

After opposing the coup d'état of 1851, Hugo went into exile in Brussels and Jersey, launching fierce literary attacks on the Second Empire in *Napoleon the Little, Chastisements,* and *The Story of a Crime.* Between 1855 and 1870 he lived in Guernsey in the Channel Islands. There he was joined by his family, some friends, and his mistress, Juliette Drouet, whom he had known since 1833, when as a young actress she had starred in his *Lucrezia Borgia.* His political interests were supplemented by other concerns. From around 1853 he became absorbed in experiments with spiritualism and table tapping. In his later years he wrote *The Contemplations* (1856), considered the peak of his lyric accomplishment, and a number of more elaborate poetic cycles derived from his theories about spirituality and history: the immense *The Legend of the Centuries* (1859–1883) and its posthumously published successors, *The End of Satan* (1886) and *God* (1891). In these same years he produced the novels *Les Misérables* (1862), *Toilers of the Sea* (1866), *The Man Who Laughs* (1869), and *Ninety-three* (1873).

After the fall of the Second Empire in 1870, Hugo returned to France and was reelected to the National Assembly, and then to the Senate. He had become a legendary figure and national icon, a presence so dominating that on his death in 1885 Émile Zola is said to have remarked with some relief: "I thought he was going to bury us all!" Hugo's funeral provided the occasion for a grandiose ceremony. His body, after lying in state under the Arc de Triomphe, was carried by torchlight—according to his own request, on a pauper's hearse—to be buried in the Panthéon.

Contents

INTRODUCTION

Elizabeth McCracken

For a moment, let us forget Quasimodo.

You know him already, of course. He is one of the most famous fictional characters of all time, a creation so indelibly described that—even if you have never seen an illustration, on paper or canvas or celluloid—you would recognize him walking down the street. Like Hugo, I "shall not attempt to give the reader any idea of that tetrahedron nose, of that horseshoe mouth, of that little left eye, obscured by a bristly red eyebrow, while the right was completely overwhelmed and buried by an enormous wart; of those irregular teeth, jagged here and there like the battlements of a fortress; of that horny lip, over which one of those teeth protruded . . ." The bell ringer of Notre-Dame requires no introduction at all.

I mean to introduce the entire book, which is *a great work of literature.* Those words once suggested a book you had to read; now they suggest one you needn't bother with, because so many generations have done it for you. Surely by now the plot of *The Hunchback of Notre-Dame* (or *Robinson Crusoe,* or *A Tale of Two Cities*) is encoded in our DNA, a kind of evolutionary Cliff's Note.

The fact is, most novels, great and bad, are best read in a state of near ignorance. You are always more easily and pleasantly seduced—even by a brilliant seducer—without the voice of your mother or your eighth-grade English teacher in your ear. Perhaps the only proper introduction for a Great Novel is: Reader, here is your book. Book, here is your reader—

—except we often know just enough about great novels to dissuade us from reading them. In the case of *The Hunchback of Notre-Dame*, I blame Quasimodo. Not the one who lives between the covers of the book but the one who haunts the world at large, the sweet Beast who falls in love with the unattainable Beauty, that whiff of melodrama about him, the human heart awoken by love. Actors want to play him, in movies and musicals. They've made him into a goddamn Disney character, in a cartoon whose moral is that good triumphs, evil fails, and people will accept you for your essential niceness even if your face is, well, a little lopsided.

This book, this great book, is not nice. It is merciless. It is full of poetry and ideas, tragedy and moments of laugh-out-loud comedy. *The Hunchback of Notre-Dame* is a Gothic cathedral of a novel, as endlessly beautiful, instructive, tragic, and brilliantly formed, as darkly funny, diverting, and entertaining. It's as interested in small things as grand, as crammed with detail, and as rigorously organized: broad-shouldered, full of gargoyle-topped alcoves and saint-filled niches you can find your way back to without much trouble, if you have paid attention.

And Quasimodo is only one of these treasures. He isn't even the true eponymous hero of Victor Hugo's novel, which was called by its author *Notre-Dame de Paris.* The English title, which Hugo hated, narrows the book down to one character and one building. In fact, this is a book full of heroes and monsters, saints and gargoyles, and saints-turned-gargoyles. For quite a while, the book seems to be a wandering mass of characters, though slowly we meet the essential players: Pierre Gringoire, luckless poet, who leads us through Paris and to Esmeralda, who saves him from being ordered hanged by the King of the Tramps at the Cour des Miracles; Claude Frollo, the archdeacon of Notre-Dame, who took in the foundling Quasimodo; Frollo's dissolute younger brother, Jehan; Esmeralda's exquisite goat, Djali; and the mysterious and wrenching recluse Sister Gudule ("Sack Woman"), formerly known as Paquette la Chantefleurie, who has shut herself in the Rat Hole, a basement cell with no door that has been expressly designed for women "who should wish to bury themselves alive, on account of some great calamity or some extraordinary penance." She has cast herself out of society, which makes her somehow more monstrous than even Quasimodo.

There is, of course, no actual aimlessness—you cannot discern the architecture of a cathedral by examining the carving on one doorjamb, exquisite though it might be. Slowly, as you read along, you see the brilliant organization. The structure is one of the true pleasures of the novel. *Notre-Dame de Paris* is broken into eleven books, which are in turn broken into smaller titled chapters. Some titles are charming and comic—for instance, "The Danger of Trusting a Goat with a Secret"—and others named for characters or locations whose natures are described therein. Some cover essential plot points and some are more digressive, some are a single page, and some thirty pages long, but each is beautifully shaped and satisfying. Your tour guide will lead you up a circular stone staircase, or into the rose-window-lit apse; he will point out the smallest cautionary serpent carved into a threshold stone. Serpent, stained glass, the iron bars over a window: no one can say exactly what architectural detail holds a cathedral up, what makes it a cathedral and not a warehouse. Not just size, not just decoration; not merely those spaces that remind us of God because they leave us awestruck, nor those that are homely and holy. *Every* detail is essential, though they seem too numerous to absorb.

Which is, after all, why you need a tour guide. Hugo's narrator is funny and mocking and mordant, and one of the first things that is lost in movie adaptations. That's the problem with filmed versions of books: they take out the poetry and replace it with recorded music. Here on every page is Hugo's brilliance with metaphor (Quasimodo looks like "a giant who had been broken in pieces and badly soldered together again"); his attention to his characters' physicality, whether Clopin Trouillefou, King of the Tramps, or Louis XI, King of France; his ability to be simultaneously chilling and laugh-provoking with the merest twist of tone, to educate and to mock—I don't even know how to begin to catalog all he accomplishes in one paragraph composed of a single sentence in a chapter discussing the former public gallows at La Place de Grève, which ends explaining that in civilized nineteenth-century Paris, there is "but one miserable, furtive, timid, shamefaced guillotine, which always seems as if fearful of being taken in the act, so speedily does it hurry away after striking the fatal blow."

It is a wicked, compassionate, enticing voice.

When you have finished reading the novel, you can go back. I always do. I love to revisit the third book, which is composed of the chapters "Notre-Dame" and "A Bird's-eye View of Paris." No human characters appear in Book III; no dialogue is spoken; the plot is not, it seems, advanced a pace. Mostly the narrator laments urban renewal, renovation, man's need to tear down the old and replace it, the "thousand various barbarisms" visited upon Notre-Dame, the fact that Paris is "deformed day by day." The narrator's voice is sometimes didactic, sometimes satirical—there's a long and hilarious riff on buildings in Hugo's own nineteenth-century Paris. He jumps over steeples and centuries, and sometimes he seems to do so only because he can.

But something happens at the end of "A Bird's-eye View of Paris." The voice turns seductively imperative. He instructs the reader, the very dear reader, to "build up and put together again in imagination the Paris of the fifteenth century," and then, step by step, the voice tells you how. It shows what a narrator like this can do: all those imperative verbs are like a great pianist taking your hands in his, and placing your fingers on the keys, and—look! what extraordinary music you can make: you almost believe that you've done it yourself, dear reader, most beloved reader. In a book full of sadness and sudden death and good, futile human works and cruelty and fear and disappointment, all those reliable jerkers of tears, it is the end of the bird's-eye view— accompanied by the bird's-tongue song of church bells (written long before bird's-eye views were as cheap and easy to obtain as footage shot from a plane)—that reliably makes me cry, for its beauty, and its brilliance, and the loss of that world, and then again for its beauty.

Small wonder Hollywood's so fond of this book; for those of us born since the dawn of cinema, it's hard to not think, from time to time, What a movie this would make! We'd recognize single-handedly staving off the Tramps who are attempting to storm the cathedral: that is what the hero of an action movie *always* does. We instinctively hear dramatic music as Claude Frollo hangs from the edge of the cathedral, begging his adopted son for rescue.

But, of course, this is not cinema: this is genius. It's the kind of peculiar mobile imagination that is rare enough throughout history and may now be rendered *impossible*, now that we have seen how plausibly (though imperfectly) cameras can mimic it. Can a post-1900 intellect think without being informed by camera angles? Hugo's eye and sensibility went everywhere. He saw things from Quasimodo's monocular point of view, and through the Recluse's barred windows; he could think like the frivolous and yet endearing Gringoire; he could think like an educated goat; he could be sympathetic with an entire mob of people; and he could distance himself from all of these points of view and mock them or instruct the reader. He could think like Paris itself: he could fly over rivers and creep behind gargoyles.

Cinema has other flaws. With enough pancake and spirit gum and prosthetics, any actor can turn himself into a credible Quasimodo: physical ugliness is easier to mimic than physical beauty. Which is, of course, the problem. So much of Hugo's book, it seems to me, is about how we are imprisoned by our physicality (how else do you explain Frollo's descent from earnest, loving priest to Esmeralda's tormenting admirer?) but also how we transcend it. In the movies we are always reminded of Quasimodo's ugliness and Esmeralda's beauty: he is always half-made, she always a shining gem, as their names suggest.

But Quasimodo is sometimes beautiful, and not just metaphorically. In one of the book's most famous scenes, he rescues Esmeralda from the gallows and spirits her into the cathedral, yelling, "Sanctuary! Sanctuary!" And, says Hugo, "at that moment Quasimodo was really beautiful. Yes, he was beautiful—he, that orphan, that foundling, that outcast." The crowd outside the cathedral sees it, and cries and laughs and cheers.

This is something a movie can never accomplish: he *really is beautiful*. Everyone sees it.

I recommend the 1939 Charles Laughton version for Laughton himself, who acts more with his one visible eye in five seconds than most other men with their whole bodies in three hours. He is extraordinary. But I cannot forgive the makers of the movie for letting him live, or for sending Esmeralda off in the arms of—good grief!—Gringoire.

In the book, Gringoire's fate is Djali, the goat. It's the only happy marriage of two living things in the entire book. Do not scorn the love of a goat: it is a powerful, touching thing, at least in Hugo's hands. Flaubert, some years later, named Madame Bovary's lap dog Djali, and small wonder: Djali is one of the greatest animal characters in all of literature, the role any goat actor would give up a hoof to play. (The best portrayal of Djali is in the 1957 Anthony Quinn *Hunchback*, which has little else to recommend it, apart from Gina Lollobrigida's really impressive corseted torso; Quinn plays Quasimodo like a five-year-old with a backache.) When Gringoire and Djali are reunited near the end of the book, she rubs against his knees, "covering the poet with caresses and white hairs." Anyone can see this is true love. When he is faced with the choice of saving the goat or his former wife from the now quite mad Frollo, Gringoire's eyes fill with tears. The goat will be hanged alongside Esmeralda. In anguish, he looks into his heart and finds the answer: he shakes off Esmeralda's pleading grip and spirits away the goat. It's such an odd moment, comic and moving at once. Hugo manages to suggest that only a much more noble man would have tried to save the woman, and that the much more noble man would then have paid with his life. And who's to say that a man who lives with a goat is less admirable than a man who dies with his dignity?

But to unite in love Gringoire and Esmeralda? It's ludicrous in the way of all forced happy endings, because it ignores the Greek word carved on the wall of Claude Frollo's cell: ΑΝΑΓΚΗ. Fate. Doom. Necessity. In a preface written for the book, Hugo said he'd seen that particular graffito on a visit to the cathedral; after the success of the book, tourists added it themselves so often the various *fates* began to obscure each other.

Fate is powerful, and its greatest weapon—not a gift, *never* a gift in the book—is love. In a book full of prisons and pseudo-prisons—Frollo's cell, the Recluse's rat hole, the pillories, the bell tower, Quasimodo's own body—love of another person is the worst.

Love is lethal. Love will pick you up and fling you from Paris's tallest building. It will lead you to the gallows. It will lock you in a tower, and when it finally releases you, it will smash your head on a paving stone. If you love your brother, he will disappoint you at every turn; if you love your baby, she will be taken from you. If you love Esmeralda, you will be tortured and rebuked, and then you will die for love.

No Hollywood happy endings here.

———

There is one beautiful love story in the book—far lovelier than anyone's pining over the beautiful gypsy girl, more moving than the Recluse's love for her daughter—and that's the romance between

Quasimodo and his bells. It is returned, it is not fruitless, it has lasted, when the book begins, for years.

"He loved them, he caressed them, he talked to them, he understood them"—and they do so likewise. The bell ringer and the rung bells shout endearments to each other in the bell tower—they have to shout, because the bells deafened Quasimodo some years before. A small price to pay for requited love, though he's already half-formed and half-blind. He can still hear the bells, just not human beings. Perhaps they have deafened him out of jealousy.

And then he meets Esmeralda, and forsakes them.

For me, the most tragic moment of the book comes when Quasimodo, at the top of the north bell tower, looks down and sees Esmeralda on the gallows and says, "There is all I ever loved!" It is awful because it isn't true: behind him are six of his once beloved bells. Across from him, in the south tower, is his favorite, the largest, Mary, and her sister, Jacqueline. He has forgotten them; they would take him back even now. But Hugo has already foreseen the cathedral's own heartbreak: after Quasimodo, Notre-Dame seems dead: "It is like a skull: the sockets of the eyes are still there, but the gaze has disappeared." If he, like Gringoire, had honored requited love, he would not need to die for love at all.

But it is his fate to do so. Love makes him no better than any of those people with more usual souls housed in more usual bodies.

Which is, in the end, why Quasimodo haunts us, as he haunts the cathedral and the book itself. He embodies a basic human fact: we are neither the container nor the thing contained. We exist somewhere on the pulsating edge between the two. "His spirit expanded in harmony with the cathedral," Hugo writes of Quasimodo. "His sharp corners dovetailed, if we may be allowed the expression, into the receding angles of the building, so that he seemed to be not merely its inhabitant but its natural contents." Our salient angles are always shaped by the physical world, by our bodies and the spaces our bodies inhabit. Our souls change when our bodies do, as we age and improve and decline, when we suffer accidents and when we heal, when people look at us and judge us beautiful or abnormal—whether we are awarded the Golden Porpoise or the crown of the Pope of Fools. When Pierre Gringoire happens into the Cour des Miracles and finds, there in the middle of the forest, beggars casting off afflictions, blind men seeing, the legless acquiring legs, it as though he really *is* watching miracles, and not the end of a long day of fraud. And he is: they are different people when they see and walk, as surely transformed as if they'd been truly afflicted, and truly cured. How people look at you changes everything, no matter how you may wish otherwise.

We are more than our bodies, always; but we require them to bind us to the earth, and each body is binding in a different way. The body is a bucket; without it, we would be nothing but puddles on the paving stones, noble puddles, beneath notice, beneath use.

———

So Quasimodo's deformed body is what we first see in Hugo's novel; it is pages and pages before we see his soul. Hugo's patience with his characters is astonishing. Frollo is drawn the opposite way, a human who eventually turns monstrous. They are both more moving and realistic for being inconsistent, though *The Hunchback of Notre-Dame* would probably never be considered a realistic novel. It is too unlikely. These days novels tend to be classified as either Realistic Fiction—books that take place in an average world, with average characters—or Unrealistic: magic realism, science fiction, our old fables, our new ones. I wonder, really, whether that's an offshoot of several generations of readers and writers raised on the movies. Having seen the fantastic on the movie screen, people better looking than our neighbors, richer, in more peril, in deeper love—maybe now we're more likely to go to books to learn about people somewhat like ourselves, people who are neither vagabonds nor kings but somewhere between the two.

But there is a much wider spectrum. Real people, actual living people, are bizarre, full of eccentricities (both physical and spiritual) and sudden hatred and wells of love. Quasimodo has an actual hump, but we are all deviant somehow. We are not average. We are not normal. I can't imagine why we spend so much time trying.

Every day on this planet is full of occurrences and people so unlikely that we would not believe them for a moment unless presented with concrete evidence. What we think of as realism—in books and in movies—is too often a very sad kind of averaging of the human experience. It is plot based on statistical probability, personality shaped out of what feels familiar. And, strangely enough, that means that the element so-called realism most often removes from the world of the book is Hugo's ANÁΓKH. Fate. Things happen because there's no reason—

if we examine the actuarial tables—for them *not* to happen. Perhaps we don't believe in Fate anymore, now that we are able to run so many numbers in so many ways.

But Fate—that which must come to pass, despite our best wishes for a happy ending—occurs to the individual, not the demographic group, and great art is *about* what occurs to the individual, not the demographic group. Just because something happens less often, does that make it less realistic?

Life is implausible. Novels distill what is possible, what is inevitable, what is shocking, what is true, so that at the end we are clobbered over the head by ΑΝΆΓΚΗ. Fate: that which is surprising and inevitable. Fate is different in every work of art, will play out on stages as small as kitchens or as large as Paris, will exact its price subtly or explicitly, will save one character and kill another, and there is no way to tell, on page one, how it will happen. That is realism. We may have fate inscribed upon us when we are born, but we will be ignorant of the details.

The characters in *The Hunchback of Notre-Dame* suffer at the hands of their passions, and their passions change in an instant—which is, in fact, human nature; only in fiction are characters so resolute that they are not able to despise someone half a second after they have declared their love, as Frollo does; or vice versa, as does the Recluse of the Rat Hole. Do I believe that every day a superhumanly strong hunchback falls in love with the beautiful dark-haired girl who is also beloved by his adoptive father, the priest? Do I believe that a woman who has imprisoned herself in a tower grabs her mortal enemy by the wrist and discovers that her enemy is in fact her long-lost daughter? Do I believe that two brothers are killed falling from the same cathedral, that two people die because they have clung to the same woman, or that a goat will fling herself into the arms of the poet she loves?

Not every day, or course, or every year, or every century. But that it happened almost six hundred years ago, beginning on the sixth of January, 1482: yes. I do believe it happened.

———

"The book will kill the building," Frollo declares in Book V, Chapter I, and then Hugo's narrator elucidates in the next chapter. The printing press will change everything, has changed everything, is an endless architectural monument producing bricks for a tower, and replaces monuments like Notre-Dame itself. And, of course, he is right, be-cause here is this novel, safe from weather, fire, revolutions, renova-tions, earthquakes. It cannot be blown up by man or toppled over by God; it fits in your hand but is larger than a cathedral.

Reader, here is your book.

———

ELIZABETH MCCRACKEN is the author of *Niagara Falls All Over Again* and *The Giant's House*. She lives in Massachusetts.

Translator's Preface

Catherine Liu

By updating and revising the Modern Library's anonymous translation of Victor Hugo's *Notre-Dame de Paris,* I have made the novel more
accessible to a contemporary audience, but I have also made the original translation with all its mistakes and prejudices disappear. There are
two major changes that have been made. The original translation was
hasty and prudish to the extreme. Not only were descriptions of La
Esmeralda's heaving bosom and graceful legs simply dropped, Claude
Frollo's erotic obsession and sadism were veiled in Anglo-Saxon eu-
phemisms that Hugo would have ridiculed. The novel is much more
sensual, much earthier, and much more troubling when this erotic language is restored to Hugo's portrait of unreciprocated love, for not
only is Claude Frollo more monstrous, La Esmeralda's own orgasmic
swoon and her inability to give up her Captain make her less innocent
than most English readers have believed her to be. Contemporary
readers will be more shocked by Hugo's obvious prejudices against
gypsies, Jews, and other ethnic and religious European minorities.
Hugo's use of the term "Egyptian" for gypsy betrays the Western European geography: decadence, paganism, and nomadism originate in
the "East." I have dropped "Egyptian" in favor of gypsy, but the usage
is an example of nineteenth-century Orientalism and the fantasy of an
East that was both reviled and desired.

Most English readers think of the Hunchback as the protagonist of the novel: this is probably due to the fact that the French title, *Notre-Dame de Paris,* has been translated as *The Hunchback of Notre-Dame.* Architecture is the real hero of the novel. Hugo's descriptions of Parisian places and palaces, and his account of the history of the city, are impassioned, awkward, and monstrously overburdened, like the Cathedral itself, with details. Architectural archaeology becomes the most important structuring theme of the novel. The original translator left out two crucial chapters that he or she must have believed to have not been important to the plot. These two chapters, which are included here in Book V, are "Abbas Beati Martini" and "This Will Kill That." The first is about the alchemical formulae that are thought to be inscribed upon the portals of the Cathedral of Notre-Dame, the second about the displacement of architecture as the most important aesthetic and cultural enterprise of pre-Modern Europe by the book, whose dissemination and reproduction was made possible by the invention of the printing press and movable type. Hugo makes the wonderful argument that the book will kill the building because, in the time of the Cathedral's construction, architecture was the highest cultural achievement and people gave to it all of their energies. Not only was architecture celebratory of the Christian deity, it preserved all sorts of heretical and mystical knowledge. Hugo predicts that with the invention of the printing press by Gutenberg, the energies formerly channeled into architecture would go into the production of books. The age of great Gothic architecture is over: all subsequent styles are ridiculous to Hugo, for whom the soaring, impossible lines of Notre-Dame de Paris incarnate in stone the impassioned aspirations of generations of craftsmen and architects.

This conceptualization of history shows that Hugo was a theoretical and reactionary thinker: Paris is debased by the architecture that comes after the grand achievements of the anonymous architects and masons who constructed the Cathedral of Notre-Dame. In this novel, the person who most understands the Cathedral is Quasimodo, who lives in it like a snail in its shell. When he finally leaves the Cathedral at the end of the novel, he is doomed to die. The central couple of the novel is not Quasimodo/Esmeralda, but Quasimodo/the Cathedral of Notre-Dame. According to Hugo, the Cathedral itself loses its life and luster after it is abandoned by its bell ringer. Not only is Quasimodo made deaf by its bells, and so has to live with this handicap that the building has given him, he also assumes the building's craggy shape. *Notre-Dame de Paris* mourns the Paris of the past, and at the same time is fascinated with the palimpsestic qualities of a city that consumes its neighborhoods and buildings to re-create itself over and over again. Quasimodo's love of the labyrinthine Cathedral can be likened to Hugo's love of a city that is convulsed by the rapid changes of modernity. Students of urban planning and architecture might do well to read this book that paints in caricatural and broad strokes the portrait of a city of political unrest, abject poverty, prejudice, bourgeois smugness, moral decrepitude, religious hypocrisy, and ruined beauty. If there is a love story here, it is a love story with Paris, with the Cathedral itself, both of which are given a density and a complexity that the human characters often lack. Quasimodo lies somewhere between the human and the architectural and as such is an allegory of modernity's monstrosities: this is one of the novel's most compelling ideas, and one that might lead the reader of Hugo to confront the transformation of the archive of human knowledge and striving in the context of technological progress. Making the connection between architecture and printing, Hugo theorizes and fictionalizes issues and problems that continue to haunt us. What is also exciting about this novel is its passion for the city of Paris itself. It will be impossible to look at the City of Light in the same way after reading Hugo's novel, for he not only tells its story, he mourns its darkness and mysteries.

———

CATHERINE LIU is an associate professor in comparative literature at the University of Minnesota. Her books include *Copying Machines: Taking Notes for the Automaton* and a novel, *Oriental Girls Desire Romance.* She is also the translator of Gérard Pommier's *Erotic Anger: A User's Manual.*

AUTHOR'S PREFACE

A few years ago, when the author of this book was visiting or, better yet, rummaging around Notre-Dame, he discovered in an obscure corner of one of the towers this word, carved into the wall by hand:

ΑΝΆΓΚΗ[1]

These capital letters in Greek blackened by age were deeply engraved in stone with I am not sure what marks that belong to Gothic calligraphy imprinted in their forms and shapes, as if to reveal that it was a hand from the Middle Ages that had written them there. Above all, the author was struck by the ominous and fatal feeling emanating from this writing. He wondered, and tried to guess, what kind of tortured soul would not want to depart this world without leaving behind this stigmata of either crime or unhappiness on the brow of an old church.

Since then, there has been some whitewashing or scraping (I do not know which) of the wall, and the inscription has disappeared. For a hundred years now, this is what we do with the marvelous medieval churches. They are mutilated from all sides, from within and without. The priest whitewashes, the architect scrapes, and then the people show up and demolish them.

Therefore, except for the fragile memory to which the author dedicates this book, there exists no other trace of this mysterious word inscribed in a dark tower of Notre-Dame. Nothing else remains of the unknowable fate that this word summarized so tragically. The man who wrote this word on the wall disappeared many centuries ago, the word in its turn has disappeared from the wall of the church, the church itself will perhaps soon disappear from the face of the earth.

It was upon this word that this book was written.

THE HUNCHBACK
OF NOTRE-DAME

BOOK I

CHAPTER I

THE GREAT HALL OF THE PALACE OF JUSTICE

Three hundred and forty-eight years, six months, and nineteen days ago, the good people of Paris awoke to the sound of all the bells pealing in the three districts of the Cité, the Université, and the Ville. The sixth of January, 1482, was, however, a day that history does not remember. There was nothing worthy of note in the event that set in motion early in the morning both the bells and the citizens of Paris. It was neither an assault of the Picards nor one of the Burgundians, nor a procession bearing the shrine of some saint, nor a student revolt in the vineyard of Laas,[1] nor an entry of "our most feared Lord, Monsieur the King," nor even a lovely hanging of thieves of either sex before the Palace of Justice of Paris. It was also not the arrival of some bedecked and befeathered ambassador, which was a frequent sight in the fifteenth century. It was barely two days since the last cavalcade of this kind had been seen, as the Flemish ambassadors commissioned to conclude a marriage between the Dauphin and Margaret of Flanders[2] had entered Paris, to the great annoyance of the Cardinal de Bourbon, who, in order to please the King, had been obliged to receive the entire rustic crew of Flemish burgomasters with a gracious smile, and to entertain them at his Hôtel de Bourbon with "very elaborate morality plays, mummery, and farce," while pouring rain drenched the magnificent tapestry at his door.

On the sixth of January, what moved the entire population of Paris was the double solemnity, as Jehan de Troyes describes it,[3] united from time immemorial, of the Epiphany and the Festival of Fools.[4] On that day there were to be fireworks on the Place de Grève, a may tree planted at the chapel of Braque, and a play performed at the Palace of Justice. Proclamation had been made to this effect on the preceding day, to the sound of trumpets in the public squares, by the Provost's officers in fair coats of purple camlet, with large white crosses on the breast.

That morning, therefore, all the houses and shops remained shut, and crowds of citizens of both sexes could be seen wending their way toward one of the three places mentioned above. Each person had made a choice, for fireworks, may tree, or play. It must be observed, however, to the credit of the taste of Parisian riffraff, that the greater part of the crowd was proceeding toward the fireworks, which were quite appropriate to the season, or the play, which was to be represented in the great hall of the palace, which was well covered and protected, and that the curious agreed to let the poor leafless may tree shiver all alone beneath a January sky in the cemetery of the chapel of Braque.

All the avenues leading to the Palace of Justice were particularly crowded, because it was known that the Flemish ambassadors, who had arrived two days before, planned to attend the performance of the play, and the election of the Pope of Fools, which was also to take place in the great hall.

On that day, it was no easy matter to get into this great hall, though it was then reputed to be the largest covered space in the world. (It is true that Sauval[5] had not yet measured the great hall of the Château of Montargis.) To the spectators at the windows, the palace yard crowded with people looked like a sea, into which five or six streets, like the mouths of so many rivers, disgorged their living streams. The waves of this sea, incessantly swelled by new arrivals, broke against the corners of the houses, projecting here and there like promontories into the irregular basin on the square. In the center of the lofty Gothic[6] facade of the palace, the crowds moved relentlessly up and down the grand staircase in a double current interrupted by the central landing, and they poured incessantly into the square like a cascade into a lake. The cries, the laughter, and the trampling of thousands of feet produced a great din and clamor. From time to time this clamor and noise were redoubled; the current that propelled the crowd toward the grand staircase turned back, grew agitated, and whirled around. Sometimes it was a push made by an archer, or the horse of one of the Provost's sergeants kicking and plunging to restore order—an admirable tradition, which the Provosty bequeathed to the constablery, the constablery to the *maréchaussée*, and the *maréchaussée* to the present *gendarmerie* of Paris.

At doors, windows, garret windows, on the rooftops of the houses, swarmed thousands of calm and honest bourgeois faces gazing at the palace and at the crowd, and desiring nothing more; for most of the good people of Paris are quite content with the sight of the spectators; a blank wall, behind which something or other is going forward, is to us an object of great curiosity.

If we could, mortals living in this year of 1830, imagine ourselves mixed up with those fifteenth-century Parisians, and if we could enter with them, shoved, elbowed, hustled, that immense hall of the palace so tightly packed, on the sixth of January, 1482, the sight would not be lacking in interest or in charm; and all that we should see around us would be so ancient as to appear absolutely new. If the reader pleases, we will endeavor to retrace in imagination the impressions that one would have experienced with us on crossing the threshold of the great hall, in the midst of this motley crowd, coated, gowned, or clothed in the paraphernalia of office.

In the first place, how one's ears are stunned by the noise! How one's eyes are dazzled! Overhead is a double roof of pointed arches, with carved wainscoting, painted sky blue, and studded with golden fleurs-de-lis; underfoot, a pavement of alternate squares of black and white marble. A few paces from us stands an enormous pillar, then another, and another; in all, seven pillars, intersecting the hall longitudinally, and supporting the thrust of the double-vaulted roof. Around the first four pillars are shops, glittering with glass and jewelery; and around the other three, oak benches worn and polished by the hosiery of the plaintiffs and the gowns of the attorneys. Along the lofty walls, between the doors, between the windows, between the pillars, is ranged the interminable series of all the kings of France ever since Pharamond: the indolent kings with pendant arms and downcast eyes; the valiant and warlike kings with heads and hands boldly raised toward heaven. The tall, pointed ogival windows are glazed with panes of a thousand hues; for exits there are rich doors, finely carved. The whole thing—ceiling, pillars, walls, wainscot, doors, statues—is covered from top to bottom with beautiful blue and gold paint, which was already somewhat faded at the time we are looking at it. It was almost entirely buried in dust and cobwebs in the year of grace 1549, when du Breul still admired it by tradition.[7]

Now imagine that immense oblong hall, illuminated by the pale light of a January day, invaded by a motley and noisy crowd, pouring in along the walls and circling the pillars, and you will have a faint idea of the general whole of the picture, the curious details of which we shall endeavor to sketch in more precisely.

It is certain that if Ravaillac had not assassinated Henry IV there would have been no documents of his trial deposited in the Rolls Office of the Palace of Justice, and no accomplices interested in the destruction of those documents; consequently no obligatory fire, for lack of better means, to burn the Rolls Office in order to burn the documents, and to burn the Palace of Justice in order to burn the Rolls Office; therefore, there would have been no fire in 1618. The old palace would still be standing with its old great hall; and I might then say to the reader, "Go, look at it," and thus we should both be spared trouble, myself the trouble of writing, and the reader that of perusing, a banal description. This demonstrates the novel truth—that great events have incalculable consequences.

It is, indeed, possible that Ravaillac had no accomplices and that even if he did, these accomplices had no hand in the fire of 1618. There are two other plausible explanations:[8] first, the great "star of fire, a foot broad, and a foot and a half high," which fell, as everybody knows, from the sky onto the Palace on the seventh of March, after midnight; second, this stanza of Théophile.

> *Certes, ce fut un triste jeu,*
> *Quand à Paris dame Justice,*
> *Pour avoir mangé trop d'épice,*
> *Se mit tout le palais en feu.*[9]

Whatever one may think of this threefold explanation, political, physical, and lyrical, of the burning of the Palace of Justice in 1618, the fact of which we may unfortunately be certain is that there was a fire. Owing to this catastrophe, and, above all, to the successive restorations that have swept away what it spared, very little is now left of this elder Palace of the Louvre, already so ancient in the time of Philip the Fair that one had to search there for the traces of the magnificent buildings erected by King Robert and described by Hegaldus. Almost everything has vanished. What has become of the Chancery Chamber, where St. Louis consummated his marriage? The garden where, reclining on carpets with Joinville, he administered justice, dressed in a camlet coat, an overcoat of sleeveless woolsey and, over all of this, a mantle of black serge? Where is the chamber of the Emperor Sigismond? That of Charles IV? Or that of Jean sans Terre? Where is the flight of steps from which Charles VI announced his edict of amnesty? The slab upon which Marcel murdered, in the presence of the Dauphin, Robert de Clermont and the Maréchal de Champagne? And the wicket where the Anti-Pope Benedict's bulls were torn into pieces, and from which those who had brought them were seized, coped, and mitered in derision, and carried in procession through all Paris? And the great hall, with its gilding, its azure, its pointed arches, its statues, its pillars, its immense vaulted ceiling, broken up by and covered with carvings? And the gilded chamber? And the stone lion at the gate, kneeling, with head lowered and tail between his legs, like the lions of King Solomon's throne, in the reverential attitude that befits strength in the presence of justice? And the beautiful doors? And the stained glass windows? And the wrought iron that discouraged Biscornette? And du Hancy's delicate woodwork?[10] What has time, what have men, wrought with these wonders? What has been given to us, in exchange for all this—for the history of the Gauls, for all this Gothic art? For the heavy, low arches of Monsieur de Brosse, for the clumsy architecture of the main entrance of St.-Gervais? So much for art! And as for history, we have the voluble memory of great pillar, which still reverberates with the gossip of the Patrus.[11]

This is no great matter. Let us return to the veritable great hall of the veritable old palace.

One of the extremities of this prodigious parallelogram was occupied by the famous table, hewn out of a single piece of marble, so long, so broad, and so thick that, as the ancient land gods say, in a style that might have whetted Gargantua's appetite, "never was there seen in the world a slice of marble to match it"; and the other by the chapel where Louis XI placed a sculpture of himself kneeling before the Virgin, and where he placed statues of Charlemagne and St. Louis, which he had recklessly removed from the lineup of royal statues, leaving two empty spots there, because he thought of them as saints who possessed great influence in heaven as Kings of France. This chapel, still new, scarcely six years old, was constructed in that charming style of delicate architecture and wonderful sculpture, and sharp, deep carving, that marks the end of the Gothic era persisting until about the middle of the sixteenth century in the fairy-tale fantasies of the Renaissance. The small rose window over the main entrance was in particular a masterpiece of lightness and grace; it looked like a lacework star.

In the middle of the hall, opposite the great door, an enclosed platform lined with gold brocade was erected expressly for the Flemish envoys and the other distinguished personages invited to the representation of the mystery; it was backed up against a wall, and a private entrance had been made by means of a window from the passage to the gilded chamber.

It was on the marble table that, according to tradition, the mystery was to be performed. It had been prepared for this since early in the morning. The rich marble floor, scratched all over by the heels of the clerks of the Basoche, supported a woodwork cage of considerable height, the upper floor of which, exposed to view from every part of the hall, was to serve as the stage while the lower, masked by hangings of tapestry, formed a sort of dressing room for the actors. A ladder, naïvely exposed, served to connect the stage and dressing room, and its rude steps were to furnish the only medium for entrances as for exits. There was no unexpected arrival, no plot twist or special effect that could avoid the use of the ladder. It was the innocent and venerable infancy of the art of theatrical illusion.

Four sergeants of the Bailiff of Paris were stationed one at each corner of the marble table. They were guardians of all the amusements of the people, at festivals as well as executions.

The play was not to begin till the great clock of the palace had struck the hour of twelve—a late hour, to be sure, for a theatrical performance, but it had been arranged according to the convenience of the ambassadors.

Therefore, the whole assembled multitude had been waiting since the morning. Many of these good, curious people had, indeed, been shivering from daybreak before the steps of the palace; some declared that they had spent the night under the great gate of the main entrance to make sure of getting in first. The crowd increased every moment and, like the water that overflows, began to ascend along the walls, to swell around the pillars, to overflow on the friezes, the cornices, the windowsills, and every architectural protuberance, and on every sculptural relief. Thus, there was an irritation, an impatience, boredom, and a sense of freedom because it was a holiday, and the quarrels that broke out every moment because of a sharp elbow or a hobnailed shoe, and the tediousness of a wait, gave, long before the hour at which the ambassadors were to arrive, a sharp, surly note to the clamor of the populace, kicked, cuffed, jostled, squeezed, and wedged together almost to suffocation. Nothing was to be heard but complaints and insults against the Flemish, the Provost of the Merchants, the Cardinal de Bourbon, the Bailiff of the Palace, Madame Margaret of Austria, the constables, the cold, the heat, the bad weather, the Bishop of Paris, the Pope of Fools, the pillars, the statues, this closed door, that open window—all to the great amusement of the groups of students and lackeys scattered through the crowd, who injected into all this discontent their sarcasms and malicious sallies, which, like pins thrust into a wound, produced no small aggravation of the general ill humor.

There was among others a knot of these high-spirited rascals who, after knocking the glass out of one of the windows, had boldly seated themselves on the sill, and from there cast their eyes and their jokes alternately within and without, toward the crowd in the hall and the crowd in the square. From their parodic gestures, their peals of laughter, and the jeers they exchanged from one end of the hall to the other with their comrades, it was evident that these young scholars felt none of the weariness and ennui that overpowered the rest of the assembly, and that they knew well how to extract from the scene before them sufficient amusement to enable them to wait patiently for the promised spectacle.

"Why, upon my soul, it's you, Joannes Frollo de Molendino!" cried one of them to a young rascal with blond hair, good looks, and an air of malice, perched on the acanthi of a capital. "You are well named, Jehan du Moulin, for your arms and legs are exactly like the four sails of a windmill spinning in the wind. How long have you been here?"

"Devil have mercy," replied Joannes Frollo, "it has been more than four hours, and I hope they will be counted into my time in purgatory. I heard the King of Sicily's eight singers strike up the first verse of High Mass at seven o'clock in the Ste.-Chapelle."

"Rare singers!" rejoined the other. "With voices sharper than their pointed caps! The King, before he dedicated a Mass to Monsieur St. John, should have made sure that Monsieur St. John is fond of Latin chanted with a Provençal twang."

"And it was to hire those cursed singers of the King of Sicily that he did it!" cried an old woman among the crowds at the foot of the window. "Only think! A thousand pounds Parisis for one Mass, taken out of the tax on the fish sold in the market of Paris!"

"Silence, old woman!" cried a portly and serious character who was holding his nose next to the fishwife. "A Mass was needed! Do you want the King to fall ill again?"

"Admirably spoken, Sire Gilles Lecornu, master furrier of the King's robes!" shouted the little scholar clinging to the capital.

A general peal of laughter from his comrades greeted the unlucky name of the poor master furrier of the King's robes.

"Lecornu! Gilles Lecornu!"[12] cried some of them.

"*Cornutus et hirsutus,*"[13] said another.

"Yes, no doubt," replied the little demon of the capital. "What is there to laugh at? An honorable man, Gilles Lecornu, brother of Master Jehan Lecornu, provost of the King's household, son of Master Mahiet Lecornu, first porter of the wood of Vincennes, all good citizens of Paris, all married from father to son!"

A fresh explosion of mirth followed; all eyes were fixed on the fat master furrier, who, without uttering a word in reply, strove to withdraw himself from the public gaze. But in vain he puffed and struggled till he was covered with perspiration; the efforts he made served only to wedge in his bloated, apoplectic face, purple with rage and irritation, the more firmly between the shoulders of his neighbors.

Eventually one of these, short, fat, and venerable as himself, had the courage to come to his defense.

"What an abomination! That students should dare to talk that way to a citizen! In my time they would have been beaten with bundles of kindling and then burned on them afterward."

The whole band burst out, "Hoho! Who sings that tune! What screech owl of ill omen is that?"

"Stay; I know him," said one; "it is Master Andry Musnier."

"One of the four sworn booksellers to the Université," said another.

"Everything goes by fours at that shop," cried a third, "the four nations,[14] the four faculties, the four festivals, the four proctors, the four electors, the four booksellers."

"Musnier, we will burn your books!"

"Musnier, we will beat your valets!"

"Musnier, we will tear your wife's rags off her back!"

"The good, fat Mademoiselle Oudarde."

"Who is as fresh and as buxom as though she were a widow."

"The devil take you all!" muttered Master Andry Musnier.

"Master Andry," rejoined Jehan, still perched on his capital, "hold your tongue, man, or I will throw myself on your head!"

Master Andry lifted his eyes, appeared to be measuring for a moment the height of the pillar, the weight of the joker, and mentally multiplying this weight by the square of the velocity, and he held his tongue.

Jehan, master of the field of battle, triumphantly continued, "That's what I would do, even though I am the brother of an archdeacon."

"Fine lords, the gentlemen of the University! They cannot even enforce respect for our privileges on a day such as this!"

"Down with the Rector, the electors, and the proctors!" cried Joannes.

"Let us make a bonfire tonight with Master Andry's books in the Champ Gaillard!" exclaimed another.

"And the desks of the scribes!" said his neighbor.

"And the wands of the beadles!"

"And the chair of the Rector!"

"Down," responded little Jehan, "down with Master Andry, the beadles, and the scribes! Down with the theologians, the physicians, and the decretists! Down with the proctors, the electors, and the Rector!"

"This must surely be the end of the world!" murmured Master Andry, putting his hands over his ears.

"The Rector! There goes the Rector!" cried one of those at the window.

All eyes were instantly turned toward the square.

"Is it really our venerable Rector, Master Thibaut?" inquired Jehan Frollo du Moulin, who, from his position on the pillar within, could not see what was passing outside.

"Yes, yes," replied the others. "It's Master Thibaut, the Rector! Old imbecile! Old gambler!"

It was, in fact, the Rector and all the dignitaries of the Université, filing in procession to meet the ambassadors, who were at that moment crossing the palace yard. The students who had taken posts at the window greeted them as they passed with sarcasm and ironical plaudits.

The Rector, who was at the head of his company, received the first volley, which was a sharp one.

"Good day, Mr. Rector! Ho ho! Good day, then!"

"How has he managed to get here—the old gambler? How could he leave his dice?"

"Ho, there! Monsieur Rector Thibaut, how often did you throw double sixes last night?"

"Oh, what a decrepit face—all haggard and wrinkled and wizened with the love of gaming and dicing!"

"Where are you going like that *'Tybalde ad dadus,'*[15] turning your back on the University and trotting toward the city?"

Presently it came the turn of the other dignitaries.

"Down with the beadles! Down with the mace bearers!"

"Robin Poussepain, who is that over there?"

"It is Gilbert le Suilly, Chancellor of the College of Autun."

"Here, take my shoe. You are better placed than I am; throw it at his head."

"Saturnalitias mittimus ecce nuces."[16]

"Down with the six theologians in their white surplices!"

"Are they theologians? Why, I took them for the six white geese given by Ste.-Geneviève to the Cité for the fief of Roogny."

"Down with the physicians!"

"Down with the Cardinal and theological debates!"

"Hats off to you, Chancellor of Ste.-Geneviève. You passed me illegally on my exam! It's true! Then he gave my place in the nation of Normandy to little Ascanio Falzaspada, who is from the province of Bourges, since he's Italian!"

"That was not fair," all the students cried. "Down with the Chancellor of Ste.-Geneviève!"

"Hey ho! Master Joachim Ladehors! Hey ho! Louis Dahuille! Hey! Lambert Hoctement!"

"Devil take the procurer of the nation of Germany!"

"And the chaplains of the Ste.-Chapelle, with their gray tunics! *Cum tunicis grisis!*"

"Seu de pellis grisis fourratis!"[17]

"Ho, there, Masters of Arts! You in sharp black capes, and you in sharper red ones!"

"That one is hightailing it to the Rector!"

"You would think he was a Doge of Venice going to marry the sea."[18]

"Hey Jehan! The canons of Ste.-Geneviève!"

"To hell with the canons!"

"Abbé Claude Choart! Doctor Claude Choart! Are you looking for Marie la Giffarde?"

"She is on the Rue de Glatigny."

"She makes the King of the Crooks' bed!"

"She pays four deniers."

"*Aut unum bombum.* Or a bomb."

"Do you want her to pay you on the nose?"

"Comrades! Master Simon Sanguin, the Elector of Picardy, who has his wife on the saddle."

"*Post equitem sedet cura.* Behind the ride, dark worry is seated, as Horace says in his *Odes.*"

"Brave Master Simon!"

"Hello, Monsieur the Elector!"

"Good night, Madame the Electrice!"

"They are so happy to be seeing all this," sighed Joannes de Molendino, still perched in the foliage of his capital.

Meanwhile, Master Andry Musnier, sworn bookseller to the Université, bending toward the ear of Master Gilles Lecornu, master furrier of the King's robes, whispered, "I tell you, sir, it is the end of the world. Never were such excesses known among students; it is the cursed inventions of the age that ruin everything—artillery, serpentines, mortars and, above all, printing, that other pestilence from Germany. No more manuscripts! No more books! Printing is ruining the bookselling trade. The end of the world is certainly at hand."

"I agree," said the master furrier, "because I have noticed that velvets have become common."

At this moment, the clock struck twelve.

"Aha," said the whole assembled multitude with one voice. The students were silent, and there ensued a prodigious bustle, a general movement of feet and heads, a great explosion of coughing and nose blowing; each individual took his post and established his rights. Profound silence fell over the crowd; every neck was outstretched, every mouth open, every eye fixed on the marble table; but nothing was to be seen, except the four sergeants of the Bailiff, who stood there, stiff and motionless as four pointed statues. Every face then turned toward the platform reserved for the Flemish ambassadors; the door remained shut and the platform empty. The crowd had been waiting ever since morning for three things: noon, the Flemish ambassadors, and the play. Noon alone had arrived on time. This was too much.

They waited one, two, three, five minutes, a quarter of an hour; nothing came. Not a creature appeared either on the platform or on the stage. Meanwhile impatience grew into anger. Angry words circulated at first, it is true, in a low tone. "The play! The play!" was faintly muttered. A storm, which as yet only rumbled at a distance, began to gather over the crowd. It was Jehan du Moulin who drew down the first spark.

"The play, and let the Flemish go to the devil!" he shouted with all his might, twisting like a snake around his capital. The crowd clapped their hands. "The play!" they repeated, "and send Flanders to all the devils!"

"We want the play right away!" resumed the student, "or we will hang the Bailiff of the Palace in the name of comedy and morality."

"Well said!" cried the people. "And let us begin with hanging the constables!"

Thunderous acclaim ensued. The four poor devils turned pale and began to look at each other. The crowd moved toward them, and they saw the frail wooden balustrade that separated them from the people already bending and giving way to the pressure of the multitude.

The moment was critical. "Down, down with them!" was the cry, which resounded from all sides. At this instant the tapestry of the dressing room, which we have described above, was thrown open, and a character emerged, the mere sight of whom suddenly appeased the crowd and, as if by magic, changed its indignation into curiosity.

"Silence! Silence!" was the universal cry.

The character in question, shaking with fear in every limb, advanced to the edge of the marble table with a flourish of bowing, which, as he approached the edge, resembled more and more genuflections. Meanwhile, calm was pretty well restored; nothing was to be heard but that slight noise that can always be heard from a silent crowd.

"*Messieurs les bourgeois,* and *mesdemoiselles les bourgeoises,*" he said, "we are to have the honor of declaiming and performing, before His Eminence Monsieur the Cardinal, a very goodly morality play, called *The Good Judgment of Madame the Virgin Mary*. The part of Jupiter will be enacted by myself. His Eminence is at this moment with the most honorable ambassador, Monsieur the Duke of Austria, who has been detained till now to hear the speech of Monsieur the Rector of the Université, at the Porte Baudets.[19] The moment His Eminence the Cardinal arrives we shall begin."

It is very certain that nothing but the interposition of Jupiter saved the necks of the four unlucky sergeants of the Bailiff of the Palace. Even if we had the honor of inventing this true story, and were consequently responsible for it before the tribunal of criticism, it is not against us that the classic precept of antiquity *Nec Deus intersit*[20] could at this moment be adduced. In any case, Lord Jupiter's costume was superb and contributed not a little to quiet the crowd by engrossing all their attention. He was attired in a brigandine of black velvet with golden studs; on his head he wore a helmet, adorned with silver gilded buttons; and, except for the rouge and the thick beard, which each covered half his face, and the roll of gilded cardboard that he held, which was sewn with sequins and covered with quill-like strips of tinsel that the practiced eye could easily recognize as a thunderbolt, except for the flesh-colored stockings and feet beribboned in a Greek fashion, he might have sustained a comparison, because of the stiffness of his posture, with a Breton archer in the corps of Monsieur de Berry.

CHAPTER II

PIERRE GRINGOIRE

While he was speaking, however, the general satisfaction and admiration inspired by his costume were dispelled by his words; and when he arrived at that unfortunate conclusion, "The moment His Eminence the Cardinal arrives we shall begin," his voice was drowned by the thunderous hooting of the multitude.

"Begin right now! The play! The play!" shouted the people. And, above the tempest of voices, one could hear Joannes de Molendino's, which cut through the uproar like a fife in a musical riot in Nîmes. "Begin right now!" yelped the young student.

"Down with Jupiter and the Cardinal de Bourbon!" clamored Robin Poussepain and the other students perched in the window.

"The morality play right now!" repeated the populace. "This instant! Or the sack and the cord for the actors and the Cardinal!"

Poor Jupiter, terrified, aghast, pale beneath his rouge, dropped his thunderbolt, took off his helmet, and bowed, trembling and stammering. "His Eminence—the ambassadors—Madame Margaret of Flanders—" He didn't know what to say. Finally, he was afraid of being hanged—hanged by the populace for waiting, hanged by the Cardinal for not waiting: in either case, he saw the abyss, that is to say, the gallows. Luckily for him, someone came forward to save him from this dilemma and to assume the responsibility.

An individual who had stationed himself inside the balustrade, in the vacant space left by the marble table, and whom no one had yet perceived, so completely was his tall, slender figure hidden from sight by the diameter of the pillar against which he had been leaning—this individual, tall and slender, fair, pale, still young, though his forehead and cheeks were already wrinkled, with sparkling eyes and smiling lips, dressed in black serge that shone with wear, approached the marble table and made a sign to the horror-stricken actor, who was too much in a state of shock to notice him.

He advanced a step farther. "Jupiter!" he said. "My dear Jupiter!" The other did not hear him. Finally, the tall, blond man lost his patience and called out almost under his very nose, "Michel Giborne!"

"Who calls me?" said Jupiter, starting like one suddenly awakened.

"Me," replied the personage in black.

"Aha!" said Jupiter.

"Begin right now," rejoined the other. "Comply with the wish of the audience. I will take care of pacifying Monsieur the Bailiff, who will pacify Monsieur the Cardinal."

Jupiter breathed again.

"Gentlemen citizens," he cried with all the force of his lungs to the crowd who continued to hoot him, "we shall begin forthwith."

"Evoe, Jupiter! Plaudite cives!"[21] shouted the scholars.

"Hurrah! Hurrah!" cried the populace.

The applause that followed was absolutely deafening; and, after Jupiter had retired behind his tapestry, the hall still shook with cheers.

Meanwhile the unknown character, who had so magically quieted the tempest and "made calm the sea," in the words of our dear old Corneille, had modestly withdrawn into his pillar's shadow, where he would have remained invisible, motionless, and mute as before if it were not for two young women, who, being in the front row of the spectators, had noticed his conversation with Michel Giborne—Jupiter.

"Master!" said one of them, beckoning him to come to her.

"Be quiet, my dear Liénarde," said her neighbor, pretty, fresh-faced, and all dressed up in her Sunday best. "He is not a clergyman, but a layman; you must call him not *master* but *messire*."

"Messire!" said Liénarde.

The stranger approached the balustrade. "What do you want with me, mesdemoiselles?" he inquired eagerly.

"Oh, nothing," said Liénarde, quite flustered. "It is my neighbor, Gisquette la Gencienne, who wants to speak to you."

"Not so," replied Gisquette, blushing. "It was Liénarde who called you *master,* and I told her she must say *messire*."

The two young women cast down their eyes. The young man, who desired nothing better than to engage them in conversation, looked at them with a smile.

"Then you have nothing to say to me?"

"Oh nothing at all," answered Gisquette.

"Nothing," said Liénarde.

The tall, blond young man took a step back, but the two inquisitive women were not going to let him go so easily.

"Messire," said Gisquette, with the impetuosity of a floodgate suddenly opened, or of a woman who has made up her mind, "you must know that soldier who is to play the part of the Virgin Mary in the play?"

"You mean the part of Jupiter?" replied the unnamed man.

"Ah, yes!" said Liénarde. "She is so stupid! You know Jupiter, then?"

"Michel Giborne?" answered the blond man. "Yes, madam."

"Quite a beard he has!" said Liénarde.

"Will it be beautiful—what they are going to perform up there?" inquired Gisquette timidly.

"Mighty beautiful, I assure you," replied the stranger without the least hesitation.

"What will it be?" said Liénarde.

"*The Good Judgment of Madame the Virgin*, a morality play,[22] may it please you, mademoiselle."

"Ah! that's different," rejoined Liénarde.

A short silence ensued; it was broken by the stranger. "This morality play is quite a new piece; it has never been performed."

"Then," said Gisquette, "it is not the same one that was performed two years ago, at the entry of Monsieur the Legate, in which three handsome young girls enacted the parts of—"[23]

"Of sirens," continued Liénarde.

"In the butt," added the young man.

Liénarde modestly cast down her eyes; Gisquette looked at her and did the same. He then proceeded, with a smile. "That was a pleasant sight. This morality play today was composed expressly for the Princess of Flanders."

"Will there be any love songs?" asked Gisquette.

"What! In a morality play! Do not confuse the genres. If it were a farce, you would have love songs soon enough."

"What a pity!" exclaimed Gisquette. "On that day there were wild men and women at the fountain of Ponceau, who fought together and made a great many faces while singing motets and love songs."

"What is fit for a legate," replied the stranger drily, "may not be fit for a princess."

"And near them," resumed Liénarde, "was a band of musicians playing delightful tunes on deep-sounding instruments."

"And, for the refreshment of passersby," continued Gisquette, "from the fountain gushed wine, milk, and mulled wine, through three different mouths, and whoever liked could drink from it."

"And a little below the Ponceau," proceeded Liénarde, "at the Trinity, the Passion play was played as a pantomime."

"If I remember correctly," cried Gisquette, "it was Christ on the cross, and the two thieves on the right and left."

Here the young gossips, warming at the recollection of the entry of Monsieur the Legate, began to speak to each other.

"And farther on, at the Porte aux Peintres, there were other characters magnificently dressed."

"And at the fountain of St.-Innocent a hunter chased a doe with a great noise of dogs and horns."

"And then, at the butcher of Paris, there were scaffolds representing the prison at Dieppe!"

"And when the Legate passed, you know, Gisquette, our people attacked it, and all the English had their throats cut!"

"And then the superb characters at the Porte du Châtelet!"

"And the Pont au Change was completely covered by an awning!"

"And as the Legate passed on the bridge, more than two hundred dozen birds of all sorts were released. What a fine sight that was, Liénarde!"

"It will be more beautiful today," remarked their interlocutor, who seemed to listen to them with impatience.

"You promise us, then, that this play will be a very fine one?" said Gisquette.

"Certainly," he replied, adding, with a degree of emphasis, "Mesdemoiselles, I am the author of this piece."

"Really?" exclaimed the girls in amazement.

"Really!" responded the poet, bridling a little. "That is to say, there are two of us, Jehan Marchand, who sawed the planks and put together the woodwork of the theater, and I, who wrote the piece. My name is Pierre Gringoire."

The author of *The Cid* could not have said with greater pride: "Pierre Corneille."

Our readers probably have noticed that some time must have elapsed between the moment when Jupiter disappeared behind the tapestry and that in which the author of the new morality play revealed himself so abruptly to the simple admiration of Gisquette and Liénarde. It was an extraordinary thing that the crowd, a few minutes before so tumultuous, now waited most meekly on the faith of the actor, which proves that everlasting truth, confirmed by daily experience in our theaters, that the best way to make the public wait patiently is to affirm that you are just about to begin.

At any rate, the young student Joannes did not fall asleep at his post.

"Hey there!" he shouted suddenly, amid the quiet expectation that had succeeded the disturbance. "Jupiter, Madame the Virgin, puppets of the devil, are you making fun of us? The play! the play! Start at once, or we will start up again!"

This was quite enough to produce the desired effect. A group of instruments, both high and low, in the interior of the theater began to play; the tapestry was raised, and four persons emerged, made up and dressed in various colors. They climbed the rude stage ladder and, on reaching the upper platform, stood in a row before the audience, to whom they paid the usual tribute of a deep bow. The orchestra grew quiet, and the mystery began.

The performers, having been liberally repaid for their bows with applause, began, in religious silence on the part of the audience, a prologue that we will gladly spare the reader. On this occasion, as often happens even today, the public bestowed much more attention on the costumes of the performers than on the speeches they had to deliver; and, to confess the truth, the audience was right. All four were dressed in robes half white and half yellow, which differed only in material. The first was of gold and silver brocade, the second of silk, the third of wool, and the fourth of linen. The first of these characters carried a sword in the right hand; the second, two gilded keys; the third, a pair of scales; and the fourth, a spade. And, to assist those lazy minds that might not have seen clearly through the transparency of their attributes, there was embroidered in large black letters at the bottom of the robe of brocade, MY NAME IS NOBILITY; at the bottom of the robe of silk, MY NAME IS CLERGY; at the bottom of the robe of wool, MY NAME IS TRADE; and at the bottom of the linen robe, MY NAME IS LABOR. The sex of the two male characters, Clergy and Labor, was sufficiently indicated to every intelligent spectator by the shortness of their robes and the shape of their caps, while the two allegorical females had longer garments and hoods on their heads.

One had to be exceedingly perverse or impenetrably obtuse not to gather from the prologue that Labor was wedded to Trade, and Clergy to Nobility; and that the two happy couples were the joint possessors of a magnificent golden dolphin, which they intended to bestow upon the most beautiful of women. Accordingly, they were traveling through the world in quest of this beauty; and, after successively rejecting the Queen of Golconda, the Princess of Trebizond, the daughter of the great Khan of Tartary, and many others, Labor and Clergy, Nobility and Trade had come to rest themselves on the marble table of the Palace of Justice, at the same time bestowing on the honest audience as many maxims and aphorisms as could in those days have been picked up at the Faculty of Arts, in the examinations; there were sophisms, arguments, figures of speech, and other wordplay by which masters acquired their caps and their degrees.

All this was really very beautiful.

Nevertheless, in the entire crowd on whom the four allegorical characters were unleashing with great enthusiasm torrents of metaphors, no ear was more attentive, no heart throbbed more deeply, no eye was more wild, no neck more tense, than the eye, the ear, the neck, and the heart of the author, of the poet, of the worthy Pierre Gringoire, who a few moments before could not deny himself the pleasure of telling his name to two pretty girls. He had retreated a few paces from them, behind his pillar; and there he listened, he watched, he exulted. The hearty applause that had greeted the opening of his prologue still rang in his ears, and he was completely absorbed in that kind of ecstatic contemplation with which an author sees his ideas drop one by one from the lips of the actor, amid the silence of a vast assembly. The worthy Pierre Gringoire!

It pains us to record it, but this first ecstasy was soon disturbed. Scarcely had Gringoire raised to his lips the intoxicating cup of joy and triumph than it was dashed with a drop of bitterness.

A ragged beggar, who was not having a good day, lost as he was among the crowd, and who had, probably, not found enough to make up for it in the pockets of his neighbors, got the idea to perch himself on some conspicuous point for the purpose of attracting notice and alms. During the delivery of the prologue he had managed to scramble, by the aid of the pillars of the reserved platform, up to the cornice that ran around it below the balustrade, and there he seated himself silently, soliciting the notice and pity of the crowd with his rags and a hideous sore that covered his right arm.

He said not a word. Because of this the prologue was undisturbed, but, as luck would have it, Joannes Frollo, from the top of his pillar, spotted the beggar and his grimaces. An outrageous fit of laughter seized the young joker, who, caring little about interrupting the performance and disturbing the profound attention of the audience, merrily cried, "Look at that sad sack begging up there!"

Reader, if you have ever thrown a stone into a pond swarming with frogs, or fired a gun at a flock of birds, you may have some idea of the effect produced by this incongruous exclamation amid the general silence and attention. Gringoire started as at an electric shock; the prologue stopped short, and every head turned tumultuously toward the beggar, who, far from being disconcerted, regarded this incident as a favorable opportunity for making a profit and began to drawl out, in a doleful tone, and with half-closed eyes, "Charity, if you please!"

"Why, upon my soul," resumed Joannes, "it is Clopin Trouillefou! Hey! My fine fellow, the wound on your leg got in the way, and so you've clapped it on your arm, have you?"

As he spoke, he threw, with the dexterity of a monkey, a small coin into the greasy hat that the beggar held out with his ailing arm. The latter pocketed, without batting an eyelash, both the money and the sarcasm, and continued in a lamentable tone, "Charity, if you please!"

This episode considerably distracted the attention of the audience, and a number of the spectators, with Robin Poussepain and all the students at their head, loudly applauded this improvised duet, performed in the middle of the prologue by the student with his squeaking voice and the beggar with his monotonous incantation.

Gringoire was very displeased. On recovering from his initial stupefaction, he yelled at the four actors on the stage, "Why the devil are you stopping? Go on! Go on!" without even condescending to cast a look of disdain at the two interrupters.

At this moment he felt a pull on the skirt of his overcoat; he turned around in an ill humor and had some difficulty in raising a smile, which, however, he could not suppress. It was the handsome arm of Gisquette la Gencienne, thrust through the balustrade, that solicited his attention.

"Sir," said the young lady, "will they go on with the play?"

"Most certainly," replied Gringoire, rather shocked by the question.

"In that case, messire," she resumed, "will you have the courtesy to explain to me—"

"What they are going to say?" asked Gringoire, interrupting her. "Well, listen."

"No," rejoined Gisquette, "but what they have been saying so far."

Gringoire started, like a person whose wound had been probed to the quick.

"A plague on the stupid wench!" he muttered between his teeth.

From that moment on Gisquette was ruined in his good opinion.

The actors had, meanwhile, obeyed his injunction; and the public, seeing that they had resumed the performance, began again to listen, but not without losing a great many beautiful bits because of the abrupt division of the piece into two parts, and the sort of soldering that they had to undergo. Such, at least, was the painful reflection mentally made by Gringoire. Calm, however, was gradually restored; the student held his tongue, the beggar counted the money in his hat, and the piece proceeded swimmingly.

It was, in truth, a masterly work, and we sincerely believe that it could be made into a success today with a few changes. The prologue was long-winded and empty of meaning, which is to say that it obeyed the rules of drama. The plot was simple; and Gringoire, in the candid sanctuary of his own bosom, admired its clarity. As we might imagine, the four allegorical characters were somewhat tired after having traveled three-fourths of the world, without being able to rid themselves, graciously and according to their intentions, of their golden dolphin. There followed a panegyric of the marvelous fish, with a thousand delicate allusions to the young bridegroom of Margaret of Flanders, at that moment sadly shut up in Amboise[24] and never dreaming that Labor and Clergy, Nobility and Trade had been making a tour of the world on his account. The said dolphin, then, was young, handsome, bold and, above all—magnificent origin of every royal virtue!— the son of the Lion of France. I declare that this bold metaphor is truly admirable; and that the natural history of the theater is not at all startled, on a day of allegory and in celebration of a royal wedding, that a dolphin should be the offspring of a lion. It is precisely these rare and Pindaric mélanges that give proof to enthusiasm. Critical justice, nevertheless, requires the admission that the poet ought to have developed this original idea within two hundred lines of verse. It is true that the mystery was to last from the hour of twelve until that of four, according to the ordinance of Monsieur the Provost, and that it was absolutely necessary to say something or the other. Besides, the audience listened very patiently.

All at once, in the midst of a quarrel between Mademoiselle Trade and Lady Nobility, at the moment when Sir Labor was delivering this emphatic line:

More stately beast was ne'er in forest seen,

the door of the reserved platform, which had until then remained so inappropriately shut, was still more inappropriately thrown open, and the sonorous voice of the usher abruptly announced, *"His Eminence Monseigneur the Cardinal de Bourbon!"*

CHAPTER III

THE CARDINAL

Poor Gringoire! The noise of all the giant double firecrackers at St. John's, the discharge of a hundred muskets, the detonation of that famous cannon of the Tour de Billy, which, at the siege of Paris,[25] on the twenty-ninth of September, 1465, killed seven Burgundians by one shot, no, the explosion of all the gunpowder stockpiled at the Porte du Temple would have given his ears less of a shock than the solemn and dramatic moment when these few words were uttered by the lips of an usher: *"His Eminence Monseigneur the Cardinal de Bourbon!"*

Not that Pierre Gringoire either feared or disdained Monsieur the Cardinal; he had neither that weakness nor that arrogance. A genuine eclectic, as we would say nowadays, Gringoire possessed one of those firm and elevated, calm and moderate minds that always know how to steer a middle course and are full of reason and liberal philosophy, at the same time that they make much of cardinals—an admirable race, very different from the philosophers; to whom Wisdom, like another Ariadne, seems to have given a ball of thread that they keep winding up from the beginning of the world, through the labyrinth of human affairs. We find them in every age and everywhere the same, that is to say, ever accommodating themselves to the times. And, without counting our Pierre Gringoire, who might be their representative in the fifteenth century, if we were to bestow on him the description that he deserves, it was certainly their spirit that animated Father du Breul when he wrote, in the sixteenth, these simply sublime words, worthy of all ages: "I am a Parisian by nation, and a parrhisian by speech; for *parrhisia,* in Greek, signifies liberty of speech, which I have used even to Messeigneurs the Cardinals, uncle and brother of Monseigneur the Prince of Conty: at the same time with respect for their high dignity, and without giving offense to anyone of their retinue, which, I believe, is no small feat."

There was, then, neither hatred of the Cardinal nor disdain of his presence in the disagreeable reaction experienced by Pierre Gringoire. On the contrary, our poet had too much good sense, and too threadbare a frock, not to feel particularly anxious that the many allusions in his prologue, and particularly the eulogy to the dolphin, the son of the Lion of France, should find its way to the Most Eminent ear. But it is not interest that dominates the noble nature of poets. Let us say that the being of the poet is to be represented by the number 10; it is certain that a chemist, on analyzing or pharmacoplizing it, in the words of Rabelais, would find it composed of one part interest and nine parts vanity. Therefore, when the door opened for the Cardinal, the nine parts of Gringoire's vanity, swollen and inflated by the breath of popular admiration, were in a state of such prodigious enlargement that they completely smothered that imperceptible particle of interest that we just now discovered in the constitution of poets; a most valuable ingredient, and the ballast of reality and of humanity, without which they would never descend to this lower world. Gringoire was delighted to see, to feel, in some measure, a whole assembly, of scoundrels, it is true—but what does that signify?—stupefied, petrified, and stricken dumb as it were by the immeasurable speeches that succeeded each other throughout his epithalamium. I affirm that he participated in the general happiness, and that, unlike La Fontaine, who, at the first performance of his comedy *The Florentine,* inquired, "What idiotic scribbler wrote this rhapsody?"[26] Gringoire would gladly have asked his neighbor, "Who is the author of this masterpiece?" Now, imagine what must have been the effect produced on him by the abrupt and untimely arrival of the Cardinal.

What he had reason to fear was only too soon realized. The entry of His Eminence upset the audience. All heads turned mechanically toward the platform. Not another word was to be heard. "The Cardinal! The Cardinal!" was on every tongue. The unfortunate prologue was cut short a second time.

The Cardinal paused for a moment on the threshold of the platform, and with an indifferent gaze surveyed the public. Meanwhile the tumult increased. Everyone wanted a better view, so everyone tried to climb up on his neighbor's shoulders.

He was, in fact, a very distinguished personage, the sight of whom was well worth any other play. Charles, Cardinal de Bourbon, Archbishop and Count of Lyons, Primate of the Gauls, was at once allied to Louis XI through his brother Pierre, Lord of Beaujeu, who was married to the King's eldest daughter, and to Charles the Bold by his mother, Agnes of Burgundy. Now the predominant, the distinctive trait in the character of the Primate of the Gauls was the spirit of the courtier and a devotion to power. The reader may form some conception of the numberless embarrassments in which he had been involved by this twofold relationship, and of the temporal rocks among which his spiritual bark had been obliged to navigate lest it be wrecked either against Louis or against Charles, that Charybdis and Scylla that had devoured the Duke of Nemours and the Constable of St.-Pol. Thank heaven, he had contrived pretty well to escape the dangers of the voyage and had arrived in Rome without obstruction. But, though he was in port, and precisely because he was in port, he could never call to mind without agitation the various risks to his political life, for so long dominated by drudgery and danger. Accordingly, he was accustomed to say that the year 1467 had been to him both black and white; thereby meaning that he had lost in that year his mother, the Duchess of Bourbonnais, and his cousin the Duke of Burgundy, and that one mourning had consoled him for the other.

In other respects he was a good sort of man; he led a jovial life as cardinal, loved to make merry with the harvest of the royal vineyard of Chaillot, did not hate the jocund Richarde la Garmoise and Thomasse la Saillarde, bestowed alms on pretty girls rather than on wrinkled hags, and for all these reasons was a great favorite with the populace of Paris. Wherever he went he was surrounded by a little court of bishops and abbots of high families, womanizers and boon companions, who had no objection to joining a party; and more than once the pious souls of St.-Germain d'Auxerre, as they passed in the evening under the bright windows of the Cardinal's residence, had been scandalized on hearing the same voices that had chanted vespers to them a few hours before lustily singing, to the clatter of glasses, the bacchanalian song of Benedict XII, that Pope who added a third crown to the tiara—*Bibamus papaliter.*[27]

It was no doubt this popularity, to which he was so justly entitled, that preserved him at his entrance from any unfavorable reception by the crowd, which a moment before had been so dissatisfied and was by no means disposed to pay respect to a cardinal on the very day that they were going to elect a Pope. But the Parisians are not apt to bear a grudge; and besides, by forcing the performance to begin, the honest citizens had gained a victory over the Cardinal, and this triumph was enough for them. Moreover, Monsieur the Cardinal de Bourbon was a handsome man; he had a superb scarlet robe, which he wore very gracefully. Of course he had in his favor all the women, that is to say, the better half of the audience. It would be decidedly unjust and in bad taste to boo a cardinal for coming late to the play when he is a handsome man and wears his scarlet robe so well.

He entered, therefore, bowed to the audience with that hereditary smile which the great have for the people, and proceeded slowly toward his armchair covered with scarlet velvet, apparently thinking of something very different from the scene before him. His retinue, which we should nowadays call his staff, of abbots and bishops, followed him as he advanced to the front of the platform, which inspired no small increase of the tumult and curiosity in the audience. Each was eager to point them out, and to recognize at least one of them by name—some called out the name of Monsieur the Bishop of Marseilles, Alaudet, if I recollect rightly; or the Dean of St.-Denis; or the Abbot of St.-Germain-des-Prés, that libertine brother of one of the mistresses of Louis XI. All of this was done in a cacophony of mockery and jeering. As for the students, they swore heartily. It was their day, their Feast of Fools, their saturnalia, the annual festival of the Basoche, the company of clerks of the Parliament of Paris, and of the schools. On that day every turpitude was permitted and even held sacred. Was it not then the least they could do to swear as much as possible, and to curse a little in the name of God, on so fine a day, in the good company of churchmen and loose women? Accordingly they made good use of the license, and amid the general uproar there was a horrible clamor of blasphemies and outrages uttered by the loosened tongues—the tongues of clerks and students restrained during the rest of the year by the fear of the red-hot iron of St. Louis. Poor St. Louis! How they mocked him at his own Palace of Justice. Among the new occupants of the platform, every student chose a black, gray, white, or purple cassock as the butt of all jokes. As for Joannes Frollo de Molendino, as brother of an archdeacon he boldly attacked the scarlet robe and, fixing his gaze on the Cardinal, he sang at the top of his lungs, *"Cappa repleta mero."*[28]

All these circumstances, which we reveal here for the edification of the reader, were so lost in the general tumult that they passed unnoticed by the reverend group on the platform. Had it, indeed, been otherwise the Cardinal would not have heeded them, so deeply were the liberties of that day a part of the customs of the age. He was, moreover, wholly preoccupied—and his countenance showed it—by another concern, which closely pursued him and, indeed, had entered the platform at almost the same time as he did, namely, the Flemish ambassador.

Not that he was a profound politician, calculating the possible consequences of the marriage of his cousin Margaret of Burgundy to his cousin Charles Dauphin on Vienna; or how long the good understanding patched up between the Duke of Austria and the King of France was likely to last; or how the King of England would take the slight suffered by his daughter. These matters worried him little, and he enjoyed himself every evening with the royal vintage from Chaillot without ever dreaming that a few bottles of the same wine—first a bit doctored, it is true, by Coictier the physician—and cordially presented to Edward IV by Louis XI would one day rid Louis XI of Edward IV.[29] The presence of the most honored ambassador Monsieur the Duke of Austria brought on the Cardinal none of these cares; but it vexed him in another way. It was in truth rather hard, as we have already observed at the beginning of this book, that he, Charles de Bourbon, should be obliged to give hearty welcome and good entertainment to mere bourgeois; he, a cardinal, to plebeian magistrates; he, a Frenchman, a witty and discerning lover of life, had to entertain Flemish beer lovers—and all of that in public. This was certainly one of the most unpleasant masks he had ever put on to please the King.

When the usher with his resounding voice announced Messieurs the Envoys of Monsieur the Duke of Austria, he turned toward the door, and as graciously as possible—so well had he studied his part. It is scarcely necessary to remark that all the spectators did the same.

The forty-eight ambassadors of Maximilian of Austria, led by the reverend father in God, Jehan, Abbot of St.-Bertin, Chancellor of the

Golden Fleece, and Jacques de Goy, Sieur Dauby, High Bailiff of Ghent, then entered two by two, with a gravity that formed a remarkable contrast to the volatile ecclesiastical retinue of Charles de Bourbon. Deep silence descended on the assembly, broken only by stifled laughter at the absurd names and all the petty titles that each of these personages repeated with imperturbable solemnity to the usher, who then announced them, names and titles all mixed up and cruelly mangled, to the crowd. There was Master Loys Roelof, *échevin* of the city of Louvain; Messire Clays d'Etuelde, *échevin* of Brussels; Messire Paul de Baeust, Sieur de Voirmizelle, Justice of Flanders; Master Jehan Coleghens, burgomaster of the city of Antwerp; Master George de la Moere, and Master Gheldolf van der Hage, *échevins* of the city of Ghent; and the Sieur de Bierbecque, Jehan Pinnock, Jehan Dymaerzelle, et cetera, bailiffs, *échevins,* burgomasters; burgomasters, *échevins,* bailiffs; all stiff, starched, formal, decked out in velvets and damasks, wearing caps of black velvet with prodigious tassels of Cyprus gold thread; fine Flemish heads after all, with austere but goodly faces, of the same family as those that Rembrandt cast in relief, so grave and so expressive, against the dark ground of his *Ronde de Nuit*,[30] personages who all had it written on their foreheads that Maximilian of Austria had good reason "to place full confidence," as his manifesto declared, "in their discretion, firmness, experience, loyalty, and rare qualities."

There was, however, one exception. There was a sharp, intelligent, crafty-looking face, with a mug that combined something of the monkey and the diplomat, before whom the Cardinal advanced three steps with a low bow, and whose name, nevertheless, was plain Guillaume Rym, councillor and resident of the city of Ghent.

Few knew who this Guillaume Rym was. He was a man of rare genius, who in times of revolution would have raised himself to distinction but was forced in the fifteenth century to resort to subterranean intrigues and to live in the trenches, as the Duke of St.-Simon put it. In any case, he was duly admired by the first trench fighter in Europe; he machinated in familiar concert with Louis XI and frequently lent a helping hand to the King in his secret activities. The crowd knew nothing of this: they were amazed at the respect paid by the Cardinal to so insignificant a person as a Flemish citizen.

CHAPTER IV

Master Jacques Coppenole

While the resident of Ghent and His Eminence were exchanging low bows and a few words in a still lower tone, a man of lofty stature, with jolly face and broad shoulders, stepped forward for the purpose of entering abreast with Guillaume Rym; he looked for all the world like a bulldog following a fox. His felt cap and leather vest were conspicuous amid the velvets and silks that surrounded him. Assuming that he was some groom who had lost his way, the usher stopped him.

"No admittance here, my friend," he said.

The man in the leather vest pushed him back.

"What does the fellow want with me?" he cried in a voice that drew the attention of the whole hall to this strange encounter. "You don't see that I belong to them?"

"Your name?" asked the usher.

"Jacques Coppenole."

"Your titles?"

"Hosier; at the sign of the Three Chains in Ghent."

The usher was staggered. To have to announce bailiffs and burgomasters and *échevins* was bad enough, but a hosier!—no—he could not make up his mind to that. The Cardinal was on thorns. The whole assembly was all eye and ear. For two days His Eminence had been taking pains to tame these Flemish bears, in order to make them a little more presentable in public, and his failure was galling. Meanwhile Guillaume Rym, with his sly smile, stepped up to the usher and said in a very low whisper, "Announce Master Jacques Coppenole, clerk to the *échevins* of the city of Ghent."

"Usher," said the Cardinal in a loud voice, "announce Master Jacques Coppenole, clerk to the *échevins* of the most noble city of Ghent."

This was a mistake. Now, it is very certain that Guillaume Rym, had he been left to himself, would have shrugged off the correction, but Coppenole had heard the Cardinal.

"No, by God!" he cried, with his voice of thunder. "Jacques Coppenole, hosier. Do you hear me, Usher? Neither more nor less. By God!

Hosier—that's good enough! Monsieur the Archduke has more than once sought his gloves among my hose."

A burst of laughter and applause exploded. A witticism is instantly understood in Paris, and consequently always applauded. Coppenole was of the people, and the assembly that surrounded him was made up of the people. As a consequence, the communication between them was immediate, electric, and unencumbered. The arrogant bravado of the Flemish hosier, at the same time that it humbled the courtiers, awakened in all those plebeian minds a sense of dignity, still but vague and indistinct in the fifteenth century. This hosier, who had just defied Monsieur the Cardinal, was their equal—a soothing thought to poor devils accustomed to obeying and respecting the valets of the very sergeants of the bailiff of the Abbot of St.-Geneviève, the train bearer of the Cardinal.

Coppenole bowed haughtily to His Eminence, who returned the obeisance of the high and mighty burgher, dreaded by Louis XI. Then, while Guillaume Rym, a "cunning, spiteful man," according to Philippe de Comines, looked at both with a mocking smile of conscious superiority, they proceeded to their places—the Cardinal mortified and disconcerted; Coppenole, calm and proud, thinking, no doubt, that his title of hosier was as good as any other, and that Mary of Burgundy, the mother of that Margaret whose marriage Coppenole had come to negotiate, would have feared him less as a cardinal than as a hosier; for it was not a cardinal who had raised the people of Ghent against the favorites of the daughter of Charles the Bold; it was not a cardinal who had steeled the crowd against her tears and her entreaties by a single word when the Princess of Flanders proceeded to the very foot of the scaffold to beg their lives of her subjects. The hosier had only to lift his finger and off went your heads, most illustrious gentlemen, Guy d'Hymbercourt and Chancellor Guillaume Hugonet![31]

The poor Cardinal's ordeal, however, was not yet over; he was doomed to drink to the very dregs the cup of penance for being in such bad company. The reader has, perhaps, not forgotten the impudent beggar, who at the opening of the prologue perched himself beneath the fringe of the Cardinal's gallery. The arrival of the illustrious guests had not dislodged him from his roost, and while the prelates and the ambassadors were packing themselves, like real Flemish herrings, in the boxes of the gallery, he had settled himself at his ease and carelessly crossed his legs over the architrave. Nobody, however, had at first noticed this extraordinary piece of insolence, the general attention being directed to another quarter. Neither was he, for his part, aware of what was going on in the hall; there he sat, rocking back and forth with Neapolitan indifference, repeating, from force of habit, the refrain "Charity, if you please!" It is certain that he was the only one in the whole assembly who had not paid attention to the altercation between Coppenole and the usher. Now, as luck would have it, the hosier of Ghent, with whom the people already sympathized so strongly, and on whom all eyes were fixed, took his seat in the first row in the gallery, just above the mendicant. Great was, nevertheless, their astonishment at seeing the Flemish ambassador, after taking a survey of the fellow nestled under his nose, slap him familiarly on his rag-covered shoulder. The beggar turned sharply around; surprise, recognition, pleasure, were expressed in both faces; and then, entirely ignoring the spectators, the hosier and the scurvy rogue shook hands and began to talk in a low tone, while the rags of Clopin Trouillefou, draped against the cloth of gold with which the gallery was hung, produced the effect of a caterpillar on an orange.

The novelty of this singular scene excited such a burst of merriment in the hall that the Cardinal could not help but notice it. He leaned forward, and as, from the place where he sat he had only a very imperfect view of the squalid figure of Trouillefou, he naturally supposed that the beggar was soliciting alms. Incensed at his audacity, he cried, "Monsieur Bailiff of the Palace, throw that scoundrel into the river."

"For God's sake! Monseigneur the Cardinal!" exclaimed Coppenole. "That scoundrel is a friend of mine."

"Hurrah! Hurrah!" shouted the crowd. From that moment Master Coppenole gained "great credit with the people of Paris, as well as of Ghent; for," adds Philippe de Comines, "men of that kind are sure to win it, since they are so unruly."

The Cardinal bit his lips. Turning to his neighbor, the Abbot of St.-Geneviève, he said in an undertone, "Monsieur the Archduke certainly sent us a nice bunch of ambassadors to announce Madame Margaret!"

"Your Eminence," replied the Abbot, "is throwing away your civilities on these Flemish hogs: *margaritas ante porcos.*"[32]

"Say rather," answered the Cardinal, with a smile, *"porces ante Margaritam."*[33]

The entire little cassocked Court was in raptures at this wordplay. The Cardinal felt somewhat relieved; he was now even with Coppenole; he too had gained applause for his witticism.

Now, of our readers who are capable of generalizing an image and an idea, to adopt the phraseology of the present day, permit us to ask if they have formed a clear image of the spectacle presented at the moment to which we are calling their attention, of the vast parallelogram of the great hall of Paris. In the middle of the hall, backed against the western wall, a wide and magnificent gallery hung with gold brocade, into which, through a small doorway with pointed arch, advances in procession a number of grave personages successively announced by the resounding voice of an usher. In the first row are already many venerable figures, muffled in ermine, velvet, and scarlet. On the floor of the hall, in front and on either side of the gallery, which maintains a dignified silence, a great crowd and a great uproar. A thousand vulgar eyes fixed on every face in the gallery, a thousand whispers at every name. The scene certainly is a curious one, and well deserving the attention of the spectators. But what is that kind of scaffold at the far end, on which are seen four puppetlike figures in motley colors? And who is that pale-faced man in a black frock at the foot of it? Why, dear reader, that is Pierre Gringoire and his prologue. We had all completely forgotten him. This was exactly what he was afraid of.

As soon as the Cardinal entered, Gringoire tried everything to save his prologue. At first he begged the actors, who were in a state of suspense, to proceed and to raise their voices; then, perceiving that nobody listened to them, he ordered them to stop; and for the quarter of an hour that the interruption lasted he struggled, calling on Gisquette and Liénarde to encourage their neighbors to call for the continuation of the prologue—but all in vain. Not a creature would turn away from the Cardinal, the ambassadors, and the balcony, the sole center of that vast circle of gazes. There is also reason to believe, and we record it with regret, that the audience was beginning to be somewhat tired of the prologue at the very moment when His Eminence arrived and created a terrible diversion. After all, the balcony exhibited precisely the same spectacle as the marble table—the conflict between Labor and Clergy, Nobility and Trade. And many people preferred to see them without disguise, living, breathing, moving, elbowing one another in flesh and blood in the Flemish ambassadors, the episcopal court, in the Cardinal's robe, in Coppenole's jacket, than talking in verse, painted, dressed up, resembling effigies of straw stuffed into the yellow and white tunics in which Gringoire had encased them.

When, however, our poet perceived that some degree of tranquillity was restored, he devised a stratagem for regaining the public attention. "Sir," he said, turning to a jolly citizen, whose face was the image of patience, "don't you think they had better go on?"

"With what?" asked the other.

"Why, with the play," replied Gringoire.

"Whatever you say," rejoined his neighbor.

This demi-approbation was quite enough for Gringoire. Mingling as much as possible with the crowd, he began to shout with all his might, "The play! The play! Go on with the play!"

"The devil!" said Joannes de Molendino. "What is it they are singing down there?" (Gringoire was, in fact, making as much noise as half a dozen persons.) "I say, comrades, the play is over, isn't it? They want to begin it again. We won't put up with that!"

"No, no," cried all the students. "Down with the play! Down with it!"

This only served to increase Gringoire's struggles, and he yelled louder than ever, "Go on! Go on!"

This clamor drew the attention of the Cardinal. "Bailiff of the Palace," he said to a stout man in black, stationed a few paces from him, "what is going on down there? It sounds like the infernal racket the devil's minions would make if they were trapped in a font of holy water!"

The Bailiff of the Palace was a sort of amphibious magistrate, a kind of bat of the judicial order, something between a rat and a bird, a judge and a soldier. He approached His Eminence and, greatly fearing his anger, explained to him with faltering tongue the impropriety of the people, how noon had arrived before His Eminence, and the actors had been forced to begin without waiting for him.

The Cardinal laughed outright. "By my faith!" he exclaimed. "The

Rector of the Université should have done the same! What do you say, Master Guillaume Rym?"

"Monseigneur," answered Master Guillaume Rym, "we ought to be glad that we have escaped half the play. The loss is so much gained."

"May those fellows continue their farce?" asked the Bailiff.

"Go on, go on," said the Cardinal, "it's the same to me. I'll read my breviary."

The Bailiff advanced to the front of the balcony and gestured for silence by a motion of his hand. "Citizens and peasants," he cried, "to satisfy those who wish the piece to proceed, and those who desire that it should end, His Eminence orders it to be continued."

Both sides had to resign themselves, but the author and the audience resented the Cardinal long afterward. The characters on the stage resumed their cue, and Gringoire hoped that at any rate the rest of the piece would be heard out. This hope, however, was destined, like his other illusions, very soon to be dashed. Silence was, indeed, to some degree restored among the audience, but Gringoire had not observed that, just when the Cardinal ordered the play to be continued, the balcony was far from full, and that after the Flemish envoys had taken their seats other persons, forming part of the retinue, kept coming in, and the names and titles of these, proclaimed every now and then by the bawling voice of the usher, broke in on the dialogue and made great havoc with it.

Try to imagine in the middle of a theatrical performance, between two rhymes and sometimes between two halves of a line, the shrill voice of the usher adding parenthetically, "Master Jacques Charmolue, the King's procurer for church courtyards!"

"Jehan de Harlay, squire, guard in the office of the night watch for the city of Paris!"

"My Lord Galiot de Genoillac, chevalier, Lord of Brussae, master of the King's artillery!"

"My Lord Treux-Raquier, overseer of waterworks and forests of our Lord the King, in the following regions of France, Champagne and Brie."

"My Lord Louis de Graville, chevalier, counselor, and chamberlain of the King, Admiral of France, warden of the forest of Vincennes."

"Master Denis Le Mercier, guard at the Home for the Blind!" et cetera, et cetera, et cetera.

It became unbearable.

Gringoire was even more incensed by this strange accompaniment, which rendered it difficult to follow the piece, because he felt that the interest increased as it proceeded, and that his work needed nothing but to be heard. Indeed, a more ingenious and more dramatic plot could scarcely be invented. The four characters of the prologue were bewailing their mortal embarrassment when Venus appeared to them in person, *vera incessu patuit dea*,[34] attired in a robe embroidered with the arms of the Cité of Paris. She came to make her claim to the dolphin promised to the most beautiful female. She was supported by Jupiter, whose thunder was heard rumbling in the dressing room, and the goddess had nearly prevailed and literally established her right to the hand of Monsieur the Dauphin when a child, in a dress of white damask and holding a daisy (diaphanous personification of the Princess of Flanders), arrived to vie against Venus. This unexpected event produced an instant change in the state of affairs. After some controversy, Venus, Margaret, and the whole party agreed to refer the matter to the good judgment of the Holy Virgin. There was another striking part, that of Don Pedro, King of Mesopotamia, but because of so many interruptions it was difficult to understand his role in the plot. All of these characters had to climb the ladder.

But the damage had been done. All these beauties were unfortunately neither appreciated nor understood. The moment the Cardinal entered it was as if an invisible and magic thread had suddenly drawn all eyes from the marble table to the balcony, from the southern extremity to the western side of the hall. Nothing could break the spell thrown over the audience. Every eye remained fixed on one point, and the newcomers and their accursed names, their faces, and their clothing created an endless diversion. This was most mortifying. Except for Gisquette and Liénarde, who turned around from time to time when Gringoire pulled on their sleeves, and their fat, patient neighbor, no one listened, or even looked at the poor forsaken play. Gringoire could see only profiles.

With what bitterness did he see his whole edifice of glory and poetry tumbling down piece by piece! To think that this same audience, which had been on the point of rebelling against Monsieur the Bailiff from impatience to see his work, now that they had it before them, cared nothing at all about it! A performance, too, that had begun amid such unanimous acclaim! Oh! The fickleness of popular opinion! How near they had been to hanging the sergeants of the bailiff! What would he not have given for the return of that delicious moment!

The brutal monologue of the usher ceased at last. Everyone had arrived. Gringoire breathed once more. The actors continued bravely. Suddenly, what should Master Coppenole the hosier do but rise from his seat? And Gringoire stood aghast to hear him, to the breathless attention of the spectators, begin this abominable speech.

"Gentleman citizens and squires of Paris, I know not, by God, what we are doing here. Down there, on that stage, there are some folks who appear ready for a fight. I cannot tell whether this is what you call a play. Let it be what it will, it is not amusing. They are mouthing off at each other, and that is all. Here I have been waiting for a quarter of an hour for the first blow, but nothing comes of it. They are a bunch of cowards who scratch each other with insults. You should have sent to London or Rotterdam for real fighters, and, I swear, you would have had punches that could be heard throughout the hall, but this bunch is pathetic. At least they should have given us a dance or some pantomime. No one told me about this. They promised me a Festival of Fools and the election of a Pope. We have our Pope of Fools in Ghent too, and, by God, in this respect we are behind your famous city! But here is what we do: we gather a crowd, such as this. Then everyone who wants to puts his head through a hole and makes a face at the others. He who makes the ugliest face is chosen Pope by popular vote—that's it. It is very amusing, I assure you. Shall we choose your Pope after the custom of my country? It will be less boring at any rate than listening to those loudmouths. If they would like to come and grin through the hole, why, let them. What do you say, gentleman citizens? We have here sufficiently grotesque samples of both sexes so that we can have a hearty laugh in the Flemish fashion, and we have ugly faces enough among us to expect an excellent grimace."

Gringoire wanted to respond, but stupefaction, outrage, and indignation rendered him speechless. Besides, the gesture of the popular hosier was hailed with such enthusiasm by the citizens, flattered to be called yeomen, that resistance was useless. All that he could now do was swim with the current. Gringoire hid his face in his hands because he was not fortunate enough to have a cape with which he might cover his head like Agamemnon of Timanthe.

CHAPTER V

QUASIMODO

In the blink of an eye everything was ready for carrying out Coppenole's idea. Townsmen, students, and lawyers' clerks had fallen to work. The little chapel opposite the marble table was chosen for the theater of the grimaces. Having broken the glass in the pretty little rose window over the door, they agreed that the competitors should put their heads through the circle of stone that was left. To enable them to reach it, two barrels were brought out and set one on top of the other. It was decided that all candidates, whether men or women—for women were eligible—should hide their faces and keep them covered in the chapel till the moment of exhibiting them so that the first impression of the grimace might be the stronger. In a few minutes the chapel was full of competitors, and the door was shut on them.

From his place Coppenole ordered, directed, and oversaw all the arrangements. During the uproar the Cardinal, not less dismayed than Gringoire, having excused himself on the plea of business and vespers, retired with his retinue while the crowd that had been so excited by his arrival was entirely indifferent to his departure. Guillaume Rym was the only person that noticed the embarrassment of His Eminence. Popular favor, like the sun, continued to move on; having set out from one end of the hall, after pausing some time in the middle, it was now at the other end. The marble table, the brocade balcony, each had had its moment; it was now the turn of Louis XI's chapel. The field was open to every sort of madness; the Flemish and the rabble alone remained.

The grimaces began. The first face presented itself at the window with its red eyes and gaping mouth, and forehead wrinkled like hussar boots in the time of the Emperor. It caused such convulsions of inextinguishable laughter that Homer[35] would have taken these wretches for immortal gods. Gringoire's Jupiter knew this fate only too well. A second and a third grimace followed—then another and another, inspiring redoubled shouts of laughter and stampings and clatterings of glee. The crowd was seized with a sort of frantic intoxication, a supernatural kind of fascination, of which it would be difficult to convey any idea to the reader of our day. Imagine a series of faces successively presenting every geometric shape, from the triangle to the trapezium—from the cone to the polyhedron; every human expression, from rage to lechery; every age, from the wrinkles of the newborn infant to those of the hag at death's door; all the religious phantasmagoria from Faunus to Beelzebub; every animal profile, from the distended jaw to the beak, from the snout of the hog to the muzzle of the bull. Imagine all the grotesque heads of the Pont Neuf, those nightmares petrified under the hand of Germain Pilon, suddenly starting into life, and coming one after another to stare you in the face with flaming eyes. All the masks of the carnival of Venice passed in succession before your eyeglass—in a word, it was a human kaleidoscope.

The frantic revel became more and more wild. Teniers could have given but an imperfect idea of the scene. Imagine Salvator Rosa's battle turned into a bacchanalian play.[36] There were no more students, ambassadors, men, or women—all were lost in the general license. The great hall was one vast furnace of effrontery and merriment. Every mouth was a cry, every eye a flash, every face a contortion, every individual a poser. Everyone howled and roared. The extraordinary faces that in turn presented themselves at the window acted like kindling thrown on a blazing fire, and from this volatile crowd issued, like steam from a furnace, a dull roar, a low hiss or whistling like the noise made by the wings of a monstrous gnat.

"Curses!"

"Look at that face!"

"That one is worthless."

"Next!"

"Guillemette Maugerepuis, look at that bull's muzzle. Only the horns are missing. Isn't that your husband?"

"Next!"

"What the hell is that face?"

"Whoa there! That's cheating! You can only show your face!"

"Damn that Perrette Callebote!"

"She can do that?"

"Hurrah! Hurrah!"

"I can't breathe!"

"His ears don't fit!"

Et cetera, et cetera.

We have to give credit to our friend Jehan. In the middle of all this, we could still see him on top of his pillar, like a ship boy on the topsail. He was going wild. His mouth was wide open, and from it escaped an inaudible sound, inaudible not because it was lost in the general clamor but because it was so intense that he must have surpassed Sauveur's frequency of twelve thousand vibrations or the eight thousand of Biot.[37]

Meanwhile Gringoire, the first moment of dejection over, had recovered his spirits; he had braced himself against adversity. "Go on!" he said for the third time to his actors, his speaking machines. Then he paced back and forth, with long strides, before the marble table. He almost felt tempted to take his turn to exhibit himself at the round window of the chapel, just for the pleasure of making a face at the ungrateful populace. But no, he said to himself, no revenge! That would be unworthy of us. Let us struggle manfully to the last: the power of poetry is mighty over the people. I will win them back. We shall see which will conquer—grimaces or belle-lettres.

Alas, poor Gringoire! He was left to be the only spectator of his play. Every back was turned on him.

I am wrong: the fat, patient man whom he had previously consulted in a critical moment was still turned toward the theater. As for Gisquette and Liénarde, they had long deserted.

Gringoire was touched to the bottom of his heart by the constancy of his only spectator. He went up and spoke to him while gently shaking his arm because the good man was leaning on the balustrade and napping a little.

"Sir," said Gringoire, "I am exceedingly obliged to you."

"Sir," replied the fat man, with a yawn, "for what?"

"I see," rejoined the poet, "that you are quite annoyed by all this noise, which prevents your listening with ease. But never mind; your name will be handed down to posterity. May I ask what it is?"

"Renauld Château, Keeper of the Seal of the Châtelet of Paris, at your service."

"Sir, you are the only representative of the Muses in this assembly," said Gringoire.

"You are too polite, sir," replied the Keeper of the Seal of the Châtelet.

"You are the only one," resumed Gringoire, "who has paid any attention to the play. What do you think of it?"

"Why, to tell the truth," answered the fat magistrate, only half awake, "it is lively enough."

Gringoire was forced to be content with this praise, for thunders of applause, mingled with prodigious shouts, cut short their conversation. The Pope of Fools was elected. "Hurrah! Hurrah! Hurrah!" cried the people on all sides.

It was, in truth, a countenance of miraculous ugliness that at this moment shone forth from the rose window. After the succession of faces, pentagonal, hexagonal, and heteroclite at this opening, none of which had realized the idea of the grotesque that the crowd had set up in its feverish imagination, it required nothing short of the sublimely monstrous grimace that had just dazzled the multitude to win their votes. Master Coppenole himself applauded; and Clopin Trouillefou, who had been a candidate—and God knows what intensity of ugliness his features could attain—confessed himself beaten. We shall do the same: we shall not attempt to give the reader any idea of that tetrahedron nose, of that horseshoe mouth, of that little left eye, obscured by a bristly red eyebrow, while the right was completely overwhelmed and buried by an enormous wart; of those irregular teeth, jagged here and there like the battlements of a fortress; of that horny lip, over which one of those teeth protruded, like the tusk of an elephant; of that hooklike chin; and, above all, of the expression, that mixture of spite, astonishment, and melancholy, spread over all these features. Imagine such an object, if you can.

The acclamation was unanimous: the crowd rushed to the chapel. The lucky Pope of Fools was brought out in triumph, but it was not till then that surprise and admiration reached their height. The grimace was his natural visage. His whole person was a grimace. His prodigious head was covered with red bristles; between his shoulders rose an enormous hump, which was counterbalanced by a protuberance in front; his thighs and legs were so strangely put together that they touched only at the knees and, seen from the front, resembled two sickles joined at the handles. His feet were immense, his hands monstrous; but, with all this deformity, he possessed a formidable air of strength, agility, and courage, constituting a singular exception to the eternal rule which ordains that force, as well as beauty, shall result from harmony. This was the Pope of Fools chosen by the crowd. He looked like a giant who had been broken in pieces and badly soldered together again.

When this sort of Cyclops appeared on the threshold of the chapel, motionless, squat, almost as broad as high, "the square of his base," as a great man has put it,[38] the populace instantly recognized him by his coat, half red and half purple, sprinkled with silver bells, and, more especially, by the perfection of his ugliness, and cried out with one voice: "It is Quasimodo the bell ringer! It is Quasimodo the hunchback of Notre-Dame! Quasimodo the one-eyed! Quasimodo the bowlegged! Hurrah! Hurrah!" The poor devil, it seems, had plenty of surnames to choose among.

"Let pregnant women take care!" cried the students. Women actually covered their faces.

"Oh, the ugly ape!" cried one.

"And as evil as he is ugly," said another.

"It is the devil himself!" exclaimed a third.

"I am so unlucky as to live near Notre-Dame, and I hear him at night prowling around in the gutters."

"What! With the cats?"

"He casts spells on us through our chimneys!"

"The other night he came and grinned at me through my garret window. I thought it was a man: I was terrified."

"I am sure he attends the witches' sabbaths. He once left a broom on my lead shots."

"Oh, the ugly hunchback!"

"Faugh!"

The men, on the contrary, were delighted and applauded. Quasimodo, the object of all the tumult, stood at the door of the chapel, gloomy and grave, exhibiting himself to the popular admiration. Suddenly, Robin Poussepain came up close to him and laughed in his face. Quasimodo, without uttering a word, caught him up by the belt and hurled him to the distance of ten paces through the crowd.

Master Coppenole, astonished at the feat, approached him. "By God!" he exclaimed. "Holy Father! Why you are the finest piece of ugliness I ever beheld. You deserve to be Pope in Rome as well as in Paris."

As he said this he cheerfully clapped his hand on the monster's shoulder. Quasimodo did not stir. Coppenole continued: "My fine fellow, I feel like having a wrestle with you, were it to cost me a new *douzain* of twelve Tournois. What do you say?"

Quasimodo made no reply. "By God!" cried the hosier, "are you deaf?" Quasimodo really *was* deaf.

Nevertheless he began to feel annoyed by Coppenole's gestures and turned toward him with so formidable a grinding of teeth that the Flemish giant recoiled, like a bulldog from a cat. A circle of terror and respect, having a radius of at least fifteen geometric paces, was left vacant around this strange personage.

An old woman informed Coppenole that Quasimodo was indeed deaf.

"Deaf!" cried the hosier, with a Flemish horse laugh. "By God, he is an accomplished Pope!"

"Ha!" said Jehan, who had at length descended from his pillar to obtain a closer view of the new Pope, "it's my brother's bell ringer! Good day, Quasimodo!"

"A devil of a fellow!" sighed Robin Poussepain, aching all over from the effects of his fall. "He appears—he is a hunchback. He walks—he is bowlegged. He looks at you—he is one-eyed. You talk to him—he is deaf! And what use does this Polyphemus make of his tongue, I wonder?"

"He can talk when he likes," said the old woman. "He became deaf with ringing the bells. He is not mute."

"That is what he is missing," observed Jehan.

"And he has one eye too many," added Robin Poussepain.

"Not so," rejoined Jehan tartly. "A one-eyed man is more incomplete than one who is quite blind. He knows what he is missing."

Meanwhile all the beggars, all the lackeys, all the thieves, along with the students, went in procession to the storeroom of the Basoche to get the pasteboard tiara and the mock robe of the Pope of Fools. Quasimodo allowed them to be put on him with a kind of proud docility. Then he was required to sit in a colorful litter. Twelve officers of the

Fraternity of Fools hoisted it up on their shoulders, and a sort of bitter and disdainful exultation spread over the morose countenance of the Cyclops when he saw beneath his feet all those heads of straight, handsome, well-shaped men. The roaring and ragged procession then moved off to parade, as was the custom, through the galleries inside the palace before it proceeded to the streets and public squares of the Cité.

CHAPTER VI

La Esmeralda

We are very happy to report to the reader that, during the whole of this scene, Gringoire and his play had stood their ground. His actors, spurred on by him, had continued the performance, and he had continued to listen to them. In spite of the uproar he was determined to go through with it, and did not give up hope of being able to regain the public's attention. This glimmer of hope became brighter when he saw Quasimodo, Coppenole, and the deafening retinue of the Pope of Fools leaving the hall. The crowd rushed out after them. "Excellent!" he said. "We shall get rid of all those troublemakers!" Unfortunately, these were the whole assembly. In the twinkling of an eye the great hall was empty.

To tell the truth, a few spectators still lingered behind, some alone, others in groups around the pillars, old men, women, or children who had had enough of the uproar and tumult. Some of the students too remained astride the entablature of the windows, where they had a good view of the square.

"Well," thought Gringoire, "there are quite as many as I want to hear the conclusion of my play. They are few, but they are an elite, a literate, audience."

At that moment a symphonic overture, destined to produce a striking effect upon the arrival of the Holy Virgin, was not forthcoming. Gringoire saw that his musicians had been pressed into the service of the Pope of Fools. "Skip that part," he said, with the composure of a stoic.

He approached a knot of citizens who seemed to be talking about his play. He overheard this fragment of their conversation:

"Master Cheneteau, you know the Hôtel de Navarre, which belonged to Monsieur de Nemours?"

"Yes, facing the chapel of Braque."

"Well! The exchequer has just leased it to Guillaume Alexandre, the historian, for six pounds eight sols Parisis a year."

"How rents are rising!"

"Bah!" cried Gringoire, with a sigh. "The others are listening, at any rate."

"Comrades," one of the young rascals at the windows suddenly shouted, "La Esmeralda! La Esmeralda in the square!"

This announcement produced a magical effect. All who were left in the hall ran to the windows, clambering up the walls to obtain a view and repeating, "La Esmeralda! La Esmeralda!" Thunderous applause arose at the same moment from the square.

"What can they mean by La Esmeralda?" said Gringoire, clasping his hands in despair. "Gracious heaven! It seems to have become the windows' turn now!"

Turning toward the marble table, he perceived that the performance was at a standstill. It was precisely the moment when Jupiter should have appeared with his thunderbolt, but Jupiter was standing stock-still at the foot of the stage.

"Michel Giborne!" cried the incensed poet. "What are you doing? What is your part? Get up there!"

"Alas!" replied Jupiter, "one of the students has run away with the ladder."

Gringoire looked: it was so. There was no way to reach the stage. "The scoundrel!" he murmured. "And why did he take the ladder?"

"To go to see La Esmeralda," answered Jupiter, in a doleful tone. "He must have said to himself, 'Here's a ladder that's of no use,' and off he scampered with it."

This was the final blow. Gringoire received it with resignation.

"The devil take you!" he said to the performers. "If I am paid you shall be."

With lowered head he then made his retreat, but at the very end, like a general who has been soundly beaten. "A nice pack of asses and boobies, these Parisians!" he muttered between his teeth as he descended the winding staircase of the palace. "They come to hear a play and will not listen to it. They will pay attention to everything and everybody—to Clopin Trouillefou, to the Cardinal, to Coppenole, to Quasimodo, to the devil! But on the Holy Virgin they have none to bestow. Had I known, I would have given you Virgin Maries, Gaping oafs! I came to see faces and I saw only backs. To be a poet, and to face the fate of an apothecary! Homer, it is true, begged for his bread in the Greek towns; and Naso[39] died in exile among the Muscovites. But the devil flay me if I understand what they mean by their La Esmeralda. And what kind of word is it to begin with? It must surely be Egyptique!"[40]

BOOK II

CHAPTER I

FROM CHARYBDIS INTO SCYLLA

Night comes on early in the month of January. It was already dusk when Gringoire left the palace. To him the nightfall was doubly welcome, as he sought out some obscure and deserted street where he might muse undisturbed, and where philosophy might apply the first dressing to the poet's wound. In fact, philosophy was his only refuge; he did not know where he would find lodging. After the great failure of his dramatic endeavor, he did not dare return to his lodging on the Rue Grenier-sur-l'Eau, opposite the Port au Foin. He had counted on being paid by Monsieur the Provost so that he could, in turn, pay Master Guillaume Doulx-Sire (licensed farmer of livestock with cloven hoofs) for the six months' rent that he owed him; that is to say, twelve sols Parisis—twelve times the value of all that he possessed in the world, including his hose, shirt, and doublet. Having all the sidewalks of Paris to choose from, he considered for a moment, seeking temporary shelter under the little gateway of the prison of the treasurer of the Ste.-Chapelle. He remembered having noticed, in the preceding week, a stepping stone at the door of a Parliamentary counselor on the Rue de la Savaterie. He thought to himself at that time that this stone would be, in case of emergency, an excellent pillow for a beggar or a poet. He thanked Providence for having sent this excellent idea, but, as he was preparing to cross the palace yard, for the purpose of entering the tortuous labyrinth of the Cité, with its ancient winding streets of la Barillerie, la Vielle-Draperie, la Savaterie, la Juiverie,[1] and others, still standing, and their houses nine stories high, he saw the procession of the Pope of Fools coming out of the palace and advancing across the courtyard toward him with loud shouts, the glow of numerous torches, and his own band of musicians. This sight tore open afresh the wounds of his self-love; he took to his heels. In the keen mortification of his dramatic failure everything that reminded him of the festival was salt in his wounds.

He wanted to reach the Pont St.-Michel. Boys were running back and forth with sparklers and setting off firecrackers. "Curse the fireworks!" Gringoire said, and he headed for the Pont au Change. To the houses at the end of the bridge were attached three large pieces of canvas, with likenesses of the King, the Dauphin, and Margaret of Flanders; and six smaller, on which were portrayed the Duke of Austria, the Cardinal de Bourbon, Monsieur de Beaujeu, Madame Jeanne of France, Monsieur the Bastard of Bourbon, and I know not whom besides—it was all illuminated by torches. A crowd of spectators was admiring these performances.

"Happy painter, Jehan Fourbault!"[2] said Gringoire with a deep sigh as he turned his back on the canvases. There was a street just before him: it appeared so dark and so deserted that he hoped there to be out of hearing as well as out of sight of all the festivities. He entered it. Suddenly his foot struck some obstacle; he stumbled and fell. It was the trunk of the may tree, which the clerks of the Basoche had placed that morning "in honor of the day" at the door of a member of the Parliament. Gringoire bore with fortitude this new misfortune; he picked himself up and reached the river. Leaving behind him the Civil and Criminal Court of the Parliament, he followed the high wall of the King's gardens, on the unpaved riverbank where he was ankle-deep in mud. He arrived at the western point of the Cité and surveyed for some time the islet of Passeur aux Vaches,[3] which has since disappeared beneath the Pont Neuf with its bronze horse. Beyond the white, narrow stripe of water that separated him from it, the islet appeared to him in the dark like a black mass. By the glimmer of a faint light he could make out a kind of hut in the shape of a beehive that afforded shelter to the ferryman during the night.

"Happy ferryman!" thought Gringoire. "You do not dream of glory, you write no epithalamiums! What are the marriages of kings and duchesses of Burgundy to you! You know no other jewels than the daisies of the meadows, which offer themselves to your grazing cattle! While I, a poet, am hooted, and shiver with cold, and owe twelve sous, and the sole of my shoe is so thin that it might serve as your lampshade! Thank you, ferryman! Your hut consoles the eye and makes me forget Paris."

He was awakened from his almost lyric ecstasy by the explosion of a double firecracker, suddenly fired from the happy cabin. It was the ferryman taking his share in the rejoicings of the day. The explosion made Gringoire shudder.

"Accursed festival!" he cried. "Will you pursue me wherever I go, even to the cabin of the cattle ferryman?" Then he looked at the Seine flowing at his feet, and a horrible temptation came over him. "Ah!" he said, "how gladly would I drown myself, only the water is so cold!"

Then he formed a desperate resolution. Since he found it impossible to escape the Pope of Fools, the paintings of Jehan Fourbault, the may trees, the sparklers, and the firecrackers, he determined to head for the Place de Grève and to penetrate boldly into the very heart of the rejoicings. "At any rate," he thought, "I shall be able to get warm at the bonfire, and perhaps dine on some of the crumbs of the meal provided at the public larder of the city."

CHAPTER II

The Place de Grève

Today only a pitiful vestige of the Place de Grève, as it then existed, remains. This is the charming turret that occupies the north corner of the square, and that, already buried beneath the ignoble plaster that encases the fine outlines of its sculptures, will probably soon disappear, engulfed by the wave of new buildings that is so rapidly swallowing up all the ancient facades of Paris.

Those who, like ourselves, cannot pass through the Place de Grève without bestowing a look of pity and sympathy on that poor turret, cooped up between two paltry erections of the time of Louis XV, may easily imagine the general aspect of the edifice to which it belonged and reconstruct in imagination the entire old Gothic square of the fifteenth century.

It was then, as at present, an irregular trapezoid, bordered on one side by the quay and on the three others by a series of lofty, narrow, and gloomy houses. By day, the viewer might admire the variety of buildings, covered with sculptures or carving and displaying a complete array of the various styles of domestic architecture of the Middle

Ages, the period between the fifteenth and the eleventh century, from the casement window, which had already begun to supersede the ogive, from the Romanesque arch, which had been supplanted by the ogive, and which still existed on the ground floor of that ancient building of the Tour-Roland, on the corner of the square next to the Seine, by the Rue de la Tannerie. By night, all that could be distinguished of that mass of buildings was the dark, jagged outline of the roofs stretching their chain of sharp corners around the square. For one of the radical differences between the cities of that time and the cities of the present day is that now the fronts face the streets and squares, whereas then it was the gables. During the last two centuries houses have turned around.

In the center of the east side of the square rose a heavy and hybrid structure in three distinct sections. It was called by three names, which explain its history, its intention, and its architecture: the Maison au Dauphin, because Charles V as Dauphin had resided there; La Marchandise, because it served as the Hôtel de Ville; and the Maison aux Pilliers (*domus ad piloria*), from the row of massive pillars that supported its three stories. One could have found there all that is requisite for a good city like Paris; a chapel for praying God in, a hall for holding audiences and occasionally snubbing the servants of the King, and, in the attic, there was an arsenal well stocked with artillery. For the citizens of Paris know that it is not sufficient on every occasion to beg and to pray for the freedom of the Cité, and therefore they always keep in reserve a good rusty musket or two in an attic in the Hôtel de Ville.

The Grève wore at that time the same sinister aspect that it still retains, because of the unpleasant ideas it inspires and because of the gloomy Hôtel de Ville of Dominique Bocador,[4] which occupies the site of the Maison aux Pilliers. A permanent gallows and a pillory, or, as they were called in those days, "a justice and a ladder," placed side by side in the middle of the pavement, conferred no particular attractions on this fatal spot, where so many human beings full of health and life had suffered. Fifty years later the fever of St. Vallier was born here.[5] This disease produced by fear of the scaffold was the most monstrous of all illnesses because it came not from God but from man.

Let us say in passing that it is of some consolation that the death penalty with its iron wheels, its stone gallows, and all its equipment for executions, permanently embedded in the pavement, which three hundred years ago still had its place in the Grève, the Halles, the Place Dauphin, the Croix du Trahoir, the Swine Market, the hideous Montfaucon, the barrier of the Sergens, the Place aux Chats, the Porte St.-Denis, Champeaux, the Porte Baudets, and the Porte St.-Jacques (without taking into consideration the numberless "ladders" of the Provosts, the Bishop, the chapters, the abbots, the priors, who all possessed the power of life and death, not to mention the judicial drownings in the river Seine), it is of some consolation, I repeat, to think that today this hoary feudal lord, stripped gradually of all the pieces of its armor, has had to renounce its luxury of pains and penalties, its imaginative punishments and its various tortures, for which cause a new leather bed was made every five years at the Grand Châtelet. This feudal sovereign is almost banished; it is pursued in our books of law, driven from square to square, and would occupy in our immense Paris merely a shabby corner of the Grève, one miserable, furtive, worried, shamefaced guillotine, which always seems as if fearful of being caught in the act, so speedily does it disappear after striking the fatal blow.

CHAPTER III

BESOS PARA GOLPES[6]

When Pierre Gringoire reached the Place de Grève, he was quite numb with cold. He had gone over the Pont aux Meuniers to avoid the crowd at the Pont au Change and the flags of Jehan Fourbault, but the wheels of all the Bishop's windmills had splashed him so unmercifully as he passed that his cloak was drenched; it seemed, moreover, as if the failure of his play had made him more chilly than ever. Accordingly, he hastened toward the bonfire that blazed magnificently in the middle of the square. A large crowd of people formed a circle around it.

"Damned Parisians!" he said to himself, for Gringoire, like a genuine dramatic poet, was addicted to soliloquies, "there they are, keeping me out from the fire! And yet I am in great need of a comfortable chimney corner. My shoes leak, and all those infernal windmills rained on me! The devil take the Bishop of Paris and his windmills! I would like to know what a bishop has to do with a windmill! Does he expect to become a miller bishop some day or other? If he needs nothing but my malediction, I will give it to him readily, and to his cathedral, and to his windmills. Let's see if these boobies will take notice! But what are they doing there, I want to know. Warming themselves—fine amusement! Gaping at the bonfire burning—what a pretty sight!"

On looking more closely, he perceived that the circle was much larger than it needed to have been had the persons composing it been desirous only of warming themselves at the King's fire; and that the assemblage of spectators had not gathered only to admire the beauty of the hundred blazing bundles of wood. In the vast space left open between the crowd and the fire there was a young girl dancing.

Gringoire, skeptical philosopher and satirical poet that he was, could not immediately decide whether this young girl was a human being, a fairy, or an angel, so completely was he fascinated by the dazzling vision. She was not tall, though she appeared to be so from the slenderness and elegance of her figure. Her complexion was dark, but it was easy to divine that by daylight her skin must have had the beautiful golden tint of the Roman and Andalusian women. Her small foot was Andalusian as well. She danced, whirled, turned around, on an old Persian carpet, carelessly thrown under her feet. Every time her radiant face passed before you as she turned, her large, black eyes flashed lightning.

Every eye was fixed on her, every mouth open; and, in truth, while she was dancing this way, to the sound of the tambourine, which her two round and exquisitely shaped arms held above her head, she was thin, frail, and volatile like a wasp. With her smooth bodice of gold, her colorful dress that swelled with the rapidity of her motions, with her bare shoulders, her finely turned legs that her skirt now and then revealed, her black hair, her flaming eyes, she was a supernatural creature.

"In truth," thought Gringoire, "she is a magical creature, a nymph, a goddess, a bacchanae of Mount Menelaeus!"[7] At that moment one of the magical creature's tresses came loose, and a piece of yellow brass that had been fastened to it fell to the ground. "But no," he said, "she is a gypsy!" The illusion was shattered.

She began dancing again. She picked up from the ground two swords, which she balanced on their points on her forehead and made them turn around one way while she turned the other. She was in fact a gypsy, neither more nor less. Though the spell was broken, the whole scene was not without fascination and charm for Gringoire: the bonfire threw a crude red, trembling light on the wide circle of faces and on the tawny brow of the girl. At the far end of the square, it cast a faint glow, mingled with the wavering shadows, on the ancient, black, and furrowed worn-out facade of the Maison aux Pilliers on the one hand and on the stone arms of the gallows on the other.

Among the thousand faces on which this light cast a scarlet hue, there was one that seemed to be more deeply absorbed in the contemplation of the dancer than any of the others. It was the face of an austere, calm, and somber man. This man, whose outfit was hidden by the crowd who surrounded him, appeared to be no more than thirty-five years of age. He was, nevertheless, bald and had at his temples a few tufts of thin and already gray hair. His ample and lofty brow was creased with wrinkles, but in his deep-sunk eyes there was an expression of extraordinary youth, ardent life, and deep passion. He kept his eyes intently fixed on the Bohemian, and while the lively girl of sixteen danced and whirled to everyone else's delight, his reverie seemed to become more and more gloomy. At times a smile and a sigh would cross his lips, but the smile was by far the more pained of the two. The girl eventually paused, out of breath, and the people applauded with love.

"Djali!" said the Bohemian. Gringoire saw a pretty little white goat emerge, a nimble, lively, glossy creature with gold horns, gold hoofs, and a gold collar, which he had not noticed before and which had, till then, been lying at the corner of the carpet watching her mistress dance. "Djali," said the girl, "it is your turn now"; and, seating herself, she gracefully held the tambourine before the animal. "Djali," she continued, "what month are we in?" The goat raised her foreleg and struck one stroke on the tambourine. It was in fact the first month. The crowd applauded. "Djali," said the girl, turning the tambourine a different way, "what day of the month is this?" Djali again raised her little gold hoof and struck six blows on the instrument. "Djali," continued the gypsy, again changing the position of the tambourine, "what time is it?" Djali gave seven blows. At that very moment the clock of the Maison aux Pilliers struck seven. The people were astounded.

"There is sorcery at the bottom of this!" said a sinister voice in the crowd. It was that of the bald man, who never took his eyes off the

Bohemian. She shuddered and turned away, and thunderous applause burst forth and drowned the sinister exclamation. The applause had the effect of effacing it so completely from her mind that she continued to question her goat.

"Djali, show me what Master Guichard Grand Remy, captain of the city pistoleers, does in the Candlemas procession." Djali raised herself on her hind legs and began bleating and walking with such comic gravity that the whole circle of spectators roared with laughter at this parody of the theatrical devotion of the captain of the pistoleers.

"Djali," resumed the girl, emboldened by the increasing applause, "show me how Master Jacques Charmolue, the King's Proctor in the Ecclesiastical Court, preaches." The goat sat down on her rump and began bleating and shaking her forepaws in such a grotesque way that, in gesture, accent, attitude, everything except bad French and worse Latin, it was Jacques Charmolue to a tee. The crowd applauded more loudly than ever.

"Sacrilege! Profanation!" shouted the bald man. The gypsy turned around once more. "Ah!" she said, "it is that hateful man!" Then, lengthening her lower lip beyond the upper, she gave a pout that seemed to be habitual to her, turned on her heel, and began to collect the donations of the multitude in her tambourine. Silver and copper coins of all sorts and sizes showered into it. She came to Gringoire, who so readily thrust his hand into his pocket that she stopped. "The devil!" muttered the poet, fumbling in his pocket and finding the reality, that is, the void. The graceful girl stood still before him, looking at him with her large eyes and holding out her tambourine. Perspiration fell from Gringoire's brow. If he had had Peru in his pocket he would certainly have given it to the dancer, but Gringoire had no Peru there, and, besides, America was not yet discovered. An unexpected incident luckily came to his rescue.

"Get out of here, locust of Egypt," cried a sharp voice from the darkest corner of the square. The young girl turned around terrified. It was not the voice of the bald man; it was the voice of a woman, it was a devout and spiritual voice. This exclamation, which frightened the gypsy, excited the merriment of a troop of boys who were strolling near the spot. "It is the crazy woman in the Tour-Roland," they cried, with shouts of laughter. "It's Sad Sack who is complaining. Perhaps she has had no supper. Let us run to the buffet and see if we can get something for her!" And away they scampered to the Maison aux Pilliers.

Meanwhile, Gringoire had taken advantage of the girl's agitation to sneak off. The shouts of the boys reminded him that he had not eaten either. He thought that he too might as well try his luck at the buffet. But the young rogues ran too fast for him; when he arrived everything was cleared away; there was not a scrap of any kind left. There wasn't even a miserable five sous sandwich. All that was left were some lovely fleurs-de-lis on the wall, with garlands of roses. These were painted by Matthew Biterne in 1434. It made for a meager meal.

It is not pleasant to be obliged to go to bed without supper, and still less agreeable to have no bed to go to as well as no supper to eat. Such was Gringoire's predicament. He found himself closely pressed on all sides by necessity, and he thought necessity unnecessarily harsh. He had long since discovered this truth, that Jupiter created man in a fit of misanthropy, and that, throughout the whole life of the philosopher, his destiny keeps his philosophy in a state of siege. For his own part, he had never seen the blockade so complete: he heard his stomach make a battle cry, and he declared it very inappropriate of malicious destiny to conquer his philosophy with famine.

He was becoming more and more absorbed in this melancholy reverie when a strange kind of song, though remarkably sweet, roused him from it. It was the gypsy girl who was singing. Her voice, like her dancing and her beauty, was indefinable, something pure, sonorous, aerial, winged, as it were. There was a continual expansion of melodies, unexpected cadences, then simple phrases interspersed with harsh and whistling notes. And then there were leaps across the octaves that would have confused a nightingale but in which harmony was nevertheless preserved. Soon, soft undulations of octaves rose and fell like the bosom of the young singer. Her fine face followed with extraordinary versatility all the variations of her song and moved from the wildest inspiration to the most chaste dignity. You could have taken her at one moment for a madwoman, at another for a queen. Gringoire did not recognize the language of the songs she sang, and it seemed unknown to her as well since her expression had little to do with the words. Therefore these four lines from her mouth were sung with mad joy:

Un cofre de gran rigueza
Hallaron dentro un pilar
Dentro de, nuevas banderas
Con figuras de espantar.

And then a moment afterward:

Alarabes de cavallo
Sin poderse manear,
Con espadas, y los cuellos
Ballestas de buen char.[8]

Gringoire felt tears sting his eyes. Her song, however, was a joyful one, and she seemed to sing like a bird, from happiness and insouciance.

The song of the gypsy had disturbed Gringoire's reverie but like the swan disturbs the water: he listened with a kind of rapture and a forgetfulness of everything. It was the first respite from suffering that he had enjoyed for several hours. It did not last long. The same female voice that had interrupted the dancing of the gypsy was now raised to interrupt her singing. "Stop chirping, cricket of hell!" it cried, still from the darkest corner of the square. The poor cricket stopped short. "Damned screeching of a saw! You have broken the lyre!" exclaimed Gringoire, pressing his hands to his ears. The other spectators also began to murmur. "Devil take the old hag!" and the invisible spoilsport might have regretted her aggression against the Bohemian had not the crowd's attention at that moment been diverted by the procession of the Pope of Fools, which, after parading through the main thoroughfares, was now entering the Place de Grève with all its torches and its clamor.

This procession, which set out, as the reader saw, from the palace, was joined in its progress by all the ragamuffins, thieves, and tramps in Paris; accordingly it exhibited a most respectable appearance when it reached the Grève.

Egypt marched in first, headed by the Duke of Egypt on horseback, with his counts on foot, holding his bridle and stirrups. They were followed by gypsies of both sexes, pell-mell, with their babies crying on their shoulders; all of them—duke, counts, and commoners—were in rags and tatters. Next came the kingdom of Slang, that is to say, all the rogues and thieves in France, drawn up according to their respective titles, the lowest walking first. They moved past, four by four, with the different insignia of their degrees in this strange group, most of them cripples, the legless, the lame, the one-armed, the chronically unemployed, an assortment of fake pilgrims, fake epileptics, and drunkards, who exhibited their counterfeit ailments when begging, fake lepers, orphans, pickpockets, et cetera, enough in any case to exhaust even Homer's powers of imagination.[9] Amid the conclave of grand dignitaries, it was difficult to distinguish the King of these ruffians, crouched in a little cart drawn by two huge dogs. After the kingdom of Slang came the empire of Galilee. The Emperor, Guillaume Rousseau, marched majestically in his purple robe stained with wine, preceded by dancers performing military dances and scuffling with one another, and surrounded by his mace bearers and underlings. Last came the Basoche, the company of lawyers' clerks, with their may trees garlanded with flowers, in their black gowns, with music worthy of the Sabbath, and large candles of yellow wax. In the center of the crowd the officers of the Fraternity of Fools bore on their shoulders a litter, more overburdened with tapers than Ste.-Geneviève's shrine during the page. On this throne glittered, with crosier, cope, and miter, the new Pope of Fools, the bell ringer of Notre-Dame, Quasimodo the hunchback.

Each of the divisions of this grotesque procession had its particular band of music. The gypsies played on their African balafos and tambourines. The men of Slang, a race by no means musical, had advanced no farther than the viol, or the goat's horn, and the Gothic rebec, or bull's horn of the twelfth century. The empire of Galilee was only a bit more advanced; one could barely make out some pathetic and primitive tune, something on the order of do, re, mi. It was around the Pope of Fools that the highest musical achievement of the age was commingled in one magnificent cacophony. It consisted only of horns, treble, alto, and tenor, besides flutes and instruments of brass. Our readers may recall that this was poor Gringoire's orchestra.

It is difficult to convey an idea of the beatific look of pride and self-complacency that had settled on Quasimodo's sad and hideous countenance during this triumphal procession from the palace to the Grève. It was the first gratification of self-love that he had ever experienced.

Until then he had encountered nothing but humiliation, contempt for his condition, and disgust for his person. Thus, deaf as he was, like a real Pope, he enjoyed the acclamations of that crowd that he hated because he knew he was hated by it. It did not matter to him that his subjects were a mob of cripples, beggars, thieves, and ruffians—they were still his subjects and he was a sovereign. He took seriously all the ironic applause, all that mock reverence and respect, with which, we must however observe, there was mingled a certain degree of real fear. The hunchback was strong, the bowlegged one was agile, the deaf bell ringer was spiteful. These three qualities tend to temper ridicule.

It is far from certain that the new Pope of Fools was aware of his own feelings or of those that he inspired. The mind that was lodged in that defective body was necessarily imperfect and a bit deaf to the world. He had therefore only a vague, indistinct, and confused idea of what he felt at that moment. Joy penetrated the fog, and pride prevailed. Around that gloomy and unhappy visage showed a halo of delight.

At the moment when Quasimodo, in this state of half intoxication, was carried triumphantly past the Maison aux Pilliers, it was, therefore, not without surprise and fear that his attendants saw a man suddenly dart from the crowd and with an angry gesture snatch from his hands his crosier of gilded wood, the mark of his newly conferred dignity. This rash man was the bald character who, mingled in the group of spectators, had terrified the poor gypsy girl by his threatening and hateful words. He was dressed in an ecclesiastical habit. When he darted out of the crowd, Gringoire, who had not noticed him before, recognized in him an old acquaintance. "Hold on there!" he said, with a cry of astonishment. "It is my master in Hermes,[10] Dom Claude Frollo the Archdeacon! What the hell does he want from that one-eyed monster? He will be devoured."

Shrieks of terror burst from the crowd as the formidable Quasimodo leaped from the litter to the ground, and the women turned away their faces so that they would not see the Archdeacon torn to pieces. With one bound he was before the priest; he looked at him and dropped on his knees. The priest pulled off his crown, broke his crosier, and tore his cape of tinsel. Quasimodo remained kneeling, bowed his head, and clasped his hands. Then they began a strange dialogue of signs and gestures, for neither of them spoke: the priest erect, irritated, threatening, imperious—Quasimodo at his feet, humble, submissive, a suppliant. And yet it is certain that Quasimodo could have crushed the priest with his thumb.

Eventually the Archdeacon, shaking the brawny shoulder of Quasimodo, motioned him to rise and follow him. Quasimodo rose. The Fraternity of Fools, overcoming their initial stupor, wanted to defend their Pope, who had been so unceremoniously dethroned. The gypsies, the beggars, and the lawyers' clerks crowded yelping around the priest. Quasimodo, stepping before the priest, clenched his muscular fists. As he eyed the assailants, he gnashed his teeth like an angry tiger. The priest resumed his somber gravity, made a sign to Quasimodo, and withdrew in silence. Quasimodo went before him, opening a passage for him through the crowd.

When they were clear of the populace and had crossed the square, a number of curious and idle persons began to follow them. Quasimodo then fell into the rear, and, facing the enemy, walked backward after the Archdeacon, square, massive, bristly, picking up his limbs, licking his tusk, growling like a wild beast. He produced immense waves of movement in the crowd with a gesture or a look. They entered a dark and narrow street into which no one dared venture to follow them. The image of Quasimodo baring his teeth was enough to put everyone off.

"That was amazing!" exclaimed Gringoire. "But where the devil shall I find supper?"

CHAPTER IV

The Unfortunate Consequences of Following a Pretty Girl in the Street at Night

Gringoire took it into his head to follow the gypsy girl at all costs. He saw her turn with her goat into the Rue de Coutellerie, and to the same street he directed his steps.

"Why not?" he said to himself.

Gringoire, a practical philosopher of the streets of Paris, had remarked that nothing is so conducive to reverie as following a pretty woman without knowing where she is going. In this voluntary resignation of free will, in this submission of one whim to another, there is a mixture of absolute independence and blind obedience, something between slavery and liberty, which was pleasing to Gringoire, whose mind was essentially divided, indecisive, and complicated. He was always suspended between all human passions and propensities, and incessantly neutralizing one with another. He was fond of comparing himself with the tomb of Mohammed, attracted in contrary directions by two lodestones and eternally wavering between the high and the low, between rising and sinking, between zenith and nadir. If Gringoire lived in our day, how beautifully he would be able to occupy the middle ground between classicism and romanticism! But he was not hearty enough to live for three hundred years. His absence in our times leaves a terrible void.

In any case, nothing tends so much to produce a disposition to follow passersby, and especially those of the fair sex, in the streets as the circumstance of having neither home nor shelter. Gringoire, therefore, walked pensively on after the girl, who quickened her pace and made her pretty little goat trot along by her side when she saw the residents of the Cité returning home and the tavern keepers, who had alone opened shop on that day, closing up for the night. "After all," he thought, "she must lodge somewhere. Gypsies are very generous. Who knows . . ." The ellipsis was filled by I cannot tell what pleasant visions.

Meanwhile, from time to time, as he passed the last groups of tradesmen shutting their doors, he caught some fragments of their conversation, which broke the chain of his pleasing hypotheses. Two old men, for instance, would accost one another in this manner:

"Master Thibaut Fernicle, do you know that it is very cold?" Gringoire had known that ever since the beginning of winter.

"It is, indeed, Master Boniface Disome! Are we going to have another winter like we had three years ago, in 'eighty, when wood cost six sous a cord?"

"Pooh! That is nothing, Master Thibaut, to the winter of 1407, when the frost lasted from Martinmas to Candlemas and the cold was so bitter that the pen of the clerk of the Parliament froze in the great chamber every three words he wrote!"

Farther on a couple of female neighbors chatted at their windows while the fog made their candles crackle.

"Did your husband tell you about the accident, Mademoiselle La Boudrague?"

"No. But what is it, Mademoiselle Turquant?"

"You know Monsieur Gilles Godin's horse—he is notary to the Châtelet; well, the horse had a scare at the Flemish and their procession and knocked over Master Philippot Avrillot, the lay brother of the Célestins."

"Indeed!"

"Absolutely!"

"A commoner's horse! That's a bit much. If it had been a cavalry horse, I could understand!"

The windows closed again, but Gringoire had, nevertheless, lost the thread of his ideas. Luckily, however, he soon recovered and quickly rediscovered it, thanks to the gypsy girl and her Djali, who were still walking before him—two elegant, delicate, charming creatures, whose small feet, handsome shapes, and graceful manners he admired, almost confusing them in his imagination. He regarded them both as young girls for intelligence and their fondness for each other, and thought of them both as young goats for their agility and lightness of step.

The streets, in the meantime, became every moment darker and more deserted. Curfew had long since rung, and it was only at rare intervals that a passerby was seen on the pavement, or a light at the windows. Gringoire, in following the gypsy, had entered that inextricable labyrinth of lanes and alleys and crossways surrounding the ancient sepulchre of the Holy Innocents. The streets resembled a skein of thread entangled by a playful cat. "Here are streets that have very little logic!" said Gringoire, lost in their thousand meanders, through which, however, the girl proceeded along a path that seemed familiar to her, and at a more and more rapid pace. For his part, he would not have had the remotest conception of where he was had he not perceived, on turning a corner, the octagonal shape of the pillory of the Halles, the black form of which was distinctly defined against a window still lighted in the Rue Verdelet.

He had, by this time, begun to attract the notice of the young girl; she had more than once turned her head and looked at him with some uneasiness. She had even stopped short and taken advantage of a ray of light from the half-open door of a bakery to stare at him attentively from head to foot. Gringoire had seen her, after this scrutiny, pout her lip as she had done before; then she moved on.

The face she made piqued Gringoire's curiosity about what it might mean. It certainly conveyed an expression of disdain and dislike. He began, as a consequence, to hang his head, as if to count the paving stones, and to drop farther behind when, on reaching the corner of a street into which she had turned, he was startled by a piercing shriek. He hurried forth. The street was extremely dark; a wick steeped in oil, burning in an iron cage at the foot of the Blessed Virgin at the corner, nevertheless enabled Gringoire to distinguish the gypsy girl struggling in the grasp of two men, who were trying to stifle her cries. The poor little goat, terrified at this attack, dropped her head, aimed her horns, and bleated.

"Watch yourselves, gentlemen!" shouted Gringoire, boldly advancing. One of the men who held the girl turned on him. It was the formidable face of Quasimodo. Gringoire did not run away, neither did he advance another step. Quasimodo went up to him and dealt him a backhanded blow that sent him reeling three or four yards and stretched him sprawling on the pavement. Then, darting back, Quasimodo caught up the young girl and carried her off across one of his arms like a silken scarf. His companion followed, and the poor goat ran after the three, bleating in a most plaintive manner.

"Murder! Murder!" cried the unfortunate gypsy girl.

"Halt, scoundrels, and let the girl go!" suddenly roared, in a voice of thunder, a horseman who came dashing out from the next street. It was the captain of the archers of the King's Order, armed from head to toe. He snatched the gypsy out of the grasp of the stupefied Quasimodo, laid her across his saddle, and just when the formidable hunchback, recovering from his surprise, would have rushed on him to regain his prey, fifteen or sixteen archers who followed close on the heels of their captain came up armed with quarterstaves. It was part of a company of the King's Order that performed the counterwatch, by the order of Messire Robert d'Estouteville, Keeper of the Provosty of Paris.

Quasimodo was surrounded, seized, and bound. He bellowed, he foamed, he kicked, he bit. Had it been daylight no doubt his face alone, rendered doubly hideous by rage, would have sufficed to scare away the whole squadron; but night disarmed him of his most formidable weapon, his ugliness. His companion disappeared during the struggle.

The Bohemian gracefully raised herself up on the officer's saddle. Pressing her hands on his shoulders, she looked at him intently for a few moments, as if hypnotized by his handsome face and grateful for the timely salvation that he had afforded her. Then, giving a sweeter tone than usual to her sweet voice, she inquired, "What is your name, sir?"

"Captain Phœbus de Châteaupers, at your service, my dear," replied the officer, drawing himself up to his full height.

"Thank you," she said; and while the captain was twirling his whiskers *à la bourguignonne* she slid down the horse's side to the ground and disappeared faster than lightning.

"Damnation!" said the captain, as he tightened the straps binding Quasimodo. "I would have preferred to keep the girl!"

"What do you want, Captain?" said a soldier. "The songbird has escaped. The bat remains."

CHAPTER V

A CHAPTER OF ACCIDENTS

Gringoire, stunned by his fall, was lying on the pavement before the good Virgin at the corner of the street. By degrees he came to himself. At first he floated for a while in a kind of dreamy reverie, which was rather soothing, though the aerial figures of the Bohemian and her goat were coupled with the weight of Quasimodo's fist. This state lasted a short while. A painful sensation of cold in that part of his body which was in contact with the pavement suddenly awoke him and he regained consciousness. "Where does this cold come from?" he said sharply to himself. He saw that he was almost in the middle of the gutter.

"Devil of a hunchbacked Cyclops!" he muttered, and he tried to rise, but he was so stunned and bruised that he was forced to remain where he was. His hand, however, was free. He held his nose and resigned himself to his fate.

"The mud of Paris," he thought—for he had decidedly made up his mind that the gutter would be his bed—"the mud of Paris has a particular stink: it must contain a great deal of volatile and nitrous salt. Besides, it is the opinion of Nicolas Flamel and of the alchemists..."

The word *alchemists* suddenly reminded him of the Archdeacon Claude Frollo. He remembered the violent scene that he had just witnessed; he remembered that the Bohemian was struggling between two men, that Quasimodo had a companion; and the stately and morose figure of the Archdeacon passed confusedly before his memory. "That would be incredible!" he thought. And with this fact and on this foundation he began to erect the fantastic edifice of hypothesis, that card house of philosophers. Then, suddenly recalled once more to reality, "By God!" he cried. "I am freezing!"

The place, in fact, was becoming less and less bearable. Each molecule of the water in the gutter carried off a particle of radiating heat from Gringoire's loins, and the equilibrium between the temperature of his body and the temperature of the gutter began to be established in a way that was far from agreeable. Suddenly he was assailed by an annoyance of a totally different kind.

A party of children, of those little bare-legged savages called gamins, who have in every age beaten the pavement of Paris and who when we too were boys threw stones at us in the evening as we left school because our trousers were not in tatters like their own, a band of these ragged urchins ran toward the spot where Gringoire lay, laughing and whooping it up, and caring very little whether they disturbed the neighborhood or not. They were dragging after them something like an enormous bag, and the mere clattering of their wooden clogs would have been enough to wake the dead. Gringoire, who was not absolutely dead, propped himself up a little to see what was going on.

"Hey there! Hennequin Dandèche! Hey there, Jehan Pincebourde," they bawled at the top of their voices. "Old Eustache Moubon, the ironmonger at the corner, has just died. We have got his straw mattress and are going to make a bonfire!"

Saying this, they threw the straw mattress down right on Gringoire, next to whom they had stopped without seeing him. At the same time one of them took a handful of straw and went to light it at the Virgin's lamp.

"Christ Almighty!" grumbled Gringoire. "Now am I going to be too hot?"

Between fire and water he was caught in a critical situation. He made a superhuman effort, the effort of a counterfeiter who is about to be boiled and tries to escape. He raised himself to his feet, threw back the straw mattress on the urchins, and hobbled away as fast as he could.

"Holy Virgin!" cried the boys. "It is the ironmonger's ghost!" And off they scampered in turn.

The straw mattress was left in possession of the field of battle. Belleforêt, Father Le Juge, and Corrozet[11] relate that on the following day it was picked up with great pomp by the neighborhood clergy and carried to the treasure house of the church of Ste.-Opportune, where the sacristan, until the year 1789, made a very handsome income with the great miracle performed by the statue of the Virgin at the corner of the Rue Mauconseil. It is said that the statue had, by its mere presence, on the memorable night between the sixth and the seventh of January, 1482, exorcised the spirit of Eustache Moubon, which, to hide from the devil, had when he died maliciously hid itself in his straw mattress.

CHAPTER VI

THE BROKEN JUG

After running for some time as fast as his legs would carry him, without knowing where he was going and knocking his head against many a corner of a street, plunging into many a gutter, dashing through many a lane, turning into many a blind alley, seeking a passage through all the meanders of the old pavement of the Halles, exploring, in his panic, what is termed in the exquisite Latin of the charters *tota via, cheminum, et viaria,*[12] our poet stopped short, in the first place for want of breath, and in the second seized, as it were, by a dilemma, which had just occurred to him. "It seems to me, Master Pierre Gringoire," he said to himself, placing his finger on the side of his nose, "that you are running around like a brainless wonder. The young rogues were not a bit less afraid of you than you of them. It seems to me that you heard their wooden shoes clattering off to the south, while you are heading to the north. Now, either they have run away, and then the straw mattress, which they have no doubt left behind in their fright, is precisely the hospitable bed for which you have been running around ever since morning, and which the Virgin—blessed be her name!—miraculously sends to reward you for having composed in honor of her a play accompanied by pomp and circumstance; or the boys have not run away. In that case they have set fire to the straw mattress, and a good fire is the very next thing you want to warm, to dry, and to cheer you. In either case, a good fire, or a good bed, the straw mattress is a gift from heaven. It was perhaps for this very reason that the Virgin at the corner caused the death of Eustache Moubon; and it is stupid of you to run your legs off this way, like a Picard from a Frenchman, leaving behind what you are running after. You are an idiot!"

He turned and, with eyes and ears on the alert, tried to steer his steps back to the lucky straw mattress. But in vain. There were only intersections of houses, blind alleys, forks in the road where he was forced to pause in doubt and hesitation, more perplexed and more entangled in the intricacies of those dark, narrow lanes and courts than he would have been in the maze of the Hôtel des Tournelles itself. Finally, he lost all patience and cried out solemnly, "Curse these streets! The devil must have made them in the image of his fork."

This exclamation consoled him a little, and a kind of reddish light, which he perceived at the end of an alley, helped to boost his morale. "God be praised!" he said. "There it is. There is my straw mattress burning!" And comparing himself with the mariner who is wrecked in the night, *"Salve,"* he piously ejaculated, *"salve maris stella!"*[13]

Whether this fragment of the seaman's hymn was addressed to the Blessed Virgin or to the straw mattress we do not know.

Before he had proceeded many steps down the alley, which sloped downward and was unpaved, and which became more and more muddy the farther he went, he perceived something most extraordinary. The alley was not deserted. Here and there crawled a number of indistinct and shapeless masses. Like heavy insects who fly from one stalk of grass to another toward a papier-mâché fire, they were headed toward the light at the bottom of the lane.

Nothing makes a man so adventurous as an empty wallet. Gringoire continued to advance and soon came up to the laggard who had fallen behind the others and was crawling lazily along after them. When

Gringoire overtook him he saw that it was only a wretched legless cripple, who was hopping along on both hands. At the moment when he was passing this sort of spider with human face it accosted him in a lamentable tone: *"La buona mancia, signor! La buona mancia!"*[14]

"The devil take you," said Gringoire, "and me along with you if I know what you mean!" And he walked on.

He overtook another of those walking shapes. He was a cripple too—a one-armed lame man who had to use such a complicated system of crutches and wooden legs that he looked like a walking scaffold. Gringoire, who was fond of lofty and classic comparisons, likened him in imagination to the living tripod of Vulcan.

This living tripod took off its hat to him as he passed but held it up under Gringoire's chin, like a barber's basin, at the same time yelling in his ear, *"Señor caballero, para comprar un pedaso de pan!"*[15]

"This fellow," said Gringoire, "seems to be talking too; but he speaks a rough language, and he must be cleverer than I am if he understands it." Then he slapped himself on the forehead at a sudden thought. "And what did they mean when they said this morning *their* Esmeralda?"

He wanted to walk more quickly, but for the third time something obstructed the way. This something, or rather this somebody, was a little blind man, with a Jewish face and long beard, who felt his way along with his stick and, towed by a great dog, sang out with nasal twang and Hungarian accent, *"Facitote caritatem."*[16]

"Finally," said Pierre Gringoire, "here is someone at least who speaks a Christian language. I must have a most benevolent look for people to ask charity of me in this manner, in the present meager state of my purse. My friend," he continued, turning toward the blind man, "last week I sold my last shirt or, as you understand no language but Cicero's, *Vendidi hebdomade nuper transita meam ultimam chemisam.*"

This said, he turned his back on the blind man and pursued his way. But the blind man quickened his pace; at the same time suddenly up came the two cripples, in great haste, with a tremendous clatter of bowls and crutches on the pavement. All three, jostling each other at poor Gringoire's heels, began to sing their song.

"Caritatem!" sang the blind man.

"La buona mancia!" sang the legless one.

The other cripple joined in the concert with *"Un pedaso de pan!"*

Gringoire covered his ears. "Oh, tower of Babel!" he exclaimed.

He began to run for it. The blind man ran. The lame man ran. The legless man followed. Soon he was surrounded by the lame and the blind, by the one-armed and the one-eyed, and by lepers with their sores, some coming out from houses, others from the adjoining streets, and still others from cellars, howling, bellowing, yelping, hobbling, rushing toward the light and wallowing in the mire like snails after the rain.

Gringoire, still followed by his three persecutors, and not knowing what to think of the matter, continued with some fear amid the others, turning and, passing the cripples on crutches, stepping over the heads of the legless, he was entangled in this crowd of limping, shuffling wretches like the English captain who found himself suddenly surrounded by a prodigious host of land crabs.

The idea occurred to him to try to turn back. But it was too late. The entire legion had closed behind him, and his three beggars stuck to him. He proceeded, therefore, propelled at once by this irresistible tide, by fear, and by a dizziness, which made the whole scene appear to him like a horrible dream.

Eventually he reached the end of the alley. It opened into a spacious square where a thousand scattered lights flickered in the muddled fog of night. Gringoire pushed his way into it, hoping by the lightness of his heels to escape from the three infirm specters who stuck so closely to him.

"Onde vas, hombre?"[17] cried the cripple on crutches, throwing them down and running after him on two legs as goodly as ever stepped on the pavement of Paris. At the same moment the legless cripple, standing bolt upright on his feet, clapped his heavy iron bowl on Gringoire's head, and the blind man stared him in the face with a pair of flaming eyes.

"Where am I?" cried the terrified poet.

"In the Cour des Miracles," replied a fourth specter, who had joined them.

"Miracles, upon my soul!" rejoined Gringoire. "Here the blind see, and the lame run."

A sinister laugh was their only answer.

The poor poet looked around him. He was actually in that dreaded Cour des Miracles, into which no honest man had ever penetrated at such an hour. It was a magic circle, which, when the officers of the Châtelet and the sergeants of the Provost had ventured there, had disappeared into thin air. It was a den of thieves, a hideous wart on the face of Paris. It was a sewer disgorging every morning and receiving every night that fetid torrent of vice, mendacity, and vagabondage that always overflows the streets of great capitals. It was a monstrous hive, to which all the hornets of the social order retired at night with their booty; the hospital of imposture, where the gypsy, the defrocked monk, the ruined scholar, the rejects of every nation—Spaniard, Italian, German—of all religions—Jews, Christians, Mohammedans, idolaters—covered with painted wounds, beggars by day, transmogrified themselves into bandits at night. It was an immense dressing room, in short, where all the actors of that eternal comedy that theft, prostitution, and murder play in the streets of Paris took refuge in those days to dress and undress.

It was a spacious area, irregular and ill-paved, like all the open squares of Paris of the time. Fires, around which swarmed strange-looking groups, were blazing here and there. All was bustle, confusion, uproar. Coarse laughter, the crying of children, the voices of women, were intermingled. The hands and heads of this multitude, black in relief against a luminous ground, made a thousand antic gestures. A dog that looked like a man, or a man who looked like a dog, might be seen from time to time crossing the square on which trembled the reflection of the fires, interrupted by broad, ill-defined shadows. The limits between races and species seemed to be done away with in this city, as in a pandemonium. Men, women, brutes, age, sex, health, disease, all seemed to be in common among these people. They were jumbled, huddled together, one on top of another; each partook of everything.

The faint and flickering light of the fires enabled Gringoire to distinguish, despite his fear, a hideous circumference of old houses, with decayed, worm-eaten, ruined facades all around the immense square. Each of them was perforated by one or two small lighted windows, and they appeared to him in the dark like enormous heads of old hags ranged in a circle who winked their eyes as they watched the rites of the witches' sabbath. It was like a new world, unexplored, unheard of, deformed, reptilian, swarming, fantastic.

Gringoire—more and more terrified, held by the three beggars as by three vises—was deafened as a crowd of other faces gathered around him, shouting. The unlucky Gringoire strove to rally his presence of mind, and to recollect whether it was Saturday or not. But his efforts were vain; the thread of his memory and of his thoughts was broken, and, doubting everything, floating between what he saw and what he felt, he asked himself this puzzling question: "If I am, can this be? If this is, can I be?"

At this moment a distinct shout arose from amid the buzzing crowd by which he was surrounded: "Lead him to the King! Lead him to the King!"

"Holy Virgin!" muttered Gringoire. "The King of this place! Why, he can be nothing but a goat."

"To the King! To the King!" repeated every voice.

He was hustled away. The rabble rushed to lay hands on him, but the three beggars held him fast in their grip, tearing him away from the others and bawling, "He is ours!" The poor poet's doublet, previously in wretched condition, was utterly ruined in this struggle.

While they were crossing the horrible square, the vertigo that had confused his senses was dispelled. After a few steps a sense of the reality flashed upon him. He became used to the atmosphere of the place. At first, there had risen from his poetic brain and perhaps, to speak quite simply and prosaically, from his empty stomach, a fume, a vapor, which, spreading itself between objects and him, had permitted him to catch a glimpse of them only in the distorting haze of the nightmare, in that darkness of dreams that makes all contours shaky. All forms seemed to be grinning, all objects heaped together in preposterous groups; things were transformed into chimeras and men into phantoms. By degrees this hallucination gave way to visions that were less wild and hyberbolic. Reality dawned on him, paining his eyes, treading on his toes, and demolishing piecemeal the whole terrifying poetry by which he had at first fancied himself to be surrounded. He could not help perceiving that he was walking not in the river Styx but in mud; that he was elbowed not by demons but by robbers; that his soul was not in danger but merely his life, because he lacked that excellent mediator between the criminal and the honest man—the purse. In short, on examining the scene more closely and more coolly, he fell from the witches' sabbath down to the tavern. The Cour des Miracles was in fact nothing but a tavern, a tavern for criminals, quite as much stained with blood as with wine.

The sight that presented itself when his ragged escort had eventually brought him to the place of his destination was not calculated to carry back to poetry, even if it were the poetry of hell. It was more than ever the prosaic and brutal reality of the tavern. If we were not in the fifteenth century, we would say that Gringoire had descended from Michelangelo to Callot.

Around a great fire that burned on a large circular hearth, whose flames rose among the red-hot bars of a trivet unoccupied at the moment, a few worm-eaten tables were haphazardly scattered. No geometrically inclined waiter had deigned to study symmetry in their arrangement, or to take care at least that they would not cut each other off at too unusual angles. On these tables shone pots flowing with wine and beer, and around these pots were grouped a great many drunken faces, empurpled by fire and by drink. There was a man with a huge paunch and jovial face noisily kissing a thick and fleshy strumpet while he took off the bandages from a false wound and removed the wrappers from a sound and vigorous knee, which had been swathed since morning in a dozen ligatures. He was a fake soldier with fake war wounds. Behind him was a shriveled wretch, preparing with suet and bullock's blood his *jambe de Dieu*[18] for the next day. Two tables off a con artist, in the full dress of a pilgrim, was singing a religious hymn without missing a word or beat. Elsewhere, another impostor was taking a lesson in how to fake epilepsy from an old cadger, who showed him how to foam at the mouth by chewing a bit of soap. Beside them a dropsical man was draining his protuberance, while four or five thieves quarreled over a child they had stolen in the course of the evening. All these details would, two centuries later, "appear so amusing to the Court," as Sauval tells us, "that they furnished pastime for the King and were introduced into a royal ballet, called *Night*, divided into four parts and performed on the stage of the Petit-Bourbon."[19] "Never," adds a spectator of this performance, "were the sudden metamorphoses of the Cour des Miracles more successfully represented. Beuserade paved the way for them with a few gallant stanzas."

Coarse laughter and obscene song could be heard everywhere. Each did just as he pleased, swearing and carping, without listening to his neighbor. The pots clanked against each other, and quarrels arose; the cracked pots led to the tearing of rags.

A large dog was sitting on his tail looking at the fire. Young children were mixed up in the chaos. The stolen child was crying bitterly. Another, a stout fellow about four years old, was sitting on a high bench, dangling his legs at the table, which reached up to his chin, and not saying a word. A third was gravely spreading with his finger the melted tallow that ran from a candle on the table. The last, a little urchin crouching in the dirt, was almost lost in a kettle, which he was scraping with a tile and from which he was extracting sounds that would have made Stradivarius swoon.

Near the fire stood a cask, and on this cask was seated a beggar. This was the King upon his throne. The three tramps who held Gringoire led him before the cask, and for a moment the whole motley assemblage was silent, except the kettle inhabited by the boy. Gringoire did not dare breathe or raise his eyes.

"Hombre, quita tu sombrero,"[20] said one of the three fellows who had him in his clutches, and before he understood what he meant one of the others took off his hat—a shabby cap, it is true, but still useful against either sun or rain. Gringoire sighed.

"What scoundrel do we have here?" asked the King. Gringoire shuddered. This voice, though it now had a threatening tone, reminded him of another that had that very morning struck the first blow to his play by whining to the audience, "Charity, if you please!" He raised his eyes. It was Clopin Trouillefou himself.

Clopin Trouillefou, invested with the insignia of royalty, had not a rag more or a rag less than usual. The sore on his arm had disappeared. He held in his hand one of the whips composed of thongs of white leather that were used by the sergeants in those days to keep back the crowd. On his head he wore a cap of such a peculiar form that it was difficult to tell whether it was a child's padded cap or a king's crown—so much are the two things alike. Gringoire, however, had regained some hope, though without knowing why, on recognizing in the King of the Cour des Miracles the accursed beggar of the great hall.

"Master," he stammered forth, "My Lord—Sire—what should I call you?" he eventually asked, having arrived at the culminating point of his crescendo and not knowing how to get higher or to descend again.

"Call me Your Majesty, or comrade, or whatever you like. But make it quick. What do you have to say in your defense?"

"In your defense!" thought Gringoire. "I don't like that one bit." "It

was I—I—I—" he resumed, with the same hesitation as before, "who, this morning—"

"By the devil's hoofs!" cried Clopin, interrupting him. "Your name, knave, and nothing more. Listen to me. You are in the presence of three mighty sovereigns—myself, Clopin Trouillefou, King of Thunes, and supreme ruler of the realm of Slang; Matthias Hunyadi Spicali, Duke of Egypt and Bohemia, that sallow old crone whom you see yonder, with a clout around his head; and Guillaume Rousseau, Emperor of Galilee, the fat man who is too busy caressing that strumpet to pay attention to us. We are your judges. You have entered our territories without being one of our subjects; you have violated the privileges of our city. You must be punished, unless you are a cheat, a con artist, or a faker—or, to use the gibberish of those who call themselves honest people, a thief, a beggar, or a vagrant. Are you any of these? Justify yourself. State your qualities."

"Alas!" sighed Gringoire. "I have not that honor. I am the author—"

"Enough!" exclaimed Trouillefou, without letting him proceed. "You shall be hanged. And quite right, too, messieurs bourgeois citizens! As you deal by our people among you, so we will deal by yours among us. The law that you make for the Tramps, the Tramps will enforce with you. It is your fault if it is a harsh one. It is only proper that an honest man should now and then be seen grinning through a hemp necklace—that makes the thing honorable. Come, my friend, divide your rags with good grace among these girls. I will have you hanged to amuse the tramps, and you shall give them your purse to drink. If you want to play around and make your last confession, go down into the cellar; there is a crucifix in stone, which we picked up at St.-Pierre-aux-Bœufs. You have four minutes to settle the affairs of your soul."

This was an alarming announcement.

"Well said, upon my life! Clopin Trouillefou preaches like His Holiness the Pope," cried the Emperor of Galilee, breaking his pot to prop up his table.

"Most powerful Emperors and Kings," said Gringoire quite coolly—I never could make out how he recovered sufficient firmness to talk so resolutely—"you cannot mean what you say. My name is Pierre Gringoire; I am the poet whose play was performed this morning in the great hall of the Palace."

"Oho! Master!" said Clopin. "I was there too. But, comrade, because we were bored by you in the morning, is that any reason you should not be hung tonight?"

"I don't know how I am going to get myself out of this," thought Gringoire. Nevertheless he made another effort.

"I do not see," he said, "why poets should not be classed among the tramps. Aesop was a tramp, Homer a beggar, Mercury a thief."

Clopin interrupted him. "I truly believe you are trying to bamfloozle us with your nonsense. By God! Let yourself be hanged and make no more fuss."

"Pardon me, most illustrious King of Thunes," replied Gringoire, disputing the ground inch by inch, "is it worthwhile—only one moment—you will not condemn me unheard—"

His voice was absolutely drowned by the uproar that prevailed around him. The little urchin continued to scrape his kettle with greater energy than ever, and, to mend the matter, an old woman had just placed on the red-hot trivet a frying pan full of fat, which yelped and cackled over the fire like a troop of mischievous boys.

Clopin Trouillefou appeared to be conferring for a moment with the Duke of Egypt and the Emperor of Galilee, who was quite drunk. He then cried out sharply, "Silence!" And, as the kettle and the frying pan paid no attention to him but continued their duet, he leaped from his cask, gave one kick to the kettle, which rolled away ten paces with the boy still in it, and another to the frying pan, which upset all the fat into the fire. Then he gravely reascended his throne, caring no more for the smothered crying of the child than for the grumbling of the hag, whose supper had gone up in a blaze.

Trouillefou made a sign, and the Duke, the Emperor, and their court of high dignitaries ranged themselves around him in a semicircle, the center of which was occupied by Gringoire, who was still held fast by his captors. It was a semicircle of rags and tatters and tinsel, of forks and hatchets, of bare, brawny arms and legs, of sordid, bloated, stupid-looking faces. In the middle of this roundtable of ragamuffins, Clopin Trouillefou, like the Doge of this senate, like the King of this peerage, like the Pope of this conclave, towered over it by the whole height of his cask, and by a certain haughty, ferocious, and formidable look, which made his eye sparkle, and held in check the bestial tendencies of his criminal race and his savage profile. You would have taken him for a wild boar among domestic swine.

"Listen," he said to Gringoire, stroking his deformed chin with his callused hand. "I see no reason why you should not be hanged. You seem, indeed, to have a dislike for it, but that is natural enough; you bourgeois are not used to it. You have too frightful an idea of the thing. After all, we mean you no harm. There is one way to get out of the scrape for the moment. Will you be one of us?"

The reader may conceive what effect this proposition must have produced on Gringoire, who had thought that his life was over, and had begun to make up his mind to the worst. He grasped eagerly at the proposed alternative.

"Certainly, most assuredly I will," he said.

"You consent," rejoined Clopin, "to enroll yourself among the men of little blades?"

"The men of the little blades,[21] decidedly so," answered Gringoire.

"You acknowledge yourself one of the crew?" proceeded the King of Thunes.

"One of the crew."

"A subject of the kingdom of Slang?"

"Of the kingdom of Slang."

"A Tramp?"

"A Tramp."

"With all your soul?"

"With all my soul."

"Take notice," said the King, "you shall nevertheless be hanged."

"The devil!" cried the poet.

"Only," continued Clopin, with imperturbable gravity, "you will be hanged a little later, and with more ceremony, at the cost of the good city of Paris, on a fair stone gallows, and by the hands of honest men. That is some consolation."

"As you say," replied Gringoire.

"There are some other advantages that you will enjoy. As one of the crew you will not have to pay taxes, for light, waste collection, or the poor, to which the honest citizens of Paris are liable."

"Be it so!" said the poet. "I am a Tramp, a pickpocket, one of the crew, a man of Slang, anything you please; no, I was all of these before, august King of Thunes, for I am a philosopher; *et omnia in philosophia, omnes in philosopho continentur,*[22] you know."

The august King of Thunes knitted his brow. "What do you take me for, my friend? What Hungarian Jewish gibberish are you talking now? I know nothing of Hebrew. One may be a ruffian without being a Jew."

Gringoire strove to slip in an excuse between these brief, angry, choked out words. "I beg Your Majesty's pardon. It is not Hebrew but Latin."

"I tell you," rejoined Clopin furiously, "I am not a Jew, and I will have you hanged, scoundrel, ay, and with you that little merchant of Judea whom I hope someday to see nailed to a counter, like the piece of counterfeit coin that he is."

As he spoke he pointed to the little bearded Hungarian Jew, who, acquainted with no language but that in which he had accosted Gringoire, was surprised at the ill humor that the King of Thunes appeared to be venting on him.

Eventually King Clopin became somewhat more calm. "Scoundrel," he said to our poet, "you want to become a crook?"

"Undoubtedly," replied Gringoire.

"It is not enough to want to," said his surly Majesty. "Goodwill puts not one more onion into the soup. To be admitted into our brotherhood, you have to prove that you are fit for something. Show us your skill at picking a pocket."

"Anything you please," said the poet.

Clopin made a sign. Several of the Tramps left the circle and presently returned. They brought two poles, each having a flat, horizontal piece of wood fastened at the base, on which it stood upright on the ground. Into the upper ends of these two poles the bearers fitted a crossbar, and the whole then formed a very handy portable gallows, which Gringoire had the satisfaction to see set up before his face in the blink of an eye. Nothing was lacking, not even the cord, which dangled gracefully from the crossbar.

"What are they doing now?" said Gringoire to himself, while his heart sank within him. A tinkling of small bells put an end to his anxiety. It was the figure of a man, a kind of scarecrow, in a red suit so profusely bestudded with little bells that they would have sufficed for harnessing thirty Castilian mules. The Tramps were suspending it by the neck from the rope. The tinkling of these thousand bells, occasioned by the swinging of the rope, gradually subsided, and eventually ceased entirely when the dummy stopped swinging.

Clopin pointed to an old, wobbly stool placed under the figure.

"Get up on it!" he said to Gringoire.

"Damnation!" the poet objected. "I'll break my neck. Your stool wobbles like a distich of Martial's; it has one hexameter and one pentameter foot."

"Get on it!" repeated Clopin.

Gringoire mounted the stool and, after some oscillation of head and arms, recovered his center of gravity.

"Now," continued the King of Thunes, "cross your right leg over the left and stand on tiptoe."

"My Lord!" cried Gringoire. "You absolutely insist on my breaking one of my limbs?"

Clopin shook his head. "Listen, friend, you talk too much for me. In two words this is what you have to do. You must stand on tiptoe as I tell you, so as to reach the pocket of the dummy. You must remove the purse that is in it, and if you can do this without making any of the bells speak, it is good: you shall be a Tramp. We shall then have nothing to do but to beat you soundly for a week or so."

"My God!" exclaimed Gringoire. "And if the bells should ring in spite of me?"

"Why, then you shall be hanged. Do you understand?"

"Not at all," answered Gringoire.

"Well then I tell you one more time. You must pick the pocket of that dummy, and if a single bell stirs while you are about it you shall be hanged. Do you understand that?"

"I do," said Gringoire. "And then?"

"If you are clever enough to take the purse out without setting the bells aclattering, you are a crook and shall be soundly thrashed every now and then for a week. You understand that, no doubt?"

"But what better shall I be? Hanged in one case, beaten in the other?"

"And a Tramp!" rejoined Clopin. "A Tramp! Is that nothing? It is for your own good that we shall beat you, to inure you to blows."

"Many thanks to you!" replied the poet.

"Come on, hurry up!" said the King, pounding on his cask, which sounded like a big drum. "To your task, knave! And remember, if I hear even a single bell you shall exchange places with that dummy."

The crew applauded Clopin's words and ranged themselves in a circle around the gallows with so pitiless a laugh that Gringoire saw he amused them too much not to have to fear the worst from them. The only hope he had left was the smallest chance of succeeding in the daunting task imposed on him. Before he set about it he addressed a fervent prayer to the dummy he was going to rob, and whom he could have moved more easily than the Tramps. The myriad bells with their little copper tongues seemed to him like many gaping jaws of serpents, ready to bite and to hiss.

"Oh!" he said softly, "is it possible that my life depends on the slightest vibration of the smallest of these bells?" He tried one more time with Trouillefou. "And if a gust of wind should blow?"

"You will be hanged," replied the King of Thunes without hesitation.

Finding that there was neither respite nor reprieve, nor any possible escape for him, he went resolutely to work. Crossing his right leg over the left, and raising himself on tiptoe, he stretched out his arm; but at the moment when he touched the effigy he found himself tottering on the stool, which had just three legs. He lost his balance, reflexively reached for the dummy, and fell heavily on the ground, stunned by the fatal jingle of the mannequin's thousand bells, as the figure, yielding to the pressure of his hand, first turned around on itself and then swung majestically between the two poles.

"Curses!" he cried as he fell, and he lay like a cadaver, with his face toward the ground. He heard, however, the horrid chime above his head, the diabolical laugh of the Tramps, and the voice of Trouillefou, who said, "Pick up the scoundrel and hang him!"

He got up. They had already taken down the dummy to make room for him. The Tramps made him mount the stool once more. Clopin stepped up to him, put the rope around his neck and, patting him on the shoulder, said, "Farewell, my friend! You cannot escape now, even with the devil's luck plus your own."

The word *"Mercy!"* died away on Gringoire's lips. He looked around him, but there was no hope. They were all laughing.

"Bellevigne de l'Étoile," said the King of Thunes to a huge tramp, who stepped forth from the ranks, "scramble up to that crossbar." Bellevigne de l'Étoile climbed lightly up the scaffold, and Gringoire, raising his eyes, beheld him with terror crouching on the crossbeam over his head.

"Now," resumed Clopin, "when I clap my hands, Andry the Red, kick away the stool; François Chante-Prune, pull the scoundrel's legs, and you, Bellevigne, jump on his shoulders—all three at once, do you understand?"

Gringoire shuddered.

"Are you ready?" said Clopin Trouillefou to the three ruffians, ready to jump on the unfortunate poet like spiders on a fly. The wretched man had a moment of horrible suspense while Clopin carelessly kicked into the fire a few twigs that the flame had not consumed. "Are you ready?" he repeated, opening his hands for the decisive clap.

He stopped short, as if a sudden thought had occurred to him. "Wait a moment!" he said. "I forgot. . . . It is customary with us not to hang a man till the women have been asked whether any of them will have him. Comrade, this is your last chance. You can marry a Tramp or the rope." This gypsy law, as bizarre as it may seem to the reader, is recorded in the ancient British code of law. Look it up in *Burington's Observations.*[23]

Gringoire breathed once more. It was the second time that he had come to life within the last half hour. He did not dare, therefore, trust very much this reprieve.

Clopin again mounted his cask. "This way, ladies!" he cried. "Is there anyone among you, from the witch to her cat, who will have this scoundrel? Colette la Charonne! Elisabeth Trouvain! Simone Jodouyne! Marie Mudfoot! Tall Thonne! Bévarde Fanouel! Michelle Genaille! Claude Itchy Ear! Mathurine Twirligig! Isabeau la Thierrye! Come forward and look! A husband for nothing! Who wants one?"

Gringoire, in this wretched plight, looked far from tempting. The female Tramps showed no eagerness to accept the offer. The unhappy man heard them answer one after another, "No, no, hang him, and there will be pleasure for everyone."

Three of them, however, stepped forward from among the crowd to sniff at him. The first was a strapping, square-jawed girl. She closely examined the philosopher's deplorable doublet and threadbare frock. She shrugged her shoulders. "Strange threads!" she grumbled. Then, turning to Gringoire, "Where is your cloak?"

"I lost it," he answered.

"Your hat?"

"They have taken it from me."

"Your shoes?"

"They are nearly worn out."

"Your purse?"

"Alas!" stammered Gringoire. "I have not a cent left."

"Hang then, and be thankful!" replied the girl, turning on her heel and striding away.

The second, an old, wrinkled hag, dark and hideously ugly, walked around Gringoire. He almost trembled for fear she would take a fancy to him. At length she muttered to herself, "He is too thin," and away she went.

The third was young, fresh-looking, and not too ugly. "Save me!" the poor devil whispered to her. She surveyed him with a look of pity, cast down her eyes, twitched her skirt, and stood for a moment undecided. He closely watched all her gestures. It was the last glimmer of hope. "No," she said at last. "No. Guillaume Saggy-Cheek would beat me," and she rejoined the crowd.

"Comrade," said Clopin, "you are unlucky." Then, standing up on his cask, "Will nobody bid?" he cried, imitating the manner of an auctioneer, to the great amusement of the crew. "Will nobody bid? Once, twice, three times!" And then, turning to the gallows, with a nod of the head, "Gone!"

Bellevigne de l'Étoile, Andry the Red, and François Chante-Prune again surrounded the scaffolding. At that moment cries of "La Esmeralda! La Esmeralda!" arose among the Tramps. Gringoire shuddered and turned toward the source of the clamor. The crowd opened and made way for a bright and dazzling figure. It was the gypsy girl.

"La Esmeralda!" cried Gringoire, struck in his agitation by the sudden manner in which that magic name connected his scattered recollections of the events of the day. This extraordinary creature appeared by her charm and beauty to exercise sovereign sway over the Cour des Miracles itself. Tramps of both sexes respectfully drew back for her to pass, and at the sight of her their brutal faces assumed a softer expression. With a light step she approached the victim. Her pretty Djali followed at her heels. Gringoire was more dead than alive. She eyed him for a moment in silence.

"Are you going to hang this man?" she said gravely to Clopin.

"Yes, sister," replied the King of Thunes, "unless you will take him for your husband."

She pouted prettily.

"I will take him," she said.

Gringoire was now thoroughly convinced that he had been in a dream ever since morning, and that this was just a continuation of it. The shock, though agreeable, was violent. The noose was removed, and the poet was dismounted from the stool, on which he was obliged to sit, so intense was his agitation.

The Duke of Egypt, without uttering a word, brought out an earthenware jug. The gypsy girl handed it to Gringoire. "Throw it on the ground," she said to him. The jug broke into four pieces.[24]

"Brother," said the Duke of Egypt, placing a hand on the head of each, "she is your wife. Sister, he is your husband. For four years. Go."

CHAPTER VII

A WEDDING NIGHT

In a few moments our poet found himself in a small room with a vaulted ceiling, very snug and very warm, seated at a table, which appeared to want nothing more than to draw a few loans from a cupboard, suspended close by, having a prospect of a good bed, and in a tête-à-tête with a handsome girl. The adventure was an absolute enchantment. He began to take himself seriously for the hero of some fairy tale and looked around from time to time to see whether the chariot of fire drawn by griffins, which could alone have conveyed him with such rapidity from Tartarus to Paradise, was still there. Now and then, too, he would stare at the holes in his doublet, as if to satisfy himself of his identity. His reason, tossed around in imaginary spaces, had only this thread to hold on to.

The girl appeared not to notice him; she moved back and forth, knocking against a stool, talking to her goat, and now and then pouting a bit. At length she sat down near the table, and Gringoire had the chance to take a good look at her.

Dear reader, you have been a child, too, and you are perhaps still happy enough to be one. I daresay you have often (I know I have, for whole days together, and some of the best-spent days of my life) followed from bush to bush on the bank of a stream, on a fine sunshiny day, some beautiful green-and-blue *demoiselle*,[25] darting off every moment at sharp angles and kissing the ends of all the branches. You remember with what ardent curiosity your attention and your eyes were fixed on those fluttering wings of purple and azure, amid which floated a form rendered indistinct by the very rapidity of its motion. Confusedly perceived, the aerial creature, through this flickering of wings, appeared to you chimerical, imaginary, a thing to be neither touched nor seen. But when at length it settled on the end of a reed and, holding your breath awhile, you could examine those delicate wings of gauze, that long, glossy robe, those two globes of crystal, what astonishment you felt, and what fear that this beautiful figure might again vanish into an airy, undefinable phantom! Remember these experiences and you will easily conceive what Gringoire felt on contemplating in a visible and palpable form that Esmeralda of whom he had till then had but a glimpse in the midst of a whirlwind of song and dance and through a crowd of spectators.

He became more and more absorbed in his reverie. "This, then," he thought, while his eye vaguely followed her motions, "is La Esmeralda! A celestial creature! A street dancer! So much and so little. It was she who struck the last blow to my play this afternoon, and it is she who saves my life tonight. My evil genius! My good angel! A pretty woman, upon my word! And who must love me to distraction to have taken me in this manner. For," he said, rising suddenly with that candor that formed the groundwork of his character and of his philosophy, "I don't know exactly how it has come to be, but I am her husband."

With this idea in his head and in his eyes, he approached the girl in such a military and gallant manner that she drew back. "What do you want with me?" she inquired.

"How can you ask such a question, adorable Esmeralda?" rejoined Gringoire in so impassioned a tone that he was astonished at it himself.

The gypsy's eyes widened. "I do not know what you mean," she said.

"What!" replied Gringoire, becoming more and more excited, and thinking that after all he was merely dealing with the feminine virtue of the Cour des Miracles. "Am I not yours, my sweet friend? Are you not mine?" He simply pulled her to him by the waist.

The bodice of the Bohemian glided through his hands like the skin of an eel. She jumped to the other end of the tiny room and stood up, with a little dagger in her hand, before Gringoire could see from where it came. She was angry and proud, her lips were swollen, her nostrils flared, and her cheeks apple red. Her eyes flashed lightning. At the same moment the little white goat placed itself before her, ready to attack, presenting to Gringoire two very pretty but very sharp gold horns. All this was done in an instant.

Our philosopher stood petrified, alternately eyeing the goat and her mistress. "Holy Virgin!" he at last ejaculated, when surprise allowed him to speak. "What a pair of vixens!"

"And you," said the Bohemian, breaking silence on her part, "must be a very impudent fellow."

"Pardon me," replied Gringoire, smiling. "But why did you take me for your husband?"

"Should I have let you be hanged?"

"Then," rejoined the poet, somewhat disappointed in his amorous hopes, "you had no other intention in marrying me than to save me from the gallows?"

"And what other intention do you suppose I could have had?"

Gringoire bit his lips. "All right," he said to himself, "I am not so triumphant in love as I had imagined. But then, why break the poor jug?"

Meanwhile Esmeralda's dagger and the horns of her goat were still on the defensive.

"Madamoiselle Esmeralda," said the poet, "let us call a truce. I am not an officer of the Châtelet, and shall not make you carry a dagger in Paris, against the Provost's ordinances and prohibitions. You must, nevertheless, be aware that Noël Lescrivain was sentenced a week ago to pay a fine of ten sous Parisis for having carried a short sword. But that is no business of mine, so, to return to the point—I swear to you by my share of Paradise not to approach you without your permission and consent, but for heaven's sake give me some supper."

In reality Gringoire, like Despreaux, was not of a very amorous temperament. He did not belong to that chivalric and military class who take young women by assault. In love, as in all other affairs, he was for temporizing and pursuing the middle course; and to him a good supper with an agreeable companion appeared, especially when he was hungry, an excellent interlude between the prologue and the conclusion of an amorous love adventure.

The gypsy made no reply. She pouted disdainfully, lifted her head like a bird, and burst into a loud laugh. The pretty little dagger vanished as it had come, so that Gringoire could not discover where the bee concealed its sting.

In a moment a loaf of rye bread, a slice of bacon, some wrinkled apples, and a jug of beer were set out on the table. Gringoire began eating with great enthusiasm, as if all his love had been changed into appetite. His hostess, seated before him, looked on in silence, visibly engaged with some other thought, at which she smiled from time to time, while her soft hand stroked the head of the intelligent goat, closely pressed between her knees. A candle of yellow wax lighted this scene of voracity and reverie.

The first cravings of his stomach being appeased, Gringoire felt a degree of false shame on perceiving that there was only one apple left. "Are you not eating, Mademoiselle Esmeralda?" he said. She replied in the negative by a shake of the head, and her pensive looks were fixed on the vaulted ceiling of the tiny room.

"What the devil can she be thinking of?" said Gringoire to himself, turning his eyes in the same direction as hers. "It is impossible that that ugly dwarf's head carved on the point of the vault can so engross her attention. Surely I could bear a comparison with that."

"Mademoiselle," he said, raising his voice. She appeared not to hear him. "Mademoiselle Esmeralda!" he began again in a still louder tone, with just as little success. The young woman's mind was elsewhere, and Gringoire's voice lacked the power to recall it. Luckily for him the goat intervened and began to pull her mistress gently by the sleeve. "What do you want, Djali?" said the gypsy girl sharply, starting like one awakened out of a sound sleep.

"She is hungry," said Gringoire, delighted at the opportunity of opening the conversation.

La Esmeralda began crumbling some bread, which Djali gracefully ate out of the hollow of her hand. Gringoire, without giving her time to resume her reverie, ventured to ask a delicate question. "Then you will not have me for your husband?" he said.

The girl looked at him intently for a moment, and then replied, "No."

"For your lover?" asked Gringoire.

She pouted her lip and again replied, "No."

"For your friend?" continued Gringoire.

She again fixed her eyes steadfastly on him. "Perhaps," she said, after a moment's reflection.

This *perhaps,* so dear to philosophers, emboldened Gringoire. "Do you know what friendship is?" he inquired.

"Yes," replied the gypsy. "It is to be as brother and sister, two souls that touch each other without uniting, like two fingers of the same hand."

"And love?" proceeded Gringoire.

"Oh! Love!" she said, and her voice trembled, and her eye sparkled. "It is to be two and yet but one—it is a man and a woman melting into an angel—it is heaven itself."

The street dancer, as she uttered these words, appeared invested with a beauty that powerfully struck Gringoire, and seemed in perfect unison with the almost Oriental exaggeration of her language. A faint smile played on her pure and rosy lips; her bright and serene brow was now and then clouded for a moment, according to the turn of her thoughts, as a mirror is by the breath; and from her long, dark, downcast eyelashes emanated a sort of ineffable light, which imparted to her profile that ideal sweetness that Raphael subsequently found at the mystical conjunction of virginity, maternity, and divinity.

Gringoire nevertheless proceeded. "And what should one be," he said, "to please you?"

"A man."

"What am I, then?"

"A man has a helmet on his head, a sword in his fist, and gold spurs at his heels."

"So then," rejoined Gringoire, "without a horse one cannot be a man. Do you love anyone?"

She remained pensive for a moment, and then said with a peculiar kind of expression, "I shall soon know that."

"Why not tonight?" replied the poet tenderly. "Why not me?"

She eyed him with a serious look. "Never can I love any man but one who is able to protect me."

Gringoire blushed and received the blow. It was evident that the girl was alluding to the little help he had afforded her in the critical situation in which she had found herself two hours before. At the memory of this circumstance, which his own subsequent adventures had banished from his mind, he struck his forehead.

"Indeed," he said, "I ought to have begun with that subject. Forgive the confusion of my ideas. How did you manage to escape from Quasimodo's clutches?"

This question made the gypsy girl shudder. "Oh, the horrid hunchback!" she exclaimed, covering her face with her hands, and she shivered as from the effect of intense cold.

"Horrid, indeed!" said Gringoire, without relinquishing his idea. "But how did you get away from him?"

La Esmeralda smiled, sighed, and made no reply.

"Do you know why he followed you?" resumed Gringoire, seeking to return to his question by a roundabout way.

"I do not," said the girl. "But," she added sharply, "you followed me too; why did you follow me?"

"In truth," replied Gringoire, "I do not know either."

Both were then silent. Gringoire took up his knife and began to carve the table. The girl smiled and seemed to be looking at something through the wall. Suddenly she began singing in a voice scarcely articulate:

> *Quando las pintadas aves*
> *Mudas están, y la tierra.*[26]

Then she abruptly broke off and began to caress her Djali.

"That is a pretty creature of yours," observed Gringoire.

"She is my sister," she replied.

"Why are you called La Esmeralda?" inquired the poet.

"I can't tell."

"No, sure!"

She drew from her bosom a small, oblong sachet on a string of adrezarach, or small red beads. It gave off a very strong scent of camphor. It was made of green silk, and in the middle of it there was a large bead of green glass in imitation of an emerald.

"Perhaps it is on account of this," she said.

Gringoire wanted to take hold of the sachet, but she started back. "Don't touch it," she said. "It is an amulet. You might do an injury to the spell, or the spell to you."

The poet became more and more curious. "Who gave you that?" he asked.

She laid her finger on her lips and replaced the amulet in her bosom. He asked further questions but could scarcely obtain answers to them.

"What is the meaning of La Esmeralda?"

"I do not know," she said.

"To what language does the word belong?"

"It is Egyptian, I believe."

"I thought so," said Gringoire. "You are not a native of France?"

"I don't know."

"Are your parents living?"

She began singing to the tune of an old song:

> *Mon père est oiseau,*
> *Ma mère est oiselle,*
> *Je passe l'eau sans nacelle,*
> *Je passe l'eau sans bateau,*
> *Ma mère est oiselle,*
> *Mon père est oiseau.*[27]

"That's good. How old were you when you came to France?"

"I was quite a child."

"And to Paris?"

"Last year. At the moment we were entering the Papal Gate I saw the warblers flying in a line over our heads. It was the end of August, and I said, 'We shall have a harsh winter.'"

"And so we have," said Gringoire, delighted with this conversational opening. "I have done nothing but blow on my fingers since it set in. Why, then, you possess the gift of prophecy?"

"No," she replied, relapsing into her laconic manner.

"The man you call the Duke of Egypt is the chief of your tribe, I presume?"

"Yes."

"And yet it was he who married us," timidly observed the poet.

She pouted prettily as was her habit. "I don't even know your name," she said.

"My name, if you wish to know it, is Pierre Gringoire."

"I know a much finer," she said.

"How unkind!" replied the poet. "Never mind, you shall not make me angry. You will, perhaps, love me when you know me better. And you have told me your story with so much trust that I cannot withhold mine from you.

"You must know then that my name is Pierre Gringoire, and that my father was a farmer-notary in Gonesse. He was hanged by the Burgundians, and my mother was murdered by the Picards, during the siege of Paris twenty years ago. So, at six years of age, I was left an orphan with no other sole to my foot but the pavement of Paris. I do not know how I survived the interval between six and sixteen. Sometimes a fruit woman gave me an apple or a plum; other times, a baker tossed me a crust of bread; at night I threw myself in the way of the watchmen, who picked me up and put me in prison, where I found at least a bundle of straw. In spite of this kind of life, I grew tall and slim, as you see. In winter I warmed myself in the sunshine, in the doorway of the Hôtel de Sens, and I thought it very absurd that the bonfires of St. John[28] should take place in the dog days of summer. At sixteen I began to think of adopting a profession and tried my hand at everything. I turned soldier but was not brave enough; I became a monk but was not devout enough, and, besides, I could not drink hard enough. In despair I apprenticed myself to a carpenter but was not strong enough. I had a much greater fancy to be a schoolmaster. True, I had not learned to read, but so what? That did not discourage me. After some time I discovered that, owing to some deficiency or other, I was fit for nothing, and I decided to be a poet and composer of rhymes. This is a profession to which a man who is a tramp may make a claim, and it is better than to thieve, as some young rogues of my acquaintance advised me to do. One day, as good luck would have it, I met Dom Claude Frollo, the reverend Archdeacon of Notre-Dame, who took a liking to me, and to him I owe it that I am this day a learned man. I know my Latin from Cicero's *De officiis*[29] to the Mortuologue of the Heavenly Fathers. I am not unpracticed in scholastics, poetics, or rhythmics, nor even in hermetics, that sophism of all sophisms. I am the author of the play that was performed today before a prodigious audience, with immense applause, in the great hall of the Palace of Justice. I have also written a book of six hundred pages on the prodigious comet of 1465, which drove a man mad. And I have distinguished myself in other ways. Being somewhat of an artillery carpenter, I assisted in making the great mortar that, you know, exploded at the bridge of Charenton on the day it was tested, and killed twenty-four of the curious. So you see I am not a bad match. I know a great many very curious tricks, which I will teach your goat: for instance, to mimic the Bishop of Paris, that cursed Pharisee whose mills splash the passengers all along the Pont aux Meuniers. And then my play will bring me in a good deal of hard cash, if I can get paid for it. In short, I am wholly at your service, my lady, my body and soul, my science and my learning, ready to live with you in any way you please, chastely or joyfully, as husband and wife, if you think proper, as brother and sister, if you like it better."

Gringoire paused, waiting for the effect of his speech on the young woman. Her eyes were fixed on the ground.

"Phœbus," she said in an undertone, and then turning to the poet, "Phœbus, what does that mean?"

Gringoire, though unable to discover what connection there could be between the subject of his speech and this question, was not displeased to have an opportunity to display his erudition. "It is a Latin word," he said, "and means the sun."

"The sun!" she exclaimed.

"It is the name of a certain handsome archer, who was a god," added Gringoire.

"A god!" repeated the gypsy, and there was in her tone something pensive and impassioned.

At this moment one of her bracelets, having accidentally become loose, fell to the ground. Gringoire instantly stooped to pick it up; when he stood up the girl and the goat were gone. He heard the sound of a bolt, on a door leading no doubt to an adjoining room, which fastened on the inside.

"No matter, at least she left me a bed!" said our philosopher. He explored the room. The only piece of furniture it contained that was fit to lie down on was a long chest. Its lid was carved in such a manner as to communicate to Gringoire, when he stretched himself on it, a sensation similar to that experienced by Micromégas[30] when he lay at his full length on the Alps.

"Well," he said, settling in as well as he could, "I must resign myself. But at any rate this is a strange wedding night! It's too bad. There was something naïve and antediluvian about this broken jug wedding that I liked."

BOOK III

CHAPTER I

NOTRE-DAME[1]

The church of Notre-Dame in Paris is doubtless still a sublime and majestic edifice today. But notwithstanding the beauty that it has retained even in its old age, one cannot help feeling grief and indignation at the numberless injuries and mutilations that time and man have inflicted on the venerable structure, without any respect for Charlemagne, who laid the first stone of it, and for Philip Augustus, who laid the last.

On the face of this aged queen of our cathedrals we always find a scar beside a wrinkle. *Tempus edax, homo edacior*—which I would translate "Time is blind, man stupid."

If we had leisure to examine with the reader, one by one, the different traces of destruction left on the ancient church, we would find that Time had had much less hand in them than men, and especially men of art. I must call them men of art because there were individuals during the last two centuries who took up the title of architect.

In the first place, to mention only some of the most important examples, there are assuredly few more beautiful specimens of architecture than that facade, with the three doorways with their pointed arches; the border embroidered and fretted with twenty-eight royal niches; the immense central stained glass window, flanked by its two lateral windows, like the priest by the deacon and the subdeacon; the lofty and light gallery of open-work clover arcades supporting a heavy platform on its slender pillars; last, the two dark and massive towers with their slate porches—harmonious parts of a magnificent whole, placed one above another in five gigantic stories—present themselves to the eye as a mass yet without confusion, with their innumerable details of statuary, sculpture, and carving powerfully contributing to the tranquil grandeur of the whole—a vast symphony of stone, if we may be allowed the expression. It is the colossal work of a people and one man, like the *Iliad* or the Romanceros, of which it is a sibling. It is the prodigious product of the forces of the age in which the fancy of the workman, chastened by the genius of the artist, is seen surging forth in a hundred ways on every stone. In short, it is a sort of human Creation, powerful and fertile as the Divine Creation, from which it seems to have borrowed its twofold character of variety and eternity.

What we say here of the facade must be said of the whole church, and what we say of the cathedral of Paris must be said of all the churches of Christendom in the Middle Ages. Everything about the self-contained work is logical and well-proportioned. To take its measure from head to toe is to take the measure of a giant. But to return to the facade of Notre-Dame, as it appears to us at present, when we piously go there to admire the solemn and gorgeous cathedral, which, to use the language of the chroniclers, "by its vastness struck terror into the spectator."

That facade, as we now see it, is missing three important features: in the first place, the flight of eleven steps that raised it above the level of the ground; in the next, the lower range of statues that filled the niches of the three doorways; and the upper range of twenty-eight ancient sovereigns of France that adorned the gallery of the first story, beginning with Childebert and ending with Philip Augustus, holding in his hand "the imperial globe."

Time, by a slow and irresistible progress raising the level of the city, occasioned the removal of the steps; but if this rising tide of the pavement of Paris has swallowed up, one after another, those eleven steps that added to the majestic height of the edifice, Time has given to the church more perhaps than it has taken away; for it is Time that has imparted to the facade that somber hue of antiquity that makes the old age of buildings the period of their greatest beauty.

But who has knocked down the two rows of statues? Who has left the niches empty? Who has inserted that new and bastard pointed arch in the middle of the beautiful central doorway? Who has dared to set up that tasteless and heavy wooden door, carved in the style of Louis XV, beside the arabesques of Biscornette?[22] The men, the architects, the artists, of our own day.

And, if we step within the edifice, who has taken down that colossal St. Christopher that was famous among statues for the same reason that the great hall of the palace is renowned among halls, and the steeple of Strasbourg among steeples? Who has brutally swept away the multitude of statues, kneeling, standing on horseback, men, women, children, kings, bishops, soldiers, of stone, marble, gold, silver, copper, and even wax that peopled the spaces between the columns of the nave and the choir? It was not Time.

And who has replaced the old Gothic altar, splendidly decorated with shrines and reliquaries, that heavy sarcophagus of marble with its cherubs and its clouds, looking for all the world like a stray specimen from the Val-de-Grâce or the Invalides? Who has stupidly inserted that clumsy anachronism of stone in the Carlovingian pavement of Hercandus? Is it not Louis XIV fulfilling the vow of Louis XIII?[3]

Who has installed cold white glass in the place of those stained glass windows that caused the astonished eyes of our ancestors to pause between the rose window of the main entrance and the pointed arches of the apse? What would a choir member of the sixteenth century say on beholding the lovely plaster with which our Vandal archbishops have bedaubed their cathedral? He would remember that this was the color with which the executioner painted over the houses of criminals; he would remember the Hôtel du Petit-Bourbon, beplastered with yellow because of the Constable's act of treason, "and a yellow of so good quality," said Sauval, "and so well laid on, that more than a century has not yet faded its color"; he would imagine that the sacred place had become desecrated, and flee from it as fast as he could.

And if we go up into the cathedral, without pausing over the thousand different barbarisms, what has been done with that charming little belfry that stood over the point of intersection of the transept, and that, neither less light nor less bold than its neighbor, the steeple of the Ste.-Chapelle (likewise destroyed) rose, light, elegant, and sonorous, into the air, topping the towers? It was amputated (1787) by an architect of taste, who deemed it sufficient to cover the wound with that large plaster of lead that looks for all the world like the lid of a saucepan.[4]

It is thus that the wonderful art of the Middle Ages has been treated in almost every country, especially in France. In its ruins we may distinguish three kinds of injuries, which have affected it in different degrees: in the first place Time, which has here and there damaged and worn away its surface; second, revolutions, political and religious, which, blind and furious by nature, attacked it tumultuously, stripped it of its rich garb of sculptures and carvings, broke its rose windows, and tore apart its chains of arabesques and fanciful figures, pulled down its statues, sometimes on account of their miters, sometimes on account of their crowns; last, fashions, more and more silly and grotesque, which since the splendid deviations of the Renaissance have succeeded each other in the inevitable decline of architecture. The fashions have in fact done more mischief than revolutions. They have cut to the quick; they have attacked the very bones of architecture; they have hacked, hewn, mangled, murdered the building, in form as well as in symbol, in logic not less than in beauty. And then they have done the work of restoration. At least Time and revolutions never had such pretensions. In the name of *good taste,* fashion has impudently dressed the wounds of Gothic architecture with the miserable baubles of a day, in ribbons of marble, pompons of metal, a true leprosy of egg molding, scrolls, spirals, draperies, garlands, fringes, flames of stone, clouds of bronze, a plethora of Cupids, chubby cherubs, which begin to eat into the face of art in the chapel of Catherine de Medici and put it to death two centuries later, writhing and grinning in the boudoir of the Dubarry.

Thus, to sum up the points to which we have directed attention, three kinds of ravages nowadays disfigure Gothic architecture: wrinkles and warts on the skin—these are the work of Time; wounds, contusions, fractures, from brutal violence—these are the work of revolutions from Luther to Mirabeau; mutilations, amputations, dislocations of limbs, *restorations*—this is the barbarous Greek and Roman work of professors, according to Vitruvius and Vignole.[5] That magnificent art that the Vandals produced the academies have murdered. Time and revolutions, whose ravages are, at any rate, marked by impartiality and grandeur, have been joined by a host of architects, licensed, certified, and sworn, destroying with the discernment of bad taste, replacing Gothic lacework with the chicories of Louis XV for the greater glory of the Parthenon. This is truly the ass's kick to the dying lion. The old oak grows its magnificent foliage so that it can be bitten, gnawed, and torn apart by caterpillars.

How far we are from the time when Robert Cenalis,[6] comparing Notre-Dame of Paris with the famous temple of Diana in Ephesus, "so highly extolled by the ancient heathen," pronounced the Gallic cathedral "more excellent in length, breadth, height, and structure."

Notre-Dame, however, is not what may be called a complete, defined, and classifiable monument. It is not a Romanesque church, neither it is a Gothic church. This building cannot be categorized. Notre-Dame has not, like the abbey of Tournus, the heavy, massive squareness, the round, wide domes, the cold nakedness, the majestic simplicity, of edifices that are based on the circular arch for their generative principle. It is not, like the cathedral of Bourges, the magnificent, light, multiform, efflorescent, highly decorated production of the pointed arch. It cannot be classed among that ancient family of churches, gloomy, mysterious, low, and crushed as it were by the circular arch; quite hieroglyphic, sacerdotal, symbolic; exhibiting in their decor more diamonds and zigzags than flowers, more flowers than animals, more animals than human figures. This is more the work of the architect than of the bishop; it demonstrates the first transformation of the art, still marked by theocratic and military discipline, that began in the Lower Empire and ended with William the Conqueror. Neither can our cathedral be placed in that other family of churches, light, lofty, rich in stained glass and sculptures; sharp in form, bold in attitude; free, capricious, unruly, as works of art. These churches demonstrate the second transformation of architecture, no longer hieroglyphic, unchangeable, and sacerdotal, but artistic, progressive, and popular, beginning with the return from the Crusades and ending with Louis XI. Notre-Dame is not purely Roman, like the former, nor is it purely Arab, like the latter.[7]

It is a transitional edifice. The Saxon architect raised the first pillars of the nave, when the pointed style, brought back from the Crusades, seated itself like a conqueror on those broad Roman capitals designed to support only domes. The ogive, or pointed style, dominant from then on, shaped the construction of the rest of the church. But inexperienced and timid at its outset, it expanded, enlarged, and then contained its sphere of influence and did not yet dare launch itself into steeples and pinnacles as it would do later in so many wonderful cathedrals. You might say that it was affected by the vicinity of the heavy Romanesque pillars.

In any case, these transitional edifices between the Romanesque and the Gothic style are not less valuable as studies than the pure types of either. They express a shade of the art that would be lost except for them—the grafting of the pointed arch onto the dome style.

Notre-Dame of Paris is a particularly curious specimen of this variety. Every face, every stone of the venerable structure is a page not only of the history of the country but also of the history of art and science. Thus, to point out only the principal details: while the little Porte Rouge almost reaches the height of Gothic delicacy of the fifteenth century, the pillars of the nave by their bulk and heaviness take us back to the time of the Carlovingian abbey of St.-Germain-des-Prés. One might believe that there were six centuries between that doorway and those pillars. Alchemists themselves find in the symbols of the main entrance a satisfactory compendium of their science, of which the church of St.-Jacques-de-la-Boucherie was so complete a hieroglyphic. Thus the Romanesque abbey and the philosophical church, Gothic art and Saxon art, the heavy round pillar, which reminds you of Gregory VII, Papal unity and schism, St.-Germain-des-Prés and St.-Jacques-de-la-Boucherie—are all blended, combined, amalgamated, in Notre-Dame. This central and fertile church is a sort of chimera among the ancient churches of Paris; it has the head of one, the limbs of another, the trunk of a third, and something of them all.

These hybrid structures, as we have observed, are no less interesting to the artist, the antiquarian, and the historian. They show how deeply primitive architecture is, since these hybrids demonstrate (what can also be seen in the ruins of Cyclops, the Pyramids of Egypt, the gigantic Hindu pagodas) that the grandest productions of architecture are not so much individuals as social works. They are the products of people's labor rather than the inventions of a single genius. They are the deposits left by a people, the accumulations of the ages, the remains of the successive disappearances of human society—in short, of a species in formation. Every wave of time superimposes its alluvium, every generation deposits its stratum on the monument, every individual brings his stone. Beavers work like this, so do bees and human beings. The great symbol of architecture, the Tower of Babel, is a beehive.

Great buildings, like great mountains, are the work of ages. Often art changes while they are still works in progress. *Pendent opera interrupta.*[8] The buildings continue to evolve peacefully according to the changes. The new art takes the structure as it finds it, encrusts itself on it, assimilates itself to it, does with it according to its own fancy, and completes it if it can. The thing is completed without disturbance, without effort, without reaction, as if according to a natural and quiet law. There are grafts that take hold. The sap circulates, and another form of vegetation emerges. Certainly there is material for very thick books in those successive weldings together of various styles at various heights on the same monument and containing the universal history of humanity. The man, the artist, and the individual disappear in these vast, unsigned structures, while human intelligence is condensed and concentrated in them. Time is the architect, the people are the mason.

To limit ourselves to Christian European architecture, that younger sister of the grand works of the East, it appears to us like an immense formation divided into three totally distinct zones laid one upon another: the Roman zone, the Gothic zone, and the zone of the Renaissance,[9] which we could call Greco-Roman. The Roman stratum, which is the most ancient and the deepest, is occupied by the dome, which reappears, supported by the Greek column, in the modern and uppermost stratum of the Renaissance. The ogive, or pointed arch, lies between the two. The buildings belonging exclusively to one of these three strata are absolutely distinct, unified, and complete. Such are the abbey of Jumièges, the cathedral of Reims, the church of St.-Croix in Orléans. But the three zones blend and intermingle at their borders, like the colors in the solar spectrum. Thus the complex monuments, the transitional and more nuanced buildings. One is Roman at the foot, Gothic in the middle, Greco-Roman at the top. The reason is that it was six centuries in building. This variety is rare; the castle of Étampes is a specimen of it. But the monuments composed of two formations are frequent. Such is Notre-Dame in Paris, an ogival building whose first pillars grow out of the Roman zone, like the entrance of St.-Denis, and the nave of St.-Germain-des-Prés. Such too is the charming semi-Gothic capitular hall of Bocherville, whose Roman stratum goes up to its middle. Such is the cathedral of Rouen, which would be entirely Gothic were it not for the extremity of its central steeple, which penetrates into the zone of the Renaissance.[10]

For the rest, all these shades, all these differences, affect only the surface of buildings. It is art that has shed its skin. The construction of the Christian church itself is not affected by them. There is always the same internal structure, the same logic of disposition of its parts. Whatever the sculptured and embroidered exterior of a cathedral may be, we invariably find underneath it, at least in a germinating or rudimentary state, the origins of the Roman basilica. It occupies space on the ground according to the same laws. There are always two naves, intersecting each other in the form of a cross, the upper extremity of which, rounded into an apse, forms the chancel. There are always two aisles for processions and for chapels, sorts of lateral walkways, into which the principal nave flows by the intercolumniations. These points being settled, the number of chapels, doorways, towers, pinnacles, is infinitely variable, according to the taste of the times, of the nation, and of art. Accommodation for the rites of religion once provided a certain set of limits, now architecture does just as it pleases. Statues, stained glass windows, rose windows, arabesques, carving, capitals, bas-reliefs—it combines all these devices according to the formula that best suits it. Thus the prodigious external variety in those edifices within which reside such order and unity. The trunk of the tree is unchangeable, the foliage capricious.

CHAPTER II

A Bird's-eye View of Paris

We have just attempted to repair for the reader the admirable church of Notre-Dame of Paris. We have briefly touched on most of the beauties that it possessed in the fifteenth century, and that it no longer possesses today. But we have omitted the most important thing, namely, the view of Paris then enjoyed from the top of the towers.

It was in fact that, after groping your way up the dark spiral staircase that vertically penetrates the thick wall of the bell towers, and exiting suddenly on one of the two high platforms bathed with light and air, a beautiful scene dominated your entire vision—a spectacle sui generis, of which our readers might have some idea if they have had the good fortune to see one of the few Gothic towns still left intact, complete, and homogeneous, such as Nuremberg in Bavaria, Vittoria in Spain, or even smaller specimens, provided they are in good preservation, as Vitré in Bretagne, and Nordhausen in Prussia.

The Paris of three hundred and fifty years ago, the Paris of the fifteenth century, was already a gigantic city. We modern Parisians are much mistaken about the amount of ground that we imagine it has gained. Since the time of Louis XI, Paris has not grown more than one-third,[11] and certainly it has lost much more in beauty than it has acquired in magnitude.

Paris was born, as everybody knows, in that ancient island in the shape of a cradle that is now called the Cité. The banks of that island were its first enclosure; the Seine was its first moat. For several centuries Paris was confined to the island, having two bridges, the one on the north, and the other on the south, and two *têtes-de-ponts,* which were at once its gates and its fortresses—the Grand Châtelet on the right bank and the Petit Châtelet on the left. In time, under the kings of the first dynasty, too crowded on the island and unable to turn itself around, Paris crossed the water. A first enclosure of walls and towers then began to invade the countryside on either bank of the Seine beyond the two Châtelets. Of this ancient enclosure some vestiges were still remaining in the past century; now nothing is left of it but the memory and here and there a traditional name: the Porte Baudets, or Baudoyer, Porta Bagauda. By degrees the flood of houses, always pushing from the heart of the city to its limits, wore away and overflowed this enclosure. Philip Augustus surrounded Paris with new ramparts. He imprisoned the city in a circular chain of large towers, high and massive. For more than a century the houses, crowding closer and closer in this basin, rose like water in a reservoir. They began to grow higher; story was piled on story; they shot high, like any compressed fluid, and each one tried to lift its head above its neighbor's in order to get a little fresh air. The streets became deeper and deeper, and narrower and narrower; every vacant square was occupied and disappeared. The houses eventually leaped over Philip Augustus's wall, and merrily scattered themselves at random over the plain, like escaped prisoners. There they installed themselves where they liked and carved themselves gardens out of the fields. As early as 1367 the suburbs of the city had spread so far as to need a fresh enclosure, especially on the right bank: this was built by Charles V. But a place like Paris is perpetually growing. It is such cities alone that become capitals of countries. They are reservoirs, into which flow all the geographical, political, moral, and intellectual tributaries of a country, and all the natural inclinations of its population. They are wells of civilization, so to speak, and drains as well, where commerce, industry, intelligence, population, that is all that constitutes the sap, the life, the soul of a nation, is incessantly collecting and filtering, drop by drop, century by century. The walls of Charles V consequently shared the same fate as those of Philip Augustus. By the end of the fifteenth century they were crossed over, and the neighborhoods kept traveling on. In the sixteenth the walls seemed to be visibly receding more and more into the ancient city, so rapidly did the new town grow dense on the other side. Thus, from the fifteenth century, to go back no farther, Paris had already worn out the three concentric circles of walls that, from the time of Julian the Apostate, lay in embryo, so to speak, in the Grand Châtelet and the Petit Châtelet. The mighty city had successively burst its four mural belts, like a growing boy bursting the garments made for him a year ago. Under Louis XI there were still to be seen ruined towers of the ancient walls, rising at intervals above this sea of houses, like the tops of hills from a flood, as if the archipelagos of old Paris were submerged beneath the new.

Since that time Paris has, unluckily for us, undergone further transformation, but it has leaped over only one more enclosure, that of Louis XV, a miserable wall of mud and dirt, worthy of the king who built it and the poet by whom it was celebrated:

Le mur murant Paris rend Paris murmurant.[12]

In the fifteenth century Paris was still divided into three totally distinct and separate cities, each having its own physiognomy, specialty, manners, customs, privileges, and history: the Cité, the Université, and the Ville. The Cité, which occupied the island, was the mother of the two others, and cooped up between them, like—reader, forgive the comparison—like a little old woman between two handsome, strapping daughters. The Université occupied the left bank of the Seine from the Tournelle to the Tour de Nesle, points corresponding with the Halle aux Vins and the Mint, of modern Paris. Its enclosure encroached considerably on the plain where Julian had built his baths. It included the hill of Ste.-Geneviève. The highest point of this curve of walls was the Papal Gate, which stood nearly on the site of the present Panthéon. The Ville, the most extensive of the three divisions, stretched along the right bank. Its quay ran, with several interruptions, along the Seine, from the spot where the Grenier d'Abondance now stands to that occupied by the Tuileries. These four points at which the Seine intersected the enclosure of the capital, the Tournelle and the Tour de Nesle on the left, and the Tour de Billy and the Tour du Bois on the right, were called the four towers of Paris. The Ville penetrated still farther into the fields than the Université. The culminating point of the enclosure of the Ville was at the gates of St.-Denis and St.-Martin, the sites of which remain unchanged to this day.

Each of these great divisions of Paris was, as we have observed, a city, but a city too specialized to be complete, a city that could not do without the two others. They had three totally different looks. The Cité, properly so called, abounded in churches; the Ville contained the palaces; and the Université, the colleges. Setting aside secondary jurisdictions, we may assume generally that the island was under the Bishop, the right bank under the Provost of the Merchants, the left under the Rector of the Université, and the whole under the Provost of Paris, a royal and not a municipal officer. The Cité had the cathedral of Notre-Dame; the Ville, the Louvre and the Hôtel de Ville; and the Université, the Sorbonne. The Ville contained the Halles; the Cité, the Hôtel-Dieu; and the Université, the Pré-aux-Clercs. For offenses committed on the left bank in the Pré-aux-Clercs, the students were tried at the Palace of Justice on the island and punished on the right bank in Montfaucon, unless the Rector, finding the Université strong and the King weak, chose to interfere. For it was the privilege of the scholars to be hung in their own neighborhood.

Most of these privileges, one should note, and some of them were more valuable than that just mentioned, had been extorted from different kings by revolts and insurrections. This is the way things go: the King never grants any favor that is not wrung from him by the people. *"Le roi ne lache que quand le peuple arrache."* There is an old saying on the topic of loyalty that puts it more naïvely, *"Civibus fidelitas in reges, quae tamen aliquoties seditionibus interrupta multa peperit privilegia."*[13]

In the fifteenth century that part of the Seine flowed between five islands within the enclosure of Paris: the Ile Louviers,[14] then covered with trees, and now with timber; the Ile aux Vaches and the Ile de Notre-Dame, both uninhabited and belonging to the Bishop (in the seventeenth century these two islands were converted into one, which has been built on and is now called the Ile St.-Louis); last, the Cité; and at its extremity the islet of the Passeur aux Vaches, since buried under the platform of the Pont Neuf. The city had at that time five bridges: three on the right, the Pont Notre-Dame and the Pont au Change of stone, and the Pont aux Meuniers of wood; two on the left, the Petit Pont of stone, and the Pont St.-Michel of wood, all of them covered with houses. The Université had six gates, built by Philip Augustus; these were, starting from the Tournelle, the Porte St.-Victor, the Porte Bordelle, the Papal Gate, and the Porte St.-Jacques, Porte St.-Michel, and Porte St.-Germain. The Ville had six gates, built by Charles V; they were, beginning from the Tour de Billy, the Porte of St.-Antoine, the Temple, St.-Martin, St.-Denis, Montmartre, and St.-Honoré. All these gates were strong and beautiful too, a fact that did not detract from their strength. A wide, deep moat, into which flowed water from the Seine, which was swollen by the floods of winter, encircled the foot of the walls all around Paris. At night the gates were closed, the river was dammed up at the two extremities of the city by great iron chains, and Paris slept in peace.

A bird's-eye view of these three neighborhoods—the Cité, the Université, and the Ville—presented to the eye a complex weave of streets strangely knit together. It was apparent, however, at first sight that these three fragments of a city formed a single body. One could see right away two long, parallel streets without break or interruption crossing the three cities, nearly in a straight line, from one end to the other, from south to north, perpendicular to the Seine, incessantly pouring the people of the one into the other. They connected, blended, crossed, infused together, and made the three parts into one. The first of these streets ran from the gate of St.-Jacques to the gate of St.-Martin; it was called in the Université Rue St.-Jacques, in the Cité Rue de la Juiverie, and in the Ville Rue St.-Martin; it crossed the river twice by the name of Petit Pont and Pont Notre-Dame. The second, named Rue de la Harpe on the left bank, Rue de la Barillerie on the island, Rue St.-Denis on the right bank, Pont St.-Michel over one arm of the Seine, and Pont au Change over the other, ran from the gate of St.-Michel in the Université to the gate of St.-Denis in the Ville. Still, though they bore so many different names, they formed in reality only two streets, but the two mother streets, the two great arteries of Paris.

All the other veins of the triple city were fed by or flowed into them.

Besides these two principal diametrical streets crossing Paris breadthwise and common to the entire capital, the Ville and the Université each had its main street running parallel with the Seine, and intersecting the two arterial streets at right angles. Thus in the Ville you might go in a direct line from the Porte St.-Antoine to the Porte St.-Honoré; and in the Université from the Porte St.-Victor to the Porte St.-Germain. These two great thoroughfares, crossed by the two former, constituted the frame on which rested the labyrinthine web of the streets of Paris, knotted and jumbled together in every possible way. In the unintelligible plan of this labyrinth might also be distinguished, on closer examination, two clusters of wide streets, which ran, expanding like sheaves of grain, from the bridges to the gates. Something of this geometrical plan survives to this day.

Now what did this all look like, when seen from the top of the towers of Notre-Dame in 1482? That is what we shall now attempt to describe. The spectator, on arriving breathless at that peak, was dazzled by the chaos of roofs, chimneys, streets, bridges, belfries, towers, and steeples. All burst at once upon the eye—the carved gable, the sharp roof, the turret perched on the corners of the walls, the stone pyramid of the eleventh century, the slated obelisk of the fifteenth, the round and naked keep of the castle, the square and fretted tower of the church, the great and the small, the massive and the light. The eye was long bewildered by this labyrinth of heights and depths where everything had its originality, its reason, its genius, its beauty, everything originated in art, from the humblest dwelling, with its painted and carved wooden facade, low doorway, and overhanging stories, to the royal Louvre, which then had a colonnade of towers. But when the eye began to reduce this tumult of edifices to some kind of order, the principal masses that stood out from among them were the following.

To begin with, the Cité. "The island of the Cité," says Sauval, who in all his rubbish has occasionally some good ideas, "the island of the Cité is shaped like a great ship that has run aground and is stuck fast in the mud, almost in the middle of the Seine." We have already stated that in the fifteenth century this ship was moored to the two banks of the river by five bridges. This resemblance to a vessel had struck the

writers of those times; for it is to this, and not because of the siege of
the Normans, that, according to Favyn and Pasquier, the ship blazoned
in the ancient arms of Paris owes its origin. To those who can decipher
it, heraldry is an algebra, a language. The entire history of the second
half of the Middle Ages is written in heraldry, as the history of the first
half is inscribed in the imagery of the Roman churches; thus the hieroglyphics of the feudal system succeed those of theocracy.

The Cité, then, offered itself first to one's view, with its stern to the
east and its prow to the west. Turning toward the west, you had before
you a countless multitude of old roofs, above which rose like the back
of an elephant supporting its castle the round, swelling lead cupola of
the Ste.-Chapelle. Only here, the castle was occupied by the boldest,
the most finely wrought, the most elegant steeple that had ever allowed the sky to be seen through its cone of lacework. Just in front of
Notre-Dame three streets flowed into the Parvis; it was a handsome
square of old houses. On the south side of this square was the Hôtel-
Dieu, with its grim and wrinkled facade and a roof that seemed to be
covered with warts and pimples. Then, to the right and to the left, to
the east and to the west, within the narrow compass of the Cité rose
the steeples of its twenty-one churches of every epoch, of all forms, of
all dimensions, from the low and crazy Roman campanile of St.-Denis-
du-Pas to the slender spires of St.-Pierre-aux-Bœufs and St.-Landry.
Behind Notre-Dame, to the north, the cloisters unfolded themselves
with their Gothic galleries; to the south the semi-Roman palace of the
Bishop; to the east the open area called the Terrain. Amid this jumble
of buildings the eye might still distinguish the lofty miters of carved
stone that crowned even the topmost windows of the palaces, the mansion that the city in the time of Charles VI gave to Juvénal des Ursins.
A little farther on, the tarred sheds of the Paluse Market; beyond them
the new apse of St.-Germain-le-Vieux, lengthened in 1458 at the expense of one end of the Rue aux Febues; and then, at intervals, an open
space crowded with people. Then we see a pillory erected at the corner of a street, a fine piece of the pavement of Philip Augustus, composed of magnificent flagstones, with a central grooved path for the
horses' hooves that was replaced in the sixteenth century by a vacant
back courtyard of gravel called "Paré de la Ligue." There is one of
those external spiral staircases from the fifteenth century that can still
be seen in the Rue des Bourdonnais. Last, on the right of the Ste.-

Chapelle, toward the west, the Palace of Justice with its group of towers was settled on the bank of the river. The high trees of the King's gardens, which covered the western point of the Cité, blocked the view of the islet of the Passeur. As for the water, it was scarcely visible at either end of the Cité from the towers of Notre-Dame; the Seine was hidden by the bridges, and the bridges by the houses.

When the eye passed beyond these bridges, whose roofs were moldy before their time from the humidity and green with moss, if one looked to the left, toward the Université, the first striking building was a clump of towers, the Petit Châtelet, whose yawning gateway swallowed up the end of the Petit Pont. If we followed the bank of the river from east to west, from the Tournelle to the Tour de Nesle, we could see a long line of houses with carved beams, stained glass windows, story on top of story over the pavement, an interminable zigzag of bourgeois houses, frequently interrupted by the end of a street, and from time to time also by the front or perhaps the corner of some spacious stone mansion, seated at its ease, with its courts and gardens amid this multitude of narrow, closely crowded dwellings, like a great lord in a crowd of his dependents. There were five or six of these mansions on the quay, from the Logis de Lorraine, which divided with the Bernardines the extensive enclosure contiguous to the Tournelle, to the Hôtel de Nesle,[15] whose main tower was the boundary of Paris, and whose pointed roofs for three months of the year eclipsed with their black triangles parts of the scarlet disk of the setting sun.

This side of the Seine was the least mercantile of the three neighborhoods of Paris. The students made more noise and bustle there than the artisans, and there was no quay, properly speaking, except from the bridge of St.-Michel to the Tour de Nesle. The rest of the bank of the Seine was in some places a naked sandy beach, as it is beyond the Bernardines. In some places a jumble of houses stood on the brink of the water, as if between the two bridges.

The washerwomen made a great din. They gabbed, shouted, sang from morning till night along the bank, and soundly beat their sheets, much the same way they do today. Among the sights of Paris this is by no means the dullest.

The Université brought the eye to a full stop. From one end to the other it is a homogeneous, compact whole. Those thousand roofs, close, angular, adhering together, almost all composed of the same geometrical element, seen from above, presented the appearance of a crystallization of one and the same substance. The capricious ravines of the streets did not cut this mass of houses into pieces that were too disproportionate. The forty-two colleges were distributed among them in a rather even manner. The curious and varied rooftops of these beautiful buildings were the production of the same art as the simple roofs over which they towered. In fact, they were simply the square or the cube of the same geometrical figure. Therefore they complicated the whole without overburdening it; they completed without overloading it. Geometry is harmony. Some superb mansions, too, made here and there magnificent inroads among the picturesque garrets of the left bank: the Logis de Nevers, the Logis de Rome, the Logis de Reims,[16] which have all disappeared. There was the Hôtel de Cluny, which still survives for the consolation of the artist although its tower was so stupidly uncrowned some years ago. That Roman palace with beautiful circular arches near Cluny was the Baths of Julian. There were also many abbeys, of a more severe beauty than the great houses, but neither less handsome nor less spacious. Those that first struck the eye were the Bernardines with their three steeples and Ste.-Geneviève, the square tower[17] of which exists still and inspires great regret for the loss of the rest. The Sorbonne was there, half college, half monastery, whose admirable nave still survives. There was the beautiful rectangular cloister of the Mathurins, and its neighbor, the cloister of St.-Benoît, in whose walls was thrown up a theater between the seventh and eighth printings of this book. The Cordeliers was there, with its three enormous gables, side by side, and the Augustines,[18] the graceful steeple of which made the second denticulation (the Tour de Nesle being the first) on the western side of Paris. The colleges, which are in fact the intermediate link between the cloister and the world, occupied the middle ground in the series of buildings between the mansions and the abbeys, with an austerity full of elegance, a sculpture less gaudy than that of the palaces, and an architecture less serious than that of the convents. Unfortunately, scarcely any vestiges are left of these edifices, in which Gothic art steered with such precision a middle course between luxury and economy. The churches—and they were both numerous and splendid in the Université, and of every period of architecture, from the domes of St.-Julian to the ogives of St.-Severin—the churches dominated everything. And, like an additional melody in this mass of harmonies, they shot up everywhere above the slashed gables, the open-work pinnacles and belfries. They had slender spires whose line was but a magnificent exaggeration of the acute angles of the roofs.

The site of the Université was hilly. To the southeast the hill of Ste.-Geneviève formed an enormous mound, and it was a curious sight to see from the top of Notre-Dame that multitude of narrow, winding streets, now called *le pays latin,* those clusters of houses, which, scattered in all directions from the summit of that hill, confusedly covered its sides down to the water's edge, seeming some of them to be falling, others to be climbing up again, and all to be holding tightly to one another. An incessant stream of thousands of black points crossing each other on the pavement made everything appear to be in motion: these were the people seen from high above.

Last, in the intervals between those roofs, those spires, and those numberless peculiarities of buildings, which folded, notched, twisted the outline of the Université in so whimsical a manner, one could see, here and there, the mossy fragment of a massive wall, a solid round tower, a crenellated doorway, reminiscent of a fortress that was part of a gateway of Philip Augustus's wall. Beyond these were green fields, beyond which led the roads. Along these roads were a few straggling houses, which became more infrequent the farther out one traveled. Some of these suburban hamlets were already places of consequence. Setting out from the Tournelle, there was first the Bourg St.-Victor, with its bridge of one arch over the Bièvre, its abbey, where one could read the epitaph of Louis the Fat. His church had an octagon steeple flanked by four belfries of the eleventh century; then the Bourg St.-Marceau, which already possessed three churches and a convent; then, leaving the Gobelins windmill and its four white walls on the left, there was the Faubourg St.-Jacques, with its beautiful sculptured cross; the church of St.-Jacques-du-Haut-Pas, a charming pointed Gothic structure; St.-Magloire, a beautiful nave of the fourteenth century converted by Napoleon into a hayloft; and Notre-Dame-des-Champs, containing Byzantine mosaics. Last, after leaving in the open country the Chartreux convent, a rich structure from the same period as the Palace of Justice with its formal gardens, and the haunted ruins of Vauvert, the eye fell, to the west, on the three Roman steeples of St.-Germain-des-Prés. The village of St.-Germain, already a large parish, was composed of fifteen or twenty streets in the back; the sharp spire of St.-Sulpice marked one of the corners of the neighborhood. Close to it, one could make out the rectangular enclosure of the Fair of St.-Germain, the site of today's market. Farther on, there was the pillory of the abbey, a pretty little circular tower well covered with a cone of lead; the tile kiln was farther off; so were the Rue du Four, which led to the everyday oven, the mill, and the isolated, almost hidden hospital for lepers. But what particularly attracted attention was the abbey itself. It is certain that this monastery, which had an air of importance both as a church and as a lordly residence, this abbatial palace, where the bishops of Paris deemed themselves fortunate to be entertained for a night, that refectory to which the architect had given the air, the beauty, and the splendid window of a cathedral, that elegant chapel of the Virgin, that noble dormitory, those spacious gardens, that portcullis, that drawbridge, that girdle of battlements cut out to the eye on the greenery of the surrounding fields, those courts where men-at-arms glistened with their capes of gold—the whole collected and grouped around three lofty spires with circular arches, firmly seated on a Gothic apse, formed a magnificent object against the horizon.

When, after attentively surveying the Université, you turned to the right bank, to the Ville, the character of the scene suddenly changed. The Ville, in fact, much more extensive than the Université, was also less compact. At first sight you perceived that it was composed of several remarkably distinct parts. In the first place, to the east, in that part of the town that is still named after the marsh into which Caesar was enticed by Camulogenes, there was a series of palaces. Four nearly contiguous mansions, the Hôtels de Jouy, Sens, Barbeau, and the Logis de la Reine, mirrored their slate roofs, broken by slender turrets, in the waters of the Seine. Those four buildings filled the space between the Rue des Nonaindières and the abbey of the Célestins, the spire of which gracefully relieved their line of gables and battlements. Some greenish walls on the water's edge, in front of these buildings, did not prevent the eye from catching the beautiful angles of their facades. Their large rectangular windows with stone frames and transoms, the pointed arches of their entranceways, covered with statues, and all those charming freaks of architecture make Gothic art seem as if it invents fresh combinations in every building. In the rear of these palaces ran in all directions, sometimes palisaded and crenellated like the

ramparts of a castle keep, sometimes hidden in great trees like a char-
terhouse, the immense and multiform enclosure of that marvelous
Hôtel de St.-Pol, where the King of France could superbly accommo-
date twenty-two princes equal in rank to the Dauphin and the Duke of
Burgundy, with their attendants and retinues, without counting distinguished nobles, or the Emperor when he visited Paris, or the lions that
had their own residence next to the royal domicile. We should point
out that the apartments of a prince in those days consisted of not fewer
than eleven rooms, from the great reception hall to the oratory, without counting galleries and baths and saunas, and other "superfluous
places" attached to each set of apartments. We do not count the private
gardens of each of the King's guests, or the kitchens, the cellars, the
servants' rooms, the general refectories of the household; the lower
courtyards, where there were twenty-two general workrooms, from the
bakery to the wine cellar; places appropriated to games of every sort, the
mall, the tennis court, the riding ring, aviaries, fishponds, menageries,
stables, libraries, arsenals, and foundries. Such was then the palace of a
king, a Louvre, a Hôtel de St.-Pol. It was a city within a city.

From the tower where we have stationed ourselves, the Hôtel de
St.-Pol, though almost half concealed by the four great buildings mentioned above, was still a marvelous sight. The three mansions that
Charles V had incorporated into his palace, though skillfully united to
the principal building by long galleries with windows and small pillars,
could be perfectly distinguished. These were the Hôtel du Petit-
Muce, with the light balustrade that gracefully bordered its roof, and
the residence of the Abbot of St.-Maur, which looked like a castle, with
a strong tower, portcullises, slits, bastions, and over the large Saxon
doorway the escutcheon of the Abbots. There was the mansion of the
Count d'Étampes, the dungeon of which, in ruins at the top, appeared
jagged to the eye like a cockscomb. Clumps of old oaks here and there
formed tufts like enormous cauliflowers. Swans played in the clear
water of the fishponds, streaked with light and shade. The dwelling of
the lions had low pointed arches supported by short Saxon pillars; one
could hear its iron grating perpetually roaring. Beyond all these stood
the scaled spire of the Ave Maria. On the left was the residence of the
Provost of Paris, flanked by four turrets of delicate workmanship; at
the bottom, in the center, the Hôtel de St.-Pol, properly named, with
its numerous facades, its successive embellishments from the time of

Charles V, the hybrid ornaments with which the whims of architects had loaded it in the course of two centuries, with all the apses of its chapels, all the gables of its galleries, a thousand weathervanes, and its two lofty, contiguous towers, whose conical roofs, surrounded at their base with battlements, looked like sharp-pointed hats with the brims turned up.

Continuing to ascend that amphitheater of palaces spread out far over the land, after crossing a deep ravine dividing the roofs of the Ville, the eye arrived at the Logis d'Angoulêm, a vast mass of buildings erected at various periods, parts of which were quite new and white and blended in no better with the whole than a red patch on a blue doublet. At the same time the remarkably sharp and elevated roof of the modern palace was covered with gutters made of lead, on which were woven glittering encrustations of gilded copper that rolled themselves in a thousand fantastic arabesques, that roof so curiously embroidered gracefully lifted itself from amid the brownish ruins of the ancient building whose old clumsy towers, swollen like casks and cracked from top to bottom, were ready to burst to pieces like round bellies popping buttons. In the rear rose the forest of spires of the Palais des Tournelles. There was not a view in the world, not excepting Chambord or the Alhambra, that was more aerial, more impressive, more magical, than this forest of pinnacles, belfries, chimneys, weathervanes, spirals, screws, lanterns, perforated as if they had been struck by a hole puncher, pavilions and turrets, all differing in form, height, and attitude. One might have mistaken it for an immense chessboard of stone.

To the right of the Tournelles there was a cluster of enormous towers, black as ink, running into one another and bound together, as it were, by a circular moat. That keep contained many more slits than windows. The drawbridge was always up, that portcullis always down—that was the Bastille. Those black muzzles sticking out between the battlements, which could be mistaken at a distance for gutters, are cannons.

At the foot of the formidable edifice, just under its guns, was the gate of St.-Antoine, hidden between its two towers.

Beyond the Tournelles, as far as the wall of Charles V, the royal parks were spread out, diversified with rich patches of verdure and flowers, amid which might be recognized by its labyrinth of trees and alleys the famous maze garden that Louis XI gave to Coictier. The doctor's observatory rose above the maze like a detached massive column, with a small house at the very top. In this laboratory were concocted terrible astrological predictions. The site of it is today occupied by the Place Royale.

As we have already observed, the section of palaces that we have tried to describe to the reader filled the corner that the wall of Charles V formed with the Seine to the east. The center of the Ville was occupied by a tumble of common houses. Here in fact the three bridges of the Cité flowed on the right bank, and bridges make houses before palaces. This accumulation of dwellings of tradesmen and artisans, jammed together like cells in a hive, had its own beauty. There is something grand in the houses of a capital as in the waves of the sea. In the first place the streets, crossing and entwining, formed a hundred amusing figures. Around the Halles, it looked like a star with a thousand rays. The streets of St.-Denis and St.-Martin, with their countless twists and turns, ran up one after the other like two thick trees intermingling their branches. And then the streets of la Plâtrerie, la Verrerie, and la Tisseranderie wound themselves over the whole. There were some handsome buildings that overlooked the petrified undulation of this sea of gables. At the head of the Pont aux Changeurs, behind which the Seine was seen foaming under the wheels of the Pont aux Meuniers, there was the Châtelet, no longer a Roman castle, as in the time of Julian the Apostate, but a feudal castle of the thirteenth century, and of stone so hard that in three hours a pickax could not chip off a piece larger than your fist. There too was the rich, square clock tower of St.-Jacques-de-la-Boucherie,[19] with its corners all blunted by sculptures, and already an object of admiration, though it was not finished till the fifteenth century. It lacked then those four monsters that, perched to this day at the corners of the roof, look like four sphinxes, giving to modern Paris a riddle from Antiquity to unravel. They were not erected till the year 1526 by Rault, the sculptor, who got twenty francs for his labor. There was the Maison aux Pilliers, which we have described to the reader; there was St.-Gervais, since spoiled by an entrance *in good taste;* there was St.-Méry, whose old pointed arches were almost all domes; there was St.-Jean, whose magnificent spire was proverbial; there were twenty other buildings that did not disdain to bury their marvels in this chaos of deep, black, narrow streets. Add to these the sculptured stone crosses, more numerous even than the scaffolds, the cemetery of the Innocents, the architectural enclosure of which was to be seen at a distance above the roofs; the pillory of the Halles, the top of which was perceptible between two chimneys of the Rue de la Cossonerie; the "ladder" of the Croix du Trahoir, in its crossing always black with people; the circular walls of the Halle au Blé; the remains of the ancient walls of Philip Augustus, to be distinguished here and there, drowning in the houses, towers overgrown with ivy, gates in ruins, crumbling and shapeless fragments of walls; the quay, with its thousand shops and its bloody slaughterhouses; the Seine covered with boats, from the Port au Foin to the For-L'Évêque, and you will have a faint image of the central trapezoid section of the Ville as it was in 1482.

Besides these two neighborhoods, one of palaces, the other of houses, the Ville presented a third feature—a long section of abbeys that ran along almost the entire circumference from west to east and formed a second wall of convents and chapels within that of the fortifications that encompassed Paris. Thus, immediately adjoining the park of Tournelles, between the Rue St.-Antoine and the old Rue du Temple, there was the church of Ste.-Catherine, with its immense gardens and cultivated grounds, which were bordered only by the wall of Paris. Between the old and the new Rue du Temple there was the Temple,[20] a grim, tall cluster of gloomy towers standing in the center of a vast enclosure of ramparts. Between the Rue Neuve du Temple and the Rue St.-Martin was the abbey of St.-Martin, amid its gardens—a superb fortified church, whose girdle of towers and tiara of steeples were surpassed in strength and splendor by St.-Germain-des-Prés alone. Between the streets of St.-Martin and St.-Denis was the enclosure of the Trinity. Finally, between the streets of St.-Denis and Montorgueil, there was the convent of Filles Dieu. Beside the latter were to be seen the rotting roofs and the unpaved area of the Cour des Miracles. It was the only profane link that interrupted this chain of convents.

The fourth section, which is sufficiently distinctive in the agglomeration of buildings on the right bank that occupied the western corner within the city walls and covered the banks of the river below, was a new knot of palaces and mansions that had sprung up at the foot of the Louvre. The old Louvre of Philip Augustus, that extravagant building whose great tower gathered around itself twenty-three other towers, without counting the turrets, appeared at a distance to be set in the Gothic heights of the Hôtel d'Alençon and of the Petit-Bourbon. That hydra of towers, the giant guardian of Paris, with its twenty-four heads ever erect, with its monstrous cupolae, cased in lead or scaled with slate, and glistening all over with a metallic shine, marked the western edge of the Ville in a striking manner.

Thus, there was an immense "island," or *insula* as the Romans called it, of common houses, flanked on the right and left by clusters of palaces, crowned, the one by the Louvre, the other by the Tournelles, girded on the north by a long belt of abbeys and cultivated enclosures. The whole blended and melted together before the eye. Above these thousands of buildings, whose tiled and slated roofs formed so many strange chains, the tattooed, honeycombed, carved steeples and spires of the forty-four churches of the right bank towered. Myriad streets running in all directions, bounded on the one hand by a high wall with square towers (the wall of the Université had circular towers), on the other by the Seine intersected by bridges and studded with craft—such was the Ville in the fifteenth century.

Beyond the walls there were suburbs crowding around the gates, but the houses there were less numerous and more scattered than those belonging to the Université. Behind the Bastille twenty hovels were clustered around the curious sculptures of the Croix Faubin. There was the abbey of St.-Antoine-des-Champs, with its flying buttresses; then Popincourt, lost in the cornfields; and then La Courtille, a jovial hamlet of taverns. The Bourg St.-Laurent came next, with its church, whose steeple seemed at a distance to belong to the gate of St.-Martin, with its pointed towers. There was the Faubourg St.-Denis, with the vast enclosure of St.-Ladre.[21] Beyond the gate of Montmartre lay La Grange Batelière, enclosed by white walls. Behind that, Montmartre, with its chalky slopes, which had then almost as many churches as windmills but has retained the mills only. Today society demands only the bread for the body. Last, beyond the Louvre one could see the Faubourg St.-Honoré, already a very considerable place. And beyond that there was the greenery of La Petite Bretagne, and the Marché aux Pourceaux, in the center of which stood the horrible cauldron for boiling counterfeiters. Between La Courtille and St.-Laurent the eye has already remarked, on the summit of a plateau squatting on desert plains, a kind of building resembling at a distance a colonnade in ruins. This was neither a Parthenon nor a temple of the Olympian Jupiter—it was Montfaucon.

Now if the enumeration of so many buildings, concise as we have purposely made it, has not effaced in the mind of the reader the general image of old Paris as fast as we constructed it, we will condense our description into a few words. In the center, the island of the Cité resembling in form an enormous tortoise; its slate bridges protruding like scaly feet beneath the gray carapace of roofs. On the left, the dense, compact, bristling trapezoid of the Université; on the right, the vast semicircle of the Ville, in which gardens and buildings were much more intermingled. The three divisions, Cité, Université, and Ville, veined by countless streets; the Seine, the "nourishing Seine," as Father du Breul calls it, studded with boats and islands and crossed by bridges. All around an immense plain broken up by a thousand different farms and sown with some villages; on the left Issy, Vanvres, Vaugirard, Montrogue, Gentilly, with its round tower and its square tower; on the right twenty others, from Conflans to Ville-l'Évêque. On the horizon a chain of hills arranged in a circle, like the rim of the basin. Last, in the distance, to the east, Vincennes and its seven rectangular towers; to the south, Bicêtre and its pointed turrets; to the north, St.-Denis and its spire; to the west, St.-Cloud and its keep. Such was Paris seen from the top of the towers of Notre-Dame by the ravens living in the year 1482.

However, Voltaire said of this city that before Louis XIV it possessed only four beautiful monuments: the dome of the Sorbonne, the Val-de-Grâce, the modern Louvre, and I am not sure of the fourth, perhaps it was the Luxembourg Palace. Luckily, Voltaire wrote *Candide*, and he is still one in a series of human beings through the ages who was capable of devilish laughter. His judgment demonstrates that one can be a genius and understand nothing of an art that is not one's own. Did not Molière believe that he was paying a high compliment to Raphael and Michelangelo by calling them the "Mignards of their times"?[22]

Let us return to Paris of the fifteenth century.

The Paris of that time was not merely a beautiful city; it was a homogenous city, an architectural and historical product of the Middle Ages, a chronicle of stone. It was a city formed of two strata only, the bastard Roman and the Gothic, for the pure Roman had long before disappeared, except at the Baths of Julian, where it pierced the thick crust of the Middle Ages. As for the Celtic stratum, no specimens of that were to be found even when digging wells.

Fifty years later, when the Renaissance came to blend with this unity so severe and yet so diversified the dazzling luxury of its fantasies and its systems, its extravagant Roman arches, Greek columns, and Gothic ellipses, its sculpture so delicate and so idealized, its particular style of arabesques and acanthi, its architectural paganism contemporaneous with Luther, Paris became perhaps still more beautiful, though less harmonious to the eye and the mind. But this splendid moment did not last long; the Renaissance was not impartial; it was not content with building up, it wanted to destroy as well. It is true enough that it needed room. Thus Gothic Paris was complete for but a minute. St.-Jacques-de-la-Boucherie was scarcely finished when the demolition of the old Louvre was begun.

Since that time the great city has been deformed day by day. The Gothic Paris, which swept away the bastard Roman, has been in its turn swept away, but can anyone tell what Paris has replaced it?

There is the Paris of Catherine de Medici at the Tuileries,[23] the Paris of Henry II at the Hôtel de Ville; two edifices still in a grand style. The Paris of Henry IV can be found at the Place Royale— facades with stone corners and slated roofs—tricolored houses. The Paris of Louis XIII is at Val-de-Grâce—a squat, clumsy style with vaulted ceilings that look like basket handles with something pot-bellied about the columns and hunchbacked in the dome. There is the Paris of Louis XIV at the Invalides, grand, rich, gilded, and cold. There is the Paris of Louis XV at St.-Sulpice—volutes, knots of ribbons, clouds, vermicellies, chicories, and Lord knows what else, all in stone. There is the Paris of Louis XVI at the Panthéon—a bad copy of St. Peter's in Rome. The Paris of the Republic is found at the School of Medicine— a poor Greek and Roman style. It looks as much like the Coliseum or the Parthenon as the constitution of the year 3 resembles the laws of Minos—it is called in architecture *the Messidor style.*[24] The Paris of Napoleon is to be found at the Place Vendôme—this is sublime—a column of bronze made of cannons. The Paris of the Restoration is at the Stock Exchange—a very white colonnade supporting a very smooth frieze; the whole thing is square and cost 20 million.

Each of these characteristic monuments is connected to a certain number of houses scattered over the different neighborhoods by a taste, fashion, and attitude: these are easily distinguished and dated by the eye of the connoisseur. Possessing this skill, you discover the spirit of an age and the physiognomy of a king even in the knocker of a door.

The Paris of the present day has no general physiognomy. It is a collection of specimens of various periods, the finest of which have disappeared. The capital increases only in houses, and what houses! At the rate Paris is now going on it will be rebuilt every fifty years. Thus the historical signification of its architecture is daily becoming obliterated. The monuments of the past are becoming more and more rare, and sometimes it seems as if one can see them engulfed one after another in the deluge of houses. Our fathers had a Paris of stone; our children will have a Paris of plaster.

As for the modern monuments of new Paris, we would rather abstain from any mention of them. Not that we admire them quite as much as is fitting. Monsieur Soufflot's Ste.-Geneviève is certainly the most beautiful Savoy cake that ever was made in stone. The Palais de la Légion d'Honneur is also a most remarkable piece of pastry. The dome of the Halle au Blé is an English jockey cap on a grand scale. The towers of St.-Sulpice are two giant clarinets, and that is as good a shape as any other: the telegraph, writhing and grinning, forms a charming accessory on its roof.[25] St.-Roch has an entrance comparable for magnificence to that of St.-Thomas d'Aquin alone. It also has an embossed scene of the Calvary in the cellar, and a sun of gilded wood. These are absolute marvels. The lantern in the labyrinth of the Jardin des Plantes is also a most ingenious work. As for the Stock Exchange, which is Greek in its colonnade, Roman in the circular arches of its doors and windows, and Renaissance in its great flattened, vaulted ceiling—it is indubitably a most pure and classic monument. The proof of this lies in the fact that it is crowned by an attic, such as was never seen in Athens—a beautiful straight line, gracefully broken here and there by stovepipes. In addition, if it is a rule that the architecture of a building should be adapted to its purpose in such a manner that this purpose may be obvious in the appearance of the building, we cannot too highly admire a structure that is equally suitable for a king's palace, a House of Commons, a town hall, a college, a riding stable, an academy, a warehouse, a court of justice, a museum, a barrack, a sepulchre, a temple, and a theater. After all it is the Stock Exchange. A building ought in addition to be adapted to the climate. This one is evidently designed expressly for our cold and rainy skies. It is almost as flat as Eastern ones, so that in winter, after a snow, it is necessary to sweep the roof, and it is most certain that a roof is made to be swept. As for that purpose we mentioned earlier, it fulfills it marvelously well: in France it is a Stock Exchange, in Greece it would have been a temple. The architect clearly had difficulty disguising the dial of the clock, which certainly would have destroyed the purity of the beautiful lines of the facade but, luckily, we have the colonnade that circles the monument, behind which, with the religious solemnity of holy days, agents of exchange and courtiers of commerce majestically work out their theories.

These are no doubt the most splendid structures. Add to them a great many handsome streets, amusing and diversified as the Rue de Rivoli, and I do not despair that Paris, viewed from a balloon, may someday present to the eye that richness of line, that luxury of detail, that diversity of aspect, a certain combination of the grand with the simple, of the beautiful with the unexpected, which characterizes a drawing board.

Admirable, however, as the Paris of the present day appears to you, reconstruct in your imagination the Paris of the fifteenth century and look at the light through that surprising line of steeples, towers, and belfries; spread out in the immense city, knock up against the points of its islands, fold the arches of the bridges, look at the current of the Seine, with its large patches of green and yellow, more changeable than a serpent's skin. Mark clearly the Gothic profile of this old Paris on a horizon of azure, make its contour float in a wintry fog that clings to its innumerable chimneys; drown it in deep night, and observe the extraordinary play of darkness and light in this dark labyrinth of buildings. Throw into it a ray of moonlight, which shall show its faint outline and make distinct the huge heads of the towers in the mist. Or take up again that dark silhouette, touch up with shade the thousand acute angles of the spires and gables, and make them soar, more jagged than a shark's teeth, on the copper-colored sky of evening. Now compare the two.

And if you would receive from the ancient city an impression that the modern cannot provide, go up (on the morning of some high holiday, at sunrise on Easter or Pentecost) to some elevated point from which you may overlook the whole capital, and listen to the awakening of the bells. Behold at a sign from heaven, because it comes from the Sun itself, those thousand churches trembling all at once. At first a faint tinkling passes from church to church, as when musicians give notice that they are going to begin. Then see, for at certain times the ear too seems to be endowed with sight—see how, all of a sudden, at the same moment, there rises from each steeple as it were a column of sound, a cloud of harmony. At first the vibration of each bell rises straight, pure, and in a manner separate from that of the others, into the splendid morning sky; then, swelling by degrees, they blend, melt, intermingle, and amalgamate into a magnificent concert. It is now but one mass of sonorous vibrations, coming out of the innumerable steeples incessantly; and it floats, undulates, leaps, and swirls over the city, and expands far beyond the horizon the deafening circle of its oscillations. That sea of harmony, however, is not a chaos. Vast and deep as it is, it has not lost its transparency: you see in it each group of notes that has wound its way up from the belfries. You can follow the dialogue, by turns deep and high. You can see the octaves leaping from steeple to steeple; you can watch them springing light, winged, sonorous, from the silver bell, dropping dull, faint, and limping from the wooden. You can admire the rich gamut ascending and descending without end the seven bells of St.-Eustache. You can see clear and rapid notes dart around in all directions, making three or four luminous zigzags, and vanishing like lightning. There the abbey of St.-Martin sends forth its harsh, sharp tones; here the Bastille raises its sinister and husky voice. At the other end of the city it is the great tower of the Louvre, with its countertenor. The royal chimes of the palace launch tirelessly on all sides their resplendent trills, on which falls, at measured intervals, the heavy tolling from the belfry of Notre-Dame, which makes them sparkle like an anvil under the hammer. From time to time you see tones of all shapes, proceeding from the triple peal of St.-Germain-des-Prés, passing before you. Then again, at intervals, this mass of sublime sounds opens and makes way for the finale of the Ave Maria, which glistens like a plume of stars. Beneath, in the deepest part of the concert, you can distinguish with some confusion the singing inside the churches, which rises through the vibrating pores of their vaults. This is truly an opera that is well worth listening to. Normally the noises that Paris makes in the daytime represent the city talking; at night the city breathes. In this case the city sings. Lend your ear then to this *tutti* of steeples; listen to the buzzing of half a million human beings, the eternal murmur of the river, the infinite breathing of the wind, the grave and distant quartet of the four forests placed like immense organs on the four hills of the horizon. Soften, as with a demi-tint, all that is too shrill and too harsh in the central mass of sound—and say if you know anything in the world more rich, more joyful, more golden, more overwhelming than that tumult of bells, than that furnace of music, than those ten thousand voices of bronze singing all at once from flutes of stone three hundred feet high, than that city which has become an orchestra, than that symphony which roars like a storm.

BOOK IV

CHAPTER I

GOOD SOULS

Sixteen years before the period of the events recorded in this history, one fine morning—it happened to be Quasimodo Sunday—a living creature was laid after Mass in the church of Notre-Dame in the wooden bed built into the left-hand side of the open sanctuary, opposite the great image of St. Christopher that faced the kneeling figure sculpted in stone of Antoine des Essarts, knight, till 1413, when both saint and sinner were destroyed. On this wooden bed it was customary to leave foundlings to public charity. Anyone who wanted to, took them. In front of the wooden bed was a copper basin to receive alms.

The living creature that lay on this hard couch on the morning of Quasimodo Sunday, in the year of our Lord 1467, appeared to excite a high degree of curiosity in the considerable crowd of persons who had collected around it. They consisted chiefly of the fair sex, almost all of them old women.

In the front row, leaning over the bed, were four who from their gray cassocks you would judge to belong to some religious sisterhood. I see no reason why history should not transmit to posterity the names of these four discreet and venerable matrons. They were Agnès la Herme, Jehanne de la Tarme, Henriette La Gaultière, and Gauchère la Violette, all four widows, and sisters of the chapel of Étienne Haudry, who had left their house with the permission of their superior, and in accordance with the statutes of Pierre d'Ailly, for the purpose of attending the sermon.

If, however, these good creatures were observing the statutes of Pierre d'Ailly, they were certainly violating at the moment those of Michel de Brache and the Cardinal of Pisa, which imposed upon them the most inhuman law of silence.

"What is that, my sister?" said Agnès to Gauchère, looking intently at the little creature, crying and writhing on the wooden couch and terrified at the number of strange gazes.

"What is the world coming to," said Jehanne, "if that is the way they make children nowadays?"

"I don't pretend to know much about children," rejoined Agnès, "but it must be a sin to look at that thing."

"It's not a child, Agnès—it is a misshapen ape," observed Gauchère.

"It's a miracle!" ejaculated Henriette La Gaultière.

"Then," remarked Agnès, "this is the third since Lætare Sunday,[1] for it is not a week since we had the miracle of the mocker of the pilgrims, who was punished by Our Lady of Aubervilliers, and that was the second miracle of the month."

"This so-called foundling is a real monster of abomination," resumed Jehanne.

"He brays loud enough to deafen a chanter," continued Gauchère.

"And to pretend that Monsieur de Reims could send this fright to Monsieur de Paris!" added La Gaultière, clasping her hands.

"I cannot help thinking," said Agnès la Herme, "that it is some brute, something between a Jew and a sow—something in short that is not Christian, and ought to be drowned or burned."

"I do hope," resumed La Gaultière, "that nobody will apply for it."

"Good God!" exclaimed Agnès. "How I pity the poor nurses at the foundling hospital in the lane going down to the river by the archbishop's, if this little monster should be carried to them to be suckled! Why, I declare, I would rather suckle a vampire!"

"Poor la Herme! What a simpleton she is!" rejoined Jehanne. "Don't you see, sister, that this little monster is at least four years old, and that he would like a piece of meat a good deal better than your breast?"

In fact, "this little monster"—we find it difficult to call it anything else—was not a newborn infant. It was a little, shapeless, moving mass, tied up in a canvas bag, marked with the initials of Guillaume Chartier, the then Bishop of Paris. Its head alone was exposed. And that head was so deformed as to be absolutely hideous: nothing was to be seen on it but a forest of red hair, one eye, a mouth, and teeth. The eye wept, the mouth cried, and the teeth seemed sadly wanting of something to bite. He was struggling in the sack with his entire body, to the great amazement of the crowd that gathered and grew around him.

Dame Aloïse de Gondelaurier, a noble and wealthy lady, who held by the hand a sweet little girl about six years old and had a long veil hanging from the gold peak of her bonnet, stopped before the bed and for a moment surveyed the unfortunate creature, while her charming little daughter Fleur-de-Lis, dressed entirely in silk and velvet, pointing with her delicate finger to each letter of the permanent inscription on the wooden bed, spelled out the words ENFANTS TROUVÉS [FOUNDLINGS].

"I really thought," said the lady, turning away with disgust, "that only children were left here."

As she turned her back she threw into the basin a silver florin, which rang among the copper coins and made the poor sisters of the chapel of Étienne Haudry open their eyes wide in astonishment.

A moment afterward the grave and learned Robert Mistricolle, the King's first notary, passed with an enormous mass book under one arm and his wife, Demoiselle Guillemette la Mairesse, under the other, thus having at his side two regulators, the one spiritual, the other terrestrial.

"A foundling!" he exclaimed, after intently examining the object. "Found apparently on the bank of the Phlegeton."[2]

"He seems to have only one eye," observed Demoiselle Guillemette. "There is a great wart over the other."

"That is no wart," replied Master Robert Mistricolle, "but an egg, which contains another demon exactly like this, with another little egg, containing a third devil, and so on."

"How know you that?" asked Guillemette.

"I know it with certainty," replied the first notary.

"Monsieur, the first notary," inquired Gauchère, "what do you predict from this kind of foundling?"

"The greatest calamities," replied Mistricolle.

"Good heaven!" exclaimed an old woman who stood by, "no wonder that we had such a pestilence last year, and that the English, it is said, are going to land in force at Harfleur!"[3]

"Perhaps that may not prevent the Queen from coming to Paris in September," rejoined another. "Trade is very flat already."

"I am of the opinion," cried Jehanne de la Tarme, "that it would be better for the people of Paris if that little sorcerer were lying on a pile of burning wood than on a plank."

"Yes, a nice blazing one!" added the old dame.

"That might be more prudent," observed Mistricolle.

For some moments a young priest had been listening to the comments of the women and the first notary. He was a man of an austere countenance, with a wide brow and piercing gaze. Pushing aside the crowd without speaking, he examined "the little sorcerer" and extended his hand over him. It was high time, for all the pious bystanders were eager for the "bonny blazing burning at the stake."

"I adopt this child," said the priest.

He wrapped him in his cassock and carried him away. The bystanders looked after him with horror, till he had passed the Porte Rouge, which then led from the church to the cloisters, and was out of sight.

When they had recovered from their first astonishment, Jehanne de la Tarme, bent toward the ear of La Gaultière, whispered, "Sister, didn't I tell you that young priest, Monsieur Claude Frollo, is a sorcerer?"

CHAPTER II

CLAUDE FROLLO

Claude Frollo was, in fact, no ordinary character. He belonged to one of those families who, in the impertinent language of the last century, were called indiscriminately *haute bourgeoisie* or *petite noblesse*. This family had inherited from the Paclets the fief of Tirechappe, which was held under the Bishop of Paris, whose twenty-one houses had been in the thirteenth century the subject of so many suits before the official. Claude Frollo, as possessor of this fief, was one of the one hundred and forty-one seigneurs who claimed manorial rights in Paris and its suburbs, and as such his name was long to be seen registered between the Hôtel de Tancarville, belonging to Master François le Rez, and the Collège de Tours in the book of deeds preserved in the church of St.-Martin-des-Champs.

Claude Frollo had from his childhood been destined by his parents for the Church. He was taught to read Latin, to cast down his eyes, and to speak softly. While he was still quite a boy, his father had placed him in the Collège de Torchi in the Université; and there he had grown up on the mass book and the Lexicon.

He was a sad, grave, serious boy, who studied assiduously and learned quickly. He was not enthusiastic about recreations, had mingled only a little in the bacchanals of the Rue du Fouarre, and did not know much about *dare alapas et capillos laniare.*[4] He had not cut a figure in that revolt of 1463, which the chroniclers have gravely recorded under the title "Sixth Disturbance of the Université." He had scarcely ever been known to make fun of the poor students of Montaigu for their little hoods, after which they were nicknamed (Capettes), or the scholarship students of the Collège de Dormans for their tonsures and their tricolored frock of gray, blue, and purple cloth—*azurini coloris et bruni,* as says the charter of the Cardinal des Quatres-Couronnes.

On the other hand, he was assiduous in his attendance at the upper and lower schools of the Rue St.-Jean-de-Beauvais. He was the first student the Abbé of St.-Pierre-de-Val saw when he began his lecture on the canon law. Claude Frollo was invariably stationed opposite the Abbé's chair, next to a pillar of the school of St.-Vendregesile. He was armed with his inkstand made of horn, chewing his pen, scribbling on his knee, and in winter blowing on his fingers. Claude Frollo was the first auditor Messire Miles d'Isliers, doctor of divinity, saw entering every Monday morning, quite out of breath, on the opening of the door of the school of Chef-St.-Denis. Accordingly, at the age of sixteen the young clerk could hold his own with a father of the Church on the subjects of mystic theology, with a father of the council on canonical theology, with a doctor of the Sorbonne on scholastic theology.

Having mastered theology, he had fallen on the "Capitularies of Charlemagne," and, with his keen appetite for knowledge, had devoured decrees after decrees, those of Théodore Bishop of Hispala, of Bouchard Bishop of Worms, of Yves Bishop of Chartres; then the decree of Gratian, which succeeded the "Capitularies of Charlemagne." He read the collection of Gregory IX, then Honorius III's epistle *Super Specula* or *On the Mirror,* till he made himself perfectly familiar with that long and tumultuous period, in which the canon law and the civil law struggled and labored in the chaos of the Middle Ages—a period opening with Théodore in 618 and closing with Pope Gregory in 1227.[5]

Having digested the decrees, he proceeded to medicine and the liberal arts. He studied the science of herbs and the science of unguents; he became skillful in the cure of fevers and of contusions, of wounds and of boils. He was qualified alike to practice in medicine and in surgery. He passed through all the degrees of licentiate, master, and doctor of arts. He studied the learned languages, Latin, Greek, Hebrew, the triple sanctuary at that time but little frequented. He had a real fever for acquiring and hoarding up knowledge, and it seemed to the young man as if life had but one object, namely, to know.

It was about this time that the intense heat of the summer of 1466 generated that destructive plague that swept away more than forty thousand human beings in the county of Paris, among others, writes Jean de Troyes, "Master Arnoul, the King's astrologer, an honest, wise, and agreeable man." A rumor reached the Université that the Rue Tirechappe in particular was devastated by this malady. There, in the midst of their fiefdom, dwelled the parents of Claude. The young scholar hastened in great alarm to the paternal residence. On reaching it, he learned that his father and mother had died the preceding night. An infant brother in swaddling was still alive and crying, abandoned in his cradle. This babe was the only member of Claude's family that was left to him; he took the child in his arms and left the house absorbed in thought. Until now he had lived only in learning and science; now he began to live in life.

This catastrophe was a crisis in Claude's existence. An orphan and head of a family at nineteen, he felt himself rudely roused from the reveries of the schools to the realities of the world. Moved with pity, he conceived a passionate fondness for this helpless infant brother—a strange and sweet thing, this human affection, to him who previously had loved nothing but books.

This affection developed itself to an extraordinary degree. In a soul so new to feeling, it was like a first love. Separated from childhood from his parents, whom he had scarcely known, cloistered and as it were spellbound by his books, eager above all things to study and to learn, exclusively attentive till then to his intelligence, which expanded itself in science; to his imagination, which developed in literature, the young scholar had not yet had time to find out where his heart lay. That little brother, without father or mother, that infant that dropped suddenly from the sky into his arms, made a new man of him.

He perceived that there was something in the world besides the speculations of the Sorbonne and the verses of Homer; that human beings have need of affections; that life without love is only a dry wheel, creaking and grating as it revolves. He fancied, it is true, for he was at an age when one illusion only gives place to another, that the family affections, the ties of blood, were the only things he needed, and that the love of his little brother was sufficient to fill his heart for his whole life.

He gave himself up therefore to the love of his little Jehan with the passion of a character already deep, ardent, and intense. This poor, frail, fair, delicate creature, this orphan without any protector but another orphan, moved him to the bottom of his soul; and, grave thinker that he was, he began to think of Jehan with feelings of infinite compassion. He bestowed on him all possible care and attention, just as if he had been something exceedingly fragile and exceedingly valuable. He was more than a brother to the child: he became a mother to him.

Little Jehan was still nursing when he lost his mother: Claude put him out to nurse. Besides the fief of Tirechappe he had inherited from his father the fiefdom of Moulin, next to the square towers of Gentilly. The property was on a hill, near the Château de Bicêtre. The miller's wife was just nursing a fine boy; it was not far from the Université. Claude carried little Jehan to her himself.

From then on, feeling that he had responsibility to bear, he took life seriously. The thought of his little brother became not only a recreation but even the object of his studies. He resolved to devote himself entirely to his care, and never to have any other wife, or any other child, but the happiness and prosperity of his brother. He attached himself therefore more strongly than ever to his clerical vocation. His merit, his learning, his condition as immediate vassal of the Bishop of Paris threw the doors of the Church wide open to him. At the age of twenty, by a special dispensation of the Holy See, he was a priest, and as the youngest of the chaplains of Notre-Dame he performed the service of the altar called, on account of the lateness of the Mass said there, *altare pigrorum,* or the altar for the lazy.

There, more than ever absorbed by his beloved books, which he abandoned only to run for an hour to the mill, this mixture of learning and austerity, so uncommon at his age, quickly earned him the admiration and the respect of the convent. From the cloister his reputation for learning spread among the people, and among some of them it even earned him the reputation of sorcerer—a frequent circumstance in that superstitious age.

It was at the moment when he was returning on Quasimodo Sunday from saying Mass at "the altar of the lazy," which stood by the door of the choir on the right, near the image of the Blessed Virgin, that his attention was attracted by the group of old women screeching around the bed of the foundlings. He approached the unfortunate little creature, so hated and so threatened. Its distress, its deformity, its destitution, the thought of his young brother, the idea that suddenly flashed across his mind, that if he were to die his poor little Jehan too might be mercilessly thrown on the same spot, assailed his heart all at once; it melted with pity, and he carried the boy away.

When he had taken the child out of the sack he found him to be, in fact, a monster of deformity. The poor little wretch had a prodigious wart over his left eye, his head was close to his shoulders, his back arched, his breastbone protruded, and his legs were twisted. But he appeared lively, and though it was impossible to tell what language he tried to speak, his cry indicated a tolerable degree of strength and health. This extreme ugliness only served to increase Claude's compassion, and he vowed in his heart to bring up this boy for the love of his brother, that, whatever the faults little Jehan might possess, he could have the benefit of this act of charity performed on his behalf. It was a humane act, placed, as it were, in his brother's account, one in a small stock of good works that he determined to store up for his brother in advance, in case the young rogue should someday run short of that kind of currency that is the only one accepted at the tollgate of Paradise.

He baptized his adopted child and named him Quasimodo, either to commemorate the day on which he had found him or to express the incomplete and scarcely finished state of the poor little creature. In truth, Quasimodo, with one eye, hunchback, and crooked legs, was only a quasi person.[6]

CHAPTER III

Immanis Pecoris, Custos Immanior Ipse[7]

Now, by the year 1482 Quasimodo had grown up. He had been for several years bell ringer of the cathedral of Notre-Dame, thanks to his foster father, Claude Frollo, who had become Archdeacon of Josas, thanks to his lord, Louis de Beaumont, who had been appointed Bishop of Paris in 1472, thanks to his patron Olivier le Daim,[8] barber to Louis XI, by the Grace of God, et cetera, et cetera. So Quasimodo became bell ringer of Notre-Dame.

In the course of time a curious attachment grew up between the bell ringer and the church. Cut off forever from society by the double fatality of his unknown parentage and his distorted form, imprisoned from childhood within this closed circle, the poor fellow was accustomed to see nothing in the world beyond the religious walls that had taken him under their shadow. Notre-Dame had been successively to him, as he grew up and developed, his egg, his nest, his home, his country, the universe.

A sort of mysterious and preexistent harmony had grown up between this creature and this building. While still quite a child he dragged himself around with difficulty, twisting and hopping in the shade of its arches; he appeared, with his human face and his bestial body, to be a reptile indigenous to those dark, damp paving stones, among the bizarre forms cast by the shadows of the capitals of the Roman pillars.

Later, as he grew up, the first time he mechanically grasped the rope in the tower and, hanging on it, set the bell in motion, his foster father reacted like a parent to the first articulate sounds uttered by his child.

Thus, little by little, his spirit expanded in harmony with the cathedral; there he lived, there he slept; scarcely ever leaving it, and, being perpetually subject to its mysterious influence, he came at last to resemble it, to be encrusted with it, to form, as it were, an integral part of it. His sharp corners dovetailed, if we may be allowed the expression, into the receding angles of the building, so that he seemed to be not merely its inhabitant but its natural contents. One could almost say that he had taken on its form like a snail assumes the shape of its shell. It was his home, his hole, his container. Between the ancient church and him there was an instinctive sympathy so deep, and so many magnetic and material affinities, that he stuck to it in some measure as the tortoise to its shell. The craggy cathedral was his carapace.

It would be useless to warn the reader not to take literally all the metaphors we are obliged to use here to describe the singular, symmetrical, immediate, and almost consubstantial coupling of a man and a building. It is scarcely necessary to say how familiar he had made himself with the whole cathedral in so long and so intimate a cohabitation. There was no depth that Quasimodo had not fathomed, no height that he had not scaled. Many times had he climbed up the facade with only the help of the projections of the sculptures. Often he could be seen crawling up the outside of the towers, like a lizard up a perpendicular wall; those twin giants, so tall, so threatening, so formidable, produced in him neither vertigo, fear, nor dizziness. So gentle did they appear under his hand, and so easy to climb, that you would have said he had tamed them. By leaping, scrambling, gliding, and groping among the chasms of the venerable cathedral, he had become something between a monkey and a mountain goat, like the boy from Calabria who swims before he can walk and plays as a child in the sea.

Not only the person but also the mind of Quasimodo appeared to be molded by the cathedral. What manner of soul was his? What line had it acquired, what form had it received, within its gnarled envelope, in the course of his wild life? It would be difficult to say. Quasimodo was born one-eyed, humpbacked, and lame. It was not without great difficulty and great patience that Claude Frollo had taught him to speak. But a grim tale was attached to the unhappy foundling. Since he had become bell ringer of Notre-Dame at the age of fourteen, a new infirmity had come upon him: the bells had broken his eardrums, and he became deaf. Thus the only gate that nature had left wide open between him and the world was suddenly closed forever. In closing, it shut out the only ray of light and joy that still reached his soul, which was now wrapped in profound darkness. The melancholy of the poor fellow became as incurable and complete as his deformity. His deafness rendered him in some measure dumb. For, the moment he lost his hearing, he resolved to avoid the ridicule of others by a silence that he never broke except when he was alone. He voluntarily tied up that tongue that Claude Frollo had taken such pains to loosen; from then on, when necessity forced him to speak, his tongue was swollen and awkward, and like a door whose hinges have grown rusty.

If then we were to attempt to penetrate this thick and hardened bark to find Quasimodo's soul, if we could sound the depths of this badly put together organism, if we were enabled to hold a torch behind these opaque organs to explore the gloomy interior of this dense being, to illuminate its obscure corners and its absurd cul-de-sacs, and to throw all at once a brilliant light on the spirit imprisoned at the bottom of all this, we should doubtless find the wretch in some miserable pose, stunted and blighted, like prisoners under the Leads of Venice, who grow old, doubled up in a box of stone, too low to stand up in and too short to lie down in.

It is certain that the spirit atrophies in a misshapen body. Quasimodo scarcely felt within him the blind movements of a soul made in his own image. The impressions of objects underwent a considerable refraction before they reached the seat of thought. His brain was a peculiar medium: the ideas that entered it came out quite twisted. The reflection resulting from this refraction was necessarily distorted and twisted. Thus the thousand optical illusions, the thousand aberrations of judgment, the thousand byways into which his sometimes silly, sometimes crazy imagination would wander.

The first effect of this fatal organism was to confuse his vision of the world. He received scarcely a single direct perception. The exterior world appeared to him at a greater distance than it does to us. The second result of his misfortune was that it made him bad. He was, in truth, bad because he was wild; he was wild because he was ugly. There was logic in his nature, as there is in ours. His strength, developed in a most extraordinary manner, was another cause of his propensity to mischief. *Malus puer robustus,* or "The energetic child is full of mischief," says Hobbes. We must nevertheless do him justice: malice was probably not innate in him. From his earliest interactions with men he had felt, and afterward he had seen himself, despised, rejected, cast off. Human speech had never been anything to him but a jeer or a curse. As he grew up he had found nothing but hatred around him. He had adopted it. He had acquired the general malevolence. He had picked up the weapon with which he had been wounded.

After all, he turned toward humankind only with reluctance; his cathedral was enough for him. It was peopled with figures of marble, with kings, saints, bishops, who at least did not laugh in his face and looked on him only with an air of tranquillity and benevolence. The other statues, those of monsters and demons, bore no malice against him. They resembled him too much for that. Their mockery was rather directed against other men. The saints were his friends and blessed him; the monsters were his friends and protected him; he would therefore pass whole hours squatting before one of these statues and conversing in a solitary manner with it. If anyone came by he would run off like a lover surprised in a serenade.

The cathedral was not only his society but his universe—in short, all of nature to him. He dreamed of no other trees than the painted windows, which were always in blossom; of no other shade than the foliage of stone adorned with birds in the Saxon capitals; of no other mountains than the colossal towers of the church; of no other ocean than Paris, which roared at their feet.

But what he loved most of all in the maternal building; what awakened his soul and made it spread its poor wings, otherwise so miserably folded up in its prison; what even gave him at times a feeling of happiness, were the bells. He loved them, he caressed them, he talked to them, he understood them—from the chimes in the steeple of the transept to the great bell above the main entrance. The belfry of the transept and the two towers were like three immense cages, in which the birds that he had reared sang for him alone. It was these same birds, however, that had deafened him: but mothers are often fondest of the child that has caused them the greatest pain. It is true that theirs were the only voices he could still hear. On this account the great bell was his most beloved. He preferred her to all the other sisters of this noisy family, who swung around him on holidays. The name of this great bell was Marie. She was placed in the southern tower, along with her sister Jacqueline, a medium-sized bell enclosed in a smaller cage of less magnitude by her side. This Jacqueline was named after the wife of Jehan Montague, who gave her to the church, a gift that did not prevent his losing his head at Montfaucon. In the second tower were six other bells; and, last, the six smallest dwelled in the steeple of the transept, with the wooden bell, which was rung only between noon on Holy Thursday and the morning of Easter Eve. Thus

Quasimodo had fifteen bells in his seraglio, but big Marie was his favorite.

It is impossible to imagine his joy on the days of the great peals. The instant the Archdeacon released him and said "Go," he ran up the winding staircase of the belfry quicker than another could have gone down. He hurried, out of breath, into the aerie chamber of the great bell, looked at her attentively and lovingly for a moment, then began to talk kindly to her, and patted her with his hand, as you would a good horse on which you are going to take a long ride. He would pity her for the labor she was about to perform. After these first caresses he shouted to his assistants in a lower story of the tower to begin. They seized the ropes, the windlass creaked, and slowly and heavily the enormous capsule of metal was set in motion. Quasimodo, with heaving bosom, watched the movement. The first shock of the clapper against the wall of brass shook the woodwork on which it was hung. Quasimodo vibrated with the bell. "Vah!" he would cry, with a burst of idiot laughter. Meanwhile the motion of the bell was accelerated and, as the angle at which it swung became sharper, the eye of Quasimodo flamed and shone brighter and brighter. At length the grand peal began: the whole tower trembled; rafters, leads, stones, all groaned together, from the piles of the foundation to the trefoils of the parapet. Quasimodo then boiled over with delight; he foamed at the mouth; he ran backward and forward; he trembled from head to foot with the tower. The great bell, let loose and, as it were, furious with rage, turned its enormous throat first to one side and then to the other side of the tower, and from it issued a roar that might be heard four leagues around. Quasimodo placed himself in front of this open mouth; he crouched down and rose up, as the bell swung to and fro, inhaled its boisterous breath, and looked alternately at the abyss two hundred feet below him and at the enormous tongue of brass that came closer and closer to bellow in his ear. This was the only word that he could hear, the only sound that broke the universal silence to which he was doomed. He took wing in it like a bird in the sun. All at once the frenzy of the bell would seize him; his look became wild: he would watch the rocking engine, as a spider watches a fly, and suddenly leap on it. Then, suspended over the abyss, carried back and forth in the formidable oscillation of the bell, he seized the bronze monster by the handles, pressed it between his knees, kicked it with his heels, and with the whole weight and force of his body increased the fury of the peal. While the tower began quaking he would shout and grind his teeth, his red hair would bristle up, his breast would heave and puff like the bellows of a forge, his eye would flash fire, and the monstrous bell would neigh breathless under him. It was then no longer the bell of Notre-Dame and Quasimodo: it was a dream, a whirlwind, a tempest, vertigo astride an uproar; a spirit clinging to a winged monster, a strange centaur, half man, half bell; a species of horrible Astolpho, carried off by a prodigious hippogriff[9] of living brass.

The presence of this extraordinary being seemed to infuse some sort of breath of life into the whole cathedral. A mysterious emanation seemed—at least so the superstitious multitude imagined—to come out of him, to animate the stones of Notre-Dame, and to make the very entrails of the old church heave and palpitate. When it was known that he was there it was easy to imagine that the thousand statues in the galleries and over the entranceways were moving and alive. In fact, the cathedral seemed to be a docile and obedient creature in his hands, waiting only for his will to raise her mighty voice, being possessed and filled with Quasimodo as with a familiar spirit. He might be said to have made the immense building breathe. He was, in fact, everywhere; he multiplied himself at all the points of the edifice. Sometimes one would be seized with fear, on beholding at the top of one of the towers an odd-looking dwarf, climbing, twining, crawling on all fours, descending externally into the abyss, leaping from one projecting point to another, and fumbling in the body of some sculptured Gorgon. It was Quasimodo unnesting the crows. At other times the visitor stumbled, in some dark corner of the church, upon a crouching, grim-faced creature, a sort of living chimera—it was Quasimodo thinking. At another time one might see under a belfry an enormous head and a bundle of ill-adjusted limbs furiously swinging at the end of a rope—it was Quasimodo ringing the vespers or the angelus. Frequently, at night, a hideous figure might be seen wandering on the delicate open-work balustrade that crowns the towers and runs around the apse—it was still the hunchback of Notre-Dame. At such times, according to the reports of the gossips of the neighborhood, the whole church took on a fantastic, supernatural, horrible look: eyes and mouths opened here and there; the dogs, and the dragons, and the griffins of stone, which keep watch day and night with outstretched necks and open jaws around the monstrous cathedral, were heard to bark and howl. If it was Christmas, while the great bell, which seemed to gasp, summoned the pious to the midnight Mass, the gloomy facade of the cathedral wore such a strange and sinister air that the grand entrance seemed to swallow the multitude, while the rose window above it looked on. All this came from Quasimodo. Egypt would have taken him for the god of the temple; the Middle Ages believed him to be its demon. He was its soul. To such a point was he, that those who knew that Quasimodo once existed, now find that the cathedral seems deserted, inanimate, dead. You feel that there is something missing. This immense body is empty; it is a skeleton. The spirit has departed; you see the place it left, and that is all. It is like a skull: the sockets of the eyes are still there, but the gaze has disappeared.

CHAPTER IV

THE DOG AND HIS MASTER

There was, however, one human being whom Quasimodo excluded from his hatred and malice, and whom he loved as much as, perhaps more than, his cathedral—that being was Claude Frollo.

The thing was perfectly simple. Claude Frollo had taken pity on him, adopted him, supported him, brought him up. It was between Claude Frollo's legs that, when quite small, he had been accustomed to seek refuge when teased by boys or barked at by dogs. Claude Frollo had taught him to speak, to read, to write. To crown it all, Claude Frollo had made him bell ringer.

The gratitude of Quasimodo was therefore profound, impassioned, unbounded; and though the countenance of his foster father was frequently gloomy and severe, though his way of speaking was habitually short, harsh, and imperious, never had this gratitude failed him for even a moment. The Archdeacon had in Quasimodo the most submissive of slaves, the most docile of attendants, the most vigilant of wardens. After the poor bell ringer had lost his hearing, Claude Frollo and he conversed in a language of signs, mysterious and understood by themselves alone. Thus the Archdeacon was the only human creature with whom Quasimodo had kept up communication. There were only two things in the world with which he still had a relationship—Notre-Dame and Claude Frollo.

Nothing on earth can be compared with the power of the Archdeacon over the bell ringer, and the attachment of the bell ringer to the Archdeacon. A sign from Claude, and the idea of pleasing him would have been enough to make Quasimodo throw himself from the top of the towers of Notre-Dame. It was truly extraordinary to see all that physical strength, which had developed in such an extraordinary way in Quasimodo, placed absolutely at the disposal of another. It was undoubtedly filial submission, domestic attachment, but it proceeded also from the fascination that one mind exercises upon another. It was an imperfect, distorted, defective creature, with head lowered and supplicating eyes, before a superior, a lofty, a commanding intelligence. But, above all, it was gratitude—albeit gratitude so carried to its extreme limit that we do not know what to compare it with. This virtue is not one of those of which the most striking examples are to be sought among men. We shall therefore say that Quasimodo loved the Archdeacon as never dog, never horse, never elephant loved his master.

CHAPTER V

CLAUDE FROLLO CONTINUED

In 1482 Quasimodo was about twenty, Claude Frollo about thirty-six. The one had grown up, the other began to grow old.

Claude Frollo was no longer the simple student of the Collège de Torchi, the tender protector of an orphan child, the young and thoughtful philosopher, so learned and yet so ignorant. He was an austere, grave, morose churchman, responsible for souls, second chaplain to the Bishop, Archdeacon of Josas, having under him the two deaneries of Montlhéry and Châteaufort, and one hundred and seventy-four parish priests. He was a somber and awe-inspiring character, before whom the choirboys in albs and long coats, the altar boys, the brothers of St.-Augustin, the clerk who officiated at the morning services at Notre-Dame, all trembled as he stalked slowly along beneath the lofty arches of the choir, majestic, pensive, with arms folded and head so bowed on his bosom that one could see only his great bald forehead. Meanwhile, Dom Claude Frollo had not abandoned either the sciences or the education of his young brother, those two occupations of his life; but time had added some bitterness to those sweet things. With time, as Paul Diacre[10] puts it, even the best land goes bad. Little Jehan de Frollo, surnamed du Moulin because of the place where he had been nursed, did not develop in the direction that Claude would have liked. His brother had counted on a pious, docile, studious, and honorable pupil. But the younger brother, like those young trees that, in spite of all the gardener's efforts, obstinately turn toward the air and sun, grew and flourished, and threw out luxuriant branches toward idleness, ignorance, and debauchery alone. Reckless of all restraint, he was a downright devil, who often made Dom Claude frown, but he was also full of mischief and drollery, which as often made him laugh. Claude had placed him in the same Collège de Torchi where he had passed his early years in study and retreat, and it was mortifying to him that this sanctuary, formerly honored by the name of Frollo, should now be scandalized by it. On this subject he frequently gave Jehan very severe and very long lectures, to which the latter listened with exemplary composure. After all, the young rascal had a good heart, as is always the case in comedies. But when the lecture was over he returned quietly to his profligacy and extravagances. Once he harassed a new student into paying him admission fees—a precious tradition that has been carefully handed down to the present day. Another time he instigated a party of students to make a classic attack on some tavern, where, after beating the keeper with bludgeons, they merrily looted the place and even broke the wine casks in the cellar. Then again there would be a long report in Latin, which the submonitor of Torchi carried pitifully to Dom Claude with this painful marginal annotation: *Rixa; prima causa vinum optimum potatum,* "Fight caused by good wine imbibed." Last, it was asserted—oh, horror of horrors in a lad of sixteen—that his excesses often carried him into the Rue de Glatigny itself.

Grieved and thwarted by these circumstances in his human affections, Claude had thrown himself with all the more ardor into the arms of science, who at least does not laugh in your face, and always repays you, though sometimes in rather hollow coin, for the attentions you have bestowed on her. Thus he became more and more learned and at the same time, by a natural consequence, more and more rigid as a priest and more and more gloomy as a man.

As Claude Frollo had from his youth traveled through almost the entire positive, external, and lawful, circle of human knowledge, he was forced, if he could not make up his mind to stop where he was, to seek further nourishment for the insatiable cravings of his under-standing. The antique symbol of the serpent biting its tail is peculiarly appropriate to science, and it appears that Claude Frollo knew this from experience. Several serious persons affirmed that after exhaust-ing the *fas* of human knowledge he had dared to penetrate into the *nefas*.[11] He had, it was said, tasted successively all the apples of the tree of knowledge and had at last bitten into the forbidden fruit. He had taken his place by turns, as our readers have seen, at the conferences of the theologians in the Sorbonne, at the meetings of the philoso-phers at the image of St.-Hilaire, at the disputes of the decretists at the image of St.-Martin, at the congregations of the physicians at the holy-water font of Notre-Dame. All the allowable and approved dishes that those four great kitchens, called the four faculties, could concoct and set before the understanding he had feasted on, and sati-ety had supervened before his hunger was appeased. He had then dug further and deeper, beneath all that finite, material, limited science; he had perhaps risked his soul, and had seated himself in the cave at that mysterious table of alchemists and astrologers, one end of which is occupied in the Middle Ages by Averroës, Guillaume de Paris, and Nicolas Flamel, while the other, lighted by the chandelier with seven branches, extends to Solomon, Pythagoras, and Zoroaster.[12] So one conjectured, either rightly or wrongly.

It is certain that the Archdeacon frequently visited the churchyard of the Innocents, where, to be sure, his parents lay buried with the other victims of the plague of 1466. But then he appeared to take much less notice of the cross at the head of their grave than of the tomb erected close by it for Nicolas Flamel and his wife, Claude Per-nelle.

It is certain that he had often been seen walking along the Rue des Lombards and stealthily entering a small house at the corner of the Rue des Écrivains and the Rue Marivaulx. It was the house built by Nicolas Flamel in which he died about the year 1411 and which, being since uninhabited, was beginning to fall to ruin, so worn were the walls by the alchemists and the professors of the occult sciences from all countries who came there and scratched their names on them. Some of the neighbors even affirmed that they had once seen through a hole the Archdeacon digging and turning over the earth in the two cellars, the planks of which had been covered with verses and hieroglyphics by Flamel himself. It was thought that Master Nicolas had buried the philosophers' stone in one of these cellars; and for two centuries the alchemists, from Magistri to Father Pacifique,[13] never ceased cruelly digging and rummaging, until the house, weakened and undermined by their excavations, at last collapsed around their ears.

It is certain, moreover, that the Archdeacon was smitten with a strange passion for the symbolic great entrance of Notre-Dame, that book of spells written in stone by Bishop Guillaume of Paris, who has no doubt been damned for having attached so infernal a frontispiece to the sacred poem forever chanted by the rest of the building. It was also believed that the Archdeacon had discovered the hidden meaning of the colossal St. Christopher, and of the other tall, mysterious statue that then stood at the entrance of the public sanctuary, or Parvis, and that the people called in derision Monsieur Legris. But everybody could see Claude Frollo sitting for hours without number on the parapet of the Parvis, contemplating the sculptures of the entrance, sometimes examining the foolish virgins with their upside down lamps, sometimes the wise virgins with their lamps right side up; at others calculating the angle of the raven's gaze on the left-hand side of the entrance, that raven looking at some mysterious spot in the church, where the philosophers' stone is certainly hidden, if it is not in Nicolas Flamel's cellar. It was, by the way, a singular destiny for the church of Notre-Dame at that period to be so loved in different degrees and with such ardor by two beings as dissimilar as Claude and Quasimodo—loved by the one, scarcely more than half man, for its beauty, its majesty, the harmonies resulting from its grand whole; loved by the other, with a learned and passionate imagination, for its mystical signification, for the meaning it conceals, for the symbols hidden beneath the sculptures of its facade, like the original text under the second in a palimpsest, in short, for the riddle that it eternally offers to human understanding.

Last, it is certain that the Archdeacon had made for himself in the tower nearest the Grève, close to the belfry, a small and secret room, which none, it was said, but the Bishop dared enter without his permission. In the past this room, almost at the top of the tower, among the ravens' nests, had been used by Bishop Hugo of Besançon, who had there practiced the black art in his time. None knew what that room contained; but from the Terrain there had often been seen at night, through a small window at the back of the tower, a strange, red, blinking light, appearing, disappearing, and reappearing at short and equal intervals, apparently governed by the blast of a bellows, and coming from the flame of a fire rather than that of a lamp or candle. In the dark this had a singular effect at that height, and the women would say, "There's the Archdeacon puffing away again: hell is crackling up there!"

These, after all, were not very strong proofs of sorcery; still there was sufficient smoke to authorize the conclusion that there must be some fire. At any rate the Archdeacon had that forbidding reputation. We must mention that the science of Egypt, necromancy, magic, even the whitest and the most innocent, had not a more inveterate enemy, a more pitiless accuser, before the officials of Notre-Dame. Whether this horror was sincere or merely the game played by the criminal who is the first to cry, "Stop thief!" it did not prevent his being considered by the learned heads of the chapter as a soul lost in the mazes of the Cabala, groping in the darkness of the occult sciences, and already in the vestibule of hell. The people held much the same opinion; all who possessed any wisdom regarded Quasimodo as the demon and Claude Frollo as the conjurer. It was obvious that the bell ringer had been engaged to serve the Archdeacon for a specific time, at the expiration of which he would be sure to steal his soul by way of payment. Accordingly the Archdeacon, in spite of the extreme austerity of his life, was on the outs with all good Christians, and there was not a devout nose among them that could not smell the magician.

And if, as he grew older, gaps opened up in his science, they did in his heart as well; at least there was good reason to believe so on surveying that face in which his soul was discernible only through a dark cloud. Where did that bald forehead come from, that head always bent down, that bosom forever heaved by sighs? What secret thought caused his lips to smile with such a bitter expression at the very moment when his knitted brows approached one another like two bulls preparing for the fight? Why was the rest of his hair already gray? What inward fire was it that at times burst from his eyes, making them look like holes in the wall of a furnace?

These symptoms of a violent moral preoccupation had acquired an unusual degree of intensity at the period of the events related in this story. More than one of the choirboys had fled terrified on meeting him alone in the church, so strange and alarming were his looks. More than once, during the service in the choir, the priest in the stall next to his had heard him mingle unintelligible parentheses with the responses. More than once the laundress of the Terrain, employed to wash for the chapter, had observed, not without horror, marks as if scratched by claws or fingernails on the surplice of Monsieur the Archdeacon of Josas.

In other respects his austerity was intensified, and never had he led a more exemplary life. From disposition as well as profession he had always kept aloof from women; he seemed now to hate them more than ever. At the mere rustling of a silk petticoat his hood was over his eyes. On this point he was so strict that when the King's daughter, the Lady of Beaujeu, came in the month of December 1481 to see the cloisters of Notre-Dame, he seriously opposed her admission, reminding the Bishop of the statute of the Black Book, dated on the vigil of St. Bartholomew, 1334, which forbids access to the cloister to every woman "whatsoever, whether old or young, mistress or servant." So the Bishop was forced to appeal to the ordinance of Odo the Legate, which excepts "certain great ladies, who cannot be refused without scandal"—*aliquæ magnates mulieres quæ sine scandalo evitari non possunt.* Still the Archdeacon protested, alleging that the ordinance of the legate, from 1207, antedated by one hundred and twenty-seven years the Black Book, and was consequently abrogated by the latter. He actually refused to appear before the princess.

It was moreover remarked that his horror of the gypsy girls and Zingari seemed to have become more vehement for some time past. He had solicited from the Bishop an edict expressly prohibiting the Bohemians to come and dance and play in the area of the Parvis; and he had recently taken the pains to search through the musty archives of the official law books for cases of wizards and witches sentenced to the flames or the gallows for practicing the black art in association with cats, swine, or goats.

CHAPTER VI

Unpopular

The Archdeacon and the bell ringer, as we have already mentioned, were not very well loved by the great and small people of the neighborhood surrounding the cathedral. When Claude and Quasimodo went out together, which happened quite often, and the people saw them, the valet following the master going through the cool, narrow, dark streets around Notre-Dame, more than one bad word, ironic comment, or insult could be heard in their wake, unless Claude Frollo walked with his head straight and erect so that his severe and almost noble brow were visible to the speechless deriders. But this was rare.

In their neighborhood, both of them were like the poets of whom Régnier writes,

> *Toute sortes de gens vont après les poètes*
> *Comme après les hiboux vont criant les fauvettes.*[14]

Sometimes it was a sneaky mischief maker who risked his skin and bones for the ineffable pleasure of sticking a pin in Quasimodo's hunchback. Sometimes it was a beautiful young girl, bolder and more flirtatious than she should have been, who brushed up against the priest's black robes, singing right under his nose, *"Niche, niche, le diable est pris."*[15] Sometimes, a squalid group of old women, squatting in a row in the shadows of a doorway, would murmur and buzz loudly at the passing of the Archdeacon and the bell ringer. They would utter as a curse this encouraging welcome, "Hmm! Here comes one whose soul looks like the other's body!" Or at times it was a group of schoolboys and street urchins playing hopscotch who would get up en masse to greet the pair in unison with a Latin jeer *"Elia! Elia! Claudius cum claudo!"*[16]

But more often than not, the insult passed unnoticed by both priest and bell ringer. Quasimodo was too deaf to hear these gracious words, and Claude too lost in thought.

BOOK V

CHAPTER I

ABBAS BEATI MARTINI[1]

Dom Claude's renown was widespread. It earned him, around the time that he refused to see Madame de Beaujeu, a visit that he long remembered.

It was evening. He was retiring after his duties to his canonical cell of the cloister of Notre-Dame. This cell, except for a few phials of an equivocal powder, which looked like an alchemical formula, revealed nothing strange or mysterious. There were here and there several inscriptions on the wall, but they were purely sentences of science or piety extracted from good authors. The Archdeacon had sat down in the light of a three-wicked brass lamp before a large trunk full of manuscripts. He had leaned his elbow on the open book of Honorius of Autun, *De prædestinatione et libero arbitrio*,[2] and was turning over with deep reflection a printed folio, the only product of the press his cell contained. In the middle of his reverie, a knock sounded at his door. "Who's there?" challenged the priest in the gracious tones of a starving dog disturbed at its bone. A voice answered from without: "Your friend, Jacques Coictier." He went and opened the door.

It was indeed the royal physician, a man of some sixty years, whose harsh features were not softened by his cunning look. Another man accompanied him. Both wore long slate-colored robes, with gray fur, belted and buttoned tight, with caps of the same stuff and color. Their hands were out of sight in their sleeves, their feet under their robes, their eyes beneath their hats.

"Heaven help me, sir!" said the Archdeacon, letting them in. "I did not expect so honorable a visit at such an hour." And while thus courteously speaking, he swept from the physician to his companion a look uneasy and scrutinizing.

"It is never too late to visit so learned a man as Dom Claude Frollo de Tirechappe," rejoined Doctor Coictier, whose Franc-Comtois accent made him drag his sentences with the majesty of the train of a court dress.

Then the physician and the Archdeacon began one of those congratulatory prologues that preceded in that age, according to custom, all conversations between learned men, which did not prevent them heartily hating one another. However, it is the same today, every mouth of a distinguished man complimenting another of his rank is a vessel of honeyed gall.

Claude Frollo's felicitations to Jacques Coictier dealt mainly with the temporal advantages the worthy doctor had managed to extract in the course of his envied career from each ailment of the King, an alchemical operation better and more certain than the search for the philosophers' stone.

"Truly, Doctor Coictier, I have great joy in learning the accession to that bishopric of your nephew, my reverend lord Pierre Verse. Is he not Bishop of Amiens?"

"Yes, Monsieur the Archdeacon; it is a blessing of heaven."

"You must know that you looked fine on Christmas Day, at the head of your company of the Chamber of Accounts, Monsieur President?"

"Vice president, Dom Claude. Alas, nothing more!"

"And there's your superb mansion in the Rue St.-André-des-Arcs. It is a Louvre! I very much like the apricot tree sculpted over the door with the pleasant play on words: A L'ABRI-COTIER."[3]

"Alas, Master Claude, all this masonry is expensive. As the house is built, so I am proportionately ruined."

"What, don't you have your revenues from the jail and bailiwick of Paris and the rent of all the houses and buildings of every kind in the Cloture?"

"My castellany of Poissy brings me nothing this year."

"But your tollhouses of Triel, St.-James, and St.-Germain-en-Laye—they are good."

"Twenty-six pounds, not even Parisis."

"You have your office of King's counselor—that's settled."

"Yes, Brother Claude; but the cursed estate of Poligny that they talk so much about is worth only sixty gold crowns, taking the good with the bad."

There was in the compliments that Dom Claude paid Jacques Coictier that sardonic tone, delicately sneering, that sad, cruel smile of a superior but unfortunate man who makes fun of the heavy prosperity of a common man. The other did not notice it.

"On my soul," said Claude finally, shaking his hand, "I am delighted to see you in good health!"

"Thank you, Master Claude."

"By the way," cried Claude, "how is your royal patient?"

"He does not pay his physician well enough," replied the doctor, glancing aside at his companion.

"Do you think so, Compère Coictier?" said the latter.

This speech, pronounced in a tone of surprise and reproach, brought the Archdeacon's attention back to the stranger; in reality it had not been diverted from him for a single moment after he had crossed the threshold of the cell. To receive the stranger, he needed to remind himself of every reason he had to be polite to Doctor Jacques Coictier, Louis XI's all-powerful physician. So his countenance was in no way very cordial when Coictier said, "Dom Claude, I bring you a brother, who, hearing your renown, desired to see you."

"Is your friend one of us, of science?" the Archdeacon inquired, riveting on Coictier's companion his penetrating eye. He did not meet under the stranger's brows a gaze less piercing and defiant than his own. He was, as well as the lamp's pale flicker would allow us to decide, a man of some sixty winters, of middling stature, who appeared broken in health. His profile, although of a very bourgeois like, had something stern and powerful about it; his eyes gleamed below a deep brow, like a light at the end of a beast's den, and, shaded by the fur cap pulled down to his nose, might be seen the broad forehead of a man of genius.

He took upon himself the reply to the Archdeacon's question: "Reverend master," he said gravely, "your fame reached me, and I determined to consult you. I am only a humble country gentleman, who is proud to enter into the presence of a learned man. You may like to know my name—I call myself compère Tourangeau."[4]

"A strange name for a gentleman!" thought the archdeacon. He felt himself before something strong and serious. The instinct of his high intelligence led him to divine one no less lofty under Tourangeau's furred cap, and on considering that grave, morose figure, the ironic laugh that had covered his face on seeing Jacques Coictier faded gradually away, like twilight on the horizon. He sat down again silently on his large armchair, his elbow resumed its usual place on the table, and his forehead on his hand. After some moments' meditation, he made a sign for his two visitors to take seats and addressed Tourangeau.

"Do you come to consult me, my master, with regard to what science?"

"Your Reverence," responded Tourangeau, "I am ill, very ill. They say you are a great Esculapian, and I have come to gain your medical advice."

"Medical advice!" echoed the Archdeacon, shaking his head. He seemed to collect himself for an instant; then he went on: "My friend, Tourangeau, since that is your name, turn your head. You will see my answer written on the wall."

Tourangeau obeyed and read above his head the following inscription inscribed on the stone: MEDICINE IS THE DAUGHTER OF DREAMS.— *JAMBLIQUE.*[5]

Meanwhile, Doctor Jacques Coictier had heard his companion's question with irritation, which Dom Claude's answer had redoubled. He bent over to Tourangeau's ear and whispered, too low for the Archdeacon to hear him: "I warned you he was mad. But you wanted to see him!"

"This madman of yours is very reasonable, Doctor Jacques!" returned the other in the same voice, with a bitter smile.

"Have it your own way," replied Coictier drily. Then, addressing the Archdeacon, he said: "You are hasty in your work, Dom Claude, but you cannot do away with Hippocrates as an ape might with a hazelnut. Medicine a dream! Why, apothecaries would stone you to death if they were here! Do you deny the influence of philters on the blood, unguents on the flesh? Do you deny that eternal pharmacy of herbs and metals, the world, made expressly for its eternal patient—man?"

"I deny," said Dom Claude coldly, "neither pharmacy nor patient. I deny the physician."

"Then it is not true," resumed Coictier heatedly, "that a gunshot wound may be healed with a roast mouse, that young blood infused in an old person's veins will rejuvenate him; it is not true that two and two make four, and that *emprosthotonos* succeeds *ophisthonos?*"[6]

The Archdeacon rejoined without emotion. "There are certain things of which I think in a certain way."

Coictier reddened with rage.

"Come, come, my good Coictier, do not let us get angry," broke in Tourangeau. "The Archdeacon is our friend."

Coictier calmed himself, though growling in an undertone: "After all he is mad!"

"*Pasque Dieu,* Master Claude," resumed Tourangeau after a pause, "you have troubled me. I had two consultations to have with you, one regarding my health, the other my star."

"Sir," replied the Archdeacon, "if such is your thought, you would have spared yourself this by not ascending the steps of my staircase. I do not believe in medicine, or in astrology."

"Really?" asked the other in surprise.

Coictier let out a forced laugh. "You see clearly he is crazed," he whispered to Tourangeau. "He does not believe in astrology!"

"How could one imagine," pursued Dom Claude, "that every astral-ray is a thread connected to a man's head?"

"In what do you believe?" asked Tourangeau.

The Archdeacon was for a moment indecisive, then let a gloomy smile escape him that belied his reply, which was: "*Credo in Deum* (I believe in God)."

"*Dominum nostrum* (and our Lord)," added Tourangeau, with a sign of the Cross.

"Amen," concluded Coictier.

"Reverend Master," said his companion, "I am charmed to find you so religious. But, learned man that you are, have you arrived at the point of not believing in science?"

"Not so," responded the Archdeacon, grasping the arm of Tourangeau, and a flash of enthusiasm kindled his dull eye. "No, I do not deny science. I have not so long crawled, dragging myself with nails in the earth, through the endless windings of the cavern, without perceiving, far off from me, at the end of the obscure gallery, a light, a flame, something, the reflection no doubt of the dazzling central laboratory where the patient and the wise have surprised God."

"And finally," interrupted Tourangeau, "what do you uphold as true and certain?"

"Alchemy."

Coictier broke in: "Of course, Dom Claude, alchemy has its reason, but why scoff at medicine or astrology?"

"Your science of man is empty! Empty is your science of the heavens!" said the Archdeacon imperiously.

"This is brushing away altogether Epidaurus and the Chaldeans," replied the physician sneeringly.

"Listen, Messire Jacques. This is spoken in good faith. I am not physician to the King, and His Majesty has not given me a Dædalian garden to observe constellations. Do not be angry, but listen to me. What truth have you drawn, I will not say from physics, which is too unlikely a thing, but from stargazing? Cite to me the virtues of the vertical boustrophedon, the labors of the number ziruph and the number zephirod."[7]

"Do you deny," asked Coictier, "the sympathetic force of the clavicle[8] and the cabalistic derived from it?"

"Error, Master Jacques! None of your formulas leads to reality, while alchemy has its discoveries. Can you contest results like these? That ice buried underground for a thousand years is transformed into rock crystal; that lead is the foundation of all metals, for gold is not a metal but light, lead requires only four periods of two hundred years each to pass successively from its state of lead to red arsenic, from that to tin, from tin to silver. Are these not facts? But to believe in the clavicle, in the straight line and the stars, is as ridiculous as to believe, with the people of Great Cathay, that the oriole changes into the mole, and grains of wheat turn into goldfish."

"I have studied hermetics," cried Coictier, "and I affirm—"

The angry Archdeacon would not let him finish.

"And I have studied medicine, astrology, and hermetics. Here only is truth (while saying this, he picked up out of the trunk a phial full of the powder before mentioned), here only is light! Hippocrates, it is a dream; Urania—likewise; Hermes—is a thought. Gold is the sun—to make gold is to be God. This is the only science. I have fathomed medicine and astrology, I tell you! Emptiness, emptiness! The human body, shadows! The stars, the same!"

He fell back on his chair in a powerful, inspired attitude. Tourangeau had watched him in silence. Coictier forced a laugh, slightly shrugged his shoulders, and in a low voice repeated: "He is mad!"

"And," said Tourangeau all of a sudden, "have you touched this? Have you made gold?"

"Had I done so," responded the Archdeacon, uttering his words slowly like a pensive man reflecting, "the King of France would be named Claude, not Louis."

His listener frowned.

"What do I say?" went on Dom Claude with a scornful smile. "What would I care for the throne of France when I might rebuild the Empire of the East!"

"Well and good!" exclaimed the other.

"Oh, the poor lunatic!" muttered Coictier.

The Archdeacon proceeded, appearing only to answer his own thoughts: "But no, I still crawl; scratching my face and hands on the sharp stones of the subterranean way. I catch a glimpse, I cannot steadily gaze! I do not read but only spell!"

"And when you have read," inquired Tourangeau, "can you make gold?"

"Who doubts it?"

"In that case, our Lady knows I have great need of money. I would like to learn to read in your books. Tell me, Reverend Master, is your science inimical or displeasing to our Lady?"

To this question, Dom Claude merely replied with haughty tranquillity: "Whose archdeacon am I?"

"True, my master. Well, are you willing to initiate me? Let me spell with you."

Claude assumed the majestic, pontifical attitude of a Samuel.

"Old man, one needs a longer span of years than is left to you to undertake that voyage on the mysterious sea. Your head is quite gray! Out of the cave one may not come except with white hair, but it cannot be entered except with dark hair. Science can wrinkle, bleach, and wither human faces—it wants none already furrowed. Yet, if the desire possesses you at your age to undergo discipline, and decipher the fearful alphabet of sages, come to me, it is well, I will try. I will not say to you, poor old man, go visit the sepulchral chambers of the Pyramids that Herodotus speaks of, or the brick Tower of Babylon, or the immense marble sanctuary of the Indian Temple of Ecklinga.[9]

"I have, no more than have you, seen the Chaldean masonry built according to the sacred shape of the Sikra, or Solomon's temple, which is destroyed, or the stone doors of the sepulchres of Israel's Kings, which are broken. We will content ourselves with the fragments of Hermes' book that we have here. I will explain to you the statue of

St. Christopher, the symbol of the Sower, and that of the two angels that are on the portal of Holy Chapel, one of whom has her hand in a vase, and the other in a cloud—"

Here, Jacques Coictier, whom the Archdeacon's fiery replies had unhorsed, leaped again to the saddle and interrupted him in the triumphant tone of one man of learning correcting another: "*Erras, amice Claudo,* you are wrong, friend Claude. The symbol is not the number. You mistake Orpheus for Hermes."

"It is you who err," gravely retorted the Archdeacon. "Dædalus is the foundation; Orpheus the wall; Hermes the building, the whole. You may come when you will," he continued, turning to Tourangeau. "I will show you the particles of gold remaining at the bottom of Nicolas Flamel's crucible, and you may compare it with the gold of William of Paris. I will teach you the secret virtues of the Greek word *peristera.*[10] But, before all, I would have you read the letters of the marble alphabet, the leaves of the granite book. We will go to the gate of Bishop William and St. Jean le Ronde's at the Holy Chapel, then to Nicolas Flamel's house in the Rue Marivaulx, to his tomb, which is in the Holy Innocents, to his two hospitals, Rue de Montmorency. I will have you read the hieroglyphics covering the four large iron clamps of the gateway of St. Gervais's Hospital and of the Rue de la Ferronerie. We will together spell out the facades of St.-Come, Ste.-Geneviève-des-Ardents, St.-Martin, St.-Jacques-de-la-Boucherie."

For a long time, his listener, however intelligent was his look, had not seemed to understand Claude. He interrupted him: "*Pasque Dieu!* What are your books?"

"Here is one," said the Archdeacon.

And, throwing open the window of his cell, he pointed with his finger to the immense church of Notre-Dame, which, with the black outline of its towers cut on a starlit sky, its stone sides and monstrous body, seemed a double-headed sphinx seated in the middle of the city.

The Archdeacon for a while considered the gigantic edifice, then, stretching with a sigh his right hand toward the printed book that lay open on the table, while his left hand pointed at Notre-Dame, he said, "Alas! This will kill that!"

Coictier, who had eagerly approached the book, could not help crying: "Why, what is so frightening about this? 'Glossa in epistolas D. Pauli, Norimbergæ, Antonius Roburger, 1474?'[11] It is not new. It is a book of Pierre Lombard, the master of sentences. Is it because it is printed?"

"You have said it," rejoined Claude, who seemed absorbed in deep meditation and stood erect, with his forefinger bent on the folio from the famed Nuremberg presses. Then he added these words: "Alas, alas! The smallest things are the death of the greatest. The rat of the Nile kills the crocodile, the swordfish the whale, the book will kill the building!"

The cloister curfew tolled at the moment Doctor Jacques repeated to his companion his eternal refrain: "He is mad." To which the latter this time replied, "I think so."

This was an hour when no stranger might remain in the cloister. "Master," said Tourangeau on taking leave of the Archdeacon, "I delight in learned men and great geniuses. Come tomorrow to the Palace des Tournelles and ask for the Abbot of St.-Martin-of-Tours."

The Archdeacon returned to his room stupefied, at last comprehending who Tourangeau was, by recollecting this passage from the cartulary of St.-Martin-of-Tours: *"Abbas beati Martini, SCILICET REX FRANCIÆ, est canonicus de consuetudine et habet parvam præbendam quam habet sanctus Venantius et debet sedere in sede thesaurarii."*[12]

It was affirmed that since that event, the Archdeacon had frequent conferences with Louis XI, whenever His Majesty came to Paris, and that Claude's credit eclipsed that of Olivier le Daim and Jacques Coictier, who, in his own way, made the King pay for it.

CHAPTER II

"THIS WILL KILL THAT"

Our readers will pardon us for stopping a moment to seek what may have been the thought hidden by the Archdeacon's enigmatic words: "This will kill that. The book will kill the building."

For us, the thought has two faces. First, the priestly side. The fear of the priesthood before a new agent, printing. It is the dread of the man of the sanctuary before Gutenberg's press. The flesh and the manuscript, the spoken and the written word, being terrified at the printed word, something like the stupor of a sparrow that might see the Legion of Angels unfolding its six thousand wings. It was the cry of the prophet who already hears emancipated humanity buzzing and humming, who sees in the future intelligence undermine faith, opinion dethrone belief, the world shake Rome. It is the prognostic of the philosopher who sees the human mind, made volatile by the press, evaporate from the theocratic confinement. It is the terror of the soldier who examines the bronze-headed ram and exclaims: "The tower must crumble." It signified one power was to succeed to another. It meant: "The printing press will kill the church."

But behind this thought, the first and simplest no doubt, in our opinion lay another, a corollary of the first less easy to perceive, and easier to contest, a perspective as philosophical, not of the priest only but of the man and the scholar. The foreshadowing that the human mind in changing its form would change its mode of expression, that the foremost idea of every generation would no longer be written on the same material, with the same manner; that the stone book, so solid and lasting, would give way to the paper book, still more solid and lasting. Under this heading, the Archdeacon's vague speech had a second sense: it signified that one art was to overturn another. That printing would kill architecture.

In truth, from the creation of things to the fifteenth century of the Christian era, architecture was the great book of humanity, the principal expression of the human being in his various states of development, whether as force or as intelligence.

When the memory of the first races grew overburdened, when the baggage of the recollections of the human species became so weighty and unwieldy that the speech, naked and fleeting, ran the risk of losing it on the way, it was transcribed on the ground in the most visible, durable, and natural fashion. Each tradition was sealed with a monument.

The first were simple rock quarries that, in the words of Moses, "iron has not touched." Architecture began like writing. It was at first an alphabet. A stone was stood upright and it was a letter; and each letter was a hieroglyphic, and on each of them rested a group of ideas as the capital on a pillar. The first races, everywhere, at the same moment, the whole surface of the earth over did the same thing. The raised stone of the Celts is in Asiatic Siberia as on the American pampas.

Later, they made words. They laid stone on stone, linked syllables of granite, the word attempted some combinations. The Celtic cairns and cromlechs, Etruscan tumuli, Hebrew galgal, are words. Some, especially the tumuli, are proper names. Sometimes, when much stone and a broad space was convenient, a phrase would be built up. The immense heap of Karnac is a whole formula.

Finally, they made books. Traditions had brought forth symbols, under which they disappeared, as under leaves the trunks of trees; all these symbols, in which men had faith, crossed and multiplied, and became more and more complicated: the first monuments no longer sufficed to contain them, they spread on all sides; those works could barely express the primeval traditions, like themselves, simple, naked, and groveling on the ground. The symbol needed a building. Thereupon, architecture revealed itself to the human mind; it became a many-headed giant with innumerable arms, and fixed in an eternal, visible, palpable shape the floating symbols. Dædalus, which is limited force; Orpheus, which is intelligence singing; the pillar, which is a letter, the arcade, which is a syllable; the pyramid, which is a word—set in motion at once by a law of geometry and poetry, grouped, combined, amalgamated, descended, ascended, fell into juxtaposition on the ground, rose in stages to the sky, until were penned, under the dictation of the general idea of an epoch, those marvelous books that are marvelous buildings as well—namely: the Tower of Ecklinga, the works of Ramses in Egypt, the Temple of Solomon.

The original idea, the word, not only is in all these edifices but shows itself in the form. Solomon's Temple, for instance, was not merely a part of a holy book but the book itself. On each of its concentric circles the priests might read the manifest translation to the eyes, and thus follow its transformations from sanctuary to sanctuary until they found it in the last tabernacle under its most concrete form, architecture's, also: the arch. So the word was enclosed in the building, but its image showed through its envelope, as the human form is visible through the wrapper of a mummy.

Not only the form of structures but the site selected reveals the thought they stand for. Greece crowned its mountaintops with temples harmonious to the view, India split up its symbol to chisel out its deformed pagodas carried by gigantic rows of granite elephants.

So, during the world's first six thousand years, from the first im-memorial pagoda of Hindustan to the Cathedral of Cologne, architecture has been the great writing of the human species. And so true is this that not only every religious symbol but every human thought has its page in the immense book and its monument.

Civilization always begins with theocracy and ends in democracy. This law of liberty succeeding unity is engraved in architecture. For let us insist on this point, it must not be believed that masonry had power only to construct the building, to express the myth and sacred symbol, to transcribe on those stone pages the mystic tables of the law. Were it so, as in every human society there comes a moment when the sacred symptom is worn away and blotted out beneath the free thought, when man tears the gown off the priest, when the develop-ment of philosophy and its systems eats into the face of religion—architecture could not reproduce this new state of the human mind; its pages, written on their front page, would be empty on the reverse, its work would fail, its book would be incomplete. But, no.

Take for example the Middle Ages, which we may see more clearly from its being nearer. During its first period, while theocracy domi-nated Europe, while the Vatican rallied around it and classed the ele-ments of an already built Rome with a Rome that had fallen to ruin around the Capitol, while Christianity sought in the ruins of anterior civilization all the stages of society and rebuilt with its ruins a new hi-erarchical universe of which priesthood is the keystone, a dull rumble could be heard through the chaos. Then gradually was seen to arise under the breath of Christianity and the hand of barbarians, heaving up the remains of dead architecture, Greek or Roman, that mystic Roman architecture, sister to the theocratic masonry of Egypt and India, unalterable emblem of pure Catholicism, immovable hiero-glyphic of Papal unity. All thoughts of those days were handed down through that gloomy Roman style. Everywhere was felt authority, unity, impenetrability, absoluteness, Gregory VII, everywhere the priest, never the man; it was the caste, not the people. But the Crusades arrived. It was a great popular movement, and all such movements whatever their cause and design, always liberate the spirit of freedom. New acts saw the light. It opened the stormy period of the Jacqueries, Pragueries, and Leagues. Authority was split, unity was divided into two parts. Feudalism demanded a share with theocracy, forestalling the people, who would inevitably come to claim the lion's share: *quia nominor leo.*[13] The lords brushed past the priests, the people pushed up the lords. Europe's face changed. So did that of architecture. Like civilization, it turned over a new leaf, and the fresh spirit of the age found it blank to be written on at its dictation. It came with the Crusades, as nations with liberty. Then, while Rome was gradually dismembered, Roman architecture died. Hieroglyphics deserted the cathedral and went to emblazon the castle to give feudalism prestige. The cathedral itself, that edifice formerly so dogmatic, invaded henceforth by the common people, by liberty, left the priest and fell into the artist's power. He built it in his own way. Farewell to mystery, myth, law. Welcome whims and fantasy. Provided the priest had his altar and his basilica, nothing could be dictated. The four walls were the artist's. The architectural book belonged no more to religion or Rome but to imagination, poetry, and the people. Thus the rapid, countless transformations of the style lasting only three centuries, so striking after the stagnant immobility of the Roman taste of six or seven. Art strode on with giant steps. Genius and originality went on past the priest's work. Each race wrote as it passed its line on the book; it scratched off the old hieroglyphics on the frontispiece of cathedrals, and seldom could you see the dogma penetrate the new symbols laid over it. The popular garment nearly shrouded completely the religious skeleton. One can hardly imagine the license architects then displayed, even toward the church. There are capitals carved with monks and nuns assembled together shamefully, as at the Salle-des-Cheminées of the Palace of Justice of Paris. There is Noah's adventure sculpted *literally* under the main portal of Burgos. It is a Bacchic monk with ass's ears and a glass in his hand, laughing in the face of a whole community, as on the sink of Bocherville Abbey. There existed at that period for thoughts on stone a privilege quite comparable to our actual freedom of the press—the liberty of architecture.

It went very far. Sometimes, a doorway, a facade, a whole church would present a symbolic meaning absolutely foreign to the worship, or even hostile to the church. In the thirteenth century, William of Paris, Nicolas Flamel in the fifteenth, wrote such seditious pages. St.-Jacques-de-la-Boucherie is entirely a church of opposition.

Thought then was free only in that way: so it wrote solely in the books called churches. It would have been burned by the executioner's hand in manuscript form had it been so imprudent as to risk it. Thus, having only that road to daylight, it rushed into it from every side. From then on the immense number of cathedrals that covered Europe, so prodigious a quantity that it can hardly be believed, even after having proved it. All the material and intellectual force of society converged on the same point—architecture. In this manner, under the pretext of raising churches to God, art developed itself in magnificent proportions.

Then, anyone born a poet became an architect. Genius scattered among the masses, pressed down in all parts by feudalism as under the *testudo*[14] of bronze shields, finding no release but through the architectural side, escaped through it, and *Iliad*s took the form of cathedrals. All the other arts obeyed and submitted under the discipline of architecture. The builder, the poet, the master, uniting in his person sculpture that chiseled the facades, painting that illuminated the windows, music that rang the bells and breathed into the organs. Poor poetry, properly so called, which obstinately refused to vegetate in manuscripts, was obliged, to be something, to encase the edifice under the form of hymn or to *prose;* the same part, after all, as Aeschylus' tragedies played in the holy feasts of Greece, and Genesis in Solomon's Temple.

Thus, until Gutenberg, architecture was the principal and universal writing. This granite book began in the East, was continued by Greek and Roman antiquity—the Middle Ages wrote the last page. The phenomenon of an architecture of caste, which we have noted in the Middle Ages, was reproduced with analogous movement in human intelligence in the other great epochs of history. So, merely to summarize a law that would require volumes to develop, in the Orient cradle of primitive times, after Hindu and Phœnician architecture, that opulent mother of Arabian architecture, in Antiquity, after Egyptian architecture, of which the Etruscan style and the Cyclopean are but varieties, the Greek, of which the Roman branch is but a prolongation loaded with the Carthaginian dome; in modern times, after Roman architecture the Gothic. And, if we double these three series, we will find, on the three elder sisters, the Hindu, the Egyptian, and the Roman, the same symbol: namely of theocracy, caste, unity, dogma, myth, God; and on the three younger sisters, the Phœnician, Greek, and

Gothic, whatever the diversity of form inherent in their nature, the same signification: that is, liberty, the people, man.

Let it be called Brahmin, or Maga, in Hindu, Egyptian, or Roman architecture, it is always about the priest, and nothing but the priest. The people's architecture is not the same, it is richer and less saintly. In the Phœnician, one feels the trader; in the Greek, the republican; in the Gothic, the citizen.

The general characteristics of all theocratic architecture are immobility, horror of progress, preservation of traditional lines, consecration of the primitive types, the constant bending of every form of man and nature to the incomprehensible caprices of the symbol. They are obscure works that the initiated alone can decipher. Every form, every deformity even has there a meaning that makes it inviolable. Do not require Hindu, Egyptian, or Roman masonry to reform its design or ameliorate its statuary. Anything perfecting them would be impious. In those architectures, the rigidness of the dogma seems to stiffen the stone like a second petrifaction. The general character of popular buildings on the other hand is variety, progress, originality, wealth, perpetual movement. They were already detached enough from religion to think of their beauty, to care for it, to correct without hesitation their decor of statues or arabesques. They are of their age. They possess something human that unceasingly blends with the divine symbol under which they are produced. From then on buildings understandable to every soul, and intelligence and imagination, still symbolic but as easily understandable as nature. Between theocratic architecture and this there is the difference between a sacred language and a vulgar tongue, between hieroglyphics and art, between Solomon and Phidias.

If what we have before mentioned is summed up, it will bring us to this, neglecting a thousand proofs and as many objections in the details: that architecture has been until the fifteenth century the principal register of humanity: that in that interval there appeared no complicated thought that did not make itself a building; that every popular idea has, like all religion's laws, its monuments; that, in short, human beings thought of nothing of importance that they did not write on stone. And why? Because every thought, whether religious or philosophical, is interested in perpetuating itself; because what has moved one generation thirsts to move others, and leaves its mark. Now, how precarious is the immortality of the manuscript? A building is an extraordinarily solid, durable, and resistant book! To destroy the written word a torch and a Turk suffice. To demolish the constructed word, one needs a social revolution, or an earthquake. The barbarians passed over the Coliseum, perhaps the deluge over the Pyramids.

In the fifteenth century, everything changed.

Human thought discovered a means of perpetuating itself in a more lasting and resistant form than architecture. It was simpler and easier as well. Architecture was dethroned. To Orpheus's stone letters succeeded Gutenberg's leaden type.

"The book will kill the building."

The invention of printing is the greatest event of history. It is the Revolution's mother. It is humanity's mode of expressing, totally renewed, it is man's thought shedding one form and arraying itself in another, the complete, definite casting off of the skin of that symbolic serpent which, since Adam, has stood for intelligence.

In the printed form the mind is more imperishable than ever: it is volatile, not to be grasped or destroyed. It mingles with the air. In the days of architecture it had grown to a mountain and powerfully weighed on a century and a place. Now, it has become a flock of birds, scattered on the four winds and at once filling every point of the air and space.

We repeat, who does not see that in this shape it is indelible? From solid that it was it has become lifelike. It has passed from duration to deathlessness. A mass may be ground to dust, but how can ubiquity be extirpated? If a flood comes, the mountain will be long covered by the waves while the birds are in the air; and let only a single ark float over the flood and they will light on it, drifting with it, witness with it the "drying up of the waters," and the new world heaving up out of the chaos, they would see as its birth, while soaring over it, winged and alive, the thought of the globe engulfed.

And, when one observes that this mode of expression is not only the best for preservation but, besides, the simplest, handiest to all, when one thinks how he does not drag a heavy burden or an unwieldy train, when one compares the thought obliged to translate itself into a building, to set in motion four or five arts and tons of gold, a mountain of stone, a forest of trees, a race of workmen—when this is compared with the thought that makes a book, requiring but a little paper, ink, and a pen—is it astounding that architecture was thrust aside for printing? Cut the primeval bed of a stream by a canal dug below it and the water will desert its traditional channel.

See how, on the discovery of printing, architecture dried up gradually, withered and was laid bare! How the fresh, diverted water coursed, which the thoughts of the time and people had drawn from it! The flow was barely noticeable in the fifteenth century; the press was still too weak and relinquished to architecture a superabundance of life. But in the sixteenth century, the wasting away of architecture was visible; it no longer expressed the essence of society; it wretchedly cleaved to classic art; from being Gallic, European, and offspring of the soil, it became Greek and Roman, from true and modern, pseudo-antique. This is that decadence called the Renaissance. A magnificent decay, nevertheless, for the old Gothic genius, the sun that had set behind the gigantic press of Mayence still cast a few of its last beams on that hybrid collection of Latin arcades and Corinthian colonnades.

It is the setting sun that we mistook for the aurora.

From the moment when architecture was no more than any other art, no longer the total, sovereign, tyrannical one, it had lost the strength to rein in the others. They were emancipated, they burst the yoke, and each flew its way, gaining every one by their divorce. Isolation increased everything. Sculpture became statuary, imagery painting, the canon became music. One would have said, it is an empire, dismembered by its Alexander's death; the provinces make themselves into kingdoms.

From this, Raphael, Michelangelo, Jean Goujon, Palestrina, the splendors of the dazzling sixteenth century.

At the same times as arts, thought liberated itself on every side. The heretics of the Middle Ages had already wrought broad gaps in Catholicism. The sixteenth century broke religious unity. Before printing, reform would have been merely a schism; printing made it a revolution. Without the press, heresy was enervated. Be it fatal or providential, Gutenberg was the forerunner of Luther.

When the sun of the Middle Ages entirely set, when Gothic genius was forever extinguished in the horizon of art, architecture was tarnished, discolored, and more and more effaced. The printed book was the consuming worm of the edifice, the devourer. The building grew thin visibly, was impoverished, came to naught. It no longer expressed anything, not even the remembrance of art and another time. Reduced to itself, cast off by the other arts because human thoughts abandoned it, it summoned workmen in place of artists. The glazier succeeded the decorator and stainer, the stonecutter followed the sculptor. Farewell to all flow of originality, life, intelligence. It dragged itself along like a beggar, from studio to studio, from copy to copy. Michelangelo, who, in the sixteenth century, felt that it was dying, doubtless had a last despairing idea. This Titan of art piled the Pantheon on the Parthenon and made St. Peter's of Rome. A great work that deserves to stand unique, the last original work of architecture, the giant artist's signature at the foot of the colossal stone register it closed. Michelangelo dead, what made this miserable architecture that survived itself look like a specter and a shade? It took St. Peter's of Rome, copied and parodied it. It was a mania, and a pity. Every century has its St. Peter's; the seventeenth, the Val-de-Grâce, the eighteenth, Ste. Geneviève—every country its St. Peter's; London and St. Petersburg have theirs; Paris has two or three. An insignificant testament, last dotage of grand decrepit art falling to childhood before dying.

If, instead of the characteristic monuments like those we have mentioned, we examine the general aspect of art in the seventeenth and eighteenth centuries, we will remark the same phenomena of waning and decline. Starting with Francis II, the architectural form of the edifice was rubbed off and allowed the geometrical forms to become visible, like the bony frame of a sick person wasted away. The sweeping lines of art were replaced by geometry's cold, inexorable ones. A building became a polyhedron.

Nevertheless, architecture writhed to conceal this nakedness. Look at the Greek facade inscribed over the Roman, and vice versa. It is ever the Pantheon in the Parthenon, St. Peter's of Rome. Look at the brick houses of Henry IV, with stone cornices; the Place Royale, the Place Dauphine. Look at the churches of Louis XIII, heavy, thickset, massed together, loaded with a dome like a hump. Look at the Mazarin architecture, the wretched Italian pasticcio, or pasty, of the Four Nations. Consider the palaces of Louis XIV; they are long barracks for courtiers, stiff, glacial, and boring. Finally, Louis XV, with its chicories, vermicelli, and all the worms and fungi that disfigure this decrepit, toothless, precious architecture. From Francis II to Louis XV, the evil increased by geometrical progression. Art was left only skin on its bones—its agony was wretched.

Meanwhile, what of printing? All the life leaving architecture came to it. Proportionately to architecture's demise, it breathed and grew. The capital of strength that the human mind expended in buildings it now spent in books. Thus, the press in the sixteenth century, rising to the level of declining architecture, grappled with it and killed it. In the seventeenth, it was already so sovereign and triumphant, and settled in its victory, as to give to the world the festival of a great literary age. In the eighteenth, well rested in the Court of Louis XIV, it grasped Luther's old sword, armed Voltaire, and ran tumultuously to the attack on that ancient Europe whose architectural expression it had slain. By the end of the eighteenth century, it had destroyed everything. In the nineteenth, it set to the work of rebuilding.

Now, we ask, which of the two arts really represented, during three centuries, human thought? Which translated it? Which not only gave expression to manias both literary and scholarly, but also to its vast, profound universal movement? Which consistently laid the ground, without interruption or break, for the thousand-legged monster called humanity?

Printing. Let no one be deceived, architecture is dead, with no ghost to return, killed by the printed book because it did not last as long and cost more. Every cathedral is a thousand million. Calculate how much money it would require to rewrite the architectural book; to erect anew on the sites of the various buildings; to return to those periods when the throng of buildings swarmed on the earth so that an eyewitness says, "One would have said, the world has shaken off its old clothes to wrap itself in a white vestment of churches. (*Erat enim ut si mundus, ipse excutiendo semet, rejecta vetustate, candidam ecclesiarum vestum indueret.*"—Glaber Radulphus).[15]

A book is quickly made, costs so little, and may go so far! Is it surprising all human thought should flow down that slope? Not that architecture has not left here and there a fine structure, an isolated masterpiece. There may still be, under the reign of printing, a column set up, I suppose, by a whole army, cast of melted cannon, as there were, under architecture's rule, *Iliad*s and romances, *Mahabarata*s and

Nibelungen, made by an entire people with mingled rhapsodies. The great accident of an architect of genius may survive to the twentieth century, as Dante's to the thirteenth. But architecture will no more be the social, collective, dominant art. The great poem, the great work of humankind will never again be built but printed.

Henceforth, if architecture rises up again accidentally, it will not be a master. It will suffer from the law of literature, which it received from it in the past. The respective standing of the two arts will be inverted. In architectural ages, poems (rare, it is true) resembled buildings. In India, Vyasa[16] is uneven, strange, impenetrable as a pagoda. In the Egyptian East, poetry has, like the buildings, grandeur and quietness of lines; in ancient Greece, beauty, serenity, calmness; in Christian Europe, Catholic majesty, popular simplicity, the rich and luxuriant vegetation of an era of renewal. The Bible resembles the Pyramids, the *Iliad* the Parthenon; Homer has Phidias; Dante the thirteenth century—the last Roman church; Shakespeare the sixteenth—the last Gothic cathedral.

So, to sum up what we have previously mentioned in a necessarily broken and incomplete fashion, human beings have two books, two registers, two testaments, masonry and printing, the stone and the paper Bible. No doubt, when the two are contemplated, so widely open in every epoch, we can regret the visible majesty of the granite writing, the gigantic alphabets formed in colonnades, in pylons, in obelisks, that kind of human mountain that covers the world, passing from the pyramid to the steeple, from Cheops to Strasbourg. The past must be read on its marble pages. The book written by architecture must be admired and constantly perused, yet the grandeur of the building erected by printing in its turn must not be denied.

That edifice is colossal. A compiler of statistics, whom I do not know, has calculated that if piled one on another, all the volumes produced by the press since the time of Gutenberg would reach from the earth to the moon. But it is not of such a kind of greatness that we would speak. When one tries to grasp a complete image of all the products of printing to our days, does not the whole appear to us like an immense construction, resting on the world, at which man is constantly working, and the monstrous head of which is lost in the future's dense mist? It is the anthill of intelligence. It is the hive to which every kind of imagination, those golden bees, brings its honey. The building has a thousand floors. Here and there may be seen yawning on its sides the shadowy caverns science drills in them. Everywhere over the surface art blossoms to the eye in arabesques, rose windows, and open work. There each individual work, however capricious and isolated, has its place. Harmony results from it all. From Shakespeare's cathedral to Byron's mosque, a thousand spires encumber this metropolis of universal thought. At its base are inscribed some ancient titles of humanity, which architecture had not recorded. To the left of the entranceway is fastened the old white marble bas-relief of Homer, to the right the Polyglot Bible rears its seven heads. The hydra of romance bristles farther on, with several other hybrid forms, the Vedas and *Nibelungen.* The prodigious edifice, however, remains always unfinished. From the press, the giant machine unceasingly pumping out the intellectual sap of society, continually gushes new materials for its work. The entire human race is on the scaffold; every mind is a mason; the humblest bores his hole or lays his stone. Retif de la Bretonne brought his basket of plaster. Every day a new layer is laid down. Independently of the original and individual layer of each writer, there are collective contingents. The eighteenth century gave the Encyclopedia, the Revolution the *Moniteur.*[17] It is also a construction that ascends in endless spirals; it has a confusion of tongues, incessant activity, unwearied labor, eager competition involving all of humanity, promised refuge to intelligence against another deluge, against a flood of barbarism. It is the second Tower of Babel of the human species.

BOOK VI

CHAPTER I

AN IMPARTIAL LOOK AT THE ANCIENT
ADMINISTRATION OF JUSTICE

In the year of grace 1482, Robert d'Estouteville, knight, Sieur of Beyne, Baron of Ivry and St.-Andry in La Marche, councillor and chamberlain of the King, and Keeper of the Provosty of Paris, was a very happy character. Nearly seventeen years ago, on the seventh of November, 1465, the year of the great comet, the King had appointed him Provost of Paris, which was considered more a lordship than an office. *"Dignitas,"* says Joannes Lœmnœus, *"quae cum non exigua potestate politiam concernente, atque praerogativis multis et juribus conjuncta ist."*[1] It was a marvelous thing that in '82 there should still be a gentleman holding a King's commission whose appointment dated from the time of the marriage of the natural daughter of Louis XI to the Bastard of Bourbon. On the same day that Robert d'Estouteville had succeeded Jacques de Villiers in the provostship of Paris, Master Jean Dauvet superseded Messire Hélye de Thorrettes as first president of the Court of Parliament, Jean Jouvénel des Ursins supplanted Pierre de Morvilliers in the office of Chancellor of France, and Regnault des Dormans turned Pierre Puy out of the post of Master of Ordinary Requests to the King's household. And how many judges, chancellors, and masters had Robert d'Estouteville seen since he held the provostship of Paris? It was "given to him to keep," said the letters patent, and he had kept it well ever since. So closely had he clung to it, so completely had he identified himself with it, that he had escaped the results of that mania for changing his servants that possessed Louis XI, a jealous, niggardly, and slave-driving sovereign, who thought he could keep up the elasticity of his power by frequent removals and appointments. In addition, the gallant knight had obtained the guarantee that his son would inherit his position, and for two years already the name of the noble

Jacques d'Estouteville, Esquire, figured beside his own on the letter-head for the register of the Provosty of Paris. Rare indeed, and signal favor! It is true that Robert d'Estouteville was a good soldier, that he had loyally raised the banner against the *league of public welfare*,[2] and that he had presented the Queen with a most wonderful stag made of sweetmeats on the day of her entry into Paris. He was, moreover, on terms of friendship with Messire Tristan l'Ermite, Provost of the Marshals of the King's household. Messire Robert led a very pleasant and enjoyable life. In the first place, he earned a handsome salary, on which hung, like extra grapes on his vine, the revenues of the civil and criminal registries of the provostships, and also the civil and criminal revenues of the Court of the Châtelet, to say nothing of the tolls collected at the bridge of Mante and Corbeil, and other taxes in Paris, such as those on the millers of logs and the weighers of salt. Add to this the pleasure of riding in the city cavalcades and processions, and showing off in the half-scarlet, half-tanned robes of the city officers his fine military armor, which you may still admire sculptured on his tomb in the abbey of Valmont in Normandy, and his morion, which was dented at Montlhéry. And then, was it nothing to have absolute authority over the sergeants, the warden, the jailer, and the two auditors of the Châtelet, the sixteen commissaries of the sixteen quarters, the hundred and twenty horse patrols, the hundred and twenty archers, and the whole of the watch of the city? Was it nothing to administer justice, civil and criminal, to have a right to burn, to hang, to draw, besides the inferior jurisdiction "in the first instance," as the charters express it, in that viscounty of Paris with its seven noble bailiffs? Can you conceive anything more gratifying than to issue orders and pass sentence, as Messire Robert d'Estouteville daily did in the Grand Châtelet beneath the wide, low arches of Philip Augustus? Or to go, as he was accustomed, every evening to that charming house on the Rue Galilee, within the Palais Royal, which he owned because of his wife, Madame Ambroise de Loré, to rest from the fatigue of having sent some poor devil to pass the night in "that little lodge in the Rue de l'Escorcherie, which the provosts and *échevins* were in the habit of making their prison, being eleven feet long, seven feet four inches in width, and eleven feet high."

Not only did Messire Robert d'Estouteville have his particular court as Provost and Viscount of Paris but he also had a finger in the infliction of the sentences decreed by the King himself. There was not a head of any distinction but passed through his hands before it was delivered up to the executioner. It was he who fetched the Duke de Nemours from the Bastille St.-Antoine to convey him to the Halles, and Monsieur de St.-Pol, who, on his way to the Grève, exclaimed loudly and bitterly against his fate, to the great delight of the Provost, who was no friend to the Constable.

Here was more than enough then to make up both a happy and an illustrious life, and to earn a page in the fascinating book of the Provosts of Paris, where one could learn that Oudard de Villeneuve had a house on the Rue des Boucheries, that Guillaume de Hangest had both the Grande and the Petite Savoie, that Guillaume Thiboust left to the nuns of Ste.-Geneviève his houses on the Rue Clopi, and that Hughe Aubriot lived in the Hôtel du Porc-Epic, as well as other domestic details.

Here certainly were reasons more than sufficient to make a man take life with both patience and joy, and yet on the morning of January 7, 1482, Messire Robert d'Estouteville awoke in a terrible mood. Where did this bad mood come from? Was it because the sky was gloomy? Did his old belt of Montlhéry constrict with too military a pressure his provostship's plumpness? Had he seen a troop of ragamuffins in doublets without shirts, in hats without crowns, with wallet and flask at their side, passing along the street under his window? Did he have a vague presentiment of the three hundred and seventy pounds, sixteen sols, eight deniers, which the future King Charles VIII would deduct from the revenues of the provostship next year? The reader can decide; for our own part we are inclined to believe that he was in a bad mood because he was in a bad mood.

Besides, it was the day after a public holiday, a day of annoyance to everybody, and more especially to the magistrate whose duty it was to clear away all the filth, literal and figurative, made by a festival in Paris. And then, too, he had to sit for the trial of offenders at the Grand Châtelet. Now we have noted that judges in general arrange matters so that the days when they have to perform their judicial functions are their days of ill humor, so that they may be sure to have somebody on whom they can conveniently vent it in the name of the King, of the law, and of justice.

Meanwhile, the proceedings had begun without him. His deputies in civil and criminal court did the business for him, according to custom, and since eight in the morning dozens of citizens of both sexes, crowded into a dark corner of the court of the Châtelet, between a strong oak barrier and the wall, gazed with great fascination at the spectacle of civil and criminal justice administered somewhat haphazardly and arbitrarily by Master Florian Barbedienne, auditor to the Châtelet and lieutenant of Monsieur the Provost.

It was a small, low room, with a vaulted ceiling; at the farther end stood a table draped in fleurs-de-lis, a large empty armchair of carved oak, reserved for the Provost, and on the left a stool for the auditor, Master Florian. Below was the clerk busily writing. In front were the people, and before the door and the table a squadron of the Provost's men in frocks of purple camlet with white crosses. Two sergeants of the Parloir aux Bourgeois, in their jackets half scarlet and half blue, stood sentry before a low closed door, which was seen behind the table. A single small, ogival window, set in the thick wall, threw the faint light of a January morning on two grotesque figures—the capricious demon of stone sculptured as a sconce into the deepest recess of the vaulted ceiling and the judge seated at the extremity of the hall.

Imagine a figure seated at the Provost's table, leaning on his elbows between two piles of papers, his feet on the skirt of his plain brown robe, furred with white lambskin, which encircled his jolly, rubicund visage with red eyebrows that seemed glued on, winking and majestically swinging jowls that met under his double chin, Master Florian Barbedienne, auditor to the Châtelet.

Now this auditor was deaf. A small defect in an auditor. Master Florian, nevertheless, gave judgment without appeal, and very consistently too. It is most certain that it is quite enough for a judge to appear to listen, and this condition, the only essential one for strict justice, the venerable auditor fulfilled even more exactly since no noise could distract him.

He had among the audience a merciless comptroller of his sayings and doings in the person of our young friend Jehan Frollo du Moulin, who was sure to be seen everywhere in Paris except before the professors' chairs.

"Look," he said in a low tone to his companion, Robin Poussepain, who was grinning beside him while he commented on the scenes that were passing before them—"there is the pretty Jehanneton du Buisson of the Marché Neuf! Upon my soul he condemns her too, the old brute! He must have no more eyes than ears. Fifteen sous four deniers Parisis for having worn two strings of beads! It's a bit much! *Lex horrendi carminis erat.*[3] Who are they? Robin Chief-de-Ville, armor maker, for passing himself off as a master of his craft! He has to pay entry! Aiglet de Soins, and Hutin de Mailly—two gentlemen among these rascals, Corpus Christi! Ha! They have been dicing. When shall we see our Rector here? To pay a fine of one hundred pounds to the King! Bravo, Barbedienne! Deals blows like a deaf man—that he is! May I be my brother the Archdeacon if this shall prevent me from gambling by night, gambling while I live, gambling till I die, and betting my soul after my shirt! Holy Virgin! what girls! one after another, my pretty lambs! Ambroise Lécuyère, Isabeau la Paynette, Bérarde Gironin, I know them all, by God! Fined, fined, fined! That will teach you to wear golden belts! Ten sous Parisis, coquettes! Oh, the old, deaf imbecile of a judge! Oh, Florian the blockhead! Oh, Barbedienne, the booby! There he is at his feast! He eats plaintiffs, he eats trials, he chews, he stuffs himself until he is full. Fines, taxes, charges, damages, interest, stocks, pillory, jail, are Christmas cakes and St. John's marzipan to him! Look at him, the pig! Go on! What, another woman in love! Thibaud la Thibaude, no less! For being seen out of the Rue de Glatigny! Who is that son? Gieffroy Mabonne, one of the bowmen of the guard—for taking the Lord's name in vain! A fine for you, La Thibaude! A fine for you, Gieffroy! But ten to one the old idiot will confuse the two charges and make the woman pay for the oath and the soldier for love! Look, look, Robin! What are they bringing in now? There are an awful lot of sergeants. By Jupiter, there are all the hounds in the pack! That must be a fine head of game! A wild boar, surely! And so it is, Robin, so it is! And a rare one too, by Hercules! It is our prince, our Pope of Fools, our bell ringer, our one-eyed, hunchbacked, lame Quasimodo!"

Sure enough it was Quasimodo, bound, corded, tied up. The squadron of the Provost's men who surrounded him were accompanied by the captain of the watch in person, wearing the arms of France embroidered on the breast of his coat and those of the city on the back. At the same time there was nothing about Quasimodo, except his deformity, which could justify this display of halberts and muskets; he was silent, sullen, and quiet. His only eye merely gave from time to time an angry glance at the cords that bound him. He cast this same gaze around him from time to time, but he was so subdued that women pointed at him only to laugh.

Meanwhile, Master Florian was intently perusing the file containing the charges alleged against Quasimodo, which had been handed to him by the clerk. By means of this precaution, which he was accustomed to take before he proceeded to an examination, he acquainted himself beforehand with the name, condition, and offense of the prisoner, and was enabled to have in readiness replies to expected answers, and succeeded in extricating himself from all the vicissitudes of an interrogation without too grossly exposing his deafness. To him therefore the file was like the dog to the blind man. If, however, his infirmity chanced to betray itself now and then by some incoherent apostrophe or some unintelligible question, with the many it passed for profundity, with some few for stupidity. In either case the honor of the magistracy remained unimpeached; for it is better that a judge should be thought profound or stupid than deaf. Accordingly he took great pains to conceal his deafness from observation, and normally he was so successful that he was able to deceive himself on this point. This is easier than one might think. Every hunchback holds his head erect, every stammerer is fond of holding forth, every deaf person speaks softly. For his part he believed that he was somewhat hard of hearing, and this was the only concession that he made on this point to public opinion in moments of perfect frankness and self-examination.

After ruminating awhile on Quasimodo's affair, he threw back his head and half-closed his eyes, to make himself look more majestic and impartial, so that at that moment he was both deaf and blind—a twofold condition without which there is no perfect judge. In this magisterial attitude he opened the interrogation.

"Your name?"

Now, here was a case that the law had not provided for—the deaf interrogating the deaf.

Quasimodo, unaware of the question addressed to him, continued to look steadfastly at the judge without answering. The deaf judge, equally unaware of the deafness of the accused, conceiving that he had answered, as persons in his situation generally did, went on agreeably with mechanical and stupid aplomb. "Very well. Your age?"

Quasimodo maintained the same silence as before. The judge, again supposing that he had answered his question, continued, "Now your business?"

Still Quasimodo was silent. The people who witnessed this curious scene began to whisper and to look at one another.

"That will do," rejoined the imperturbable auditor when he presumed that the accused had finished his third answer. "You are accused before us, in the first place, of making a nighttime disturbance; second, of an assault on the person of a loose woman *in praejudicium meretricis;*[4] third, of disloyalty, sedition, and resistance to the archers of the guard of our Lord the King. What do you have to say for yourself on these points? Clerk, have you taken down the prisoner's answers thus far?"

At this unlucky question a roar of laughter burst from both clerk and audience, so vehement, so loud, so contagious, so universal, that neither of the deaf men could help but notice it. Quasimodo merely turned around and shrugged his hump with disdain, while Master Florian, equally astonished, and supposing that the mirth of the spectators had been provoked by some irreverent reply of the prisoner's, made visible to him by the rising of his shoulders, indignantly exclaimed, "For that answer, fellow, you deserve a halter. Do you know to whom you speak?"

This sally was not likely to check the explosion of general mirth. So odd and so ridiculous did it appear to all that the fit of laughter spread even to the sergeants of the Parloir aux Bourgeois, armed with pikes and spades, proverbial for their stupidity. Quasimodo alone preserved his gravity, for this very good reason, that he had not the least idea what was going on around him. The judge, more and more exasperated, thought fit to proceed in the same strain, hoping to strike the prisoner with a terror that would reverberate on the audience and make everyone more respectful.

"How dare you thus insult the auditor of the Châtelet, the deputy superintendent of the police of Paris, appointed to investigate all crimes, offenses, and misdemeanors; to control all trades; to prevent monopolies; to maintain the pavements, to check the black-marketing of poultry and game; to cleanse the city of filth and the air of contagious diseases; in short, to care for the public welfare, and all that without wages or hope of salary! Do you know that I am Florian

Barbedienne, own lieutenant of Monsieur the Provost, and, moreover, Commissary, Comptroller, examiner . . ."

The Lord knows when Master Florian would have finished this flight of eloquence had the low door behind him not suddenly opened and revealed the Provost himself. Master Florian did not stop short at his entrance but, turning half around on his heel, abruptly directed to the Provost the harangue that a moment before he was launching forth against Quasimodo. "Monseigneur," he said, "I demand what punishment it pleases you to pronounce on the prisoner here for audacious and heinous contempt of justice."

Out of breath with the exertion, he sat down and began to wipe off the perspiration that trickled from his forehead and fell in big drops on the parchments spread out before him. Messire Robert d'Estouteville frowned and commanded attention with a gesture so imperious and expressive that Quasimodo had some inkling of what was meant.

"What have you done to be brought here, scoundrel?" said the Provost sternly.

The poor devil, supposing that the Provost was inquiring his name, broke his usual silence and in a harsh and guttural voice replied, "Quasimodo."

The answer was so incongruous with the question that it once more excited laughter in the audience when Messire Robert, flushed with rage, exclaimed, "Are you making fun of me too, you arrant knave?"

"Bell ringer at Notre-Dame," replied Quasimodo, conceiving that the judge had inquired his profession.

"Bell ringer!" roared the Provost, who had got up that morning, as we have observed, in such an ill humor as not to need the further provocation of these strange responses. "Bell ringer! I'll have such a carillon rung with switches in every corner of Paris. Do you hear, scoundrel?"

"If you want to know my age," said Quasimodo, "I believe I shall be twenty next Martinmas."

This was too provoking—the Provost lost all patience. "What, wretch! Do you defy the Provost! Here, archers, take this fellow to the pillory of the Grève; let him be flogged and then turn him for an hour. By God, he shall pay for his insolence, and my pleasure is that this sentence be proclaimed by four trumpeters in the seven castellanies of the Viscounty of Paris."

The clerk instantly fell to work to record the sentence.

"*Ventre-Dieu!* Well sentenced!" cried Jehan Frollo du Moulin from his corner.

The Provost turned around and again fixed his flashing eyes on Quasimodo. "I truly believe," he said, "that the knave has dared to swear '*Ventre-Dieu*' in our presence. Clerk, add a fine of twelve deniers Parisis for the oath, and let half of it be given to the church of St.-Eustache. I have a prayer said at St.-Eustache."

In a few minutes the sentence was drawn up. The language was simple and concise. The practice of the Provosty and Viscounty of Paris had not then been laid down by the Judge Thibaut Baillet, and Roger Barmne, King's advocate; it was not then obstructed by that forest of quirks, cavils, and quibbles that these two lawyers planted before it at the beginning of the sixteenth century. Everything about it was clear, explicit, expeditious. It was all straightforward work, and you saw at once at the end of every path, uninterrupted by bushes or detours, the pillory, the gallows, and the wheel. You knew at least what to expect.

The clerk handed the sentence to the Provost, who affixed his seal and left the hall to continue his round of the courts in a mood that was likely to fill all the jails of Paris. Jehan Frollo and Robin Poussepain laughed in their sleeves, while Quasimodo looked on with an air of calm indifference.

While Master Florian Barbedienne was in his turn reading the sentence, before signing it, the clerk, feeling compassion for the wretched victim and hoping to obtain some mitigation of his punishment, approached as near as he could to the ear of the auditor and said, pointing at the same time to Quasimodo, "The poor fellow is deaf."

He conceived that this community of infirmity might awaken Master Florian's lenience in favor of the culprit. But, in the first place, as we have already mentioned, Master Florian was by no means anxious to have it known that he was deaf; and, in the next, he was so hard of hearing that he didn't catch a single syllable of what the clerk said to him. Pretending, nevertheless, to hear, he replied: "Aha! That is a different thing. I did not know that. In this case let him have another hour in the pillory"; and he signed the sentence with this revision.

"That's right!" cried Robin Poussepain, who bore Quasimodo a grudge. "This will teach him to rough people up."

CHAPTER II

THE RAT HOLE

With the reader's permission, we shall bring him back to the Place de Grève, which we yesterday left with Gringoire to follow La Esmeralda.

It is ten in the morning. The square looks as it does the day after a holiday. The pavement is strewn with garbage—rags, ribbons, feathers, drops of wax from the torches, crumbs from the public banquet. A good many citizens are strolling around, kicking the half-consumed cases of fireworks, admiring the Maison aux Pilliers, extolling the beautiful hangings of the preceding day, and looking at the nails that had held them, a last pleasure. The vendors of cider and beer are trundling their barrels through the groups. A few passersby, on business, come and go. The shopkeepers are calling to one another from their doors and conversing. The festival, the ambassadors, Coppenole, the Pope of Fools, are on every tongue, each striving to crack the best jokes and to laugh the loudest. And yet four sergeants on horseback, who have just posted themselves at the four sides of the pillory, have already attracted around them a considerable portion of the populace, who are crowded together on the square, ready to suffer immobility and boredom in the hope of enjoying a small execution.

Now, if the reader, after surveying this lively and noisy scene that is taking place all over the square, turns his eye toward the ancient half-Gothic, half-Roman building called the Tour-Roland, which forms the corner of the quay to the west, he may perceive at the angle of the facade a large public breviary, richly illuminated, sheltered from the rain by a small awning, and protected from thieves by an iron grating, which, nevertheless, does not prevent one's turning its pages. Beside this breviary is a narrow-pointed, unglazed window, looking out on the square and defended by two crossbars of iron—the only aperture for the admission of air and light to a small cell without a door, formed in the basement of the wall of the old building and full of a quiet more profound, a silence more melancholy, from its very proximity to a public square, the most populous and the most noisy in Paris, which is buzzing all around it.

This small room had been noted in Paris for three centuries, ever since Madame Rolande of the Tour-Roland, out of affection for her father, who had fallen in the Crusades, caused it to be cut out of the wall of her own house, for the purpose of shutting herself up in it forever, keeping no part of her mansion but this hole, the door of which was walled up and the window open winter and summer, and giving all the rest to the poor and to God. In this anticipated tomb the disconsolate lady had awaited death for twenty years, praying night and day for the soul of her father, lying on ashes without so much as a stone for a pillow, dressed in black sackcloth, and subsisting solely on the bread and water that the passersby, inspired by pity, left on her windowsill, thus living on charity after having performed it. At her death, at the moment of leaving this room for her last sepulchre, she bequeathed it forever to afflicted women, maids, wives, or widows, who should have occasion to pray much for themselves or others, and who should wish to bury themselves alive, on account of some great calamity or some extraordinary penance. The tears and blessings of the poor embalmed her memory, but to their great disappointment their pious benefactress could not be canonized for lack of sufficiently powerful patronage. Those who were a bit impious had hoped that the thing would be more easily accomplished in Paradise than in Rome, and had therefore at once prayed to God instead of the Pope on behalf of the deceased. Most of them had been content to hold her memory sacred and to make relics of her rags. The city had endowed in honor of this lady a public breviary, which was sealed to the wall near the window of the cell, so that passersby might stop from time to time, if not to pray so that prayer might induce them to think of giving alms so that the poor recluses, heirs of Madame Rolande, would not die of hunger.

In the cities of the Middle Ages tombs of this sort were not rare. In the busiest street, in the most crowded and noisy market, in the midst of the highways, almost under the horses' feet and the cart wheels, you frequently met with a cellar, a cave, a well, a walled and grated cabin, in which a human being, devoted to some everlasting sorrow, to some signal expiation, spent night and day in prayer. And none of those reflections that would be awakened in us at the present time by this strange sight, this horrid cell, a sort of intermediate link between a house and a grave, between the cemetery and the city; that being cut off from all community with mankind and henceforth numbered among the dead; that lamp consuming its last drop of oil in obscurity; that spark of life glimmering in a grave; that voice of incessant prayer in a cage of stone; that face forever turned toward the next world; that eye already lit by another sun; that ear pressed against the side of the tomb; that soul a prisoner in this body; this body a prisoner in this dungeon, and the moaning of that afflicted soul within this twofold envelope of flesh and granite—none of these ideas presented themselves to the crowd in those days. The unreasoning and far from subtle piety of that period could not see so many facets in a religious act. It took the thing as a whole and honored, venerated, on occasion sanctified the sacrifice, but without analyzing the suffering, or bestowing on it more than a moderate degree of pity. It carried from time to time a scrap to the wretched penitent, peeping through the hole to see if he were still alive; but it knew not his name; it scarcely knew how many years it was since he had begun to die; and to the stranger's inquiries about the living skeleton who was rotting in such a cave or cellar the neighbors merely replied, "It is the recluse."

Thus in that day people saw everything with the naked eye, without a magnifying glass, without exaggeration, without metaphysics. The microscope had not yet been invented, either for material or for spiritual things.

As we have just observed, this kind of seclusion in the heart of cities, though it inspired only a little amazement, was common. In Paris there were a considerable number of these cells for praying to God and doing penance, and almost all of them were occupied. The clergy, it is true, disliked to see them empty, because their emptiness implied lukewarmness in their flocks; and lepers were placed in them when no penitents offered themselves. Besides the cell of the Grève there was one at Montfaucon, another at the mortuary of the Innocents; a third, I do not remember exactly where, at the Logis Clichon, I believe; and others at various places, where you still find traces of them in customs, though the buildings have been swept away. On the hill of Ste.-Geneviève a kind of medieval Job sang for thirty years the seven penitential psalms on a dunghill at the bottom of a cistern, starting over as soon as he had finished and raising his voice highest at night; and to this day the antiques dealer imagines that he hears his voice as he enters the Rue du Puits-qui-parle, or the Street of the Talking Well.

But to return to the cell of the Tour-Roland. It is right to mention that since the death of Madame Rolande it had seldom been unoccupied for any length of time. Many a woman had come there to mourn, some their indiscretions and others the loss of parents or lovers. Parisian gossip pervades everything, even things that least concern it, and it was declared that very few widows had been seen among the number.

According to the fashion of the age, a Latin legend inscribed on the wall indicated to the literate passerby the pious function of this cell. Until the middle of the sixteenth century it was customary to explain the object of a building by a short motto placed over the door. Thus in France there may still be read over the side entrance of the seigneurial house of Tourville, *Sileto et spera,* or "Be quiet and hope"; in Ireland, beneath the coat of arms over the grand entrance to Fortescue castle, *Forte scutum salus ducum,* "A good coin, hail to the Chief"; in England, over the principal door of the hospitable mansion of Earl Cowper, *Tuum est,* or "This castle is yours." In those days every building was a thought.

Because there was no door to the cell of the Tour-Roland, there had been engraved in great Roman capital letters underneath the window these two words, *Tu, ora,* "Pray, you."[5]

Thus the people, whose plain common sense never looks for profound meanings in things, and who do not hesitate to translate *Ludovico Magno* "To Louis the Great," by Porte St.-Denis, gave to this dark, damp, loathsome place the name of "Rat Hole," an interpretation less sublime perhaps than the other but certainly more picturesque.

CHAPTER III

The Story of a Cake

During the time when our story took place, the cell of the Tour-Roland was occupied. If the reader wants to know by whom, he has only to listen to the conversation of three honest gossips, who, at the very moment at which we have directed his attention to the Rat Hole, were going to the very spot, heading up from the Châtelet along the riverside toward the Grève.

Two of them were dressed like wives of respectable citizens of Paris. Their fine white neckerchiefs; their linsey-woolsey petticoats, striped red and blue; their white worsted stockings, with colored clocks, pulled up tight on the leg; their square-toed shoes of tawny leather with black soles; and above all their headdress, a sort of high cap of shiny material covered with ribbons and lace, still worn by the women of Champagne, and also by the grenadiers of the Russian Imperial Guard—indicated that they belonged to that class of wealthy trades-folk that comes between what lackeys call a woman and what they style a lady. They wore neither gold rings nor gold crosses, evidently not on account of poverty but simply for fear of the sumptuary laws. Their companion was attired nearly in the same fashion, but in her dress and manner there was something that said "wife of a country no-tary." The height of her belt above the hips told that she had not been long in Paris. Add to this a plaited neckerchief, bows on her shoes, the stripes of her petticoat running breadthwise instead of lengthwise, and various other outrages equally abhorrent to good taste.

The first two walked with the step peculiar to the women of Paris who are showing the city to their provincial friends. The third held a big boy by one hand, while he carried a large cake in the other. We regret to report that because of the season, he used his tongue as a hand-kerchief. The boy let himself to be dragged along, *"non passibus aguis,"*[6] in the words of Virgil, and stumbled every moment, to the great irritation of his mother. It is true that he paid much greater attention to the cake than to the pavement. Some weighty reason no doubt prevented his taking a bite, for he did no more than look wistfully at it. His mother should have carried the cake. It was cruel to make a Tantalus of the chubby-cheeked rascal.

Meanwhile the three demoiselles—for the term *dames* was then re-served for noble females—were talking all at once.

"Let us hurry, Demoiselle Mahiette," said the youngest, who was also the lustiest of the three, to her country friend. "I am afraid we shall be too late. We were told at the Châtelet that he was to be put in the pillory right away."

"Bah! What are you talking about, Demoiselle Oudarde Musnier?" replied the other Parisian. "He is to stay two hours in the pillory. We shall have plenty of time. Have you ever seen anyone in the pillory, my dear Mahiette?"

"Yes," answered Mahiette, "in Reims."

"Your pillory in Reims! Why, what is that? A wretched cage, where they pillory only peasants!"

"Peasants, indeed!" rejoined Mahiette. "At the Linen Market in Reims we have seen some very good criminals—people who murdered both father and mother. Peasants, indeed! What do you take us for, Gervaise?"

It is certain that the provincial lady was about to become angry in defense of the honor of her pillory. Luckily the discreet Demoiselle Oudarde gave a discreet turn to the conversation.

"What do you say, Mahiette," she asked, "to our Flemish ambassadors? Have you ever had any like them in Reims?"

"I confess," replied Mahiette, "that Paris is the only place for Flemish like them."

"Did you see among the ambassadors the big one who is a hosier?"

"Yes," said Mahiette, "he looks rather like Saturn."

"And the big one whose face looks like a stomach?" Gervaise asked.

"And the little one whose little eyes are so red-rimmed that they look like two pieces of burning charcoal?"

"And their horses, what beautiful animals, decked out as they are in the fashion of their country!"

"Ah, my dear!" exclaimed Mahiette, assuming in her turn an air of superiority, "what would you say if you had been in Reims at the coronation in '61, and seen the horses of the princes and of the King's retinue! There were saddles and trappings of all sorts; some of damask cloth and fine cloth of gold lined with sable; others of velvet furred with ermine; others all covered with jewelry and large gold and silver bells. Think of the money all that must have cost! And then the beautiful pages that were on them!"

"That doesn't prevent the Flemish from having beautiful horses," replied Demoiselle Oudarde drily, "and it also doesn't make it any less true that they had a superb supper yesterday at Monsieur the Provost's at the Hôtel de Ville, where they served them candy-covered almonds, mulled wine, spices, and other unusual delicacies."

"What are you saying, my dear?" cried Gervaise. "It was at Monsieur the Cardinal's at the Petit-Bourbon that the Flemish ate."

"Not at all! At the Hôtel de Ville."

"No, at the Petit-Bourbon."

"It was certainly at the Hôtel de Ville," Oudarde continued sharply. "Doctor Scourable made a speech in Latin, with which they were very pleased. My husband, who is a licensed bookseller, told me so."

"It was at the Petit-Bourbon," answered Gervaise no lcss hotly, "and here is what Monsieur the Cardinal's procurer presented them with— a dozen double quarts of white mulled wine, claret and red wine, twenty-four loaves of gilded double marzipan from Lyon, as many torches at two pounds a piece, and six half barrels of wine from Beaune, both white and claret, of the best variety they could find. I hope that is proof positive for you. I have it from my husband, who works at the Parloir-aux-Bourgeois, who was just this morning comparing the Flemish ambassadors with the Abyssinian Prete-Jan and the Emperor of Trebisonde, who came from Mesopotamia to Paris under the last King. They had rings in their ears."

"It is so true that they dined at the Hôtel de Ville," replied Oudarde, who was a bit disturbed by this display, "that there had never been seen such a triumph of meats and candy-covered almonds."

"I tell you that they were served by Le Sec, sergeant of the City, at the Hôtel du Petit-Bourbon, and that you are the one who is wrong."

"At the Hôtel de Ville, I say."

"At the Petit-Bourbon, my dear! They even engraved magic glasses with the word *hope,* which is inscribed on its main entrance."

"At the Hôtel de Ville! The Hôtel de Ville! Husson le Voir even played the flute!"

"I say no!"

"I say yes!"

"I say no!"

The good, plump Oudarde was about to reply and headgear might have become involved in the quarrel if Mahiette had not suddenly cried, "What is going on there? See what a crowd is collected at the foot of the bridge? There seems to be something in the middle that they are looking at."

"Surely I hear the sound of a tambourine," said Gervaise. "I daresay it is young Esmeralda performing tricks with her goat. Quick, Mahiette, and pull your boy along. You have come to see the curiosities of Paris. Yesterday you saw the Flemish; today you must see the gypsy."

"The gypsy!" exclaimed Mahiette, starting back and forcibly grasping the arm of her son. "God forbid! She might steal my boy! Come, Eustache!"

With these words she began to run along the quay toward the Grève, till she had left the bridge a considerable distance behind her. Soon the boy, whom she dragged after her, tripped and fell on his knees. She stopped breathless, and Oudarde and Gervaise overtook her.

"That gypsy steal your boy," said Gervaise, "that is a strange idea!"

Mahiette shook her head with a pensive look.

"And what is still more strange," observed Oudarde, "the Sack Woman[7] has the same notion of the gypsies."

"Who is the Sack Woman?" inquired Mahiette.

"You must be vastly ignorant in your Reims not to know that," replied Oudarde. "Why, the recluse of the Rat Hole."

"What! The poor woman to whom we are carrying the cake?"

Oudarde nodded affirmatively. "Just so. You will see her soon at her window on the Grève. She has the same idea as you of those gypsy tramps, who go around drumming on tambourines and telling fortunes. Nobody knows why she has such a horror of the Zingari and gypsies. But you, Mahiette, why should you take to your heels that way at the mere sight of them?"

"Oh!" said Mahiette, clasping her boy's head in both her hands, "I would not for the world have the same thing happen to me as befell Paquette la Chantefleurie."

"Ah! You must tell us that story, good Mahiette," said Gervaise, taking her by the arm.

"I will," answered Mahiette. "But how ignorant you must be in your Paris not to know that! But we don't have to stop while I tell you the story. You must know, then, that Paquette la Chantefleurie was a handsome girl of eighteen just when I was so myself, that is, eighteen years ago, and it is her own fault that she is not at this day, like me, a hearty, comely mother of six and thirty, with a husband and a boy. She was the daughter of Guybertaut, minstrel of Reims, the same one that played before King Charles VII at his coronation, when he went down our river Vesle from Sillery to Muison, and the Maid of Orléans was in the barge with him. Paquette's father died while she was still an infant; so she had only her mother, who was the sister of Monsieur Matthieu

Pradon, master brazier here in Paris, on the Rue Parin-Garlin, who died only last year. You see she came of a good family. The mother was unluckily a kind, easy woman and taught Paquette nothing but to do a little needlework and make herself finery, which helped to keep them very poor. They lived in Reims, along the river, on the Rue de Folle Peine. In '61, the year of the coronation of our King Louis XI, whom God preserve! Paquette was so lively and so handsome that everybody called her La Chantefleurie. Poor girl! What beautiful teeth she had! And how she would laugh so that she might show them! Now a girl that laughs a great deal is on the way to crying, fine teeth spoil fine eyes. Chantefleurie and her mother had great difficulty earning a livelihood; since the death of the minstrel their circumstances had been getting worse and worse; their needlework brought them no more than six deniers a week. How different from the time when old Guybertaut received twelve sols Parisis for a single song, as he did at the coronation! One winter—it was that of the same year '61—when the poor creatures had neither cordwood nor kindling, the weather was very cold, which gave Chantefleurie such a beautiful color that the men called her Paquette, and this led to her ruin.—Eustache, don't play with the cake!—We all knew that she was lost as soon as we saw her come to church one Sunday with a gold cross on her neck. At fourteen! Can you believe it? Her first lover was the young Vicomte de Cermontreuil, whose castle is about three-quarters of a league from Reims. And then My Lord Henri de Triancourt, cavalryman of the King, and then always descending, Chiart de Beaulion, sergeant at arms, and then falling some more, Guery Aubergeon, King's valet, and then Macé de Frépus, barber to Monsieur the Dauphin, and then Thévenin le Moine, train bearer of the King, and then always older and less noble, she fell on Guillaume Racine, minstrel, and Thierry de Mer, lantern maker. Then, poor Chantefleurie, all men became the same to her. She had come to her last gold coin. What can I say, my ladies? At the coronation of '61, she shared a bed with the king of the petty criminals. In the same year!" Mahiette sighed, brushing away a tear that started from her eye.

"There is nothing very extraordinary in this history," said Gervaise, "nor, as far as I can see, has it anything to do with gypsies or children."

"Have patience," replied Mahiette. "You will soon see that it has. In '66, it will be sixteen years this very month on St. Paul's Day, Paquette brought into the world a little girl. How delighted she was, poor thing! She had long been wishing for a child. Her mother, poor soul, who had always turned a blind eye to her ways, was now dead; so Paquette had nothing in the world to love, and none to love her. For five years, ever since her fall, she had been a miserable creature, poor Chantefleurie! She was alone, alone in this life, pointed at and hooted in the streets, cuffed by the beadles, teased by little ragged urchins. By this time she was twenty—an age at which, it is said, loose women begin to be old. Her way of life scarcely brought her more than her needlework had formerly done. For every new wrinkle, she earned a cent less. The winter had set in sharp, and wood was again rare on her hearth, and bread in her cupboard. She could no longer work, for in becoming decadent she had become lazy, and she suffered all the more for it because in becoming lazy she became more decadent. She was, of course, very sorrowful, very miserable, and her tears wore deep channels in her cheeks. But in her degraded and forlorn condition it seemed to her that she should be less degraded and less forlorn if she had anything or anyone in the world that she could love, and that could love her. She felt that this must be a child, because nothing but a child could be innocent enough for that. Women of her class must have either a lover or a child to engage their affections or they are very unhappy. Now, since Paquette could not find a lover she set her whole heart on a child, and prayed to God night and day for one. And he took compassion on her, and gave her a little girl. Her joy is not to be described. How she hugged and fondled her infant! It was quite a fury of caresses and kisses. She nursed it herself, made it swaddling out of her own covers, and after that felt neither cold nor hunger. Her beauty returned. An old maid makes a young mother. In a short time she again pursued the life of gallantry and spent all the money she made on frocks and caps and lace and little satin bonnets and all sorts of finery for her child. Monsieur Eustache, haven't I told you not to eat that cake? It is certain that little Agnes—that was the name given to the child at her christening—was more decorated with ribbons and embroidery than a princess. Among other things she had a pair of little shoes, such as I'll be bound Louis XI never had. Her mother had made and embroidered them herself with the utmost art and skill of her needle. A prettier pair of little pink slippers was never seen. They were not longer than my thumb, and you had to have seen the child's feet come out of them or you would never believe they could go into them. But then those feet were so small, so pretty, so rosy—more than the satin of the shoes. When you have children, Oudarde, you will know that nothing is so pretty as those delicate little feet and hands."

"I desire nothing better," said Oudarde with a sigh, "but I must wait till it is the good pleasure of Monsieur Andry Musnier."

"Paquette's baby," resumed Mahiette, "had not merely handsome feet. I saw her when she was only four months old. Oh! She was a love! Her eyes were larger than her mouth, and she had the most beautiful dark hair, which already began to curl. What a superb brunette she would have made at sixteen! Her mother became every day more and more mad about her. She hugged her, she kissed her, she washed her, she tickled her, she dressed her up—she was ready to eat her. In the wildness of her joy she thanked God for the gift. But it was her tiny pink feet above all that she was never tired of admiring. She marveled at them, held them up to the light, pitied them when she walked the baby across the bed. She could not get over their tininess. She could have spent her whole life on her knees, putting on and taking off shoes from those little feet as if they were the feet of the baby Jesus himself."

"This is a very good story," said Gervaise in an undertone, "but where are the gypsies in all of this?"

"Why, here," replied Mahiette. "One day a party of very strange-looking people on horseback arrived in Reims. They were beggars and tramps who roved around the country, headed by their duke and their counts. They were swarthy; they had curly hair and wore silver rings in their ears. The women were uglier than the men. Their complexion was even darker. They went bareheaded; a shabby mantle covered the body, an old piece of sackcloth was tied around the shoulders, and their hair was worn in ponytails. The children, who were squirming around on their laps, were enough to frighten apes. They were a group of excommunicated people. These hideous people had come—so it was said—straight from Egypt to Reims through Poland; the Pope had confessed them and ordered them by way of penance to wander for seven years through the world without sleeping in beds. They were called Penanciers, and they stank. They claimed ten pounds Tournois of all archbishops, bishops, and crosiered and mitered abbots, by virtue of a Bull of the Pope. They came to Reims to tell fortunes in the name of the King of Algiers and the Emperor of Germany. This was quite enough, as you may suppose, to cause them to be forbidden to enter the city. The whole band then camped out at the Porte de Braine, on the mill hill, by the old chalk pits, and all Reims went to see them. They looked at your palm and foretold wonderful things. At the same time there were various reports about their stealing children, cutting purses, and eating human flesh. Prudent persons said to the simple, 'Don't go near them,' yet went themselves in secret. It was quite the rage. The fact is, they told things that would have astonished a cardinal. Mothers were not a little proud of their children after the gypsies had read all sorts of marvels written in their hands in Pagan and Turkish. One had an emperor, another a Pope, a third a great captain. Poor Chantefleurie was seized with curiosity; she was anxious to know her fortune, and whether little Agnes would one day be Empress of Armenia or something like that. She carried her to the gypsies. The women admired the infant, they fondled her, they kissed her with their dark lips, they were astonished at her tiny hand, to the great delight of the poor mother. But above all they praised her delicate feet and her pretty little shoes. The child was not quite a year old. She had begun to lisp a word or two, laughed at her mother like a little madcap, and was plump and fat and had a thousand charming, angelic gestures and tricks up her sleeve. But she was frightened by the gypsies and began crying. Her mother kissed and cuddled her, and away she went, overjoyed at the good luck the fortune-tellers had promised her Agnes. She was to be a beauty, a paragon, a queen. She returned to her garret in the Rue de Folle Peine quite proud to have brought home a queen. The next day she softly slipped out for a moment while the infant lay asleep on the bed, leaving the door slightly open, and ran to tell an acquaintance in the Rue de la Séchesserie how there would come a time when her dear little Agnes would have the King of England and the Archduke of Ethiopia to wait on her at her table and a hundred other marvelous things. On her return, not hearing the child cry as she went upstairs, she said to herself, 'That's lucky! Baby is still asleep.' She found the door wider open than she had left it; she went in hastily and ran to the bed. Poor mother! The infant was gone, and nothing belonging to it was left except one of its pretty little shoes. She rushed out of the room, darted downstairs, screaming, 'My child! My child! Who has taken my child?' The house stood by itself, and the street was empty; nobody could give her any clue. She went through the town, searching

every street; she ran back and forth the whole day, distracted, mad-
dened, glaring in at the doors and windows like a wild beast that has
lost her young. She was panting, disheveled, she was fearful to see, and
there was a fire in her eyes that dried up her tears. She stopped the
passersby, crying, 'My little girl! My little girl! My pretty little girl!
Tell me where to find my child, and I will be your dog's servant, you
can eat my heart out.' She ran into Monsieur le curé de St. Rémy and
said to him, 'I will work the earth with my fingernails, please give me
back my daughter.' It was quite pitiful, Oudarde, and I assure you I
saw a very hard-hearted man, Master Ponce Lacabre, the attorney,
shed tears at it. Poor, poor mother! In the evening she went home.
While she was away a neighbor had seen two gypsy women slip secretly up her stairs with a large bundle and immediately come down
again, shut the door, and hurry off. After they were gone cries as if of
a child had been heard coming from Paquette's lodging. The mother
laughed with joy, flew upstairs, dashed open the door, and went in. The
thing was, Oudarde, instead of her lovely baby, so smiling, and so
plump, and so ruddy, who was a gift from God, she found a sort of little monster, a hideous, deformed, one-eyed, limping thing, squalling
and creeping around the floor. She covered her eyes in horror. 'Oh,' she
said, 'can it be that the witches have changed my Agnes into this frightful animal?' Her neighbors took the little clubfoot away immediately;
he would have driven her mad. He was the monstrous child of some
gypsy or other, who had given herself up to the devil. He appeared
to be about four years old and spoke a language that was not a human
language—such words were never before heard in this world. Chantefleurie snatched up the tiny shoe, all that was left her of all that she had
loved. She lay so long, without moving, without speaking, apparently
without breathing, that everybody thought she was dead. All at once
she trembled in every limb; she covered the precious relic with passionate kisses and burst into a fit of sobs, as if her heart was going to
break. I assure you we all wept along with her. 'Oh, my baby!' she said,
'my dear little baby! Where are you?' It made one's heart bleed. I can't
help crying still at the thought of it. Our children, you see, are like the
very marrow of our bones. Oh, my Eustache, my poor Eustache, if I
were to lose you, what would become of me! Eventually Chantefleurie
sprang up and ran through the streets of Reims, shouting, 'To the
camp of the gypsies! Let the witches be burned!' The gypsies were

gone. It was a dark night; nobody could tell which way they had gone. The next day, which was Sunday, they found on a heath between Gueux and Tilloy, about two leagues from Reims, the remains of a large fire, a few ribbons that belonged to Paquette's child, and several drops of blood and goat droppings. There could be no further doubt that the gypsies had Saturday night held their Sabbath on this heath and devoured the child in the company of their master, Beelzebub, as is the custom among Mahometans. When Chantefleurie heard these horrid things she did not weep; she moved her lips as if to speak, but could not. The day after her hair was quite gray, and on the next she disappeared."

"A frightful story indeed," exclaimed Oudarde, "and enough to draw tears from a Burgundian!"

"I am no longer surprised," said Gervaise, "that you are so terribly afraid of the gypsies."

"You are quite right," replied Oudarde, "to get out of their way with Eustache, especially because these are gypsies from Poland."

"Not so," said Gervaise. "It is said that they come from Spain and Catalonia."

"Catalonia?" replied Oudarde.

"It's possible, Catalonia, Wallonia, Polonia, I always confuse those three places. What is certain is that they are gypsies."

"And not less certain," continued Gervaise, "that their teeth are long enough to eat little children. And I would not be surprised if La Esmeralda were to pick a bit now and then, though she has such a small, pretty mouth. Her white goat plays so many marvelous tricks that there must be something wrong at bottom."

Mahiette walked on in silence. She was absorbed in that reverie that is a sort of prolongation of a doleful story, and that continues till it has communicated its vibration to every fiber of the heart. "And did you never know what became of Chantefleurie?" asked Gervaise. Mahiette made no reply. Gervaise repeated the question, gently shaking her arm and calling her by her name.

"What became of Chantefleurie?" she said, mechanically repeating the words whose impression was still fresh upon her ear. Then, making an effort to recall her attention to the sense of those words: "Ah!" said she sharply. "It was never known what became of her."

After a pause she added, "Some said they saw her leave Reims in the dusk of the evening by the Porte Fléchembault; and others at daybreak by the old Porte Basée. Her gold cross was found hanging on the stone cross in the field where the fair is held. It was this trinket that occasioned her fall in '61. It was a present from the handsome Vicomte de Cermontreuil, her first admirer. Paquette would never part with it, distressed as she had often been. She clung to it as to life. Of course, when we heard how and where it was found, we all concluded that she was dead. Yet there are people who declared they had seen her on the road to Paris walking barefoot on the stones. But, in this case, she must have gone out at the gate of Vesle, and all these accounts cannot be true. My own opinion is that she did actually go by the gate of Vesle, not only out of the town but out of the world."

"I don't understand you," said Gervaise.

"The Vesle," replied Mahiette, with a melancholy smile, "is our river."

"Poor Chantefleurie!" said Oudarde, shuddering. "Drowned!"

"Drowned!" replied Mahiette. "Ah! How it would have spoiled good Father Guybertaut's singing, while floating in his rowboat beneath the bridge of Tinqueux, had he been told that his dear little Paquette would someday pass under that same bridge, but without song and without a boat!"

"And the little shoe?" said Gervaise.

"Disappeared with the mother," replied Mahiette.

Oudarde, a comely, tenderhearted woman, would have been satisfied to sigh along with Mahiette; but Gervaise, who was of a more inquisitive disposition, had not got to the end of her questions.

"And the monster?" she said all at once, resuming her inquiries.

"What monster?" asked Mahiette.

"The little gypsy monster, left by the witches at Chantefleurie's in exchange for her child. What was done with it? I hope you drowned that too."

"Oh, no!" replied Mahiette.

"Burned then, I suppose? The best thing that could be done with a witch's child."

"Not that either, Gervaise. The Archbishop had compassion on the gypsy boy; he carefully took the devil out of him, blessed him, and sent him to Paris to be left in the wooden cradle at Notre-Dame as a foundling."

"Those bishops," said Gervaise grumblingly, "because they are learned men, never do anything like other people. Only think, Oudarde, to pop the devil into the place of the foundlings! For it is quite certain that this little monster could be nothing else. Well, Mahiette, and what became of him in Paris? No charitable person would look at him, I suppose."

"I don't know," replied her country friend. "Just at that time my husband bought the notary's position in Beru, about two leagues from Reims, and we had nothing more to do with this story. In front of Beru, there are the two hills of Cernay that block the view of the church towers of Reims."

Still chatting like this, the worthy trio reached the Place de Grève. Engrossed by the subject of their discourse, they had passed the public breviary in the Tour-Roland without being aware of it and turned mechanically toward the pillory, around which the crowd was every moment increasing. It is probable that the scene which at this moment attracted their attention would have made them completely forget the Rat Hole and their intention of calling there had not Eustache, whom Mahiette still led by the hand, as if apprised by some instinct that the Rat Hole was behind them, cried, "Mother, now may I eat the cake?"

Had the boy been less hasty, that is to say, less greedy, he would have waited till the party had returned to the house of Master Andry Musnier, Rue Madame la Valence in the Université, when there would have been the two branches of the Seine and the five bridges of the Cité between the cake and the Rat Hole, before he had ventured the timid question, "Mother, now may I eat the cake?"

That very question, an imprudent one when it was asked by Eustache, roused Mahiette's attention.

"Upon my word," said she, "we are forgetting the recluse. Show me your Rat Hole, that I may give her the cake."

"Let's go at once," said Oudarde. "It is an act of charity."

This was not what Eustache wanted. "She can't have my cake," he said, dashing his head against his two shoulders by turns, which in a case of this kind is a sign of displeasure.

The three women turned back, and, having arrived at the Tour-Roland, Oudarde said to the other two: "We must not all look in at the hole at once or we'll frighten Sachette. You two pretend to be reading the Dominus in the breviary while I peep in at the window—she knows me a little. I will tell you when to come."

She went up by herself to the window. The moment she looked in, a profound pity took possession of her every feature, and her open, good-humored face changed color and expression as suddenly as if it had passed out of the sunshine into the moonlight; a tear trembled in her eye and her mouth was contracted as when a person is going to weep. A moment afterward she put her finger on her lips and made a sign for Mahiette to come and look.

Mahiette went in silence and on tiptoe, as though approaching the bed of a dying person. It was in truth a sad sight that presented itself to the two women, while they looked in without stirring or breathing at the barred window of the Rat Hole.

The cell was small, wider than deep, with a vaulted ceiling, and seen from within resembled the hollow of a large episcopal miter. On the stone floor, in one corner, a woman was seated or, rather, crouched. Her chin rested on her knees, while her arms and clasped hands encircled her legs. Doubled up in this manner, wrapped in brown sackcloth, her long, lank gray hair falling over her face down to her feet, she presented at first sight a strange figure standing out from the dark ground of the cell, a sort of blackish triangle that the ray entering at the window revealed like one of those specters seen in dreams or in Goya's extraordinary paintings, half shadow and half light, pale, motionless, gloomy, cowering on a grave or before the grating of a dungeon. It was neither woman, nor man, nor living creature. It had no definite form; it was a shapeless figure, a sort of vision in which the real and the fantastic were contrasted like light and shade. Scarcely could you distinguish under her streaming hair the forbidding profile of an emaciated and severe face; scarcely did the ample robe of sackcloth that enfolded her permit the toes of a bare foot to be seen peeping from beneath it and curling up on the hard, cold pavement. The faint likeness of the human form discernible under this garb of mourning made one shudder.

This figure, which you would have supposed to be embedded in the stone floor, appeared to be deprived of motion, breath, and thought. With only the sackcloth for clothing, in the month of January, barefoot on a pavement of granite, without fire, in the gloom of a dungeon, whose oblique window admitted only the chill breeze but not the cheering sun, she seemed not to suffer, not even to feel. You would have thought that she had turned herself to stone with the dungeon, to ice with the season. Her hands were clasped, her eyes fixed. At first glance you would have taken her for a specter, at second for a statue.

At intervals, however, her livid lips opened for the purpose of breathing, and quivered; but they looked as dead and as will-less as leaves driven by the blast. Meanwhile those haggard eyes cast a look, an ineffable look, a profound, melancholy, imperturbable look, steadfastly fixed on a corner of the cell that could not be seen from outside; a look that seemed to connect all gloomy thoughts of that afflicted spirit with some mysterious object.

Such was the creature to whom was given from her garb the familiar name of Sachette, and from her dwelling that of the recluse.

The three women—for by this time Gervaise had joined Oudarde and Mahiette—peeped in at the window. Their heads cut off the faint light that entered the dungeon, but the wretched being whom they deprived of it appeared not to notice them. "Let us not disturb her," said Oudarde softly; "she is praying."

Mahiette scrutinized all this time, with an anxiety that increased every moment, that wan, withered, deathlike head under its veil of hair. Her eyes filled with tears. "It would be most extraordinary!" she muttered. Putting her head between the bars of the aperture, she was able to see the corner on which the eye of the unhappy recluse was still riveted. When she drew back her head from the window, her cheeks were bathed with tears.

"What do you call this woman?" she said to Oudarde, who replied, "We call her Sack Woman."

"For my part," rejoined Mahiette, "I call her Paquette la Chantefleurie."

Then, laying her finger on her lips, she made a sign to the astonished Oudarde to put her head through the aperture and look. Oudarde did so, and saw in the corner on which the eye of the recluse was fixed in gloomy ecstasy a tiny shoe of pink satin, embroidered all over with gold and silver. Gervaise looked in after Oudarde, and the three women began weeping at the sight of the unfortunate mother. Neither their looks, however, nor their tears, were noticed by the recluse. Her hands remained clasped, her lips mute, her eyes fixed, and that look bent on the little shoe was enough to break the heart of anyone who knew her story.

The three women gazed without uttering a word; they dared not speak even in a whisper. This profound silence, this intense sorrow, this utter forgetfulness of all but one object, produced on them the effect of a high mass at Easter or Christmas. It awed them too into silence, into devotion; they were ready to fall on their knees.

At length Gervaise, the most inquisitive, and of course the least tenderhearted of the three, called to the recluse, in hopes of making her speak, "Sack Woman!" Three times she repeated the call, raising her voice every time. The recluse did not stir; it drew from her neither word, nor look, nor sigh, nor sign of life.

"Sack Woman!" said Oudarde in turn, in a kinder and more soothing tone. The recluse was silent and motionless as before.

"A strange woman!" exclaimed Gervaise. "I truly believe that a bombardment would not awaken her."

"Perhaps she is deaf!" said Oudarde, sighing.

"Perhaps blind," added Gervaise.

"Perhaps dead," ejaculated Mahiette.

It is certain that if the spirit had not yet left that inert, lethargic, and apparently inanimate frame, it had at least retired to and shut itself up in recesses that the perceptions of the external organs could not reach.

"What shall we do to rouse her?" said Oudarde. "If we leave the cake in the window, some boy will run away with it."

Eustache, whose attention had till this moment been taken up by a little cart drawn by a great dog that had just passed by, suddenly perceived that his mother and her friends were looking through the window at something, and, curious to learn what it was, he clambered up on a post, and, thrusting his red, chubby face in at the aperture, he cried, "Just look, Mother! Who is that?"

At the sound of the child's clear, fresh, sonorous voice, the recluse started. She instantly turned her head with the sharp movement of a steel spring, her long, bony fingers drew back the hair from her face, and she fixed her astonished, bitter, desperate eyes on the boy. That look was like lightning. "Oh, my God!" she instantly exclaimed, burying her face in her lap, and it seemed as if her harsh voice ripped open her chest, "at least keep those of others out of my sight!"

This shock, however, had awakened the recluse. A long shudder thrilled her whole frame; her teeth chattered; she half-raised her head, and, taking hold of her feet with her hands as if to warm them, she cried, "Oh! How cold it is!"

"Poor creature," said Oudarde, with deep compassion, "would you like a little fire?"

She shook her head in sign of refusal.

"Well, then," rejoined Oudarde, offering her a bottle, "here is some mulled wine, which will warm you."

Again she shook her head, looked steadfastly at Oudarde, and said, "Water!"

Oudarde remonstrated. "No, Sack Woman," said she, "that is not fit drink for January. Take some of this mulled wine and a bit of the cake we have brought you."

She pushed aside the cake, which Mahiette held out to her. "Some brown bread," was her reply.

"Here," said Gervaise, catching the charitable spirit of her companions and taking off her wool cloak. "Here is a cloak that is a bit warmer than yours. Put it over your shoulders."

She refused the cloak, as she had the bottle and the cake, with a single word, "Sackcloth."

"But surely," resumed the kindhearted Oudarde, "you must have noticed that yesterday was a festival."

"Ah! Yes, I did," replied the recluse. "For the last two days I have had no water in my pitcher." After a pause she added, "Why should the world think of me when I do not think of it? When the fire is out the ashes get cold."

As if tired by the effort of speaking, she dropped her head onto her knees. The simple Oudarde conceived that in the concluding words she was again complaining of cold. "Do have a fire, then," she said.

"Fire!" exclaimed the recluse, in a strange tone. "And would you make one for the poor baby who has been underground these fifteen years?"

Her limbs shook, her voice trembled, her eyes flashed; she raised herself up on her knees; suddenly she extended her white, skinny hand toward the boy. "Take away that child," she cried. "The gypsy will soon pass."

She then sank on her face, and her forehead struck the floor with a sound like that of a stone falling on it. The three women concluded that she was dead. Soon, however, she began to stir, and they saw her crawl on hands and knees to the corner where the little shoe was. She was then out of their sight, and they didn't dare look after her; but they heard a thousand kisses and a thousand sighs, mingled with piercing shrieks, and dull, heavy thumps, as if from a head striking against a wall. At last, after one of these blows, so violent as to make all three start, they heard nothing more.

"She must have killed herself!" said Gervaise, venturing to put her head in at the aperture. "Sack Woman!"

"Sack Woman!" repeated Oudarde.

"Good God!" exclaimed Gervaise, "she does not stir. She must be dead! Sack Woman! Sack Woman!"

Mahiette, shocked to such a degree that she could scarcely speak, made an effort. "Wait a moment," she said. Then, going close to the window, "Paquette!" she cried, "Paquette la Chantefleurie!"

A boy who thoughtlessly blows on a badly lit firecracker and makes it explode in his eyes is not more frightened than was Mahiette at the effect of this name so abruptly pronounced.

The recluse shook all over, sprang up on her feet, and bounded to the window, her eyes at the same time flashing fire, with such vehemence that the three women retreated to the parapet of the quay. The haggard face of the recluse appeared pressed against the bars of the window. "Aha!" she cried, with a horrid laugh. "It is the gypsy who calls me!"

The scene that was just then unfolding at the pillory caught her eye. Her brow wrinkled with horror, she stretched both her skeleton arms out of her cell and cried with a voice unlike that of a human being: "So it is you, gypsy woman, it is you, child stealer, who calls me. Curse you! A curse upon you!"

CHAPTER IV

A TEAR FOR A DROP OF WATER

These words were, if we may so express it, the point of junction of two scenes that had thus far been developing simultaneously, each on its particular stage; the one, which has just been described, at the Rat Hole; the other, which we are about to describe, at the pillory. The first had been witnessed only by the three women whom the reader has just met; the spectators of the other consisted of the crowd we saw a little while ago gathering in the Place de Grève around the pillory and the gallows.

This crowd, to whom the appearance of the four sergeants posted at the four corners of the pillory ever since nine in the morning intimated that some poor wretch was about to suffer, if not capital punishment, then a flogging, the loss of ears, or some other infliction—this crowd had increased so rapidly that the sergeants had been obliged more than once to keep it back by means of their horses' heels and the free use of their whips.

The mob, accustomed to wait whole hours for public executions, did not show too much impatience. They amused themselves with gazing at the pillory, a very simple contrivance, consisting of a cube of masonry some ten feet high, hollow within. A rude flight of steps of rough stone led to the upper platform, on which was seen a horizontal wheel of oak. On this wheel the culprit was bound on his knees with his hands tied behind him. An axle of timber, moved by a capstan concealed from sight in the little building, caused the wheel to revolve in the horizontal plane, and thus exhibited the culprit's face to every point of the square in succession. This was called turning a criminal.

Thus, you see, the pillory of the Grève was by no means as interesting an object as the pillory of the Halles. There was nothing architectural, nothing monumental about it: it had no roof with iron cross, no octagon lantern, no slender pillars spreading from the edge of the roof into capitals of acanthi and flowers, no fantastic and monstrous waterspouts, no carved woodwork, no delicate sculpture deeply cut in stone.

Here the eye was forced to be content with four flat walls and two buttresses of unhewn stone, and a plain, bare gibbet, likewise of stone, standing beside it. The treat would have been a sorry one for the lovers of Gothic architecture. It is true, however, that no people ever held works of art in less estimation than the Parisian populace in the Middle Ages, and that they cared very little about the beauty of a pillory.

The culprit, tied to the tail of a cart, was eventually brought forward; and when he had been hoisted onto the platform, where he could be seen from all points of the square, bound with cords and thongs on the wheel of the pillory, a prodigious hooting, mingled with laughter and acclamations, burst from the mob. They had recognized Quasimodo.

It was in fact he. It was a strange reversal for the poor fellow to be pilloried on the same spot where the preceding day he had been hailed and proclaimed Pope and Prince of Fools, escorted by the Duke of Egypt, the King of Thunes, and the Emperor of Galilee. This much is certain, that there was not a creature in that crowd, not even himself, alternately the object of triumph and of punishment, who could clearly make out the connection between the two situations. Gringoire and his philosophy were missing from this spectacle.

Presently Michel Noiret, sworn trumpeter of our Lord the King, commanded silence and proclaimed the sentence according to the ordinance of the Provost. He then fell back behind the cart with his men in their official liveries.

Quasimodo never stirred; he did not so much as frown. All resistance, indeed, on his part was rendered impossible by what was then called in the language of criminal jurisprudence "the vehemence and the firmness of the bonds," which means that the chains and the thongs probably cut into his flesh. He had suffered himself to be led, and pushed, and carried, and lifted, and bound again and again. His face betrayed no other emotion than the astonishment of a savage or an idiot. He was known to be deaf; you would have supposed him to be blind also.

He was placed on his knees on the circular floor. His doublet and shirt were taken off, and he allowed himself to be stripped to the waist without opposition. He was enmeshed in a fresh series of thongs: he let himself be bound and buckled; only from time to time he breathed hard, like a calf whose head hangs dangling over the tail of a butcher's cart.

"The stupid idiot!" exclaimed Jehan Frollo du Moulin to his friend Robin Poussepain, for the two students had followed the culprit as a matter of course. "He has no more idea of what they are going to do than a ladybird shut up in a box."

A loud laugh burst from the mob when they beheld Quasimodo's naked hump, his camel breast, and his scaly and hairy shoulders. Amid all this mirth a man of short stature and robust frame, clad in the livery of the city, ascended the platform and placed himself by the side of the culprit. His name was quickly circulated among the crowd. It was Master Pierrat Torterue, sworn torturer of the Châtelet.

The first thing he did was to set down on one corner of the pillory an hourglass, the upper division of which was full of red sand that flowed into the lower half. He then threw back his cloak, and over his left arm was seen hanging a whip composed of long white, glistening thongs, knotted, twisted, and tipped with sharp bits of metal. With his left hand he carelessly turned up the right sleeve of his shirt as high as the elbow. At length he stamped with his foot. The wheel began to turn. Quasimodo shook in his bonds. The amazement suddenly expressed in his hideous face drew fresh shouts of laughter from the spectators.

All at once, at the moment when the wheel in its revolution presented the mountainous shoulders of Quasimodo to Master Pierrat, he raised his arm; the thin lashes hissed sharply in the air like so many vipers and descended with fury on the back of the unlucky man.

Quasimodo started like one awakened from a dream. He began to comprehend the meaning of the scene, he writhed in his bonds; a violent contraction of surprise and pain distorted the muscles of his face, but he heaved not a single sigh. He merely turned his head, first one way, then the other, balancing it all the while like a bull stung in the flank by a gadfly.

A second stroke succeeded the first, then came a third, and another, and another. The wheel continued to turn and the blows to fall. The blood began to trickle in a hundred little streams down the swarthy shoulders of the hunchback; and the slender thongs, whistling in the air in their rotation, sprinkled it in drops over the gaping crowd.

Quasimodo had fallen back, in appearance at least, into his former apathy. He had endeavored, at first quietly and without great external effort, to burst his bonds. His eye was seen to flash, his muscles to swell, his limbs to gather themselves up, and the thongs, cords, and chains to stretch. The effort was mighty, prodigious, desperate; but the old shackles of the Provost proved too tough. They cracked, and that was all. Quasimodo sank down exhausted. Stupor gave way in his countenance to an expression of deep despondency. He closed his only eye, dropped his head onto his breast, and counterfeited death.

From then on he did not stir again. Nothing could make him

flinch—neither the blood that oozed from his lacerated back, nor the lashes that fell with redoubled force, nor the fury of the executioner, roused and heated by the exercise, nor the hissing and whizzing of the horrible whips. At length an usher of the Châtelet, dressed in black and mounted on a black horse, who had taken his station by the steps at the commencement of the flogging, extended his ebony wand toward the hourglass. The executioner held his hand; the wheel stopped; Quasimodo's eye slowly opened.

Two attendants of the sworn torturer's washed the bleeding back of the sufferer, rubbed it with a sort of ointment, which in an incredibly short time closed all the wounds, and threw over him a kind of yellow frock shaped like a priest's cope; in the meantime Pierrat Torterue drew through his fingers the thongs saturated with blood, which he shook off onto the pavement.

Quasimodo's punishment was not yet over. He still had to remain in the pillory that hour that Master Florian Barbedienne had so judiciously added to the sentence of Messire Robert d'Estouteville; to the great glory of the old physiological pun: *Surdus absurdus,* or "A deaf man is absurd." The hourglass was therefore turned and the hunchback left bound as before, that justice might be fully satisfied.

The populace, especially in a half-civilized era, are in society what the boy is in a family. As long as they continue in the state of primitive ignorance, of moral and intellectual immaturity, you may say of them as of the mischievous urchin, "That age is without pity." We have already shown that Quasimodo was generally hated, for more than one good reason, it is true. There was scarcely a spectator among the crowd who had either had or imagined that he had ground to complain of the malicious hunchback of Notre-Dame. His appearance in the pillory had excited universal joy; and the severe punishment that he had undergone, and the pitiful condition in which it had left him, so far from softening the populace, had only rendered their hatred more malevolent by arming it with the sting of mirth.

Thus when the "public vengeance" was satisfied—according to the jargon still used by the gowned—it was the turn of private revenge to seek gratification. Here, as in the great hall, the women were most vehement. All bore him some grudge—some for his mischievous disposition and others for his ugliness: the women were the most furious.

"Oh, Mask of the Antichrist!" cried one.

"Broomstick rider!" cried another.

"The beautiful tragic grimace," cried a third, "that got you crowned Pope of Fools. If only today were yesterday!"

"That is good," continued an old woman. "Here is a face for the pillory. And do we get a face for the gallows?"

"When will you be knocked out by your great church bells a hundred feet underground, damned bell ringer?"

"It is a devil who rings in the angelus."

"Deaf, one-eyed, hunchbacked! A monster!"

"A face to end a pregnancy better than all medicines or other concoctions."

The two students, Jehan du Moulin and Robin Poussepain, sang at the top of their lungs the popular refrain:

> *Une hart*
> *Pour le pendard*
> *Un fagot*
> *Pour le magot!*[8]

A thousand other insults rained down on his head with the booing, the cursing, the laughter, the stones here and there.

Quasimodo was deaf. But he was sharp-sighted, and the fury of the populace was expressed no less energetically in their countenance than in their words. Besides, the pelting of the stones explained the meaning of the bursts of laughter. This annoyance passed for a while unheeded, but by degrees that patience that had braced itself up under the lash of the executioner gave way under all these stings of petty insects. The bull of the Asturias, which scarcely deigns to notice the attacks of the picador, is exasperated by the dogs and the banderillos.

At first he cast a threatening look at the crowd; but, shackled as he was, this look could not drive away the flies that galled his wound. He then struggled in his bonds, and his furious contortions made the old wheel of the pillory creak upon its axle. This served only to increase the jeers and derisions of the populace.

The wretched sufferer, finding, like a chained beast, that he could not break his collar, again became quiet, though at times a sigh of rage heaved all the cavities of his chest. Not a blush, not a trace of shame was to be discerned in his face. He was too far from the social state and too near to the state of nature to know what shame is. Besides, is it possible that disgrace can be felt by one cast in a mold of such extreme deformity? But rage, hatred, despair, slowly spread over that hideous face a cloud that gradually became more and more black, more and more charged with an electricity that exploded in a thousand flashes from the eye of the Cyclops.

This cloud, however, cleared off for a moment at the appearance of a mule bearing a priest. The instant he caught a glimpse of this mule and this priest in the distance, the face of the poor sufferer assumed a look of gentleness. The rage that had contracted it was succeeded by a strange smile, full of ineffable meekness, kindness, tenderness. As the priest approached this smile became more expressive, more distinct, more radiant. The prisoner seemed to be anticipating the arrival of a deliverer; but the moment the mule was near enough to the pillory for its rider to recognize the sufferer the priest cast down his eyes, wheeled around, clapped spurs to his beast, as if in a hurry to escape a humiliating appeal, and by no means wanting to be recognized or addressed by a poor devil in such a situation. This priest was the Archdeacon Claude Frollo.

Quasimodo's brow was overcast by an even darker cloud. For some time a smile mingled with the gloom, but it was a smile of bitterness, disappointment, and deep despair. Time passed. For an hour and a half at least he had been exposed to incessant ill usage—lacerated, jeered, and almost stoned. Suddenly he again struggled in his chains with a redoubled effort of despair that made the whole platform shake; and, breaking the silence that he had kept until then, he cried in a hoarse and furious voice, more like the bark of a wild beast than in the articulate tones of a human tongue, "Water!"

This cry of distress, heard above the shouts and laughter of the crowd, so far from exciting compassion only served to heighten the mirth of the good people of Paris, who surrounded the pillory and who, to tell the truth, were in those days not much less cruel or less brutalized than the disgusting crew of tramps whom we have already introduced to the reader; these merely formed, in fact, the lowest stratum of the populace. All the voices raised around the unhappy sufferer were scornful and derisive of his thirst. It is certain that at this moment he was more grotesque and repulsive than pitiable; his face empurpled and trickling with perspiration, his eye glaring wildly, his mouth foaming with rage and agony, with his tongue lolling out of it. It must also be confessed that had any charitable soul of either sex been tempted to carry a draft of water to the wretched sufferer, the notion of infamy and disgrace hung over the ignominious steps of the pillory so strongly that it would have effectually deterred the Good Samaritan.

In a few minutes Quasimodo surveyed the crowd with an anxious eye and repeated in a voice rougher than before, "Water!" He was answered with peals of laughter.

"There is water for you, deaf idiot," cried Robin Poussepain, throwing in his face a sponge soaked in the gutter. "I owe it to you!"

A woman hurled a stone at his head. "That will teach you to wake us at night," she said, "with your cursed bells."

"Hey there, son!" cried a lame man who tried to reach him with his cane. "Are you still going to cast spells on us from high up on your towers of Notre-Dame?"

"Here's a bowl to drink from!" said a man who threw a broken jug against his chest. "You're the one who, in passing my wife, made her give birth to a two-headed child!"

"And you made my cat give birth to a kitten with six legs!" yelped an old woman who threw a tile at him.

"Water!" roared the panting Quasimodo for the third time.

At that moment he saw the crowd part. A strangely young girl approached the pillory. She was followed by a little white goat with gilded horns, and she carried a tambourine in her hand. Quasimodo's eye sparkled. It was the Bohemian whom he had tried to carry off the night before, and he had a confused notion that for this prank he was being punished, though in fact it was only because he had the misfortune to be deaf and to be tried by a deaf judge. He thought that she was coming to take revenge also, to add her blow to the rest.

He watched her ascend the steps with nimble feet. He was choked with rage and vexation. Had the lightning of his eye possessed the power, it would have blasted the gypsy into nothingness before she reached the platform. Without uttering a word she approached the victim, who vainly writhed away from her, and, taking a gourd from her belt, she gently lifted it to the parched lips of the exhausted wretch. A big tear flowed out of his dry and bloodshot eye, and it trickled slowly down his deformed face so long contracted by despair. It was perhaps the first tear that he had shed since he arrived at manhood.

Meanwhile he forgot to drink. The gypsy pouted prettily with impatience, then put the neck of the gourd between Quasimodo's jagged teeth; he drank greedily. His thirst was great.

When he had finished the hunchback puckered his dark lips, no doubt to kiss the kind hand that had brought such welcome relief; but the girl, perhaps remembering the violent assault of the previous night, quickly drew back her hand with the same start of terror that a child does when he is afraid of being bitten by a beast. The poor fellow then fixed on her a look full of reproach and unutterable woe.

Anywhere else, it would have been a touching sight to see this girl, so fresh, so pure, so lovely, and at the same time so weak, hastening to the relief of so much distress, deformity, and malice. On a pillory this sight was sublime. The people themselves were moved by it and began clapping their hands and shouting, "Hurrah! Hurrah!"

It was precisely at this moment that the recluse perceived from the window of her den the gypsy on the pillory and pronounced on her that bitter imprecation—"Curse you, gypsy woman! A curse upon you!"

CHAPTER V

The End of the Story of the Cake

La Esmeralda turned pale and with faltering step descended from the pillory. The voice of the recluse still pursued her, "Get down from there! Get down, gypsy child stealer! You will have to go up again one of these days!"

"Sachette is in one of her moods today," said the people, grumbling; and they did nothing else. Women of her class were then deemed holy and revered accordingly. Nobody liked to attack people who were praying night and day.

The time of Quasimodo's punishment having ended, he was released, and the mob dispersed.

Mahiette and her two companions had reached the foot of the Grand Pont on their return, when she suddenly stopped short. "Goodness!" she exclaimed. "What has become of the cake, Eustache?"

"Mother," said the boy, "while you were talking with the woman in that dark hole, a big dog came and bit a great piece out of it, so I ate some too."

"What, sir," she asked, "have you eaten it all?"

"It was the dog, Mother. I told him to leave it alone, but he didn't listen to me—so I just took a bite too."

"You're a sad, greedy boy!" said his mother, smiling and scolding at once. "Look, Oudarde, not a cherry or an apple in our garden is safe from him; so his grandfather says he will make a rare captain. I'll make you pay, Monsieur Eustache! Go on, you great lion!"

BOOK VII

CHAPTER I

The Danger of Trusting a Goat with a Secret

Several weeks had elapsed. It was now the beginning of March. The sun, which Dubartas, that classic ancestor of periphrasis, had not yet styled "the grandduke of candles," shone brightly and cheerily. It was one of those spring days that are so mild and so beautiful that all Paris pours into the public square and promenades on Sundays and holidays. On days so brilliant, so warm, and so serene there is a particular hour when one should go to admire the entrance of Notre-Dame. It is when the sun, already sinking in the west, looks the cathedral almost full in the face. Its rays, becoming more and more horizontal, slowly withdraw from the pavement of the square and rise along the pinnacled facade, causing its thousands of figures in relief to stand out from their shadows, while the great central rose window glares like the eye of a Cyclops, tinged by the reflections of the forge. It was now just that hour.

Across from the lofty cathedral, glowing in the sunset on a stone balcony, over the porch of a rich Gothic building at the corner of the square and the Rue du Parvis, some lovely young women were chatting and laughing in a lively manner. By the length of their veils, which fell from the tops of their pointed caps, encircled with pearls, to their heels; by the fineness of the embroidered shawls that covered their shoulders, but without wholly concealing according to the style of the times the contours of their virgin bosoms; by the richness of their petticoats, which surpassed that of their upper garments; by the gauze, the silk, the velvet, with which their dresses were trimmed; and above all by the whiteness of their hands, which showed them to be idle and unused to labor it was easy to guess that they belonged to noble and wealthy families. It was, in fact, Demoiselle Fleur-de-Lis de Gondelaurier and her companions, Diane de Christeuil, Amelotte de Montmichel,

Colombe de Gaillefontaine, and little de Champchevrier, who were visiting at the house of the Dame de Gondelaurier, a widow, because of the expected visit of Monseigneur de Beaujeu and his wife, who were to come to Paris in April for the purpose of selecting ladies of honor for the Dauphiness Marguerite. Now, all the gentry for a hundred miles around were anxious to obtain this favor for their daughters, and with this in mind many had already brought or sent them to Paris. The young ladies were placed by their parents under the care of the discreet and venerable Dame Aloïse de Gondelaurier, widow of an officer of the King's crossbowmen, who lived with her only daughter in her own house in the Place du Parvis of Notre-Dame in Paris.

The balcony opened onto an apartment hung with rich fawn-colored Flanders leather stamped with gold borders. The parallel beams that crossed the ceiling amused the eye by a thousand bizarre carvings that were gilded and painted. Richly carved coffers shimmered everywhere with splendid coats of arms, while a boar's head in Delft ware crowned a magnificent buffet, indicating that the mistress of the house was the wife or widow of a knight. At the farther end, by a high fireplace, with escutcheons and armorial insignia from top to bottom, sat, in a rich armchair of crimson velvet, the Dame de Gondelaurier, whose fifty-five years were as legibly inscribed on her dress as on her face. By her side stood a young man, of a bold but somewhat vain and swaggering look—one of those handsome fellows to whom all the women take a liking, though the serious man and the physiognomist shrug their shoulders at them. This young cavalier wore the brilliant captain's uniform of the archers of the King's Ordnance, which so closely resembled the costume of Jupiter described at the beginning of this story that we do not need to tire the reader with a second description of it.

The young women were seated partly in the room, partly on the balcony, some on cushions of Utrecht velvet with golden feet, others on oak stools, carved with flowers and figures. Each of them held on her lap a portion of a large piece of tapestry, on which they were all working together, while the other part lay on the matting that covered the floor.

They were chatting together, in those whispers and with those half-stifled giggles so common in a party of young girls when there is a young man present. The young man, whose presence was enough to put into play all this feminine vanity, appeared to care very little about it. And while these beauties were all striving to engage his attention he seemed to be busily engaged in polishing the buckle of his belt with his leather glove.

Now and then the old lady spoke to him in a very low tone, and he answered as well as he could, with a sort of awkward and forced politeness. From her smiles, and from the nods and winks that Dame Aloïse directed toward her daughter, Fleur-de-Lis, while softly speaking to the Captain, it was easy to see that a match had been made between the young officer and Fleur-de-Lis and that it would be speedily concluded. It was easy too to see from his coldness and embarrassment that, on his side at least, love was no longer involved. His face expressed a kind of irritation and boredom that our garrisoned sublieutenants would translate admirably today as "What a bitch of a job!" The good lady, who, poor mother that she was, doted on her daughter, did not notice the Captain's indifference, and strove by her words and gestures to make him notice the grace with which Fleur-de-Lis plied her needle and wound her skein.

"Look, little cousin," she said, plucking him by the sleeve in order to whisper in his ear. "Look at her now, as she bends over her work."

"Yes, indeed," replied the young man, relapsing into his former cold and distracted silence.

A moment afterward he was required to lean over once more. "Did you ever," said Dame Aloïse, "see a more charming and engaging face than your betrothed? Is it possible to be fairer? Aren't her hands and arms perfect shapes? And her neck, doesn't it have all the elegance of a swan's? At times I envy you. How happy you must be, miserable libertine that you are. I think my Fleur-de-Lis has become more beautiful for being adored—you must be madly in love."

"No doubt," he replied, meanwhile thinking of something else.

"Why don't you go and talk to her then?" retorted the lady, pushing him toward Fleur-de-Lis. "Go and say something to her. You have become very shy."

Now we can assure the reader that neither shyness nor modesty was to be numbered among the Captain's faults. He attempted, however, to do what was demanded of him.

"Fair cousin," he said, stepping up to Fleur-de-Lis, "what is the subject of this tapestry you are working on?"

"Fair cousin," answered Fleur-de-Lis, irritated, "I have told you three times already that it is Neptune's grotto."

It was evident that the Captain's cold and absent manner had not escaped the keen observation of Fleur-de-Lis, though it was not noticed by her mother. He felt the necessity of making an attempt at conversation.

"And for whom is this Neptunery?" he inquired.

"For the abbey of St.-Antoine-des-Champs," replied Fleur-de-Lis without raising her eyes.

The Captain lifted a corner of the tapestry. "And pray, my fair cousin," he said, "who is this big fellow blowing the trumpet with puffed up cheeks?"

"That is Triton," she answered.

In the tone of Fleur-de-Lis's brief replies there was still something that betrayed displeasure. The young man understood that he had to whisper something into her ear, any nonsense, a compliment, anything. He leaned over, but he could find nothing more tender or intimate to say than the following: "Why does your mother always wear that armored petticoat from the time of our grandmothers and the reign of Charles VII? Tell her, lovely cousin, that it is out of style now, and that the hinges and laurels embroidered and emblazoned on her dress make her look like a walking chimney mantel. We don't sit on our flags like that anymore, I swear to you."

Fleur-de-Lis raised her beautiful, reproachful eyes to look at him. "Is that what you have to swear to me?" she asked in a low voice.

In spite of this, the good Lady Aloïse was overjoyed to see them leaning over each other whispering and said, playing with the cover of her book of hours, "What a touching tableau of love!"

The Captain was more and more at a loss for what to say. He stooped down over the tapestry. "Really charming piece of work!" he cried.

At this exclamation, Colombe de Gaillefontaine, another beautiful blonde, of a delicately fair complexion, in a dress of blue damask, timidly ventured to address a question to Fleur-de-Lis in the hope that the handsome Captain would answer it. "My dear Gondelaurier," she said, "have you seen the tapestries in the Hôtel de la Roche-Guyon?"

"Isn't that the hôtel next to the garden of the Lingère?" asked Diane de Christeuil, with a laugh. This young lady had remarkably beautiful teeth and consequently laughed at every occasion.

"And near the great old tower of the ancient wall of Paris?" inquired Amelotte de Montmichel, a charming brunette with a lovely complexion and dark curls, who had a habit of sighing as the other of laughing, without knowing why.

"My dear Colombe," continued Lady Aloïse, "don't you want to tell us about the hôtel that belonged to Monsieur de Bacqueville under King Charles VI? There are very beautiful, superb tapestries of the finest quality there."

"Charles VI! Charles VI!" grumbled the young captain while playing with his mustache. "My God, the good lady has a long memory!"

Madame de Gondelaurier went on, "Beautiful tapestries, truly. The work is so respected that it is believed to be absolutely unique!"

At this moment Bérangère de Champchevrier, a little sylph of seven years, looking down on the square through the rails of the balcony, cried, "Oh! Look, Godmother Fleur-de-Lis! Look at that pretty dancer on the pavement playing the tambourine among the people down there!"

"Some gypsy, I daresay," replied Fleur-de-Lis, carelessly turning her head toward the square.

"Let's see! Let's see!" cried her lively companions, running to the front of the balcony while Fleur-de-Lis, thinking of the coldness of her lover, slowly followed, and the Captain, released by this incident, which cut short a conversation that embarrassed him not a little, returned to the farther end of the apartment with the satisfaction of a soldier relieved from duty. Being at the service of the gentle Fleur-de-Lis was nevertheless charming and delightful; and so it had formerly seemed to him. But now the prospect of an impending marriage left him colder and colder every day. The fact is, he was of a rather inconstant disposition and, if the truth must be told, rather vulgar in his tastes. Though of high birth, he had contracted more than one of the habits of the common soldier. He was fond of the tavern and everything that goes with it. He felt comfortable only among coarse language, military flirtations, easy beauties, and easy conquests. He had received from his family some education and polish, but he had been thrown into the army too young, too young placed in garrison, and the varnish of the gentleman was being worn off by the hard friction of his guardsman's leather belt. Though he still paid occasional visits to Fleur-de-Lis, he found himself doubly embarrassed when he called on her, in the first place, because he distributed his love so promiscuously in all sorts of places that he reserved a very small portion of it for her; and, second, because in the company of so many handsome, well-bred, and modest women he was constantly on his guard lest his tongue, used to oaths and imprecations, should get the better of him and launch out into the language of the tavern. You could imagine what sort of scene that might make! All of this was mixed up in his pretensions of elegance, dress, and good looks. The readers must reconcile these things for themselves; I am but a historian.

The Captain, then, had stood for some moments, lost in thought, or not thinking at all, leaning in silence on the carved mantelpiece, when Fleur-de-Lis, suddenly turning around, addressed him. After all, she sulked at him unwillingly.

"Did you not tell us, cousin, of a little Bohemian you rescued one night, about two months ago, from the hands of a dozen robbers?"

"I think I did, lovely cousin," replied the Captain.

"Perhaps," she resumed, "it was the Bohemian dancing down there in the Parvis. Come and see whether you know her, Cousin Phœbus."

In this gentle invitation to come to her and the tone in which it was uttered he detected a secret desire of reconciliation. Captain Phœbus de Châteaupers—for this is the personage whom the reader has had before him since the beginning of this chapter—advanced with slow steps toward the balcony. "Look," said Fleur-de-Lis, softly grasping the Captain's arm, "look at the girl dancing in that circle. Is she your Bohemian?"

Phœbus looked. "Yes," he said. "I know her by her goat."

"Oh! What a pretty little goat!" exclaimed Amelotte, clapping her hands in admiration.

"Are its horns of real gold?" asked Bérangère.

Without moving from her armchair, Lady Aloïse spoke. "Isn't she one of those Bohemians who arrived last year by the Porte Gibard?"

"Mother," Fleur-de-Lis said sweetly, "this gate is now called the Porte d'Enfer."

Mademoiselle de Gondelaurier knew how shocked the Captain was by her mother's outmoded ways of speaking. He started laughing and saying between his teeth, "Porte Gibard! Porte Gibard! It was made for Charles VI!"

"Godmother," Bérangère asked, having suddenly raised her bright eyes, which were in constant motion, to the top of the towers of Notre-Dame, "who is that man in black up there?"

All the young ladies looked up. A man was indeed leaning on his elbows on the topmost balustrade of the northern tower, overlooking the Grève. It was a priest, as might be known by his dress, which was clearly distinguishable, and his head was supported by both hands. He was motionless as a statue. He stared at the square as intently as a hawk who has discovered a sparrow's nest.

"It's the Archdeacon of Josas," said Fleur-de-Lis.

"You must have good eyes to recognize him at this distance," observed Gaillefontaine.

"How he looks at the dancing girl!" exclaimed Diane de Christeuil.

"Let the gypsy beware!" said Fleur-de-Lis. "The Archdeacon is not fond of Egypt."

"It is a pity that man looks at her so," added Amelotte de Montmichel, "for she dances delightfully."

"Good Cousin Phœbus," abruptly cried Fleur-de-Lis, "since you know this Bohemian, tell her to come up. It will amuse us."

"Yes, do!" exclaimed all the young ladies, clapping their hands.

"That would be madness," rejoined Phœbus. "She has no doubt forgotten me, and I do not even know her name. However, as you wish it, ladies. I will try." Leaning over the balustrade of the balcony, he called out, "Little girl!"

The dancer had paused for a moment. She turned her head in the direction from which the voice proceeded; her sparkling eye fell on Phœbus, and she stood stock-still.

"Little girl!" repeated the Captain, beckoning her to come to him.

The girl still looked steadfastly at him; then she blushed deeply, as if every drop of blood had rushed to her cheeks and, taking her tambourine under her arm, she made her way through the circle of astonished spectators toward the house to which she was summoned with slow, faltering steps and with the agitated look of a bird unable to resist the fascination of a serpent.

A moment afterward the tapestry hung before the door was raised, and the Bohemian appeared at the threshold of the room, out of breath, speechless, and flushed, with her large eyes fixed on the floor; she dared not advance a step farther. Bérangère clapped her hands.

Meanwhile, the dancer stood motionless at the door of the room. Her appearance had produced a singular effect on the party of young ladies. It is certain that all of them were more or less influenced by a certain vague and indistinct desire of pleasing the handsome officer; that the splendid uniform was the point at which all of their flirtatiousness was aimed, and that ever since his entrance there had been a sort of secret rivalry between them, of which they were themselves scarcely conscious but which nevertheless betrayed itself every moment in all they said and did. Because, however, they all possessed nearly the same degree of beauty, they fought with equal weapons, and each could cherish a hope of victory. The coming of the Bohemian suddenly destroyed this balance of power. Her beauty was so rare that when she appeared at the entrance of the room she seemed to shed over it a sort of light peculiar to herself. In this crowded room, beneath the wall hangings and carvings, she appeared incomparably more beautiful and radiant than in the public square. It was like a torch that is carried out of the broad daylight into the dark. In spite of themselves, the young ladies were dazzled. Each felt wounded, as it were, in her beauty. Their battlefront—reader, excuse the term—was changed accordingly, though not a single word passed between them. The instincts of women apprehend and answer one another much more readily than the intelligence of men. An enemy was in their midst; they all felt it, and therefore they all rallied together. One drop of wine is sufficient to redden a whole glass of water; to taint an entire company of pretty women with a certain degree of ill humor merely introduce an even prettier woman, especially when there is only one man in the party.

The reception of the Bohemian was of course marvelously cold. They surveyed her from head to foot, then looked at each other. Everything had been said. Meanwhile the stranger waited for someone to speak to her, so terrified that she dared not look up.

The Captain was the first to break silence. "A charming creature!" he cried with his intrepid stupidity. "What do you think of her, my pretty cousin?"

This observation, which a more delicate admirer would at least have uttered in a less audible tone, was not likely to diminish the feminine jealousies arrayed against the Bohemian.

"Not bad," replied Fleur-de-Lis to the Captain's question, with
sweetly affected disdain. The others whispered together.

At length Madame Aloïse, who was no less jealous because she felt
it on behalf of her daughter, accosted the dancer. "Come here, little
girl," she said. The gypsy advanced to the lady.

"Come here, little girl!" repeated Bérangère with comic dignity.
She would have been as tall as the gypsy's hip.

"Lovely child," said Phœbus, taking a few steps toward her, "I do not
know if I have the supreme pleasure of being recognized by you—"

"Oh, yes!" she said, interrupting him, with a smile and a look of inexpressible sweetness.

"She has a good memory," observed Fleur-de-Lis.

"How was it," resumed Phœbus, "that you slipped away in such a
hurry the other night? Did I frighten you?"

"Oh, no!" said the Bohemian.

In the accent with which this "Oh, no!" was uttered immediately
after the "Oh, yes!" there was an indefinable something that wounded
Fleur-de-Lis to the quick.

"In your place," continued the Captain, whose tongue was loosened
enough in talking to a girl of the streets, "you left me a surly, one-eyed,
hunchbacked fellow—the Bishop's bell ringer, I think they say. Some
will have it that the Archdeacon, and others that the devil, is his father.
He has a funny name—I have forgotten it—taken from some festival
or other. Four Seasons, Blooming Easter, Mardi-Gras. He was trying to
kidnap you, as if you were destined for beadles. What the devil did that
monster of a fellow want with you?"

"I don't know," she answered.

"Can you imagine his impudence! A bell ringer kidnap a girl, as if
he were a viscount! A common fellow poach on the game of gentlemen! Who ever heard of such a thing! But he paid dearly for it. Master
Pierrat Torterue is the roughest groom that ever beat a scoundrel, and
I assure you, if that can do you any good, he tanned the bell ringer's
hide most soundly."

"Poor fellow!" said the Bohemian, who at the Captain's words could
not help calling to mind the scene at the pillory.

"Bulls' horns!" cried the Captain, laughing outright. "That pity is as well placed as a feather on a pig's ass. May I be as potbellied as a Pope, if—" He stopped short. "I beg your pardon, ladies, I was going to talk folly."

"My goodness, sir!" said Gaillefontaine.

"He is only talking to that creature in her own language," said Fleur-de-Lis in an undertone, her irritation increasing every moment. Nor was it diminished when she saw the Captain, enchanted with the Bohemian and still more with himself, make a pirouette, repeating with blunt, soldierlike gallantry, "A fine girl, on my soul!"

"But very uncouthly dressed," said Diane de Christeuil, smiling to show her beautiful teeth.

This remark was a new light to her companions. It showed them the vulnerable side of the gypsy; since they could not attack her beauty, they fell on her outfit.

"How does it happen, child," said Montmichel, "that you run around the streets in this manner, without veil or ruff?"

"That's an alarmingly short skirt," exclaimed Gaillefontaine.

"My dear," said Fleur-de-Lis, in a tone of anything but kindness, "the officers of the Châtelet will arrest you for wearing that gold belt."

"Child, child," resumed Christeuil, with an implacable smile, "if you were to cover your arms decently with sleeves they would not be so sunburned."

It was in truth a sight worthy of a more intelligent spectator than Phœbus to see how these fair damsels, with their keen and poisoned tongues, twisted, glided, and writhed around the dancing girl; they were at once cruel and graceful. They maliciously made fun of her poor but whimsical toilet of sequins and spangles. Their arrogant benevolence and evil looks and sarcasms rained down on the gypsy girl. You would have taken them for some of those young Roman ladies who amused themselves by thrusting gold pins into the breasts of a beautiful slave; or they might be compared to elegant greyhounds, turning, with flared nostrils and ardent eyes, around a poor fawn, which the look of their master forbids them to devour.

What after all was a poor street dancer to these daughters of distinguished families! They seemed to take no account of her presence and talked of her before her face, and even to herself, as of an object at once rather abject, dirty, and pretty.

The Bohemian was not insensible to their stinging remarks. From time to time the glow of shame or the flash of anger flushed her cheek or lit up her eye; a disdainful word seemed to hover on her lips; her contempt expressed itself in that pout with which the reader is already acquainted. She stood motionless, fixing on Phœbus a resigned and yet gentle look. In that look there was also an expression of tenderness and happiness. You would have said that she restrained her feelings for fear of being chased out.

Meanwhile Phœbus laughed and began with a mixture of impertinence and pity to take the side of the Bohemian. "Let them talk as they like, my dear," he said, clicking together his gold spurs. "Your dress is certainly somewhat extravagant and a bit wild, but for such a charming creature as you are, what can that do?"

"Dear me!" exclaimed the fair Gaillefontaine, stretching her swan's neck with a sarcastic smile. "How soon the gentlemen archers of the King's Ordnance take fire at bright gypsy eyes!"

"Why not?" said Phœbus.

At this reply, carelessly uttered by the Captain, Colombe laughed, so did Diane, so did Amelotte, so did Fleur-de-Lis, though not without a tear in her eye. The Bohemian, who had hung down her head at the remark of Colombe de Gaillefontaine, raised her eyes glistening with joy and pride, and again fixed them on Phœbus. She was extremely beautiful at that moment.

The old lady, who watched this scene, felt offended, though she did not know why. "Holy Virgin!" she cried suddenly, "what have I between my legs? Ah! The nasty beast!"

It was the goat, which, in springing toward her mistress, had entangled her horns in the load of drapery that kept about the feet of the noble lady when she was seated. This was a diversion. The Bohemian without a word disengaged the animal.

"Oh! Here is the pretty little goat with golden feet!" cried Bérangère, leaping for joy.

The Bohemian bent on her knees and pressed her cheek against the head of the nuzzling goat while Diane, stooping to the ear of Colombe, whispered, "How very stupid of me not to think of it sooner! Why, it is the gypsy with the goat. It is reported that she is a witch, and that her goat performs the most amazing tricks."

"Well," said Colombe, "the goat must perform one of its miracles and amuse us in its turn."

Diane and Colombe eagerly addressed the gypsy. "Child," they said, "make your goat perform a miracle for us."

"I don't know what you mean," replied the dancer.

"A miracle, a piece of magic, or witchcraft, in short."

"I don't understand you," she rejoined, and again began fondling the pretty creature, repeating, "Djali! Djali!"

At this moment Fleur-de-Lis noticed a small embroidered leather bag hung around the goat's neck. "What is that?" she asked the gypsy.

The girl raised her large eyes toward her and gravely answered, "That is my secret."

"I would like to know what your secret is," thought Fleur-de-Lis.

The good lady had meanwhile gotten in ill humor. "Girl," she said sharply, "if neither you nor your goat has any dance for us, why do you stay here?"

The Bohemian, without making any reply, headed slowly for the door. The nearer she approached it the more slowly she moved. An invincible magnet seemed to detain her. All at once she turned her eyes glistening with tears toward Phœbus and she stood still.

"Good God!" cried the Captain. "You can't leave like this. Come back and give us a dance. By the way, what is your name, my pretty dear?"

"La Esmeralda," said the dancing girl, whose eyes were still fixed on him.

At this strange name the young ladies burst into a loud laugh.

"A terrible name for a girl!" said Diane.

"You see plainly enough," observed Amelotte, "that she is a witch."

"My girl," said Dame Aloïse in a solemn tone, "your parents never found that name for you in the baptismal font."

While this scene was taking place, Bérangère had enticed the goat into a corner of the room with a piece of bread. They were immediately the best friends in the world. The curious girl loosened the little bag from the neck of the animal, opened it, and emptied its contents on the mat: they consisted of an alphabet, each letter separately inscribed on a small piece of boxwood. No sooner were these playthings spread out on the mat than, to the astonishment of the child, the goat—one of whose miracles this no doubt was—sorted out certain letters with her golden foot, arranged them, and shuffled them gently together, in a particular order, to make a word, which the animal formed with such readiness that she seemed to have had a good deal of practice in putting it together. Bérangère, clapping her hands in admiration, suddenly exclaimed, "Godmother Fleur-de-Lis, come and see what the goat has done!"

Fleur-de-Lis ran to her and shuddered. The letters that the goat had arranged on the floor spelled the name PHŒBUS.

"Was it the goat that did this?" she asked in a changed voice.

"Yes, indeed it was, Godmother," replied Bérangère. It was impossible to doubt the fact.

"The secret is out," thought Fleur-de-Lis.

At the outcry of the child, all who were present, the mother and the young ladies, and the Bohemian, and the officer, hastened to the spot. The dancing girl saw at once what a blunder the goat had made. She changed color and began to tremble, like one who had committed some crime, before the Captain, who eyed her with a smile of astonishment and gratification.

For a moment the young ladies were struck dumb. "Phœbus!" they at length whispered to one another. "Why, that is the name of the Captain!"

"You have a wonderful memory," said Fleur-de-Lis to the petrified Bohemian. Then, bursting into sobs, "Oh!" she stuttered, in a tone of anguish, covering her face with both her fair hands. "She is a sorceress!" All the while a voice cried bitterly in the depth of her heart— "She is a rival!" She sank fainting to the floor.

"My daughter! my daughter!" shrieked the terrified mother. "Get out of here, gypsy from hell!" she said to the Bohemian.

La Esmeralda picked up the unlucky letters in the twinkling of an eye, made a sign to her Djali, and left by one door while Fleur-de-Lis was borne away through another.

Captain Phœbus, being left by himself, wavered for a moment between the two doors and then followed the gypsy girl.

CHAPTER II

A PRIEST AND A PHILOSOPHER
ARE TWO DIFFERENT PEOPLE

The priest, whom the young ladies had observed on the top of the north tower leaning over the square and intently watching the Bohemian's dance, was in fact the Archdeacon Claude Frollo.

Our readers have not forgotten the mysterious cell that the Archdeacon had reserved for himself in that tower. (I do not know, by the way, whether this is not the same cell whose interior may still be seen through a small square window on the east side, at about the height of a man, on the platform from which the towers rise. It is a small room, naked, empty, dilapidated, the ill-plastered walls of which are at the present day adorned with yellow engravings representing the facades of cathedrals. This hole is, I presume, inhabited conjointly by bats and spiders, and consequently a double war of extermination is carried on there against the unfortunate flies.)

Every day, an hour before sunset, the Archdeacon ascended the staircase of the tower and shut himself up in this cell, where he frequently passed entire nights. On this day, just as he had reached the low door of his retreat and put into the lock the little complicated key that he always carried with him in the pouch hanging at his side, the sounds of a tambourine and castanet struck his ear.

These sounds came from the Place du Parvis. The cell, as we have already stated, had only one window, looking out on the roof of the church. Claude Frollo hastily withdrew the key, and the next moment he was on the top of the tower, in the attitude of profound reverie in which the young ladies had seen him.

There he was, serious, motionless, absorbed—all eye, all ear, all thought. All Paris was at his feet, with the thousand spires of its buildings, and its circular horizon of gentle hills, with its river winding beneath its bridges and its people pouring through its streets, its cloud of smoke, and its mountain chain of roofs crowding close to Notre-Dame with their double slopes of mail. In this whole city the Archdeacon's eye sought just one point of the pavement, the Place du Parvis, and among the whole multitude just one figure, the Bohemian.

It would have been difficult to decide what was the nature of that look, and of the fire that flashed from it. It was a fixed gaze, but full of trouble and perturbation. And yet, from the profound stillness of his whole body, scarcely shaken now and then by a mechanical shudder, as a tree by the wind, from the stiffness of his arms, more marblelike than the balustrade on which they leaned; from the petrified smile that contracted his face, you would have said that Claude Frollo had nothing alive about him but his eyes.

The Bohemian was dancing; she made the tambourine spin around on the tip of her finger and threw it up in the air while she danced Provençal sarabands—light, agile, joyous, and not aware of the weight of that formidable look that fell straight down on her head.

The crowd thronged around her; from time to time a man dressed in a yellow and red loose coat went around the circle of spectators to keep them back; he then seated himself in a chair, a few paces from the dancer, taking the head of the goat on his knees. This man seemed to be the companion of the Bohemian, but Claude Frollo could not from his elevated station distinguish his features.

From the moment the Archdeacon perceived this stranger his attention seemed to be divided between the dancer and him, and the gloom that overspread his countenance became deeper and deeper. All at once he started up, and a trembling ran through his whole frame. "Who can that man be?" he muttered. "Till now I have always seen her alone!"

Then he darted under the winding vault of the spiral staircase and descended. In passing the door of the belfry, which was open, he saw an object that struck him: it was Quasimodo, leaning out at one of the windows of those slated penthouses that resemble enormous blinds and intently looking down at the square. So entirely was he engrossed by the scene that he was not aware of the passing of his foster father. "Strange!" murmured Claude. "Can it be the gypsy that he is watching so earnestly?" He continued to descend. In a few minutes the Archdeacon, very preoccupied, entered the square by the door at the foot of the tower.

"What has become of the Bohemian?" he inquired, mingling with a group of spectators the tambourine had attracted.

"I do not know," replied one of them. "She has just disappeared. I rather think she went to give them a dance in that house over there. Someone called to her from there."

Instead of the gypsy, on the same carpet whose arabesques had only a moment disappeared under her brilliant dance, the Archdeacon now found only the man in the red and yellow coat, who, to earn in his turn a few small coins, moved around the circle, with his elbows against his hips, his head thrown back, his face flushed, his neck tense, and a chair between his teeth. On this chair was tied a cat, which a neighbor had lent for the purpose, and which, being frightened, was crying loudly.

"By our Lady!" exclaimed the Archdeacon at the moment when the performer passed him with his pyramid of chair and cat. "What is Pierre Gringoire doing here?"

The stern voice of the Archdeacon threw the poor fellow into such a commotion that he lost his balance, and chair and cat tumbled pell-mell onto the heads of his assistants, amid the inextinguishable laughter of the crowd.

In all probability Master Pierre Gringoire—for sure enough it was he—would have had an ugly account to settle with the mistress of the cat and the owners of all the bruised and scratched faces around him, had he not availed himself of the confusion to slip away to the church after the Archdeacon, who had motioned him to follow.

The cathedral was already dark and deserted, and the lamps in the chapels began to twinkle like stars in the gloom. The great rose window of the front alone, whose thousand colors were lit up by a ray of the setting sun, shone in the dark like a cluster of diamonds and threw its dazzling reflection on the farthest extremity of the nave.

After they had advanced a few steps from the entrance, Dom Claude, stopping short with his back against a pillar, looked steadfastly at Gringoire. In this look there was nothing to excite dread in Gringoire, deeply ashamed as he was of having been caught by a serious and learned personage in that buffoon's costume. The look of the priest had in it nothing that was sarcastic or ironic; it was serious, calm, and piercing. The Archdeacon first broke the silence.

"Come here, Master Pierre. There are many things that I want you to explain. In the first place, how is it that I have not seen you for these two months, and that I find you in the public streets, dressed in such a costume, half red and half yellow, like a Caudebec apple?"

"My Lord," replied Gringoire dolefully, "it is indeed a strange outfit, and one in which I feel about as comfortable as a cat in a coconut-shell. It is a sad thing, I admit, to let the gentlemen of the watch run the risk of belaboring under this sorry disguise the shoulders of a Pythagorean philosopher. But how can I help it, my reverend master? The blame rests with my old coat, which basely abandoned me in the depth of winter, on the pretext that it was falling to tatters. What could I do? Civilization is not yet so far advanced that one may go stark naked, as Diogenes of old wished to do. Besides, a very harsh wind was blowing at the time, and the month of January is not a likely season to attempt to introduce this new fashion with any hope of success. This cloak presented itself; I took it and gave up my old black coat, which, for a hermetic philosopher like me, was far from being hermetically sealed. So here I am in a performer's costume, like St. Genest. I have fallen in the world, to be sure. But Apollo, you know, tended swine for Admetus."[1]

"A respectable profession truly that you have taken up!" replied the Archdeacon.

"I admit, master, that it is better to philosophize or to wax poetic, to cultivate the flame in the furnace or to receive it from heaven, than to carry cats around the streets. That is why, when I heard your exclamation, I was stupid as an ass before a spit. But what would you have, my Lord? A poor devil must live, one day as well as another; and the finest Alexandrines ever penned are not worth as much as a pica of Brie when it comes to filling a hungry stomach. You know, for example, that famous epithalamium I composed for Madame Margaret of Flanders, and the Cité refuses to pay me for it on the ground that it was not good enough, as if one could furnish tragedies like those of Sophocles at four crowns apiece. Of course, I was ready to perish of hunger. Luckily, I knew that I was pretty strong in the jaw, so I said to this jaw, 'Try feats of strength and balancing; work and feed yourself.' A band of beggars, who are my very good friends, have taught me twenty different herculean feats, and now I give to my teeth every night the bread that they have helped to earn in the day. After all, I grant that it is a sorry employment of my intellectual faculties, and that man was not made to play the tambourine and to carry chairs between his teeth. But, my reverend master, in order to live one must earn a livelihood."

Dom Claude listened in silence. Suddenly his hollow eye assumed an expression so searching and so piercing that Gringoire felt that look penetrate to the inmost recesses of his soul.

"Well, Master Pierre. But how does it happen that you are now in the company of that gypsy dancing girl?"

"Mercy!" replied Gringoire. "It is because she is my wife and I am her husband."

The gloomy eyes of the priest glared like fire. "Wretch! Is this really so?" he cried, furiously grasping Gringoire's arm. "Have you so completely forsaken your God as to become the husband of that creature?"

"By my hope of Paradise, Monseigneur," answered Gringoire, trembling in every joint, "I swear that she allows me no more familiarity than if I were an utter stranger."

"What are you talking about then, husband and wife?" rejoined the priest.

Gringoire lost no time in relating to him as concisely as possible the circumstances with which the reader is already acquainted, his adventure in the Cour des Miracles, his marriage with the broken jug, and the course of life he had since followed. From his account, it appeared that the Bohemian had never shown him more kindness than she had done on the first night. "It is disappointing, though," he said, as he finished his story. "I have the misfortune of being married to a virgin."

"What do you mean?" asked the Archdeacon, whose agitation had gradually subsided during this narrative.

"It is rather difficult to explain," replied the poet. "It is a superstition. My wife, as I am informed by an old fellow we call among ourselves the Duke of Egypt, is a child that has been either lost or found, which is the same thing. She has a charm hung around her neck that, they say, will someday cause her to find her parents but that would lose its virtue if the girl were to lose hers."

"So then," rejoined Claude, whose face brightened up more and more, "you really believe, Master Pierre, that this creature is still virtuous?"

"What chance, Dom Claude, does a man have against a superstition? This, I tell you, is what she has got into her head. I consider this nunlike chastity, which keeps itself intact among those Bohemian females, who are not remarkable for that quality, a very rare circumstance indeed. But she has three things to protect her: the Duke of Egypt, who has taken her under his safeguard; her whole tribe, who hold her in extraordinary veneration, like another Notre-Dame; and a certain little dagger, which the girl always carries somewhere or other, notwithstanding the ordinances of the Provost, and which is sure to be in her hands if you just grab her waist. She is a fearless girl, I can tell you."

The Archdeacon pursued his cross-examination of Gringoire. In the estimation of the latter La Esmeralda was a charming, fascinating, inoffensive creature, with the exception of the pout peculiar to her; a simple, warmhearted girl, exceedingly ignorant and exceedingly enthusiastic; fond above all things of dancing, of noise, of the open air; a sort of human bee, having invisible wings at her feet and living in a perpetual whirl. She owed this disposition to the wandering life she had always led. Gringoire had contrived to learn as much as this, that she had traveled over Spain and Catalonia, and as far as Sicily; no, he believed that she had been carried by the caravan of Zingari to which she belonged into the Kingdom of Algiers. The Bohemians, Gringoire said, were vassals of the King of Algiers, as chief of the nation of the white Moors. So much was certain, that La Esmeralda had come to France while very young by way of Hungary. From all these countries the girl had brought scraps of odd languages, snatches of old songs, and foreign ideas, which made her language as curious a piece of patchwork as her dress, half Parisian and half African. She was a favorite with the people of those quarters of the city that she frequented, for her sweetness, her gracefulness, her personal attractiveness, her dancing, and her singing. She had a notion that in the whole city there were only two people who hated her, and of whom she often spoke with terror—the wretched recluse of the Tour-Roland, who, for some reason or other, bore an implacable enmity to the gypsies and cursed the poor dancing girl whenever she passed her cell, and a priest, whom she never encountered without being frightened by his looks and language. This last intimation disturbed the Archdeacon not a little, though Gringoire scarcely noticed his agitation so completely had the lapse of two months effaced from the memory of the thoughtless poet the singular circumstances of that night when he first met the gypsy, and the presence of the Archdeacon on that occasion. There was nothing else that the young dancer had reason to be afraid of; she never told fortunes, so she was safe from prosecutions for witchcraft, so frequently instituted against the gypsy women. And then Gringoire was as a brother to her, if not a husband. After all, the philosopher bore this kind of platonic marriage with great resignation. At any rate, he was sure of shelter and bread. Every morning he headed out from the headquarters of the Tramps, mostly in the company of the gypsy girl; he assisted her in collecting her harvest of small coins in the streets; at night he returned with her to the same room, allowed her to lock herself up in her own cell, and slept the sleep of the righteous—"a very easy life," he said, "considering all things, and very favorable for reverie." And then, in his soul and conscience, the philosopher was not sure that he was not head over heels in love with the Bohemian. He loved her goat almost as dearly. It was a charming, gentle, clever, intelligent creature—in short, a learned goat. There was nothing more common in the Middle Ages than those learned animals, which excited general wonder and frequently brought their instructors to the stake. The sorceries of the golden-hoofed goat, however, were very innocent tricks. These Gringoire explained to the Archdeacon, who appeared to be deeply interested by the details. It was enough, he said, in most cases, to hold the tambourine to the animal in such and such a way, to make it do what you wished. It had been trained in these performances by the girl, who was so extremely clever at the business that she had taken only two months to teach the goat to put together with block letters the word *Phœbus*.

"Phœbus!" exclaimed the priest. "Why Phœbus?"

"God knows," replied Gringoire. "Maybe she imagines that this word possesses some secret magic virtue. She frequently repeats it in an undertone when she thinks she is alone."

"Are you sure," inquired Claude, with his piercing look, "that it is only a word, and not a name?"

"Name! Whose name?" said the poet.

"How should I know?" rejoined the priest.

"I'll just tell you, Messire, what I am thinking. Those Bohemians are sorts of fire worshipers—thus Phœbus."

"That is not so clear to me as to you, Master Pierre."

"At any rate, it's a point I care very little about. Let her mutter her *Phœbus* as much as she pleases. This much is certain, that Djali is almost as fond of me as of her mistress."

"Who is Djali?"

"Why, that is the goat."

The Archdeacon rested his chin on the points of his fingers and for a moment appeared to be lost in thought. Then, suddenly turning toward Gringoire, "You swear," he said, "that you have never touched her?"

"What! The goat?" asked Gringoire.

"No, the girl."

"Oh! My wife! I swear I never did."

"And you are often with her?"

"Every evening for a full hour."

Dom Claude knitted his brow. "Oh! Oh! *Solus cum sola non cognitabantur orare Paternoster.* Alone with each other, we cannot believe they recite the Our Father."

"Upon my life I might say the Pater, and the Ave Maria, and the *Credo in Deum Patrem omnipotentem,* or 'I believe in God Almighty,' and she would take no more notice of me than a hen of a church."

"Swear to me, by the soul of your mother," cried the Archdeacon with vehemence, "that you have not touched this creature with the tip of your finger."

"I am ready to swear to it by the body of my father also. But, my reverend master, allow me to ask a question in turn."

"Speak."

"How can this concern you?"

The pale face of the Archdeacon crimsoned like the cheek of a bashful girl. He paused for a moment before he replied, with visible embarrassment. "Listen, Master Pierre Gringoire. You are not yet eternally lost, as far as I know. I take an interest in your welfare. Let me tell you, then, that the moment you lay a hand on that gypsy, that child of the devil, you become the vassal of Satan. It is the body, you know, that always plunges the soul into perdition. Woe betide you if you approach this creature! That is all."

"I tried once," Gringoire said, scratching his ear. "It was the first day, but I was stung."

"You had the effrontery, Master Pierre!" The priest's brow grew stormy once more.

"Another time," continued the poet with a smile, "before going to bed, I looked through the keyhole, and I saw the most beautiful woman in a nightgown who ever made a bedspring cry out under her naked foot!"

"Go to the devil! Now get out of here!" cried the priest with a terrible look and, pushing the astonished Gringoire from him by the shoulders, he retreated hastily beneath the gloomy arcades of the cathedral.

CHAPTER III

THE BELLS

Ever since the morning of the pillory the good people who lived in the neighborhood of Notre-Dame fancied that they noticed a great abatement in Quasimodo's ardor for bell ringing. Before that event the bells were going on all occasions; there were long tollings, which lasted from prime to compline, chimes for High Mass, merry peals for a wedding or a christening, mingling in the air like an embroidery of all sorts of charming sounds. The old church, all quaking and all sonorous, seemed to keep up a perpetual rejoicing. You felt incessantly the presence of a spirit of noise and caprice, speaking by all these bronze mouths. This spirit seemed now to have forsaken its abode: the cathedral appeared sullen and silent. Holidays, funerals, and the like were marked merely by the tolling that the ritual required and no more. Of the double sound that makes a church, that of the organ within and of the bells without, the former alone was left. You would have said that there was no longer a musician in the belfries. Quasimodo was still there. But what had happened to him? Was it that the shame and despair of the pillory had stayed in his heart? Did he still feel in imagination the lash of the executioner, and had the despondency caused by such treatment extinguished even his passion for the bells? Or was it possible that big Marie had a rival in the heart of the bell ringer of Notre-Dame, and that she and her fourteen sisters were neglected for a more beautiful and a more lovely object?

It so happened that in this year of grace 1482 the Annunciation fell on Tuesday the twenty-fifth of March. On that day the air was so light and serene that Quasimodo felt the love for his bells revive. So he went up into the north tower, while below the beadle threw open the doors of the church, which were at that time formed of enormous slabs of oak, covered with leather, studded with nails of gilded iron, and adorned with carvings "most cunningly wrought."

Having reached the high loft of the belfry, Quasimodo gazed for some time at the six bells with a sad shake of the head, as if lamenting that some foreign object had intruded itself into his heart between them and him. But when he had set them in motion, when he felt this bunch of bells swinging in his hand; when he saw, for he could not hear, the palpitating octave running up and down that sonorous scale, like a bird hopping from twig to twig; when the demon of Music, that demon that shakes a glittering quiver of *stretti*, trills, and *arpeggios*, had taken possession of the poor deaf bell ringer, he was once more happy. He forgot all his troubles, his heart expanded, and his face brightened up.

He paced back and forth, he clapped his hands, he ran from rope to rope, he encouraged the six chimers with voice and gesture, as the leader of an orchestra spurs on intelligent virtuosi.

"Go on, Gabrielle, go on," said he, "pour your flood of sound into the square, for it is a holiday. Don't lag, Thibault; no idling! Move, move; are you rusty, lazybones? Well done! Quick, quick! Peal it lustily: make them all deaf like me! That's right, bravely done, Thibault! Guillaume, Guillaume, you are the biggest, and Pasquier the smallest, and yet Pasquier beats you silly. Those who can hear, I wager, hear more of him than of you. Well done! Well done, my Gabrielle. Harder and harder still! Hey, you two Sparrows up there! I do not hear you give out the least chirp. Of what use is it to have those bronze mouths if you only yawn when you ought to sing? There, work away! It's the Annunciation. There is beautiful sunshine; we need a carillon. Poor Guillaume! You are quite out of breath, my big fellow!"

He was thus engaged in egging on his bells, and all six of them bounded and shook their shining haunches, like a noisy team of Spanish mules, urged first this way then that by the calls of the driver. All at once, looking down between the large slates that like scales cover the perpendicular wall of the belfry to a certain height, he saw in the square a young girl bizarrely dressed, who stopped and spread on the ground a carpet on which a little goat came and placed itself. A circle of spectators was soon formed around them. This sight suddenly changed the current of his ideas and congealed his musical enthusiasm as a breath of air congeals melted rosin. He paused, turned his back to his bells, and, leaning forward from beneath the slated penthouse, eyed the dancing girl with that pensive, kind, even tender look that had once before astonished the Archdeacon. Meanwhile the bells, left to themselves, abruptly ceased, to the great disappointment of the lovers of this kind of music, who were listening with delight to the peal from the Pont au Change, and they went away as sulky as dogs to whom you have held out a piece of meat and given a stone.

CHAPTER IV

ANÁΓKH

One fine morning in the same month of March, I believe it was Saturday, the twenty-ninth, the festival of Saint Eustache, it so happened that our young friend Jehan Frollo du Moulin noticed, while dressing himself, that his breeches, containing his purse, gave out no metallic sound. "Poor purse!" he said, drawing it out of his pocket, "not one little cent! How cruelly you have been gutted by dice, Venus, and the tavern! There you are, empty, wrinkled, flaccid. You are like the bosom of a fury. I would just ask you, Messire Cicero and Messire Seneca, whose dog-eared works lie scattered on the floor, of what use is it to me to know, better than a master of the mint or a Jew of the Pont aux Changeurs, that a gold crown is worth thirty-five unzains, at twenty-five sous eight deniers Parisis each, if I have not a single miserable black liard to risk on the double six! O Consul Cicero! This is not a calamity from which one may extricate oneself with periphrases, with *quemadmodums* and *verumenimveros*." [2]

He began to dress in silent sadness. While he was lacing his boots a thought occurred to him, but he gave it up immediately. Again it presented itself, and he put on his vest the wrong side out, an evident sign of some violent inward struggle. Eventually, throwing his cap on the ground, he exclaimed, "Too bad! Come what may I will go to my brother. I shall get a lecture, but then I shall get a crown."

Then, hastily throwing on his surcoat trimmed with fur, and picking up his cap, he rushed out of the room like a desperate man. He went down the Rue de la Harpe toward the Cité. As he passed the Rue de la Huchette his olfactory sense was gratified by the smell of the brochettes incessantly roasting there, and he cast a sheep's eye at the gigantic apparatus that one day drew from Calatagirone, the Franciscan, this pathetic exclamation: *Veramente, queste rotisserie sono cosa stupenda!* [3] But Jehan had no money to buy breakfast with, and with a deep sigh he pursued his course under the gateway of the Petit Châtelet, that enormous cluster of massive towers that guarded the entrance to the city.

He did not even take the time to throw a stone in passing, as was then customary, at the mutilated statue of Perinet Leclerc, who had surrendered the Paris of Charles VI to the English—a crime for which his effigy, defaced by stones and covered with mud, did penance for three centuries as in a perpetual pillory at the corner of the Rues de la Harpe and de Bussy.

Having crossed the Petit Pont and the Rue Neuve-Ste.-Geneviève, Jehan at length found himself before Notre-Dame. Again he wavered in his purpose, and he walked for a few moments around the statue of Monsieur Legris, repeating to himself, "I am sure of the lecture, but shall I get the crown?"

He stopped a beadle who was coming from the cloisters. "Where is the Archdeacon of Josas?" he inquired.

"I believe he is in his hideout in the tower," replied the beadle, "and I would not advise you to disturb him there, unless you have a message from a person such as the Pope or Monsieur the King."

Jehan clapped his hands. "By Jupiter!" he exclaimed, "a fine opportunity for seeing that famous den of sorcery!"

Determined by this reflection, he resolutely entered the little black door and began to ascend the winding stairs leading to the upper floors of the tower. "We shall see," he said to himself on the way. "By the whiskers of the Blessed Virgin, it must be a curious place, that cell that my reverend brother hides as carefully as his pudendum. They say that he has a roaring fire there sometimes to cook the philosophers' stone in. By God, I care no more about the philosophers' stone than about any old pebble, and I would rather find a savory omelette cooked in lard on his stove than the biggest philosophers' stone in the world!"

Having reached the pillar gallery, he stood puffing for a moment and then swore at the endless stairs by I don't know how many million cartloads of devils. Having somewhat vented his spleen, he recommenced his ascent by the little door of the north tower, which is now closed to the public. Just after he had passed the bell room, he came to a landing where there was a low arched door. Its surface was pierced by a narrow aperture that allowed him to make out a huge lock and iron armature. The curious who would like to see this door will recognize it by this inscription, carved in white letters into the dark wall, I LOVE CORALIE, 1829. SIGNED UGÈNE. *Signed* is actually in the text. "Oof!" said the scholar. "This must be the place, I suppose."

The key was in the lock, and the door unlocked, so he gently pushed it open far enough to look in.

The reader has no doubt turned over the admirable works of Rembrandt, that Shakespeare of painting. Among so many wonderful engravings there is one, representing Dr. Faustus, that you cannot look at without being dazzled. The scene is a dark cell, in the middle of which is a table covered with hideous objects—skulls, globes, alembics, compasses, parchments with hieroglyphics. Before this table is the doctor dressed in a long gown and with his fur cap pulled down to his very eyebrows. The lower part of his person is not to be seen. Half risen from his immense armchair, he leans with clenched fists on the table and is looking with curiosity and terror at a large, luminous circle, composed of magic letters, which glares on the opposite wall like the solar spectrum in a dark room. This cabalistic sun seems to the eye to tremble and fills the gloomy cell with its mysterious radiance. It is terrible, and it is beautiful.

A scene out of Dr. Faustus presented itself to Jehan when he ventured to look in the half-open door. This, too, was a gloomy hole into which the light was very sparingly admitted. It contained, too, a great armchair and a large table, compasses, alembics, skeletons of animals hanging from the ceiling, a globe lying on the floor with glass jars filled with liquids of various colors, skulls placed on parchments scrawled over with figures and letters, thick manuscripts wide open and heaped one on another—in short all the rubbish of science—and the whole covered with dust and cobwebs; but there was no circle of luminous letters, no doctor in ecstasy contemplating the flaming vision as the eagle gazes at the sun.

The cell, however, was not unoccupied. A man seated in the armchair was leaning over the table. His back was turned to Jehan, who could see no more than his shoulders and the back of his head. But he had no difficulty recognizing that bald crown, on which nature had made an everlasting tonsure, as if to mark by this outward symbol the irresistible clerical vocation of the Archdeacon.

The door had opened so softly that Dom Claude was not aware of the presence of his brother. The young rascal took advantage of this circumstance to examine the cell for a few moments. To the left of the armchair and beneath the small window was a large furnace, which he had not noticed at first glance. The ray of light that entered at the aperture passed through a circular cobweb, in the center of which the motionless insect architect looked like the hub of this wheel of lace. On the stove lay in disorder all sorts of vessels, glass phials, and retorts. Jehan noticed with a sigh that there was no saucepan. "Quite impressive, these cooking utensils." There was no fire in the furnace, nor did it appear to have been lit for quite some time. A glass mask, which Jehan observed among the implements of alchemy, and which no doubt served to protect the Archdeacon's face when he was at work on any dangerous substance, lay in one corner, covered with dust as if it were forgotten. By its side was a pair of bellows equally dusty, the surface of which bore this legend inlaid in letters of copper: *Spira, spera,* or blow and hope.

Other maxims in great number were inscribed, according to the custom of the hermetic philosophers, on the walls, some written with ink and others cut as if with a metal point. Gothic, Hebrew, Greek, and Roman letters were all mixed together; the inscriptions ran into one another, the more recent effacing the older, and all dovetailing like the boughs of a clump of trees, or pikes in a battle. They composed in fact a confused medley of all human philosophies, reveries, and knowledge. There was one here and there that was conspicuous above the rest like a pennant among the heads of lances. Most of them were short Latin or Greek mottoes, such as the Middle Ages were so clever at devising: *Unde? inde?—Homo homini monstrum.—Astra, castra; nomen, numen.—*Μέγα βιβλίον, μέγα κακόν.*—Sapere aude.—Flat ubi vult,*[4] et cetera. There were also, by the way, Hebrew scrawls, which Jehan, who knew very little of Greek, could not decipher, and the whole was crossed in all directions by stars, figures of men and beasts, and triangles, which intersected one another and contributed to make the wall of the cell resemble a sheet of paper on which a monkey has been scribbling with a pen.

In other respects the cell exhibited a general appearance of neglect and dilapidation, and from the state of the utensils it might be inferred

246 · The Hunchback of Notre-Dame

that the master had long been distracted from his usual pursuits by other occupations.

This master, meanwhile, bending over a vast manuscript adorned by grotesque paintings, appeared to be tormented by an idea that incessantly interrupted his meditations. At least this is what Jehan thought on hearing him utter this soliloquy, with the pensive pauses of one in a cave who thinks aloud:

"Yes, so Manou asserted and Zoroaster taught. The sun is the offspring of fire, the moon of the sun: fire is the soul of the universe. Its elementary atoms are incessantly overflowing and pouring on the world in innumerable currents. At the points where these currents intersect one another in the atmosphere they produce light; at their points of intersection in the earth they produce gold. Light, gold—one and the same thing! From the state of fire to the concrete state—the difference between the visible and palpable, between the fluid and solid in the same substance, between steam and ice, nothing more. This is not a dream—it is the general law of nature. But how is science to set about detecting the secret of this general law? Why, this light that floods my hand is gold! These same atoms, which expand according to a certain law, only have to be condensed according to a certain other law. How is this to be done? Some have proposed to effect it by burying a ray of the sun. Averroës—yes, it was Averroës—buried one under the first pillar on the left in the sanctuary of the Koran in the grand mosque at Córdoba; but the vault must not be opened to see whether the operation has been successful for eight thousand years."

"The devil!" said Jehan to himself. "It is a long time to wait for a crown!"

"Others have thought," continued the Archdeacon, "that it would be better to operate on a ray of Sirius. But it is very difficult to obtain one of his pure rays because of the simultaneous presence of the other stars, whose light mingles with it. Flamel conceives that it is more simple to operate on terrestrial fire. Flamel! what a predestined name! *Flamma*—yes, fire. That is all. The diamond is in charcoal, gold is in fire. But how is it to be extracted? Magistri affirms that there are certain names of women possessing so sweet and so mysterious a charm, that it is sufficient to pronounce them during the operation. Let us see what Manou says on the subject: 'Where women are honored the gods are pleased; where they are despised it is useless to pray to the gods. . . . The mouth of a woman is constantly pure; it is a running water, a ray of sunshine. . . . The name of a woman ought to be agreeable, soft, imaginary; to end with long vowels and to be like words of blessing.' Yes, the philosopher is right: thus, La Maria, La Sophia, La Esmeral—— Damnation! Always, always that thought!"

He closed the book with violence. He passed his hand over his brow, as if to chase away the idea that obsessed him. And then he took up a nail and a small hammer, the handle of which was curiously painted with cabalistic letters.

"For some time past," he said with a bitter smile, "I have failed in all my experiments. One fixed idea haunts me and pierces my brain like a red-hot iron. I have not even been able to discover the secret of Cassiodorus, who made a lamp burn without wick and without oil. A simple matter nevertheless!"

"Peste!" muttered Jehan.

"One single miserable thought, then," continued the priest, "is sufficient to make a man weak or mad! Oh! How Claude Pernelle would laugh at me! She who could not for a moment divert Nicolas Flamel from the prosecution of the great work! But don't I have in my hand the magic hammer of Zéchiélé! At every blow that the dread rabbi in the recesses of his cell struck on this nail with this hammer one of his enemies whom he had doomed to destruction sank into the earth, which eventually swallowed him up. The King of France himself, having one night knocked for an amusement at his door, sank up to his knees in the pavement of Paris. This happened less than three centuries ago. Well, I have the hammer and the nail, but then these tools are not more formidable in my hands than a ruler in the hands of a carpenter. Yet I would possess the same power if I could only discover the magic word pronounced by Zéchiélé while striking the nail."

"Nonsense!" thought Jehan.

"Let's see! Let's try!" resumed the Archdeacon with vehemence. "If I succeed, a blue spark will fly from the head of the nail. *Emen-Hétan! Emen-Hétan!*—That's not it. *Sigéani! Sigéani!*—May this nail open a grave for every man named Phœbus! . . . Curses on it! Forever and ever the same idea!"

He angrily threw down the hammer and then sank forward in his armchair on the table, so that the enormous back completely hid him from Jehan's sight. For a few minutes he saw no part of the Archdeacon except his hand convulsively clenched on a book. All at once Dom Claude rose, picked up a pair of compasses, and engraved in silence on the wall in capital letters the Greek word ΑΝΑΓΚΗ.

"My brother is mad," said Jehan to himself. "It would have been much more simple to write *Fatum*. Not everybody understands Greek."

The Archdeacon returned, seated himself again in his armchair, and laid his head on both his hands, like one whose head aches and burns to such a degree that he cannot hold it up.

The student watched his brother with astonishment. He, who carried his heart in his hand, who observed no other law in the world but the good law of nature, who let his passions run off by his inclinations, and in whom the lake of powerful emotions was always dry, so assiduous was he every morning in making new channels to drain it—he did not know how furiously this sea of human passions ferments and boils when it is refused any outlet; how it swells, how it rises, how it overflows; how it heaves in inward convulsions till it has broken down its dikes and burst its bed. The austere and icy envelope of Claude Frollo, that cold surface of inaccessible virtue, had always deceived Jehan. The jovial student never dreamed of the lava, deep and furious, that boils beneath the snowy summits of Etna.

We do not know whether these ideas occurred to him at the moment; but, volatile as he was, he apprehended that he had seen more than he ought to have seen, that he had surprised the soul of his elder brother in one of its most secret attitudes, and that he must take care not to let Claude know it. Perceiving that the Archdeacon had relapsed into his former stupor, he softly drew back his head and made some noise outside the door, that his footfall might apprise the Archdeacon of his arrival.

"Come in," cried his brother, from within the cell. "I have been waiting for you. Come in, Master Jacques."

The student boldly entered. The Archdeacon, to whom such a visitor in such a place was anything but welcome, started at the sight. "What! Is it you, Jehan?"

"It is a *J* at any rate," said the student, with his ruddy, impudent, jovial face.

The face of Dom Claude resumed its stern expression. "What brings you here?"

"Brother," replied the student, assuming as humble, modest, and decorous an air as he could, and twirling his cap on his fingers with a look of innocence, "I've come to ask of you ..."

"What?"

"A little wholesome advice, which I much need." Jehan dared not add "And a little money, which I need still more." This last half of the sentence he withheld.

"Sir," said the Archdeacon, in an austere tone, "I am highly displeased with you."

"Alas!" The student sighed.

Dom Claude turned his chair a quarter of a circle and looked steadfastly at Jehan. "I am very happy to see you," he said.

This was an ominous beginning. Jehan prepared himself for a fierce attack.

"Every day, Jehan, complaints are brought to me of your misconduct. What do you have to say for yourself about that beating you gave to the young Vicomte Albert de Ramonchamp?"

"Oh!" replied Jehan. "It was nothing! A nasty page amused himself with making his horse run in the mud to splash the students."

"And what excuse do you have," resumed the Archdeacon, "for that affair with Mahiet Targel, whose gown you tore? *Tunicam dechiraverunt*,[5] says the complaint."

"Pooh! Only one of the sorry Montaigu hoods! That's all!"

"The complaint says *tunicam* and not *capettam*. Haven't you learned Latin?"

Jehan made no reply.

"Yes," continued the priest, "the study of letters is at a low ebb now. The Latin language is scarcely understood, the Syriac unknown, the Greek so hateful that it is not called ignorance even if a great scholar skips a Greek word without pronouncing it, says, *Græcum est, non legitur.*"[6]

Jehan boldly raised his eyes. "Brother," he said, "would you like me to explain in simple French the Greek word written there on the wall?"

"Which word?"

"ΑΝΆΓΚΗ!"

A slight flush tinged the pallid cheek of the Archdeacon, like the puff of smoke that indicates the secret commotions of a volcano. The student scarcely perceived it.

"Well, Jehan," stammered the elder brother with some effort, "what is the meaning of that word?"

"Fate."

Dom Claude turned pale, and the student carelessly continued, "And that word underneath, engraved by the same hand, 'Ἀναγνεία' signifies 'impurity.' You see, I do know something of Greek."

The Archdeacon was silent. The Greek lesson had made him thoughtful. Young Jehan, who had all the art of a spoiled child, deemed it a favorable moment for hazarding his request. Assuming, therefore, as soothing a tone as possible, he began: "My good brother, surely you will not look morose and take a dislike to me merely on account of a few petty bruises and thumps given in a fair fight to a pack of boys and monkeys—*quibusdam marmosetis*.⁷ You see, I do know something of Latin, brother Claude."

But this unctuous hypocrisy failed to have its accustomed effect on the stern older brother. It did not remove a single wrinkle from the brow of the Archdeacon. "Get to the point," he said drily.

"Well, then," replied Jehan, screwing up his courage, "it is this—I need money."

At this straightforward declaration the countenance of the Archdeacon assumed a pedagogical and paternal expression.

"You know, Monsieur Jehan," he said, "that our fief of Tirechappe produces no more, deducting ground rent and other expenses for the twenty-one houses, than thirty-nine pounds, eleven sous, six deniers Parisis. This is half as much again as in the time of the Paclets, but it is not a lot."

"I need money," repeated Jehan stoically.

"You know that the official has decided that our twenty-one houses are liable to the payment of fines to the bishopric, and that to relieve ourselves from this homage we must pay the most reverend Bishop two marks in silver gilt at the rate of six pounds Parisis. Now I have not yet been able to save these two marks, as you well know."

"I know that I need money," repeated Jehan for the third time.

"And what would you do with it?"

At this question a glimmer of hope danced before Jehan's eyes. He resumed his sweet, fawning manner. "Look, my dear brother Claude, it is not for any bad purpose that I make this application. It is not to play the gallant in taverns with your money, or to parade the streets of Paris in a suit of gold brocade with a lackey at my heels. No, brother; it is for an act of charity."

"What act of charity?" inquired Claude, with some surprise.

"Two of my friends have proposed to purchase the layette for the child of a poor widow in Haudry's almshouse; it is a real charity. It would cost three florins, and I wish to contribute my share."

"What are your two friends called?"

"Pierre Knockout and Baptiste Squandergoose."

"Hmm!" said the Archdeacon. "Those are names that belong to an act of charity like a canon belongs on an altar."

Jehan had indeed picked very bad names for his two friends. He realized it too late.

The sagacious Claude continued, "What sort of layette must it be to cost three florins—and for the infant of one of the Haudry widows! Since when have those widows had young infants to provide clothes for?"

"Well, then," cried Jehan, once more arming himself with his usual impudence, "I want money to go at night to see Isabeau la Thierrye in the Val-d'Amour."

"Dissolute wretch!" exclaimed the priest.

"Ἀναγνεία," said Jehan.

This word, which stared the student in the face on the wall of the cell, produced an extraordinary effect on the priest. He bit his lips, and his anger was extinguished in a deep blush.

"Get out of here!" he said to Jehan. "I expect someone."

Jehan made another attempt. "Brother Claude, give me at least one petit Parisis to get something to eat."

"Where are you in Gratian's decrees?" asked Dom Claude.

"I have lost my exercises."

"Where are you in the Latin humanists?"

"Somebody has stolen my Horace."

"Where are you in Aristotle?"

"My goodness, brother! Which of the Fathers of the Church is it who says that heretics have in all ages sought refuge under the briars of Aristotle's metaphysics? Hang Aristotle! I will not tear my religion to rags against his metaphysics."

"Young man," replied the Archdeacon, "at the last entry of the King there was a gentleman called Philippe de Comines, who had embroidered on the trappings of his horse this motto, which I counsel you to ponder well: *Qui non laborat non manducet*. He who does not work, does not eat."

The student remained silent for a moment, with his finger on his ear, his eye on the floor, and a look of irritation on his face. Suddenly, turning toward Claude with the brisk motion of a dog wagging his tail, "Then, my good brother," he said, "you refuse me a sou to buy a crust at the baker's?"

"Qui non laborat non manducet."

At this inflexible answer of the Archdeacon's Jehan covered his face with his hands, sobbed like a woman, and cried in a tone of despair, "O το το το το τοι!"[8]

"What is the meaning of that?" asked Claude, surprised at this mischievous outburst.

"Why," said the student, after rubbing his eyes with his knuckles to give them the appearance of weeping—"it is Greek. It is an anapest of Æschylus, which expresses grief about life."

He then burst into a laugh so droll and so ungovernable that the Archdeacon could not help smiling. It was in fact Claude's fault: why had he so utterly spoiled the boy?

"Now, my good brother Claude," resumed Jehan, "only look at my worn-out boots. Did you ever see a more lamentable sight than boots whose soles stick out like tongues?"

The Archdeacon had quickly resumed his former sternness. "I will send you new boots but no money."

"Only one poor petit Parisis, brother!" besought Jehan. "I will learn Gratian by heart, I will be a good Christian, a real Pythagoras of learning and virtue. One petit Parisis, pray! Would you let me fall prey to hunger, which is staring me in the face?"

Dom Claude shook his wrinkled brow. *"Qui non laborat—"*

"Well, then," cried Jehan, interrupting him, "Long live joyfullness! I will gamble, I will fight, I will break cups, I will go see the girls!"

Saying this, he put on his cap and snapped his fingers like castanets. The Archdeacon stared at him gloomily. "Jehan, you have no soul."

"In that case, according to Epicurus, I am lacking something I cannot know that has no name."

"Jehan, you have to think seriously of mending your ways."

"Oh, that!" the student cried, looking from his brother to the still and the stove. "Everything here is of the devil, just like dice and bottles!"

"Jehan," he said, "you are on a very slippery slope. Do you know where you are heading?"

"To the tavern," said Jehan.

"The tavern leads to the pillory."

"It is a lantern like any other, and it was perhaps the one with which Diogenes found his man."

"The pillory leads to the gallows."

"The gallows is a balance, which has a man at one end and all the world at the other. It is a fine thing to be the man."

"The gallows leads to hell."

"That is a big fire."

"Jehan, Jehan, the end will be bad."

"The beginning at least will have been good."

At this moment a footfall was heard on the stairs.

"Silence!" said the Archdeacon. "Here is Master Jacques. Listen, Jehan," he added, in a lower tone, "be sure not to mention what you see and hear here. Quick! Hide under this furnace and don't so much as breathe."

The student crept under the furnace. Here an excellent idea occurred to him. "By the way, brother Claude, I must have a florin for not breathing."

"Silence! You will have it."

"But give it to me now."

"There, take it!" said the Archdeacon angrily, throwing him his purse. Jehan crawled as far as he could under the furnace, and the door opened.

CHAPTER V

The Two Men in Black

The person who entered had a black gown and a gloomy look. Our friend Jehan, who had arranged himself in his hiding place so that he could hear and see all that went on, was struck at the first glance by the perfect sadness of the visitor's garb and face. A certain gentleness at the same time covered that face, but it was the gentleness of a cat or a judge. The man was very gray, wrinkled, and close to sixty, with white eyebrows, hanging lip, and large hands. When Jehan saw that it was nobody, that is to say, in all probability some physician or magistrate, and that his nose was far from his mouth, a sure sign of stupidity, he shrank back in his hole, irritated at the prospect of having to pass an indefinite time in so confined a posture and in such bad company.

The Archdeacon meanwhile had not even risen for this visitor. He motioned to him to be seated on a stool near the door, and after a few moments' silence, in which he seemed to be pursuing a previous meditation, he said with the tone of a patron to his client, "Good day, Master Jacques."

"Good day, master," replied the man in black.

In the two ways of pronouncing on the one hand that "Master Jacques" and on the other that "master" by way of eminence, there was as much difference as between *monseigneur* and *monsieur;* it clearly indicated the master and the disciple.

"Well," resumed the Archdeacon after another silence, which Master Jacques took care not to interrupt, "have you succeeded?"

"Alas, Master," said the other with a sorrowful smile, "I keep puffing away. More ashes than I want but not an atom of gold."

A gesture of displeasure escaped Dom Claude.

"I was talking not of that, Master Jacques Charmolue, but of the proceedings against your sorcerer, Marc Cenaine, I think you called him, the butler of the Cour des Comptes. Does he confess his guilt? Has the torture produced the desired effect?"

"Alas! No," replied Master Jacques, still with his sad smile. "We don't have that consolation. The man is a rock. We could boil him in the Swine Market before he confesses. However, we are sparing no pains to get at the truth; his joints are all dislocated. We are applying all of St. John's herbs, as that old comedian, Plautus, put it.

> *Advosum stimulus, laminas, crucesque, compedesque,*
> *Nervos, catenas, carceres, numellas, pedicas, boias.*[9]

We are trying everything we can think of, but all with no effect. Oh, he is a terrible fellow! I waste my Latin on him."

"Have you found nothing further in his house?"

"Yes," said Master Jacques, groping in his pouch, "this parchment. There are words on it that are beyond our comprehension, yet Monsieur Philippe Lheulier, the criminal advocate, knows something of Hebrew, which he picked up in the affair of the Jews of Rue Kantersten at Brussels."

As he said this Master Jacques unrolled the parchment.

"Give it to me," said the Archdeacon. He skimmed it. "Pure magic, Master Jacques!" he exclaimed. "*Emen-Hétan*—that is the cry of the witches on their arrival at their sabbath meetings. *Per ipsum, et cum ipso, et in ipso*[10]—that is the command that chains down the devil in hell. *Hax, pax, max*—that belongs to medicine, a remedy for the bite of rabid dogs. Master Jacques, you are the King's Proctor in the Ecclesiastical Court: this parchment is abominable."

"We will apply the torture again. But here is something else," added Master Jacques, fumbling a second time in his pouch, "that we have found at Marc Cenaine's."

It was a vessel of the same family as those that covered Dom Claude's furnace. "Aha!" said the Archdeacon. "A crucible of alchemy!"

"I must confess," resumed Master Jacques, with his timid and awkward smile, "that I tried it on the furnace, but with no better luck than with my own."

The Archdeacon examined the vessel. "What has he engraved on his crucible? *Och, och*—the word that drives away fleas. This Marc Cenaine is an ignoramus. I can easily believe that you will not make gold with this. It is fit to put in your alcove in summer, and that is all."

"Speaking of blunders," said the King's Proctor, "I was examining the entrance below before I came up. Is Your Reverence quite sure that the one of the seven naked figures at the feet of our Lady, with wings at his heels, is Mercury?"

"Certainly," replied the priest. "So it is stated by Augustin Nypho, the Italian doctor, who had a bearded demon that revealed everything to him. But we will go down soon, and I will explain this to you by the text."

"Many thanks, master," said Charmolue, with a very low bow. "But I had nearly forgotten—when would it please you that I should order the young sorceress to be apprehended?"

"What sorceress?"

"That Bohemian, you know, who comes every day to dance in the Parvis, despite the official prohibition. She has a goat that is possessed, and has the devil's own horns, and reads, and writes, and understands mathematics, and would be enough to bring all Bohemia to the gallows. The indictment is quite ready. A handsome creature, upon my soul, that dancer! The brightest black eyes! Like a pair of gypsy jewels! When shall we begin?"

The Archdeacon turned pale as death. "I will tell you," he stammered, with a voice scarcely articulate. Then with an effort he added, "Take care of Marc Cenaine."

"Never fear," said Charmolue, smiling. "As soon as I get back I will have him strapped again to the leather bed. But he is a devil of a fellow. He tires Pierrat Torterue himself, and his hands are bigger than mine. As good Plautus says, *Nudus vinctus, centum pondo, es quando pendes per pedes.* Or, 'Naked, tied up, weighed down by a hundred pounds, tied to the feet.' The windlass will be the best thing for him."

Dom Claude appeared to be absorbed in gloomy reverie. Suddenly turning to Charmolue, he said, "Master Pierrat . . . Master Jacques, take care of Marc Cenaine."

"Yes, yes, Dom Claude. Poor man, he will have suffered a martyrdom. But then what an idea, to go to the sabbath! A butler of the Cours des Comptes, who ought to know the text of Charlemagne's ordinance. (*'Stryga vel masca?'* 'A witch or a mask?') As for the girl— Smerlarda, as they call her—I shall await your orders. Ah, true! And when we are at the entrance you will explain to me what the painted, plaster gardener is there for! Isn't it the Sower? Hey, master! What are you thinking about?"

Dom Claude, engrossed by his own thoughts, paid no attention. Charmolue, following the direction of his eye, perceived that it was mechanically fixed on a large spider's web stretched across the window. At that moment a giddy fly, attracted by the March sun, flew into the net and became entangled in it. At the shock given to his web, an enormous spider rushed from his central cell and then with one leap sprang on the fly, which he folded up in two, using his front antennae, while with his hideous sucker he attacked the head. "Poor fly!" said the Proctor and raised his hand to rescue it. The Archdeacon, suddenly starting up, held back his arm with convulsive violence. "Master Jacques!" he cried. "Let fate run its course!"

The Proctor turned around in alarm; it seemed as if his arm was held by iron pincers. The eye of the priest was fixed, wild, glaring, and gazed intently on the horrible coupling of the fly and the spider.

"Oh, yes, yes!" resumed the priest, with a voice that seemed to proceed from his very bowels. "This is a symbol of the whole affair. She is young, she flies around. She is merry, she seeks the open air, the spring sunshine, liberty. Oh, yes! But she is stopped at the fatal window; she is caught in the toils of the spider, the hideous spider! Poor dancing girl! Poor predestined fly! Be quiet, Master Jacques! It is Fate!—Alas, Claude! You are the spider. Claude, you are the fly too! You did seek science, the light, the sunshine; you only wanted to reach the open air, the broad daylight of eternal truth. But while darting toward the dazzling window, which opens into the other world, a world of brightness, intelligence, and science, blind fly, silly doctor, you did not perceive that subtle spider's web, spread by Fate between the light and you; you rushed into it, and now, with mangled head and broken wings, you struggle in the iron grip of Fate! Master Jacques! Master Jacques! Leave the spider alone!"

"I assure you," said Charmolue, who stared at him without comprehending his meaning, "that I will not meddle with it. But, for mercy's sake, master, let go of my arm! You have a hand like a vise."

The Archdeacon did not hear him. "Oh, fool! Fool," he began again, without taking his eyes for a moment off the window. "And if you could have broken through those formidable meshes with your delicate wings, do you imagine that you could then have reached the light? How would you have passed through glass that is beyond it, that transparent obstacle, that wall of crystal harder than brass, which separates all philosophies from truth? Oh, vanity of science! How many sages come fluttering from afar to dash their heads against it! How many systems come buzzing to throw themselves against this eternal window!"

He paused. The concluding reflections, which had insensibly diverted his mind from himself to science, appeared to have restored him a degree of composure. Jacques Charmolue brought him back completely to reality by asking him this question: "By the way, master, when will you come and help me make gold? I am not good at it."

The Archdeacon shook his head with a bitter smile. "Master Jacques," he replied, "read the *Dialogus de energia et operatione dœmonum*,[11] by Michael Psellus. What we are doing is not absolutely innocent."

"Speak lower, master," said Charmolue. "I thought so myself. But a man may be allowed to dabble a little in hermetics when he is merely King's Proctor in the Ecclesiastical Court at thirty crowns Tournois a year. Only let us speak more softly."

At that moment chewing sounds came from beneath the furnace and reached the alarmed ear of Charmolue.

"What is that?" he asked.

It was the student, who, cramped in his hiding place and very tired of it, found there a hard crust and a cube of moldy cheese and had started eating them without ceremony, for consolation and for breakfast. Since he was very hungry he made a great deal of noise and smacked his lips so audibly with every mouthful that he excited alarm in the Proctor.

"It's only my cat," said the Archdeacon sharply, "rewarding herself under there with a mouse."

This explanation satisfied Charmolue. "In fact, master," he replied, with a respectful smile, "every great philosopher has had his familiar beast. As Servius says, you know: *Nullus enim locus sine genio est.*"[12]

Dom Claude, apprehensive of some new prank of Jehan's, reminded his worthy disciple that they had some figures on the entrance to study together, and both left the cell, to the great relief of the student, who had begun to fear seriously that his knees and his chin would grow together.

CHAPTER VI

Consequences of Seven Oaths
Sworn in the Open Street

"Te Deum laudamus! God be praised!" exclaimed Master Jehan, climbing from his hole. "The two screech owls are gone. *Och! och! Hax! Pax! Max!* The fleas! The mad dogs! The devil! I've had quite enough of their talk! My head rings like a belfry. Moldy cheese on top of it all! Let us be off too and turn my good brother's money into bottles!"

He cast a look of kindness and admiration into the interior of the precious purse, adjusted his clothes, wiped his boots, brushed the ashes from his sleeves, whistled a tune, turned a pirouette, looked around to see if there was anything else in the cell that he could make off with, picked up here and there on the furnace some amulet of glass that could be given as a jewel to Isabeau la Thierrye, opened the door that his brother as a last indulgence had left unlocked, and that he in his turn left open as the last trick he could play on him, and descended the winding stairs, hopping like a bird.

In the shadows of the spiral staircase, he passed something that drew back grumbling and he thought it had to be Quasimodo, and this seemed so funny to him that he descended the rest of the staircase laughing his head off. He was still laughing when he entered the square.

He stamped his foot when he found himself again on the ground. "Oh, good and honorable pavement of Paris!" he exclaimed. "Cursed stairs that would make the angels of Jacob's ladder breathless! What was I thinking of to squeeze myself into that stone zigzag that pierces the sky, and all to eat moldy cheese and to see the steeples of Paris through a slit in the wall hole!"

He had advanced only a few steps when he saw the two screech owls, alias Dom Claude and Master Jacques Charmolue, contemplating one of the sculptures of the entrance. He approached them on tiptoe and heard the Archdeacon say in a very low tone to his companion, "It was Guillaume de Paris who had a Job engraved on that stone of the color of lapis lazuli, and gilded on the edges. Job represents the philosophers' stone, which must be tested and tortured in order to become perfect, as Raymond Lulle writes: *Sub conservatione formae specifi-cae salva anima.*"[13]

"What is that to me?" said Jehan to himself. "I have got the purse."

At this moment he heard a loud and sonorous voice behind him articulate a formidable volley of oaths: *"Sang Dieu! Ventre-Dieu! Bedieu! Corps de Dieu! Nombril de Belzébuth! Nom d'un pape! Corne et tonnerre!"*[14]

"Upon my soul," cried Jehan, "that can only be my friend Captain Phœbus!"

The name Phœbus struck the ear of the Archdeacon just when he was explaining to the King's Proctor the dragon hiding his tail in a bath from which smoke and a royal head issue. Dom Claude shuddered, stopped short, to the great surprise of Charmolue, turned around, and saw his brother Jehan accosting a tall officer at the door of the Gonde-laurier mansion.

It was in fact Captain Phœbus de Châteaupers. He was leaning against the corner of the house and swearing like a pagan.

"By my faith, Captain Phœbus," said Jehan, grasping his hand, "you swear with admirable verve."

"Blood and thunder!" replied the Captain.

"Blood and thunder to you!" rejoined the student. "But, I say, gentle Captain, what has occasioned this flood of fair words?"

"I beg your pardon, my good friend Jehan," cried Phœbus, shaking him by the hand, "a horse at the top of his speed cannot stop short. I was swearing at full gallop. I have just come from those affected prudes, and whenever I leave them I have my throat full of swear words. I am forced to spit them out or they would choke me outright—blood and thunder!"

"Will you come and drink with me?" asked the student.

This proposal pacified the Captain. "I would," he said, "but I have no money."

"Well, but I have."

"Aha! Let us see!"

Jehan showed the purse to the skeptical Captain. Meanwhile the Archdeacon, who had left Charmolue quite astounded, had approached and stopped within a few paces of the pair, watching both without their being aware of it, so entirely was their attention engrossed by the purse.

"A purse in your pocket, Jehan," cried Phœbus, "is like the moon in a bucket of water. You see it, but it is not there. It is only the shadow. Nothing but pebbles in it, I bet."

"These are the pebbles that I pave my pocket with," replied Jehan drily, and he emptied the pouch on a post close by, with the air of a Roman saving his country.

"By heaven!" muttered Phœbus. "Real money! It's absolutely dazzling."

Jehan retained his grave and dignified attitude. A few liards had rolled into the mud; the Captain in his enthusiasm stooped to pick them up. Jehan held him back. "Fie, Captain Phœbus de Châteaupers!" Châteaupers counted the coins and, turning with a solemn look toward his companion, said, "Do you know, Jehan, that there are twenty-three sous Parisis? Who did you rob last night in Slash a Gullet Alley?"

Jehan threw back the long, light hair that curled around his face and half-closed his disdainful eyes. "It is a good thing," he said, "to have a brother who is an archdeacon and an idiot."

"Corne de Dieu!" exclaimed Phœbus. "The worthy fellow!"

"Let us go and drink," said Jehan.

"Where shall we go?" asked Phœbus. "To Eve's Apple?"

"No, let's go to A la Vieille Science. *Une vieille qui scie une anse.*[15] It is a rebus. I like that."

"To hell with rebus, Jehan! The wine is better at Eve's Apple. And then, next to the door, there is a vine in the sun that entertains me when I drink."

"All right then, to Eve and her apple," said the student and, taking Phœbus's arm, "By the way, my dear Captain, you just said Slash a Gullet Alley. That is very bad language. We are no longer so barbarous. We say Cutthroat Alley."

The two friends then turned their steps toward the tavern known by the sign of Eve's Apple. It is unnecessary to add that they had first picked up the money, and that the Archdeacon followed them.

The Archdeacon followed them with a wild and gloomy look. Was this the Phœbus whose accursed name had, ever since his interview with Gringoire, haunted all his thoughts? He did not know, but at any rate it was a Phœbus, and this magic name was enough to lure the

Archdeacon to follow the two reckless companions with stealthy step. He listened to their conversation and watched their slightest gestures with attentive anxiety. Indeed, nothing was more easy than to hear all they said, so loudly did they carry on their conversation about duels and girls, jugs and drunken frolics.

At the turning of a street the sound of a tambourine drifted toward them from a nearby corner. Dom Claude heard the officer say to his brother, "Blood and thunder! Let us quicken our pace!"

"Why, Phœbus?"

"I am afraid the Bohemian will see me."

"What Bohemian?"

"The girl with the goat."

"La Smeralda?"

"The same, Jehan. I always forget her devil of a name. Hurry. She would recognize me. I don't want that girl to accost me in the street."

"Are you acquainted with her, Phœbus?"

Here the Archdeacon saw Phœbus grin, stoop to Jehan's ear, and whisper a few words into it. The Captain then burst into a loud laugh and tossed his head triumphantly.

"Truly?" asked Jehan.

"Upon my soul!" replied Phœbus.

"Tonight?"

"This very night."

"Are you sure she will come?"

"Are you crazy, Jehan? Does one doubt things like that?"

"Captain Phœbus, you are a lucky fellow!"

The Archdeacon heard every syllable of this conversation. His teeth chattered. A shudder, visible to the eye, thrilled his whole frame. He paused for a moment, leaned against a post like a drunken man, and again followed the trail of the two boon companions. When he rejoined them, they had moved on in the conversation. He heard them singing at the top of their lungs,

> *Les enfants des Petits-Carreaux*
> *Se font pendre comme des veaux.*[16]

CHAPTER VII

THE GOBLIN-MONK

The celebrated tavern called Eve's Apple was in the Université, at the corner of Rue de la Rondelle and Rue du Bâtonnier. There was a very spacious but very low room, with a vaulted ceiling, the central dome of which was supported by a massive wooden pillar painted yellow; the floor covered with tables, bright tin jugs hanging up against the wall, plenty of drinkers, plenty of loose women, a window on the street, a vine at the door, and over it a creaking square of sheet iron, rusted with rain and turning on an iron spike, on which were painted a woman and an apple. This kind of weathervane, which looked toward the street, was the sign of the house.

It was nightfall. The street was dark. And the tavern, full of candles, shown at a distance like a forge. The sounds of carousal, swearing, fighting, mixed with the jingle of glasses, came out from the broken panes. Through the steam that covered the window because of the heat of the room one could see swarms of confused figures, from which burst from time to time roars of laughter. The pedestrians whose business called them that way passed this noisy window without looking in, but at intervals some little, ragged urchin would stand on tiptoe to look and shout the old doggerel couplet with which it was usual in those days to greet drunkards:

> *Aux Houls,*
> *Saouls, saouls, saouls!*[17]

One man, however, kept incessantly walking back and forth before the noisy tavern, closely watching all goers and comers and never moving farther from it than a sentry from his box. He was muffled up to his eyes in a cloak. This cloak he had just bought at a shop next to the tavern, no doubt as a protection from the cold of the March evenings but perhaps also to conceal his dress. From time to time he paused before the window, looked through the small diamond-shaped panes bordered with lead, listened, and stamped his feet.

Eventually the tavern door opened. It was this that he seemed to be waiting for. Two persons who had been drinking there came out. The ray of light that escaped at the door fell for a moment on their jovial faces. The man in the cloak stationed himself in a doorway on the other side of the street to watch them.

"The clock has just struck seven," exclaimed one of the drinkers. Everyone knows that once you've ridden a bear, you are no longer afraid. But your nose follows the smell of food, like St. Jacques de l'Hôpital. "It is the time for my appointment."

"I tell you," replied his companion with a thick tongue, "that I don't live in the Rue des Mauvaises Paroles—*indignus qui inter verba mala habitat.* I live in the Rue Jean-Pain-Mollet. You are more horned than a unicorn, if you contradict me."[18]

"Jehan, my friend, you are drunk," said the other.

His companion answered, staggering, "That is what you say, Phœbus. But it is proved that Plato had the profile of a hunting dog."

The reader has no doubt already recognized our good friends the Captain and the student. The man who was watching them in the dark also appeared to have recognized them, for he slowly followed all the zigzags into which the Captain was drawn by his companion. The former, a more experienced drinker, had kept his head. The man in the cloak, listening to them attentively, was able to catch the whole of the following interesting conversation.

"Body of Bacchus! Mr. Bachelor of Arts, try to walk straight; you know I must leave you. It is seven o'clock, I tell you, and I have a date with a woman."

"Then go, leave me! I see stars and flames. You are like the castle of Dampmartin, bursting with laughter."

"By my grandmother's warts, Jehan, the nonsense you talk is too absurd. By the way, Jehan, do you have any money left?"

"Mr. Rector, there is no fault—the little butcher shop, *parva boucheria.*"

"Jehan, my friend Jehan, you know I have a rendezvous with that girl at the end of the Pont St.-Michel. You know I have to take her to Falourdel's, and I have to pay for the room in advance. The old wench with white whiskers won't let me have any credit. Surely, Jehan, we have not drunk all the priest's money. See if you don't have one Parisis left."

"The consciousness of having spent the other hours to good purpose is an excellent sauce to the table."

"Damnation! Stop this nonsense, Jehan. Tell me, do you have any money left? I must have some, or, by heaven, I will rifle your pockets, even if you were a leper like Job or mangy like Caesar."

"Why, sir, the Rue Galiache is a street that has the Rue de la Verrerie at one end, and the Rue de la Tixeranderie at the other."

"Quite right, my dear friend Jehan, so it has. But, for heaven's sake! Come to your senses. It is seven o'clock, and I want just one sou Parisis."

"Silence, now—silence to the song, and attention to the chorus:

> When it shall befall the cats
> To be eaten up by rats,
> Then the King of Arras city
> Shall be master—more's the pity!
> When at Saint John's tide the sea,
> Wide and warm although it be,
> Shall be frozen firm and fast,
> As if by winter's blast;
> Then the folks from Arras, they
> Over the ice shall trudge away.[19]

"Student of Antichrist!" cried Phœbus, "may your brains be dashed out with your own books!" At the same time he gave the intoxicated student a violent push, which sent him reeling against the wall, where he fell gently on the pavement of Philip Augustus. From a relic of that brotherly compassion that is never wholly banished from the heart of a drunkard, Phœbus rolled Jehan with his foot onto one of those pillows of the poor that Providence keeps ready in the corners of all the streets of Paris, and that the wealthy disdainfully stigmatize with the name "garbage heap." The Captain placed Jehan's head on an inclined plane of cabbage stalks, and the student instantly began snoring in a magnificent bass. Yet the Captain's heart was not wholly free from animosity. "So much the worse for you if the devil's cart picks you up as it passes!" he said to the sleeping student, and away he went.

The man in the cloak, who was still following him, paused for a moment before the helpless youth, as if undecided what to do; then, heaving a deep sigh, he continued to follow the Captain.

Like them we will leave Jehan sleeping beneath the canopy of heaven and speed after them, if it pleases the reader.

On reaching the Rue St.-André-des-Arcs, Phœbus noticed that someone was following him. Happening to turn, he saw a kind of shadow creeping behind him along the walls. He stopped; the figure stopped. He walked on; the figure walked on. He felt only little alarm at this discovery. "Pooh!" he said to himself. "I don't have a sou."

He halted in front of the college of Autun, where he had begun what he called his studies, close to the statue of Cardinal Pierre Bertrand, carved on the right of the doorway. There, out of naughty schoolboy habit, he never passed the statue without inflicting on it the offense of which Priapus so bitterly complains in Horace's satire *"Olim truncus eram ficulnus."*[20] He was so assiduous in his performance of his duty that the inscription BISHOP OF AUTUN was almost completely effaced. He stopped in front of the statue as was his habit. The street was absolutely deserted. Nothing was to be seen but the figure, which approached him with slow steps, so slow that he had abundant time to observe that it had a cloak and a hat. When very near to him it stopped and remained as motionless as the statue of Cardinal Bertrand, intently fixing on him, however, a pair of eyes glaring with that vague light that glows at night from those of a cat.

The Captain was brave and would not have cared a rush for a robber with a cudgel in his fist. But this walking statue, this petrified man, thrilled him with horror. There were at that time in circulation a number of stories of a goblin-monk who haunted the streets of Paris at night; these stories crowded confusedly on his memory. He stood stupefied for some minutes, and then broke the silence with a forced laugh. "If you are a robber, as I hope," he said, "you are somewhat like a heron attacking a nutshell. I am the son of a ruined family, my dear fellow. Seek some better game. In the chapel of that college there is some wood of the true Cross, which is kept in the treasure room."

The hand of the figure was stretched out from under the cloak and grasped Phœbus's arm with the force of an eagle's talons. "Captain Phœbus de Châteaupers," said the specter at the same moment.

"What the devil!" cried Phœbus. "You know my name!"

"Not only your name," replied the mysterious stranger in a sepulchral tone. "You have a rendezvous this evening."

"I have," answered the astounded Phœbus.

"At seven o'clock."

"In a quarter of an hour."

"At Falourdel's at the Pont St.-Michel."

"Precisely so."

"To meet a woman."

"I plead guilty."

"Whose name is . . ."

"La Smeralda," said Phœbus gaily, having by degrees recovered his levity.

At that name the specter shook the Captain's arm with violence. "Captain Phœbus de Châteaupers, you lie!"

Whoever could have seen at that moment the flushed face of the Captain, the backward bound that he made with such force that he pulled his arm from the grip in which it was held, the fierce look with which he grasped the hilt of his sword, and the motionless attitude of the cloaked figure—whoever had witnessed this would have been frightened. It was something like the battle between Don Juan and the statue.

"Christ and Satan!" cried the Captain. "That is a word to which the ear of a Châteaupers is not accustomed. You dare not repeat it."

"You lie!" the specter said drily.

The Captain gnashed his teeth. Goblin-monk, phantom, superstitious tales were all forgotten at the moment. He only saw a man and an insult. "Bravely said!" he stammered, half choked with rage. He drew his sword, and in a faltering voice—for rage makes one tremble as well as fear—cried: "Here! On the spot! This very moment! Draw your sword. Draw! Blood must be spilled on this pavement!"

Meanwhile the other neither flinched nor stirred. When he saw his adversary on guard and ready for the combat, he said, "Captain Phœbus," in a tone shaking with bitterness. "You forget your rendezvous."

In men like Phœbus gusts of passion are like boiling milk, which a drop of cold water is sufficient to calm. At those few simple words the Captain dropped the weapon that glistened in his hand.

"Captain," continued the stranger, "tomorrow, the day after tomorrow, a month, a year, ten years from now, you will find me ready to cut your throat, but first go to your rendezvous."

"In fact," said Phœbus, as if seeking to surrender it himself; "a sword and a girl are two delightful things to encounter in a meeting. But I don't see why I should give up one for the other when I can have both."

He put his sword back in the scabbard.

"Go to your rendezvous," repeated the unknown.

"Many thanks, sir, for your courtesy," replied Phœbus, with some embarrassment. "It is very true that there will be time enough tomorrow to slash and cut buttonholes in Father Adam's doublet. I am indebted to you for allowing me one more pleasant quarter of an hour. I did hope, to be sure, to put you to bed in the gutter, and yet be in time for my appointment, especially as in such cases it is stylish to make the girls wait a little. But you appear to be a hearty fellow, and it is safest to put off our meeting till tomorrow. So I shall go to my rendezvous, which is for the hour of seven, as you know." Here Phœbus tapped his forehead. "Ah! I forgot! I must have money, and I have not a single sou left to pay for the miserable room. The old hag always wants to be paid up front. She doesn't trust me."

"Here is the money," said the stranger.

Phœbus felt the cold hand of the stranger slip into his a heavy coin. He could not help taking it and pressing that hand.

"By heaven!" he exclaimed. "You are a good fellow!"

"One condition!" said the stranger. "Prove to me that I was wrong, and that you spoke the truth. Hide me in some corner, where I may see whether the girl is really the same whose name you mentioned."

"Oh!" replied Phœbus. "That will make no difference to me. We will take a room at Ste.-Marthe. You can see everything from the garret next to it."

"Come along, then," answered the figure.

"At your service," said the Captain. "For all I know, you may be the devil in person, but let us be good friends tonight; tomorrow I will pay you my debts, both of the purse and of the sword."

They walked away quickly. In a few minutes the noise of the river apprised them that they were on the Pont St.-Michel, at that time covered with houses. "I will first let you in," said Phœbus to his companion, "and then I'll go get the girl, who is to wait for me near the Petit Châtelet." That companion made no reply; since they had been walking side by side he had not uttered a word. Phœbus stopped before a low door, against which he kicked violently. A light glimmered through the crevices of the door. "Who's there?" cried a weak voice. *"Corps-Dieu! Tête-Dieu! Ventre-Dieu!"* replied the Captain. The door instantly opened and revealed an old woman and a lamp, both of which trembled. The hag was bent almost double and dressed in rags. Her head shook, and her hands, face, and neck were covered with wrinkles. She had very small eyes; her lips receded almost to her toothless gums, and all around her mouth she had long white hairs resembling the whiskers of a cat. The interior of her dwelling was no less dilapidated. The walls were of plaster; the ceiling was formed of the black rafters and floor of the room above; the fireplace was dismantled, and every corner was covered by cobwebs. Two or three rickety tables and stools occupied the middle of the floor; a dirty boy was playing in the ashes, and at the farther end the stairs, or rather ladder, led up to a trapdoor in the ceiling. On entering this den, the Captain's mysterious companion drew his cloak up to his eyes while Phœbus kept swearing like a Turk. He put into the hand of the old woman the coin that had been given to him by the stranger. He made the sun shine in an écu, as our admirable Régnier put it. "St. Martha's room," added Phœbus. The crone, who called him Monseigneur with every other word, deposited the coin in a drawer. While her back was turned the ragged urchin rose from the hearth, slowly went to the drawer, took out the piece of money, and put a dry leaf that he had pulled from the kindling in its place.

The old woman beckoned to the two gentlemen, as she called them, to follow and ascended the ladder before them. On reaching the room above she set the lamp on a trunk, and Phœbus opened a door that led to a dark closet. "This way, my good fellow," he said to his companion. The man in the cloak complied without uttering a word. The door closed after him; he heard Phœbus bolt it and a moment afterward go downstairs with the old woman. The light disappeared along with them.

CHAPTER VIII

The Usefulness of Windows Looking Toward the River

Claude Frollo—for we presume that the reader, more intelligent than Phœbus, has discovered that the specter-monk was no other than the Archdeacon—Claude Frollo groped around for a few moments in the dark hole in which the Captain had bolted him. It was in fact a loft such as builders sometimes leave in the roof above the outer walls of a house. The vertical section of this garret, as Phœbus had aptly called it, would have been a triangle. It had neither window nor loophole, and the inclined plane of the roof would not permit a person to stand upright in it. Claude therefore crouched in dust and mortar that crunched under him. His brain seemed to be on fire, but what passed at that moment in the dark soul of the Archdeacon none but God and himself could ever know.

In what fatal order did he arrange in his thoughts La Esmeralda, Phœbus, Jacques Charmolue, his young brother, whom he so loved yet whom he had left in the mud, his Archdeacon's gown, his reputation perhaps, staked as it was at Falourdel's—all these images, all these adventures? I cannot tell. But it is certain that these ideas formed in his mind a horrible constellation.

He waited a full quarter of an hour. To him this interval appeared a century. Suddenly he heard the stairs creak; someone was coming up. The trapdoor opened; a light was discernible. In the crazy door of the loft there was a crevice to which he brought his eye. It was wide enough to allow him to see all that went on in the adjoining room. The old woman appeared first, with the lamp in her hand, then Phœbus, turning up his whiskers, then a third face, that of the beautiful and graceful Esmeralda. The priest saw it rise above the floor like a dazzling apparition. Claude trembled; a cloud darkened his eyes; his arteries beat with violence; he was stunned with a rushing like a mighty wind; everything around him seemed to whirl; and suddenly sight and hearing failed him.

When he regained his senses, Phœbus and La Esmeralda were alone, sitting on the wooden chest by the side of the lamp, which threw a strong light on their two youthful faces and enabled the Archdeacon to discover a miserable bed at the far end of the garret.

Beside this bed was a window, through the panes of which, broken like a spider's web by a shower of rain, he could see a patch of sky and the moon couched on a bed of light downy clouds.

The girl was flushed, confused, trembling. Her long, downcast eyelashes shaded her crimson cheeks. The face of the officer, to which she dared not raise her eyes, was radiant with delight. Unconsciously, and with a charming clumsiness, she traced unmeaning lines on the lid of the chest with the tip of her finger and then looked at the finger that had been thus employed. Her feet could not be seen; the little goat was cowering on them.

The Captain was very elegantly dressed: he had great tufts at his collar and cuffs. This was the style of the times. Dom Claude did not manage to listen to their conversation without pain. He heard what they said through the sound of boiling blood in his veins.

An amorous conversation is very banal. It is a perpetual *I love you*— a phrase musical enough to the parties concerned but exceedingly dull and insipid to indifferent listeners when not adorned with a few rhetorical flourishes. Claude, however, was not an indifferent listener.

"Oh! Do not despise me, Monseigneur Phœbus!" said the girl, without raising her eyes. "I fear that what I am doing is wrong."

"Despise you, my pretty dear!" replied the officer, with a superior and distinguished air of gallantry. "Despise you! Why?"

"For having followed you."

"I perceive, my beauty, that we don't understand one another. I ought, by rights, not to despise you but to hate you."

The girl looked at him in alarm. "Hate me! What, then, have I done?"

"For your having needed so much wooing."

"Alas!" she said. "I am breaking a vow. . . . I shall never find my parents again. . . . The charm will lose its power. But no matter! What do I need a father or mother for now?"

As she spoke, she fixed on the Captain her large, dark eyes, moist with delight and tenderness.

"Devil take me if I understand you!" exclaimed Phœbus.

La Esmeralda was silent for a moment; a tear then trickled from her eye, a sigh burst from her lips, and she said, "Oh, my Lord, I love you!"

There was around this young girl such an air of chastity, such a spell of virtue, that Phœbus did not feel quite at ease by her side. This confession, however, emboldened him. "You do love me!" he said, with transport, throwing his arm around the waist of the gypsy. He had waited for the chance.

"Phœbus," resumed the Bohemian, gently removing from her waist his tenacious hand, "you are kind, you are generous, you are handsome; you saved me, who am but a poor orphan. I have long been dreaming about an officer saving my life. It was you that I dreamed of before I knew you; the officer of my dreams had a handsome uniform like you, the look of a gentleman, and a sword. Your name is Phœbus; it is a fine name; I love your name, I love your sword. Draw your sword, Phœbus—let me look at it."

"Strange girl!" said the Captain, unsheathing his sword with a smile. The gypsy looked at the handle and at the blade, examined with special curiosity the cipher on the hilt, and kissed the weapon, saying, "You belong to a brave man. I love my captain."

As she bent over it Phœbus availed himself of the opportunity to imprint a kiss on her beautiful neck. The girl suddenly raised her head with a face red like a cherry. The priest gnashed his teeth in the dark.

"Phœbus," the gypsy began again, "let me talk to you. Just stand up and walk, and let me hear your spurs rattle. How handsome you are!"

The Captain rose in compliance with her wish and said in a tone of rebuke, yet with a smile of satisfaction, "Why, how childish you are! . . . But, my dear, did you ever see me in my ceremonial uniform?"

"Alas, no!" she replied.

"Now that is handsome."

Phœbus went and again seated himself beside her, but much closer than before.

"Listen, my dear . . ."

The gypsy patted his lips with her pretty hand, with the grace and playfulness of a child. "No, no, I won't listen to you. Do you love me? I want you to tell me if you love me."

"Do I love you, angel of my life?" exclaimed the Captain, half-sinking on his knee. "I love you and have never loved any but you."

The Captain had so often repeated this declaration in many a similar situation that he uttered it without forgetting a word or making a single blunder. At this impassioned declaration the gypsy raised her eyes with a look of angelic happiness toward the dirty ceiling that here usurped the place of heaven. "Oh!" she softly murmured. "This is the moment when one ought to die!"

Phœbus thought it the right time for stealing another kiss, which inflicted fresh torment on the miserable Archdeacon in his hiding place.

"To die," cried the amorous Captain. "What are you talking of, my angel? Why, it is the very time to live, or Jupiter is a fake! Die at such a moment as this! A good joke, by the devil's horns. . . . No, no, that won't do. Listen, my dear Similar . . . excuse me, Esmenarda . . . but you have such a prodigiously outlandish name that I can't get it into my head. It is an obstacle that gets in my way."

"Good God!" said the poor girl. "And I thought it a pretty name just because of its outlandishness. But since you dislike it, I will change it to whatever you please."

"No, my darling, don't think about such trifles! It is a name one must get used to, that's all. When I have learned it by heart, I shall say it without a problem. But listen, my dear Similar, I passionately adore you. I cannot tell how much I love you. It is a marvel, and I know a girl who is bursting with rage about it."

"Who is that?" inquired the jealous girl.

"That has nothing to do with us," said Phœbus. "Do you love me?"

"Do I?" she said.

"Well, that is enough. You shall see how I love you too. May the great devil Neptunus impale me on his fork if I don't make you the happiest girl in the world! We will have a pretty little apartment somewhere or other. My archers shall parade under your windows. They are all on horseback, and Captain Mignon's look like fools next to them. I will take you to the Grange de Rully—it is a magnificent sight. Eighty thousand armed men; thirty thousand suits of bright armor, cuirasses or brigandines; the sixty-seven banners of all the trades; the standards of the Parliament, the Chambre des Comptes, the workers of the Mint—in short, a hell of a spectacle. I'll take you to see the lions at the Hôtel du Roi. All the women love it."

For some moments the girl, absorbed in her own charming thoughts, was drinking in the intoxicating tones of his voice without listening to the meaning of his words.

"Oh! You shall be so happy!" continued the Captain, at the same time examining the buckle of her belt.

"What are you doing?" she said sharply, roused from her reverie.

"Nothing," replied Phœbus. "I was only saying that you must abandon this strange outfit when you are with me."

"When I am with you, my Phœbus!" said the girl affectionately, and again she became silent and thoughtful. Suddenly she turned toward him. "Phœbus," she said, with an expression of infinite love, "teach me your religion."

"My religion!" cried the Captain, bursting into a laugh. "I instruct you in my religion! Blood and thunder! What do you want with my religion?"

"So that we may be married," replied the gypsy.

The Captain's face assumed a mixed expression of surprise, disdain, and licentious passion. "Pooh!" he said. "What should we marry for?"

The Bohemian turned pale and sorrowfully drooped her head on her chest.

"My sweet one," returned Phœbus tenderly, "these are silly notions. Of what use is marriage? Do people love one another the less for not having mangled Latin in the presence of a priest?" As he said this in his kindest tones, he came very close to the gypsy girl; his caressing hands reassumed their position around her narrow, supple waist. His eyes glowed more and more, and everything betrayed the fact that Monsieur Phœbus was obviously reaching one of those states in which Jupiter himself did so many foolish things that Homer was obliged to call in the clouds for help.[21]

Dom Claude, meanwhile, saw all that went on. The planks of which the door was made were so decayed that they left large gaps for his hawk's eye. The swarthy, broad-shouldered priest, who had previously known only the austere virginity of the cloister, quivered and boiled at the scene. The sight of the beautiful girl in a tête-à-tête with the ardent officer seemed to infuse molten lead into his veins. He was extraordinarily disturbed. His eye plunged with jealous desire beneath all the undone buttons. Whoever could have seen, at that moment, the face of the unhappy man closely pressed against the cracks of the door would have taken it for the face of a tiger watching from its cage a hyena devouring a gazelle. His eyes flamed like candles through the gaps of the door.

All at once Phœbus snatched away the gypsy's shawl. The poor girl, who had remained pale and dreamy, started up and hastily retreated from the enterprising officer. Casting a glance at her bare shoulders, blushing, confused, and dumb with shame, she crossed her two finely turned arms over her bosom to conceal it. Except for the flush that crimsoned her cheeks, whoever saw her so silent, motionless, and with downcast eyes, would have taken her for a statue of Modesty.

This attack of the Captain's on her outfit had uncovered the mysterious amulet that she wore around her neck.

"What is that?" he said, seizing this pretext for approaching the beautiful creature whom his vehemence had just frightened.

"Don't touch it," she answered sharply. "It is my protector. It will enable me to find my family, if I do nothing unworthy of it. Oh leave me, Captain, I beg you! Ah, Mother! My poor mother! Where are you? Help, help your child! Captain Phœbus, please give me my shawl!"

"Oh, mademoiselle!" said Phœbus, stepping back, in a tone of indifference. "I see plainly that you do not love me."

"I do not love you!" exclaimed the unhappy girl, at the same time clinging to the Captain and making him sit down by her. "Not love you, my Phœbus! Cruel man to say so! Do you want to break my heart? Take me! Take everything! . . . I am yours. Of what use to me is the amulet! What need do I have of a mother! To me you are father and mother because I love you, Phœbus, my beloved Phœbus. Look at me; you will not push away one who seeks you out of her own accord. My soul, my life, my body, my person, my all are yours. So we won't marry because it bores you. Who am I, a miserable gutter girl, while you Phœbus are a gentleman. What a marriage that would be if a street dancer were betrothed to an officer! I was mad. I will be the proudest and happiest of women. And when I grow old and ugly, Phœbus, when I am no longer fit for you to love, then permit me to be your servant. Others will then embroider scarves for you, but you will let me clean your boots and your spurs, and brush your uniform. You will grant me that indulgence, won't you, my Phœbus? Meanwhile, take me; let me belong to you and be the only object of your love. We gypsies want nothing else but air and love."

As she said this she threw her arms around the neck of the officer. She looked at him, smiling through her tears with the gaze of a supplicant. Her delicate throat was pressed against the rough cloth and embroidery of his uniform. She twisted her beautiful, half-naked body on his knees. The Captain, intoxicated, pressed ardent lips to the beautiful dark shoulders. The young girl, eyes turned toward the ceiling, fell back, trembling and palpitating under this kiss.

All at once above the head of the captain she beheld another head—a livid, green, convulsive face, with the look of one of the damned; close to this face was a hand holding a dagger. It was the face and the hand of the priest. He had broken down the door!

The girl was struck speechless and paralyzed by this terrible apparition; she was like a dove raising her head just when a falcon finds her nest. She didn't even have the power to shriek. She saw the dagger descend on the Captain and rise again bloodied. "Perdition!" he exclaimed and fell. She fainted.

When her eyes closed and her senses were forsaking her, she thought she felt a kiss, like the executioner's hot iron, impressed on her lips. On coming to herself, she was surrounded by soldiers of the watch. The Captain was carried away bathed in blood. The priest was gone. The window at the farther end of the chamber, which looked toward the river, was wide open. A cloak, supposed to belong to the officer, was picked up, and she heard the men saying to one another, "A witch has stabbed a captain."

BOOK VIII

CHAPTER I

The Coin Transformed into a Dry Leaf

For over a month Gringoire and the whole crew in the Cour des Miracles had been in a state of extreme anxiety. La Esmeralda was missing. They knew neither what had become of her, which sorely grieved the Duke of Egypt and his vagabond subjects, nor what had become of her goat, which redoubled Gringoire's sorrow. One night the girl had disappeared, and all searches had proved fruitless; no traces of her could be discovered. A few dirty beggars had told Gringoire that they had met her that evening near the Pont St.-Michel, walking along with an officer; but this husband after the fashion of Bohemia was a skeptical philosopher; and, besides, he knew better than anyone else how well his wife could defend herself. He had had abundant opportunities of judging what invincible chastity resulted from the two combined virtues of the amulet and the gypsy, and had mathematically calculated the resistance of that chastity to the second power. He was therefore quite easy on that point.

But for this very reason he was more puzzled by her disappearance. So deeply did he take it to heart that he would have worried himself thinner had it been possible for him to become skinnier than he was. He had forgotten everything else, even his literary pursuits, even his great work *De figuris regularibus et irregularibus,*[1] which he intended to get printed with the first money he got. For he was head over heels in love with printing, ever since he had seen the *Didaskalon* of Hugo St.-Victor,[2] printed with the celebrated types of Vindelin of Spire.

One day, while sorrowfully passing the Tournelle, a prison for criminals, he perceived a crowd of people around one of the doors of the Palace of Justice. "What is going on here?" he asked a young man who was coming out.

"I do not know, sir," answered the young man. "I am told that they are trying a woman for murdering an officer of the King's Ordinance. Because there seems to be something of sorcery in the business, the Bishop and the official have interfered; my brother, the Archdeacon of Josas, devotes all his time to it. I wanted to speak to him but could not get to him for the crowd, which irritated me exceedingly, because I am in great need of money."

"Alas, sir!" said Gringoire. "I wish it was in my power to lend you some, but my breeches are all in holes, not with crowns or any other coin, I can assure you."

He dared not tell the young man that he knew his brother, the Archdeacon, whom he had never called on since the scene in the church—a negligent behavior of which he felt ashamed.

The student went his way, and Gringoire followed the crowd ascending the great staircase. In his estimation there was nothing like a criminal trial for dispelling melancholy; the judges were in general so amusingly stupid. The people with whom he had mingled moved on and elbowed one another in silence. After a slow and tiresome shuffling along an endless passage, which wound through the palace like the intestinal canal of the old building, he arrived at a low door opening into a hall, which, from his stature, he was enabled to survey above the undulating heads of the crowd.

The hall was spacious and dark, which made it appear still larger. Night was falling; the long windows admitted only a faint light, which faded before it reached the vaulted roof, an enormous trellis of carved woodwork whose thousand figures seemed to move confusedly in the dark. There were already several lighted candles here and there on the tables, which threw their rays on the heads of clerks poring over heaps of papers. The back of the hall was occupied by the crowd; on the right and left were lawyers seated at tables; at the farther end, on a raised platform, a great number of judges, men with immovable and sinister-looking faces, the last rows of whom were scarcely discernible in the darkness. The walls were covered with a field of fleurs-de-lis. A large crucifix was indistinctly seen above the judges, and on every side an array of pikes and halberts, which the light of the candles seemed to tip with fire.

"Sir," said Gringoire to one of his neighbors, "who are all those people sitting in rows there, like prelates in council?"

"Sir," answered his neighbor, "those are the counselors of the great chamber on the right, and the counselors of inquiry on the left; the masters in black gowns, and the messires in red ones."

"And who is that great red thing sweating?" inquired Gringoire.

"That is Monsieur the President."

"And those sheep behind him?" continued Gringoire, who, as we have already observed, was not fond of magistrates. This was perhaps because of the grudge he bore the Palace of Justice ever since his theatrical misadventure.

"They are the Masters of Requisitions of the King's household."

"And that boar in front of them?"

"The clerk to the Court of Parliament."

"And that crocodile, on the right?"

"Master Philippe Lheulier, Special Attorney to the King."

"And that great black cat on the left?"

"Master Jacques Charmolue, the King's Proctor in the Ecclesiastical Court, with the gentlemen of the officiality."

"But, I ask you, sir, what are all these worthy folks doing here?"

"They are trying somebody."

"Who is it? I do not see the accused."

"It is a young woman, sir. She stands with her back toward us, and we can't see her for the crowd. Why, there she is, where you see that group of halberts."

"Do you know her name?" asked Gringoire.

"No, sir, I've just arrived, but I presume that there is sorcery in the case, as the clergy attends the trial."

"Come on!" said our philosopher. "Let us watch all these lawyers banqueting on human flesh! It is a spectacle as good as any other."

Here the bystanders imposed silence on the interlocutors. An important witness was under examination.

"Gentlemen," said an old woman in the middle of the hall, who was so muffled up she looked like a walking bundle of rags, "gentlemen, it is true that my name is Falourdel, and that I have kept house for forty years on the Pont St.-Michel, and regularly paid rent, taxes, and rates. My door is opposite the house of Tassin-Caillart, the fabric dyer who is upstream from me. A poor old woman now, my lords, but once a pretty girl. People had been telling me for a few days, 'La Falourdel, don't use your spinning wheel too much at night. The devil likes to comb old women's spinning with his horns.' I am sure that the goblin-monk that was wandering around the temple last year is now roaming the Cité. One night I was spinning when there was a knock at my door. I asked 'Who's there?' and there was such a swearing! I opened the door: two men came in, a man in black with a handsome officer. Nothing was to be seen of the man in black but his eyes, for all the world like two burning coals; all the rest of him was cloak and hat. 'Saint Martha's room!' they said to me. That is my room upstairs, gentlemen, my best room. They gave me a crown. I put it into my drawer, saying to myself, 'It will serve tomorrow to buy tripe at the butcher's of the Gloriette.' Well, we went upstairs, and while my back was turned the man in black disappeared. This amazed me a little. The officer, as handsome a gentleman as you would wish to set eyes on, went downstairs with me, and out he goes. By the time I had spun a quarter of a bobbin, in he comes again with a pretty doll of a girl, who would have dazzled you like the sun if she had been properly attired. She had with her a goat, a large goat; it might be black, it might be white, I don't recollect now. The girl—that was no concern of mine—but the goat, I must say . . . I don't like those animals; they have got a beard and horns . . . too like a man . . . and then the thing smells of witchcraft. However, I said nothing, and why should I? Hadn't I got the money? And all right too, my lord, wasn't it? So I took the Captain and the girl to the room upstairs and left them alone, that is to say, with the goat. I went down and began spinning again. . . . But I ought to tell you that my house has a ground floor and a floor above: the back of it looks out on the river, like all the other houses on the bridge, and the windows of both the ground floor and the chamber open toward the water. Well, as I said just now, I began spinning again. I can't tell why I thought of the goblin-monk, which the goat had put into my head—and then the girl was dressed in such a strange fashion! . . . Well, suddenly I heard such a scream upstairs, and something fall on the floor, and the window open. I ran to my window, which is under it, and saw a black figure drop before my eyes and tumble into the water. It was a specter in the habit of a priest. The moon was shining bright, so I saw it as plain as I see you now. It swam away toward the city. I was trembling all over and called the watch. When those gentlemen came in, they did not know what to make of it at first, and, being rather drunk, they began beating me. I soon set them right. We went up, and what should we find but my best room drenched with blood, the Captain lying at full length with a dagger in his bosom, the girl pretending to be dead, and the goat frightened out of its wits! 'A pretty job!' I said. 'It will take me two weeks to get the floor clean again—scour and scrub it as I must.' They carried away the officer—poor young man!—and the girl with her bosom all bare. . . . But, worse than that, the next day, when I went to the drawer for the crown to buy tripe, lo and behold! I found nothing but a withered leaf where I had left it!"

The old woman ceased speaking. A murmur of horror arose from the listeners. "The specter, the goat, and all that, look very like much sorcery," said Gringoire to a neighbor. "Oh yes, and the withered leaf," added another. "No doubt," observed a third, "it was a witch working with the goblin-monk to rob the officer." Gringoire himself could scarcely help thinking that there was some probability in the conjecture.

"Witness," said the president in a dignified manner, "have you nothing further to communicate to the court?"

"No, my lord," replied the old woman, "only that in the report my house is called a crazy, filthy hovel, which is an outrageous falsehood. To be sure, the houses on the bridge are not the best looking because there are so many people living there, but butchers like to live in them, and they are rich and some of them are married to very good looking, clean women."

The magistrate whom Gringoire had compared to a crocodile now rose. "Silence!" he said. "I beg you, my lord and gentlemen, to bear in mind that a dagger was found on the accused. Witness, have you brought with you the leaf into which the crown given you by the demon was changed?"

"Yes, sir," she replied. "Here it is."

An usher handed the dry leaf to the crocodile, who gave a sinister shake of the head and passed it to the president; and the president sent it to the King's Proctor in the Ecclesiastical Court; so it went the rounds of the hall. "Upon my word, a birch leaf!" ejaculated Master Jacques Charmolue. "More proof of sorcery!"

A counselor then rose and spoke. "Witness," he said, "two men went upstairs together in your house: a man in black, who immediately disappeared, and whom you afterward saw swimming in the Seine, in the habit of a priest, and the officer. Which of the two gave you the crown?"

The old woman considered for a moment. "It was the officer," she said.

A murmur again ran through the court. "Aha!" thought Gringoire, "that alters the case materially."

Master Philippe Lheulier, Special Attorney to the King, again interposed. "Let me remind you, my lord and gentlemen, that the officer, in his deposition, taken in writing by his bedside, while admitting that he had a confused idea when he was accosted by the man in black that it might be the goblin-monk, added that the phantom had strongly urged him to keep his appointment with the accused; and when the said Captain observed that he had no money, he gave him the crown with which the officer paid the witness Falourdel. The crown therefore is a coin of hell."

This conclusive observation appeared to dispel all the lingering doubts of Gringoire and the other skeptics among the audience.

"Gentlemen are in possession of the papers," added the King's Attorney, sitting down. "They can refer to the deposition of Captain Phœbus de Châteaupers."

At that name the accused rose. Her head was seen above the crowd. To his horror, Gringoire recognized La Esmeralda.

She was pale; her hair, once so gracefully braided and woven with sequins, was disheveled; her lips were blue, her eyes hollow. Alas! What a change!

"Phœbus!" she exclaimed wildly. "Where is he? Oh, my lords, before you put me to death, for mercy's sake tell me if he still lives!"

"Silence, woman!" replied the president. "We have nothing to do with that."

"If you have any pity, tell me if he is alive!" she resumed, clasping her beautiful, thin hands; her chains rustled along her dress.

"Well," said the King's Advocate drily, "he is dying. Are you satisfied?"

The unhappy girl sank down again on her seat, voiceless, tearless, white as wax.

The president stooped toward a man placed at his feet, who had a gold-laced cap, a black gown, a chain around his neck, and a wand in his hand. "Usher, bring in the second prisoner."

All eyes turned toward a small door, which opened and, to the extreme agitation of Gringoire, in walked a pretty goat with gilded horns and hoofs. The elegant creature stopped for a moment on the threshold, stretching out her neck as if, perched on the point of some rock, she was overlooking a vast plain beneath her. Suddenly she saw the Bohemian and, springing over the table and the head of a clerk of the court, in two leaps she was at her feet; she then nestled gracefully at the feet of her mistress, soliciting a word or a caress. But the prisoner remained motionless, and poor Djali herself could not get even a look.

"No, by my faith! It's the same nasty beast," cried old Falourdel. "I could swear positively to them both."

"If it pleases you, my lord and gentlemen," began Charmolue, "we will proceed to the examination of the second prisoner."

The second prisoner was the goat, sure enough. Nothing was more common in those days than to indict animals for sorcery. In the accounts of the provosty for 1466 we find, among others, the curious details of the costs of the trial of Gillet-Soulart and his sow, "executed for their crimes in Corbeil." Every item is there: the charge for the pigsty made for the sow, the five hundred bundles of wood carried to the port of Morsant, the three quarts of wine and the bread, the last meal of the sufferer, fraternally shared by the executioner, even the eleven days' keep and subsistence of the sow at eight deniers Parisis each. Sometimes, indeed, our pious ancestors went still farther than animals. The capitularies of Charlemagne and Louis le Débonnaire decreed the infliction of severe punishments on those luminous phantoms that have the audacity to appear in the air.

The Proctor of the Ecclesiastical Court then pronounced this solemn denunciation: "If the demon that possesses this goat, and that has withstood all the exorcisms that have been tried, persists in his wicked deeds and shocks the court with them, we forewarn him that we shall be forced to demand that he be sentenced to the gallows or the stake."

Gringoire broke out in a cold sweat. Charmolue took from a table the tambourine of the gypsy, held it in a particular way to the goat, and asked, "What time is it?"

The goat eyed him with an intelligent look, raised her gilded hoof, and struck seven strokes. It was actually seven o'clock. A shudder of terror thrilled the crowd. Gringoire could no longer contain himself. "The creature will be her own destruction!" he exclaimed aloud. "Don't you see that she knows not what she does?"

"Silence in the court!" cried the usher sternly.

Jacques Charmolue, by shifting the tambourine in various ways, made the goat exhibit several other tricks with regard to the day of the month, month of the year, and so forth, which the reader has already witnessed; and, from an optical delusion peculiar to judicial proceedings, the very same spectators, who had perhaps many a time applauded the innocent pranks of Djali in the streets, were horrified by them within the walls of the Palace of Justice. The goat was decidedly a devil.

But, worst of all, when the King's Proctor had emptied out on the table a little leather bag filled with block letters that Djali had around her neck, and the goat was seen sorting out with her foot the letters of the fatal name Phœbus, the spells to which the Captain had fallen a victim appeared to be irresistibly proven, in the opinion of all. The Bohemian, that exquisite dancer who had so often enchanted passersby with her graceful performances, was a terrifying witch.

The poor girl, meanwhile, showed not the slightest sign of life: She noticed neither Djali's fond tricks, nor the threats of the judges, nor the muttered imprecations of the audience. In order to rouse her a sergeant went to her and shook her most unmercifully while the head judge, raising his voice in a solemn tone, said, "Girl, you are of Bohemian race, given to unrighteous deeds. In company with the bewitched goat, your accomplice, implicated in this indictment, you did, on the night of the twenty-ninth of March, in concert with the powers of darkness, and by the aid of charms and unlawful practices, stab and slay Phœbus de Châteaupers, Captain of the Archers of the King's Ordinance. Do you persist in denying this?"

"Oh, horror of horrors!" exclaimed the prisoner, covering her face with her hands. "Oh, my Phœbus! This is hell indeed!"

"Do you persist in denying it?" asked the head judge coldly.

"Do I deny it!" she said in a fearful tone and with flashing eye as she rose from her seat.

"Then," proceeded the head judge calmly, "how do you explain the facts that led to these accusations?"

In broken accents, she replied: "I have already told you. I don't know. It was a priest—a priest, a stranger to me—an infernal priest who haunts me!"

"There it is!" resumed the judge—"the goblin-monk."

"Oh, sirs, have pity on me! I am but a poor girl . . ."

"A poor gypsy girl," continued the judge.

Master Jacques Charmolue, in his gentlest, softest tone, then said, "In consequence of the painful obstinacy of the prisoner, I demand the application of torture."

"Granted," said the head judge.

The unhappy girl shook all over. She rose, however, at the order of the bailiffs and, preceded by Charmolue and official priests, walked with relatively firm step between two rows of armor toward a low door, which suddenly opened, and closed after her. To Gringoire it seemed as though she had been swallowed up by the gaping jaws of some monster. As soon as she had disappeared a plaintive bleating was heard. It was the poor goat bewailing the loss of her mistress.

The proceedings were suspended. A counselor observed that the judges must be fatigued, and that they would be detained a long time if they waited for the conclusion of the torture; to which the head judge replied that a magistrate ought to have learned to sacrifice personal convenience to his duty.

"What a strange and bothersome girl," said an old judge, "to bring the torture on herself just now, when we ought to be at supper!"

CHAPTER II

THE COIN TRANSFORMED INTO A DRY LEAF, PART II

Having ascended and descended some steps in passages so dark that they were lighted in broad day by lamps, La Esmeralda, still surrounded by her dismal escort, was thrust by the sergeants of the palace into a sinister room. This circular chamber occupied the ground floor of one of the towers that still interrupt the layer of new buildings with which modern Paris has covered the old city. There were no windows in this dungeon, nor was there any aperture other than the low entrance closed by a strong iron door. At the same time there was no lack of light; in the thickness of the wall there was a furnace, in which burned a great fire that threw a red glow over the cave and quite eclipsed the light of a miserable candle placed in one corner. The iron portcullis, which served as a door to the furnace, was drawn up at that moment, so that at its flaming mouth there were to be seen only the lower extremities of its bars, resembling a row of black, sharp, parted teeth. This made the furnace look like the mouth of one of those legendary dragons who vomit fire and smoke. By the light it produced, the prisoner perceived around the room a variety of instruments, the uses of which were unknown to her. In the middle was a leather mattress laid almost flat on the floor, from which hung a whip with a buckle, fastened to a copper ring. A grotesque monster sculpted in the keystone of the vaulted ceiling held the whip between his teeth. Tongs, pincers, broad plowshares lay scattered, heating up in the fire of the furnace. Its bloodred light illuminated nothing but an assemblage of horrible objects. This hell was merely called the Chamber of the Question.

On the bed was carelessly seated Pierrat Torterue, the "official torturer." His assistants, two square-faced gnomes with leather aprons and canvas breeches, were stirring the coals under the iron implements.

In vain, the poor girl tried to be brave; on entering this room she was struck with horror. The sergeants of the Bailiff of the Palace ranged themselves on one side, and the official priests on the other. In one corner was a table, at which sat a clerk with pen, ink, and paper.

Master Jacques Charmolue approached the gypsy with one of his kindest smiles. "My dear child," he said, "do you persist in your denial?"

"Yes," she replied, in a scarcely audible voice.

"In that case," rejoined Charmolue, "it will be very painful to us to *question* you more urgently than we would like. Please sit down on this bed. Master Pierrat, make room for this young woman, and shut the door."

Pierrat rose grumbling. "If I shut the door," he muttered, "my fire will go out."

"Well, then, my good fellow," replied Charmolue, "leave it open."

Meanwhile La Esmeralda remained standing. That leather bed, on which so many wretched creatures had writhed in agony, frightened her. Horror froze the very marrow of her bones; there she stood bewildered, stupefied. At a sign from Charmolue the two assistants took hold of her and placed her in a sitting posture on the bed. Those men did not hurt her, but when they grasped her, when the leather touched her, she felt all her blood flow back to her heart. She looked wildly around the room. She imagined that she saw those ugly implements of torture leaving their places and advancing from every part of the room toward her, to crawl over her, and to bite, pinch, and sting her like bats, millipedes, and spiders.

"Where is the doctor?" asked Charmolue.

"Here," answered a man in a black gown whom she had not yet noticed.

She shuddered.

"Demoiselle," resumed the smooth tongue of the Proctor of the Ecclesiastical Court, "for the third time, do you persist in denying the charges preferred against you?"

This time her voice failed; she was able only to nod an affirmative.

"You persist!" cried Charmolue. "I am very sorry for it, but I am obliged to perform the duty of my office."

"Mr. Proctor," said Pierrat abruptly, "what shall we begin with?"

Charmolue paused for a moment, with the ambiguous grimace of a poet at a loss for a rhyme. "With the boot," he replied at length.

The unfortunate girl felt herself so totally abandoned by God and man that her head sank on her bosom, like some inert and lifeless thing. The torturer and the physician approached her together; at the same time the two assistants began to rummage in their hideous arsenal. At the clanking of the horrible irons the unhappy girl shivered like a dead frog to which one administers electric shocks. "Oh, my Phœbus!" she murmured, in so low a tone it was inaudible. Then she relapsed into her former insensibility and deathlike silence. This sight would have broken any other heart than the hearts of her judges. The wretched being to whom all this tremendous apparatus of saws, wheels, and pulleys was about to be applied, the being about to be consigned to the iron grip of executioners and pincers, was a gentle, tender, frail creature—poor grain of wheat, given up by human justice to be ground in the horrible mill of torture!

Meanwhile the callused hands of Pierrat's men had brutally stripped that lovely leg, and that small, elegant foot, which had so often delighted bystanders in the streets of Paris with its gracefulness and agility. "It's a pity!" muttered the torturer, surveying those graceful and delicate shapes. Had the Archdeacon been present, he would assuredly have thought at that very moment of his symbol of the spider and the fly. Soon the poor girl saw through the cloud before her eyes the "boot" approaching. Then her foot was hidden in the iron-bound apparatus. Terror then restored her strength. "Take it off!" she cried wildly, at the same time starting up. "Have mercy!" She sprang from the bed with the intention of throwing herself at the feet of the King's Proctor, but, her leg being confined in the heavy block of oak sheathed with iron, she sank down powerless as a bee with wings of lead. On a sign from Charmolue she was put back on the bed, and two coarse hands fastened around her slender waist the whip that hung from the ceiling.

"For the last time," said Charmolue, with his imperturbable benignity, "do you confess to the crimes of which you are accused?"

"I am innocent."

"Then how do you explain the circumstances alleged against you?"

"Alas, sir, I do not know."

"You deny them?"

"Everything!"

"Begin," said Charmolue to Pierrat.

Pierrat turned a screw; the boot became more and more contracted, and the wretched sufferer gave one of those horrible shrieks that have no spelling in any human language.

"Stop!" Charmolue said to Pierrat. "Do you confess?" he asked the gypsy.

"Everything!" cried the miserable girl. "I confess. Have mercy! Mercy!"

In defying the torture she had miscalculated her strength. Poor thing! Her life had till then been so bright, so cheerful, so joyous! The first pain defeated her.

"Humanity obliges me to inform you," observed the King's Proctor, "that, though you confess, you can expect nothing but death."

"I wish for it," she said. And she sank back on the leather bed, suspended, as if lifeless, by the thong buckled around her waist.

"So, my pretty! Hold up a little!" said Master Pierrat, raising her. "You look like the golden sheep around the neck of Monsieur of Burgundy."

Jacques Charmolue again raised his voice. "Clerk, write. Bohemian girl, you confess your participation in the feasts, sabbaths, and practices of hell, with demons, sorcerers, and witches? Answer."

"Yes," she said in a voice so soft that it disappeared into her breathing.

"You confess that you have seen the ram that Beelzebub displays in the clouds to summon his children to their sabbath, and which is visible only to sorcerers?"

"Yes."

"You confess that you have had commerce with the devil in the shape of the pet goat implicated in these proceedings?"

"Yes."

"Last, you declare and confess that, instigated by, and with the assistance of the devil and the goblin-monk, you did, on the night of the twenty-ninth of March, kill and slay a captain, named Phœbus de Châteaupers?"

She fixed her glazed eyes on the magistrate and replied, as if mechanically, without shock or convulsion, "Yes." It was evident that her spirit was utterly broken.

"Write, clerk," said Charmolue. Then turning to Pierrat's men, he proceeded, "Untie the prisoner, and let her be taken back into court." When the boot was removed the Proctor examined her foot, still swollen with the pain. "Come, come," he said, "it is not much the worse. You cried out in time. You would soon be able to dance as well as ever, my beauty!" Then, addressing the official priests, "Justice is enlightened at last," he said. "It is a consolation, gentlemen! And the girl will bear witness that we have shown her the greatest mercy."

CHAPTER III

CONCLUSION OF THE COIN TRANSFORMED
INTO A DRY LEAF

When she again entered the court, pale and limping, she was greeted with a general buzz of pleasure. On the part of the public it came from that feeling of gratified impatience that is experienced in the theater at the conclusion of the last intermission of a play, when the curtain rises and the fifth act begins. On the part of the judges, it came from the prospect of soon being dismissed to their suppers. The poor little goat too bleated for joy. She would have run to her mistress, but she had been tied to a bench.

It was now dark night. The candles, having received no supplement to their number, gave so faint a light that the walls of the court were not visible. The darkness enveloped objects in a sort of fog. Through it, a few unfeeling faces of judges alone were barely distinguishable. Opposite them, at the other end of the long hall, they could perceive a vague patch of white in relief against the dark background. It was the accused.

She advanced with faltering steps to her place. When Charmolue had magisterially resumed possession of his, he sat down; rising again, he said, without too strongly betraying the vanity of success: "The accused has confessed to everything."

"Bohemian girl," began the head judge, "you have confessed, then, all your misdeeds of magic, of prostitution, and of murder committed on the body of Phœbus de Châteaupers?"

Her heart was wrung, and she was heard sobbing in the dark. "Whatever you like," she answered faintly, "only kill me quickly!"

"Mr. Proctor of the King," said the head judge, "the court is ready to hear your requisitions."

Master Charmolue produced a tremendous roll of paper, from which he began to read with abundant gesticulation, and the exaggerated emphasis of the bar, a Latin oration in which all the evidence was built on Ciceronian periphrases, flanked by quotations from Plautus, his favorite comic writer. We are sorry that we cannot offer to the reader this delectable composition. The orator delivered it with wonderful gestures. Before he had finished big drops of perspiration trickled from his brow, and his eyes appeared to be popping from his head. Suddenly he stopped short in the middle of a sentence. His gaze, which was normally so bland, and even so stupid, became terrifying. "Gentlemen," he cried—now deigning to speak in French, for it was not in his manuscript—"to such a degree is Satan mixed up in this business that there he is personally present at our proceedings, and making a mockery of their majesty!" As he said this, he pointed at the little goat, which, observing the gesticulations of Charmolue, seated herself on her rump and was imitating as well as she could, with her forepaws and bearded head, the pathetic pantomime of the King's Proctor in the Ecclesiastical Court. The reader will remember that this was one of her most amusing tricks. This incident, the last proof, produced a powerful effect. To put an end to this scandal, the goat's legs were bound, and the King's Proctor resumed the thread of his eloquent harangue. It was very long, but the conclusion was admirable. Here is the last sentence. One must add Master Charmolue's rolling syllables and breathless gestures: *"Ideo Domini, coram stryga demonstrata, crimine patente, intentione criminis existente, in nominee sancta ecclesiae Nostré-Dominae Parisiensis, qua est in saisina habendi omnimodam altam et bassam justitiam in illa hac intemerata Civitatis insula, tenore praesentium declaramus nos requirere, primo aliquandam pecuniariam indemnitatem; secundo amendationem honorabilem ante portalium maximum Nostra-Dominae, ecclesia cathedralis; tertio, sententiam in virtute cujus ista stryga cum sua capella, seu in trivio vulgariter dicto la Grève, seu in insula exeunte in fluvio Sequanae, juxta pointam jardini reglais, executate sint."* Or, "This is why, my elders, in the presence of a confessed witch, the crime being obvious, criminal intention present, in the name of the Holy Church of Notre-Dame of Paris, which is in possession of all justice of every sort, high and low, in this spotless island of the Cité, by the tenor of those present, we declare that we require, first of all, financial restitution and the payment of a fine; second, a formal apology in front of the main entrance of the Cathedral of Notre-Dame; and third, the sentence that condemns this witch and her goat to be executed on the square, popularly known as the Grève, near the end of the island around which flows the Seine, near the edge of the Royal Gardens."

He put on his cap and sat down.

A man in a black gown, near the prisoner, then rose; it was her lawyer. The judges, feeling the lack of supper, began to murmur.

"Be brief," said the head judge.

"My lord," replied the lawyer, "since the prisoner has confessed the crime I have but a few words to offer. In the Salic law there is this clause: 'If a witch has eaten a man, and she is convicted of it, she shall pay a fine of eight thousand deniers, which makes two hundred sous in gold.' May it please the court then to sentence my client to pay this fine."

"That clause has become obsolete," said the Advocate Extraordinary to the King.

"Nego!" replied the lawyer of the prisoner.

"To the vote!" said a counselor. "The crime is obvious."

The question was put to the vote without their leaving the court. The judges decided quickly; they were pressed for time. Their capped heads were seen uncovered one after another in the shadows as the question was put to them successively in a low tone by the head magistrate. The poor prisoner appeared to be looking at them, but her eye no longer saw the objects before it.

The clerk of the court began writing and then handed a long parchment to the head judge. The unhappy girl heard a bustle among the people, pikes clashing together, and a chilling voice pronounce these words:

"Bohemian girl, on the day that shall please our Lord the King, at the hour of noon, you shall be drawn in a cart, stripped to your slip, barefoot, with a rope around your neck, to the main entrance of the church of Notre-Dame, and shall there do penance, holding in your hand a two-pound wax taper, and from there you shall be taken to the Place de Grève, and there hanged by the neck on the gallows of the Cité; and your goat likewise; and you shall pay to the official three gold lions in reparation of the crimes by you committed and by you confessed, of sorcery, magic, lasciviousness, and murder done upon the body of Sieur Phœbus de Châteaupers. May God receive your soul!"

"Oh! It must be a dream!" murmured the prisoner, and she felt rough hands bearing her away.

CHAPTER IV

Lasciate Ogni Speranza[3]

In the Middle Ages when a building was complete there was almost as much of it underground as above. A palace, a fortress, a church, always had a double basement, unless it stood on piles like Notre-Dame. Under a cathedral there was a kind of subterranean church, low, dark, mysterious, blind, and mute, beneath the upper nave, which was resplendent with light and rang with the pealing of organs and bells, night and day; sometimes it was a catacomb. In palaces, in bastilles, it was a prison, sometimes a sepulchre, and sometimes both together. These mighty edifices, the mode of whose formation and *vegetation* we have elsewhere described, had not merely foundations but, as it were, roots, which shot out into the soil in chambers, in galleries, in stair-cases, like the buildings above them. Thus churches, palaces, bastilles, were buried up to the middle in the ground. The vaults of a building were another building, to which you descended instead of ascending, and which installed their subterraneous stories beneath the exterior stories, like those woods and mountains that appear upside down in the mirror of a lake beneath the woods and mountains rising from its banks.

In the Bastille St.-Antoine, in the Palace of Justice, in the Louvre, these subterraneous edifices were prisons. The stories of these prisons became smaller and gloomier the lower you descended. They were so many zones pervaded by different shades of horror. Dante could not find anything more suitable for his hell. These craterlike dungeons usually terminated in a deep hole gradually widening from the bottom upward, in which Dante has placed his Satan but where society confined culprits under sentence of death.[4] Once a miserable wretch was buried there, farewell to light, to air, to life, to every hope; there was no leaving the place except for the gallows or the stake. Sometimes the prisoner was left there to rot; human justice called this forgetting. The condemned felt himself cut off from his kind by a gigantic mountain of stones and a host of jailers; and the entire prison, the massive fortress, was nothing but one enormous complicated lock, which shut him off from the living world.

Into a dungeon of this kind—the prison cells dug by St. Louis, the *in pace* of the Tournelle—La Esmeralda was thrust after her condemnation, no doubt for fear of escape, with the colossal Palace of Justice over her head. Poor girl! She could not have stirred the smallest of the stones of which it was built. Certainly, Fate and society had been equally unjust. Such an excess of misery and torture was not needed to crush so frail a creature.

There she was, wrapped in darkness, buried, entombed, walled up. Whoever saw her in this state after having seen her laughing and dancing in the sun would have shuddered. Cold as night, cold as death, not a breath of air in her dark locks, not a human sound in her ear, not a glimmer of light in her eyes, weighted down with chains, bent double, crouched beside a pitcher and a loaf of bread, on a little straw, in the pool formed beneath her by the water that dripped from the walls of her dungeon, motionless and scarcely breathing—she was almost beyond suffering. Phœbus, the sun, the daylight, the free air, the streets of Paris, the dances to such applause, the prattle of love with the officer; then the priest, the old woman, the dagger, the blood, the torture, the gallows; all this had again passed before her mind, sometimes like a gay and golden vision, at others like a hideous nightmare: but it was now no more than a horrible and indistinct struggle, which was veiled in darkness, or distant music played above on the earth, which was not heard at the depths to which the unfortunate creature was sunk. Since she had been there she had not awakened, she had not slept. In this profound wretchedness, in the gloom of this dungeon, she could no more distinguish waking from sleeping, dream from reality, than night from day. She had ceased to feel, to know, to think. At the very most she dreamed. Never had a living creature been plunged so deeply into nothingness.

Thus numbed, frozen, and petrified, she scarcely noticed the noise of a trapdoor, which had opened two or three times somewhere near her, but without admitting a glimmer of light, and through which a hand had thrown down to her a crust of black bread. It was nevertheless the sole communication with mankind still left to her—the periodical visit of the jailer. Only one sound automatically engaged her hearing. Above her head dampness filtered through the mossy stones of the vaulted roof, and a drop of water fell from it at equal intervals. She listened stupidly to the noise made by this drop falling into the pool of water by her side. This was the only motion still perceptible around her, the only clock that marked the lapse of time, the only noise that reached her of all the noises that are made on the face of the earth. To leave nothing out, she did indeed sometimes feel, in the dark and filthy muddiness of her abode, something cold crawling around on her foot or her arm, and she shuddered.

How long she had been in this place she did not know. She remembered a death sentence passed somewhere on somebody; she remembered that she had then been borne away, and that she had awoken frozen, in darkness and silence. She had crawled around on her hands because iron rings had then cut into her ankles and chains had rattled. She recognized that there was a solid wall all around her, that under her there were paving stones covered with water, and a bundle of straw. There was no lamp or ventilation. She had then seated herself on the straw and sometimes, for change of posture, on the lowest of the stone steps of her dungeon. At one time she had tried to count the dark minutes measured by the drop of water, but soon this melancholy task imposed by a sick mind stopped all by itself, and it left her in a stupor.

At length, one day, or one night—for midnight and noon were of the same color in this sepulchre—she heard above her a louder noise than that usually made by the jailer when he brought her loaf and her pitcher of water. She raised her head and saw a reddish ray entering through a cranny in a kind of trapdoor placed in the vault of the *in pace*. At the same time the heavy iron bars rattled; the door grated on its rusty hinges; it turned, and she saw a lantern, a hand, and the lower halves of two figures, the door being too low for her to perceive their heads. The light hurt her eyes so much that she closed them.

When she opened them again the door was shut, a lantern was placed on one of the steps, and something like a human form stood before her. A monk's black cloak descended to its feet; a hood of the same color concealed the face. Nothing was to be seen of the person, not even the hands. The figure looked like a long black winding sheet standing upright, under which something seemed to move. For some minutes she kept her eyes intently fixed on this spectral shape. Neither spoke. You would have taken them for two statues confronting each other. Only two things showed signs of life in the dungeon: the wick of the lantern, which crackled because of the humidity, and the drip of water from the roof that broke this irregular crackling with its monotonous plash, which made the light of the lantern dance in concentric rings on the oily surface of the puddle.

At length the prisoner broke silence.

"Who are you?"

"A priest."

The word, the accent, the voice made her shudder.

"Are you prepared?" asked the priest, in a low tone.

"For what?"

"To die."

"Oh!" she said. "Will it be soon?"

"Tomorrow."

Her head, which she had raised with a look of joy, again sank on her bosom. "It is a long time till then," she murmured. "Why not today? What difference could it have made to them?"

"You must be very unhappy, then?" said the priest after a moment's silence.

"I am very cold," she replied. She clasped her feet with her hands, a habit of the unfortunate victims of cold that we have already seen in the recluse of the Tour-Roland, and her teeth chattered.

The priest seemed from beneath the hood to look around the dungeon. "Without light! Without fire! In the water! It's horrible!"

"Yes," she answered, with that air of astonishment that suffering had imparted, "everybody enjoys the light. Why should I know only darkness?"

"Do you know," resumed the priest, after another pause, "why you are here?"

"I think I did know," said she, passing her attenuated fingers over her brow, as if to assist her memory, "but I don't now."

Suddenly she burst out crying like a child. "I want to leave this place, sir. I am cold, I am afraid, and there are loathsome things that crawl on me."

"Well, come along with me."

With these words the priest took hold of her arm. The wretched girl was almost chilled to the bone, but that hand produced a sensation of cold.

"Oh!" she murmured. "It is the icy hand of death! Who are you then?"

The priest pushed back his hood. She looked at him. It was that sinister face that had so long haunted her, that demon-head that had appeared to her at Falourdel's above the head of her adored Phœbus, that eye that she had last seen glistening near a dagger.

This apparition, always so fatal to her, which had thrown her from misery to misery, roused her from her stupor. The thick veil that seemed to have spread itself over her memory was torn away. All the circumstances of her dismal adventure, from the nocturnal scene in Falourdel's to her condemnation in the Tournelle, came back to her, not vague and confused as at the time of their occurrence but distinct, fresh, palpitating, terrible. These memories, almost obliterated by the excess of her sufferings, were revived by the somber figure before hers, like words written with invisible ink on white paper that stand out all fresh when the paper is held to the fire. All the wounds of her heart seemed to be torn open afresh, and to bleed once more.

"Ha!" she cried with a convulsive tremor and, holding her hands over her eyes, "It is the priest!" Then she dropped her enfeebled arms, she remained sitting, her head bent forward, her eye fixed on the ground, mute and trembling. The priest looked at her with the eye of a hawk that has long been descending in silence from the highest height of the heavens in smaller and smaller circles around a poor lark sitting in the corn, and, having suddenly pounced like winged lightning on his prey, clutches the panting victim in his talons.

She began to murmur softly: "Get it over with! Be done with it! The last blow!" and she bowed her head with terror, like the lamb awaiting the fatal stroke from the hand of the butcher.

At length he asked, "Are you horrified by me?"

She made no reply.

"Are you horrified by me?" he repeated.

Her lips were compressed as though she smiled.

"Yes," she said, "the executioner mocks the condemned. For months he has been haunting, threatening, terrifying me! Without him, oh, God, how happy I was! It was he who hurled me into this abyss. It was he who killed *him*—who killed my Phœbus!" Sobbing vehemently, she raised her eyes to the priest. "Who are you, wretch?" she exclaimed. "What have I done to you? Why should you hate me so? What do you have against me?"

"I *love* you!" said the priest.

Her tears suddenly ceased. She eyed him with the vacant stare of an idiot. He had meanwhile sunk onto his knees and gazed on her with a flaming eye.

"Do you hear? I *love* you!" he repeated.

"Ah! What love!" said the unhappy creature, shuddering.

"The love of the damned," he replied.

Both remained silent for some minutes, crushed by the weight of their emotions; he was frantic, she was stupefied.

"Listen," said the priest at length, who had suddenly recovered an amazing degree of composure. "You will know everything. I will tell you what till now I have scarcely dared tell myself when I secretly examined my conscience, during those hours of the night when it is so dark that it seems as if even God could not see us. Listen. Before I saw you I was happy."

"And I." She sighed faintly.

"Do not interrupt me. Yes, I was happy, or at least I thought that I was. Priests consulted me about chastity, and doctors consulted me on doctrine. Science was everything to me; it was a sister, and a sister was enough for me. In spite, however, of my determination to acknowledge no other influence, that power of nature which, silly youth that I was, I had hoped to crush for life, had more than once convulsively shaken the chain of those iron vows that bind me, miserable man that I am, to the cold stones of the altar. But fasting, prayer, study, the mortifications of the cloister restored to the spirit mastery over the passions. I avoided women. Besides, I needed only to open a book and all the impure vapors of my brain were dispelled by the splendor of science. In a few minutes the dark things of the earth fled far away, and I found myself calm, bedazzled, and serene in the soothing light of everlasting truth. So long as the demon sent only vague shadows of women to attack me, so long as they passed casually before my eyes, at church, in the streets, in the fields, and scarcely recurred to my thoughts, I vanquished him with ease. Alas! If victory has not remained mine, it is God's fault for not making man equal in strength to the demon. Listen. One day . . ."

The priest paused; the prisoner heard painful tears through his bosom. He resumed:

"One day I was sitting at the window of my cell. What was I doing? Oh! All of it is a blur. I was reading. The window looked out on an open square. I heard the sound of a tambourine. Irritated at being disturbed in my reverie, I looked down on the square. What I saw there, and what others besides me saw, was not a sight made for human eyes. There, in the middle of the pavement—it was noon, brilliant sunshine—a creature was dancing—a creature so beautiful that God would have preferred her to the Virgin, and would have chosen her for his mother, and would have wanted to have been born of her if she had existed when he himself was made man! Her eyes were black and splendid; amid her dark hair were locks that, reflecting the sun's beams, shone like threads of gold. Her feet disappeared in movement like the spokes of a rapidly turning wheel. Around her head, in her black braids, there were pieces of gold, which sparkled in the sun and formed a crown of stars for her brow. Her dress, sewn with a thousand sequins, glistened dark blue like a summer night. Her brown and supple arms whirled around her body like two scarves. The form of her body was astonishing in its beauty. Oh, the resplendent figure, which had something luminous about it even in the broad sunlight! . . . Alas, young woman, it was you. Surprised, charmed, intoxicated, I let myself go, watching you; I looked until I shuddered with fear. I felt that the hand of Fate was upon me."

The priest, oppressed by emotion, paused again for a moment. Then he proceeded:

"Half fascinated already, I tried to grasp at something to break my fall. I remembered the traps that Satan had previously prepared for me. The creature before me possessed that superhuman beauty that can come only from heaven or from hell. She was not a mere girl, molded of common clay and faintly illuminated from within by the flickering ray of a woman's soul. It was an angel, but an angel of darkness—of fire, not of light. At the moment when these thoughts were crossing my brain I saw near her a goat, a beast that one associates with witches. It looked at me and laughed. The noontide sun tipped the goat's horns with flame. Then I perceived the demon's trap, and had no further doubt that you were from hell, and had come for my perdition. I believed it."

The priest here looked steadfastly in the face of the prisoner and coldly added, "I believe it still.

"Meanwhile the spell began to work on me by degrees. Your dancing turned my brain. I felt the mysterious spell take hold of me. All that should have been vigilant in my soul was lulled to sleep; and, like a man dying in the snow, I took pleasure in yielding to this slumber. All at once I heard you begin to sing. What could I do? Your singing was more fascinating than your dancing. I would have fled. Impossible. I was riveted, rooted, to the spot. I was forced to remain till you had finished. My feet were ice, my head boiled. At length, perhaps out of pity for me, your song ceased, and I saw you depart. The reflection of the dazzling vision, the sounds of the enchanting music, vanished gradually from my eyes and died away in my ears. Then I sank into the corner of the window, stiffer and more helpless than a fallen statue. The vesper bell awoke me. I got up. I fled, but alas! Something had fallen within me that I could not raise up; something had come upon me from which I could not flee!"

He paused again and continued:

"Yes, from that day I was possessed with a spirit that I did not know.

I had recourse to my remedies—the cloister, the altar, work, books. Madness! Oh, how hollow science sounds when you dash against it in despair a head filled with passions. Do you know, maiden, what I always saw between the book and me from that day on? You, your shadow, the image of the luminous apparition that had one day passed before me. But that image no longer had the same color; it was dark, funereal, shadow, like the black circle that dances for a long time before the eye that has been imprudent enough to stare at the sun.

"I could not get away from it. I kept hearing your song ringing in my ears, kept seeing your feet dancing on my breviary, at night, in my dreams. I felt your body gliding against my flesh, and I wanted to see you again, to touch you, to know who you were, to determine whether you resembled the ideal image that stayed with me, perhaps to break the illusion with reality. In any event, I hoped that a new impression would efface the first; for the first had become intolerable to me. I sought you out. Again I saw you. When I had seen you twice I wished to see you a thousand times, to have you always in my sight. Then—who can stop himself on the steep descent to perdition?—then I was no longer my own master. I became a vagrant, like yourself. I waited for you in doorways. I lurked at the corners of streets, I watched you from my tower. Each night, on examining myself, I found that I was more helpless, more spellbound, more bewitched, more undone.

"I learned who you were: Gypsy, Bohemian, Gitana, Zingara. How could I doubt any longer that there was witchcraft in the case! Listen. I hoped that the law would break the charm. A sorceress had bewitched Bruno d'Ast: he had her burned and was cured. I knew it. I resolved to try the same remedy. In the first place I obtained an ordinance forbidding you to appear in the precincts of our church, hoping to forget you if I couldn't see you anymore. Ignoring this prohibition, you came as usual. Then I conceived the idea of kidnapping you. One night I attempted to make it happen. There were two of us. We already had you in our clutches when that miserable officer came up and rescued you. Thus did your sufferings, mine, and his, begin. Finally, not knowing what to do, I denounced you to the officials. I thought that I would be cured, as Bruno d'Ast was. I also had a confused notion that a trial would deliver you into my power; that in a prison I would have you, would hold you; that there you could not escape me. When one is doing evil, it is madness to stop halfway. The extremity of guilt has its delirium of rapture. In prison and on a bed of straw, a priest and a witch could discover delicious pleasures and melt into each other's arms. Therefore I denounced you. That was when I frightened you during our encounters. The conspiracy that I was brewing against you, the storm that I was going to unleash on your head escaped from my control in threats and lightning. Nevertheless, I hesitated. My plan had horrible parts that made me back off.

"I might have given up my designs; my hideous ideas would perhaps have evaporated from my brain without producing any result. I imagined that I could follow up or stop the proceedings whenever I pleased. But every wicked thought is inexorable and hurries to become a fact; and where I fancied myself all-powerful, Fate proved more mighty than I. Alas! Alas! It was Fate that caught you, and threw you among the terrible gears of the machine that I had secretly constructed. Listen to me. I am nearly done.

"One day—another day of lovely sunshine—I saw walking before me a man who pronounced your name, who laughed, and whose eyes glistened with lasciviousness. Damnation! I followed him—you know the rest."

He ceased speaking. "Oh, my Phœbus!" was all the poor girl could say.

"Not that name!" said the priest, seizing her arm with violence. "Do not say that name! Wretched as we are, it is that name that has undone us; or rather, we are undoing one another through the unaccountable game of Fate! . . . You are suffering, I know it. You are cold; the darkness blinds you; the dungeon restrains you. But perhaps you still have some light in the recesses of your soul—even if it is only your childish love for that empty man who played with your heart—while I, I carry a dungeon within me; within me is the chill of winter, ice, despair. Night is in my soul. Do you know all that I have suffered? I was at your trial. I was sitting on the officials' bench. Yes, one of those priest's cowls covered torments unequaled but by those of the damned. When they took you away, I was there. When they interrogated you, I was there—Den of wolves! It was my crime, it was my scaffold that I saw rising slowly on your face. With every proof, with every witness, I was there. I could have counted every one of your steps along that painful path. I was there when that savage beast—Oh! I did not expect torture!—bore you off to his den. I followed you into the torture chamber. I saw you stripped, and your delicate limbs manhandled by the infamous hands of the executioner. I saw your foot, which I would have given an empire to kiss, that foot by which to have been trampled upon would have been to me happiness, I saw it encased in the horrible boot that transforms the limbs of a living being into a bloody mess. Oh wretched one! While I watched that, I carried beneath my cloak a dagger that I cut my chest with. At the shriek that was forced from you, I plunged it into my bosom. If there had been a second cry of pain, it would have reached my heart. Look, I think it is still bleeding."

He threw open his cassock. His breast was lacerated as by the claws of a tiger. The prisoner recoiled in horror.

"O maiden!" said the priest. "Take pity on me! You think you are miserable. Alas! You do not know what misery is. It is to love a woman—to be a priest—to be hated—to love with all the force of your soul—to feel that you would give for the least of her smiles your blood, your life, your character, your salvation, immortality and eternity, this world and the next—to regret that you are not a king, a genie, an emperor, an archangel, a god, so that you could cast a greater slave at her feet. To clasp her night and day in your dreams and in your thoughts—to see her in love with a soldier's uniform, and to have nothing to offer her but the wretched cassock, which is to her an object of fear and disgust. To be present, with a heart bursting with jealousy and rage, while she lavishes on an idiotic braggart the treasures of love and beauty. To see the body that burns you, the sweet breast, that tender flesh palpitate and blush under another's kisses! Oh heaven! To love her foot, her arm, her shoulder, to think of her blue veins, of her brown skin until you spend entire nights writhing on the floor of your cell, and to see all the caresses you have been saving up for her lead to her torture! To have succeeded only in laying her on the leather bed! Oh, these are pincers heated in the fire of hell! Happy in comparison is he who is sawed apart between two planks, or quartered by horses! Do you know what agony it is when, during the long nights, your arteries boil, your heart is breaking, your head splitting, and your teeth tear your own flesh! Thoughts of love, jealousy, and despair are pitiless tormentors, and they turned me pitilessly on a red hot spit! Girl, have mercy! Stop for a moment! A bit of ash on that fire! Wipe, I beg you, the sweat pouring off my brow in great drops! Child! Torture me with one hand, but caress me with the other! Have pity, girl! Have pity on me!"

The priest rolled in the water on the floor and dashed his head against the stone steps of the dungeon. The gypsy listened to him, looked at him. When he ceased speaking, breathless and exhausted, she repeated in a low tone, "Oh, my Phœbus!"

The priest crawled toward her on his knees. "I implore you," he cried, "if you have any compassion, do not push me away. I love you. I am miserable. When you say that name it is as if you were tearing with your teeth all the fibers of my heart. Only have pity. If you come from hell, I will go there with you. All that I have done I have done for this. The hell where you are will be to me a Paradise; the sight of you is more charming than that of God. Oh, tell me, will you not have me? I should have thought that the day when a woman could reject such love the mountains would be moved. Oh, if you would, how happy we might yet be! We would flee. . . . I would help you to escape . . . we would seek that spot on earth where there are the most trees, the most sunshine, the most azure sky."

She interrupted him with a loud, terrible laugh. "Look, Father, you have blood on your fingers!"

The priest, motionless for some moments, as if petrified, stared at his hand.

"Why, yes," he replied at length with a strange sweetness. "Abuse me, jeer at me, overwhelm me! But come, come! Let us lose no time. It will be tomorrow, I tell you. The gallows of the Grève—you know it—it is always ready. It is horrible—to see you drawn in that cart! Oh, mercy, mercy! I never realized until now how much I love you! Oh, follow me! You will take your own time to love me after I have saved you. You can hate me as long as you like. Only come. Tomorrow! Tomorrow! The gallows! Oh, save yourself—spare me!"

In a state approaching madness, he seized her arm and would have carried her away. She stared at him. "What has become of my Phœbus?" she inquired.

"Ah!" said the priest, letting go of her arm. "You have no pity!"

"What has become of Phœbus?" she repeated coldly.

"He is dead," replied the priest.

"Dead!" she said, still cold and immobile. "Then why persuade me to live?"

He did not hear her. "Oh, yes!" he said, as if talking to himself, "he must be dead. I struck home. The point must have reached his heart. Oh, I lived at the edge of that dagger!"

The girl rushed on him like an enraged tigress and thrust him toward the steps with supernatural force. "Begone, monster! Begone, murderer! Leave me to die! May both our blood mark your brow with an everlasting stain! . . . Be yours, priest! Never! Never! Nothing will bring us together, not even hell itself. Go, accursed!—Never!"

The priest had stumbled up the steps. Silently disengaging his feet from the skirts of his cassock, he picked up his lantern and began slowly to go to the door; he opened it and went out. The prisoner gazed after him. Suddenly the girl saw his head again. His face was ghastly. With a rattle of rage and despair he cried, "I tell you he is dead!"

She fell with her face to the ground, and no sound could be heard in the dungeon except the plash of the dropping water, which made ripples in the pool in the profound darkness.

CHAPTER V

THE MOTHER

I cannot conceive anything in the world more delightful than the ideas awakened in the heart of a mother at the sight of her child's little shoe, especially if it is a holiday, a Sunday, a baptismal shoe; a shoe embroidered down to the very sole; a shoe on which the infant has never yet stepped. This shoe is so small and so pretty; it seems so impossible for it to be walked in that it seems to the mother as though she saw her child. She smiles at it, she kisses it, she talks to it; she asks herself if a foot can really be so small; and, if the infant should be absent, the pretty shoe is sufficient to make the sweet and fragile little creature appear before her eyes. She imagines she sees her—she does see her— all alive, all joyful, with her delicate hands, her round head, her pure lips, her serene eyes, the whites of which are blue. If it is winter, there she is, crawling on the carpet, climbing laboriously up on a stool, and the mother trembles lest she approach too near to the fire. If it is summer, she is wandering around in the courtyard or in the garden, looking innocently and fearlessly at the big dogs and the big horses, pulling up the grass growing between the stones, playing with the shells and the flowers, and making the gardener scold on finding sand on his borders and dirt on his paths. Everything laughs, everything shines, everything plays around the child, even the very breeze and the sunshine, which tousle the locks of her soft hair. All this the little shoe shows the mother, and it makes her heart melt like wax before the fire.

But when the child is lost these thousand images of joy, delight, and affection, which crowd around the little shoe, are transformed into as many horrible things. The pretty little embroidered shoe then becomes only an instrument of torture, which eternally racks the mother's heart. It is still the same fiber that vibrates—the deepest and the most keenly sensitive fiber—not under the caresses of an angel but in the grip of a demon.

One morning when the sun of May was rising in one of those deep blue skies beneath which Garofalo loved to picture the taking down from the Cross,[5] the recluse of the Tour-Roland heard the rumbling of wheels, the tramp of horses, and the clanking of iron in the Place de Grève. The noise scarcely roused her; she pulled her hair over her ears so that she might not hear it, and again fell on her knees gazing at the inanimate object that she had adored this way for fifteen years. To her this little shoe was, as we have already observed, the universe. Her thoughts were wrapped up in it and never to be parted from it except by death. How many bitter imprecations, how many touching complaints, how many earnest prayers she had addressed to heaven on the subject of this charming little shoe of rose-colored satin was known to the cell of the Tour-Roland alone. Never were keener sorrows poured out over an object so pretty and so delicate. On this particular morning her grief seemed to burst forth with greater violence than usual, and she was heard from outside lamenting with a loud and monotonous voice that wrung the heart.

"Oh, my daughter!" she said. "My daughter! My poor dear little daughter! Never, no never shall I see you again! And still it seems as if it had happened only yesterday. Oh, my God! My God! Better that she had not been given to me at all than to have had her taken from me so soon! And yet You must know that our children are a part of ourselves, and that a mother who has lost her child is tempted not to believe in God. . . . Ah! Wretch that I was, to go out that day! . . . Oh, Lord! Lord!

To snatch her from me that way. You could never have seen me with her, when I warmed her, all happy, before the fire, when she laughed while she nursed, when I made her little feet step up my bosom to my lips! Had You seen this—oh, my God!—You would have had pity on my joy; You would not have taken from me the only love that was left in my heart! Was I then so vile a wretch—O Lord!—that You could not look at me before condemning me? Alas! Alas! There is the shoe, but where is the foot? Where is the child? My child! My own child! What have they done with you! O Lord, give me back my child! My knees have been flayed for these fifteen years in praying to You: Is not this enough? Restore her to me for a day, an hour, a minute, only one minute, O Lord! And then cast me to the Evil One to all eternity. Oh, if I knew where to find You, I would grasp the skirts of Your garment with both these hands and not let You go till You had given me back my child! See her pretty little shoe! Have You no compassion? Can You doom a wretched mother to fifteen years of such torment? Blessed Virgin of heaven! They have stolen my child; they have devoured her on the moor; they have drunk her blood; they have gnawed her bones. Kind Virgin, have pity on me! My daughter! I want my daughter! What is it to me that she is in Paradise? I want none of your angels; I want my child. Oh, I will writhe on the ground, I will dash my head against the stones, I will gladly seal my own perdition, if You will only restore to me my child! You see how these arms are bitten! Has then the good God no compassion? Oh, let them give me nothing but black bread and salt, provided I have my daughter; she will be to me both meat and drink, and warmth and sunshine. I confess that I am only a vile sinner, but my child was making me pious. Out of love for her I was amending my life, and I saw You through her smile as through the opened heavens. . . . Oh that I could just once more, only once, put this pretty shoe on her rosy little foot, I would die blessing You, Holy Virgin! But no. Fifteen years—she must be grown up now! Unfortunate girl! It is too certain that I shall never see you again, not even in heaven, for there I shall never enter. Oh, what misery!—to say, there is her shoe and that is all."

The wretched creature threw herself on that shoe, a source of solace and of sorrow for so many years, and she sobbed as though her heart would break, just as she had done on the very first day. Grief like this never grows old. For a mother who has lost her child, it is always the first day. This pain never ages. It is useless that the colors of mourning fade. The heart remains black as ever.

At this moment the brisk and merry voices of boys passed her cell. At the sight or the sound of children, the unhappy mother would always dart into the darkest corner of her sepulchre, so quickly that you would think she was striving to bury her head in the wall, so that she might not hear them. On this occasion, contrary to her custom, she started up and listened attentively. One of the boys was just saying to another, "They are going to hang a gypsy today."

With the sudden bound of the spider, which we recently saw rushing on the fly entangled in her net, she sprang to the window, which looked, as the reader knows, toward the Place de Grève. A ladder was actually leaning against the permanent gallows, and the hangman was engaged in adjusting the chains, which had become rusty with rain. A few people were standing around.

The laughing troop of boys was already far off. The Sack Woman looked around for some passerby she might question. She perceived close to her cell a priest who pretended to be reading in the public breviary but whose thoughts were much less engaged by the book than by the gallows, toward which he glanced from time to time with a wild and gloomy look. She recognized in him the Archdeacon of Josas, an austere and holy man.

"Father," she inquired, "whom are they going to hang over there?"

The priest looked at her without answering. She repeated the question. "I don't know," he said.

"Some boys," answered the woman, "said just now that it was a gypsy."

"I believe so," replied the priest.

Paquette la Chantefleurie burst into a hysterical laugh.

"Sister," said the Archdeacon, "you seem to hate the gypsies with all your heart."

"Hate them!" cried the recluse. "Why, they are witches, child stealers! They devoured my little girl, my child, my only child! They ate my heart along with her—I have none now!" She was terrifying.

The priest eyed her coldly.

"There is one in particular," she resumed, "that I hate and that I have cursed; a young girl about the same age that my child would have been now had they not eaten her. Whenever this young viper passes my cell she disturbs my blood."

"Well, then, sister, rejoice," said the priest, cold as the statue on a sepulchre. "It is for her that these preparations are being made."

His head sank on his bosom, and he slowly withdrew.

The recluse waved her arms in triumph. "Thank you, Priest," she cried. "I told her what she would come to."

Then she began to pace back and forth before her window, her hair disheveled, her eye glaring, banging her shoulder against the wall, with the wild air of a caged she-wolf that has been hungry a long time and is aware that the hour for her meal is approaching.

CHAPTER VI

THREE HUMAN HEARTS DIFFERENTLY CONSTITUTED

Phœbus, meanwhile, was not dead. Men of that kind are hard to kill. When Master Philippe Lheulier, Special Attorney to the King, said to poor Esmeralda, "He is dying," he was either misinformed or joking. When the Archdeacon repeated to her after condemnation "He is dying," the fact was that he knew nothing about it, but he believed it, he had no doubt of it, he made sure of it, he hoped it. It would have gone too much against the grain to give good news of his rival to the woman whom he loved. Every man in his place would have done the same.

Not that Phœbus's wound was not severe, but the injury was less serious than the Archdeacon flattered himself it was. The master surgeon to whose house the soldiers of the watch had immediately carried him was for more than a week worried for his life, and had even told him so in Latin. Youth, however, enabled him to get the better of it; and, as frequently happens, notwithstanding prognostics and diagnostics, nature had amused herself in saving the patient under the doctor's nose. It was while lying on the master surgeon's pallet bed that he underwent the first interrogations of Philippe Lheulier and the inquisitors of the official, which had annoyed him exceedingly. One fine morning, therefore, finding himself better, he had left his gold spurs in payment at the surgeon's and slipped away. This circumstance, however, had not in the least affected the judicial proceedings. Justice in those days cared little about propriety and accuracy in a criminal process; provided that the accused was hung, it was perfectly satisfied. Now the judges had sufficient evidence against Esmeralda. They believed Phœbus to be dead, and that was quite enough.

Phœbus, for his part, had not fled far. He had merely rejoined his company, garrisoned in Queue-en-Brie, on the Ile de France, a few stations from Paris. He felt no inclination whatsoever to come forward personally in this trial. He had a vague impression that he should cut a ridiculous figure in it. At bottom, he did not know what to think of the whole affair. Irreligious and superstitious, like every soldier who is nothing but a soldier, when he called to mind all the circumstances of this adventure he could not tell what to make of the goat, of the odd way in which he had first met La Esmeralda, of the no less strange manner in which she had betrayed her love, of her being a gypsy, and, last, of the goblin-monk. He imagined that more magic than love was mixed up in it, and there was probably a sorceress, perhaps the devil who had gotten involved. In short, it was a comedy or, to use the language of those days, a mystery of a very disagreeable nature, in which he had played an extremely awkward part—that of the butt of all blows and jokes. The Captain was quite crushed: he felt the sort of shame that La Fontaine so admirably compares with that of a fox caught by a hen.[6] He hoped, besides, that the affair would not circulate and that in his absence his name would scarcely be mentioned in connection with it, or at any rate not beyond the pleadings in the Tournelle. Neither was he far wrong in this expectation: there were then no newspapers, and scarcely a week passed without some counterfeiter who was boiled, some witch hanged, or some heretic burned, at one of the numberless justices of Paris. People were so accustomed to see the old feudal Themis, with bare arms and rolled-up sleeves, performing her duty at the gallows and the pillory that they scarcely took any notice of such events. In those days the higher classes scarcely knew the name of the victim who was carried past to the corner of the street, and the people at most regaled themselves with this coarse fare. An execution was a familiar incident in public places, like the oven of the baker, or the butcher's slaughterhouse. The hangman was just a kind of butcher, a shade darker than the other.

Phœbus therefore soon set his mind at ease with regard to the witch

Esmeralda, or Similar, as he called her, the wound inflicted by the Bohemian or the goblin-monk—he did not care which—and the outcome of the trial. But no sooner was his heart vacant on this score than the image of Fleur-de-Lis returned to it. The heart of Captain Phœbus, like the philosophy of those times, abhorred a vacuum.

Besides, Queue-en-Brie was a very stupid place, a village of blacksmiths and dairywomen with chapped hands, a long line of crazy cottages bordering both sides of the high road for a mile. It was a *queue*. Fleur-de-Lis was his last passion but one, a handsome girl with a good dowry. One fine morning, therefore, completely recovered, and presuming that the affair with the Bohemian must after the lapse of two months be completely blown over and forgotten, the amorous knight pranced to the door of the Gondelaurier mansion. He took no notice of a large crowd assembled in the Place du Parvis, before the main entrance of Notre-Dame: he remembered that it was the month of May, and, supposing that the people might be drawn together by some religious holiday or procession, he tied his horse to the ring at the gate and gaily went upstairs to his fair betrothed.

She was alone with her mother. Fleur-de-Lis resented the scene with the sorceress, her goat, her cursed block letters, and the long absences of Phœbus: nevertheless, at the entrance of her truant he looked so handsome, had such a new uniform, such a smart shoulder belt, and so impassioned an air, that she blushed with pleasure. The noble young lady was herself more charming than ever. Her magnificent blond hair was admirably braided; she was dressed completely in sky blue, which so well suits women of a fair complexion—Colombe had taught her this technique of coquetry—and her eye swam in that languor of love that makes them even more beautiful.

Phœbus, who had for so long seen nothing superior in beauty to the girls of Queue-en-Brie, was infatuated with Fleur-de-Lis; and this imparted such a warmth and such a tone of gallantry to his manner that his peace was instantly made. Madame de Gondelaurier herself, maternally seated as usual in her great armchair, did not have the heart to scold him, and as for the reproaches of Fleur-de-Lis, they expired in tender endearments.

The young lady was seated near the window, still working away at her grotto of Neptune. The Captain leaned over the back of her chair, and in an undertone she commenced her half-caressing, half-scolding inquiries.

"What have you been doing with yourself for two whole months, you naughty man?"

"I swear," replied Phœbus, who did not relish the question, "you are so beautiful that an archbishop could not help falling in love with you."

She could not keep from smiling. "That's good! But let's leave my beauty aside for the moment! I want an answer to my question."

"Well, then, my dear cousin, I was ordered away to be garrisoned."

"Where, if you please? And why not come to bid me adieu?"

"At Queue-en-Brie."

Phœbus was delighted that the first question enabled him to shirk the second.

"But that is close by, sir. How is it that you have not been once to see me?"

Here Phœbus was seriously embarrassed. "Why . . . our duty . . . and, besides, charming cousin, I have been ill."

"Ill!" she exclaimed, in alarm.

"Yes, wounded."

"Wounded!"

The poor girl was extremely upset.

"Oh, you need not frighten yourself about that," said Phœbus carelessly. "It was nothing. A quarrel, a scratch with a sword; what is that to you?"

"What is that to me?" cried Fleur-de-Lis, raising her beautiful eyes swimming in tears. "Oh, in so saying you do not say what you are thinking. How did you get the scratch? I insist on knowing everything."

"Well then, my fair cousin, I had a quarrel with Mahé Fédy—you know him—the lieutenant of St.-Germain-en-Laye, and each of us ripped up a few inches of the other's skin. That is everything."

The mendacious Captain knew well that an affair of honor always raises a man in the eyes of a woman. Accordingly, Fleur-de-Lis turned around and looked him in the face with emotions of fear, pleasure, and admiration. Still she was not completely satisfied.

"Ah, Phœbus," she said, "how I rejoice that you are quite well again! I do not know your Mahé Fédy—but he is a miserable fellow. And what was the cause of this quarrel?"

Here Phœbus, whose imagination was not the most fertile, began to be puzzled about how to overcome his own prowess.

"Oh, what do I know? A mere nothing, a wrong word. But, fair cousin," he cried, in order to change the topic, "what is going on in the Parvis? Look," he continued, stepping to the window, "what a crowd there is in the square!"

"I don't know," replied Fleur-de-Lis. "I did hear that a witch is to do penance this morning in front of the church before they hang her."

The Captain was so sure that the affair with La Esmeralda was long since over that he was not in the least troubled by Fleur-de-Lis's news. He nevertheless asked her one or two questions.

"What is the name of the witch?"

"I do not know," she answered.

"And what do they say she has done?"

"I don't know," she said, with another shrug of her fair shoulders.

"Oh, my God!" said the mother. "There are nowadays so many sorcerers and witches that they burn them, I believe, without knowing their names. You might as well ask the name of every cloud in the sky. But why should we care? God Almighty will be sure to keep a correct list." Here the venerable lady rose and advanced to the window. "Bless me! There is indeed a crowd, as you say, Phœbus. Why, the very roofs are covered with people! Do you know, Phœbus, this reminds me of my youth, of the entry of King Charles VII, when there was as great a crowd as this—I forget what year it was—only the people were much more good looking than now. There were people on the battlements of the gate of St.-Antoine. The King had the Queen on the saddle behind him, and after Their Highnesses came all the ladies riding in the same way behind their lords. I remember everyone laughed heartily because next to Amanyon de Garlande, who was very short, there was Lord Matefelon, who was a knight of *gigantal* proportions. He had killed mountains of Englishmen. It was very beautiful. A procession of all the gentlemen of France with their banners waving in the air. There were those who had pennants and those who had banners. What do I know? The Lord of Calan had a pennant. Jean de Châteaumorant had a banner. The Lord of Coucy had a banner that was more elaborate than all the others except for the Duke of Bourbon. . . . Alas, it is so sad to think that all that existed once and is no more!"

The lovers were not listening to the worthy dowager. Phœbus had again planted himself behind his betrothed and was leaning over the back of her chair. It was a lovely position from which his libertine gaze wandered over all the openings of her décolletage. Dazzled by that skin, which shone like satin, the Captain said to himself, "How can one love anyone but a blonde?" Both kept silent. The young lady gave him from time to time a look of passion and tenderness, and their hair mingled together in the spring sunshine.

"Phœbus," said Fleur-de-Lis abruptly, in a low tone, "we are to be married in three months; swear that you never loved any other but me."

"I do swear it, beautiful angel!" replied Phœbus, and his impassioned look concurred with the emphatic accent of his words to convince Fleur-de-Lis. It is possible that at the moment he himself believed what he asserted.

Meanwhile the good mother, pleased to see the young people on such excellent terms, had left the apartment to attend to some domestic matter or other. Phœbus noticed her absence, which emboldened the enterprising Captain. Fleur-de-Lis loved him; she was betrothed to him; she was alone with him. His former fondness for her was revived, if not in all its freshness, at any rate in all its ardor. After all, it is not such a crime to taste the fruits of the orchard before their time. I do not know if such ideas crossed his mind, but this much is certain, that Fleur-de-Lis became suddenly alarmed at the expression of his gaze. She looked around her—her mother was gone!

"My God!" she said, flushed and agitated. "I am very hot!"

"Why," replied Phœbus, "I daresay it is almost noon. The sun is troublesome. I will draw the curtains."

"No, no!" cried the trembling damsel. "On the contrary, I need air." And, rising, she ran to the window and stepped out on the balcony. Phœbus followed her there.

The Place du Parvis, in front of Notre-Dame, into which, as the reader knows, this balcony looked, presented at this moment a sinister and singular spectacle, which quickly changed the nature of the timid Fleur-de-Lis's alarm. An immense crowd, which flowed back into all the adjacent streets, covered the square. The low wall that encompassed the Parvis would not have been sufficient to keep it clear had it not been thickly lined by sergeants of the Onze-vingts and musketeers, with their guns in their hands. The wide doors of the church were closed, contrasting with the numberless windows around the square, which, thrown open up to the very roofs, displayed thousands of heads heaped one above another, nearly like piles of cannonballs in an armory. The surface of this crowd was gray, squalid, dirty. The sight it was awaiting was evidently one of those that have the privilege of calling together all that is most disgusting in the population. Nothing could be more hideous than the noise that arose from this assemblage of yellowing caps and unkempt heads. In this crowd there were more women than men, more laughing than crying.

Every so often some harsh or shrill voice was heard above the general din:

"I say, Mahiet Baliffre, is she going to be hanged there?"

"No, idiot—only to do penance there in her slip. The priest is going to cough Latin in her face. It is always done here, at noon precisely. If you want to see the hanging, get over to the Grève."

"I will go afterwards."

———

"Is it true, La Boucombry, that she refused a confessor?"

"It seems so, La Bechaine."

"You see, the pagan!"

———

"It is the custom, sir. The Bailiff of the Palace is bound to deliver the culprit for execution, if of the laity, to the Provost of Paris, but if a clergyman, to the official of the bishopric."

"I thank you, sir."

———

"Oh, my God! The poor creature!" exclaimed Fleur-de-Lis, surveying the populace with a look of pain. The Captain was too much engaged with her to notice the rabble; he rubbed against her skirts from behind.

"For goodness' sake, Phœbus, leave me alone! If my mother were to return, she would see your hand!"

At this moment the clock of Notre-Dame slowly struck twelve. A murmur of satisfaction ran through the crowd. Scarcely had the last vibration of the twelfth stroke faded when the vast assemblage of heads was broken into waves like the sea in a gale of wind, and one immense shout of "There she is!" burst simultaneously from pavement, windows, and roofs.

Fleur-de-Lis covered her eyes with her hands so that she would not see.

"Charming girl, do you want to go back in?" asked Phœbus.

"No," she replied, and those eyes that she had shut for fear she opened again out of curiosity.

A cart, drawn by a strong Norman shaft-horse and completely surrounded by horsemen in purple livery, marked with white crosses, had just come from the Rue St.-Pierre-aux-Bœufs and entered the square. The sergeants of the watch opened a passage for it through the people by clubbing with their staves. Beside the cart rode officers of justice and police, who could be recognized by their black outfits and the awkward manner in which they sat in their saddles. At their head paraded Master Jacques Charmolue. In the fatal vehicle was seated a young girl, with her hands tied behind her, and no priest at her side. She was stripped to her slip; her long black hair—for it was not then customary to cut it off till the culprit was at the foot of the gallows—fell loosely over her bosom and her half-uncovered shoulders.

Through this flowing hair, more glossy than a raven's plumage, you could see a twisted, gray, rough rope, which chafed her delicate clavicle and twined itself around the neck of the poor girl like an earthworm on a flower. Beneath this cord glistened a little amulet adorned with green beads, which had been left her no doubt because one refuses nothing to those who are going to die. The spectators in the windows could see at the bottom of the cart her naked legs, which she strove to conceal beneath her, as if by a last instinct of feminine modesty. At her feet there was a little goat, also bound. The prisoner held with her teeth her slip, which was not properly fastened. Her misery seemed to be greatly aggravated by her being so exposed, nearly naked, to the public gaze. Alas! It is not for such tremors that modesty is intended!

"Jesus," said Fleur-de-Lis sharply to the Captain. "It's that miserable Bohemian with the goat."

As she said this she turned around toward Phœbus. He was staring at the cart. He was unusually pale.

"What Bohemian with the goat?" he said, faltering.

"What!" rejoined Fleur-de-Lis. "Don't you remember?"

"I don't know what you mean," said Phœbus, interrupting her.

He moved to go back in, but Fleur-de-Lis, whose jealousy, once so strongly excited by this same gypsy, was reawakened, cast on him a penetrating look full of mistrust. She remembered vaguely having heard that a Captain was implicated in the proceedings against this witch.

"What ails you?" she said to Phœbus. "One would think that the sight of this creature had given you a shock."

"Me! Not at all!" stammered Phœbus, with a forced laugh.

"Then stay!" she answered imperiously, "and let us look on until it is all over."

The unlucky Captain was forced to stay. He recovered his composure somewhat on observing that the prisoner never raised her eyes from the bottom planks of the cart. It was only too surely La Esmeralda. At the lowest point of misfortune and ignominy, she was still beautiful; her large, black eyes appeared still larger, because her cheeks were so hollow; her vivid profile was pure and sublime. She resembled what she was as a Virgin of Masaccio's resembles a Virgin of Raphael's—feebler, thinner, more frail.

Otherwise, there was nothing about her, except her modesty, that she had not abandoned to chance, so deeply was she broken by stupor and despair. At each jolt of the cart her form rebounded like a dead or broken thing; her gaze was dull and inert. A tear glistened in her eye, but it was motionless and looked as if it were frozen.

Meanwhile the somber cavalcade had passed through the crowd, through shouts of joy and looks of curiosity. In order to be faithful historians, we must record that many of the mob, and of the hardest-hearted too, on seeing her so beautiful and so overwhelmed, were moved by pity. The cart had now reached the Parvis.

It stopped before the central doorway. The escort ranged itself on either side. The mob kept silence, and amid this silence, full of solemnity and anxiety, the two doors of the great entrance turned as if spontaneously on their hinges, which creaked with the shrillness of a fife. The crowd had a view of the whole length of the church, vast, gloomy, hung with black, dimly lit by a few tapers glimmering in the distance on the high altar, and opening like the mouth of a cavern on the square, bright with the glorious sunshine. At the farthest end, in the darkness of the apse, a colossal silver cross could barely be seen in relief against a black curtain that fell behind it from the vault to the floor. The whole nave was deserted. Heads of priests were however visible confusedly moving around in the distant stalls of the choir; and at the moment when the great door opened there burst from the church a deep, loud, and monotonous chant, exploding, as it were, in gusts, fragments of lugubrious psalms on the head of the condemned one.

Non timebo millia populi circumdantis me: exsurge, Domine; salvum me fac, Deus! Salvum me fac, Deus, quoniam intraverunt aquæ usque ad animam meam. Infixus sum in limo profundi; et non est substantia.

At the same time another voice, isolated from the chorus, resounded on the steps of the high altar this melancholy offering:

Qui verbum meum audit, et credit ei qui misit me, habet vitam æternam et in judicium non venit; sed transit à morte in vitam.[7]

These songs sung by old men lost in the darkness over that beautiful creature, full of youth and life, caressed by the warm air of spring and inundated with the sunlight, belonged to the Mass for the dead. The people listened quietly.

The terrified girl, staring into the dark entrails of the church, seemed to lose both sight and thought. Her pale lips moved, as if in prayer; and, when the executioner's man went to assist her in descending from the cart, he heard her repeating in a faint voice the word *"Phœbus!"*

Her hands were unbound, and she stepped down, accompanied by her goat, which had also been untied and bleated for joy on finding itself at liberty; and she was made to walk barefoot on the hard paving stones to the foot of the steps leading to the entrance. The rope that was fastened around her neck trailed behind her; it looked like a snake that was following her.

The singing in the church ceased. A large gold crucifix and a row of candles began to move in the darkness. The sound of the armor of the Swiss guard was heard. A few moments later a long procession of priests in hoods and deacons in dalmatics slowly advanced singing toward the prisoner and spread out before her eyes and those of the mob. She stared at the one who walked at its head immediately after the bearer of the crucifix. "Oh!" she muttered to herself, shuddering. "There he is again! The priest!"

It was in fact the Archdeacon. On his left was the *sous-chantre,* and on his right the *chantre* bearing the staff of his office. He advanced, with head thrown back, and eyes staring and open, chanting with a loud voice:

De ventre inferi clamavi, et exaudisti vocem meam.
Et projecisti me in profundum, in corde maris, et flumen circumdedit me.[8]

At the moment when he appeared in the broad daylight beneath the agile arch of the door, wrapped within a cape of silver marked with a black cross, he was so pale that some in the crowd thought it must be one of the marble bishops kneeling on the sepulchral monuments in the choir who had risen and come to receive on the brink of the tomb the one who was about to die.

She, not less pale, not less statuelike, was scarcely aware that a heavy lighted candle of yellow wax had been put into her hand; she did not hear the squeaking voice of the clerk reading the fatal syllables of the penance; when told to say *Amen* she said *Amen.* When she saw the priest make a sign to those who had her in custody to retire, and advance alone toward her, she regained some signs of life. She felt the blood boil in her head, and a spark of indignation was rekindled in that soul, already so cold and numb.

The Archdeacon approached her slowly. Even in this extremity she saw him survey her nearly naked form with an eye glowing with lust, desire, and jealousy. In a loud voice he addressed her, "Young woman, have you prayed God to pardon your crimes and misdemeanors?" Then stooping—as the spectators imagined, to receive her last confession—he whispered, "Will you have me? I can still save you!"

She stared at him steadfastly. "Go to the devil, your master, or I will denounce you!"

He grinned a ghastly smile. "They will not believe you," he replied. "You will only add scandal to guilt. Answer quickly, will you have me?"

"What have you done with my Phœbus?"

"He is dead," said the priest.

At that moment the wretched Archdeacon raised his head mechanically and saw on the other side of the square the Captain standing in the balcony with Fleur-de-Lis. He shuddered, passed his hand over his eyes, looked again, muttered a malediction, and all his features contracted violently.

"Well die then!" he said. "No one shall have you." Then, lifting his hand over the gypsy, he pronounced these words in a loud and solemn tone: *"I nunc anima anceps, et sit tibi Deus misericors!"*[9] This was the dreadful formula with which it was customary to conclude these gloomy ceremonies. It was the signal given by the priest to the executioner. The populace fell on their knees.

"Kyrie eleison!"[10] said the priests, who stopped beneath the doorway.

"Kyrie eleison!" repeated the crowd with a murmur that rose above their heads like the rumbling of an agitated sea.

"Amen!" said the Archdeacon.

He turned his back on the prisoner; his head sank on his bosom; he crossed his hands. He rejoined the train of priests and a moment later disappeared with the crucifix, the candles, and the hoods, beneath the dark arches of the cathedral; and his sonorous voice faded gradually in the choir, while chanting this verse of anguish: *"Omnes gurites tui et fluctus tui super me transierunt."*[11]

At the same time the intermittent reverberation of the iron-shod lances of the halberts of the Swiss guard faded away between the columns of the nave; it sounded like a clock hammer striking the last hour of the accused.

Meanwhile the doors of Notre-Dame were left open, putting the empty church on view. It was desolate, in mourning, without candles or singing. The condemned girl stood motionless in her place, waiting for them to dispose of her. One of the guards was obliged to make a sign to Master Charmolue, who, during the entire scene, had been studying the bas-relief of the great doorway, representing, according to some, the sacrifice of Abraham, according to others, an alchemical operation, the angel represented by the sun, fire by the bundle of sticks, and the alchemist by Abraham. It was with some difficulty that he was roused from this contemplation, but at length he turned around, and at a sign he made two men in yellow suits, the executioner's assistants, approached the gypsy to tie her hands again.

When she had to get back in the fatal cart and set out for her last stop, the unfortunate creature was probably seized by some keen longing for life. She raised her dry but red eyes toward heaven, toward the sun, toward the silvery clouds, interrupted here and there with patches of azure sky, and then she cast them down around her upon the earth, upon the crowd, upon the houses.

Suddenly, while the men in yellow were tying her elbows together, she gave a startling scream, a scream of joy. In the balcony at the corner of the square she had spotted *him,* her friend, her lord, her Phœbus, just as he looked when he was alive. The judge had lied to her! The priest had lied to her! It was he himself—she could not possibly doubt it. There he was, handsome, living, dressed in his brilliant uniform, with a feather on his head and the sword by his side.

"Phœbus!" she cried. "My Phœbus!" And she would have stretched out her arms trembling with love and transport toward him, but they were bound.

Then she saw the Captain frown; a beautiful young girl who leaned on him looked at him with a disdainful mouth and angry eye. Phœbus then uttered a few words, which she was too far off to hear; both hastily retreated from the balcony into the room, and the window was immediately closed.

"Phœbus!" she cried wildly. "Do you believe it?" A horrible idea had just flashed upon her. She remembered that she had been condemned for the murder of Captain Phœbus de Châteaupers. She had borne up thus far against everything. This last shock was too violent. She fell senseless on the ground.

"Come!" said Charmolue. "Carry her to the cart, and let us put an end to the business!"

Nobody had noticed in the gallery of the royal statues, immediately above the pointed arches of the entrance, a strange-looking spectator, who had till then been watching everything impassively, head so outstretched, visage so deformed that, except for his apparel, half red and half purple, he might have been taken for one of those stone monsters out of whose mouths the long gutters of the cathedral have for these six hundred years disgorged themselves. This spectator had not lost a single detail of the tragedy that had been played out since noon in front of the main entrance of Notre-Dame. From the very beginning he had, unobserved, securely tied to one of the small pillars of the gallery a knotted rope, the end of which reached the ground. This done, he had settled in watching as quietly as before, hissing from time to time at the crows as they flew past him. Suddenly, when the executioner's assistants were preparing to obey Charmolue's order, he climbed across the balustrade of the gallery, seized the rope with his feet, knees, and hands, glided down the facade like a drop of rain down a pane of glass, ran up to the two men with the swiftness of a cat that has fallen from a roof, knocked both of them to the ground with his enormous fists, and bore off the gypsy on one arm, as a girl would a doll. With one bound he was in the church, holding the young girl up above his head and shouting with a terrific voice, "Sanctuary! Sanctuary!" This was all done with the speed of lightning.

"Sanctuary! Sanctuary!" repeated the mob, and the clapping of ten thousand hands caused Quasimodo's only eye to shine with joy and exultation.

This shock brought La Esmeralda to her senses. She opened her eyes, looked at Quasimodo, and instantly closed them again, as if horror-stricken at the sight of her deliverer.

Charmolue stood stupefied. So did the executioners and the whole escort. Within the walls of Notre-Dame the prisoner was secure from molestation. The cathedral was a place of refuge. Human justice dared not cross its threshold.

Quasimodo paused under the great entrance. His large feet seemed as firmly rooted in the pavement of the church as the massive Roman pillars. His great hairy head appeared to be set upon his shoulders like that of the lion, who too has a copious mane and no neck. He held the young girl, trembling all over, suspended from his callused hands like a piece of white cloth. But he carried her so carefully that it was as if he was fearful of breaking or bruising her. He felt, it seemed, that a thing so delicate, so exquisite, so precious, was not made for such hands as his. At times he looked as though he did not dare touch her even with his breath. Then, all at once, he would clasp her tight in his arms, against his angular bosom, as his treasure, as his all, as the mother of that girl would herself have done. His Cyclops eye bent over her, shed over her a flood of tenderness, of pity, of grief, and was suddenly raised again, flashing lightning. At this sight the women laughed and cried; the crowd stamped with enthusiasm, for at that moment Quasimodo was really beautiful. Yes, he was beautiful—he, that orphan, that foundling, that outcast; he felt himself august and strong; he looked in the face that society from which he was banished, and in which he had so powerfully intervened. He stared down the human justice from which he had snatched its victim, those judges, those executioners, all that force of the King's, which he, the meanest of the mean, had foiled with the force of God!

And then, so touching was that protection afforded by a being so deformed to a being so unfortunate as the girl condemned to die and saved by Quasimodo! It was the two extreme miseries of nature and society meeting and helping each other.

However, after a triumph of a few minutes, Quasimodo rushed suddenly into the church with his burden. The people, fond of daring deeds, followed him with their eyes along the dark nave, regretting that he had so soon withdrawn himself from their praise. Suddenly he was again glimpsed at one of the ends of the gallery of the Kings of France; he ran along it like a maniac, holding up his prize in his arms, and shouting, "Sanctuary!" The people greeted him with fresh applause. Having crossed the gallery he again plunged inside the church. A moment later, he again appeared on the upper platform, still bearing the gypsy in his arms, still running madly, still shouting, "Sanctuary." Again the mob applauded. Eventually he made his third appearance on the top of the great bell tower; there he seemed to show proudly to the whole city the girl he had saved, and his thundering voice—that voice which was heard so seldom, and which he himself never heard—made the air ring with the repeated shout of "Sanctuary! Sanctuary! Sanctuary!"

"Hurrah! Hurrah!" cried the populace; and this prodigious acclamation was heard on the other side of the river by the crowd collected in the Place de Grève, and by the recluse, who was still waiting with her eyes riveted on the gallows.

BOOK IX

CHAPTER I

A High Fever

Claude Frollo was no longer in Notre-Dame when his foster son so abruptly cut the fatal noose in which the unhappy Archdeacon had trapped the gypsy himself. On returning to the sacristy he had stripped off the alb, the cape, and the stole, thrown them all into the hands of the stupefied beadle, hurried out the private door of the cloisters, ordered a boatman of the Terrain to carry him across the river, and wandered among the hilly streets of the Université, meeting at every step groups of men and women hastening joyously toward the Pont St.-Michel, "in hopes of being in time to see the witch hanged!" Pale and haggard, blinded and more bewildered than an owl let loose and pursued by a troop of boys in broad daylight, he did not know where he was, what he did, or whether he was awake or dreaming. He walked, he ran, taking any street at random, still driven onward by the Grève, the horrible Grève, which he vaguely knew to be behind him.

In this way he went around the hill of Ste.-Geneviève and left the town by the gate of St.-Victor. As long as he could see, on turning around, the line of towers enclosing the Université and the scattered houses of the suburb, he continued on, but when at last the hilliness of the terrain had completely blocked his view of that hateful Paris, when he could pretend to be a hundred leagues off, in the country, in a desert, he paused, and felt as though he could breathe again.

A crowd of horrible ideas then came to his mind. He saw clearly into the recesses of his soul, and he shuddered. He thought of that unhappy girl who had undone him, and whom he had undone. With haggard eye he followed the double winding way along which fatality had urged their two destinies to the point of intersection, where it had pitilessly dashed them against one another. He thought of the madness of eternal vows, of the vanity of chastity, science, religion, virtue, and of the uselessness of God. He willfully plunged into evil thoughts, and as he immersed himself in them he felt a satanic laugh explode within him.

And when, while diving into his soul this way, he saw how large a space nature had prepared there from the passions, he laughed still more bitterly. He stirred up from the bottom of his heart all its hatred and its malice, and he perceived, with the cold indifference of a physician examining a patient, that this hatred and this malice were only distorted love; that love, the source of every virtue in man, was transformed into horrid things in the heart of a priest, and that someone constituted as he was, in becoming a priest made himself a demon. He then laughed more hideously than ever, and suddenly he again turned pale on considering the darkest side of his fatal passion, that corrosive, venomous, rancorous, implacable love, which had consigned the one to the gallows, the other to hell. She was condemned. He was damned.

And then he laughed again on thinking that Phœbus was not dead; that he was still alive, gay, and joyous, that he had a sharper uniform than ever, and a new mistress, whom he took to see the former one hanged. He laughed still more heartily on reflecting that, among all the living beings whose death he had wished for, the gypsy, the only creature he did not hate, was also the only one who could not escape him.

From the Captain, his thoughts turned to the people, and an unspeakable jealousy overtook him. He thought about how the woman he loved had been exposed to the gaze of the crowd, of the entire population of Paris, in her slip, half naked. He wrung his hands thinking that this woman, whose body glimpsed in the dark would have been for him the supreme happiness, had been delivered in full daylight, at noon, to an entire people dressed as if for a night of voluptuous pleasures. He cried in rage at all of these mysteries of love that were profaned, sullied, stripped bare, faded forever. He cried in rage imagining how those vulgar gazes had found their satisfaction in the badly tied slip, and that this beautiful girl, this virgin lily, this vessel of modesty and delicacy to whom he dared raise his lips only while trembling, had been transformed into a sort of whore, in whom the vile common people of Paris—robbers, beggars and lackeys alike—collectively tasted an offensive, impure, and depraved pleasure.

And when he strove to picture to himself the happiness that he might have found on earth if she had not been a gypsy, and if he had not been a priest, if Phœbus had not existed, and if she had loved him; when he considered that a life of serenity and affection might have been possible for him, too, even for him; that, at that very moment, there were here and there on the earth happy couples lost in long conversations under orange groves, on the banks of murmuring streams, in the presence of a setting sun, or of a starry sky, and that, if God had willed it, he might have formed with her one of those blessed couples, his heart dissolved in tenderness and despair.

She formed the subject of his every thought. It was this fixed idea that haunted him incessantly, that tortured him, that racked his brain and gnawed his insides. He felt no regret about anything; he felt no remorse; all that he had done he was ready to do again. He would rather see her in the hands of the hangman than in the arms of the Captain. But so acute was his anguish that at times he tore off his hair by handfuls to see if it was not turning white.

There was one moment among others when it occurred to him that possibly at that very instant the hideous cord that he had seen in the morning might be drawing tight its iron noose around that neck so frail and so graceful. This idea made perspiration start from every pore.

There was another moment when, laughing diabolically at himself all the while, he thought of La Esmeralda as she was on the first day he had ever seen her, all life, all mirth, all joy, adorned, agile, dancing, winged, harmonious, and of La Esmeralda of the last hour, stripped, the rope around her neck, slowly ascending with bare feet the rough ladder to the gallows. This twofold picture was drawn before him with such force that it extracted from him a terrible shriek.

While this storm of despair was breaking, disturbing, overthrowing, uprooting everything in his soul, his eye ranged over the scene around him. At his feet some hens were pecking in the bushes, and picking up the burnished insects that were running around in the sun; overhead groups of dappled clouds were sprinkled on an azure sky; on the horizon the steeple of the abbey of St.-Victor pierced the curve of the hill with its slate obelisk, and the miller of Copeaux watched the laboring sails of his mills turn, (whistling) all the while. This active, organized, tranquil life around him reproduced in a thousand forms gave him pain. And so he began again to flee.

He ran through the fields until nightfall. This flight from nature, from life, from himself, from man, from God, from everything, lasted till evening. Sometimes he threw himself on his face on the earth and tore up the young corn with his fingers; at other moments he paused in some lone village street, and his thoughts were so unbearable that he grasped his head with both hands and tried to wrench it from his shoulders in order to dash it against the ground.

When the sun began to set, he examined himself again; and he found that he was almost mad. The storm that had been raging within him from the moment he had lost the hope and the will to save the gypsy had not left in his mind a single healthy thought or idea. His reason was laid low, almost utterly destroyed. His mind retained only two distinct images, La Esmeralda and the gallows. All the rest was black. These two images formed a horrible pair, and the more he fixed on them what was left of his thought and attention, the more they seemed to increase, according to a fantastic progression, the one in charm, in grace, in beauty, in light—the other in horror, so that at last La Esmeralda appeared like a star, the gallows like an enormous flesh-less arm.

It is remarkable that, during the whole of this torture, he never had any serious idea of putting an end to his life. This was how he was. The wretched man was tenacious of life. Perhaps he really saw hell gaping before him.

The day, meanwhile, continued to fade. The living principle that still existed within him began to think confusedly of returning home. He thought that he was far from Paris, but on examining the objects around he found that he had done nothing but turn around the walls of the Université. The steeple of St.-Sulpice and the three tall spires of St.-Germain-des-Prés shot up above the horizon on his right. He proceeded in that direction. When he heard the "Who goes there?" of the men-at-arms of the abbot around the ramparts of the walls of St.-Germain, he turned away and took a path that presented itself between the abbey mill and the leper house of the hamlet, and soon he found himself on the edge of the Pré-aux-Clercs. This meadow was celebrated for its chaos, which lasted night and day; it was the hydra of the poor monks of St.-Germain. *"Quod monachis Sancti-Germani pratensis hydra fuit, clericis nova semper dissidiorum captia sucsitantibus."*[1] The Archdeacon was afraid of meeting someone; he was afraid of every human face. He had avoided the Université and the hamlet of St.-Germain; he wished to make it as late as possible before he entered the streets. He proceeded along the Pré-aux-Clercs, took the lonely path that separated it from the Dieu Neuf, and at last reached the bank of the river. There Dom Claude found a boatman who for a few deniers took him up the Seine to the point of the Cité and set him ashore on that vacant tongue of land where the reader has already seen Gringoire dreaming, which extended beyond the King's gardens parallel with the isle of the cattle ferryman.

The monotonous rocking of the boat and the murmur of the water had somewhat lulled the wretched Claude. When the boatman had left him, he remained standing stupidly on the beach, looking straight forward. All the objects he saw seemed to dance before his eyes, forming a sort of phantasmagoria. It is not uncommon for the fatigue of excessive grief to produce this effect on the mind.

The sun had set behind the tall Tour de Nesle. It was just twilight. The sky was white; the water of the river was white. Between these the left bank of the Seine, on which his eyes were fixed, extended its somber mass, which, gradually diminished by the perspective, pierced the haze of the horizon like a black arrow. It was covered with houses, of which nothing was distinguishable but a dark silhouette, standing out in stark relief in the dark against the light ground of the sky and the water. Lights began to glimmer here and there in the windows. This immense black obelisk, thus bound by the two white sheets of the sky and the river, very wide at this place, produced on Dom Claude a singular effect. You could compare it with what a man would experience lying down on his back at the foot of the steeple of Strasbourg Cathedral, looking at its enormous spire piercing the penumbra of the twilight above his head. Only here, Claude was standing and the obelisk lying down. But as the river, in reflecting the sky, lengthened the abyss beneath him, the immense promontory shot forth into space like any church steeple, and the impression was the same. That impression was rendered the more striking and extraordinary by the fact that this steeple was two leagues high—a colossal, immeasurable, unparalleled object; a tower of Babel. An edifice such as human eye never beheld. The chimneys of the houses, the battlements of the walls, the angles of the roofs, the steeple of the Augustines, the Tour de Nesle, all those sharp points that indented the profile of the immense obelisk, heightened the illusion by presenting to the eye a grotesque semblance of the carving of a labored and fantastic sculpture. Claude, in his hallucinatory state, imagined that he saw—saw with his own eyes—the tower of hell: the thousand lights gleaming from bottom to top of this frightful tower appeared to him to be so many entrances to the immense furnace within; and the voices and sounds that came out of it were the shrieks and moans of the damned. A deep fear came over him; he covered his ears with his hands so that he might not hear, turned his back that he might not see, and hurried away from the terrible vision. But the vision was within him.

On entering the streets the passersby who jostled one another by the light of the shop fronts appeared like specters incessantly going and coming around him. Strange noises rang in his ears; extraordinary fantasies disturbed his mind. He saw neither houses nor pavement, neither men, women, nor carriages, but a chaos of confused objects blending one with another. At the corner of the Rue de la Barillerie there was a grocer's shop, the penthouse of which was hung all along, according to immemorial custom, with tin hoops, to which were attached imitation candles of wood: these, shaken by the wind, clattered like castanets. He imagined that he heard the skeletons of Montfaucon knocking together in the dark.

"Oh!" he muttered. "The night wind is driving them against one another, and mingling the clank of their chain with the rattling of their bones. She is there too, perhaps, among them!"

Distracted, he did not know where he was going. After a few steps, he was on the Pont St.-Michel. He saw a light in the window of a ground-floor room; he approached it. Through a cracked pane he saw a sordid room, which awakened confused recollections in his mind. In this apartment, faintly lit by a lamp, he saw a blond, jovial-looking young man, who, while laughing, kissed a young woman who was dressed very provocatively. Near the lamp was seated an old woman spinning and singing in a quivering voice. Since the young man was not always laughing, the old woman's song passed through the cracks and was audible to the priest. It was something unintelligible and horrible at the same time:

> *Grève, aboye, Grève grouille!*
> *File, file ma quenouille*
> *File sa corde au bourreau*
> *Qui siffle dans le préau.*
> *Grève, aboye, Grève grouille.*
>
> *La belle corde de chanvre!*
> *Semez d'Issy jusqu'à Vanvre*
> *Du Chanvre et non pas du blé*
> *Le voleur n'a pas volé*
> *La belle corde de chanvre.*
>
> *Grève, grouille, Grève aboye!*
> *Pour voir la fille de joie*
> *Pendre au gibet chassieux*
> *Les fenêtres sont des yeux.*
> *Grève, grouille, Grève aboye.*[2]

With that the young man laughed and caressed the girl.

The old woman was Falourdel, the girl was a prostitute, and the young man was his brother, Jehan. He continued to watch them. He saw Jehan go to a window at the farther end of the room, open it, and look out on the quay, where a thousand lit windows shone in the distance; and he heard him say while shutting the window, "Upon my soul, it is a dark night. The citizens are lighting up their candles, and God Almighty his stars."

Jehan then went back to his companion and held up a bottle that stood on the table. "Damn!" he cried. "Empty already! And I have no more money. I will not be happy with Jupiter until he has changed your two white breasts into two black bottles from which I will suck night and day the wine of Beaune." This lovely joke made the girl laugh. Saying this he came out of the house. Dom Claude just had time to throw himself on the ground so that he might not be met, looked in the face, and recognized by his brother. Luckily the street was dark and the student not sober. "Oho!" he said. "Here is one who has been enjoying himself today." With his foot he shook Dom Claude, who held his breath.

"Dead drunk!" resumed Jehan. "Full enough, it seems. A real leech peeled away from a cask. Bald too!" he added, stooping. "An old man! *Fortunate senex!* Happy old man!"

Dom Claude then heard him move away, saying, "Never mind! Reason is a fine thing, though; and my brother the Archdeacon is very lucky in being prudent and having money."

The Archdeacon then rose and ran without stopping toward Notre-Dame, whose enormous towers he saw lifting themselves in the dark above the houses. At the moment when, quite breathless, he reached the Place du Parvis, he paused, and he dared not raise his eyes to the fatal edifice. "Oh!" he said, in a low tone. "Is it true, then, that such a thing could have happened here today—this very morning?"

He ventured, however, to look at the church. The facade was dark; the sky behind it glistened with stars. The crescent of the moon, which had not been long above the horizon, was seen at that moment on the top of the right-hand tower, and seemed to be perched like a luminous bird on the edge of the parapet, cut out into large trefoils.

The door of the cloisters was shut, but the Archdeacon always carried with him the key of the tower where he had his laboratory. Using it, he entered the church. He found the interior dark and silent as the grave. From the large shadows that fell from all sides in broad sheets, he knew that the hangings put up for the morning's ceremony had not been removed. The great silver cross glistened in the gloom; it was dotted with sparkling points, like the Milky Way of this sepulchral night. The tall windows of the choir shone above the black drapery the tops of their pointed arches. The panes admitted a faint ray of moonlight, and had only those doubtful colors of night, a sort of violet, white, and blue whose tint is otherwise found only on the faces of the dead. The Archdeacon, seeing all around the choir these pale points of arches, thought that it was a circle of ghastly faces staring at him.

He began to flee across the church. It seemed to him then that the church too moved, breathed, lived; that each massive column was transformed into an enormous leg, stamping the ground with its broad stone foot; and that the gigantic cathedral was a sort of prodigious elephant, puffing and walking, with pillars for legs, the two towers for trunks, and the immense sheet of black cloth for trappings.

Thus the fever or the frenzy of the wretched priest had reached such a degree of intensity that to him the external world was nothing but a kind of visible, palpable, terrifying Apocalypse.

For a moment he felt somewhat relieved. On entering one of the aisles, he saw a reddish light behind a cluster of pillars. He ran toward it as toward a star. It was the poor lamp that night and day threw a dim light on the public breviary of Notre-Dame, beneath its iron grating. He hurried to the sacred book, in hopes of finding in it some consolation or encouragement. It was open at this passage of Job, which caught his eye, "Then a spirit passed before my face; the hair of my flesh stood up."

On reading this fearful text he felt much the same as a blind man whose fingers are pricked by the staff he has picked up. His knees failed him, and he sank down on the pavement, thinking of her who had that day suffered death. He felt his brain enveloped in such monstrous, exploding fumes that it seemed as if his head had been turned into one of the chimneys of hell.

He must have remained for a long time in this posture, neither thinking nor feeling, helpless and passive in the hand of the demon. Eventually, recovering some degree of consciousness, he thought of seeking refuge in the tower, near his trusty Quasimodo. He rose and, being afraid, he took the lamp of the breviary to light his way. This was a sacrilege, but he no longer cared about such a trivial one.

He slowly ascended the staircase of the tower, filled with a secret dread, which was communicated to the passersby who now and then crossed the Parvis, on seeing the mysterious light of this lamp mounting so late from tiny window to tiny window all the way to the top of the tower.

Suddenly he felt cool air on his face and found himself under the doorway of the uppermost gallery. The night was cold. The sky was covered with clouds, the large white masses of which, overlapping each other at the edges and being compressed at the corners, resembled the ice of a river that has broken up in winter. The crescent moon, embedded in those clouds, looked like a celestial ship surrounded by aerial sheets of ice.

He looked down through the iron railing of the miniature colonnade that joins the two towers and for a moment contemplated through the veil of mist and smoke the vast extent of the roofs of Paris, sharp, countless, crowded together, and small as the ripples of a calm sea in a summer night. The moon gave only a faint light, which cast an ashy tint to earth and sky.

At this moment the clock raised its loud and solemn voice. It was midnight. The priest thought of noon: it was again twelve o'clock. "Oh!" he muttered to himself. "She must be cold by this time!"

All at once a gust of wind extinguished his lamp, and at the same moment he saw something white—a shade, a human form, a female—appear at the opposite corner of the tower. He shuddered. By the side of this female there was a little goat, which mingled her bleating with the last tones of the bell. He had the courage to look at her—it was she herself.

She was pale; she was sad. Her hair fell over her shoulders as in the morning; but there was no rope around her neck; her hands were not bound; she was free, she was dead.

She was dressed in white and had a white veil over her head. She came toward him slowly, looking up at the sky and followed by the supernatural goat. He was petrified: he would have fled but was unable to do so. All he could do was back a step away for every one that she advanced. He retreated in this manner till he was beneath the dark vault of the staircase. His blood curdled at the idea that she might come that way too; if she had, he might have died of fright.

She did in fact approach as near as the door of the staircase, where she paused for a moment; she cast a fixed look into the darkness, but without appearing to discern the priest, and passed on. She seemed to him taller than when alive; he saw the moonshine through her white robe; he heard her breath.

When she was gone he began to descend the stairs as slowly as the specter. Horror-stricken, his hair erect, still holding the extinguished lamp in his hand, he thought he was a ghost himself. While descending the spiral staircase, he heard a voice, laughing and repeating distinctly in his ear, "A spirit passed before my face; the hair of my flesh stood up."

CHAPTER II

ONE-EYED, HUNCHBACK, AND LAME

In the Middle Ages every town, and until the time of Louis XII every town in France, had its sanctuaries. Amid the deluge of penal laws and barbarous jurisdictions that inundated the division of Paris that we have called the Cité, these sanctuaries were sorts of islands, which were beyond the level of human justice. Every criminal who took refuge in them was saved. There were in a district almost as many sanctuaries as places of execution. It was the abuse of impunity going hand in hand with the abuse of punishment—two bad things, which strove to correct one another. The palaces of the King, the mansions of the princes, but above all the churches, had the right of sanctuary. Sometimes that right was conferred for a time on a whole city that needed to be repopulated. Louis XI made Paris a sanctuary in 1467.

Once he had set foot in the sanctuary, the criminal was sacred, but he could not leave. One step out of the island-asylum plunged him again into the sea. The wheel, the gallows, the rack, kept strict guard around his retreat, and they watched their prey incessantly as sharks prowl around a ship. Condemned persons thus rescued have been known to grow gray in a cloister, on the staircase of a palace, in the garden of an abbey, at the entrance of a church: in this way the sanctuary was a prison as much as any place that bore the name. It sometimes happened that a solemn ordinance of Parliament violated the sanctuary and gave up the condemned to the executioner, but this was rare. The Parliaments were afraid of the bishops, and when the gowns of the two professions got tangled in a conflict, the soutanes of the Church generally got the better of it. At times, however, as in the case of the assassins of Petit-Jean, who was the executioner of Paris, and in that of Emery Rousseau, the murderer of Jean Valleret, Justice leaped over the Church and went on to the execution of its sentences. But unless authorized by an ordinance of the Parliament, woe to him who forcibly violated the sanctuary. Everybody knows the fate of Robert de Clermont, Marshal of France, and Jean de Châlons, Marshal of Champagne; and yet the party in whose case they had intervened, one Perrin

Marc, was nothing but a moneychanger's man and a miserable assassin. But the two marshals had broken open the doors of St.-Méry.[3] That was the outrage!

Such was the respect with which sanctuaries were invested that, according to tradition, it occasionally extended to brute animals. Aymoin relates that when a stag hunted by Dagobert took refuge near the tomb of St.-Denis, the dogs stopped short and merely barked at him.

Churches had in general a place devoted to lodging fugitives. In 1407 Nicolas Flamel had built for such persons, in the church of St.-Jacques-de-la-Boucherie, a room that cost him four pounds, six sous, sixteen deniers Parisis.

In Notre-Dame it was a small cell on the top of the aisles, under the flying buttresses, facing the cloisters, on the very spot where the wife of the present keeper of the towers made herself a garden, which is to the hanging gardens of Babylon what a lettuce is to a palm tree, or a porter is to Semiramis.

It was here that, after his wild and triumphant course through towers and galleries, Quasimodo deposited La Esmeralda. As long as this race lasted the girl had not recovered her senses; half stupefied, half awake, she had the feeling that she was floating in the air, that she was floating, flying, and that something was lifting her high above the earth. From time to time she heard the loud laugh and the harsh voice of Quasimodo in her ear; she opened her eyes, and then beneath her she confusedly saw Paris inlaid with its thousand roofs of slate and tile, like red and blue mosaic work, and above her head the frightening but joyful face of Quasimodo. Again her eyes closed; she imagined that it was all over, that she had been executed during her swoon, and that the deformed spirit who had governed her destiny had seized and borne her away. She did not dare to look at it and let herself be carried away.

But when the breathless bell ringer had laid her down in the cell of sanctuary, when she felt his huge hands gently untying the cord that had rubbed her arms raw, she experienced the kind of shock that abruptly awakens those onboard a ship that runs aground in the middle of a dark night. Her ideas awoke as well and returned to her one by one. She saw that she was in Notre-Dame; she remembered having been snatched out of the hands of the executioner; that Phœbus was alive, and that he no longer loved her. As these two ideas, one of which imparted such bitterness to the other, presented themselves at once to the poor girl, she turned toward Quasimodo, who remained standing beside her, and who frightened her, and said, "Why did you save me?"

He looked anxiously at her, as if trying to guess what she said. She repeated the question. He then cast on her a deeply sorrowful look and withdrew. She was lost in astonishment.

A few moments afterward he returned, bringing a bundle, which he laid at her feet. It contained clothing that charitable women had left for her at the door of the church. She then cast her eyes down at herself, and saw that she was almost naked, and blushed. Life had fully returned. Quasimodo seemed to share this feeling of modesty. Covering his face with his large hand, he again retreated, but slowly.

She dressed herself quickly. It was a white robe with a white veil—the habit of a novice of the Hôtel-Dieu. She had scarcely finished before Quasimodo returned. He brought a basket under one arm and a mattress under the other. The basket contained a bottle, bread, and some other provisions. He set down the basket, and said, "Eat!" He spread the mattress on the floor and said, "Sleep!" It was his own dinner, his own bed, that the bell ringer had brought her.

The gypsy lifted her eyes to his face to thank him, but she could not utter a word. The poor fellow was absolutely hideous. She lowered her head with a thrill of horror. "Ah!" he said. "I frighten you, I see. I am ugly enough. Don't look at me, but listen to me. In the daytime you shall stay here; at night you can walk all over the church. But do not leave the church either by night or by day, or they will catch you and kill you, and it will be the death of me."

Moved by this speech, she raised her head to reply, but he was gone. Once more she was alone, thinking about the singular words of this almost monstrous being, and struck by the tone of his voice, at once so harsh and so gentle.

Then she began to examine her cell. It was a chamber some six feet square, with a small aperture for a window and a door opening onto the slightly inclined plane of the roof, composed of flat stones. Several gutters, terminating in heads of animals, seemed to bend down over it, and to stretch out their necks to look in at the window. On a level with its roof she perceived a thousand chimney tops, coughing up the smoke of all the fires of Paris. Melancholy prospect for the poor gypsy, a foundling, rescued from the gallows; an unfortunate young creature who had neither country nor family nor home!

When the idea of her forlorn situation wrung her heart more keenly than ever, she felt a hairy, shaggy head rubbing against her hands and her knees. She shuddered—everything frightened her now—and looked. It was the poor goat, the nimble Djali, which had escaped along with her when Quasimodo dispersed Charmolue's brigade, and had been at her feet for nearly an hour, lavishing caresses on her mistress, without obtaining a single glance. The gypsy covered the fond animal with kisses. "Oh, Djali!" she said. "How I have forgotten you! And yet you think of me. You are not an ingrate." At the same time, as if an invisible hand had removed the obstruction that had so long kept back her tears, she began to weep, and as they flowed down her cheeks, she felt the bitterest portion of her sorrows disappearing along with them.

Evening came. The night was so beautiful, the moonlight so soft, that she ventured to walk along the high gallery that runs around the church. She felt somewhat refreshed by her walk, so calm did the earth appear to her, beheld from that height.

CHAPTER III

Deaf

The next morning she noticed on awakening that she had slept. This singular circumstance astonished her—it had been so long that she had been unaccustomed to sleep! A joyful ray of the rising sun caressed her cheek. But besides the sun she saw at this garret window an object that frightened her—the unlucky face of Quasimodo. She involuntarily closed her eyes, but in vain; she still imagined that she saw through her rosy lids that visage so like an ugly mask. She kept her eyes shut. Soon she heard a hoarse voice saying very kindly, "Don't be afraid. I am your friend. I came to see you sleep. What harm can it do you, if I come to look at you when your eyes are shut? Now I am going. There, now, I am behind the wall. Now you can open your eyes."

More pathetic than these words was the tone in which they were uttered. The gypsy, affected by them, opened her eyes. He was actually no longer at the window. She went to it, looked out, and saw the poor hunchback cowering under the wall, in a posture of grief and resignation. She made an effort to overcome the aversion that he inspired. "Come!" she said kindly to him. Observing the movement of her lips, Quasimodo imagined that she was bidding him to go away. He then rose and retreated, limping with lowered head, without so much as daring to look despairingly at the girl. "Come then!" she cried, but he continued to move off. She then darted out of the cell, ran to him, and took hold of his arm. On feeling her touch, Quasimodo trembled in every limb. He lifted his supplicating eye and, finding that she drew him toward her, his whole face shone with joy and tenderness. She wanted him to go into her cell, but he insisted on staying at her threshold. "No, no," he said, "the owl never enters the nest of the lark."

Then she seated herself gracefully on her bed, with her goat at her feet. Both remained for some minutes motionless, contemplating in silence, he so much beauty, she so much ugliness. Every moment she discovered in Quasimodo some new deformity. Her gaze wandered from his knock-knees to his hunchback, from his hunchback to his only eye. She could not conceive how a creature so awkwardly put together could exist. At the same time, he had such an air of sadness and gentleness that she began to be reconciled with his appearance.

He was the first to break the silence. "You told me to come back?" he said.

"Yes!" she replied, with a nod of affirmation.

He understood the sign. "Alas!" he said, as if hesitating to finish. "You must know, I am deaf."

"Poor man!" exclaimed the Bohemian, with an expression of pity.

He smiled sadly. "You probably think that that was all I needed, don't you? Yes, I am deaf. That is the way that I am made. It is terrible, isn't it? While you—you are so beautiful!"

The tone of the poor fellow conveyed such a profound feeling of his wretchedness that she did not have the heart to utter a word. Besides, he would not have heard her. Then he resumed: "Never till now did I realize how hideous I am. When I compare myself with you, I cannot help pitying myself, poor unhappy monster that I am! I must look like a beast to you. You, you are a sunbeam, a drop of dew, a bird's song! I, I am something frightful, neither man nor animal, something harder, more shapeless, and more trampled upon than a pebble."

Then he laughed, and there was nothing in the world more heart-breaking than this laugh. He continued, "Yes, I am deaf. But you will speak to me by gestures, by signs. I have a master who talks to me in this way. And then I will know what you want from the movement of your lips, and from your gaze."

"Well, then," she replied smiling, "tell me why you have saved me."

He looked attentively at her while she spoke.

"I understand," he answered, "that you ask me why I saved you. You have forgotten a wretch who tried one night to carry you off, a wretch to whom, the very next day, you brought relief on the vile pillory. A drink of water and a look of pity are more than I could repay with my life. You have forgotten that wretch—but he has not forgotten."

She listened to him with deep emotion. A tear filled the eye of the bell ringer, but it did not fall. He appeared to make a point of holding it back. "Listen," he began again, when he was no longer afraid of that tear escaping him, "we have very high towers here; a man falling from one of them would be dead almost before he reached the pavement. When you wish to be rid of me, tell me to throw myself from the top. You have but to say the word; no, a look would be enough."

Then he rose. Unhappy as the Bohemian was, this grotesque being awakened her compassion. She made a sign for him to stay.

"No, no," he said. "I must not stay too long. I am ill at ease. It is out of pity that you do not look away from me. I will seek someplace where I can look at you without your seeing me; that will be better."

He drew from his pocket a small metal whistle. "Take this," he said. "When you want me, when you wish me to come, when you have the courage to see me, whistle with this. I shall hear that sound."

He laid the whistle on the floor and disappeared.

CHAPTER IV

EARTHENWARE AND CRYSTAL

Time passed. Tranquillity was gradually restored to La Esmeralda's spirits. Excessive grief, like excessive joy, is too violent to last. The human heart cannot continue long in either extreme. The Bohemian had suffered so much that of the feelings she had recently experienced astonishment alone remained.

With safety, hope was rekindled in her. She was outside of society, outside of life, but she had a vague feeling that it might not be impossible for her to return to them. She was like the dead who kept in reserve a key to her own tomb.

The terrible images that had so long haunted her gradually grew more distant. All the hideous phantoms, Pierrat Torterue, Jacques Charmolue, had faded from her mind—all of them, even the priest himself. And then, Phœbus was still alive: she was sure of it; she had seen him. To her the life of Phœbus was everything. After the series of fatal shocks that had laid waste all her affections, she had found only one sentiment in her soul that had not been undone—her love for the Captain. Love is like a tree: it grows by itself; it strikes its roots deep into our whole being, and frequently continues to put forth green leaves over a heart in ruins. And there is this unaccountable circumstance attending it, that the blinder that passion, the more tenacious it is. Never is it stronger than when it is most unreasonable.

No doubt La Esmeralda did not think of the Captain without pain. No doubt it was terrible that he too should have made such a mistake, that he too should have thought the thing possible, that he too should have believed the wound to be inflicted by one who would have given a thousand lives for his sake. Still there was no reason to be angry with him. Had she not confessed the crime? Had she not, frail creature that she was, yielded to the torture? All the fault was hers. She should have borne the suffering of having her fingernails torn out rather than make such an admission. After all, if only she could see Phœbus one more time, for a single minute. A word, a look, would be enough to undeceive him and bring him back to her. Of this she was absolutely certain. There were, at the same time, several unusual things that puzzled her—the accident of Phœbus's presence at the penance, the young woman in whose company he was. She was, no doubt, his sister. An improbable explanation, but she was satisfied with it, because she needed to believe that Phœbus still loved her, and loved only her. Had he not sworn it? What more could she require, naïve and credulous as she was? And then, in this affair, weren't appearances much more against her than against him? She waited therefore—she hoped.

We may add that the church, that vast church, which saved her, which enveloped her on all sides, which guarded her, was itself a great source of consolation. The solemn lines of that architecture, the religious attitude of all the objects around her, the serene and pious thoughts that transpired, as it were, through all the pores of that stone, acted on her without her knowledge. The edifice, moreover, had sounds of such majesty and such blessing that they soothed her broken spirit. The monotonous chant of the officiating priests; the responses of the congregation, sometimes inarticulate, sometimes thundering; the harmonious shiver of the windows; the organ bursting forth like a hundred trumpets; the three belfries buzzing like hives of immense bees. That orchestra, with its gigantic scales incessantly ascending and descending from the crowd below to the bell tower above, soothed her memory, her imagination, her sorrows. The bells more especially consoled her, cradled her. They were like a magnetic field whose great power spread itself over her in broad waves. So each successive sunrise found her more at peace, more comfortable, and less pale. As her inward wounds healed, her face recovered its grace and beauty but chastened by greater seriousness and more repose. Her former character returned as well—even something of her cheerfulness, her pretty pout, her love of her goat and of singing, and her modesty. In the morning she shrank into a corner of her cell to dress herself, in case an inhabitant of the neighboring garrets should spy her through the window.

When thoughts of Phœbus allowed her time, the gypsy would sometimes think of Quasimodo. He was the only bond, the only link, the only communication with mankind and the living that was left her. The unfortunate girl was more completely cut off from the world than Quasimodo. She did not know what to make of the strange friend whom chance had given her. She would frequently reproach herself for not feeling sufficient gratitude that she might be blind to his imperfections. But decidedly she could not get used to the poor bell ringer. He was too hideous.

She had left on the floor the whistle that he had given her. On the first days Quasimodo, nevertheless, looked in from time to time. She tried as much as she could to conceal her aversion when he brought her the basket of provisions or the pitcher of water, but he was sure to perceive the slightest movement of that kind, and so he went away sadly.

One day he came just when she was fondling Djali. For a while he stood full of thought before the graceful couple of the goat and gypsy. At length, shaking his huge, misshapen head, he said, "My misfortune is that I am too much like a human creature. I would prefer to be a downright beast, like that goat!"

She cast on him a look of astonishment. "Oh!" he replied to that look. "I know why," and immediately went away.

Another time, when he came to the door of the cell, which he never entered, La Esmeralda was singing an old Spanish ballad. She did not know the meaning of the words, but it stayed with her because the Bohemian women had lulled her to sleep with it when she was a small child. At the sudden appearance of that ugly face, the girl stopped short, with an involuntary start, in the middle of her song. The unhappy bell ringer dropped to his knees on the threshold of the door and with a beseeching look clasped his clumsy, shapeless hands. "Oh!" he said in pain. "Go on, I beg you, and don't drive me away." Not wishing to hurt him, the trembling girl continued the ballad. Gradually her fear subsided, and she gave herself up entirely to the impression of the melancholy tune she was singing while he remained on his knees, with his hands joined as in prayer, scarcely breathing, his look intently fixed on the sparkling eyes of the Bohemian. It seemed that he was listening to her song with his eyes.

Another time he came to her with an awkward and bashful air. "Listen," he said, with effort, "I have something to say to you." She made a sign to him that she was listening. He then began to sigh, half-opened his lips, appeared for a moment ready to speak, looked at her, shook his head, and slowly retreated, pressing his hand to his brow and leaving the gypsy in amazement.

Among the grotesque heads sculpted in the wall there was one for which he showed a particular affection, and with which he seemed to exchange brotherly looks. The gypsy once heard him say to the head, "Oh! Why am I not made of stone, like you?"

Finally, one morning La Esmeralda, having advanced to the parapet of the roof, was looking at the Square over the sharp roof of St.-Jean-le-Rond. Quasimodo was behind her. He stationed himself there on purpose to spare the girl the disagreeable spectacle of his ungainly person. Suddenly the Bohemian shuddered; a tear and a flash of joy sparkled at the same time in her eyes; she fell on her knees and extended her arms in anguish toward the square, crying, "Phœbus! Come! Come! One word, a single word, for God's sake! Phœbus! Phœbus!" Her voice, her face, her attitude, her whole figure had the agonizing expression of a shipwrecked person who is making signals of distress to a distant vessel sailing gaily along in the sunshine.

Quasimodo, bending forward, saw that the object of this wild and tender appeal was a young and handsome horseman, a captain, glistening with arms and accoutrements, who passed gallantly through the square and bowed to a fair lady smiling on her balcony. The officer was too far off to hear the call of the unhappy girl.

But the poor deaf bell ringer understood it. A deep sigh heaved his breast; he turned around; his heart was swollen with the tears that he held back. He dashed his clenched fists against his head, and when he removed them there was in each a handful of red hair.

The gypsy paid no attention to him. Gnashing his teeth, he said, in a low tone, "Damnation! That is how one should look, then! One only has to be handsome on the outside!"

She continued meanwhile on her knees and cried, with extraordinary agitation, "Oh! There he stops! He is going into that house! Phœbus! Phœbus! He does not hear me! Phœbus! Oh! That woman is so mean to talk to him at the same time! Phœbus! Phœbus!"

The deaf bell ringer watched her. He understood this pantomime. The poor fellow's eye filled with tears, but he let none of them escape. Suddenly he gently pulled her sleeve. She turned around. He had assumed a look of composure and said to her, "Shall I go and fetch him?"

She gave a cry of joy. "Oh! Go, go! Run! Quick! That captain! That captain! Bring him to me! I will love you!" She clasped his knees. He could not help shaking his head sorrowfully. "I will go and bring him to you," he said, in a faint voice. Then he retired and hurried down the staircase, stifling his sobs.

When he reached the square nothing was to be seen but the fine horse fastened to the gate of the Gondelaurier mansion. The Captain had just entered. He looked up to the roof of the church. La Esmeralda was still in the same place, in the same posture. He made her a sad sign with his head and leaned with his back against one of the pillars of the Gondelaurier doorway, determined to await the Captain's departure.

In that house it was one of those festive days before a wedding. Quasimodo saw many persons enter, but nobody came out. Every now and then he looked up at the roof; the gypsy did not stir any more than he. A groom came and untied the horse, and led him to the stable. The whole day went by this way, Quasimodo at the pillar, La Esmeralda on the roof, and Phœbus no doubt at the feet of Fleur-de-Lis.

Eventually night arrived, a night without a moon, a dark night. In vain Quasimodo kept his eye fixed on La Esmeralda; soon she appeared to be just a white spot in the twilight, which became more and more indistinct till it was no longer discernible amid the darkness.

Quasimodo saw the facade of windows at the Gondelaurier mansion lit from top to bottom; he saw the other windows of the square lit up one after another. He saw them darkened again to the very last one, for he remained the whole evening at his post. Still the officer did not come out. When all the last passersby had retired to their homes, and not a light was to be seen in any of the windows, Quasimodo was left quite alone, in absolute darkness. There were no streetlamps on the Parvis of Notre-Dame then.

The windows of the Gondelaurier mansion, however, were still illuminated, even after midnight. Quasimodo, motionless and attentive, saw a multitude of vivid and dancing shadows passing through the multicolored panes. Had he not been deaf, he would have heard more and more distinctly sounds of festivity, laughter, and music coming out of the mansion as the noises of Paris faded.

About one in the morning the party began to break up. Quasimodo, enveloped in darkness, watched all the guests as they came out the doorway lit by torches. The Captain was not among them.

He was filled with sad thoughts. At times he looked up at the sky, as if tired of waiting. Large, heavy, ragged, black clouds hung like silk hammocks beneath the starry dome of night. They looked like cobwebs of the firmament. In one of those moments he saw all at once the French doors of the balcony mysteriously open. Two persons came out and shut the doors after them without noise. It was a man and a woman. Quasimodo quickly recognized in the one the handsome Captain, in the other the young lady whom he had seen that morning welcoming the officer from the window. The square was quite dark, and a double crimson curtain, which had fallen again behind the doors when they shut, barely let a gleam of light from the apartment reach the balcony.

The young Captain and the lady, as far as our deaf watchman could judge—for he could not hear a word they said—appeared to indulge in a very tender tête-à-tête. The young lady seemed to have let the officer throw his arm around her waist and tenderly resisted a kiss.

Quasimodo witnessed from below this scene, which was all the more lovely to see since it was not intended to be witnessed. He, however, contemplated that happiness, that beauty, with bitterness. After all, nature was not silent in the poor fellow, and his vertebral column, nastily twisted as it was, nevertheless thrilled like any other. He thought of the miserable fate that Providence had allotted to him; that woman, love, and its pleasures would be forever passing before his eyes, but that he could never do more than witness the felicity of others. But what afflicted him most in this sight, and mingled anger with his resentment, was to think what the gypsy must suffer if she saw it. To be sure, the night was very dark; La Esmeralda, if she had stayed in the same place—and he had no doubt of that—was at a considerable distance; and it was all he could do himself to distinguish the lovers in the balcony. This consoled him.

Meanwhile their conversation became more and more animated. The young lady appeared to beg the officer not to demand more of her. Quasimodo could discern only her fair hands clasped, her smiles mingled with tears, her looks uplifted to the stars, and the eager eyes of the Captain lowered on her.

Luckily, for the resistance of the lady was becoming weaker and weaker, the doors of the balcony suddenly opened; an old lady appeared; the fair one was in disarray, the officer irritated, and all three went back in.

A moment afterward a horse was prancing before the doorway, and the brilliant officer, wrapped in his cloak, passed Quasimodo swiftly. The bell ringer let him turn the corner of the street, then ran after him with the agility of a monkey, crying, "Ho! Captain!"

The Captain pulled up. "What does this rascal want with me?" he said, on spying in the dark the ungainly figure limping toward him.

Quasimodo, coming up to him, boldly took hold of the horse's bridle. "Follow me, Captain," he said. "There is one who would speak with you."

"By the devil's horns!" muttered Phœbus. "I think I have seen this raggedy scarecrow somewhere before. Hey, fellow! Let the bridle go."

"Captain," replied the deaf bell ringer; "don't you want to know who it is?"

"Let my horse go, I tell you," cried Phœbus angrily. "What does the rogue want, hanging like that from my bridle rein. Do you take my horse for a gallows, knave?"

Quasimodo, far from relaxing his hold of the bridle, was preparing to turn the horse's head the opposite way. Unable to account for the Captain's opposition, he hurried to give him this explanation. "Come, Captain; it is a woman who is waiting for you—a woman who loves you."

"A rare imbecile," said the Captain, "to suppose that I am obliged to go to all the women who love me, or say they do. After all, perhaps she is like yourself with that owl's face. Tell her who sent you that I am going to be married, and that she may go to the devil."

"Listen, monseigneur," cried Quasimodo, thinking with a word to overcome his hesitation, "it is the gypsy whom you know."

This intimation made a strong impression on Phœbus, but not of the kind that the speaker anticipated. The reader will recollect that our gallant officer had retreated with Fleur-de-Lis a few moments before Quasimodo rescued the condemned girl from the clutches of Charmolue. In all his subsequent visits to the Gondelaurier mansion he had carefully abstained from mentioning that woman, whose memory was, besides, painful to him; and Fleur-de-Lis, for her part, had not deemed it politic to tell him that the gypsy was alive. Phœbus believed, therefore, that poor *Similar* was dead, and that she must have been so for a month or two. Add to this that for some moments the Captain had been thinking about the extreme darkness of the night, the supernatural ugliness and sepulchral voice of the strange messenger: it was past midnight; the street was as lonely as on the evening that the goblin-monk had accosted him, and his horse snorted at the sight of Quasimodo.

"The gypsy!" he exclaimed with almost a feeling of terror. "What, then, are you from the other world?" At the same time he grabbed the hilt of his dagger.

"Hurry! Hurry!" said the deaf man, striving to lead the horse. "This way!"

Phœbus dealt him a smart kick in the chest. Quasimodo saw stars. He made a movement, as if to attack the Captain, but, instantly restraining himself, he said, "Oh! How lucky you are that there is somebody who loves you!" laying particular emphasis on the word *somebody*. "Be gone!" he added, letting go of the bridle.

Phœbus spurred his horse, at the same time swearing lustily. Quasimodo looked after him till he was lost in the darkness. "Oh!" said the poor fellow. "To refuse such a simple thing as that!"

He returned to Notre-Dame, lit his lamp, and ascended the tower. As he expected, the Bohemian was still in the same place. The moment she saw him she ran to meet him. "Alone!" she exclaimed, sorrowfully clasping her hands.

"I could not find him," said Quasimodo dryly.

"You should have waited all night," she replied angrily.

He saw her look of displeasure and comprehended the reproach. "I will watch him better another time," he said, drooping his head.

"Go away!" she cried.

He left her. She was unhappy with him. He preferred to be mistreated by her than to give her pain. Therefore he kept all the pain to himself.

From that day he avoided the gypsy. He stopped coming to her cell. At most she sometimes caught a glimpse of the bell ringer on the top of a tower, staring in a melancholy mood at her, but the moment he was aware that she saw him he was gone.

Truth obliges us to state that she grieved very little about this voluntary absence of the poor hunchback. At the bottom of her heart she was glad of it. Quasimodo did not deceive himself on this point.

She did not see him, but she felt the presence of a good genie all around her. Her fresh supplies of provisions were brought by an invisible hand while she was asleep. One morning she found over her window a cage with birds. Above her cell there was a sculptured figure that frightened her, as she had more than once indicated to Quasimodo. One morning—for all these things were done at night—it was gone; it had been broken off. Whoever had clambered up to this piece of sculpture must have risked his life.

Sometimes, in the evening, she heard the voice of some unseen person under the penthouse of a belfry singing a wild, sad melody, as if to lull her to sleep. They were verses without rhyme, such as a deaf man might make.

> Do not look at the face,
> Young girl, look at the heart.
> The heart of a handsome young man is often deformed.
> There are hearts where love does not last.
> Young girl, the fir is not beautiful.
> It is not beautiful like the poplar,
> But it keeps its foliage in winter.
> Alas! What good is it to say this?
> That which is not beautiful is wrong to be at all.
> Beauty loves only beauty,
> April turns its back on January.
> Beauty is perfect,
> Beauty is capable of anything.
> Beauty is the only thing that does not exist in half measures.
> The crow flies only in the day.
> The owl flies only at night.
> The swan flies day and night.

One morning, on opening her eyes, she saw two bouquets of flowers in her window. One was in a bright, beautiful crystal vase, that was cracked. The water with which it was filled had run out, and the flowers were dried. The other was a pot of coarse, common stoneware, but it retained all its water, and the flowers in it were fresh and fragrant. I do not know whether it was done intentionally, but La Esmeralda took the faded nosegay and carried it all day in her bosom. On that day she did not hear the voice singing from the tower—a circumstance that gave her very little worry. She passed her days in petting Djali, watching the door of the Gondelaurier mansion, talking to herself of Phœbus, and feeding the swallows with crumbs of bread.

For some time she had neither seen nor heard Quasimodo. The poor bell ringer seemed to have entirely abandoned the church. One night, however, unable to sleep for thinking of her handsome captain, she heard a sigh near her cell. Somewhat alarmed, she rose, and by the light of the moon she saw a shapeless mass lying outside across the doorway. It was Quasimodo asleep on a stone.

CHAPTER V

THE KEY OF THE PORTE ROUGE

Meanwhile rumor had communicated to the Archdeacon the miraculous way in which the gypsy had been saved. When he learned of this, he did not know how he felt. He had reconciled himself to the death of La Esmeralda, and was therefore easy on that point: he had drained the cup of misery to the dregs. The human heart—Dom Claude had deeply meditated on these matters—cannot contain more than a certain quantity of despair. When a sponge is saturated, the sea may pass over it without introducing into it one more tear.

Now, the sponge was saturated by the death of La Esmeralda, and Dom Claude could not experience keener suffering in this world. But to know that she was alive, and Phœbus too, was to be exposed anew to the vicissitudes, the shocks, the torments of life; and Claude was weary of them all.

On hearing this news he shut himself up in his cell in the cloisters. He attended neither the conferences of the chapter nor the usual offices. He shut his door to everyone, even the Bishop. He continued to isolate himself in this way for several weeks. It was reported that he was ill. So he was.

What was he doing while shut up this way? With what thoughts was the wretched Archdeacon struggling? Was he engaged in a last battle with his indomitable passion? Was he combining a final plan of death for her and damnation for himself?

His Jehan, his beloved brother, his spoiled child, came to his door, knocked, swore, entreated, called his name ten times—Claude would not open the door to him.

He spent whole days with his face close to the panes of his window. From that window, situated as we have said in the cloisters, he could see La Esmeralda's room; he saw the girl herself with her goat, sometimes with Quasimodo. He noticed the small attentions of the clumsy hunchback, his respectful manner and his submissive demeanor toward the gypsy. He remembered—for he had a good memory, and memory is the tormentor of the jealous—he remembered the bell ringer's extraordinary gaze on the dancing girl on a particular evening. He asked himself why Quasimodo had rescued her. He witnessed a thousand little scenes between the Bohemian and the hunchback, the pantomime of which, beheld at a distance, and transformed by his passion, appeared to him extremely tender. Then he vaguely felt awakening within him an utterly unexpected jealousy, a jealousy that made him blush for shame and indignation. Toward the Captain—it was not surprising; but toward that one! The idea disturbed him.

His nights were terrible. Since he knew that the gypsy was alive, the cold ideas of specter and tomb that had haunted him for a whole day were dispelled, and the flesh regained its dominion over him. He writhed on his bed when he thought that the lovely brunette was so nearby.

Every night his frenzied imagination presented La Esmeralda to him in all those postures that had made the blood boil most vehemently in his veins. He saw her stretched on the wounded Captain, her eyes closed, her beautiful bosom covered with his blood, at the delicious moment when the Archdeacon had imprinted on her pale lips that kiss which the unfortunate girl, though half dead, had felt as a burn. Again he saw her stripped by the rough hands of the torturers; he saw them strip her finely shaped leg, and her white, supple knee, while they encased her delicate little foot in the boot. He saw that ivory knee alone left uncovered by the horrible apparatus of torture. Last, he imagined to himself the forlorn girl, the rope around her neck, with bare feet, bare shoulders, bare bosom, as he had seen her on the day of penance. These voluptuous images made his blood boil, and a thrill run through his entire spine.

One night, among others, they inflamed his virgin arteries of a priest to such a degree that he bit his pillow and leapt out of his bed. He threw a surplice over himself and left his cell, with his lamp in his hand, half naked, wild, his eyes on fire.

He knew where to find the key of the Porte Rouge, which connected the cloisters and the church; and, as the reader knows, he always carried with him a key to the staircase of the towers.

CHAPTER VI

THE KEY OF THE PORTE ROUGE, PART II

On that night La Esmeralda had fallen asleep in her little room, forgetful of the past and full of hope and pleasant thoughts. She had slept for some time, dreaming, as always, of Phœbus, when she seemed to hear a kind of noise around her. Her sleep was always light and restless—a bird's sleep; the least thing awoke her. She opened her eyes. The night was very dark. Still, she saw at the window a face looking at her; there was a lamp that threw a light on this apparition. When the figure saw that it was perceived by La Esmeralda, it blew out the lamp. The girl, however, had had time to get a glimpse of it; she closed her eyes with terror. "Oh!" she cried in a faint voice. "The priest!"

All her past miseries flashed past her again like lightning. She fell back on her bed frozen with horror. A moment afterward, she felt something touch her, which made her shudder. Furious, she sat up. The priest clasped her in both arms. She would have shrieked but could not.

"Get away from me, murderer! Get away from me, monster!" she said, in a low voice tremulous with rage and terror.

"Mercy! Mercy!" muttered the priest, pressing his lips to her shoulders.

Seizing with both hands the hair remaining on his bald head, she strove to prevent his kisses, as though they were the bites of a mad dog.

"Mercy! Mercy!" repeated the wretched priest. "If you know what my love for you is! It is fire; it is molten lead; it is a thousand daggers in my heart!" And he held her arms with superhuman force.

"Let me go!" she cried distractedly, "or I will spit in your face!"

He loosened his hold. "Strike me; heap indignities on me; do what you will! But, for mercy's sake, love me!"

Then she struck him with childish rage. "Get away from me, demon!" she said, while she clawed at him to scratch his face.

"Love me! For pity's sake, love me!" cried the wretched priest, rolling on top of her and returning her blows with kisses.

She soon found that he was too strong for her. "It's time to put an end to this!" he said, gnashing his teeth.

Palpitating, exhausted, vanquished, she made a last effort and began to cry, "Help! Help! A vampire! A vampire!"

No one came. Djali alone was awakened, and bleated with anguish.

"Shut up," said the panting priest.

Suddenly, having fallen on the floor in the struggle, the gypsy touched something cold and metallic. It was Quasimodo's whistle. She seized it with a convulsion of hope, lifted it to her lips, and whistled with all the force she had left. The whistle gave out a clear, shrill, piercing sound.

"What is that?" asked the priest.

Almost at the same moment he felt himself grasped by a vigorous arm. The cell was dark: he could not see who had seized him, but he heard teeth gnashing with rage, and there was just enough faint light in the darkness to enable him to see the broad blade of a knife glistening above his head.

The priest imagined that he saw the figure of Quasimodo. He guessed that it could be no one else. He remembered having stumbled when he entered against a bundle of something lying across the door-way outside. Still, as the newcomer uttered not a word, he did not know what to believe. He caught the arm that held the knife, crying, "Quasimodo!" forgetful, in this moment of distress, that Quasimodo was deaf.

Instantly the priest was stretched on the floor, and felt a leaden knee pressing on his breast. From the angular pressure of that knee he recognized Quasimodo. But what could he do? How was he to make himself known to the assailant? Night had made the deaf monster blind.

He gave himself up for lost. The girl, with as little pity as an en-raged tigress, did not intervene to save him. The knife was descending on his head. The moment was critical. Then his adversary appeared to hesitate. "No," said a hollow voice. "No blood on her!" It was actually the voice of Quasimodo.

The priest then felt a huge hand dragging him by the leg out of the cell; it was there that he was to die. Luckily, for him, the moon had just appeared. When they were past the door, its pale beams fell on the priest's face. Quasimodo looked at him, was seized with a trembling, relaxed his grasp, and started back.

The gypsy, who had advanced to the threshold of the cell, saw with surprise the actors suddenly exchanging roles. It was now the priest's turn to threaten, Quasimodo's to supplicate. The priest, having furiously assailed the hunchback with gestures of anger and reproach, eventually motioned for him to retreat. Quasimodo stood for a moment with bowed head, and then, falling on his knees before the door of the gypsy, said, "Monseigneur," in a tone of gravity and resignation, "kill me first, and do what you please afterward."

As he said this he offered his cutlass to the priest. Beside himself with rage, the priest grabbed at the weapon, but La Esmeralda was too quick for him. Snatching the knife from Quasimodo's hand and bursting into a hysterical laugh, she said to the priest, "Come on!"

She held the blade up. The priest wavered. She would certainly have struck. "You don't dare approach now, coward," she cried. Then, with an unpitying look, and well aware that she would pierce the heart of the priest with a thousand red-hot irons, she added, "Ah! I know that Phœbus is not dead!"

The priest, with a violent kick, knocked Quasimodo down and rushed quivering with rage into the vault of the staircase. When he was gone Quasimodo picked up the whistle that had saved the gypsy. "It was getting rusty," he said, handing it to her. Then he left her to herself.

The girl, agitated by this violent scene, sank exhausted on her bed and sobbed loudly. Her horizon had once again grown sinister.

The priest, for his part, groped his way back to his cell. The thing was sure. Dom Claude was jealous of Quasimodo! With a pensive look he repeated the fatal phrase, "Nobody shall have her!"

BOOK X

CHAPTER I

GRINGOIRE HAS SEVERAL EXCELLENT IDEAS ONE AFTER ANOTHER IN THE RUE DES BERNARDINS

As soon as Gringoire perceived the turn this whole affair was taking, and that decidedly noose, gallows, gibbet, and other unpleasant things would be the lot of the principal players in this comedy, he did not want to get involved. The Tramps, with whom he had remained, considering that after all they were the best company in Paris, had continued to worry about the gypsy. He thought this was perfectly natural in people who, like her, had no prospect other than Charmolue and Torterue, and who never soared like him into the regions of imagination between the wings of Pegasus. From them he learned that she whom he had married over the broken jug had taken sanctuary in Notre-Dame, and he was very glad of it. But he was not in the least bit tempted to go see her. He thought sometimes of the little goat, and that was all. In the daytime he performed tricks for a living, and at night he labored away at a paper against the Bishop of Paris, for he remembered the drenching he had got from his mills and bore him a grudge for it. He was also working on a commentary on the admired work of Baudry-le-Rouge, Bishop of Noyon and Tournay, *De cupa petrarum,*[1] which had awakened in him a violent passion for architecture, a passion that had superseded in his heart the passion for hermetics. The latter indeed was only a natural corollary to the former, since there is an intimate connection between hermetics and masonry. Gringoire had passed from the love of an idea to the love of the form of an idea.

One day he had stopped near St.-Germain-l'Auxerrois, at the corner of a building called the For-l'Évêque, which faced another named the For-le-Roi. At the For-l'Évêque there was a beautiful fourteenth-century chapel whose choir looked toward the street. Gringoire was intently examining the sculptures on the outside. It was one of those moments of selfish, exclusive, supreme enjoyment, when the artist sees nothing in the world but his art, and sees the world in his art. Suddenly he felt a hand fall heavily on his shoulder. He turned around. It was his old friend, his old master, the Archdeacon.

He was stupefied. It was a long time since he had seen the Archdeacon, and Dom Claude was a solemn and impassioned character. Meeting him always disturbed the equilibrium of the skeptical philosopher.

The Archdeacon kept silent for a few minutes, during which Gringoire had leisure to observe him. He found Dom Claude greatly changed—pale as a winter morning, his eyes sunken, his hair almost white. Eventually the priest broke this silence, saying, but in a calm, glacial tone, "How are things with you, Master Pierre?"

"As to my health?" said Gringoire. "Why, I may say, so-so. On the whole good. I take everything in moderation. You know, master, the secret of health recommended by Hippocrates—*cibi, potus, somni, Venus, omnia moderata sint.*"[2]

"Then you have no troubles, Master Pierre?" rejoined the Archdeacon, looking steadfastly at Gringoire.

"No, by faith, not I."

"And what are you doing now?"

"You see, master, I am examining the cut of these stones, and the way that bas-relief is chiseled."

The priest smiled. It was one of those bitter smiles that lift up only one of the corners of the mouth. "And that amuses you?"

"It's Paradise!" exclaimed Gringoire. And, turning to the sculptures, with the dazzled look of a lecturer on living phenomena, he said, "Don't you think that this metamorphosis in low bas-relief, for example, is executed with great skill, patience, and delicacy? Look at this little pillar. On what capital did you ever see foliage more elegant and more highly finished? Look at those three medallions by Jean Maillevin. They are not first-rate works of that great genius; nevertheless, the truth to nature, and the sweetness of the faces, the gaiety of the poses and draperies, and that inexplicable charm that is blended with all the defects render the miniature figures very lively and very delicate—perhaps too much. Don't you think that this is wonderful?"

"Yes, I do," said the priest.

"And if you were to see the interior of the chapel!" resumed the poet, with his garrulous enthusiasm, "sculptures all over, tufted like a cauliflower. The choir is in a very pious style; it's so peculiar that I never saw anything like it."

Dom Claude interrupted him. "You are happy, then?"

"Yes, on my honor," replied Gringoire with warmth. "At first I was fond of women, then of animals, now of stones. They are quite as amusing as women and animals, and much less treacherous."

The priest raised his hand to his brow. It was his habitual gesture. "Indeed!"

"Stay," said Gringoire. "You shall see that a man need not lack for pleasure." He took the arm of the priest, who gave no resistance, and drew him into the staircase turret of the For-l'Évêque. "There is a staircase for you! Whenever I look at it I am happy. It is the simplest of its kind, and yet the most exquisite in Paris. Every step is rounded off and beveled. Its beauty and simplicity consist in the beveling, which makes each step interlaced with the next: they are embedded, en-chained, enchased, dovetailed one into another in such a solidly won-derful way."

"And you wish for nothing?"

"No."

"And regret nothing?"

"Neither wishes nor regrets. I have arranged my life."

"Man arranges," said Claude, "circumstances derange."

"I am a Pyrrhonian philosopher," replied Gringoire, "and I keep everything in balance."

"And how do you earn a living?"

"I still write epics and tragedies now and then, but what brings in most money is the trade you have seen me ply—carrying pyramids of chairs and so forth between my teeth."

"A vulgar trade for a philosopher."

"It has to do with balance," said Gringoire. "When you take an idea into your head, you find everything in it."

"I know," replied the Archdeacon.

After a pause the priest resumed. "You are nevertheless as poor as ever?"

"Poor, yes, but unhappy, no."

At this moment the dialogue was interrupted by the trampling of horses, and a company of archers of the King's Order, with raised lances and an officer at their head, passed by at the end of the street. The cavalcade was brilliant, and the pavement rang under their tread.

"How you eye that officer!" said Gringoire to the Archdeacon.

"I think I know him."

"What is his name?"

"I believe," said Claude, "his name is Phœbus de Châteaupers."

"Phœbus, a curious name! There is also a Phœbus Comte de Foix. I once knew a girl who swore by Phœbus."

"Come this way!" said the priest. "I have something to say to you."

Ever since the appearance of the archers, some agitation was perceptible under the Archdeacon's frozen exterior. He walked on, followed by Gringoire, who was used to obeying him, like all who had ever approached him, this man of great authority. They proceeded in silence to the Rue des Bernardins, which was rather deserted. Here Dom Claude stopped short.

"What do you have to say to me, master?" inquired Gringoire.

"Don't you think," said the Archdeacon, with a look of deep reflection, "that the uniforms of those archers who have just passed is finer than yours or mine?"

Gringoire shook his head. "By my faith! I like my red and yellow jacket better than those shells of iron and steel. A sorry pleasure, to make at every step the same noise as the Ironmongers' Quay would produce in an earthquake!"

"Then, Gringoire, you have never envied those handsome fellows in their war regalia?"

"Envied them! For what, Archdeacon? For their strength, their armor, their discipline? Far preferable are philosophy and independence in rags. I would rather be the head of a fly than the tail of a lion."

"That is unusual!" said the priest thoughtfully. "A handsome uniform is handsome nevertheless."

Gringoire, seeing him absorbed in thought, left him and went up to the doorway of a neighboring house. Soon he returned, clapping his hands. "If you were not so deeply engaged with the handsome uniforms of the men-at-arms, Archdeacon, I would beg you to go and look at that door. I always said that the entrance to the Sieur Aubrey's house is the most superb in the world."

"Pierre Gringoire," said the Archdeacon, "what have you done with the young gypsy dancing girl?"

"La Esmeralda? Why, how abruptly you change the conversation!"

"Wasn't she your wife?"

"Yes, after a fashion; by means of a broken jug we were joined together for four years. By the way," added Gringoire, with a half-bantering tone and look, "you seem to be always thinking of her."

"And you never think of her now?"

"Very little. I am so busy! . . . But what a charming little goat that was!"

"Didn't that Bohemian save your life?"

"True enough, by God!"

"Well, what has become of her? What have you done with her?"

"I can't tell. I believe they hanged her!"

"You believe?"

"I am not sure. When I saw that they were determined to hang somebody, I got out of the way."

"Is that all you know about the matter?"

"Wait a moment! I was told that she had taken sanctuary in Notre-Dame, and that she was safe there, which I was very glad to hear; but I was not sure if her goat was saved along with her—and that is all I know about the matter."

"I can tell you more, then," cried Dom Claude, his voice, which had been almost a whisper, rising to the loudness of thunder. "She has actually taken sanctuary in Notre-Dame. But in three days Justice will again seize her, and she will be hanged in the Grève. The Parliament has issued a decree."

"That is a pity!" said Gringoire.

Immediately the priest had relapsed into his former coldness and tranquillity.

"And," resumed the poet, "who the devil has amused himself with soliciting an order of restitution? Why could they not let the Parliament alone? What harm is there if a poor girl seeks shelter among the swallows' nests under the flying buttresses of Notre-Dame?"

"There are Satans in the world," rejoined the Archdeacon.

"It is infernally confused!" observed Gringoire.

"Then she did save your life?" resumed the Archdeacon, after a pause.

"That was among my very good friends, the Tramps. She came in the nick of time, or I should have been hanged. They would have been sorry for it now."

"Won't you then try to do something for her?"

"I desire no better, Dom Claude, but I may get my own neck into an ugly noose!"

"What does that mean?"

"What does that mean! You are exceedingly kind, master! I have just begun two great works."

The priest struck his forehead. Despite the composure he affected, a violent gesture from time to time betrayed his inner convulsions. "What can be done to save her?"

"Master," said Gringoire, "I answer, *Il padelt*, which is Turkish for 'God is our hope.'"

"What can be done to save her?" repeated Claude thoughtfully.

Gringoire, in his turn, struck his brow. "Listen, master, I have no lack of imagination; I will devise expedients. Suppose we ask for the King's pardon."

"A pardon! Of Louis XI!"

"Why not?"

"Take the bone from the hungry tiger."

Gringoire cast about for other expedients.

"Well, stop! Shall we declare that the girl is pregnant, and demand a midwives' examination?"

The pupil of the priest's hollow eye sparkled. "Pregnant, idiot! Do you know anything about that?"

His look alarmed Gringoire. "Oh, no, not I!" he hastily replied. "Our marriage was literally *forismaritagium*[3]—for I was shut out. At any rate we could get a reprieve."

"Stupid oaf! Shut up!"

"You're wrong to be angry," muttered Gringoire. "We could get a reprieve. That would harm nobody, and it would put forty deniers Parisis into the pockets of the midwives, who are poor women."

The priest did not hear him. "At any rate," he muttered, "she has to leave that place! The order must be executed in three days! Besides, if there were no order, that Quasimodo! Who can account for the depraved tastes of women!" Then, raising his voice: "Master Pierre," he said, "I have weighed the matter well; there is only one way to save her."

"And which? I can see none."

"Listen, Master Pierre; remember that you owe your life to her. I will tell you frankly my idea. The church is watched night and day; only persons who have been seen to enter are allowed to leave again. Of course you would be allowed to go in. You must come, I will take you to her. You will change clothes with her. She'll take your jacket. You'll put on her skirt."

"So far, so good," observed the philosopher. "And then?"

"Why, then she will go away in your clothes, and you will remain in hers. You will be hanged perhaps; but she will escape."

Gringoire rubbed his brow with a profoundly serious look.

"I declare," he said, "that is an idea that would never have occurred to me."

At this unexpected proposition of Dom Claude's, the poet's open and good-humored face was overcast, like a smiling landscape of Italy when some unlucky gust of wind blows a cloud over the sun.

"Well, Gringoire, what do you say to this idea?"

"I say, master, they will not hang me perhaps, but they will hang me indubitably."

"That does not concern us."

"The devil!" exclaimed Gringoire.

"She saved your life. You are only paying a debt."

"I have plenty of other debts that I don't pay!"

"Master Pierre, you must comply."

The Archdeacon spoke with authority.

"Listen, Dom Claude," replied the dismayed poet, "you cling to this idea, but you are quite wrong. I see no reason why I should thrust my head into the noose in place of another."

"What is there, then, that so strongly attaches you to life?"

"Why, a thousand things."

"What are they? I would ask."

"What are they? The fresh air, the blue sky, morning and evening, the warm sunshine, and the moonlight, my good friends the Tramps, our romps with the good-natured girls, the beautiful architectural works of Paris to study, three thick books to write—one of them against the Bishop and his mills—and more besides. Anaxagoras said that he was in the world to admire the sun. And then I have the good fortune to spend all my days from morning till evening with a man of genius, that is, myself, and this is extremely agreeable."

"A head fit for a bell!" muttered the Archdeacon. "Well, but tell me, who saved this life which is so charming to you? To whom do you owe the fact that you still breathe this air, behold that sky, and can amuse your lark's spirit with extravagances and follies? What would you be if it weren't for her? And yet you can allow her to die—her to whom you owe your life—that beautiful, lovely, adorable creature, almost as necessary to the light of the world as the sun himself, while you, half sage, half mad, rough sketch of something or other, a species of vegetable, who imagine that you can walk and think, you will continue to live the life of which you have robbed her, as useless as a candle at noonday! No, no, have some feeling, Gringoire; be generous in your turn. It was she who set the example."

The priest was vehement. Gringoire listened to him at first with a look of indecision; then he began to relent, and at last he put on a tragic grimace, which made his wan face look like that of a colicky newborn.

"You are pathetic," he said, brushing away a tear. "Well, I will think about it. It is a funny idea of yours!" After pausing awhile, he continued. "After all, who knows! Perhaps they will not hang me. Betrothal is not always followed by marriage. When they find me up there in the little cell, so grotesquely dressed in cap and petticoat, perhaps they will only laugh. And then, if they do hang me, why, death by the noose is like any other death, or, more correctly speaking, it is not like any other death. It is a death worthy of the sage who has oscillated all his life; a death that is neither fish nor fowl, like the soul of the downright skeptic; a death impressed all over with Pyrrhonism and hesitation, which holds the middle place between heaven and earth, which leaves one in suspense. It is a philosophical death, and perhaps I was predestined to it. It is magnificent to die as one has lived."

The priest interrupted him. "Are we in agreement?"

"After all, what is death?" continued Gringoire, in the warmth of his excitement. "An unpleasant moment, a toll, a passage from little to nothing. When someone asked Cercidas of Megalopolis if he should like to die, 'Why not?' he replied, 'for, after death, I shall see those great men, Pythagoras among the philosophers, Hecatæus among the historians, Homer among the poets, and Olympus among the musicians.'"

The Archdeacon held out his hand. "It is settled, then; you will come tomorrow?"

This gesture, and the question that accompanied it, brought Gringoire back from his digression. "Heavens, no!" he said, in the tone of a man awakening from sleep. "Be hanged! It is too absurd! I don't want to."

"Farewell, then!" and the Archdeacon added, muttering between his teeth. "I will track you down again!"

"I don't want that fellow to find me again," thought Gringoire, running after Dom Claude. "Hold on, Mr. Archdeacon, no malice between old friends! You take an interest in that girl, my wife, I would say—quite right! You have devised a stratagem to withdraw her in safety from Notre-Dame, but to me your plan is extremely unpleasant. A luminous idea has just occurred to me. If I could propose a method of extricating her from the dilemma without entangling my own neck in the smallest noose whatever, what would you say to it? Would that satisfy you? Or must I absolutely be hanged before you are content?"

The priest tore off the buttons of his cassock with irritation. "Eternal babbler! What is your proposal?"

"Yes," resumed Gringoire, talking to himself, and placing his forefinger against his nose as a sign of meditation, "that's it! She is a favorite with the Tramps. They will rise at the first word. Nothing easier. A sudden attack. In the confusion, carry her away! Tomorrow night. . . . They would desire nothing better."

"Your proposal! Let us hear it!" said the priest, shaking him.

Gringoire turned majestically toward him. "Leave me alone! You see I am composing." Having considered for a few moments longer, he clapped his hands in exultation, exclaiming, "Admirable! Sure to succeed!"

"But the means?" inquired Claude angrily. Gringoire was radiant.

"Come here, then, I have to whisper it. It is an excellent counterplot, which will get all of us out of our trouble. By heaven! It must be said that I am no fool."

He stopped short. "By the way, is the little goat with the girl?"

"Yes! Devil take you!"

"They meant to have hanged her too, did they not?"

"What is that to me?"

"Yes, they meant to hang her. Why, it was only last month that they hanged a sow. The hangman likes that—he eats the meat afterwards. Hang my pretty Djali! Poor, dear, little lamb!"

"Curses!" cried Dom Claude. "You are yourself the hangman. What is your plan for saving her? Idiot! Must we tear your idea from you with forceps?"

"Gently, master, I will tell you."

Gringoire bent his lips to the Archdeacon's ear and whispered very softly, at the same time casting an uneasy look from one end of the street to the other, though no one passed by. When he had finished, Dom Claude grasped his hand and said coldly, "Good! Tomorrow?"

"Tomorrow," repeated Gringoire. The Archdeacon retreated one way while he went the other, saying to himself, in an undertone, "A tricky affair this, Monsieur Pierre Gringoire! No matter! It shall not be said that because one is little one shrinks from great undertakings. Biton carried a full-grown bull on his shoulders, the wagtail, the nightingale, and the swallow, across the ocean."[4]

CHAPTER II

BECOME A TRAMP

The Archdeacon on his return to the cloisters found his brother, Jehan, waiting for him at the door of his cell. The youth had amused himself while waiting by drawing with a piece of charcoal on the wall a profile of his elder brother, supplemented by an enormous nose.

Dom Claude scarcely looked at Jehan; his thoughts were otherwise engaged. The reckless, jovial countenance of Jehan, whose radiance had so often restored serenity to the gloomy physiognomy of the priest, was now incapable of dispelling the fog that thickened daily over his corrupt, noxious, and stagnant soul.

"Brother," said Jehan diffidently, "I have come to see you."

"What then?" replied the Archdeacon, without so much as lifting his eyes to him.

"Brother," resumed the young hypocrite, "you are so kind to me, and give me such good advice, that I cannot stay away from you."

"What then?" repeated Dom Claude.

"Alas, brother! You were right to say to me, *Cessat doctorum, doctrina, discipulorum, disciplina.*[5] 'Jehan, conduct yourself discreetly; Jehan, attend to your studies; Jehan, do not pass the night out of college without legitimate occasion and the leave of the master. Do not beat the Picards. Do not rot, like an unlettered ass, on the straw of the school. Jehan, submit to punishment at the discretion of the master. Jehan, go to chapel every evening and sing an anthem, with collect and prayer, to the blessed Virgin Mary.' Ah! What excellent advice that was!"

"Well?"

"Brother, you see before you a sinner, a grievous sinner, a wretch, a libertine, a criminal, a reprobate. My dear brother, Jehan has treated your sage advice as if it were straw and night soil and trampled on it. I am severely punished for it; God Almighty is extraordinarily just. So long as I had money, I made merry, reveled in folly, and led a joyous life. How fascinating is debauchery from the front. But oh how ugly and deformed behind! Now I do not have a cent; I have sold my linen, my shirt, and my towels. My joyous life is over. The bright taper is put out; and I have only a scurvy tallow candle, which stinks in my nostrils. The girls make fun of me. I have only water to drink. I am filled with remorse and followed by creditors."

"What more?" said the Archdeacon.

"Alas! My dear brother, I want to lead a better life. I come to you full of contrition. I repent. I confess my sins. You are right to want me to become one day licentiate and submonitor of the Collège de Torchi. At this moment I feel an irresistible calling to that office. But I have no ink, I have no pens, I have no paper, I have no books—I must buy more. To this end I am in great need of a little money, and I have come to you, brother, with a heart full of contrition."

"Is that all?"

"Yes," said the student. "A little money."

"I have none."

"Well then, brother," replied Jehan, with a grave and at the same time a determined look, "I am sorry to have to inform you that very fair offers have been made to me from another quarter. You will not give me some money?"

"No."

"Then I will become a Tramp." In uttering this monstrous resolution he assumed the look of Ajax[6] expecting the thunderbolt to descend on his head.

"Become a Tramp then," the Archdeacon replied coldly.

Jehan made a low bow and skipped whistling down the cloister stairs.

When he was passing through the court of the cloisters, beneath the window of his brother's cell, he heard it open, and, looking up, saw the stern face of the Archdeacon looking out through the aperture. "Go to the devil!" said Dom Claude. "That is the last money you will have from me."

At the same time the priest threw a purse at Jehan; it made a great bump on the student's forehead, and with it Jehan went his way, at once growling and pleased, like a dog pelted with juicy bones.

CHAPTER III

L'ALLEGRO

The reader has perhaps not forgotten that part of the Cour des Miracles was enclosed by the ancient wall surrounding the Ville, many towers of which had begun to fall to ruin even in this period. One of these towers had been converted by the Tramps into a cabaret. In the basement was a tavern, and the rest of the upper floors served other purposes. This tower was the liveliest and consequently the most disgusting part of this den of tramps. It was a kind of monstrous hive that buzzed night and day. At night, when all the rest of the colony slept, when not a single light was to be seen in the windows of the crazy buildings looking onto the square, when no sound was to be heard issuing from the innumerable dens swarming with thieves, kidnapped girls, and stolen or bastard children, you could always recognize the merry tower by the noise that was made there, by the crimson light, which, gleaming at once from the chimneys, the windows, and the crevices in the cracked walls, escaped, as it were, from every pore.

The cellar, therefore, was the tavern. The descent to it was by a low door and stairs as rugged as a classic alexandrine. Over the door there was a sign, a marvelous sketch representing a number of new coins and dead hens (*des sous neufs et des poulets tués*) with this pun underneath: *Aux sonneurs pour les trépassés.*[7]

One evening, when the curfew bell was ringing in every belfry in Paris, the sergeants of the watch, had they chanced to enter the imposing Cour des Miracles, might have noticed that there was a greater tumult than usual in the tavern of the Tramps, and that there were both more drinking and more swearing than usual. In the open space outside numerous groups were conversing in a subdued tone, as when some important plan is being hatched, and here and there a crook crouched and sharpened some rusty weapon on a paving stone.

In the tavern itself, however, wine and gaming were so powerful a diversion to the ideas that on that evening engrossed the tramps that it would have been difficult to discover from the conversation of the drinkers what their project was about. They merely appeared to be in higher spirits than normal, and between the legs of each you could see some weapon glistening—a billhook, a hatchet, a thick bludgeon, or the frame of an old musket.

The round room was very spacious, but the tables were crammed so close together, and the customers so numerous, that all the contents of the tavern, men and women, benches and beer jugs, those who were drinking, those who were sleeping, those who were gambling, the ablebodied and the cripple, seemed to be tumbled together chaotically, with just as much order and harmony as a pile of oyster shells. A few candles were burning on the tables, but the real light of the tavern, the thing that performed the part of the chandelier at the Opera House, was the fire. This cellar was so damp that the fire was never extinguished, even in summer. There was an immense fireplace, with a carved mantel, bristling with clumsy andirons and other culinary apparatus, containing one of those large fires of wood and turf mixed, which produce at night in the village streets, by their red glare on opposite walls, the glow of an ironsmith's forge. A large dog, sitting seriously in the ashes, was turning a spit laden with meats.

Despite the confusion, after the first glance you could distinguish three principal groups in this multitude; they were crowded around three characters with whom the reader is already acquainted. One of these personages, dressed grotesquely in many a piece of Oriental regalia, was Matthias Hungadi Spicali, Duke of Egypt and Bohemia.

The scoundrel was seated on a table, his legs crossed, his finger lifted, imparting in a loud voice sundry lessons in black and white magic to many a gaping face around him. Another party had drawn close around our old friend the valiant King of Thunes, who was armed to the very teeth. Clopin Trouillefou, with stern look and in a low voice, was watching over the pillage of a large barrel full of arms, which stood broken open before him. Hatchets, swords, coats of mail, hunting knives, spearheads, saws, crossbows, spilled out of it like apples and grapes from a horn of plenty. Each took from the heap what he pleased—one a helmet, another a long rapier, a third a cross-hilted dagger. The children armed themselves, and there were even little urchins cuirassed and armored, running like large beetles between the legs of the drinkers.

Last, a third party, the most noisy, the most jovial, and the most numerous, occupied the benches and tables, in the middle of which a high voice was swearing and holding forth from beneath a heavy suit of armor complete from head to toe. The individual who had thus encased himself was so overwhelmed by his martial accoutrements that no part of his person could be seen, save a saucy red snub nose, a blond curl, rosy lips, and daring eyes. He had his belt stuck full of daggers, a long sword at his thigh, a rusty crossbow on his left, a large jug of wine before him, to say nothing of a voluptuous girl with bared bosom on his right. Every mouth around him was laughing, cursing, drinking.

Add to these twenty secondary groups, the servers, male and female, running around with plates and jugs, the gamblers, leaning over the billiards, the dice, or the impassioned game of the tringlet. There were the quarrels in one corner, the kisses in another. Now you have some idea of the whole scene, over which flickered the glare of a huge blazing fire, which cast a thousand gigantic, grotesque shadows dancing on the walls of the tavern.

As for the noise, it was like being inside a pealing bell. The frying pan, where a storm of grease crackled, filled the gaps in the thousand conversations that were held at the same time in every corner of the room with the racket it made.

In all this din, on the bench in the chimney corner was seated a philosopher absorbed in meditation, his feet in the ashes and his eye fixed on the burning brands. It was Pierre Gringoire.

"Come, hurry, arm yourselves! We shall start in an hour!" said Clopin Trouillefou to his crew.

A girl sang,

> Good night, mother and father!
> The last ones are gone for curfew!

Two card players were quarreling. "Knave," cried the more inebriated of the two, waving his fist at the other, "I will club you. You will be able to succeed Mistigri[8] in the card parties of Monseigneur the King."

"Ouf," roared a Norman, who might easily be known by his nasal twang, "we are crammed together here like the saints of Caillouville!"[9]

"Boys," said the Duke of Egypt to his auditors, in his falsetto, "French witches go to the Sabbath without broom grease or saddle, armed with a few magic words; Italian witches always have a goat waiting for them at the door. They all have to get out of the house through the chimney."

The voice of the young warrior in armor rose above the uproar. "Hurrah! Hurrah!" he cried. "My first feat of arms today! A Tramp! I am a Tramp! Pour me something to drink! My friends, my name is Jehan Frollo du Moulin, and I am a gentleman. I could bet that if Jupiter were a gendarme he would be fond of plunder. We are going, brothers, on a rare expedition. We are valiant fellows. Lay siege to the church, break open the doors, carry off the girl, rescue her from the judges, save her from the priests, dismantle the cloisters, burn the bishop in his palace—why, we shall do it all in less time than a good citizen takes to eat a bowl of soup. Our cause is a righteous one; we'll plunder Notre-Dame; that's it! We'll hang Quasimodo. Do you know Quasimodo, fair gentlewomen? Have you seen him heaving at the great bell on Pentecost? By Beelzebub's horns, that is grand! He looks like a devil riding a ghoul. I say, my friends, I am a Tramp to my heart's core, a con man in my soul, a born crook. I was very rich, and have run through my fortune. My mother wanted to make me an officer, my father a deacon, my aunt a counselor of the Inquisition, my grandmother counselor to the King, my great-aunt Keeper of the Short Robe: while I—I have chosen to be a Tramp. I told my father so;

he cursed me to my face; and my mother—poor old lady—began to cry and sputter like that stake on the fire. A merry life though a short one, I say! Tavernière, my darling, let us have another wine; I have some money left yet. I don't like the Suresne; it hurts my gullet. *Corbœuf!* I'd rather gargle with a basket."

Meanwhile the rabble applauded with bursts of laughter, and as the tumult swelled around him the student shouted, "How delightful! *Populi debacchantis populosa debacchatio!*"[10] His eye swimming in ecstasy, he then started singing in the tone of a canon at vespers:

Quae cantica! Quae organa! Quae cantilenae! Quae melodiae hic sine fine decantantur! Sonant melliflua hymnorum organa, suavissima angelorum melodia, cantica canticorum mira![11]

But, suddenly stopping short, he cried, "Here, you waitress from hell, give me some supper!"

Then followed a moment of comparative quiet, during which the Duke of Egypt raised his shrill voice while instructing his Bohemians. "The weasel is called Aduine; the fox, Bluefoot; the wolf, Grayfoot or Goldfoot; the bear, the old man, or the grandfather. The cap of a gnome renders you invisible and enables you to see invisible things. Every toad that is baptized ought to be dressed in red or black velvet, with a bell around its neck and a bell on each foot. The godfather must take hold of the head; the godmother of the rump. The demon Sidragasum has the power to make girls dance naked."

"By God," Jehan interrupted, "I'd like to be the demon Sidragasum!"

The crew continued to arm itself while whispering and muttering at the other end of the pub. "Poor Esmeralda! She is our sister—we must release her."

"Is she still in Notre-Dame?" asked a Jewish-looking peddler.

"Yes, by the Mass!"

"Well then, comrades!" cried the peddler. "To Notre-Dame! The sooner the better! In the chapel of St.-Féréol and St.-Ferrution there are two statues, one of St. John the Baptist, the other of St. Anthony, both of gold, weighing together seventeen marks fifteen esterlins, and the pedestals of silver seventeen marks five ounces. I know this—I am a goldsmith."

By this time Jehan's supper was set before him. Grabbing at his neighbor's décolletage, he exclaimed, "By St. Voult-de-Lucques—the people call him St. Goguelu—I am the happiest fellow in Paris, though I have renounced the half of a well-situated house in Paradise, promised me by my brother the Archdeacon. Look at that simpleton, gazing at me with the smooth look of an archduke. There is another on my left with teeth so long that they hide his chin. I am like the Maréchal de Gié at the siege of Pontoise; my right hand squeezes a breast! Body of Mahom! Comrade! You look like a bone dealer. You dare to sit down next to me! I am noble, my friend. Trade is incompatible with nobility. Get out of here. Hey! You there! What are you fighting for? What, Baptiste Squandergoose, aren't you afraid of endangering your handsome nose against that idiot's giant fists? Don't you know, imbecile, *non cuiquam datum est habere nasum*?[12] You are truly divine, Jacqueline Itchy-Ear! It's too bad you're bald. Hey there! My name is Jehan Frollo. Everything I say is the truth! In becoming a tramp I have happily given up my half of a house in Paradise that my brother has promised me. *'Dimidiam domum in paradiso.'*[13] I cite the text itself. I have a fief on the Rue Tirechappe, and all the women are in love with me, this is as true as it is true that St. Eloy was an excellent goldsmith, and that the five professions of the good city of Paris are tanners, leathermakers, anglers, bursars, and laborers, and that Saint Laurent was burned with eggshells. I swear to you, comrades, I will drink no spice for a year if I do tell a lie! My darling, look out the window at the moonlight, how the wind sweeps through the clouds! There I am doing the same with your collar. Girls, wipe the children's noses and snuff out the candles! Christ! What am I eating here? Jupiter! The hag! The hairs you don't find on the heads of these girls, you find in your omelettes. I like my omelettes bald. May the devil make you snub-nosed! Hotel of Beelzebub, where the waitresses comb themselves with forks!"

Saying this, he threw his plate on the ground and began singing at the top of his lungs one of the peculiar songs of the lawless crew of whom he had become a worthy associate.

> I have, by God,
> No bloody Faith,
> No laws or vows,
> No hearth or house,

No God or king,
Or any such thing.

Clopin Trouillefou had meanwhile finished his distribution of arms. He went up to Gringoire, who, with his feet on the andiron, appeared to be deep in thought. "Friend Pierre," said the King of Thunes, "what the devil are you thinking of?"

Gringoire turned toward him with a melancholy smile. "I am fond of the fire, my dear sir," he said, "not for the trivial reason that it warms our feet or cooks our soup but because there are sparks in it. Sometimes I spend whole hours watching those sparks. I discover a thousand things in those stars that sprinkle the black chimney back. Those stars are worlds too."

"Thunder and death if I understand you!" cried the King of Thunes. "Do you know what time it is?"

"No," answered Gringoire.

Clopin then went to the Duke of Egypt. "Comrade Matthias," he said, "our timing is not good. I am told the King is in Paris."

"One more reason why we should get our sister out of their clutches," replied the old Bohemian.

"You speak like a man, Matthias," rejoined Trouillefou. "Besides, it will be easy. No resistance to be afraid of in the church. The canons are mere rabbits, and we are strong. The officers of the Parliament will be stumped tomorrow when they go to look for her. By the Pope's nose! I don't want them to hang that pretty girl!"

Clopin left the tavern.

Gringoire, roused from his meditations, had begun to contemplate the wild and noisy scene around him, muttering between his teeth, "*Luxuriosa res vinum et tumultuosa ebrietas.*[14] How right I am to abstain from liquor! And how admirably St. Benedict observes, *Vinum apostatare facit etiam sapientes!*"[15]

At that moment Clopin returned and shouted in a thunderous voice, "Midnight!"

At this signal all the Tramp crew, men, women, and children, poured in a torrent out of the tavern, with a loud noise of arms and the clanking of iron implements.

The moon was overcast. The Cour des Miracles was quite dark.

Not a light was to be seen. It was nevertheless far from being deserted. It was filled with a crowd of both sexes, who talked in low tones together. A vast buzz was to be heard, and all sorts of weapons were seen glistening in the shadows. Clopin mounted a huge stone. "To your ranks, denizens of Slang," he cried. "To your ranks, Egypt! To your ranks, Galilee!" There was a movement in the darkness. The immense multitude appeared to be forming a column. In a few minutes the King of Thunes raised his voice again. "Now, silence in passing through the streets! The password is *'Petite-flambe en baguenaud.'* No torch is to be lit till we are at Notre-Dame. March!"

In less than ten minutes the horsemen of the watch fled panic-stricken before a long black procession descending in profound silence toward the Pont au Change, along the winding streets that run in all directions through the massive neighborhood of the Halles.

CHAPTER IV

A CLUMSY FRIEND

That same night Quasimodo could not sleep. He had just gone on his last rounds in the church. He had not noticed that when he was locking the doors the Archdeacon had passed, or the ill humor he had shown on seeing him carefully bolting and padlocking the immense iron bars, which gave to the large panels of the door the solidity of a wall. Dom Claude appeared that night to be more deeply preoccupied than usual. Ever since the nocturnal adventure in the cell he had abused Quasimodo; but, in spite of this abuse, even though he sometimes went so far as to strike him, nothing could shake the submission, the patience, the devoted resignation of the faithful bell ringer. From the Archdeacon he would take anything—abuse, threats, blows—without murmuring a reproach or uttering a complaint. The most that he did was watch the Archdeacon with anxiety when he ascended the staircase of the tower, but Claude had himself cautiously abstained from appearing again in the presence of the gypsy.

That night, then, Quasimodo, after taking a glance at his bells, at Marie, at Jacqueline, at Thibault, whom he had lately so miserably neglected, went up to the top of the northern tower and there, placing his sealed lantern on the rooftop, he began to survey Paris.

The night, as we have already said, was very dark. Paris, which at this period was hardly illuminated at all, presented to the eye a confused collection of black forms, intersected here and there by the pallid curve of the Seine. The only light Quasimodo could see came from the window of a distant building whose vague and somber outline was visible above the roofs in the direction of the gate of St.-Antoine. There too was someone who kept vigil.

While his eye ranged over this expanse of haze and darkness, the bell ringer had an inexpressible sense of uneasiness. For the past several days he had been on his guard. He had observed suspicious-looking men prowling incessantly around the church, who stared at the young girl's place of refuge. He imagined that some plot against the unfortunate refugee might be afoot, and that the hatred of the people might be directed against her as it was against himself. So he stood on the watch, on his tower, *revant dans son revoir,*[16] as Rabelais writes, gazing by turns at the cell and at the city, keeping careful watch, like a good dog whose heart is full of distrust.

Suddenly, while he was scrutinizing the great city with the eye that Nature, by way of compensation, had made so piercing that it almost made up for the deficiency of the other organs, it seemed to him that there was something unusual about the outline of the quay of La Vielle Pelleterie. Things seemed to be in movement there. The black line of the parapet, defined on the white surface of the water, was not straight and steady like that of the other quays; it seemed to undulate like the waves of a river, or like the heads of a crowd on the move. This struck him as strange. He redoubled his attention. The movement appeared to be headed toward the Cité. It lasted some time on the quay, then subsided by degrees, as if what caused it had penetrated the Ile. Then it ceased entirely, and the outline of the quay again became straight and motionless.

While Quasimodo was trying to guess what was happening, the movement seemed to reappear in the Rue du Parvis, which runs into the Cité, perpendicular to the facade of Notre-Dame. At last, despite the intense darkness, he saw the head of a column approaching through this street, and the next moment a crowd rushed into the Place du Parvis, where nothing of it could be distinguished but that it was a crowd.

This sight was terrifying. It is probable that this singular procession, which seemed to make a point of avoiding observation, was equally careful to maintain profound silence; yet it could not help making some noise, were it only the tramping of feet. But even this sound did not reach Quasimodo's ear; and this vast crowd, of which he could scarcely see anything, and of which he heard absolutely nothing, was all bustle and motion so near to him, and it must have seemed like an army of the dead, mute, impalpable, shrouded in fog. It appeared to him as if a mist full of human beings was approaching, and that what he saw moving were shadows in shadows.

Then his apprehensions were revived, and the idea of some act against the gypsy girl again occurred to his mind. He had a confused foreboding of violence. At this critical moment, with better judgment and more quickly than might have been expected from a brain so imperfectly organized, he began to consider what course was best for him to pursue. Should he wake the gypsy? Help her to escape? How? Which way? The streets were blocked; in back of the church was the river. There was no boat, no escape. There was only one way out: to die on the threshold of Notre-Dame. At any rate, he had to stage all the resistance in his power until help arrived. He did not want to disturb the slumber of La Esmeralda. The unfortunate creature would be awakened in time to die. Once this resolution was made, he began examining the enemy with greater composure.

The crowd seemed to increase every moment in the Parvis. He presumed, however, that the noise they made must be very slight, because the windows in the streets and the square remained closed. Then a light appeared, and in an instant seven or eight torches rose above the heads of the crowd, shaking their plumes of flame in the darkness. Then Quasimodo distinctly perceived a frightful rabble of men and women in rags, armed with scythes, pikes, pickaxes, and halberts, whose thousand points glittered. Here and there black forks projected like horns over hideous faces. He had some vague recollection of this mob and fancied that he had seen those faces some months before, when he was elected Pope of Fools. A man, who held a torch in one hand and a cudgel in the other, got up on a post and appeared to be haranguing them. At the same time this strange army was on the move, as if certain divisions were taking their respective stations around the church. Quasimodo picked up his lantern and went down to the platform between the towers to get a better view and to arrange his means of defense.

Clopin Trouillefou, on his arrival before the lofty portal of Notre-Dame, had, in fact, ranged his troops in order of battle. Though he expected no resistance, yet he resolved, like a prudent general, to preserve enough order to enable him to turn around in case of need against any sudden attack of the watch or of the Onze-vingts. Accordingly, he drew up his brigade in such a way that, had you seen it from above, or at a distance, you would have taken it for the Roman triangle at the battle of Ecnomus, the boar's head of Alexander, or the famous wedge of Gustavus Adolphus. The base of this triangle rested on the farthest side of the square, to block up the Rue du Parvis; one of its sides faced the Hôtel-Dieu, and the other the Rue St.-Pierre-aux-Bœufs. Trouillefou had placed himself at the apex, with the Duke of Egypt, our friend Jehan, and the boldest of the Tramps.

An enterprise of this kind was by no means uncommon in the towns of the Middle Ages. Police, as we understand the term, did not exist. Neither was there in populous cities, and in capitals more particularly, any sole, central, regulating power. The feudal system had constituted these large communities in a strange way. A city was an assemblage of a thousand fiefdoms, which cut it up into compartments of all forms and all dimensions. Therefore, there were a thousand contradictory polices, that is to say, no police at all. In Paris, for instance, independently of the one hundred and forty-one fiefdoms claiming manorial rights, there were twenty-five who claimed the right of administering justice, from the Bishop of Paris, who had five hundred streets, down to the Prior of Notre-Dame-des-Champs, who had four. The sovereign authority of the King was only nominally recognized by all these feudal agents of the law. Louis XI, that indefatigable workman, who so ambitiously began the demolition of the feudal edifice continued by Richelieu and Louis XIV for the interest of the monarchy and completed by Mirabeau for the benefit of the people—Louis XI had certainly tried to break this web of fiefdoms spread out over Paris, by violently imposing on it two or three random ordinances of the general police. Thus, in 1465, the inhabitants were ordered as soon as it was dark to light candles in their windows and to shut up their dogs, on pain of the gallows. The same year Parisians were ordered to block off the streets at night with iron chains and forbidden to carry daggers or offensive weapons out-of-doors after dusk, but, in a short time, all these attempts at municipal legislation fell into neglect. The bourgeois let the wind blow out the candles in their windows, just as they let their dogs wander around. Iron chains were put up only during sieges. The outlawing of dagger carrying led only to the transformation of the name of Slash a Gullet Alley to Cutthroat Alley, which is an obvious sign of progress. The old structure of feudal jurisdiction was left standing. Bailiwicks and lordships without number carved out the city between them, crossing, jostling, entangling themselves with, and dovetailing into one another. There was an endless confusion of watches, underwatches, and counterwatches, in defiance of which robbery, rape, and sedition were carried on by force. In this disorder, then, it was not uncommon for a part of the rabble to make an attack on a palace, a mansion, a house in the most populous parts of the city. In most cases, neighbors abstained from interfering in the affair, unless the pillage extended to their own property. They shut their ears to the muskets, closed their shutters, barricaded their doors, left the quarrel to be settled with or without the watch; and the next morning the talk in Paris would be, "Etienne Barbette's house was broken into last night," or "the Maréchal de Clermont was kidnapped," et cetera. Thus not only the royal domiciles, the Louvre, the Palace, the Bastille, the Tournelles, but the mere seigneurial residences, the Petit-Bourbon, the Hôtel de Sens, and the Hôtel d'Angoulême, had their walls and their battlements, their portcullises and their gates. The churches were protected by their sanctity. Some of them, however, were fortified; but Notre-Dame was not among them. The abbey of St.-Germain-des-Prés had embattlements like a baronial castle, and it spent more on bronze for the cannon than on the bells.

But let us return to Notre-Dame.

As soon as the first arrangements were settled—and we must say, for the honor of the Tramp discipline, that Clopin's orders were executed in silence and with admirable precision—the worthy chief of the crew mounted the parapet of the Parvis and raised his harsh and husky voice, turning his face toward Notre-Dame and at the same time waving his torch, whose flame, blown about by the wind and almost drowning in its own smoke, illuminated in fragments the crimson facade of the church.

"To you, Louis de Beaumont, Bishop of Paris, counselor to the court of Parliament, I, Clopin Trouillefou, King of Thunes, Grand Coësre, Prince of Slang, Bishop of Fools, give this notice: Our sister, falsely condemned for magic, has taken sanctuary in your church. You owe her safeguard and protection. Now, the court of Parliament wishes to lay hold of her again, and you consent to this; therefore, O Bishop, we have come to you. If your church is sacred, our sister is sacred also; if our sister is not sacred, neither is your church. We summon you, then, to surrender the girl to us if you would save your church; or we will take the girl ourselves and plunder your church. This will be still better. In testimony of this, I plant my banner here. May God keep you, Bishop of Paris!"

Unluckily Quasimodo could not hear these words, which were pronounced with a sort of wild and somber majesty. One of the Tramps delivered his banner to Clopin, who solemnly planted it between two paving stones. It was a pitchfork, on the prongs of which hung a lump of bleeding carrion.

This done, the King of Thunes turned around and surveyed his army, a savage throng, whose eyes glistened almost as much as their pikes. After a moment's pause he gave the word. "Forward, my lads! Do your business, blackguards!" was the cry of Clopin Trouillefou.

Thirty stout men, fellows with brawny limbs and the faces of blacksmiths, sprang from the ranks, bearing sledgehammers and crowbars in their hands and on their shoulders. They made for the great door of the church, ascended the steps, and were soon crouching beneath the arch, at work with their crowbars and levers. A crowd of the Tramps followed to assist or to look on. They thronged on the eleven steps of the portal. The door, however, held firm. "By the devil!" said one. "It is tough and obstinate!" "It's old, and its joints are stiff," said another. "Courage, comrades!" replied Clopin. "I'll wager my head against an old shoe that you will have opened the door, taken the girl, and stripped the high altar before there is a beadle awake. Hold on, I think the lock is giving way."

Clopin was interrupted at this moment by a tremendous crash behind him. He turned around. An enormous beam had fallen from the sky; it had crushed a dozen of the Tramps on the steps of the church and rebounded on the pavement with the noise of a cannon, breaking a score or two of legs in the crowd of Tramps, who, with cries of horror, scampered off in every direction. The area of the Parvis was cleared instantly. The blacksmiths, though protected by the depth of the portal, abandoned the door, and Clopin himself fell back to a respectful distance from the church. "I have had a narrow escape," cried Jehan. "I felt its wind, by Jove! But Pierre the Butcher is butchered."

It is impossible to describe the fear and surprise that that beam spread through the *banditti*. They stood staring up at the sky for some minutes, more astounded at the piece of timber than they would have been by the arrival of twenty thousand of the King's archers. "The devil!" exclaimed the Duke of Egypt. "This does look like magic!" "It must surely be the moon that has thrown us this log," said Andry the Red. "Why, then, I think, the moon is a good friend to our Lady, the Virgin," observed François Chante-Prune. "Hell's bells!" cried Clopin. "You are a pack of fools!" But still he did not know how to account for the fall of the beam.

Meanwhile nothing was to be seen on the facade, whose top the light of the torches could not reach. The ponderous beam lay in the middle of the Parvis, and nothing was heard except the groans of the wretches who had received the blow and whose stomachs were cut in half against the edges of the steps. The first panic over, the King of Thunes considered that he had made a discovery, which appeared plausible to his companions. "By God!" he cried, "Are the canons defending themselves? If so, sack the church! Sack!" "Sack! Sack!" responded the whole crew, with a tremendous hurrah, and a furious discharge of crossbows and muskets was aimed at the church's facade.

The detonation of firearms awoke the peaceful inhabitants of the neighboring houses; a few windows were opened, nightcaps popped out, and hands holding candles appeared at the panes. "Fire at the windows!" roared Clopin. The windows were shut in an instant, and the poor citizens, who had scarcely had time to cast a hasty and timid glance on this scene of torches and tumult, returned to perspire with fright next to their wives, asking themselves whether the witches' sabbath was now held in the Parvis, or whether there was another attack of the Burgundians, as in '64. The men were afraid of robbery, the women of rape, and everyone trembled.

"Sack! Sack!" repeated the men of Slang, but they dared not advance. They looked first at the church and then at the beam. The beam did not stir, and the church retained its calm and lonely air, but something had frozen the courage of the Tramps.

"To work, then, scoundrels!" cried Trouillefou. "Force the door!" Not a soul moved a finger. "By God," said Clopin, "there are men who are frightened out of their wits by a bit of wood!" "Captain," rejoined an old smith, "it is not the bit of wood that frightens us, but the door is all sown up with iron bars. The crowbars are useless." "What do you need to break it open with?" inquired Clopin. "We need a battering ram." "Here it is then," cried the King of Thunes, stepping boldly up to the formidable beam and setting his foot on it. "The canons themselves have sent you one. Thank you, canons," he added, making a mock obeisance toward the church.

This bravado produced the desired effect. The beam's spell was broken; picked up like a feather by two hundred vigorous arms, it was dashed with fury against the great door, which the Tramps had attempted in vain to force. In the dim light thrown by the few torches on the square, this long beam and its supporters looked like an immense insect with thousands of legs butting its head against a giant of stone.

At the shock of the beam, the half-metallic door resounded like an immense drum; it did not yield, but the whole cathedral shook, and the innermost cavities of the edifice were heard to groan. At the same instant a shower of stones began to rain down on the assailants. "Hell and the devil!" cried Jehan. "Are the towers shaking their balustrade on us?" But the evidence was there; the King of Thunes was right; it was decidedly the Bishop defending his citadel, and the Tramps only battered the door with the more fury, in spite of the stones that were cracking skulls left and right. It is remarkable that these stones fell one by one but followed each other so closely that the assailants always felt two at a time, one at their legs, the other on their heads. Few of them were spared; already a large pile of killed and wounded lay bleeding and trembling under the feet of their comrades, who, undaunted, filled the ranks as fast as they were thinned. The long beam continued to batter at regular intervals like a clock, the door groaned, and the stones showered down. The reader need not be told that this unexpected resistance, which so exasperated the Tramps, came from Quasimodo. Chance had unluckily favored the courageous hunchback.

When he had descended to the platform between the towers, his brain was all in confusion. For some minutes he ran back and forth along the gallery like a maniac, looking down at the compact mass of *banditti* ready to burst into the church, and calling on God and the devil to save the gypsy. He had a thought of mounting to the southern belfry and ringing the alarm bell, but before he could have made big Marie utter a single sound, the church might have been broken open ten times over. It was just at this moment that the smiths were coming up to the door with their tools. What was to be done?

Suddenly he remembered that masons had been working the whole day on repairing the wall, timbers, and roof of the southern tower. Quasimodo hurried to that tower. The lower rooms were full of building materials. There were piles of stones, rolls of lead, bundles of laths, massive beams, and heaps of gravel; it was, in short, a complete arsenal.

There was no time to be lost. The crowbars and hammers were at work below. With a strength increased tenfold by the sense of danger, he hoisted up the heaviest and longest beam that he could find, shoved it out of a small window and over the angle of the balustrade surrounding the platform, and launched it into the abyss. The enormous mass, in this fall of one hundred and sixty feet, grazed the wall, breaking sculptures, and turned over and over several times in its descent. Eventually it reached the ground; terrible shrieks followed, and the black beam, bouncing against the pavement, looked like a serpent writhing and darting on its prey.

Quasimodo saw the Tramps scattered by the fall of the beam like ashes before the wind. He took advantage of their consternation, and while they fixed a superstitious stare on the log fallen from the sky, he saw them put out the eyes of the stone saints of the porch by the discharge of their arrows and firearms. Quasimodo fell to work in silence carrying stones, rubbish, gravel, and even the bags of tools belonging to the masons to the edge of the balustrade over which he had already hoisted the beam. As soon as they started battering the door, the shower of stones began to fall, and the Tramps imagined that the church was tumbling around their ears. Anyone who could have seen Quasimodo at that moment would have been seized with dread. Besides the projectiles that he had piled on the balustrade, he had carried a heap of stones to the platform itself, so as soon as the former was exhausted he would have recourse to the latter. There he was, then, stooping and rising, stooping and rising again, with an absolutely inconceivable activity. His huge head, more like that of a gnome than of a human being, was at times bent over the balustrade; then an enormous stone would fall, then another, and another. From time to time, too, he would follow a thumping stone with his eye, and when its aim was true, he would grunt out "Hun!"

The Tramps, however, were not discouraged. More than twenty times the massive door against which their attack was directed had trembled under the weight of the oaken ram, multiplied by the force of a hundred men. The panels were cracked, the carving flew off in slivers, the hinges at every blow sprang up from their pivots, the planks began to pop, and the wood was pounded to powder between the braces of iron. Luckily for Quasimodo there was more iron than wood. He was aware, nevertheless, that the door could not hold out long. Though he could not hear it, every stroke of the ram reverberated in the caverns and in the inmost recesses of the church. From on high he saw the assailants, flushed with triumph and with rage, shaking their fists at the gloomy facade, and for his own sake as well as for the gypsy's, he envied the owls their wings. They flew off in flocks above his head. His ammunition was not effective enough to repel the assailants.

At this moment of anguish he noticed, a little lower down than the balustrade from which he crushed the men of Slang, two long gutters of stone, which disgorged themselves immediately over the great door. The inner opening of these gutters opened on the level of the platform. An idea struck him. He ran to his bell ringer's lodge for a bunch of kindling, placed it over the hole of the two spouts, laid on it several bundles of laths and rolls of lead, a kind of ammunition to which he had not yet resorted; and, as soon as all was arranged, he set fire to the kindling with his lantern.

During this interval, since the stones had ceased falling, the Tramps no longer looked up; and the rogues, panting like dogs baying the wild boar in his den, crowded tumultuously around the great door, shattered by the battering engine but still standing. They awaited with a thrill of impatience the last great blow, the blow that was going to break it down. Each was striving to get nearest to the door, so that he could be first to dart into the rich storehouse of treasures, which had accumulated in the cathedral for three centuries. They roared with joy as they reminded one another of all the beautiful silver crucifixes, the rich copes of brocade, the monuments of silver gilt, the magnificence of the choir, the gorgeous festivals, at Christmas, gay with torches, at Easter, shining in the sun—all those splendid rituals when shrines, chandeliers, chalices, tabernacles, reliquaries, decorated the altars encrusted with gold and diamonds. Assuredly at this moment the crooks and con men, the hobos and beggars, the fakers and fast talkers thought much less of the rescue of the gypsy than of the plunder of Notre-Dame. In our opinion, for the majority, saving La Esmeralda was only a pretext, if thieves need any pretext.

All of a sudden, while they were grouping themselves for a last effort around the ram, each holding his breath and stiffening his muscles to throw all his strength into the decisive blow, a howling, more hideous than that which had followed the fall of the fatal beam, exploded in their midst. Those who were not yelling and still alive looked around. Two streams of molten lead were pouring from the top of the building onto the thickest part of the crowd. A sea of men had fallen beneath the boiling metal, which had made, at points where it fell, two black and smoking holes in the rabble, like hot water would make in a snowdrift. Here the dying were writhing, half-petrified and roaring with agony. All around the two main streams a shower of horrible rain was scattered over the attackers, and the drops pierced their skulls like spirals of fire. The noise was horrible. The Tramps, throwing the beam on the dead and dying, fled helter-skelter, the bold and the timid together, and the Parvis was cleared a second time.

All eyes were raised to the top of the building. They beheld an amazing sight. In the uppermost gallery, above the central rose window, a huge flame rose up, accompanied by showers of sparks, between the two towers—a fierce and irregular flame, patches of which were every now and then carried off by the wind along with the smoke. Below this fire, below the somber balustrade, with its glowing red open-work ornaments, two gutters, in the shape of the jaws of monsters, incessantly vomited two silver streams of molten lead that stood out distinctly against the shadows of the lower facade. As they reached the ground, those two streams sprayed like water poured through the holes of a watering can. Above the flames, the craggy, enormous towers, each showing two very different facades, the one quite black, the other quite red, emerged looking bigger than ever, from the immense shadows they threw toward the sky. Their countless sculptures of devils and dragons assumed a lugubrious air. The flickering of the flame made them seem as if the sculptures were alive. Gorgons seemed to be laughing, gargoyles howling, salamanders puffing fire, and griffins sneezing in the smoke. And, among the monsters awakened from their sleep of stone by the flames and by the din, there was one that moved from place to place and passed from time to time in front of the fire, like a bat before a candle.

Without a doubt this strange light was going to wake up the wood-cutter far away on the hills of the Bicêtre, who would be frightened to see swaying on his fields of heather the gigantic shadows cast by the towers of Notre-Dame.

A silence of terror fell on the army of the Tramps, through which one could hear the cries of the canons, more alarmed than horses in a burning stable, shut up in their cloisters, together with the sound of windows stealthily opened and more quickly shut, a bustle in the interior of the houses and, from the Hôtel-Dieu, the wind in the flames, the last rattle of the dying, and the continuous splattering of the leaden rain on the pavement.

Meanwhile, most of the Tramps had retreated to the doorway of the Gondelaurier mansion and were holding a meeting. The Duke of Egypt, seated on a post, contemplated with religious awe the resplendent blaze burning two hundred feet in the air. Clopin Trouillefou struck his clumsy fists together with rage. "Impossible to break in!" he muttered to himself. "There is a spell on that church!" grumbled the old Bohemian, Matthias Hunyadi Spicali. "By the Pope's whiskers," exclaimed a gray-headed fox who had been a soldier, "those two church gutters beat the fortification of Lectoure at spewing lead!" "Do you see that demon running back and forth in front of the fire?" cried the Duke of Egypt. "By God," said Clopin, "it's that cursed bell ringer, that Quasimodo." "And I tell you," replied the Bohemian, shaking his head, "it is the spirit Sabnac, the demon of fortification. He appears in the form of an armed soldier with a lion's head. He changes men into stones and builds towers with them. He commands fifty legions. I know him well. It's him, sure enough. Sometimes he's dressed in a beautiful gold robe in the style of the Turks."

"Where is Bellevigne de l'Étoile?" asked Clopin.

"He's dead," answered a tramp.

Andry the Red laughed idiotically. "Notre-Dame is making work for the Hôtel-Dieu."

"Is there no way of breaking down that infernal door?" cried the King of Thunes, stamping violently on the pavement. The Duke of Egypt pointed mournfully to the two streams of boiling lead, which continued to streak the dark facade. "Churches have been known," he observed with a sigh, "to defend themselves in this manner without the aid of man. It is now about forty years since Ste.-Sophia at Constantinople threw down the crescent of Mohammed three times running by shaking her domes, which are her heads. Guillaume de Paris, who built this church, was a magician."

"Do we have to give it up for lost, like a miserable set of cowards?" said Clopin. "Do we have to leave our sister behind, to be hanged tomorrow by these cowled wolves?"

"And the sacristy too, where there are cartloads of gold?" added a rascal, whose name we regret our inability to record.

"Beard of Mahound!" cried Trouillefou.

"Let us make one more attempt," said the preceding speaker.

Again Matthias Hunyadi shook his head. "We shall not get in by that door, that much is certain."

"I will try again," said Clopin. "Who will come with me? By the way, where is little Jehan, the student, who had himself encased up to the eyes in steel?"

"Dead, no doubt," replied someone. "I have not heard his laugh for some time."

The King of Thunes knitted his brow. "That's too bad! He had a bold heart under that iron shell. And Master Pierre Gringoire, what is become of him?"

"Captain Clopin," said Andry the Red, "he sneaked off as soon as we had reached the Pont aux Changeurs."

Clopin stamped. "Damnation! The coward! To urge us into this affair and then leave us in the lurch! Cowardly loudmouth!"

"Captain," cried Andry the Red, who was looking down the Rue du Parvis, "here comes the little scholar."

"Pluto be praised!" rejoined Clopin. "But what the devil is he dragging after him?"

It was actually Jehan, who was advancing as expeditiously as he could with his heavy armor and a long ladder, which, with the aid of half a dozen of the gang, he was trailing along the pavement, more out of breath than an ant dragging a blade of grass twenty times as long as itself.

"Victory! *Te Deum!*" shouted the student. "There is the ladder of the St.-Landry dockworkers."

Clopin went up to him. "What, in the devil's name, are you going to do with that ladder?"

"I got it," replied Jehan, breathless. "I knew where it was kept—under the shed of the lieutenant's house. I know one of the maids there, who thinks I am a perfect Cupid. The poor girl came down half naked to let me in—and here is the ladder."

"I see," said Clopin. "But what are you going to do with it?"

Jehan eyed him with a look of spite and importance, and snapped his fingers like castanets. At that moment he really was sublime. His head was cased in one of those heavy helmets of the fifteenth century, which frightened the enemy by their monstrous embellishments. His helmet was studded with ten iron pikes so that he might have made a claim to the formidable epithet δεκεμβολος[17] with Nestor's Homeric ship.

"What am I going to do with it, august King of Thunes? Do you see that row of statues, which look so much like idiots, there above the three doors?"

"Yes, what about them?"

"That is the gallery of the Kings of France."

"And what of that?" said Clopin.

"Just listen. At the end of that gallery there is a door, which is never locked. With this ladder I will get up there, and then I am in the church."

"Let me go up first, boy."

"No, no, comrade. I brought the ladder. You shall be second, if you will."

"May Beelzebub strangle you!" cried Clopin peevishly. "I will not be second to any man."

"Then, my dear fellow, get a ladder for yourself."

Jehan started off again, dragging his ladder along and shouting, "This way, lads!"

In an instant the ladder was raised and placed against the balustrade of the lower gallery, above one of the side doors, amid loud acclamations from the crowd of the Tramps, who thronged to the foot of it.

Jehan maintained his right to go up first. The gallery of the Kings of France is at this time about sixty feet above the pavement. The eleven steps up to the entranceway increased the height by as much. Jehan mounted slowly, impeded by his heavy armor, holding the ladder with one hand and his crossbow in the other. When he was about halfway up, he cast a melancholy look at the dead bodies that covered the steps and the pavement. "By my faith," he said, "a heap of carcasses that would not disgrace the fifth book of the *Iliad*." Then he continued to ascend, followed by the Tramps. If you had seen this line of armored backs undulating in the dark, you would have mistaken it for an immense serpent with iron scales rearing itself against the church.

Eventually the student reached the balcony and nimbly leaped up on it. He was greeted by a general shout from the whole gang. Thus master of the citadel, he joined in the hurrahs, but suddenly he was struck dumb with horror. He saw Quasimodo, his eye flashing fire, crouching in the dark behind one of the royal statues.

Before a second attacker could set foot on the gallery, the formidable hunchback sprang to the top of the ladder and, without uttering a word, grabbed the two poles with his powerful hands, pushing them from the wall with superhuman force. The long ladder, bending under the load of the crew, whose piercing shrieks rent the air, balanced upright for a moment and seemed to hesitate; then, taking a tremendous lurch, it fell with its load of *banditti* more swiftly than a drawbridge when the chains that held it have broken. There was much cursing. Then all was silent, and here and there a mangled wretch crawled out from beneath the heap of the dead. Quasimodo, leaning with his two elbows on the balustrade, looked quietly on. He looked like a lion-haired old king at his window.

Jehan Frollo found himself in a critical situation. Separated from his comrades by a perpendicular wall of eighty feet, he was alone in the gallery with the formidable bell ringer. While Quasimodo was playing with the ladder, the student had run to the door, which he expected to find open. He was disappointed. The deaf man had locked it after him when he went down to the gallery. Jehan then hid himself behind one of the stone kings, holding his breath and eyeing the monstrous hunchback with a look of horror, like a man who, having flirted with the zookeeper's wife, went one night to meet her and, climbing over the wrong wall, found himself suddenly face-to-face with a prodigious white bear. At first Quasimodo did not see him, but by chance, he turned around and suddenly started up. He had spotted the student.

Jehan prepared himself for a rude shock, but the hunchback stood stock-still, merely staring intently at the student. "Ho ho!" said Jehan. "Why do you look at me so sadly with your one eye?" With these words the young joker secretly cocked the crossbow. "Quasimodo," he cried, "I will change your surname; instead of the deaf you shall from now on be called the blind." The feathered shaft whizzed and pierced the bell ringer's left arm. Quasimodo did not react to it any more than King Pharamond to a scratch. He grabbed the arrow, drew it from his arm, and calmly broke it on his massive knee. Then he dropped rather than threw the pieces over the balustrade. But Jehan had no time to shoot again. Quasimodo, having broken the arrow, suddenly drew in his breath, leaped like a grasshopper, and tackled the student, whose armor was flattened against the wall by the force. By the uneven light of the torches a terrible vision could be seen.

With his left hand, Quasimodo grasped the student's two arms; Jehan did not fight back, so completely did he feel himself overpowered. With his right the hunchback took off in silence, and with ominous deliberation, the different parts of his armor one after another—helmet, cuirass, arm pieces, sword, daggers. He looked for all the world like an ape shelling a walnut. He threw the student's iron carapace piece by piece at his feet.

When Jehan found himself stripped, disarmed, powerless, in the hands of his irresistible antagonist, he began to laugh impudently in his face, with all the intrepid carelessness of a boy of sixteen. He started to sing the popular song of the times,

> *Elle est bien habillée*
> *La ville de Cambrai.*
> *Marafin l'a pillée—*

He did not get to finish the song.[18]

Quasimodo was seen standing on the parapet of the gallery, holding the student by the leg with one hand and swinging him around over the abyss like a leaf. Then you could hear a sound like that of a box of bones being dashed against a wall; something was seen falling, but it was caught one-third of the way down by a projecting part of the building. It was a dead body that stuck there, bent double, the back broken and the skull empty.

A cry of horror burst from the Tramps. "Revenge!" shouted Clopin. "Sack! Sack!" responded the multitude. "Attack! Attack!" Then followed prodigious yells, in all languages, all dialects, all accents. The death of poor Jehan kindled a fury in the crowd. They were filled with shame and indignation at having been so long held in check before a church by a hunchback. Rage found ladders and multiplied the torches, and in a few moments Quasimodo saw with consternation a fearful rabble mounting on all sides to the assault of Notre-Dame. Some had ladders, others knotted ropes; those who could not procure either scrambled up by means of the sculptures, holding on by each other's rags. There was no way to withstand this rising tide of grim faces, to which rage gave a look of doubled ferocity. The perspiration trickled down their grimy brows; their eyes flashed; all these hideous figures were now closing in on Quasimodo. You would have imagined that some other church had sent its gorgons, its demons, its dragons, its gargoyles, its most fantastic monsters, to attack Notre-Dame.

Meanwhile the square was lit by a thousand torches. A flood of light suddenly burst on the scene of confusion, which had till then been buried in darkness. The fire kindled on the platform was still burning and lit the city to a considerable distance. The enormous outline of the two towers, projected far onto the roofs of the houses, formed a large shadow in all this light. The city seemed to come alive. Distant alarm bells were proclaiming that there was something wrong. The Tramps were shouting, yelling, swearing, climbing; and Quasimodo, powerless against such a host of enemies, shuddering for the gypsy, seeing so many ferocious faces approaching nearer and nearer the gallery, prayed to heaven for a miracle, at the same time that he wrung his hands in despair.

CHAPTER V

THE RETREAT WHERE MONSIEUR LOUIS OF FRANCE SAYS HIS PRAYERS

The reader has, perhaps, not forgotten that Quasimodo, the moment before he perceived the nocturnal band of the Tramps, while surveying Paris from the top of his tower, had seen a single light, at a window in the uppermost floor of a lofty and gloomy building by the gate of St.-Antoine. This building was the Bastille. That light was the candle of Louis XI.

The King had actually been in Paris for two days. He was to leave it again on the day after for his fortress of Montilz-lès-Tours. His visits to his good city of Paris were rare and short; for there he felt that he did not have enough trap-doors, gallows, and Scottish archers around him.

He had come that day to sleep in the Bastille. He did not like the large room he had at the Louvre, five fathoms square, with its great chimney adorned with twelve great beasts and thirteen great prophets, and its enormous bed, twelve feet by eleven. He was lost in all that grandeur. This good bourgeois King preferred the Bastille, with its humble room and bed. Besides, the Bastille was more fortified than the Louvre.

This little room that the King had reserved for himself in the famous State prison was spacious and occupied the topmost floor of a turret in the keep. It was a circular apartment, the floor covered with woven straw matting; the beamed ceiling was decorated with fleurs-de-lis of pewter gilt against a painted background. The room was wainscoted with rich woods, sprinkled with rosettes of tin, painted in a light green mixed from yellow orpiment and blue woad.

There was only one ogival window, latticed with brass wire and iron bars, and darkened by beautiful stained glass, representing the arms of the King and Queen. Each pane cost twenty-two sous.

There was only one entrance, a modern door under a low arch, covered on the inside with cloth. On the outside, it was framed by one of those doorways of Irish wood, delicate structures of curious workmanship, which were still very common in old buildings one hundred and fifty years ago. "Though they disfigure and encumber the places," says Sauval peevishly, "yet our old folk will not get rid of them, but they preserve them in spite of everyone."

In this room you could not find the furniture of ordinary apartments; no tables on trestles, no stools, or common benches, in the shape of a chest, or fancier ones, supported by columns and counter-columns, at four sous apiece. There was nothing but a magnificent folding armchair; the woodwork was adorned with roses painted on a red ground, and the seat was of scarlet Spanish leather, decorated with a silk fringe and studded with a thousand golden nails. This solitary chair indicated that only one person had a right to sit down in that apartment. Near the chair and close to the window was a table covered by a carpet decorated with the figures of birds. On this table were a portfolio spotted with ink, a few parchments, pens, and a silverwork goblet. At a little distance stood a chafing dish and a prie-dieu, covered with crimson velvet embossed with studs of gold. Finally, at the farthest part of the room there was a simple bed, of yellow and scarlet damask, without lace or a trimming. The borders were very plain. This bed, famed for having witnessed the sleep or the sleeplessness of Louis XI, was still to be seen two hundred years ago in the house of a councillor of State where Madame Pilou saw it. She was immortalized in the *Cyrus*[19] under the name of Arricidie and La Morale vivante.

Such was the room commonly known as "the retreat where Monsieur Louis of France said his prayers."

When we ushered the reader into this retreat, it was very dark. An hour had elapsed since the tolling of the curfew; it was night, and there was only one flickering wax candle on the table, to cast light for five persons, who formed several groups in the chamber.

The first on whom the light fell was a superbly dressed lord in hose, scarlet jerkin striped with silver, and a coat of gold cloth with black designs, trimmed with fur. This splendid costume, on which the light played, seemed to be braided with flame in all its folds. The wearer had his arms embroidered at the breast in gaudy colors: a chevron, with a leaping deer in the base of the shield. The escutcheon was supported on the right side by an olive branch and on the left by a buck's horn. This person carried in his belt a rich dagger, whose hilt, of silver gilt, was cast in the form of a crest and terminated in a count's coronet. He carried his head high, had a haughty bearing and an ill-natured look.

At the first glance one read in his face arrogance, at the second cunning.

He stood bareheaded, with a long paper in his hand, behind the armchair, on which was seated a shabbily dressed person, his body ungracefully bent, one knee crossed over the other, and his elbow on the table. Imagine to yourself, on the seat of rich cordovan leather, a pair of skinny thighs and bony kneecaps, poorly covered by black knitted woolen hose; a body wrapped in a coat of fustian, trimmed with fur, which showed much more leather than hair. Last, to crown it all, an old greasy hat of the coarsest black cloth, in the band of which were stuck a number of small leaden figurines. This, with a dirty skullcap, which hardly let a single hair straggle from beneath it, was all that could be seen of the seated personage. His head was so bent forward on his breast that it threw into the shade his whole face, except the tip of his nose, on which a ray of light fell; it was evidently a long one. The wrinkled, attenuated hand indicated that he was old. It was Louis XI.

At some distance behind the two persons we have described, two men, dressed in the Flemish fashion, were conversing in a low voice. It was light enough where they stood that if you had attended Gringoire's play, you could have recognized them as two of the principal Flemish envoys, Guillaume Rym, the sagacious citizen of Ghent, and Jacques Coppenole, the popular hosier. Remember that these two persons were mixed up with the secret politics of Louis XI.

Finally, at the opposite end of the room, near the door, in the dark, stood, motionless as a statue, a short, thickset man in military attire, with a coat of arms embroidered on the breast, a square face without brow, eyes on a level with the top of the head, and ears hidden by two flat, wide pieces of straight hair. He looked at once like a dog and a tiger.

All were bareheaded except the King.

The nobleman standing near the King was reading to him a long memorial, to which His Majesty seemed to listen attentively. The two Flemish men were whispering together.

"By the Cross!" muttered Coppenole. "I am tired of standing. Are no chairs allowed here?"

Rym answered by a shake of the head, accompanied by a discreet smile.

"Christ!" resumed Coppenole, who was quite miserable to be obliged to speak in so low a tone. "I have a good mind to sit myself down on the floor, legs crossed, in my stockings, as I might do at my store."

"No, Master Jacques, do no such thing."

"Hey, Master Guillaume! Must one stay on one's feet the whole time one is here, then?"

"Even so, or on your knees," replied Rym.

At that moment the King raised his voice. They were silent.

"Fifty sous the gowns of our lackeys, and twelve pounds the cloaks of the clerks of our crown! Why, this is throwing gold away by tons! Are you mad, Olivier?"

As he said this the old King raised his head. Around his neck one could see glistening the golden shells of the necklace of Saint Michael. The rays of the candle fell on his skinny and morose face. He snatched the paper from the reader's hands.

"You will ruin us!" he cried, running his hollow eyes over it. "What does all this mean? What do we need such a prodigious establishment for? Two chaplains, at the rate of ten pounds each a month, and a clerk of the chapel at one hundred sous! A valet de chambre, at ninety pounds a year! Four kitchen squires, at six score pounds a year each! An overseer of the roast, another of the vegetables, another of the sauces, a head cook, a butler, and two assistants, at ten pounds each a month! Two scullions at eight pounds! A groom and his two helpers at twenty-four pounds a month! A porter, a pastry cook, a baker, two carters, at sixty pounds a year each! And the Marshal of the Forges, six score pounds! And the Master of the Chamber of our Exchequer, twelve hundred pounds! And the Comptroller, five hundred! And I don't know how many more! It's enough to drive one mad! To pay the wages of our servants France is plundered. All the ingots in the Louvre will melt away in such a fire of spending! We will have to sell our dishes! And next year, if God and our Lady [here he lifted his hat] grant us life, we will be drinking our herbal teas out of a pewter pot."

As he said this he cast a look at the silver cup that glittered on the table. He coughed and then proceeded: "Master Olivier, the princes who rule over great countries, such as kings and emperors, should never tolerate overspending in their households; for that fire runs farther and catches the provinces. Do not make me repeat this, Master Olivier. Our expenditure increases every year. We do not like it. Why, *Pasque-Dieu*! Till '79 it never exceeded thirty-six thousand pounds; in

'80 it amounted to forty-three thousand, six hundred and nineteen pounds—I have the exact sum in my head—in '81 to sixty-six thousand, six hundred and eighty; and this year, by the faith of my body, it will not be under eighty thousand! Doubled in four years! Monstrous!"

He paused for breath and then began again heatedly: "I see around me only people who grow fat upon my leanness. You suck crowns out of me from every pore!"

All present maintained a profound silence. It was one of those fits of anger that must be left to spend themselves. He continued:

"It is like that petition in Latin from the nobles of France, that we reestablish what they call the great charges of the Crown! Charges, in good sooth! Crushing charges! Ah, gentlemen! You say that we should not reign *dapifero nullo, buticulario nullo*![20] We will show you—*Pasque-Dieu!*—whether we are not a king!"

Here he smiled at the sense of his own power; his wrath was softened, and he turned toward the Flemish.

"Look, Guillaume, the Grand Master of the pantry, the Grand Chamberlain, the Grand Seneschal are of less use than the least valet. Remember that, Coppenole! They are good-for-nothings. Such useless attendants on a king are very much like the four evangelists around the dial of the great clock of the Palace, which Philip Brille has lately beautified. They are gilded, but they do not mark the hour, and the hand can turn without them."

For a moment he appeared thoughtful, and then, shaking his old head, he added, "No, no, by our Lady, I am not Philip Brille, and I will not gild the grand vassals. Go on, Olivier." The person to whom he spoke took up the paper and began reading again with a loud voice:

"To Adam Tenon, clerk to the Keeper of the Seals of the Provost of Paris, for silver, making and engraving said seals, which have been newly remade, because the former could no longer be used, by reason of their being old and worn out—twelve pounds Parisis.

"To Guillaume Frère, the sum of four pounds four sous Parisis, as his salary and wages for feeding the pigeons in the two dovecotes of the Hôtel des Tournelles, in the months of January, February, and March of this present year; and for this there have been given seven quarters of barley.

"To a Friar, for confessing a criminal, four sous Parisis."

The King listened in silence. He coughed from time to time; he would then lift the cup to his lips and swallow a mouthful, at the same time making a wry face.

"In this year there have been made by order of justice, by sound of trumpet, in the public places of Paris, fifty-six proclamations—the account to be settled.

"For having made quest and search in certain places, both in Paris and elsewhere, after moneys that were said to be concealed there, but none found—forty-five pounds Parisis."

"Bury a crown to dig up a sou!" said the King.

"For putting six panes of white glass in the place where the iron cage is at the Hôtel des Tournelles—thirteen sous.

"For two new sleeves to the King's old doublet—twenty sous.

"For a pot of grease to grease the King's boots—fifteen deniers.

"For renovation of a sty for the King's black hogs—thirty pounds Parisis.

"For sundry partitions, planks, and doors, made to shut up the lions at St.-Pol—twenty-two pounds."

"Those are expensive animals!" said Louis XI. "No matter! It is a proper magnificence in a king. There is a great red lion whom I like very much for his engaging ways. Have you seen him, Master Guillaume? It is right that princes should keep extraordinary animals. We kings ought to have lions for our dogs and tigers for our cats. What is great befits crowns. In the time of Jupiter's pagans, when the people offered to the churches a hundred oxen and a hundred sheep, the emperors gave a hundred lions and a hundred eagles. That was proud and magnificent. The kings of France have always had roaring around their thrones; nevertheless, people must do me the justice to say that I spend less money in that way than my predecessors, and that I am exceedingly moderate on the score of lions, bears, elephants, and leopards. Go on, Master Olivier. We wished to say this to our Flemish friends."

Guillaume Rym bowed deeply, while Coppenole, with his sulky mien, looked like one of those bears that His Majesty had been describing. The King did not notice this. He sipped at the cup and, spitting out the drink, exclaimed, "Pooah! The horrid infusion of herbs!" The reader proceeded:

"For the maintenance of a vagrant shut up for these six months in the lodge of the slaughterhouse, until it is decided what to do with him—six pounds four sous."

"What is that?" said the King. "Feed someone who should be hung! *Pasque-Dieu!* Not another sou will I give for *that* food. Olivier, settle that business with Monsieur d'Estouteville, and this very night make the necessary preparation for wedding this gentleman with the gallows. Go on."

Olivier made a mark with his thumbnail against the last item and proceeded:

"To Henriet Cousin, Master Executioner of Paris, the sum of sixty sous Parisis, to him adjudged and ordered by Monseigneur the Provost of Paris, for that he did buy, at the command of the said Sieur the Provost, a great sword for executing and beheading persons condemned by justice for their misdeeds, and did provide a sheath and all thereunto appertaining, and likewise did get the old sword ground and repaired, by reason that it was broken and notched in doing justice upon Messire Louis of Luxembourg, as may more fully appear—"

The King interrupted the reader. "That is enough! I order that sum with all my heart. Those are necessary expenses. I never grudge money spent in this way. Go on."

"For making a new great cage—"

"Ah!" said the King, grasping the arms of his chair with both hands. "I knew that I had come to this Bastille for something. Stop, Master Olivier, I will look at that cage myself. You shall read the items while I examine it. Gentlemen of Flanders, come and look at it—it is a curious thing."

Then he rose, leaned on the arm of the reader, motioned to the kind of mute standing before the door to precede him, to the two Flemish men to follow, and left the room.

The royal party was reinforced at the door of the retreat by men-at-arms encumbered with iron and slender pages bearing torches. It pursued its way for some time through the interior of the somber castle keep, perforated with staircases and corridors even into the thickness of the walls. The Captain of the Bastille went first, to have the passage gates opened for the old King, who, bent with age and infirmity, coughed as he walked along.

At each passage gate every head was obliged to stoop except that of the old monarch. "Hum!" he muttered between his gums—for he had lost all his teeth—"we are already not far from the door of the tomb. At a low door the passerby must stoop."

Eventually, having passed the last passage gate, which was so encumbered with locks and fastenings that it took nearly a quarter of an hour to open it, they entered a lofty and spacious hall, in the middle of which was revealed, by the light of the torches, a massive cube of masonry, iron, and timber. The interior was hollow. It was one of those famous cages for prisoners of State that were called the King's daughters. In its sides were two or three small windows, so tightly latticed with thick iron bars that the glass could not be seen. The door was a large stone slab, like a gravestone, one of those doors that are used only as entrances. Except in this case the buried person was still alive.

The King began to walk slowly around the little edifice, examining it with care, while Master Olivier, who followed him, read aloud to this effect:

"For having newly made a great wooden cage of thick joists, girders, and planks, being nine feet long by eight wide, and seven feet from floor to ceiling, planed and clamped by strong iron clamps, which have been installed in a room in one of the towers of the Bastide St.-Antoine, in which cage is put and kept, by command of our Lord the King, a prisoner who had before dwelled in a cage that was old, decrepit, and worn out. There were used for the said new cage ninety-six joists, fifty-two uprights, ten girders, three fathoms in length; and there were employed nineteen carpenters, in squaring, cutting, and working all said timber in the court of the Bastide for twenty days—"

"Nice oak!" said the King, rapping the wood with his knuckle.

"There were used for this cage," continued the reader, "two hundred and twenty thick iron clamps, of nine and eight feet, the rest of middling length, with the screws, nuts, and bands to the said clamps; the whole of the said iron weighing three thousand, seven hundred and thirty-five pounds; besides eight stout holdfasts to fasten said cage, with the nails, weighing together two hundred and eighteen pounds; without counting the iron grating to the windows of the chamber in which the cage is placed, the iron doors of that chamber, and other things—"

"A great deal of iron," said the King, "to contain the levity of one mind!"

"The whole amounts to three hundred seventeen pounds five sous seven deniers."

"*Pasque-Dieu!*" exclaimed the King. At this imprecation, which was the favorite oath of Louis XI, somebody seemed to awaken inside the cage. Chains were heard rattling on the floor, and a faint voice, which seemed to issue from a tomb, cried, "Mercy, sire! Mercy!" The person who thus spoke could not be seen.

"Three hundred seventeen pounds five sous seven deniers!" repeated Louis XI.

The sad voice that came out of the cage had frozen all present, including Master Olivier himself. The King alone appeared not to have heard it. At his command Master Olivier began reading again, and His Majesty coolly continued his examination of the cage.

"Besides the above, there has been paid to a mason who made the holes to hold the bars of the windows, and the floor of the chamber where the cage is, because the floor could not have borne this cage by reason of its weight—twenty-seven pounds fourteen sous Parisis."

The voice again began moaning. "Mercy, for heaven's sake, sire! I assure Your Majesty that it was the Cardinal d'Angers who committed the treason, and not I."

"The mason is exorbitant," said the King. "Proceed, Olivier."

Olivier continued:

"To a carpenter for windows, bedstead, and other things—twenty pounds two sous Parisis."

The voice also continued: "Alas! sire! Will you not hear me? I protest that it was not I who wrote that thing to Monseigneur de Guyenne, but Cardinal Balue!"

"The carpenter is expensive," observed the King. "Is that all?"

"No, sire. To a glazier, for the windows of the said chamber, forty-six sous eight deniers Parisis."

"Mercy, sire! Is it not enough that all my wealth has been given to my judges, my service to Monsieur de Torcy, my library to Master Pierre Doriolle, my tapestry to the Governor of Roussillon? I am innocent. For fourteen years I have shivered away in an iron cage. Mercy, sire! Mercy! You will be rewarded for it in heaven."

"Master Olivier," said the King, "the total?"

"Three hundred sixty-seven pounds eight sous three deniers, Parisis."

"By our Lady!" exclaimed the King. "An outrageous cage!"

Snatching the paper from the hand of Master Olivier, he looked back and forth at the account and at the cage, and began to count on his fingers. Meanwhile the prisoner continued wailing and sobbing. It was truly lugubrious in the dark. The bystanders looked at each other and turned pale.

"Fourteen years, sire! Fourteen long years! Since the month of April 1469. In the name of the Blessed Mother of God, sire, listen to me. Your Majesty has all this time been enjoying the warmth of the sun. Am I never more to see the daylight? Be merciful, sire! Clemency is a right royal virtue, which turns aside the current of wrath. Does Your Majesty believe that at the hour of death it is a great consolation to a king not to have left any offense unpunished? Besides, sire, it was not I, but Monsieur d'Angers, who was guilty of the treachery against Your Majesty. Would that you saw the thick chain fastened to my leg, and the great iron ball at the end of it, much heavier than it need be! Ah, sire! Take pity on me!"

"Olivier," said the King, shaking his head, "I see that I am charged twenty sous by the load for plaster, though it may be bought for twelve. Send back this account."

Turning from the cage, he began to move toward the door of the chamber. The wretched prisoner judged from the receding torches and noise that the King was going. "Sire! Sire!" he cried in tones of despair. The door shut. He saw nothing, he heard nothing but the rough voice of the jailer chanting a stanza of a song of the time on the subject of his own misfortunes:

> *Maître Jean Balue*
> *A perdu la vue*
> *De ses évêchés.*
> *Monsieur de Verdun*
> *N'en a plus pas un,*
> *Tous sont dépêchés.*[21]

The King returned in silence to his retreat, followed by his entourage, who were terrified by the last heartrending wailings of the prisoner. His Majesty turned abruptly toward the Governor of the Bastille. "By the way," he said, "wasn't there someone in that cage?"

"Indeed, sire, there was," replied the Governor, astonished at the question.

"Who, then?"

"The Bishop of Verdun."

The King knew that better than anybody else. But this was his way.

"Ah!" he said, as naturally as if he had but just thought of it. "Guillaume de Harancourt, a friend of Monsieur the Cardinal Balue's. Not a bad fellow for a bishop!"

The door of the retreat then opened, and again closed on the five personages to whom the reader was introduced at the beginning of this chapter, and who resumed their places, their whispering conversation, and their attitudes.

During the King's absence several dispatches had been laid on his table. He broke the seals himself and hastily ran over one after another. Then he made a sign to Master Olivier, who appeared to perform the office of minister, to take a pen and, without communicating to him the contents of the dispatches, began in a low tone to dictate his answers, which Olivier wrote kneeling very uncomfortably in front of the table.

Guillaume Rym watched him closely. The King spoke so softly that the Flemish could catch no more than a few detached and scarcely intelligible fragments of his dictations, such as: "To maintain the fertile places by commerce, the barren by factories." "To show the English lords our four pieces of Ordnance, the London, the Brabant, the Bourg-en-Bresse, and the St.-Omer." "The artillery now causes war to be carried on more judiciously." "To our friend, Monsieur Bressuire." "Armies cannot be kept without taxes—"

Once he raised his voice. "*Pasque-Dieu!* Monsieur the King of Sicily seals his letters with yellow wax, like a King of France. Perhaps we are wrong to permit this. The greatness of houses is assured by the integrity of their prerogatives. Note this, Olivier."

Then, "O-ho!" he said. "The big message! What does our brother the Emperor want?" Running his eye over the missive, he interrupted his reading by interjections—"Indeed, the Germans are so great and so mighty that it's hardly to be believed." "But we forget the old saying: The finest county is Flanders; the finest duchy, Milan; the finest kingdom, France. Is it not so, my Flemish friends?"

This time Coppenole as well as Rym bowed. The patriotism of the hosier was tickled.

The last dispatch made Monsieur Louis knit his brow. "What is this?" he exclaimed. "Grievances and complaints against our garrisons in Picardy! Olivier, write to Monsieur the Maréchal de Roualt right away—that discipline is relaxed—that the gendarmes of the guard, the nobles of the ban, the yeomen-archers, the Swiss guard, do infinite mischief to our lieges; that the soldier, not content with the provisions he finds in the houses of the farmers, drives them out with grievous blows of sticks and staves to the city in quest of wine, fish, groceries, and other luxurious things; that Monsieur the King is acquainted with these proceedings; that it is our intention to protect our people from molestation, robbery, and plunder; that it is our will, by our Lady! That, moreover, it pleases us not that any musician, surgeon, or man-at-arms shall be attired like a prince in velvet, silks, and rings of gold; that these vanities are hateful to God; that we ourselves, who are a gentleman, are content with a doublet of cloth at sixteen sous a yard; that messieurs the soldiers' boys may even come down to that price too. Order and command. To Monsieur de Roualt, our friend. Right!"

This letter he dictated aloud, in a firm tone. When he had finished the door opened and someone, who was visibly terrified, rushed into the room, crying, "Sire! Sire! The people of Paris have risen in revolt!"

The stern features of Monsieur Louis contracted, but all the visible signs of his emotion passed away like lightning. He restrained himself and observed with calm austerity, "Compère Jacques, you come in rather abruptly!"

"Sire! Sire! The mob is in rebellion!" replied Compère Jacques, breathless with haste and alarm.

The King, who had risen, seized him roughly by the arm and whispered so he would be heard by him alone, with concentrated anger and a sidelong glance at the Flemings, "Shut up, or speak softly!"

The newcomer understood him and began in a low tone as coherent a narrative as his fears would permit. The King listened with composure, while Guillaume Rym directed the attention of Coppenole to the face and the dress of the speaker, to his furred hood, his short cloak, and his black velvet gown, which announced a president of the Cour des Comptes.

No sooner had this personage communicated a few details to the King than Monsieur Louis burst into a loud laugh, exclaiming: "Is that all? Speak up, Compère Coictier! Don't be afraid to open your mouth! Our Lady knows that I have no secrets from our good friends of Flanders."

"But, sire . . ."

"Speak up, I tell you, man!"

Compère Coictier was dumbfounded.

"Come!" resumed the King. "Speak, sir! There is a riot of the rabble in our good city of Paris?"

"Yes, sire."

"Directed, you say, against Monsieur the Bailiff of the Palace of Justice?"

"It is, apparently," said the compère, still stammering, quite disconcerted at the abrupt and unaccountable change in the sentiments of the King.

"Where did the watch meet the mob?" inquired Louis.

"Going along the great Truanderie toward the Pont aux Changeurs. I met it myself, as I was coming here in obedience to the commands of Your Majesty. I heard some of them shouting, 'Down with the Bailiff of the Palace!'"

"And what complaint do they have against the bailiff?"

"Why," said Compère Jacques, "he is their liege lord."

"Indeed!"

"Yes, sire. They are the scoundrels of the Cour des Miracles; they have long been complaining of the bailiff, whose vassals they are. They will not acknowledge his authority either in criminal or in civil matters."

"Aha!" cried the King, with a smile of satisfaction, which he strove in vain to disguise.

"In all their petitions to the Parliament," replied the Compère Jacques, "they pretend that they have but two masters: Your Majesty and their God—who, I verily believe, is the devil."

"Hey hey!" said the King.

He rubbed his hands with an inward exultation, which glowed in his face; he could not hide his joy, though he endeavored at times to compose himself. He completely puzzled all present, including Master Olivier. He kept silent for a moment, with a look of deep thought but also of satisfaction.

"Are they numerous?" he suddenly inquired.

"Indeed they are, sire," answered Compère Jacques.

"How many?"

"Six thousand, at least."

The King could not help crying out, "Good!" Then he asked, "Are they armed?"

"With scythes, pikes, spades, harquebus—all sorts of very danger-ous weapons."

The King appeared not at all uneasy at this recapitulation. Com-père Jacques deemed it his duty to add, "If Your Majesty does not send immediate help to the bailiff, he is lost."

"We will do it," said the King, with a look of false seriousness. "That's good. Of course, we will send help. Monsieur the Bailiff is our friend. Six thousand! They are a determined bunch of rascals. Their boldness is marvelous, and has sorely offended us. But we have few people around us tonight. It will be time enough in the morning."

"Instantly, sire!" exclaimed Compère Jacques, "or they will have the time to plunder the bailiff's house, to pull down the siegneurie, and to hang the bailiff twenty times over. For the love of God, sire, send help before morning!"

The King looked him full in the face. "I tell you, I will do it in the morning." It was one of those looks to which there is no reply.

For some moments Louis was silent. "Tell me, Compère Jacques," he began again, "for you must know what was"—he corrected himself—"what *is* the feudal jurisdiction of the bailiff?"

"Sire, the Bailiff of the Palace has the Rue de la Calandre, as far as the Rue de l'Herberie, the Place St.-Michel, and the Places vulgarly called the Mureaux, near the church of Notre-Dame-des-Champs"—here the King lifted the brim of his hat—"there are thirteen mansions there; also the Cour des Miracles, the leper's house called La Banlieue, and the whole causeway beginning at this leper's house and ending at the Porte St.-Jacques. Of all these different places he is the liege lord, with the right of administering high, middle, and low justice."

"Yeees!" said the King, rubbing the side of his nose with his fore-finger. "That is a good slice of my fair city. So Monsieur the Bailiff was king of all that!"

He asked no more questions but remained absorbed in thought and talking to himself. "Very fine, Monsieur the Bailiff! You had there be-tween your teeth a nice piece of our Paris!"

Suddenly he burst forth: "*Pasque-Dieu!* What does it mean those men who pretend to be liege lords, judges, and masters here? Who have their toll bar at the end of every field? Their gallows and their hangman at every cross street among our people? So that, like the Greeks, who believed in as many gods as there were streams, and the Persians, as they saw stars, the French have as many kings as they see gallows. By God! This is a bad state of affairs. I do not like all this confusion. I want to know if it is by the grace of God that there is in Paris any other liege lord besides the King, any other justice besides our Parliament, any other emperor besides ourselves in this empire. By the faith of my soul, there must come a day when there shall be in France but one king, one liege lord, one judge, one executioner, as there is in Paradise but one God!"

Again he lifted his hat and, still musing, continued with the look and accent of a huntsman who sends off and urges on his dogs: "Good! My people! Well done! Down with these false lords! Get them! Get them! Sack, plunder, bang! You would like to be kings, my Lords, wouldn't you? Go people! Go!"

Here he stopped short, bit his lips, as if to hold back the thought that had half-escaped him, fixing his piercing eye on each of the five characters around him, and, suddenly seizing his hat with both hands, and looking steadfastly at it, he exclaimed, "Oh! I would burn you if you knew what was in my head!"

Then, casting his eyes again around him, with the keen and restless look of a fox slyly returning to his den, he said, "It does not matter. We will send help to Monsieur the Bailiff. Unluckily we have but few troops here at this moment against such a mob. We must wait till morning. Order shall be restored in the city, and they shall hang everyone who is arrested."

"By the way, sire," said Compère Coictier, "I forgot in my initial alarm—the watch has taken two stragglers from the mob. If Your Majesty pleases to see them, they are below."

"Will I see them?" cried the King. "*Pasque-Dieu!* How could you forget that! Run quick, Olivier, and fetch them!"

Master Olivier left the room and soon returned with the two prisoners surrounded by archers of the Ordnance. The first had a bloated face and stupid, idiotlike, drunken look. He was dressed in rags, and, in walking, he bent his knees and shuffled his feet. With the pale and smiling countenance of the other the reader is already familiar.

The King scrutinized them for a moment without saying a word and then abruptly asked the first, "What is your name?"

"Gieffroy Pincebourde."

"Your profession?"

"Tramp."

"What were you going to do in that damnable uprising?"

The rogue stared at the King, swinging his arms with an expression of stupidity. He had one of those deformed minds in which the understanding is almost as uncomfortable as a light beneath an extinguisher.

"I don't know," he said. "The others went, so I went along."

"Were you not going to attack and to plunder your liege lord the Bailiff of the Palace?"

"I know that we were going to take something from somebody—that is all!"

A soldier brought to the King a hoe that had been found on the prisoner.

"Does that weapon belong to you?" inquired the King.

"Yes; it's my hoe. I am a wine grower."

"Do you know this man?" said the King, pointing to the other prisoner. "Was he one of your companions?"

"No: I do not know him."

"That's enough," said the King, and, beckoning to the silent person stationed near the door. "Compère Tristan," he said, "there is a man for you."

Tristan the Hermit bowed. He gave some directions in a low tone to two archers, who took the wretched prisoner away.

The King meanwhile turned to the second prisoner, whose brow was covered with a cold sweat. "Your name?"

"Sire, Pierre Gringoire."

"Your trade?"

"A philosopher, sire."

"How dare you, knave, assault our friend Monsieur the Bailiff of the Palace, and what have you to say to this riot?"

"Sire, I had no hand in it."

"Scoundrel! So you haven't been apprehended by the watch in bad company?"

"No, sire. It is a mistake: it was quite an accident. I write tragedies. Sire, I beg Your Majesty to hear me. I am a poet. Men of my profession are addicted to walking the streets at night. It was the greatest chance in the world. I have been wrongfully apprehended; I am innocent of this civil unrest. Your Majesty found that I am not known to that tramp. I beseech Your Majesty—"

"Silence!" said the King between two gulps of his herb tea. "You're getting on my nerves."

Tristan the Hermit stepped forward and, pointing to Gringoire, asked, "Sire, shall we hang him too?" It was the first audible word that he had uttered.

"Why," replied the King, "I see no obstacles."

"Alas, sire! I see a great many!" cried Gringoire.

Our philosopher was at that moment greener than an olive. From the cold and indifferent look of the King he perceived that he could have recourse only to something unusually pathetic, and, throwing himself at his feet, he cried with vehement gesticulation: "Sire, Your Majesty will deign to hear me. Ah, sire! Let not your wrath fall upon so humble an object as I am! The thunderbolts of God are not hurled against a lettuce. You, sire, are an august and most powerful monarch. Have pity on a poor but honest man who would be more helpless in kindling an uprising than an icicle could strike a spark. Most gracious sovereign, clemency is a virtue of lions and kings; severity only drives the minds of men more indomitable. The fierce north wind cannot make the traveler throw off his cloak; the sun, little by little pouring forth his rays, warms him to such a degree that he is glad to strip himself to his shirt. I swear to you, my sovereign lord and master, that I am not of the crew of Tramps, a thief, or a disorderly person. Sedition and robbery do not belong to the train of Apollo. I am not a man to rush into those clouds that burst in thunders of insurrection. I am a faithful liege of Your Majesty. The same jealousy that a husband has for the honor of his wife, the love that a son feels in return for the affection of a father, a good subject ought to have for the glory of his king; he ought to burn with zeal for his person, his house, his prosperity, to the exclusion of every other passion. Such, sire, is my political creed. Judge me not, then, from this coat worn out at the elbows to be an accomplice in sedition and plunder. Pardon me, sire, and on my knees I will pray to God, night and morning, for you. I am not very rich, it is true; indeed I am rather poor, but not vicious for all that. It is not my fault. Everyone knows that great wealth is not to be gained by letters, and that the most learned do not always have the largest fire in winter. The lawyers run away with all the grain and leave nothing but the straw for the other scientific professions. I could repeat to you forty excellent proverbs on the ragged cloak of the philosopher. Oh, sire! Clemency is the only light that can illuminate a great soul. Clemency bears the torch before all the other virtues. Without it they are blind and grope around in the dark for God. Mercy, which is the same thing as clemency, produces love in subjects, which is the most effective protection for the person of the prince. What harm can it do to Your Majesty, who dazzles all eyes, that there is one poor man more upon the earth, one poor innocent philosopher, floundering in the darkness of calamity, with empty pocket and empty stomach! Besides, sire, I am one of the learned. Great kings add pearls to their crowns by protecting letters. Hercules disdained not the title of Musagetes; Matthias Corvinus patronized Jean de Monroyal,[22] the ornament of the mathematics. Now it is a bad way of patronizing letters to hang those who cultivate them. What a stain upon Alexander if he had hanged Aristotle! That *trait* would be not a spot on the face of his reputation heightening its beauty but a foul ulcer disfiguring it. Sire, I have composed a most pertinent epithalamium for Mademoiselle of Flanders and Monseigneur the most august Dauphin. That is not a brand of rebellion. Your Majesty perceives that I am not an ignorant rogue, that I have studied deeply, and that I have great natural eloquence. Have mercy then, sire! In doing so you will perform an act of gallantry to our Lady; and I protest to you that I am terrified of being hanged!"

As he said this the distraught Gringoire kissed the King's slippers, and Guillaume Rym whispered to Coppenole: "He does right to crawl the floor. Kings are like the Cretan Jupiter; they only have ears in their feet." The hosier, without bestowing a thought on the Cretan Jupiter, replied with a grim smile, and his eye fixed on Gringoire, "Capital, by God! I think I hear the Chancellor Hugonet[23] begging me for his life!"

When Gringoire finally stopped talking because he was out of breath, he lifted his eyes, trembling, toward the King, who was scratching with his nail a spot on the knee of his breeches; His Majesty then sipped at his drink. He uttered not a word, however, and this silence kept Gringoire on the rack. Finally, the King looked at him. "What an unbelievable chatterbox!" he said. Then, turning to Tristan the Hermit, "Bah! let the rascal go!"

Gringoire fell backward, overwhelmed with joy.

"Let him go!" grumbled Tristan. "Will it not please Your Majesty to have him shut up awhile in a cage?"

"Compère," rejoined Louis XI, "do you think it is for such birds that we make cages that cost three hundred sixty-seven pounds eight sous three deniers? Get rid of this rascal for me right now." Monsieur Louis was fond of this term, which, with *Pasque-Dieu*, constituted the whole stock of his jocularity—"and turn him out with a good beating."

"Ah!" cried Gringoire. "What a magnanimous king!" And, for fear of a counterorder, he rushed toward the door, which Tristan opened for him with very ill grace. The soldiers went out with him, driving him before them with kicks and punches, which Pierre bore like a genuine stoic.

The good humor of the King, ever since he had been informed of the insurrection against the bailiff, manifested itself in all he did. This unusual clemency was not the least sign of it. Tristan the Hermit looked as surly in his corner as a dog when you have shown him a bone and taken it away again.

The King, meanwhile, was playfully drumming the march of Pont-Audemer with his fingers on the arm of his chair. This prince was a dissembler, but he could conceal his troubles much better than his joy. These external manifestations of delight at good news were sometimes carried very far; at the death of Charles the Bold he promised to present a silver balustrade to St.-Martin-de-Tours; and at his accession to the throne, when he forgot to order his father's funeral.

"Eh, sire!" Jacques Coictier suddenly exclaimed. "What has become of the acute illness for which Your Majesty commanded my services?"

"Oh!" said the King. "I am really in great pain, compère. I have a ringing in my ears and burning flames rack my breast."

Coictier took the hand of the King and felt his pulse with a most competent air.

"See, Coppenole," said Rym, in a low tone, "there he is between Coictier and Tristan. This is his entire court. A physician for himself, a hangman for everyone else."

While feeling the King's pulse, Coictier assumed a look of greater and greater alarm. Louis eyed him with some anxiety. Coictier's countenance assumed a darker and darker shade. The worthy man had nothing to live on but the ill health of the King; he cultivated this resource with the utmost skill.

"Indeed!" he muttered eventually. "But this is serious!"

"Is it?" said the King in alarm.

"*Pulsus creber, anhelans, crepitan, irregulari.* Pulse quick, irregular, intermittent," continued the physician.

"*Pasque-Dieu!*"

"In less than three days this might prove fatal."

"Our Lady!" ejaculated the King. "And what remedy, compère?"

"I am thinking, sire."

He wanted the King to stick out his tongue, shook his head, and frowned. In the midst of these grimaces, "By God, sire!" he abruptly began. "I have to tell you that a receivership of benefices is available, and I remind you that I have a nephew."

"Your nephew shall have my receivership, Compère Jacques," replied the King; "but get rid of this fire in my chest."

"Since Your Majesty is so gracious," rejoined the physician, "you will not refuse me a little help toward the building of my house in the Rue St.-André-des-Arcs."

"Eh!" said the King.

"I am at the end of my savings," continued the doctor, "and it would indeed be a pity that the house should lack a roof: not for the sake of the house, which is quite simple and bourgeois, but for the paintings of Jehan Fourbault that decorate the ceilings. There is a Diana flying in the air, so excellent, so delicate, so tender, painted in such a natural posture with gorgeous hair and crowned with a crescent, and flesh so white that she is enough to tempt those who examine her too closely. There is a Ceres too—another goddess of rare beauty. She is seated on sheaves of wheat, having on her head a gay garland of ears woven with salsify and other flowers. Nothing is more lovely than her eyes, more neatly turned than her limbs, more noble than her air, or more graceful than her robes. She is one of the most innocent and perfect beauties that the painter's brush has ever produced."

"Bloodsucker!" muttered the King. "What do you want?"

"I need a roof for these paintings, sire, and despite the insignificance of the cost, I have no money."

"How much will it cost?"

"Why—a roof of copper, embellished with figures and gilded—two thousand pounds at the utmost."

"Ah! The murderer!" exclaimed the King. "He never draws me a tooth but he makes a diamond of it for himself."

"Shall I have my roof?" said Coictier.

"Yes; and go to the devil! But cure me first."

Jacques Coictier bowed deeply. "Sire," he said, "only an astringent can save you. We will rub your loins with that great composition made of cerate, an Armenian bolus, egg white, oil, and vinegar. You must continue to take your teas, and we will be responsible for Your Majesty."

A glowing candle attracts more than one moth. Master Olivier, seeing the generosity of the King and deeming it a favorable moment, approached in his turn. "Sire . . ."

"What is it now?" said Louis XI.

"Sire, Your Majesty knows that Simon Radin is dead."

"What then?"

"He was counselor of Justice to the Exchequer."

"Well?"

"His place is vacant, sire."

As he said this the haughty face of Master Olivier had relinquished its arrogant expression and assumed a cringing air—the only change of which a courtier's features are capable. The King looked him full in the face. "I understand," he said dryly.

"Master Olivier," he began again, after a brief pause, "Maréchal de Boucicaut used to say, 'There are no gifts to be got but from the King, no fish to be caught but in the sea.' I perceive that you are of the same way of thinking as Monsieur de Boucicaut. Now listen to this. We have a good memory. In '68 we made you groom of our chamber; in '69 keeper of the castle of the bridge of St.-Cloud, at a salary of one hundred pounds Tournois; you wanted them to be Parisis. In November '73, by letters issued in Gergeaule, we appointed you keeper of the wood of Vincennes, instead of Gilbert Acle, esquire; in '75 warden of the forest of Rouvray-les-St.-Cloud, in place of Jacques le Maire; in '78 we were graciously pleased, by letters patent with double seal of green wax, to grant a yearly interest of ten pounds Parisis to you and your wife, on the Place aux Marchands, where the school of St.-Germain is; in '79 we made you warden of the forest of Senart, in place

of poor Jehan Daiz; then captain of the castle of Loches, then governor of St.-Quentin, then captain of the bridge of Meulan, of which
you call yourself count. Out of the fine of five sous paid by every barber who shaves on a holiday, three sous go to you, and we have the rest.
We have been pleased to change your name from *le Mauvais,* or the
Bad, which went too well with your look. In '74 we granted you, to the
great displeasure of our nobility, coat armor of a thousand colors,
which makes your breast look like a peacock's. *Pasque-Dieu!* Are you
still not content? Is your catch of fish not miraculous enough? Are
you not afraid that another salmon would sink your boat? Pride will be
your downfall, compère. Pride always has ruin and shame close at its
heels. Think of this, and shut up."

These words, uttered with a severe look, brought back the former
look of insolence on the angry face of Master Olivier. "It is obvious,"
he murmured, almost aloud, "that the King is ill today. He gives everything to the physician."

Louis, far from being exasperated at this impertinence, began again
with some mildness: "Hold on, I forgot that I made you my ambassador
to Ghent for Madame Marie. Yes, gentlemen," added the King, turning
toward the Flemish, "this man was my ambassador. There now, compère," he continued, addressing Master Olivier, "we will not be angry;
we are old friends. It is very late; we have finished our business. Shave
me."

Our readers were probably not prepared till this moment to recognize in "Master Olivier" that terrible Figaro whom Providence, the
great playwright, so curiously mixed up with Louis XI's long and
bloody comedy. We will not attempt here to describe that singular
face. This royal barber had three names. At court he was politely
called Olivier le Daim; by the people, Olivier the Devil. His real name
was Olivier le Mauvais.

Olivier le Mauvais, then, stood motionless, pouting at the King and
stealing sidelong glances at Jacques Coictier. "Yes, yes! The physician!"
he muttered between his teeth.

"Ah, yes, the physician!" repeated Louis XI, with singular mildness.
"The physician has more influence than you. And very naturally.
He has our whole body in his grip, while you lay hold of us only by
the chin. Come, my poor barber, think no more of it. What would
you say, and what would become of your office, if I were a king like

Chilperic, who had a beard that he was in the habit of grasping in his hand? Now, compère, get your things and shave me."

Olivier, seeing that the King was determined not to be put out of temper, left the room grumbling to comply with his orders.

The King rose, went to the window and, hastily opening it, cried, clapping his hands, and with extraordinary agitation, "Ah, yes! The sky over the city is all aglow. The bailiff's house must be on fire. It cannot be anything else. Well done, my good people! You help me to crush their lordships." Then, turning toward the Flemish, "Only come and look, gentlemen. Isn't that a fire out there?"

The two citizens of Ghent approached. "It is a great fire too," said Guillaume Rym.

"Oh!" cried Coppenole, whose eyes all at once sparkled. "That reminds me of the burning of the Seigneur d'Hymbercourt's house. There must be a fine insurrection over there."

"Do you think so, Master Coppenole?" said the King, with a look of scarcely less delight than that of the hosier. "It will be difficult to quell, no doubt."

"By God, sire, Your Majesty will get a great many companies of men-at-arms thinned in doing it."

"Ah! I! That alters the case!" rejoined the King. "If I wanted . . ."

"If this riot is what I suppose," the hosier boldly replied, "your wanting will be useless."

"Compère," said Louis XI, "with two companies of the King's guard and one cavalry regiment, I could put down the rabble quickly."

The hosier, regardless of the signs made to him by his colleague, appeared determined to contradict the King. "The Swiss guard too were rabble," he said. "The Duke of Burgundy, being a proud gentleman, underestimated them. At the battle of Grandson, he cried, 'Gunners, fire on the base-born rascals!' and he swore by St. George. But Scharnachthal, the avenger, rushed on the goodly Duke with his mace and his men; and at the onslaught of peasants clad in buffalo hides, the shining Burgundian army was exploded like a pane of glass under the impact of a pebble. I do not know how many knights were slain by the scoundrels; and Monsieur de Château-Guyon, the most illustrious of the Burgundian nobles, was found dead with his tall gray charger in a small meadow."

"My friend," rejoined the King, "you are talking of a battle; we are dealing with a riot. Why, I would put an end to it in the twinkling of an eye."

"It may be, Sire," replied the other, with indifference, "but in that case the people's time has not come."

Guillaume Rym thought it right to interfere. "Master Coppenole, you are speaking to a mighty monarch."

"I know it," gravely replied the hosier.

"Let him talk away, my friend Rym," said the King. "I like this frankness. My father, Charles VII, was accustomed to say that Truth was sick. Now, I fancied that she was dead, and had not found a confessor. Master Coppenole is making me realize my mistake."

Then, laying his hand familiarly on Coppenole's shoulder, he proceeded: "You were saying, Master Jacques ..."

"I was saying, sire, that perhaps you are right—that the hour of the people here has not yet come."

Louis fixed on him his piercing eye. "And when will that hour arrive?"

"You will hear it strike."

"By what clock, pray?"

Coppenole, with a grave but tranquil look, drew the King close to the window. "Listen, sire. Here is a castle keep, there a bell tower, cannon, bourgeois, soldiers. When the bell tower buzzes, when the cannon roar, when the keep collapses with a mighty crash, when the bourgeois and the soldiers shout and slay one another, then the hour will have struck."

The face of Louis XI became gloomy and thoughtful. For a moment he was silent; then he patted the thick wall of the tower as though it were the flank of a favorite charger. "Oh, no!" he said. "You will not fall so easily, my good Bastille!" Then, turning sharply toward the bold Fleming, he said, "Master Jacques, have you ever seen an insurrection?"

"I have raised one," answered the hosier.

"How do you set about raising an insurrection?" inquired the King.

"Why," replied Coppenole, "the thing is not at all difficult. There are a hundred ways. In the first place the city must be discontented. That is not a rare circumstance. And then the character of the inhabitants. Those of Ghent are disposed to rebellion. They always love the son of the reigning prince, but never the prince himself. Well, suppose some morning someone comes into my shop and says to me: 'Father Coppenole, there is this, and there is that; the maid of Flanders is determined to save her ministers; the high bailiff has doubled the tax for grinding corn'—or anything else for that matter. That's all we need. I leave my work, and I go out into the street and shout, 'To arms!' There is always some cask or barrel lying around. I leap up on it, and cry out in the first words that come to mind what I have upon my heart; and when one belongs to the people, sire, one always has something upon the heart. Then everyone assembles, they shout, they ring the alarm bell, they arm themselves with weapons taken from the soldiers, the market people join them, and they go to work. And this will always be the way, while there are lords in the seigneuries, bourgeois in the cities, and peasants in the country."

"And against whom do you rebel?" inquired the King. "Against your bailiffs? Against your liege lords?"

"Sometimes one, sometimes the other; sometimes it is against the Duke."

Monsieur Louis returned to his chair. "Aha!" he said, with a smile. "Here they have got no farther than the bailiffs!"

At that moment Olivier le Daim returned. He was followed by two pages bearing the necessary items for the King's toilet; but what struck Louis XI was the circumstance of his also being accompanied by the Provost of Paris and the officer of the watch, who seemed very worried. The face of the spiteful barber also wore a look of dismay, but an expression of pleasure lurked beneath it. It was he who spoke. "Begging Your Majesty's pardon," he said, "I bring calamitous tidings."

The King, turning sharply around, tore the mat on the floor with the legs of his chair. "What do you have to say?"

"Sire," replied Olivier le Daim, with the malignant look of a man who rejoices in the opportunity of striking a severe blow, "it is not against the Bailiff of the Palace that the insurrection of the populace is directed."

"And against whom, then?"

"Against yourself, sire!"

The aged monarch started up on his feet, upright as a young man. "Explain yourself, Olivier, explain yourself! And beware of your head, compère; for I swear by the cross of St.-Lo[24] that if you are lying to us the sword that cut off the head of Monsieur de Luxembourg is not so dull that it cannot still saw yours off!"

This was a formidable oath. In all his life Louis XI had sworn only twice by the cross of St.-Lo. Olivier opened his lips to reply. "Sire—"

"Down on your knees!" cried the King vehemently, interrupting him. "Tristan, watch this man!"

Olivier fell on his knees. "Sire," he said coldly, "a witch has been sentenced to death by your court of Parliament. She has taken sanctuary in Notre-Dame. The people have risen to remove her by force. The Provost and the officer of the watch, who have just come from the spot, are here to contradict me if I do not speak the truth. It is to Notre-Dame that the rabble are laying siege."

"Aha!" cried the King, in a low tone, pale and trembling with rage. "Notre-Dame, is it? They are besieging our Lady, my good mistress, in her own cathedral! Rise, Olivier. You are right. I give you Simon Radin's place. You are right. It is myself they are assailing. The witch is under the safeguard of the church, the church is under my safeguard. I truly believed that the bailiff was the object of their attack. It is myself, after all!"

Then, as if his passion had suddenly restored to him the vigor of youth, he began to pace the floor with hasty strides. He no longer laughed; he was terrible to behold as he stalked back and forth. The fox had turned into a hyena. He seemed to be choked and incapable of speech; his lips moved, and his skinny fists were clenched. Suddenly he raised his head; his hollow eye glared, and his voice exploded like the blast of a trumpet: "Cut them to pieces, Tristan! Cut all those scoundrels to bits! Go, my friend Tristan! Slay, and kill! Kill!"

This explosion over, he returned to his seat and said with cold, concentrated rage: "Here, Tristan! We have with us in this Bastille the Vicomte de Gif's fifty lances, making together three hundred horses: take them. There is also Captain de Châteaupers's company of the archers of our Order: take them. You are provost of the marshals; you have your own people: take them. At the Hôtel de St.-Pol you will find forty archers of the new guard of Monsieur the Dauphin: take them. And with all these troops hurry to Notre-Dame. So, so, messieurs of the mob of Paris, it is at the crown of France, at the sanctity of our

Lady, and at the peace of this commonwealth that your blows are aimed! Exterminate them, Tristan! Exterminate them! Make sure that none of them escapes, except to Montfaucon!"

Tristan bowed. "It shall be done, sire." After a pause he asked, "What shall I do with the witch?"

"Ah!" he said, musing at this question. "The witch! Monsieur d'Estouteville, what do the people want with her?"

"Sire," replied the Provost of Paris, "I should imagine that, as the people have gone to take her from her sanctuary in Notre-Dame, they are offended because she is unpunished and mean to hang her."

For a while the King appeared to be lost in thought; then, turning to Tristan, he said, "Compère, exterminate the people, and hang the witch."

"Excellent!" whispered Rym to Coppenole. "Punish the people for their intention, and carry that intention out!"

"It is enough, sire," answered Tristan. "But if the witch is still in Notre-Dame, is she to be removed in spite of sanctuary?"

"*Pasque-Dieu!* Sanctuary!" ejaculated the King, rubbing his forehead. "The witch must be hanged."

Here, as if seized by a sudden idea, he fell on his knees before his chair, took off his hat, laid it on the seat, and devoutly fixed his eyes on one of the lead figurines with which it was adorned. "Oh!" he began with clasped hands. "My gracious patroness, our Lady of Paris, forgive me. I will do it just this once. That criminal must be punished. I assure you, Holy Virgin, my good mistress, that she is a witch who is not worthy of your kind protection. You know, madam, that many very pious princes have transgressed the privilege of churches for the glory of God and the necessity of the State. St. Hugh, a bishop of England, allowed King Edward to take a magician in his church. St. Louis of France, my master, violated for the same purpose the church of Monsieur St. Paul; and Monsieur Alphonse, son of the King of Jerusalem, the church of the Holy Sepulchre itself. Forgive me then for this time, our Lady of Paris! I will never do so again, and I will give you a beautiful statue of silver, just like the one I gave last year to our Lady of Ecouys. Amen!"

He made the sign of the Cross, rose, put on his hat, and said to Tristan, "Hurry, compère. Take Monsieur de Châteaupers along with you. Let the alarm bell be rung. Crush the people. Hang the witch. That is settled. I expect you to bear the costs of the execution. You shall make a report to me. Come, Olivier, I shall not get to bed tonight. Shave me."

Tristan the Hermit bowed and retired. The King then motioned Rym and Coppenole to withdraw. "God keep you, my good friends of Flanders. Go, get a little rest: the night is late; indeed we are nearer to morning than evening."

Both accordingly retired, and on reaching their apartments, to which they were escorted by the captain of the Bastille, Coppenole said to Guillaume Rym, "By God! I have had enough of this coughing king. I have seen Charles of Burgundy drunk; he was less mean than Louis XI sick."

"Master Jacques," replied Rym, "that is because for kings, wine is not as cruel as herbal infusions."

CHAPTER VI

Petite Flambe en Baguenaud

On leaving the Bastille, Gringoire went down the Rue St.-Antoine with the swiftness of a runaway horse. When he had reached the Porte Baudoyer, he walked straight up to the stone cross that stood in the middle of the open space, as though he had been able to discern in the darkness the figure of a man in a black cloak and cowl, seated on the steps. "Is it you, master?" said Gringoire.

The black figure started up. "Death and perdition! You make my blood boil, Gringoire. The man on the tower of St.-Gervais has just cried half past one."

"Why," replied Gringoire, "it is not my fault but that of the watch and the King. I have had a narrow escape. I was on the point of being hanged. I am predestined to it, I imagine."

"You are never in time for anything," said the other, "but let us be gone. Do you have the password?"

"Only think, master. I have seen the King! I have just come from him. He wears fustian breeches. It was quite an adventure!"

"Blabbermouth! What do I care for your adventures! Do you have the password of the Tramps?"

"Don't worry, I have it. *Petite flambe en baguenaud.*"

"That's good. Otherwise, we would not be able to reach the church. The Tramps have blocked all the streets. Luckily they seem to have met with resistance. We may yet arrive in time."

"Yes, master, but how are we to get into the church?"

"I have a key to the towers."

"And how shall we get out?"

"Behind the cloisters there is a door that opens on the Terrain, and so to the river. I have the key, and I moored a boat there this morning."

"I have had a most lucky escape from the gallows indeed!" said Gringoire exultingly.

"Never mind that now! Come along, quick!" the other answered.

Both then proceeded at a rapid pace toward the Cité.

CHAPTER VII

CHÂTEAUPERS TO THE RESCUE!

The reader probably remembers the critical situation in which we left Quasimodo. The brave hunchback, assailed on all sides, had lost, if not all courage, at least all hope of saving, not himself—he never once thought of himself—but the gypsy. He ran desperately to the gallery. The church was on the point of being taken by the mob. Suddenly the tramp of horses in full gallop was heard in the neighboring streets, and soon a wide column of horsemen riding at full speed and a long file of torches poured with a tremendous noise into the square like a hurricane. "France! France! Châteaupers to the rescue! Down with the rascals!" The frightened Tramps turned around.

Quasimodo, who could not hear the din, saw the naked swords, the torches, the pikeheads, the whole column of cavalry, at the head of which he recognized Captain Phœbus. He observed the confusion of the rabble, the consternation of some and the alarm of the bravest; and, at the sight of this unexpected help, he mustered strength enough to throw down the first of the assailants, who were already running through the gallery.

The mob defended themselves with the valor of despair. Taken on the flank by the Rue St.-Pierre-aux-Bœufs and in the rear by the Rue du Parvis, with their backs toward Notre-Dame, to which they still lay siege and which Quasimodo defended, at once besiegers and besieged, they were in the singular situation in which Count Henri d'Harcourt subsequently found himself at the famous siege of Turin, in 1640, between Prince Thomas of Savoy, whom he was besieging, and the Marquis de Leganez, who was blockading him; *Taurinum obsessor idem et obsessus;* or "He oppressed the people of Turin and was oppressed by them," his epitaph has it.

It was a terrible struggle. As Father Mathieu observes, "Wolf's flesh requires dogs' teeth." The King's troops, amid whom Phœbus de Châteaupers conducted himself valiantly, gave up nothing: what escaped the point of the sword was cut down by its blade. The rabble, badly armed, foamed and bit. Men, women, children, darting at the flanks and chests of the horses, clung to them like cats by tooth and nail. Some thrust torches into the faces of the archers, while others, catching them by the neck with iron hooks, pulled them from their horses and cut them in pieces. One man in particular was seen with a huge scythe, mowing away at the legs of the horses. It was a fearful sight. He sang in a nasal twang, while he kept his scythe incessantly going. At each stroke he traced around himself a large semicircle of dismembered limbs. In this way he advanced into the thickest pace of the cavalry with the deliberate movement, the swaying of the head, and the regular breathing of a mower cutting a field of clover. It was Clopin Trouillefou. Musket fire laid him low.

Meanwhile windows were thrown open. The neighbors, hearing the shouts of the men-at-arms, took part in the affair, and showers of bullets were discharged from every window onto the rabble. The Parvis was filled with a dense smoke, which the musketry cut through with tongues of flame. Through this smoke, you could barely make out the façade of Notre-Dame, and the decrepit Hôtel-Dieu, where a number of pale-faced patients looked out from the rooftop studded with garret windows.

The Tramps eventually gave way. Exhaustion, the lack of proper weapons, the panic of that surprise attack, the firing from the windows, and the furious onslaught of the King's troops defeated them. Forcing the line of their assailants, they fled in all directions, leaving the Parvis strewn with dead.

When Quasimodo, who had been busily engaged the whole time, saw their defeat, he fell on his knees and lifted his hands to heaven;

then, frantic with joy, he flew with the swiftness of a bird to the little cell, the access to which he had so gallantly defended. He had now only one thought—to throw himself at the feet of the woman whom he had saved for the second time. When he reached the cell, he found it empty.

BOOK XI

CHAPTER I

The Little Shoe

When the Tramps attacked the church, La Esmeralda was asleep. It was not long before she was roused by the constantly increasing noise surrounding the cathedral and the uneasy bleating of her goat, which had awoken before her. She sat up, listening and looking around; then, alarmed by the light and the uproar, she hurried out of the cell to see what was the matter. The scene she saw in the square, the confusion of this nocturnal assault, the hideous appearance of the rabble, hopping around like a host of frogs, faintly discerned in the dark, the harsh cries of this uncouth mob, the few torches dancing back and forth in the obscurity, like will-o'-the-wisps skipping over the misty surface of bogs, produced all together the effect of a mysterious battle between the phantoms of the witches' sabbath and the stone monsters of the church. Imbued from infancy with the superstitions of the gypsy tribe, she first thought that she had caught the strange beings of the night at their unholy pranks. Then she hurried back in fear to her cell, to bury her face in the bedclothes, and to shut out if possible the terrific vision.

The first sense of fear having gradually been dispersed, she found, from the incessantly increasing din and other signs of reality, that what she had seen were not specters but creatures of flesh and blood. Her terror then, without being augmented, changed its form. She had imagined the possibility of a popular uprising to tear her from her asylum. The prospect of losing once again her life, her hopes, her Phœbus, which her imagination held forth to her, the absolute nothingness of her own strength, her forlorn situation, cut off from all support, all chance of flight—these and a thousand other thoughts overwhelmed her. She fell on her knees, laying her head covered with her clasped hands on the bed, filled with anxiety and fear; and, gypsy, idolater, and pagan that she was, she began with heavy sobs to implore the mercy of the God of Christians and to pray to our Lady, her protectress. For, whatever one's creed, there are moments in life when one is always of the religion of the nearest temple.

She remained in this position for a considerable time, trembling indeed more than she prayed, her blood curdling at the ever-approaching sounds of that infuriated multitude. She was utterly at a loss as to their origin and ignorant of what they were doing and what they meant to do. She anticipated some terrible catastrophe.

In this anguish she heard a footstep close to her. She looked up. Two men, one of whom carried a lantern, had just entered her cell. She gave a faint shriek.

"Fear nothing," said a voice, which was not unknown to her. "It is I."

"And who are you?" she inquired.

"Pierre Gringoire."

That name gave her fresh courage. She lifted her eyes and saw that it actually was the poet. But at his side stood a black figure, muffled from head to foot, which struck her dumb.

"Ah!" resumed Gringoire, in a tone of reproach. "Djali knew me before you did!"

The little goat had, in fact, not waited for Gringoire to mention his name. No sooner did he enter than she fondly rubbed against his knees, covering the poet with caresses and white hair, for she was shedding her coat. Gringoire returned her affection.

"Who is that with you?" said the gypsy, in a low tone.

"Don't worry," answered Gringoire. "It is one of my friends."

The philosopher, setting down the lantern, crouched on the floor, clasped Djali in his arms, and cried with enthusiasm, "Oh! She is an adorable creature, with her engaging ways, as shrewd, ingenious, and learned as a grammarian! Come, my Djali, let us see if you have not forgotten your amusing tricks. How does Master Jacques Charmolue do—?"

The man in black would not let him finish. He stepped up to Gringoire and roughly pushed him on the shoulder. Gringoire rose. "Ah! True!" he said. "I had almost forgotten that we are in a hurry. But yet, master, that is no reason for hurting people. My poor dear child, your life is in danger, and Djali's too. They mean to hang you again. We are your friends and have come to save you. Follow us."

"Is it true?" she cried in extreme agitation.

"Quite true, I assure you. Come quick!"

"I will," she stammered. "But how is it that your friend does not speak?"

"Why," said Gringoire, "the fact is that his father and mother were strange people, and made him taciturn."

She had to be satisfied with this explanation. Gringoire took her by the hand; his companion picked up the lantern and walked in front. The young creature was stupefied with fear. She let Gringoire lead her away. The goat went with them, skipping around and so overjoyed to see the poet again that she rubbed her head every moment against his legs with such force that she made him stagger. "Such is life," said the philosopher, whenever he had almost fallen. "It is often our best friends who knock us down!"

They rapidly descended the tower stairs, passed through the church, dark, solitary, but echoing the uproar, which produced a fearful contrast, and went out by the Porte Rouge into the cloister court. The cloisters were deserted; the canons had fled to the Bishop's palace, where they were praying together; the courtyard was empty, with the exception of a few frightened lackeys squatting in the dark corners. Gringoire and his companions headed toward the little door leading out to the Terrain. The man in black unlocked it with a key that he had brought with him. The reader is aware that the Terrain was a slip of land, enclosed with walls, belonging to the chapter of Notre-Dame, forming the eastern end of the island, in the rear of the cathedral. They found this spot entirely deserted. At that distance, there was less tumult in the air. The various noises of the assault reached them more blended, more muted. The breeze that followed the current of the river shook the leaves of the only tree standing on the point of the Terrain, whose rustling was audible. But they were not far from danger. The buildings nearest to them were the Bishop's palace and the cathedral. There was evidently a great bustle inside the former. Its gloomy facade was streaked with lights that flashed from window to window. When you have burned a sheet of paper there remains a dark edifice of ashes on which bright sparks make a thousand capricious runs. Beside it, the enormous towers of Notre-Dame, seen from behind, with the long nave from which they rise, standing out in black relief from the red glare that filled the Parvis, looked like the two gigantic andirons of a fire of the Cyclops.

What could be seen of Paris oscillated to the eye in a chiaroscuro that we can find in the backgrounds of Rembrandt's paintings.

The man with the lantern proceeded directly to the point of the Terrain. At that spot there was, at the water's edge, a decayed fence, composed of stakes crossed by lattices, on which a few sickly branches of a low vine were spread like the fingers of an open hand. Behind, and in the shadow cast by this trellis, lay a small skiff. The man made a sign to Gringoire and his companion to get in. The goat followed him. The man then stepped in himself, cut the rope that moored the skiff, pushed off from the shore with a long pole, seated himself in the fore, and, taking up two oars, began to row out toward the middle of the river. In this place the Seine is very rapid, so he had some difficulty getting away from the point of the island.

The first thing Gringoire did, after getting into the boat, was to take his seat at the stern and lift the goat up on his knees. Her mistress, in whom the stranger excited unspeakable apprehensions, sat down by the poet, pressing close to his side.

When our philosopher felt the boat moving, he clapped his hands and kissed Djali's forehead. "Oh!" he exclaimed. "We are all four saved!" With the look of a profound thinker, he added, "One is indebted sometimes to fortune, sometimes to stratagem, for the successful outcome of great undertakings."

The skiff slowly pursued its way toward the right bank. The girl watched the mysterious stranger with a secret terror. He had carefully masked the light of his dark lantern, and he was faintly seen in the fore of the skiff, like a specter. His cowl, still down, formed a sort of visor, and every time that, in rowing, he opened his arms, from which hung wide, black sleeves, they looked like two prodigious bat's wings. He had not yet uttered a word, or let a breath escape. He made no other noise in the boat except the working of the oars, which blended with the rush of the thousand folds of water against the side of the vessel.

"By my soul!" exclaimed Gringoire suddenly. "We are as merry as so many Ascalaph![1] Mute as Pythagoreans or fish! *Pasque-Dieu*, my friends, I wish somebody would talk to me. The human voice is music to the human ear. By the way, that saying belongs not to me but to Didymus of Alexandria, and a most pertinent one it is. For certain, Didymus of Alexandria was no ordinary philosopher. One word, my dear child!

Speak to me, I beseech you. By the way, you have a very very singular pout. Do you still do it? Do you know, my love, that the Parliament has supreme jurisdiction over sanctuaries, and that you ran as much risk in your cell in Notre-Dame as the little bird trochylus, which builds its nest in the jaws of the crocodile?[22] The moon is breaking out again, master! I hope we shall not be seen. We are doing a praiseworthy thing in saving the young lady, yet we should be hanged in the King's name if they were to catch us. Alas! Human actions always have two handles by which they can be grasped. What is condemned in one is applauded in another. Many a man censures Catiline and admires Cæsar. Is it not so, master? What do you say to that philosophy? For my part, I possess the philosophy of instinct, of nature, *ut apes geometriam,* or 'as the bees do geometry.' What, will nobody answer me? You are both in bad moods! I have to talk to myself. That is what we call in tragedy a soliloquy. *Pasque-Dieu!* Let me tell you I have just seen Louis XI and have learned that oath from him. *Pasque-Dieu!* Then, what an uproar they are still making in the Cité! He is a mean old king, that Monsieur Louis. He has not yet paid me for my epithalamium, and it was a mere chance that he did not order me to be hanged tonight, which would have greatly annoyed me. He is stingy toward men of merit. He ought to read the four books by Salvianus of Cologne, *Adversus avaritiam.*[3] Frankly, he is a stingy king in his dealings with men of letters, and commits very barbarous cruelties. He is a sponge in sucking up the money drained from the people. His savings are like the belly swelling on the leanness of all the other members. Complaints of the hardness of the times are therefore treated as murmurs against the prince. Under this sweet, pious lord, the gallows crack with the weight of the condemned, the blocks are clotted with putrefying gore, the prisons are bursting like cows in a clover field. This king has a hand that takes and a hand that hangs. He is the procurer for Monseigneur Gallows and My Lady the Salt Tax. The great are stripped of their dignities, and the humble incessantly loaded with fresh burdens. He is an exorbitant prince. I cannot love this monarch. What do you say, master?"

The man in black let the garrulous poet babble on. He continued to struggle against the violence of the current that separates the prow of the Cité from the stern of the Ile de Notre-Dame, which we now call the Ile de St.-Louis.

"By the way, master," Gringoire began again abruptly, "when we passed through the enraged rabble and reached the Parvis, did you notice that unlucky little devil whose brains your hunchback was in the midst of dashing out against the balustrade of the gallery of the kings? I am too nearsighted to recognize him. Perhaps you know who it was."

The stranger did not answer a word. But he suddenly ceased rowing, his arms sank, as if broken, his head drooped on his breast, and La Esmeralda heard him sigh convulsively. She had heard sighs of that kind before.

The skiff, left to itself, drifted for some moments at the will of the current. Eventually the man in black roused himself, and again began pulling against the current. He passed the point of the Ile de Notre-Dame and rowed toward the landing place of the Port au Foin.

"Ah!" said Gringoire. "There is the Logis Barbeau. Only look, master, at that group of black roofs that form such singular angles—there, under that pile of low, stringy, dirty-looking clouds, where the moon appears smashed and spread around like the yolk of a broken egg. That's a good house! It has a chapel with vaulted roof, decorated with excellent sculptures. You can see above it the belfry, with its rare and delicate carvings. There is also a pleasant garden, containing a fishpond, an aviary, a mall, a maze, a menagerie, and many shady alleys particularly agreeable to Venus. There is also a devil of a tree called the Lovers' Tree, because it served as the trysting place of a famous princess and a romantic and witty Constable of France. Alas! We poor philosophers are to a constable what a bed of cabbages or turnips is to a grove of laurels. What does it matter after all! For the great, as for us, life is a mixture of good and ill. Pain is ever by the side of pleasure as the spondee is by the dactyl. I must tell you the history of the Logis Barbeau, master; it has a tragic ending. It was in 1319, under Philip V, who ruled longer than any other King of France. The moral of the story is that the temptations of the flesh are hurtful and pernicious. Beware of looking too hard at the wife of your neighbor, much as your senses may be susceptible to her beauty. Fornication is a very libertine idea. Adultery is curiosity about the pleasures of others. Hey! It is getting noisier by the second over there. Hey! What an uproar they are making!"

The tumult around Notre-Dame was in fact raging with increased vehemence. They heard distinctly the shouts of victory. Suddenly a hundred torches, which made the helmets of the men-at-arms gleam, appeared in every part of the church, on the towers, the galleries, the flying buttresses. These torches seemed to be searching for something, and soon distant shouts of "The gypsy! The sorceress! Death to the gypsy!" were plainly heard by the fugitives.

The unhappy girl let her head fall on her hands, and the unknown began to row furiously toward the shore. Our philosopher was meanwhile musing. He hugged the goat in his arms and sidled gently away from the Bohemian, who pressed closer and closer to him, as to the only asylum that was now left her.

Gringoire was certainly in a cruel dilemma. He considered that, as the law then stood, the goat would be hanged too if she were retaken; that it would be a great pity—poor, dear Djali! Two condemned ones clinging to him was more than he could manage. However, his companion desired nothing better than to take charge of the gypsy. A violent conflict took place in his thoughts, in which, like Homer's Jupiter, he weighed by turns the gypsy and the goat; and he looked first at one and then at the other with eyes full of tears, muttering at the same time between his teeth: "And yet I cannot save you both!"

A bump apprised them that the skiff had reached the shore. The Cité was still filled with the appalling uproar. The stranger rose, stepped up to the gypsy, and offered her his arm to help her to land. She refused it and clung to the sleeve of Gringoire, who, for his part, engaged with the goat, almost pushed her away. She then sprang without help out of the boat. She was so alarmed that she did not know what she was doing or where she was going. She stood stupefied for a moment, with her eyes fixed on the water. When she came to herself a little, she was alone on the quay with the stranger. It appeared that Gringoire had taken advantage of the instant of landing to steal away with the goat among the cluster of houses composing the Rue Grenier-sur-l'Eau.

The poor gypsy shuddered on finding herself alone with that man. She wanted to speak, to cry out, to call Gringoire; but her tongue was inert, and not a sound came out of her mouth. Suddenly she felt the stranger's hand on hers. It was a cold, strong hand. Her teeth chattered, and she turned paler than the moon's ray that illuminated her. The man did not speak a word. He began to move toward the Place de Grève, drawing her along by the hand. At that moment she had a vague feeling that Fate was an irresistible power. She had lost all motivation and followed mechanically, running while he walked. The quay at this spot goes uphill; to her it seemed as if she were running downhill.

She looked around on all sides. Not a passerby was to be seen. The quay was absolutely deserted. She heard no sound, she saw no movement of men except in the tumultuous and roaring Cité. There was only an arm of the Seine that separated her from the battleground. From there her name, mingled with cries of death, reached her ear. The rest of Paris spread itself out before her as massive, shadowy blocks.

Meanwhile the stranger continued to drag her along in the same silence and with the same rapidity. She had no recollection of the places through which he took her. In passing a lit window she suddenly made an effort to resist, and cried, "Help! Help!"

The window opened; the occupant of the room appeared at it in his shirt and nightcap, with a lamp in his hand, looked out with drowsy eyes on the quay, muttered a few words, which she could not catch, and reclosed the window. She felt as though the last glimmer of hope was extinguished.

The man in black did not say a word; he held her tightly and began to quicken his pace. She stopped resisting and followed him helplessly.

From time to time she mustered a little strength, and in a voice broken from the jolting of the rugged pavement and from her being out of breath, because of the rapid rate at which she was drawn along, she asked, "Who are you? Who are you?" He made no reply.

Proceeding this way along the quay, they arrived at a large open space. The moon shone faintly. It was the Grève. In the middle of it stood a sort of black cross—it was the gallows. Now she knew where she was.

The man stopped, turned toward her, and raised his cowl. "Oh!" she stammered, petrified with horror. "I knew that it must be you!"

It was in truth the priest. He looked like a phantom. Moonlight produces this effect. It seemed as if by that light one could see only the specters of objects.

"Listen to me!" he said, and she shuddered at the sound of that fatal voice, which she had not heard for such a long time. He continued, with frequent pauses and in broken sentences that revealed violent inward agitation. "Listen to me! Here we are. I want to talk to you. This is the Grève. We go no farther. Fate delivers us up into the hands of each other. Your life is at my disposal; my soul at yours. Here is a place and a night beyond which one sees nothing. Listen to me, then. I am going to tell you . . . but not a word about your Phœbus." As he spoke he paced back and forth, like a man who cannot remain quietly in one spot, and pulled her after him. "Do not talk to me about him. If you utter that name, I do not know what I shall do; it will be terrible."

Having said this, like a body recovering its center of gravity, he stood still, but his words did not betray less agitation. His voice became softer and softer.

"Do not turn your head from me like that. Listen to me. This is serious business. First, I will tell you what has happened. It is no laughing matter, I swear to you. But what was I saying? Ah, yes! An order has been issued by the Parliament that condemns you again to the gallows. I have rescued you from their hands. But there they are searching for you. Look."

He pointed toward the Cité. It was evident, in fact, that the search continued. The noise drew nearer. The tower of the lieutenant's house, facing the Grève, was full of bustle and lights, and the soldiers could be seen running on the opposite quay with torches, shouting, "The gypsy! Where is the gypsy! Death! Death!"

"You see that they are in pursuit of you, and that I am not deceiving you. I love you! Do not say anything; do not answer me if it is to tell me that you hate me. I am determined not to hear that. I have helped you escape. Let me complete the work. I can save you. Everything is prepared. All depends on your will. Whatever you want shall be done."

He interrupted himself violently. "No! That is not what I meant to say." Then running, and pulling her along after him, for he still kept hold of her, he went straight to the foot of the gallows, and, pointing to it, said coldly, "Choose between the two of us."

She tore herself from his clasp and fell at the foot of the gallows and kissed the deadly contraption; then, half-turning her head, she looked over her shoulder at the priest. The priest stood like a statue, motionless, his finger still raised toward the gallows.

"This horrifies me less than you," the gypsy said at last.

He slowly dropped his arm and looked down at the pavement, overwhelmed. "Yes," he said; "if these stones could speak, they would say, 'There is the most miserable of men!'

"I love you," he again began. The girl, kneeling before the gallows, covered by her long, flowing hair, allowed him to proceed without interruption. His accent was now soft and plaintive, woefully in contrast to the arrogant harshness of his features.

"I love you. Nothing can be more true. No fire can be fiercer than that which consumes my heart. Ah! Maiden, night and day—yes, night and day—does this deserve no pity? It is a love, torture, night and day, I tell you. Oh! My poor child, I suffer too much. This is an agony worthy of compassion, I assure you. I want to speak gently to you. I do not want you to be horrified by me. And then, if a man loves a woman, it is not his fault. What! You will never have compassion for me, then? You will hate me forever? This is what makes me cruel—ay, hateful to myself! You will not even look at me. You are thinking perhaps of something else, while I am talking to you and trembling, while we both are on the brink of death! Just don't talk to me of your officer! I would throw myself at your knees; I would kiss, not your feet—you would not let me—but the ground beneath them. I would sob like a child, and tear from my bosom not words but my heart and my entrails, to tell you how I love you. But it would all be in vain And yet you have in your soul only what is kind and tender. You are all goodness, all gentleness, all compassion, all sweetness. Alas! To me alone you are cruel. Oh! What a terrible fate."

He buried his face in his hands. La Esmeralda heard him weep. It was the first time. His figure, so upright and shaken by sobs, was more pitiable and more humble than if he had knelt. He continued to weep for some time.

"Alas!" he proceeded, this first paroxysm over. "I am at a loss for words. And yet I had pondered well what I would say to you. Now I tremble and shudder; I shrink back at the decisive moment; I feel some superior power that overwhelms me and makes me stammer. Oh! I shall sink on the pavement unless you take pity on me, on yourself. Do not condemn both of us. If you only knew how much I love you, and what a heart is mine. Oh! What an abandonment of all virtue, what a desperate desertion of myself! I make a mockery of learning; I destroy my good name; as a priest, I make of the most holy vows the resting place of sensuality, and renounce my God! And all for your sake, enchantress, and all this to make myself worthy of your hell. And still you reject me. Oh! I must tell you all—still more, something even yet more horrible—most horrible!"

As he uttered the concluding words, he began to look quite wild. He kept silent for a moment, and then started again, as if speaking to himself, in a loud tone, "Cain, what have you done with your brother?"

Again he paused, and then continued: "What have I done with him, Lord? I have taken him to me, I have fed him, I have brought him up, I have loved him, I have idolized him, and—I have slain him! Yes, Lord, it was he whose head was just now dashed before my eyes against the stones of your temple, and it was on my account, and on account of this woman, because of her . . ."

His eye flashed wildly. His voice became more and more faint: he repeated several times, and with pauses of some length, like a bell prolonging its last vibration: "Because of her . . . because of her . . ." His lips continued to move, but his tongue ceased to articulate any audible sound. Suddenly he sank down and remained motionless on the ground, with his head bowed to his knees.

A slight movement made by the girl to draw her foot from under him brought him to himself again. He passed his hand slowly over his hollow cheeks and looked vacantly for some moments at his fingers, which were wet. "What!" he muttered. "Have I wept?"

Turning abruptly toward the gypsy, with irrepressible anguish, he said, "And have you coldly watched me weep? Do you know, girl, that those tears are lava? Is it then true that women are not moved by anything that happens to the man they hate? If you were to see me die, you would laugh. But I—I do not wish for your death! One word! A single word of kindness! Do not tell me that you love me; say only that you wish me well: it shall suffice—I will save you. Otherwise . . . Oh! The time passes. I implore you by all that is sacred, do not wait until I am again transformed into stone, like that gallows, which also claims you! Consider that I hold both our fates in my hand, that I am mad—Oh! It is terrible—that I may let all drop, and that there is beneath us a bottomless abyss, down which I shall follow you in your fall to all eternity! One kind word! One word! But a single word!"

She opened her lips to answer. He fell on his knees before her, to catch with adoration the words, perhaps of sympathy, that might fall from her mouth. "You are a murderer!" she said.

The priest clasped her furiously in his arms and burst into a terrific laugh. "Murderer though I be," he cried, "I will have you. You will not have me for a slave; you shall have me for a master. You shall be mine. I have a den to which I will drag you. You will come, you must come with me, or I will give you up! You must die, my beauty, or be mine— be the priest's, the apostate's, the murderer's! Do you understand? Come now! Kiss me, darling! The tomb or my bed! The choice rests with yourself—decide instantly."

His eye sparkled with passion and rage. The girl's neck was flushed under the touch of his burning lips. She struggled in his arms. He covered her in foaming kisses.

"Stop biting me, monster!" she cried. "Oh! The hateful poisonous monk! Let me go, or I will tear out your disgusting gray hair and throw it in your face!"

He reddened, turned pale; he released her from his grip and eyed her with a somber look. She considered herself victorious and continued: "I tell you, I belong to my Phœbus, it is Phœbus I love, it is Phœbus who is handsome! As for you, priest, you are old, you are ugly! Go away!"

He gave a violent shriek, like a wretch to whose flesh a red-hot iron is applied. "Die then!" he said, gnashing his teeth. She noticed the diabolical malevolence of his look and would have fled. He grabbed her, shook her, and with rapid strides proceeded toward the corner of the Tour-Roland, dragging her after him along the pavement by her beautiful arms.

On reaching that point he turned toward her. "Once more," he said, "will you be mine?"

She replied firmly, "No."

Then he cried aloud: "Sack Woman! Sack Woman! Here is the gypsy! Revenge yourself on her!"

The girl felt herself suddenly seized by the wrist. She looked; it was a skeleton arm, thrust through a hole in the wall, which held her like a vise.

"Hold fast!" said the priest. "It is the gypsy, who has gotten away. Do not let her escape. I will get the sergeants; you will see her hanged."

These inhuman words were answered by a guttural laugh from within the wall. "Ha! Ha! Ha!" The gypsy saw the priest run off toward the bridge of Notre-Dame. The tramp of cavalry horses was heard in that direction.

The girl immediately recognized the malicious recluse. Panting with terror, she strove to get away. She writhed, she twisted with a bound of agony and despair, but the recluse held her with supernatural force. The bony fingers meeting around her wrist clasped her so firmly they dug into her arm. More efficient than a chain or an iron ring, they were a pair of living and intelligent clamps that came out of the wall.

Against that wall La Esmeralda sank exhausted, and then the fear of death came over her. She thought of the pleasure of life, of youth, of the view of the sky, of the beauty of nature, of love, of Phœbus, of all that was past and all that was to come, of the priest who had gone to denounce her, of the gallows that stood there, and the hangman who would soon arrive. Then she felt the horror mounting to the roots of her hair, and she heard the sinister laugh of the recluse, who said in a low tone, "You are going to be hanged! Ha! Ha! Ha!"

She turned half dead toward the opening and saw the wild face of the recluse between the bars. "What have I done to you?" she said faintly.

The recluse made no reply but began to mutter, with a singing, irritating, and jeering intonation, "Gypsy girl! Gypsy girl! Gypsy girl!"

The wretched Esmeralda let her head drop; she realized that she was not dealing with a human being.

Suddenly the recluse exclaimed, as if she had taken all this time to understand the girl's question, "What harm have you done to me, you ask? What have you done to me, gypsy! Why, listen. I had a child, you see? A little child, a baby, I tell you—a pretty little girl. My Agnes," she resumed, kissing something in the dark. "Well, they stole my child; they took my child away; they ate my child. That is what you have done to me."

The young girl replied, like a lamb, "I was not even born then."

"Oh, yes!" rejoined the recluse, "you must have been born. You were one of them. She would be about your age. Just! It's been fifteen years that I have been here: fifteen years I have suffered, fifteen years I have prayed, fifteen years I have dashed my head against these four walls. I tell you the gypsies stole my baby, and ate her afterward. Do you have a heart? Then imagine what it is to have a child who nurses, sleeps, and plays! It is so innocent! Well, it was such an infant that they stole from me and killed, God knows it well. Now it is my turn; I will feast on the gypsy. Oh, I would bite you if I could get my head between the bars! Only think—while the poor little thing was asleep! And if they had woken her up when they took her, her crying would have been useless; I was not there. Ah, you gypsy mothers! You ate my child! Come and see how I will serve yours."

Then she began to laugh or to gnash her teeth—for both had nearly the same expression on that furious face. The day began to dawn. An ashen light illuminated faintly this scene, and the gallows in the middle of the square became more and more distinct. From the other side, toward the bridge of Notre-Dame, the poor condemned girl imagined that she heard the tramp of horses approaching.

"Madame!" she cried, clasping her hands and sinking on her knees, disheveled, overwhelmed, distracted with terror. "Take pity on me. They are coming. I never harmed you. Would you have me die that horrid death before your face? You are compassionate, I am sure. It is too frightful! Let me go—let me try to escape. Have mercy! I would not like to die in this way!"

"Give me back my child," said the recluse.

"Mercy! Mercy!"

"Give me my child."

"Let me go, for heaven's sake!"

"Give me my child."

The poor girl sank down, overcome, exhausted, with the glazed eye of one who is already in the grave. "Alas!" she stammered. "You seek your child, and I seek my parents!"

"Give me my little Agnes," continued the recluse. "You don't know where she is? Then die! I tell you, I was a harlot; I had a child; they took it away—those accursed gypsies! It is plain then you must die. When your gypsy mother comes to ask for you I will say to her, 'Mother, look at that gallows!' Or, give me back my child—do you know where she is, where my little daughter is? Stay, I will show you. There is her shoe, all that is left to me of her. Do you know where its mate is? If you do, tell me, and if it is at the end of the world, I will fetch it, if I have to crawl there on my hands and knees."

As she said this, she reached her other hand out of the opening and showed the little embroidered shoe to the gypsy. It was already light enough for her to distinguish its form and colors.

"Let me look at that shoe," said the girl, shuddering. "Gracious God!" At the same time, with her free hand, she tore open the little bag adorned with green beads that she wore around her neck.

"Go ahead! Go ahead!" muttered Sack Woman. "Fumble away in your devilish amulet!" Then, stopping short and trembling in every joint, she cried with a voice that came out of her very bowels, "My child! My child!"

The gypsy had taken out of the bag a little shoe that was the precise mate to the other. To this little shoe was attached a piece of parchment, on which was written this rhyme:

When its mate thou shalt find,
Thy mother is not far behind.

In a flash the recluse had compared the two shoes, read the inscription on the parchment, and, thrusting her face, beaming with celestial joy, against the bars of the window, shouted, "My daughter! My daughter!"

"My mother! My mother!" responded the gypsy.

Who could describe such a scene?

The wall and the iron bars were between them.

"Oh! This wall!" cried the recluse. "To see her, yet I cannot clasp her to my heart! Your hand! Give me your hand!"

The girl put her hand through the window; the recluse seized it, fastened her lips to it, and stood absorbed in that kiss, giving no other sign of life but a sigh, which from time to time shook her entire body. Meanwhile torrents of tears gushed from her eyes, in silence, and in the dark, like a rain shower at night. The poor mother poured on that adored hand the dark, deep wellspring of tears that was within her, and from which her sorrows had filtered drop by drop for fifteen years.

Suddenly she raised her head, threw back the long, gray hair from her face, and, without saying a word, began to shake the bars of her window more furiously than a lioness. The bars defied her utmost strength. Then she went to a corner of her cell, got a large paving stone that had been her pillow, and dashed it against them with such violence that she broke one of them into several pieces. A second blow drove out the old iron cross that barricaded the window. With both hands she then removed the rusty fragments of the bars. There are moments when the hands of a woman possess superhuman force.

The passage being cleared—and this was accomplished in less than a minute—she clasped her daughter in her arms and drew her into the cell. "Come!" she murmured. "Let me drag you from the abyss!"

She set her down gently on the floor, then caught her up again, and, carrying her in her arms, as if she were still her baby Agnes, she paced her narrow cell, intoxicated, frantic with joy, shouting, singing, kissing the girl, talking to her, laughing, weeping, suddenly and with vehemence.

"My child! My dear child!" she cried. "I have got my child! Here she is! The gracious God has restored her to me. Come, all of you, and see that I have got my daughter again! Lord Jesus, how beautiful she is. The Almighty made me wait fifteen years, but it was to give her back to me in beauty. After all then the gypsies did not eat you! Who could have predicted it? My child, my dear little child, kiss me! Oh, those good gypsies! How I love the gypsies! And it is you yourself! And this was the reason why my heart always leaped within me whenever you passed. Fool that I was to take this for hatred! Forgive me, my Agnes, forgive me! You must have thought I was very nasty, didn't you? Ah! How I love you! And the beauty mark on your neck! Do you still have it? Let us see. Yes, there it is! Oh! How beautiful you are! It is from your mother you have those large bright eyes! Kiss me, darling! I love you! What do I care if other mothers have children! I can laugh at them now. Let them come. Here is mine. Here is—her neck, her eyes, her hair, her hand. Show me anything more charming than this! Yes, yes, she will have plenty of lovers, I will answer for it. I have mourned for fifteen years. All my beauty has left me and gone to her. Kiss me, love!"

In this strain she ran on, uttering a thousand extravagant things, disheveling the poor girl's dress so as to make her blush, stroking her silken hair with her hand, kissing her foot, her knee, her brow, her eyes, and extolling every feature. The girl let her do as she pleased, repeating at intervals, in a low and infinitely sweet tone, "Oh, Mother!"

"Ah, my darling," the recluse began again, interrupting herself at every word with kisses, "how I shall love you! We will leave this place. How happy we shall be! I have some property in Reims, in our own country. Do you remember Reims? Ah, no! How could you! You were still an infant. If you knew how pretty you were at four months old! Tiny feet that people came to see all the way from Epernay out of curiosity. It is fifteen miles away! We shall have a house and a field. You shall sleep in my bed. My God! My God! Who would have believed it! I have got my daughter again!"

"Oh, Mother!" said the girl, eventually recovering power to speak amid her emotion. "The gypsy woman told me this. There was a good woman of our tribe who died last year, and who always took care of me like a nurse. It was she who fastened this little bag around my neck. She always said, 'My dear, never part with this trinket. It is a treasure. It will enable you to find your mother again. You carry your mother around your neck.' The gypsy woman foretold it, you see."

The recluse again clasped her daughter in her arms. "Come, let me kiss you! How sweetly you said that! When we go to the country we will give those little shoes to an infant Jesus in the church. We certainly owe that to the kind Holy Virgin. But what a charming voice you have! When you were speaking to me just now, it was like music. Ah! Lord God! I have found my child again! And yet who would believe the story! Surely nothing can kill me, since I have not died of joy."

She then began to clap her hands, laughing, and exclaiming, "How happy we shall be!"

At that moment the cell rang with the clank of arms and the tramp of horses, which seemed to be advancing from the bridge of Notre-Dame along the quay. The gypsy threw herself in unutterable anguish into the arms of the recluse.

"Save me!" she shrieked. "Save me, Mother! They are coming!"

The recluse turned pale. "Oh, heavens! What are you saying! I had forgotten! They are searching for you! What have you done, then?"

"I do not know," answered the unfortunate girl, "but I am condemned to die."

"Die!" cried the recluse reeling, as if stricken by a thunderbolt. "Die!" she slowly repeated, fixing her glazed eye on her daughter.

"Yes, Mother," replied the frightened girl, "they mean to put me to death. They are coming to take me. That gallows is for me. Save me! Save me! They are coming! Save me!"

For some moments the recluse remained motionless as a statue; then she shook her head doubtingly and suddenly burst into a loud laugh, her old terrific laugh: "No, no, you must be dreaming. It cannot be. To lose her for fifteen years, and then to find her for a single minute! And they would take her from me again, now that she is grown up and handsome, and talks to me and loves me! They would now come to devour her before my face—mine, who am her mother! Oh, no! Such things are not possible. God Almighty would not permit such doings."

By this time the cavalry had apparently halted. A distant voice was heard calling out, "This way, Messire Tristan! The priest says that we shall find her at the Rat Hole." The sound of the horses resumed.

The recluse started up with a shriek of despair. "Away! Save yourself, my child! I remember now. You are right. It is for your death. Curses on them! Get out of here!"

She put her head out the window and quickly drew it back again. "Stay!" she said, in a low, pained voice, convulsively grasping the hand of the gypsy, who was more dead than alive. "Stay! Hold your breath! The square is full of soldiers. You cannot escape. It is too light."

Her eyes were dry and burning. For a moment she remained silent, but she rapidly paced up and down her cell, stopping now and then, and tearing out handfuls of her gray hair, which she threw on the floor.

"They are coming!" she exclaimed suddenly. "I will talk to them. Hide yourself in this corner. They will not see you. I will tell them that I let you go, that you have run away—that's what I'll do!"

She carried the girl to a corner of the cell that was not visible from outside. Here she made her crouch down, taking care that neither foot nor hand should protrude beyond the dark shadow, loosened her black hair, which she spread over her white dress in order to conceal it, and placed before her the water jug and paving stone, the only furniture she possessed, imagining that they would help to hide her. This done, she was more calm, knelt down, and prayed. Day had just broken, but shadows still pervaded the Rat Hole.

At that moment the voice of the priest, that infernal voice, passed very close to the cell, crying, "This way, Captain Phœbus de Châteaupers!"

At that name, at that voice, La Esmeralda made a slight movement. "Don't move!" said Sack Woman.

She had scarcely uttered the words when a tumult of horses and men was heard outside the cell. The mother hastily rose and posted herself before the window to block their view of the interior. She saw a great troop of armed men, on foot and horseback, drawn up in the Grève. Their commander descended and advanced toward her. He looked horrible. "Old woman," he said, "we are looking for a witch to hang her; we were told that you had her."

The poor mother, assuming a look of as much indifference as she could, answered, "I don't know what you mean."

"By God!" cried the other. "What kind of story did that crazed Archdeacon tell us? Where is he?"

"Monseigneur," said one of the soldiers, "he has slipped away."

"Come, come, old crone," resumed the commandant, "let us have the truth! A witch was given to you to hold. What have you done with her?"

The recluse, apprehensive that by denying everything she might awaken suspicion, replied in a tone of affected sincerity and surliness, "If you mean a tall young girl that I was told to hold just now, all I can tell you is that she bit me, and I let her go. Leave me alone, I beg you."

The commandant's expression betrayed his disappointment.

"Tell me no lies, old scarecrow," he rejoined. "I am Tristan the Hermit, the compère of the King. Tristan the Hermit, do you hear? It is a name," he added, looking around at the Place de Grève, "that has an echo here."

"If you were Satan the Hermit," replied Sack Woman, regaining some hope, "I should have nothing else to tell you, nor should I be afraid of you."

"My God!" cried Tristan. "There's a hag for you! So, the young witch has escaped! And which way has she gone?"

"Down the Rue du Mouton, I believe," answered Sack Woman in a careless tone.

Tristan turned his head and motioned to his troop to prepare to start. The recluse began to breathe again.

"Monseigneur," said one of the archers suddenly, "ask the old witch why the bars of her window are broken like that."

That question once more overwhelmed the wretched mother's heart with anguish. Nevertheless she retained some presence of mind. "They were like that," she stammered.

"Bah!" replied the archer. "Only yesterday they formed a fair black cross, fit to remind a man of his prayers."

Tristan cast a sidelong glance at the recluse. "By my faith," he said, "the hag does begin to look confused."

The wretched woman felt that all depended on keeping up a bold face, and, while her soul was racked with mortal anguish, she began to laugh. Mothers have this kind of force. "Pshaw!" she said. "That fellow is drunk. It is more than a year since the tail of a cart laden with stones was backed against my window and broke the grating. How I insulted the driver!"

"That's true enough," said another archer, "I was there."

Wherever you may be you are sure to meet people who have seen everything. This unexpected testimony somewhat revived the recluse, who felt during this interrogation like one forced to cross an abyss on the edge of a knife. But she was doomed to go from hope to panic.

"If it was a cart that did this," replied the first soldier, "the stumps of the bars would be driven inward, whereas these are bent outward."

"Aha!" said Tristan to the archer. "You have a nose like an inquisitor of the Châtelet. What do you say to that, woman?"

"Good God!" she exclaimed, driven to extremity, and in a voice in spite of herself akin to that of weeping. "I assure you, monseigneur, that it was a cart which broke those bars. That man saw it, you hear. Besides, what does . . . this have to do with your gypsy?"

"Hum!" grumbled Tristan.

"The devil!" resumed the first soldier, flattered by the compliment of the Provost. "The fractures of the iron are quite fresh."

Tristan shook his head. The recluse turned pale. "How long is it, do you claim, since this affair of the cart?"

"A month—a fortnight perhaps, monseigneur. I cannot remember exactly."

"She said at first above a year," observed the soldier.

"That looks suspicious," said the Provost.

"Monseigneur," she exclaimed, still standing close to the window and trembling in fear that they would think of putting in their heads and looking around the cell, "monseigneur, I swear to you that it was a cart which broke this ironwork. I swear it by the angels in Paradise. If it was not a cart, may I deny God, and may eternal perdition be my lot!"

"You swear with enthusiasm," said Tristan, with the look of an inquisitor.

The poor creature felt her assurance forsaking her by degrees. She was so confounded that she made awkward blunders, and she saw with terror that she was not saying what she ought to have said.

A soldier now came up, crying, "Monseigneur, the old witch lies. The girl has not been on the Rue du Mouton. The chain has been up all night, and the keeper has not seen a creature pass."

Tristan, whose look became every moment more threatening, turned to the recluse. "What do you have to say to this?"

"I do not know, monseigneur," she replied, still striving to make headway against this new incident. "I may be mistaken. In fact, I almost think she must have crossed the river."

"Why, that is the very opposite way," said the Provost. "Besides, it is not likely that she would have gone back to the Cité, where the search was on for her. You lie, hag!"

"And then," added the first soldier, "there is no boat, either on this side of the water or on the other."

"She must have swum over," replied the recluse, defending the ground inch by inch.

"Who ever heard of women swimming!" cried the soldier.

"By God, old woman, you lie! You lie!" exclaimed Tristan with vehemence. "I have a good mind to let the young witch go, and to take you instead. A quarter of an hour's torture will bring the truth out of your throat. Come, you shall go with us."

"As you please, monseigneur," she said, eagerly catching at these words. "Hurry, hurry! The torture! I am ready. Take me. Let us go right away!" Meanwhile, she thought, my daughter will have an opportunity to escape.

"Christ!" cried the Provost. "What an appetite for torture! The mad creature completely puzzles me."

An old gray-headed sergeant of the watch advanced from the ranks. "Mad indeed, monseigneur," he said, addressing the Provost. "If she has let the gypsy go, it is not her fault, for she is not fond of the gypsies. For these fifteen years that I have belonged to the watch, I have heard her every night cursing the Bohemian women with bitter and endless execrations. If the one we are seeking is, as I suppose, the dancing girl with the goat, I know that she hates her above all."

The recluse made an effort and repeated, "Above all."

The unanimous testimony of the men belonging to the watch confirmed the words of the old sergeant. Tristan the Hermit, despairing of being able to extract any information from the recluse, turned his back on her, and with inexpressible anxiety she watched him slowly heading toward his horse. "Come," he muttered between his teeth, "let us be off and pursue our search. I will not sleep till the gypsy is hanged."

Nevertheless he paused for some time before he mounted his horse. Sack Woman wavered between life and death, on seeing him cast around the square the restless look of a hound, which is aware that the lair of the game is nearby and is unwilling to leave the spot. Eventually he shook his head and vaulted onto the saddle. The recluse's heart, so cruelly oppressed, once more expanded, and, casting an eye on her daughter, at whom she had not dared to look while the soldiers were there, she said in a soft voice, "Saved!"

The poor girl had remained all this time in her corner, without stirring, without breathing, with the image of death before her eyes. She had not missed a single detail of the scene between Sack Woman and Tristan, and she had shared all the agonies endured by her mother. She had heard the successive snappings of the threads by which she was suspended over the abyss; twenty times she expected to see them all break; then she began again to breathe and to feel herself on solid ground. At this moment she heard a voice saying to the Provost, "*Corbœuf!* Mr. Provost, it is no business of mine, who am a soldier, to hang witches. That is beneath me. I leave you to attend to it alone. You must let me go and rejoin my company, because it is without a captain." That voice was the voice of Phœbus de Châteaupers. What she felt then is not to be described. He was there, then, her friend, her protector, her refuge, her Phœbus! She sprang up and, before her mother could prevent her, darted to the window, crying, "Phœbus! My Phœbus! Come here!"

Phœbus was gone; he had just turned at a gallop the corner of the Rue de la Coutellerie. But Tristan was there still.

The recluse rushed to her daughter with the roar of a wild beast. Striking her nails into her neck, she drew her back with violence. A mother tigress is not very particular. But it was too late. Tristan had seen her.

"Hey ho!" he cried, with a grin that revealed all his teeth and made his face resemble the muzzle of a wolf. "Two mice in the trap!"

"I suspected as much," said the soldier.

"You are an excellent cat!" replied Tristan, patting him on the shoulder. "Come," he added, "where is Henriet Cousin?"

A man who had neither the garb nor the look of a soldier stepped out of the ranks. He wore a dress half gray and half brown, with leather sleeves; had lank hair; and carried a coil of rope in his huge fist. This man always accompanied Tristan, who always accompanied Louis XI.

"My friend," said Tristan the Hermit, "I presume that there is the witch we are seeking. You will hang her right away. Do you have your ladder?"

"There is one under the shed of the Maison aux Pilliers," replied the man. "Is it at this *justice* that we are to do the business?" he continued, pointing to the stone gallows.

"Yes."

"Ho ho ho!" rejoined the man, with a more vulgar, more bestial grin than even that of the Provost. "We don't have far to go."

"Hurry up," said Tristan, "you can laugh afterward."

Ever since Tristan had seen the girl, and all hope was at an end, the recluse had not uttered a word. She had thrown the poor gypsy, half dead, in the corner of the cell and posted herself again at the window, with her two hands like claws resting on the corner of the entablature. In this posture her eyes, which had again become wild and fierce, wandered fearlessly over the surrounding soldiers. When Henriet Cousin reached the cell, her look was so ferocious that he started back.

"Monseigneur," he said, returning to the Provost, "which are we to take?"

"The young one."

"So much the better; for that old hag looks uneasy."

"Poor dancing girl with the goat!" sighed the veteran sergeant of the watch.

Once more Henriet Cousin approached the window. His eye quailed before that of the mother. "Madam . . . ," he began very timidly.

"What do you want?" she cried, interrupting him in a low but resolute tone.

"I don't want you," he said, "I want the other one."

"What other?"

"The young one."

She shook her head, crying, "There is nobody, I tell you—nobody! Nobody!"

"There is," replied the executioner, "and you know it. Let me take the girl. I will not harm you."

"Oh! You will not harm me!" she said, with a terrible laugh.

"Let me take the other, madam; it is by the order of Monsieur the Provost."

Panic-stricken, she repeated, "There is nobody! Nobody!"

"I tell you there is," replied the executioner. "We all saw that there were two of you."

"Look then!" said the recluse, grinning. "Stick your head in at the hole."

The hangman eyed her nails and dared not venture further.

"Hurry!" cried Tristan, who had drawn up his men in a semicircle around the Rat Hole and posted himself on horseback near the gallows.

Henriet returned once more to the Provost, quite at a loss for how to proceed. He had laid his rope on the ground and, with a clownish air, twirling his hat on his hand, he asked, "Monseigneur, how are we to get in?"

"By the door."

"There is none."

"By the window."

"It is too small."

"Enlarge it then," said Tristan angrily. "Don't you have pickaxes?"

The mother watched them from her den, still leaning against the windowsill. She had ceased to hope; she did not know what she would do, but she would not let them take her daughter from her.

Henriet Cousin went to the shed of the Maison aux Pilliers to fetch his tools. He also brought a ladder, which he immediately set up against the gallows. Five or six of the Provost's men armed themselves with picks and crowbars, and Tristan proceeded with them to the cell.

"Old woman," said the Provost in a stern voice, "give up the girl to us quietly."

She looked at him as if she did not understand what he was saying.

"By God!" resumed Tristan. "Why do you want to prevent us from hanging the witch according to the King's will?"

The wretched woman burst into one of her wild laughs. "Why? Why? She is my *daughter!*" The tone with which she uttered that word made even Henriet Cousin himself shudder.

"I am sorry about that," replied the Provost, "but it is by order of the King."

"What is your King to me?" cried she, redoubling her terrible laugh. "I tell you, she is my daughter!"

"Break down the wall," said Tristan.

Nothing more was required to make the opening sufficiently wide than to remove one massive stone from under the window. When the mother heard the picks and the crowbars attacking her fortress, she gave a terrific scream and then began to run around her cell with frightful swiftness—one of the habits of a wild beast that she had contracted from confinement. She said nothing, but her eyes flashed fire. The soldiers were terrified to their hearts' core. Suddenly she picked up her paving stone in both hands, laughed, and hurled it at the workmen. The stone, feebly thrown—for her hands trembled—missed them all and rolled to the feet of Tristan's horse. She gnashed her teeth.

Meanwhile, though the sun had not yet risen, it was broad daylight; the old mossy chimneys of the Maison aux Pilliers were tinged a beautiful pinkish hue. It was the hour when the earliest windows of the great city open cheerfully on the rooftops. Certain inhabitants—fruit sellers and other merchants riding on their asses to the markets—began to cross the Grève. They paused for a moment in front of the party of soldiers collected around the Rat Hole, surveyed them with looks of astonishment, and went on their way.

The recluse had sat down in front of her daughter, covering her with her body, listening to the poor girl, who did not stir, who did not speak, except to murmur in a low tone, "Phœbus! Phœbus!"

As the besiegers' work seemed to advance, the mother mechanically drew back and pressed the girl closer and closer against the wall. Suddenly she saw the stone shake—she kept strict watch, and never took her eyes from it—and she heard the voice of Tristan encouraging the laborers. This roused her from the stupor into which she had sunk for some minutes, and she cried—her voice sometimes tore the ear like a saw; sometimes it stammered as if all the curses filling her throat were jostling one another on her lips—"Ho ho ho! But this is horrible. Robbers, do you really mean to take my daughter from me? I tell you it is my daughter! Oh, the cowards! Oh, the hangman's lackeys! Oh, the assistant murderers! Help! Help! Fire! Will they rob me of my child in this manner? Can such a thing be allowed by the Almighty?"

Then, turning to Tristan, with foaming lips, glaring eyes, on all fours like a panther, and bristling with rage: "Come a little nearer to rob me of my daughter! Do you not understand that this woman is telling you it is her daughter! Do you know what it is to be the mother of a child? And if you have young ones, when they howl do you not have within you something that is moved by their cry?"

"Remove the stone!" said Tristan. "It is loose."

The crowbars displaced the heavy stone. It was, as we have said, the mother's last rampart. She threw herself on it; she would have held it fast; she scratched it with her nails; but the massive block, set in motion by six men, slipped from her grasp and glided gently to the ground along the iron levers.

The mother, seeing an entry made, threw herself across the opening, barricading the breach with her body, waving her arms, striking her head against the top of the window, and shouting with a voice so husky with fatigue that it could scarcely be heard, "Help! Fire! Fire!"

"Now take the girl," said Tristan, as cool as ever.

The mother glared at the soldiers so fiercely that they were much more disposed to fall back than to advance.

"Go on!" shouted the Provost. "Henriet Cousin!"

Not a creature stirred a step.

The Provost exclaimed, "What! Men-at-arms afraid of a woman!"

"Monseigneur," said Henriet, "you call that a woman?"

"She has the mane of a lion," said another.

"Advance!" replied the Provost. "The opening is large enough. Enter three abreast, as at the breach of Pontoise. Let us finish the business. By the death of Mahound! The first one who retreats I will cut in two."

Placed between the Provost and the mother, and threatened by both, the soldiers hesitated for a moment; then, making their choice, they advanced toward the Rat Hole.

When the recluse saw this she suddenly raised herself up on her knees, threw back her long hair from her face, and dropped her lank and lacerated hands onto her thighs. Tears sprang into her eyes, trickling down one by one the wrinkles in her cheeks, like a stream along the riverbed that it has made for itself. At the same time she began to speak, but in a voice so suppliant, so meek, so subdued, so cutting, that more than one old trooper who could have eaten human flesh had to wipe his eyes.

"Gentlemen, and Messieurs Sergeants, one word! There is one thing that I must tell you. It is my daughter—my dear little girl, whom I had lost. Listen—it is a strange story. I am no stranger to messieurs the sergeants. They were always very kind to me when the boys in the streets pelted me with stones, because I was a streetwalker. You will leave me my child when you know all. I was a poor unfortunate girl. The Bohemians stole my infant. Look, here is her shoe, which I have kept for fifteen years. Her foot was no bigger than that. La Chante-fleurie, Rue de Folle-Peine, in Reims—perhaps you know that name. Well, I was she. You will take pity on me, won't you, gentlemen? The gypsies stole her from me and hid her away for these fifteen years. I thought she was dead. Only think, my good friends, I thought she was dead. I have lived here these fifteen years, in this den, without fire in winter. It is hard, is it not? The poor dear little shoe! I have prayed so earnestly that God Almighty has heard me. This very morning He has restored my daughter to me. It is a miracle of His doing. She was not dead, you see. You will not take her from me, I am sure. If it were myself I would not say a word—but as for her, a girl of sixteen, give her time to see the sun! What harm has she done to you? None whatever. Nor I either. If you only knew that I have none but her, that I am getting old, that she was a blessing bestowed on me by the Holy Virgin herself! And then you are all so kindhearted! You did not know that it was my daughter, till I told you. Oh! How I love her! Monseigneur High Provost, I would rather be stabbed in the heart than have a scratch upon her finger! You look like a good, kind gentleman. What I tell you explains everything—no? Oh, my lord! If you ever had a mother! You are the captain; leave me my child! Consider that I am praying to you on my knees, as one prays to Jesus Christ. I ask nothing of anyone. I am from Reims, gentlemen. I have a little spot left me by my uncle, Matthieu Pradon. I am not a beggar. I want nothing but my child! God Almighty, who is the Master of us all, did not give her to me for nothing. The King, you say! The King! How could it please him for you to kill my daughter! And then the King is merciful! It is my daughter! Mine, I tell you! She is not the King's! She is not yours. I will be gone; we will both go. Who would stop two weak women, one of them the mother, the other the daughter. Let us pass, then! We are from Reims. Oh! You are very kind, Messieurs Sergeants; I love you all. You will not take my darling from me—it is impossible. Isn't it? Quite impossible! My child! My own dear child!"

We shall not attempt to convey any idea of her gestures, of her tone, of the tears that she swallowed as she spoke, of her hands, which she clasped and then wrung, of the devastating smiles, the moans, the sighs, the heartrending shrieks that she blended with this wild, rambling, and incoherent harangue. When she was done Tristan the Hermit frowned, but it was to conceal a tear that rolled from his tigerlike eye. Overcoming this weakness, however, he said in a dry tone, "The King wills it."

Then, bending to the ear of Henriet Cousin, he whispered, "Finish this business!" Perhaps the terrifying Provost himself felt even his own heart fail him.

The hangman and the sergeants entered the cell. The mother made no resistance; she merely crawled toward her daughter and threw herself headlong on her. The gypsy girl saw the soldiers approaching. The horror of death roused her. "Mother," she cried, in a tone of inexpressible anguish, "Mother, they are coming; save me!" "Yes, my love, I will defend you," replied the mother in a faint voice, and, clasping her tight in her arms, she covered her with kisses. Mother and daughter, as they lay on the ground, presented a sight that was truly pitiable.

Henriet Cousin grabbed hold of the girl around the waist. When she felt the touch of his hand she shuddered, cried "Ugh!" and fainted. The hangman, from whose eyes big tears fell drop by drop on her, attempted to lift her but was prevented by the mother, who had entwined her arms around her daughter's body and clung so firmly to her child that it was impossible to part them. Henriet Cousin, therefore, dragged the girl out of the cell and the mother after her—the latter, too, with her eyes shut, and apparently unconscious.

The sun was just then rising, and a considerable number of people collected this early in the square were trying to make out what the hangman was dragging along the pavement toward the gallows. It was Tristan's way to prevent the approach of the gawkers at executions.

There was not a creature at the windows. On the top of that tower of Notre-Dame that overlooks the Grève, two men could be seen in dark relief against the clear morning sky. They appeared to be looking on.

Henriet Cousin stopped with what he was dragging when he reached the foot of the fatal ladder and, scarcely breathing, so deeply was he affected, he slipped the cord about the girl's lovely neck. The unfortunate creature felt the horrid touch of the rope. She opened her eyes and saw the hideous arm of the stone gallows extended over her head. Rousing herself, she cried in a loud and heartrending voice, "No! No! I will not." The mother, whose face was buried in her daughter's garments, did not utter a word; her whole body trembled, and she was heard to kiss her child even more intensely. The hangman took advantage of this moment to wrench open her arms, with which she had clung to the condemned girl. From either exhaustion or despair, she did not resist. Then he lifted the girl on his shoulder, from which the charming creature hung gracefully folded in two, and began to ascend the ladder.

At that moment the mother, crouched on the pavement, opened her eyes. Without uttering any cry, she sprang up with a terrific look; then, like a beast of prey, she seized the hand of the hangman and bit him. It was like lightning. The executioner roared with pain. Some of the sergeants ran to him. With difficulty they extricated his bleeding hand from the teeth of the mother. She maintained profound silence. They thrust her back brutally, and her head fell heavily on the pavement. They lifted her up, but again she sank to the ground. She was dead.

The hangman, who had not set the girl down, continued to mount the ladder.

CHAPTER II

LA CREATURA BELLA BIANCO VESTITA[4]

When Quasimodo saw that the cell was vacant, that the gypsy was not there, and that while he was defending her she had been kidnapped, he grasped his head with both hands and stamped the ground with rage and astonishment. Then he began to run all over the church in search of the Bohemian, sending up strange shouts at every corner and sowing his red hair on the ground. When the King's archers entered the cathedral victorious, also seeking the gypsy, Quasimodo helped them, having no suspicion—poor deaf creature!—of their fatal intentions; it was the crew of Tramps whom he regarded as the enemies of the girl. He himself conducted Tristan the Hermit to every possible hiding place, opened for him all the secret doors, the double-bottomed altars, and the back sacristies. Had the unfortunate girl still been there, he would inevitably have betrayed her. When Tristan was tired of the unsuccessful search—and on such occasions he was not soon tired—Quasimodo continued it alone. He crossed the church twenty times, a hundred times, length and breadth, from top to bottom, mounting, descending, running, calling, crying, shouting, ferreting, rummaging, poking his head into every hole, thrusting a torch into every dark corner, distracted, mad. A male beast who has lost his mate could not have been more distraught or desperate. At last, when he was sure, quite sure, that she was no longer there, that she had been stolen away from him, he slowly ascended the tower stairs, those stairs that he had mounted with such transport and exultation on the day he saved her. He passed that way again, with drooping head, speechless, tearless, almost unbreathing. The church was once more empty, and silence again reigned within it. The archers had left the sacred edifice to track the witch in the Cité. Quasimodo, left alone in the vast cathedral, ringing but a few moments before with the clamor of the besiegers, returned toward the cell where the gypsy had slept for so many weeks under his guardianship. As he approached it he could not help imagining that he might find her there again. When, at the turn of the gallery that opens on the roof of the aisles, he saw the narrow room with its small window and its little door, wedged under a great flying buttress, like a bird's nest under a bough, his heart failed him, poor fellow! He leaned against a pillar, in case he should fall. He imagined that she might have returned there, that a good genie had no doubt brought her back, that this little cell was too quiet, too safe, too charming for her not to be there; and he dared not take another step for fear of destroying the illusion. "Yes," he said to himself, "perhaps she is asleep, or praying. Let us not disturb her." Eventually he mustered courage, advanced on tiptoe, looked in, entered. Empty! The cell was still empty! The unhappy hunchback slowly paced around it, lifted up the bed and looked under it, as though she could have been hidden between the mattress and the floor. He shook his head and remained for a while in a state of stupor. Then he furiously stamped out his torch, and without a word or sigh he dashed his head with all his strength against the wall and fell in a dead faint on the ground.

When his senses returned he threw himself on the bed, he rolled on it, he wildly kissed the spot where La Esmeralda had lain; he remained there for some time as motionless as if life had left him. Then he rose, bathed in perspiration, panting, beside himself, and began to beat his head against the wall with the frightful regularity of a pendulum, and the resolution of one who is determined to dash out his brains. After a while he fell a second time, exhausted. Then he crawled on his knees out of the cell and crouched opposite the door in an attitude of despair. In this state he continued for more than an hour, without moving, his eye fixed on the vacant cell, more gloomy and more thoughtful than a mother seated between an empty cradle and a full coffin. He did not say a word; only at long intervals a sob violently shook his whole body, but it was a sob without tears, like summer lightning that makes no noise.

It seems that then, trying in his doleful reverie to figure out who the surprise kidnapper might be, he thought of the Archdeacon. He remembered that no one but Dom Claude had a key to the staircase leading to the cell; he remembered his nocturnal attempts upon the young girl, in the first of which he, Quasimodo, himself had assisted, and the second of which he had prevented. He remembered a thousand other things and soon felt not the least doubt that it was the Archdeacon who had taken the girl from him. Such, however, was his respect for the priest, so deeply had gratitude, devotion, and love for that man taken root in his heart, that even at this moment they withstood the pull of jealousy and despair.

He considered that the Archdeacon had done this, and instead of the mortal rancor that he would have felt for anyone else, he was even more pained. When the dawn began to whiten the flying buttresses, he saw on a higher story of the cathedral, at a corner formed by the outer balustrade that runs around the apse, a moving figure. The face of this figure was turned toward him. He recognized the person. It was the Archdeacon. Claude's step was grave and deliberate. He did not look ahead as he walked toward the north tower; his face was turned toward the right bank of the Seine, as if he were trying to see something over the intervening roofs. The owl frequently assumes this oblique posture, flying in one direction while looking in another. The priest passed above Quasimodo this way without seeing him.

The hunchback, petrified by this sudden apparition, watched until he lost sight of him at the door of the staircase of the north tower. The reader already knows that this is the tower that commands a view of the Hôtel de Ville. Quasimodo rose and followed the Archdeacon.

He went up the stairs to climb the tower, in order to find out why the priest had gone up. The poor bell ringer did not know what he would do, or what he wanted. He was full of rage and apprehension. In his heart, the Archdeacon and the gypsy clashed.

When he reached the top of the tower, before he emerged from the darkness of the staircase and stepped out onto the platform, he looked cautiously around to find out where the priest was. Claude had his back to him. A balustrade of openwork surrounds the platform of the steeple. The priest, whose eyes were bent on the town, was leaning with his breast against that corner of the balustrade that looks down on the bridge of Notre-Dame.

Quasimodo stole up behind him to see what he was looking at. The priest's attention was so completely engrossed that he did not notice the hunchback's approach.

Paris, viewed from the towers of Notre-Dame in the cool light of a summer morning, is a magnificent and lovely sight. It must have been the month of July. The sky was perfectly serene. A few lingering stars were going out in different places, and there was still a very bright one in the east, in the lightest part of the sky. The sun was just rising. Paris began to stir. A very white and a very pure light touched the eastward faces of its countless houses and made them stand out. The giant shadows of the steeples extended from roof to roof, from one end of the great city to the other. There were neighborhoods that had already begun to make noise and bustle. Here was heard the hammer of the smith, there that of the carpenter, and beyond that the complicated creaking of a cart as it passed along the street. A few columns of smoke rose out of different places in this vast terrain of roofs, as from the fissures of an immense solfatara. The river that flowed against the arches of so many bridges, and the points of so many islands, was streaked with silver. Around the Cité, beyond the ramparts, the horizon melted into a wide circle of fleecy clouds, through which could be faintly discerned the indefinite line of the plains and the graceful swelling of the hills. All sorts of sounds floated confusedly over this half-awakened city. Toward the east the morning breeze drove across the sky a few white strands of mist torn from the mantle of fog that enwrapped the hills.

In the Parvis certain housewives, with milk jugs in their hands, pointed out to each other with astonishment the shattered state of the great portal of Notre-Dame, and the two streams of lead congealed in the interstices between the stones of the pavement. These were the only vestiges of the tumult of the past night. The fire kindled by Quasimodo between the towers was extinguished. Tristan had already ordered the square to be cleared and the dead to be thrown into the Seine. Kings such as Louis XI take care to have the pavement speedily washed after a massacre.

Outside the balustrade of the tower, below the exact point where the priest had stopped, there was one of those stone gutters, fantastically carved, with which Gothic edifices bristle, and in a crevice of this gutter were two fine gillyflowers in full bloom, which moved, as if they were animated by the breeze and seemed to be playfully bowing to each other. Above the towers, high in the air, small birds were heard twittering and screaming.

But the priest neither heard nor saw any of these things. He was one of those who take no notice either of mornings or of birds or of flowers. His attention was engrossed by only one point on that immense horizon, which presented so many things to him.

Quasimodo burned with impatience to ask what he had done with the gypsy, but the Archdeacon seemed at that moment to be somewhere else. With him it was evidently one of those critical moments of life, when a man would not feel the earth crumbling beneath his feet. He remained motionless and silent, with his eyes unwaveringly fixed on a particular spot. The silence and the motionless attitude were so formidable that the savage bell ringer himself shuddered before it and dared not disturb it. All he could do, therefore, and this was one way of questioning the Archdeacon, was to follow the direction of his eye. Thus guided, the unhappy hunchback's gaze fell on the Place de Grève.

He now saw what the priest was looking at. The ladder was set up against the permanent gallows. There were a few people in the square and a great number of soldiers. A man was dragging along the pavement something white, to which something black was clinging. This man stopped at the foot of the gallows. What then took place he could not clearly make out; not that the sight of his only eye was at all impaired but a party of soldiers prevented his distinguishing what was going on. Besides, at that moment the sun came out and poured such a flood of light above the horizon that every point of Paris—steeples, chimneys, gables—seemed to be set on fire at the same moment.

Meanwhile the man began to mount the ladder. Quasimodo now saw distinctly again. He carried across his shoulder a woman, a young woman dressed in white; this young woman had a rope around her neck. Quasimodo knew her. It was the gypsy!

The man reached the top of the ladder. There he arranged the rope. The priest, in order to see better, now knelt down on the balustrade.

The man suddenly kicked away the ladder, and Quasimodo, who had not breathed for some moments, saw the unfortunate girl, with the man mounted on her shoulders, dangling at the end of the rope within two or three yards of the pavement. The rope spun around several times, and Quasimodo saw the body of the gypsy shaken by terrible convulsions. The priest, for his part, with outstretched neck and eyes staring from his head, contemplated the terrifying couple—the man and the young girl, the spider and the fly.

At this most awful moment, a demon laugh, a laugh such as only one who has ceased to be human is capable of, burst across the livid face of the priest. Quasimodo did not hear this laugh, but he saw it. The bell ringer recoiled a few steps from the Archdeacon, then, rushing furiously on him, thrust him with his two huge hands into the abyss, over which Dom Claude was leaning. "Damnation!" cried the priest as he fell.

The gutter beneath caught him and broke the fall. He clung to it with desperate hands and was just opening his mouth to give a second cry when he saw the formidable and avenging face of Quasimodo over the balustrade above his head. He was then silent.

The abyss was beneath him—a fall of more than two hundred feet—and the pavement! In this terrible situation, the Archdeacon uttered neither word nor groan. He writhed on the edge of the gutter and made astonishing efforts to hoist himself onto it. But his hands had no hold of the granite, and his toes merely scratched the blackened walls without finding the least support. All who have ever been up the towers of Notre-Dame know that the stone bulges immediately under the balustrade. It was against this slope that the wretched Archdeacon exhausted himself in fruitless efforts. He was dealing not with a perpendicular wall but with a wall that receded from him.

Quasimodo might have saved him from the abyss merely by extending to him his hand, but he did not so much as look at him. He looked at the Grève. He looked at the gypsy. He looked at the gallows. The hunchback was leaning on the balustrade, at the very spot that the Archdeacon had just before occupied. And there, never turning his eye from the only object that existed for him at that moment, he was motionless and mute as one thunderstruck while a stream flowed in silence from that eye that till then had not shed a single tear.

The Archdeacon meanwhile began to pant. The perspiration trickled from his bald brow; the blood oozed from his fingers' ends; the skin was rubbed from his knees against the wall. He heard his cassock, which hung by the gutter, crack and rip at every movement he made. To crown his misery, that gutter ended in a lead pipe that was bending with his weight. The Archdeacon felt it slowly giving way. The wretched man said to himself that when his cassock was torn, when the lead pipe yielded, he would fall, and fear took hold of his entrails. At times he wildly eyed a sort of narrow ledge, formed about ten feet below him by the sculpture of the church, and in his distress he prayed to heaven in the recesses of his soul to permit him to end his life on this space of two square feet, even if it were to last a hundred years. Once he glanced at the abyss beneath him; when he lifted his head his eyes were closed and his hair standing erect.

There was something frightful in the silence of these two men. While the Archdeacon, a few feet away, was experiencing the most horrible agonies, Quasimodo kept his eye fixed on the Grève and wept.

The Archdeacon, seeing that all his exertions served but to shake the only frail support that was left him, determined to move no more. There he was, clasping the gutter, scarcely breathing, absolutely motionless except for that automatic convulsion of the abdomen that you feel in your sleep when you dream you are falling. His staring eyes were open in a wild and ghastly manner. Meanwhile he began to lose his hold; his fingers slipped down the gutter: he felt his arms becoming weaker and weaker, and his body heavier and heavier. The lead pipe that supported him bent more and more every moment toward the abyss. Beneath him he saw—fearful sight!—the roof of St.-Jean-le-Rond, diminutive as a card bent in two. He looked one after another at the pitiless sculptures of the tower, suspended like himself over the abyss, but without fear for themselves or pity for him. All around him was stone: before his eyes, gaping monsters; under him, at the bottom of the gulf, the pavement; over his head, Quasimodo weeping.

In the Parvis several groups of curious spectators were calmly wondering who could be the maniac that was amusing himself in this strange manner. The priest heard them say, for their voices reached him, clear and sharp, "He's going to break his neck!"

Quasimodo wept.

Finally the Archdeacon, foaming with rage and terror, realized that everything was useless. He nevertheless gathered all his remaining strength for a last effort. Setting both his knees against the wall, he hooked his hands into a cleft in the stones and succeeded in raising himself about a foot; but this struggle caused the lead beak that supported him to give way suddenly. His cassock was torn from the same cause. Feeling himself sinking, having only his stiffened and crippled hands to hold by, the wretched man closed his eyes, and soon his fingers relaxed their grasp. Down he fell!

Quasimodo watched him fall.

A fall from such a height is rarely perpendicular. The Archdeacon, launched into the abyss, fell at first head downward and with outstretched arms, then whirled several times over and over; dropping on the roof of a house and breaking some of his bones. He was not dead when he reached it, for the bell ringer saw him try to grab the ridge with his fingers; but the slope was too steep, and his strength utterly failed him. Sliding rapidly off the roof like a loose tile, down he went, and bounced on the pavement. Then he moved no more.

Quasimodo raised his eye to the gypsy, dangling from the gallows.

At that distance he could see her quiver beneath her white robe in the last convulsive agonies of death; then he looked down at the Archdeacon, stretched at the foot of the tower, looking hardly human at all, and, heaving a deep sigh, he cried, "There is all I ever loved!"

CHAPTER III

THE MARRIAGE OF CAPTAIN PHŒBUS

Toward the evening of the same day, when the judicial officers of the Bishop came to remove the mangled corpse of the Archdeacon from the pavement of the Parvis, Quasimodo was not to be found in Notre-Dame.

Many rumors circulated respecting this affair. The general opinion was that the day had arrived when, according to agreement, Quasimodo, or the devil, was to carry away Claude Frollo, the sorcerer. It was presumed that he had smashed the body to get at the soul, just as monkeys crack the shell of a nut to get at the kernel. For this reason the Archdeacon was not buried in sacred ground.

Louis XI died in the month of August in the following year, 1483.

As for Pierre Gringoire, he tried to save the goat, and to gain applause as a tragic writer. It appears that, after dabbling in astrology, philosophy, architecture, alchemy, and all sorts of vain pursuits, he reverted to tragedy, which is the most vain of all. This he called "having come to a tragic end." In the accounts of the Ordinary for 1483 may be found the following entry relative to his dramatic triumphs:

> To Jehan Marchand and Pierre Gringoire, carpenter and composer, who made and composed the play enacted at the Châtelet of Paris at the entry of Monsieur the Legate, and arranged the characters, dressed and equipped as by the said play was required; and also for having made the scaffolds that were necessary thereto, one hundred pounds.[5]

Phœbus de Châteaupers likewise "came to a tragic end": he got married.

CHAPTER IV

THE MARRIAGE OF QUASIMODO

We have just said that on the day the gypsy and the Archdeacon died Quasimodo was not to be found in Notre-Dame. He was never seen afterward, nor was it ever known what became of him.

The night after La Esmeralda's execution, the hangman and his assistants took her body down from the gallows, and transported it, according to custom, to the vault of Montfaucon.

Montfaucon, as we are told by Sauval, was "the most ancient and the most superb gallows in the kingdom." Between the faubourgs of the Temple and St.-Martin, about one hundred and sixty fathoms from the walls of Paris, and a few crossbow shots from La Courtille, was seen at the top of a gentle, imperceptible rise, yet sufficiently elevated to be visible for several leagues around, a building of strange form, almost like a Celtic cromlech where human victims were also sacrificed.

Imagine on the top of a mound of chalk, a clumsy rectangular piece of stone masonry, fifteen feet high, forty long, and thirty wide, with a door, an outer railing, and a platform. Upon this platform sixteen massive pillars of unhewn stone, thirty feet high, ranged in the form of a colonnade around three of the four sides of the stonework that supported them, connected at the top by strong beams, from which at certain distances hang chains, each with a skeleton dangling at the end of it. There on the flat surface a stone cross and two gallows of secondary rank seem to spring up like shoots from the central fork. Above all this, in the air, crows perpetually fly—now you have a picture of Montfaucon.

At the end of the fifteenth century, this terrifying gallows, which dated from 1328, was already very decrepit: the beams were rotten, the chains eaten up with rust, the pillars green with moss; there were wide gaps between the blocks of the stone. Grass grew on the deserted platform. The silhouette of this edifice against the sky was a horrible one, especially at night, when the faint moonlight fell on those bleached skulls, or when the night breeze, shaking the chains and the skeletons, made them rattle in the dark. The presence of this gallows was enough to make you believe that the entire area was haunted.

The stonework that served as a base to the odious building was hollow. Here a vast vault had been formed, shut in by an old crazy iron gate, into which were thrown not only the human remains taken from the chains of Montfaucon but the bodies of all the wretches executed at the other permanent gallows of Paris. In this vast mortuary, in which so many corpses and so many crimes have rotted together, many of the great of the world, and many innocent people, have successively been laid to rest, from Enguerraud de Marigni, who made a present of Montfaucon to the King, and who was a good man, to the Admiral de Coligni,[6] who was the last to be brought there, and who also was a good man.

With regard to the mysterious disappearance of Quasimodo, all that we have been able to discover is this:

About a year and a half or two years after the events with which this story concludes, when a search was made in the vault of Montfaucon for the body of Olivier le Daim,[7] who had been hung two days before, and to whom Charles VIII had granted the favor of being in better company at St.-Laurent, among these hideous corpses two skeletons were found in an unusual posture. One of the skeletons, which was that of a woman, still had on it some rags of a dress that had once been white; and around the neck was a necklace of the seeds of adrezarach, and a little silk bag embroidered with green beads, which was open and empty. These things were of so little value that the hangman no doubt had not thought it worth his while to take them. The second, which embraced the first tightly, was the skeleton of a man. It was noticed that the spine was crooked, the head jammed between the shoulder blades, and one leg shorter than the other. There was, however, no rupture of the vertebræ of the neck, and it was obvious that the person to whom it belonged had not been hanged. He must have come there and died in the place. When those who found this skeleton attempted to disengage it from the one it embraced, it fell to dust.

Notes

Hugo's principal historical sources for The Hunchback of Notre-Dame *were the following:*

du Breul, P. Jacques. *Le Théâtre des Antiquités de Paris* (Paris: Chez Pierre Chevalier, 1622).

de Commyne, Phillipe. *Mémoires* (Paris: Éditions J. Calmette, 1924–25).

Dictionnaire infernal. 2d ed. 4 vols. (Paris: n.p., 1825–26).

Matthieu, Pierre. *Histoire du Louis XI, roi de France* (Paris: 1610).

Attributed to de Roye, Jean (Hugo refers to him as Jehan de Troyes). *Chroniques scandaleuses* (Paris: Édition Lenglet-Dufresnoy, 1747).

Sauval, Henri. *Histoires et Recherches des Antiquités de la Ville de Paris.* 3 vols. (Paris: Moette et Chardon, 1724). *Comptes de la Prévôté,* often cited by Hugo, is in vol. 3.

Tristan, L'Hermite de Soliers. *Le Cabinet du roi Louis XI* (Paris: 1661).

AUTHOR'S PREFACE
1. *ANÁΓKH: ANÁΓKH* signifies fatality. Hugo wrote this preface after he completed the novel.

BOOK I
1. *vineyard of Laas:* In 1548 a student revolt led by the humanist Ramus took place in the *terroir des vignes.* The monks of St.-Germain-des-Prés took over this part of the Pré-aux-Clercs. See du Breul.
2. *the Dauphin and Margaret of Flanders:* The Dauphin (who would be crowned Charles VIII), as the heir apparent to the throne was called, was twelve years old in 1482. Marguerite of Austria (or Flanders) was three. The Treaty of Arras, which stipulated their marriage, was

signed on December 23, 1482. In 1493, Charles VIII annulled his engagement with this princess.

3. *as Jehan de Troyes describes it:* Jehan de Troyes was the author of the *Chroniques scandaleuses,* detailing events of 1460–1483. Victor Hugo drew on many historical details from de Troyes's chronicle in writing this novel.

4. *Festival of Fools:* The Festival of Fools is celebrated on different dates in different places, but it usually takes place between the feast of Saint Stephen (December 26) and January 14. Outlawed by Charles VII in 1445, it was still celebrated under Louis XI, and traces can be found until the seventeenth century.

5. *Sauval:* Henri Sauval, nineteenth-century historian of Paris. Hugo consulted Sauval's article "Deux in-folio, traitant des antiquités et de l'histoire de la ville de Paris," which appeared in the *Journal* of July 21, 1830.

6. *Gothic:* The word *Gothic* in the general sense is perfectly incorrect but has been consecrated by general use. We therefore accept it, and we adopt it like everyone else to characterize the architecture of the second half of the Middle Ages. The ogival [or pointed] arch is its principal motif, and it replaces the architecture of the first period, for which the full dome was the most important feature. [Hugo's note]

7. *when du Breul still admired it by tradition:* This entire passage follows closely the writing of du Breul, who describes in detail many of the architectural features that Hugo enumerates here in his *Le Théâtre des Antiquités de Paris* (1622).

8. *two other plausible explanations:* Hugo takes three explanations of the cause of the fire from Sauval's work.

9. Certes . . . en feu: In Paris it was a sorry sport/When Lady Justice, prey to greediness/Consumed too many bribes in excess/And set fire to her own High Court.

10. *du Hancy's delicate woodwork:* Du Hancy was a famous woodworker under Louis XII.

11. *Patrus:* Olivier Patru (1604–81) was a famous lawyer and Boileau's master.

12. *Gilles Lecornu!:* Lecornu means "the horned one"; this can refer to the horns of the devil and the horns of the cuckold, the man whose wife is cheating on him.

13. Cornutus et hirsutus: Horned and hairy.

14. *the four nations:* The four nations were France, Picardy, Normandy, and Germany, among whom the students of the university were divided.
15. Tybalde ad dadus: Corrupted Latin for "Thibaut, you dice player."
16. Saturnalitias mittimus ecce nuces: Citation from Martial's *Epigrams,* VII, 91, "Look, I send to you the nuts of Saturnalia." During the saturnalian festivities, the partygoers bombarded each other with nuts.
17. Seu de pellis grisis fourratis: "Or lined with gray fur!"
18. *a Doge of Venice going to marry the sea:* Every year on Pentecost the Doge of Venice married the sea symbolically by throwing a ring into the Adriatic.
19. *Porte Baudets:* The Porte Baudets was on Philip Augustus's fortified walls, at the corner of the Rue St.-Antoine and the Rue des Barres.
20. Nec Deus intersit: "Never let a god intervene, unless the situation is worthy of him," from Horace's *Poetics.*
21. Evoe, Jupiter! Plaudite cives!: "Hurrah, Jupiter! Applaud, citizens!"
22. *a morality play:* Hugo did not distinguish between the play, which was religious, and the morality play, which was allegorical and didactic. We begin by translating *mystère* as "play," and will use "play" for the sake of readability, but Hugo's attempt to give his novel a medieval "feeling" should be heard in the question of the play, which in the fifteenth century was almost always based on either a religious or an allegorical theme. [translator's note]
23. *in which three handsome young girls enacted the parts of:* The Cardinal Julien de la Rovère entered Paris as the papal legate on September 4, 1480. But it was actually at the entry of Louis XI into Paris that there was a performance of naked women, at least according to the *Chroniques scandaleuses.*
24. *shut up in Amboise:* At the Château d'Amboise, Louis XI shut up his son, the Dauphin Charles, to protect him from illnesses, kidnapping, and bad influences.
25. *siege of Paris:* During the War of the Bien Public, Paris was under siege during August and September 1465.
26. *wrote this rhapsody: La Florentine* was attributed to La Fontaine, and this witticism became part of the legend around the poet. The play was in fact, however, written by Champmeslé and first performed on July 23, 1685.
27. Bibamus papaliter: "Drink like a Pope." Benedict XII was pope at Avignon from 1334 to 1342. He was a pious Benedictine, a good administrator and a lover of fine wines.

28. Cappa repleta mero: "The Cardinal's cape refills the wine."

29. *Edward IV:* Edward IV died in April 1483. Hugo interprets his death as a poisoning at the hands of Louis XI because the French King supported Warwick and the Lancasters against the house of York.

30. *Ronde de Nuit:* Rembrandt's famous 1642 painting, known as *The Night Watch* in English. Hugo understood Rembrandt as having been a genius at being able to capture the rich complexity of bourgeois psychology in his paintings of the prosperous and newly confident Flemish merchant class.

31. *Guy d'Hymbercourt and Chancellor Guillaume Hugonet:* Guy de Brimeu and Guillaume Hugonet, Chancellors of Burgundy, were executed on April 3, 1477, in Ghent. Marie de Bourgogne did beg for their lives, but three days before their execution. This mistake comes from Hugo's reading of Commynes.

32. margaritas ante porcos: "Pearls before swine."

33. porces ante Margaritam: "Swine before a pearl" (a pun on the meaning of the word Margaret, "a pearl").

34. *Vera incessu patuit dea:* "In her step alone, the goddess was revealed." Virgil describes Venus in this way in the *Aeneid,* I, 405.

35. *Homer:* In the *Iliad,* Homer describes the gods' laughter at the sight of Hephaestus.

36. *bacchanalian play:* The artist Salvator Rosa (1615–73) painted many battle scenes that Hugo could have seen at the Louvre.

37. *eight thousand of Biot:* An anachronistic reference to nineteenth-century science.

38. *as a great man has put it:* Hugo's manuscript indicates that he referred to Napoleon, who used "the square of his base" in a moral sense to describe people.

39. *Naso:* Naso, or Ovid (P. Ovidius Naso), died in exile among the Getes, not the Muscovites.

40. *Egyptian:* Hugo uses *Egyptian* in the sense of *gypsy.* References to Egypt allude to the land of gypsies and Bohemians and have little to do with the reality of a place in the Middle East. The fear of and prejudice against gypsies, who were seen as un-Christian, is assimilated to a fear of the "East" in general.

BOOK II

1. *la Barillerie . . . la Juiverie:* These streets were all destroyed during the renovations of Paris during the Second Empire.

2. *Jehan Fourbault:* Hugo borrows details of the banners and flags made by Jehan Fourbault from *Comptes de la Prévôté,* textile maker to whom the banners are attributed.

3. *Passeur aux Vaches:* The Passeur aux Vaches or "Cattle Ferry" was a small island that has since become a part of the Ile de la Cité. Today the Square du Vert-Galant occupies the place where the island was.

4. *Dominique Bocador:* Hugo takes these details from Sauval, who describes Dominique Bocador's expansion of the Hôtel de Ville at the expense of the nearby bourgeois homes.

5. *fever of Saint Vallier:* A fever that was said to strike those who were condemned to death by hanging.

6. *Besos para Golpes:* Incorrect Spanish, it should read "Besos por Golpes" meaning "kisses for blows."

7. *Mount Menelaeus:* In Greek mythology, this island was where Bacchus was worshiped.

8. Un cofre . . . buen char: These lines are taken from a romance published by Abel Hugo in 1821. Victor replicates his brother's mistakes in Spanish. A rough translation would be "A very valuable trunk/was found in a pillar/inside were new banners/decorated with frightening figures/Arab riders/Incapable of moving/Armed with swords/And around their necks sharpshooting crossbows."

9. *next came the kingdom of Slang . . . powers of imagination:* Hugo's description of the medieval Parisian underworld, or the Kingdom of Slang, is taken from Sauval. Many of the terms are very picturesque but untranslatable. To give an idea, *coquillard* referred to the false pilgrims of St. Jacques or St. Michel, saints who are distinguished by *coquilles* or shells worn by those devoted to them. The *saboleux* were fake epileptics who ate soap to simulate foaming at the mouth.

10. *Hermes:* Greek god of commerce, eloquence, invention, travel, and theft, who serves as herald and messenger of the other gods. Hermes Trismegistus was a legendary author of works on alchemy, astronomy, and the occult.

11. *Belleforêt, Father Le Juge, and Corrozet:* François de Belleforêt, Pierre Le Juge, and Gilles Corrozet were sixteenth-century chroniclers of history.

12. tota via, cheminum, et viaria: "Every path, way, and passage."

13. *Salve maris stella:* Hugo's incorrect version of "Ave, maris stella" or "Hail, star of the sea!," the opening line of a well-known hymn to the Virgin Mary.

14. La buona mancia, signor! La buona mancia!: Incorrect Italian for "Sir, good charity, good charity!"

15. Señor caballero, para comprar un pedaso de pan!: Incorrect Spanish for "Sir Knight, to buy a piece of bread!"

16. Facitote caritatem: "Give alms."

17. Onde vas, hombre?: Incorrect Spanish for "Where are you going, man?"

18. jambe de Dieu: Sauval describes the *jambe de Dieu* as a beggar's leg dressed to look infected or diseased in order to inspire the pity and charity of passersby.

19. *performed on the stage of the Petit-Bourbon:* In 1653, at the Court of Louis XIV, the Royal Ballet performed the metamorphoses of the con men and tricksters of the Parisian underworld for the King's entertainment.

20. Hombre, quita tu sombrero: "Take off your hat, man."

21. *the little blades:* The little blade, or *petite flambé,* was the tool of the trade of pickpockets and purse cutters.

22. et omnia in philosophia, omnes in philosopho continentur: "Philosophy contains everything and the philosopher all men."

23. Burington's Observations: Daines Burington published in English in 1766 *Observations on the statutes chiefly the most ancient from the Magna Carta.*

24. *The jug broke into four pieces:* Marriage by a broken jug among gypsies is mentioned in the *Dictionnaire Infernal* under the term *bohemian.*

25. demoiselle: Hugo is playing on the double meaning of *demoiselle* in French: it refers both to a dragonfly and to a young girl.

26. Quando . . . tierra: "When the colorful birds fall silent/and the earth . . ."

27. Mon . . . oiseau: "My father is a bird/And my mother as well/I crossed the water without a skiff/I crossed the water without a boat/My father is a bird/And my mother as well."

28. *St. John:* The feast of St. John the Baptist was celebrated by bonfires on June 24.

29. De officiis: Cicero's *On Duty.*

30. *Micromégas:* Micromégas is the hero of Voltaire's story by the same name; he was a giant who was eight miles tall.

BOOK III

1. *Notre-Dame:* Most of the details of this chapter are taken from the work of du Breul and Sauval.

2. *Biscornette:* An ironworker who made many of the wrought-iron ornaments for the cathedral.

3. *Louis XIII:* According to du Breul, the construction of the cathedral was begun by Hercandus under Charlemagne. In 1638, Louis XIII declared that he desired repairs on the main altar of Notre-Dame. Louis XIV began the restoration in 1699.

4. *lid of a saucepan:* The thirteenth-century steeple was replaced by Viollet-le-Duc in 1859.

5. *Vitruvius and Vignole:* Jacques Barozzio (1507–73), called Vignole, was the Italian architect who, after Michelangelo's death, completed St. Peter's Basilica in Rome. He was a reader of Marcus Vitruvius Pollio or Vitruvius (88–26 B.C.) and author of *De architectura.*

6. *Robert Cenalis:* Robert Cenalis, Bishop of Aurenche, reported that Notre-Dame of Paris was more harmonious and spacious than the temple of Diana in Ephesus.

7. *Notre-Dame . . . like the latter:* Gothic architecture, based on the pointed or ogival arch, was said to have come to Europe by way of the East, or the Arabs. The heavy Romanesque architecture of the early Middle Ages was dominated by low domes and rounded arches. Hugo will make constant reference to the tensions between these two styles.

8. Pendent opera interrupta: "Interrupted work remains suspended" (Virgil, *Aeneid,* IV, 88).

9. *the Roman zone . . . the zone of the Renaissance:* This is called, depending on the country, climate, and genre of building, Lombard, Saxon, and Byzantine. These three are parallel and related styles, each with its particularities, but they are all derived from the same principle—the circular arch. *Facies non omnibus una/Non diversa tamen, qualem, etc.,* "Their appearances are not the same, but still not different" (Ovid, *Metamorphoses,* II, 13). [Hugo's note]

10. *the extremity of its central steeple, which penetrates into the zone of the Renaissance:* It was precisely this part of the steeple, which was made of wood, that was destroyed by the fire from the sky of 1823. [Hugo's note]

11. *Paris has not grown more than one-third:* According to Marius-François Guyard, editor of the Garner Frères edition of *Notre Dame de Paris,* this version of the limited scope of Parisian expansion is highly exaggerated. Paris in the time of Louis XI comprised only the first four of the

arrondissements. The Paris of Hugo's time had expanded to include the eighth, ninth, tenth, and eleventh arrondissements, or more than double what it was in the sixteenth century.

12. Le mur murant Paris rend Paris murmurant: "The wall enclosing Paris makes Parisians murmur." An epigram against the wall of the Farmer Generals, begun in 1784 and completed in 1790 under Louis XVI.

13. Civibus . . . privilegia: The loyalty of kings, interrupted by some revolts here and there, granted the citizens many privileges.

14. *Ile Louviers:* The Ile Louviers was connected to the right bank in 1843. It used to lie between what are today the Boulevard Morland and the Quai Henri IV.

15. *Hôtel de Nesle:* In 1572, Louis Gonzague, the Duke of Nevers, bought the Hôtel de Nesle, which then took his name. This building has disappeared. A Hôtel de Nevers remains on the Rue Colbert.

16. *Logis de Reims:* In the cul-de-sac du Paon, the Parisian home of the Bishop of Reims, near the Rue Hautefeuille.

17. *the square tower:* The square tower, or Tour Clovis, is located today in the group of buildings that make up the Lycée Henri IV.

18. *Augustines:* Construction on the Church of the Augustines was begun in 1368. The church, located on the Quai des Grands Augustins, was demolished in the beginning of the nineteenth century.

19. *St.-Jacques-de-la-Boucherie:* All that remains of this church, demolished in 1797, is the Tour St.-Jacques.

20. *Temple:* The fortified enclosure of the Temple occupied the area defined by the Rues du Temple, de Bretagne, de Picardie, and Dupetit-Thouars, in what is today known as the neighborhood of the Marais.

21. *St.-Ladre:* St.-Ladre, or St.-Lazare, was a lepers' colony and then a women's prison. Today it is on the Rue du Faubourg St.-Denis.

22. *Mignards of their times:* Molière, in *La Gloire du Val-de-Grâce,* calls Raphael and Michelangelo the Mignards of their times. *Mignard* means "a precious, affected person obsessed with trivialities and mincing in manner."

23. *Tuileries:* It is with pain and anger that we have witnessed the desire to enlarge, recast, remake, which is to say destroy, this admirable palace. Today's architects are too heavy-handed to touch these delicate Renaissance buildings. We hope that they will not dare take such a step. Besides, not only would the demolition of the Tuileries now be an act that would make a drunken Vandal blush but it would be an act

of treason. The Tuileries are not only a masterpiece of sixteenth-century art but a page of history of the nineteenth century. This palace does not belong to the King. It belongs to the people. Let us leave it as it is. Our revolution has twice marked its brow. On one of its two facades, it bears the bullet holes of August 10, on the other the bullet holes of July 21. It is sacred. —Paris, April 7, 1831. [Hugo's note in the fifth edition]

24. the Messidor style: The French Revolution redrew the calendar and modeled itself after the ancient Romans and Greeks in both style and substance when it established what is now known as the First Republic. The revolutionaries renamed the months and began counting the years from the date of the fall of the King. Classicism in architecture and painting came into vogue to replace what was seen as the decadent style of the Old Regime. Hugo mocks the revolutionary pretensions, but he makes a mistake in dating this building. The School of Medicine was not constructed under the First Republic but was built under Louis XV. In 1794, however, under the First Republic, the bas-relief on the facade representing the good works of Louis XV was taken down.

25. *The telegraph . . . on its roof:* The telegraph towers on Saint-Sulpice inspired Hugo's poem "Le Télégraphe."

BOOK IV

1. *Lætare Sunday:* Laetare Sunday is the fourth Sunday of Lent, and its name comes from the first word of the Mass for that day, *Laetare,* or "Rejoice." It occurs four weeks before Quasimodo Sunday.

2. *Phlegeton:* Phlegeton is the Greek name of one of the rivers of hell that flow into the Acheron and around Tartarus.

3. *Harfleur:* The seige of Harfleur, which occurred between August 19 and September 22, 1415, was Henry V's first military undertaking after he resumed the Hundred Years' War against France. Dysentery among the English soldiers and the city's impressive fortifications enabled the French to hold out for more than a month.

4. *dare alapas et capillos laniare:* "Slapping and hair pulling," a phrase from Matthew Paris's *History of England* regarding a student revolt in 1229.

5. *in which the canon law . . . in 1227:* According to du Breul, whom Hugo follows faithfully in his version of history, in the year 1216, Pope Honorius III forbade the reading of civil law in Paris. Papal decrees alone

were to be obeyed. It was Bishop Isidore, not Theodore, who kept a faithful collection of decrees beginning in the year 618. In 1227, Pope Gregory IX had a diligent record of all Papal decrees made. In any case, Hugo sought to illustrate the struggle between civil law and religious decrees that raged in Europe during the Middle Ages.

6. *quasi person:* The first words of the first Mass following Easter are *Quasimodo geniti infantes,* "Like newborn babes," hence Quasimodo Sunday. In French *quasi* means both "almost" and "as if."

7. *Immanis Pecoris, Custos Immanior Ipse:* "For a monstrous herd, an even more monstrous guardian." From Hugo's own phrase, in the manuscript of *Hernani,* this line is a parody of Virgil's "For a beautiful herd, a guardian even more beautiful," from his *Bucolics,* V, 44.

8. *Olivier le Daim:* Olivier le Daim was Louis XI's barber, upon whom the King showered great honors. He will appear later in the novel.

9. *hippogriff:* The hippogriff is the half horse, half griffon that Astolpho rides to the moon in Ariosto's *Orlando furioso.*

10. *Paul Diacre:* Paul Warnefrid, historian and poet of Latin (740–801).

11. fas... nefas: *Fas* means "licit," *nefas* "illicit."

12. *Averroës . . . Zoroaster:* Averroës, an Arab philosopher of the twelfth century known for his commentary on Aristotle. Guillaume de Paris was a philosopher and Bishop of Paris, author of *De universo.* Nicolas Flamel (1330–1418) was a wealthy *écrivain-juré* at the University who made a number of donations to his parish, St.-Jacques-de-la-Boucherie. It was said that he had discovered the secrets of alchemy and sorcery, which were purported to be the sources of his great riches. Solomon is mentioned here as the supposed ancestor of the Knights Templars and the Masons. Pythagoras was a philosopher of the sixth century B.C. and Zoroaster or Zarathustra was the Persian founder of Zoroastrianism, a religion based on the conflict between good and evil, light and dark.

13. *Magistri to Father Pacifique:* By Magistri, Hugo may be referring to Rodolphe Magister de Tonnerre. Father Pacifique was a Capucine missionary and a chemist (1575–1653). Hugo makes him a contemporary of Claude Frollo.

14. Toutes sortes ... fauvettes: Slightly modified, from Régnier's *Satires:* "All sorts of people follow poets/like the small wild animals that come crying after owls."

15. Niche, niche, le diable est pris: "Trapped, tricked, the Devil is caught!"

16. Elia! Elia! Claudius cum claudo!: "Here comes Claude and the lame

one." In French and Latin, there is a play on *claudo* or *claudicant*, or "the lame one," "the limping one."

BOOK V

1. *Abbas Beati Martini:* The Abbey of St. Martin.
2. *De prædestinatione et libero arbitrio: On Predestination and Free Will.* Honorius d'Autun (d. ca. 1130) wrote this treatise in which he examines the problem of predestination in relation to free will.
3. A L'ABRI-COTIER: a play on words: it means literally "At the Apricot Tree," but *a l'abri* can be translated as "in the shelter of" and *cotier* as "of the coast."
4. *Compère Tourangeau:* In Sir Walter Scott's *Quentin Durward*, Louis XI appears to the hero disguised as a merchant.
5. JAMBLIQUE: Jamblic (233–333 B.C.) was a Greek philosopher very interested by mystic cults.
6. *emprosthotonos* succeeds *ophisthonos: Emprosthotonos* describes the contraction of the muscles of the trunk of the body that allows us to bend forward. *Ophisthonos* is an advanced form of tetanus and manifests itself when the body and head bend backward.
7. *vertical boustrophedon . . . zephirod:* It seems that *vertical boustrophedon* is something Hugo made up to sound astrological. *Zephiroth* is the name given by cabalists to the ten perfections of divine essence.
8. *clavicle: Clavicle* is the name of a book of magic falsely attributed to Solomon.
9. *Indian Temple of Ecklingar:* Hugo synthesizes Egyptian and Indian imagery and symbols to concoct his fictional version of occult mysteries.
10. peristera: Greek word for verbena, a sacred plant, said to be able to cast out evil spirits and reunite lovers.
11. *Norimbergae, Antonius Roburger, 1474:* "Commentary on the epistles of Saint Paul, Nuremberg, Antoine Koburger 1474." Koburger published in 1474 a commentary on the Psalms of Father Lombard; Hugo invented the title of this book.
12. Abbas . . . thesaurarii: "The Abbey of St.-Martin, that is the King of France, is according to custom canon: he has the little prebend of St.-Venant and must be seated at the seat of the treasurer."
13. quia nominor leo: From Phaedrus, *Fables,* I, 5, 7. The complete citation is *Ego primam tollo nominor quia nominor quia leo,* or "I take the first part because I am called lion."

14. testudo: A *testudo* describes the attack formation of Roman soldiers who made a vault by raising their shields above their heads.
15. *Glaber Radulphus:* According to Georges Huard, a Hugo scholar, this reference comes from Alain Deville's monograph on Saint Georges de Boscherville. Glaber, who died in 1050, was the author of a chronicle describing history between 900 and 1046.
16. *Vyasa:* Indian ascetic poet.
17. Moniteur: The *Moniteur* was founded in 1789 and reported in vivid detail the goings-on of the Assemblée Constituante.

BOOK VI

1. Dignitas . . . ist: "Dignity is associated with great police power and many rights and privileges," cited in Sauval to describe the power of the Provost.
2. league of public welfare: The League of Public Welfare was composed of powerful vassals of the King who allied themselves against him in 1464. The King gave in to their demands in 1465 with the Treaty of Conflans.
3. Lex horrendi carminis erat: "The text of the law was terrifying," a citation of Titus-Livy.
4. in praejudicium meretricis: "Against a courtesan."
5. Tu, ora, *"Pray, you": Tu, ora* is almost an anagram for Trou aux Rats, or "Rat Hole."
6. *"non passibus aguis":* Virgil, "with uneven steps."
7. *the Sack Woman:* Sachette, or Sack Woman, from *sac,* because penitents often wore sackcloth.
8. Une hart . . . magot!: "A rope/For the hanged man/A bunch of kindling/For the ape!"

BOOK VII

1. *tended swine for Admetus:* Apollo tended horses and cattle for Admetus, King of Thessalia, in expiation for the murder of the Cyclops.
2. quemadmodums *and* verumenimveros: *quemadmodums,* "in any case," and *verumenimveros,* "in truth."
3. Veramente, queste rotisserie sono cosa stupenda!: "This rotisserie is truly a stupendous thing!"
4. Unde . . . vult: "From where? From there?" "Man is a monster to men." "The stars my camp, the name my god." "The bigger the book, the greater the evil." "To learn, listen." "It blows where it flows."

5. Tunicam dechiraverunt: "They have torn the robe."

6. Græcum est, non legitur: "It is Greek, it is not read."

7. quibusdam marmosetis: "for certain marmots."

8. Ο το το το το τοῦ!: A corruption of an exclamation in Aeschylus in the form of an anapest, which is a foot of verse made up of two short followed by one long syllable.

9. Advosum . . . boias: From Plautus, *Asinaria*, 549–550, "With needles, red-hot irons, crosses and double rings/Ties, chains, prisons, shackles, and iron collars."

10. Per ipsum, et cum ipso, et in ipso: "By him, and with him, and in him," words from the Canon of the Mass. Hugo uses details of the witches' sabbath garnered from the *Dictionnaire infernal* under the entry "magic words."

11. Dialogus de energia et operatione dœmonum: *Dialogue of Energy and the Operation of Demons*, by Michael Psellus (1010–78), a Byzantine writer considered a great scholar of his times.

12. Nullus enim locus sine genio est: "There is no place without its genie," Servius Honoratus, grammarian and scholar of the fourth century A.D.

13. Sub conservatione formae specificae salva anima: "Preserved in its specific form, the soul is intact." Raymond Lulle was a Spanish priest and author of an *Ars magna* (1275) that purported to offer an infallible method of reasoning.

14. Sang Dieu . . . tonnere!: These picturesque oaths can be roughly translated as "Bloody hell! God's stomach! Body of God! Belly button of Beelzebub! Name of the Pope! Horn and thunder!"

15. *A la Vieille Science;* "Une vieille qui scie une anse": A play on "A la vieille science," or "The old science," and the tavern's sign, which shows an old woman sawing a handle, or *une vieille qui scien une anse*.

16. Les enfants . . . veaux: "The children of the Petits-Carreaux/Get themselves hung like veal cattle."

17. Aux Houls/Saouls, saouls, saouls!: To the Houls! Drunk! Drunk! Drunk!

18. *Rue des Mauvaises . . . contradict me:* Rue des Mauvaises Paroles can be literally translated as "Street of Bad Words." The Latin aphorism can be translated as "Unworthy are those who live among bad words." Rue Jean-Pain-Mollet can be translated as "John Soft Bread Street." Jehan is playing with the names of streets. St.-Jacques de l'Hôpital faces the Rue de l'Ours, or Bear Street.

19. *When it shall . . . trudge away:* From Tristan, L'Hermite de Soliers, *Le Cabinet du roi Louis XI* (1661).

20. Olim truncus eram ficulnus: The title of the satire "I was once the trunk of a fig tree" should clue us in to the nature of the offense—Phœbus urinated on the statue of the Bishop of Autun.

21. *call in the clouds for help:* In the *Iliad*, Zeus hides himself in a golden cloud in order to make love to Hera on Mount Ida.

BOOK VIII

1. De figuris regularibus et irregularibus: *Of Regular and Irregular Figures.*

2. Didaskalon of Hugo St.-Victor: Hugo seems to mention Hugo St.-Victor (or Hugh of St.-Victor, 1096?–1141), an obscure medieval figure, only because he could not resist making the pun on his own name, and in doing so, inserting himself into his novel. The *Didascalicon* was a very influential medieval work of Christian educational philosophy written by Hugh sometime between 1225 and 1330.

3. *Lasciate Ogni Speranza:* "Leave all hope behind," a fragment of the inscription engraved on the gates of hell in Dante's *Divine Comedy.*

4. *sentence of death:* This is another reference to Dante's *Inferno,* in which one finds a detailed description of hell.

5. *Garofalo loved to picture the taking down from the Cross:* Benvenuto Tisi, called Garofalo (1481–1559), an imitator of Raphael, painted a *Descent from the Cross* and other religious subjects concerning the Crucifixion.

6. *La Fontaine . . . fox caught by a hen:* La Fontaine's fable "The Fox and the Stork" is about a fox who becomes the victim of his prey.

7. Non . . . vitam: From Psalms, "I am not afraid of the thousands who surround me, arise, Lord and save me!/Save me, O Lord, because the waters have penetrated my soul./I am caught in the deep mire of the abyss. There is no help for me." . . . "Whoso hears my word and believes in the One who sent me will have eternal life and know no judgment. He will go from death to life."

8. De . . . me: "I called from the deep and You heard my voice. You did plunge me into the deep, in the heart of the sea, and the floods surrounded me."

9. I nunc . . . misericors: "Go trembling soul. May God have mercy on you!"

10. Kyrie eleison!: Greek response to the greeting of the Mass, "Have mercy, Lord."

11. Omnes gurites tui et fluctus tui super me transierunt: "All Your whirlpools and all Your waves have gone over me!"

BOOK IX

1. Quod . . . sucsitantibus: "Which for the monks of St.-Germain-des-Prés was a hydra, the clerics were always finding new subjects for disputes." The Latin plays on the word *capita,* which means both "subjects" and "heads," as in the many heads of the hydra.

2. Grève . . . aboye: "Grève bark, Grève crawl/Spin, spin my spindle/Spin the hangman's noose/That whistles in the courtyard/Grève bark, Grève crawl/The beautiful hempen rope/Sow d'Issy until Vanvre/Of hemp and not of wheat/The robber has not robbed us of/The beautiful rope of hempen rope/Grève crawl, Grève bark/To see the harlot/Hung on the gallows/The windows are eyes/Grève crawl, Grève bark."

3. *the doors of St.-Méry:* In 1324 Perrin Marc murdered the treasurer of the Duke of Normandy (the future Charles V). That night the Maréchal of Normandy and Jean de Chalon (not Champagne) went into the Church of St.-Méry, brought Marc out, and hanged him. The two of them were ordered killed by Etienne Marcel, but this has little to do with the history of sanctuary.

BOOK X

1. De cupa petaraum: *The Stone Cup.*

2. cibi, potus, somni, venus, omnia moderata sint: "In food, drink, sleep, and love let there be moderation."

3. forismaritagium: Marriage forced by external forces.

4. *across the ocean:* Biton was a Greek mathematician who lived in the third century B.C.

5. Cessat doctorum, doctrina, discipulorum, disciplina: "The doctrine of the indoctrinated and the discipline of the disciples deteriorate."

6. *Ajax:* Ajax is taken here as the symbol of resentment: Homer and Sophocles represent this hero as being humiliated when he did not receive the arms of the fallen Achilles.

7. Aux sonneurs pour les trépassés: "The bell ringers for those passed away."

8. *Mistigri:* Mistigri is the name of the Jack of Clubs.

9. *Caillouville:* In Notre-Dame de Caillouville there were, until the Revolution, five hundred statues of the saints.

10. Populi debacchantis populosa debacchatio: "The ravings of the people, popular fury!"

11. Quae . . . mira: "What songs, what instruments! What singing! What

melodies one sings without end! They resonate as sweet as honey, the instruments of the hymns, the very smooth harmonies of the angels, the admirable song of songs!" Citation from St. Augustine on Paradise.

12. non cuiquam datum est habere nasum: "It is not given to everyone to have a nose."

13. Dimidiam domun in paradiso: "Half of a house in Paradise." This phrase comes from du Breul, whose *in paradiso* referred to "on the parvis," or the square in front of a church. Hugo's notes say that "*Parvis* comes from Paradise."

14. Luxuriosa res vinum et tumultuosa ebrietas: "Wine and drunkenness are luxurious things."

15. Vinum apostatare facit etiam sapientes: "Wine makes even wise men apostates."

16. revant dans son revoir: "Dreaming in his dream place."

17. δεκεμβολος: "Armed with ten spurs."

18. Elle . . . pillée: "The City of Cambray/Is very well dressed/Marafin has pillaged it." In Tristan, Louis Marafin put pressure on Cambray in 1477, and after the death of its ruler, Téméraire, he governed it in the name of Louis XI.

19. Cyrus: The *Cyrus* was a seventeenth-century roman à clef by Mademoiselle Scudéry in which members of aristocratic literary circles were allegorized.

20. dapifero nullo, buticulario nullo: "Without an attending squire or butler."

21. Maître . . . dépêchés: Master John Balue/Has lost his view/Of his bishoprics./Monsieur de Verdun/Has not even one/All of them have been dispatched.

22. *Hercules . . . Jean de Monroyal:* Hercules was called Musagetes, or "guide of the muses," because in destroying the reign of monsters, he prepared the way for the Muses to reestablish harmony and order. Matthias Corvinus ruled Hungary in 1482. Much of this speech, like most of this scene, is borrowed from Pierre Matthieu's *Histoire de Louis XI, roi de France.*

23. *Chancellor Hugonet:* Guillaume Rym had the Chancellor Hugonet executed at Ghent. *See Book I, note 31.*

24. *cross of St.-Lo:* Those who swore by the cross of St.-Lo were supposed to die within the year.

BOOK XI

1. *Ascalaph:* The ascalaph is an insect. Gringoire refers to Ascalalphe, son of Acheron, who was buried under a rock and transformed into an owl.

2. *jaws of the crocodile:* This bird often forages for food in the mouths of crocodiles.

3. Adversus avaritiam: "Against avarice."

4. *La Creatura Bella Bianco Vestita:* "The beautiful creature dressed in white." Dante describes with these words the Angel of Humility in the *Purgatorio.*

5. *To Jehan Marchand . . . pounds:* The collaboration between Jehan Marchand and Pierre Gringoire is mentioned in the *Comptes de la Prévôté,* but it took place between 1502 and 1531. Hugo changed the dates to suit his needs.

6. *Coligni:* Admiral Coligni (1519–72) was murdered during the Saint Bartholomew's Massacre.

7. *Olivier le Daim:* Olivier le Daim, the King's barber, was hung on May 21, 1484. *See Book IV, note 8.*